The O. Henry Prize Stories 2002

PRIZE STORIES 2002

The O. Henry Awards

Edited and with an introduction
by Larry Dark

ANCHOR BOOKS
A Division of Random House, Inc.
New York

AN ANCHOR ORIGINAL, SEPTEMBER 2002

Copyright © 2002 by Anchor Books, a division of Random House, Inc.

All rights reserved under International and Pan-American Copyright Conventions.
Published in the United States by Anchor Books, a division of Random House, Inc.,
New York, and simultaneously in Canada by Random House of Canada Limited, Toronto.

Anchor Books and colophon are registered trademarks of Random House, Inc.

Owing to limitations of space, permissions appear on pages 474–76.

Library of Congress Cataloging-in-Publication Data is on file.

Book design by Debbie Glasserman

www.anchorbooks.com

Printed in the United States of America

10 9 8 7 6 5 4 3 2 1

Publisher's Note

WILLIAM SYDNEY Porter, who wrote under the pen name O. Henry, was born in North Carolina in 1862. He started writing stories while in prison for embezzlement, a crime for which he was convicted in 1898 (it is uncertain if he actually committed the crime). His writing career was short and started late, but O. Henry proved himself a prolific and widely read short story writer in the twelve years he devoted to the craft, and his name has become synonymous with the American short story.

His years in Texas inspired many lively Westerns, but it was New York City that galvanized his creative powers, and his New York stories became his claim to fame. Loved for their ironic plot twists, which made for pleasing surprise endings, his highly entertaining tales appeared weekly in Joseph Pulitzer's *New York World*.

His best known story, "The Gift of the Magi," was written for the *World* in 1905 and has become an American treasure. Dashed off past deadline in a matter of hours, it is the story of a man who sells his watch to buy a set of hair combs as a Christmas present for his wife, who in the meantime has sold her luxurious locks to buy him a watch chain. "The Last Leaf" is another O. Henry favorite. It is the story of a woman who falls ill with pneumonia and pronounces that she will die when the last leaf of ivy she sees outside her Greenwich Village window falls away. She hangs on with the last stubborn leaf, which gives her the resolve to recover. She eventually learns that her inspirational leaf wasn't a real leaf at all, but rather a painting of a leaf. Her neighbor, who has always dreamed of painting a masterpiece, painted it on the wall and caught pneumonia in the process.

His work made him famous, but O. Henry was an extremely private man who, sadly, preferred to spend his time and money on drink, and ultimately it was the bottle that did him in. He died alone and penniless in 1910. O. Henry's legacy and his popularization of the short story was such that in 1918 Doubleday, in conjunction with the Society of Arts and Sciences, established the O. Henry Awards, an annual anthology of short stories, in his honor. Anchor Books is proud, with the eighty-second edition of the series, to continue the tradition of publishing this much beloved collection of outstanding short stories in O. Henry's name.

Publisher's Note: An Update

The twenty stories included in *Prize Stories 2002: The O. Henry Awards* were chosen by the series editor, Larry Dark, from among the three thousand or so short stories published during the course of the previous year in the magazines consulted for the series listed on page 434. Blind copies of these stories, that is, copies with the names of the authors and magazines omitted, were then sent to the prize jury members. Each juror was instructed to vote for his or her top three choices, and the first-, second-, and third-prize winners were determined as a result of these votes. The jurors for the 2002 volume were Dave Eggers, Joyce Carol Oates, and Colson Whitehead. An introduction by one of the three jurors precedes each of the top-prize stories selected.

A shortlist of fifty other stories given serious consideration for *Prize Stories 2002: The O. Henry Awards*, along with brief summaries of each, can be found on page 422.

The Magazine Award is given to the magazine publishing the best fiction during the course of the previous year. This is determined by (1) the number of stories selected for *Prize Stories 2002: The O. Henry Awards*, (2) the number and placement of stories among the top-prize winners, and (3) the number of short-listed stories. The Magazine Award winner for 2002 is *The New Yorker*. A citation for this award is provided on page 432.

Acknowledgments

Thanks, as always, to Alice Elliott Dark, to Jenny Minton and Megan Hustad at Anchor Books, and, for their valuable and greatly valued assistance, to Augustine Chan and Denise Delgado.

Contents

Introduction

Each year, out of the seeming chaos of thousands of short stories published in hundreds of magazines, a tidy collection of twenty or so stories emerges, laying claim to representing the best of what was published during the course of the previous year. Over time, a given volume tends even to take on an air of inevitability. But there is nothing simple or remotely inevitable about the choices that go into narrowing an enormous field down to such a small sampling. Hundreds of O. Henry Awards–worthy stories are written and published annually. In the end, order is imposed simply by the necessary act of choosing.

The world, it turns out, is not so tidy as we would like to believe, either. The twenty pieces included in *Prize Stories 2002: The O. Henry Awards* were all published in 2001, a year that will long be remembered for the catastrophic events of early fall and the sorrow, fear, and anger that followed. Nowhere in this collection will you see any of this reflected because most—if not all—of these stories were written before any of it happened. To ask readers to forgive the stories in this collection their personal concerns in light of these events, however, would be missing the point. The personal, the emotional, the psychological, the train of thought, the gesture, the moment, the smallest choice—these will remain the stuff of short stories. What gives this form its power is that, no matter what happens, human beings experience the world on the intimate level at which stories offer their insights. And this, most likely, is the approach short story writers will take to the events of September 11 and beyond when they turn their attention to the subject.

Because stories are written on a personal level, even the most astute readers, including the eminent authors who serve as top-prize jurors for the O. Henry Awards, react to stories in this way. As a result, any attempt I make to anticipate which story each juror will like best is usually in vain. For one, my view of the writers serving as jurors is inevitably based on my encounters with their work. I've learned, however, that the kind of work a writer produces doesn't always match his or her taste in reading. It wasn't until I saw the introductions Dave Eggers, Joyce Carol Oates, and Colson Whitehead each wrote for the stories they championed that I fully understood their individual choices. Each was very passionate about his or her favorite, and what they've written reveals this. Oddly enough, Joyce Carol Oates selected a story from *McSweeney's,* which is edited by Dave Eggers, and Eggers chose a story from the *Ontario Review,* which happens to be edited by Oates and her husband, Raymond Smith. This can only be taken for what it is: a coincidence. As always, the three jurors read blind, which meant they didn't know what magazines the stories were first published in or the names of the authors. In fact, both Eggers and Oates recused themselves from voting for work from their own magazines, and neither had previously encountered the stories they ultimately selected.

The traditional scope of this series and other annual "best of" collections often favors realistic, literary fiction. However, as Joyce Carol Oates points out in her introduction, the First Prize–winning "The Ceiling" by Kevin Brockmeier is more stylistically expressive, along the lines of a dark fairy tale. The stories in this volume by David Foster Wallace, Jonathan Nolan, and David Leavitt likewise stretch the form in nontraditional directions. The inclusion of such work enriches what I believe is a nicely balanced collection on several levels. For one, there are an equal number of stories by men and women. And there's a good mix of established and lesser-known writers from a range of different backgrounds. In part, the book has kind of a retro feel, circa 1985, with stories by Ann Beattie, Deborah Eisenberg, Richard Ford, David Leavitt, and Alice Munro, all of whom were celebrated for short stories they published around that time. The 2002 volume also features the work of several writers under the age of thirty: Kevin Brockmeier, Anthony Doerr, Mark Ray Lewis, Jonathan

Nolan, and Mary Yukari Waters. And two of this year's contributors, Leavitt and Heidi Jon Schmidt, provide a connection between the old and the new in that both had stories in the influential 1980s anthology *Twenty Under Thirty.* Even in the interest of balance, however, it's impossible in so few stories to represent the full spectrum of fiction published each year, or the diversity of writers contributing short stories to magazines. Nor should an ideal balance be imposed too forcibly because what this collection is ultimately about is publishing what the editor honestly feels are the year's best stories.

Aside from the common element of accomplished work, there are a few themes that connect several of the stories. The most obvious one is that a lot of them revolve around travel—thirteen of the twenty, in fact. In the past, I've often decided early in the year to include a particular story, which then strikes a chord that affects many of my choices thereafter. For this volume, that story was Deborah Eisenberg's "Like It or Not," about a divorced woman visiting a friend in Rome who ends up taking a trip to the coast with a stranger. After that, I found myself drawn to Ann Beattie's "That Last Odd Day in L.A.," in which a man flies to Los Angeles to visit his niece and nephew and has an interesting poolside epiphany. Travel is an excellent literary subject because the situation itself—displacement, being somewhere unfamiliar, or returning to a familiar place after many years—heightens and sometimes even creates the conflict that is at the heart of any good story. In Bill Roorbach's "Big Bend," for instance, a well-off, retired widower takes a low-wage job as a volunteer in Big Bend National Park. This displacement from his ordinary existence makes possible a romantic relationship with a younger, married woman. In Richard Ford's "Charity," a husband and wife, who are trying to figure out whether to continue their lives together or apart, take a trip up the coast of Maine that brings many of the issues between them into sharper focus. Chitra Banerjee Divakaruni's "The Lives of Strangers" concerns an American-born Indian woman who embarks on a pilgrimage to Kashmir with her aunt and encounters what she considers to be native superstition that nonetheless still holds some power over her. In "Do Not Disturb" by A.M. Homes, a doctor afflicted with cancer and her husband travel to Paris to sort out their marital problems, only to find their incompatibilities beyond cure. Edwidge Danticat's "Seven" concerns a Haitian woman who travels to New York to be with a husband she hasn't seen in seven years and who faces a new existence in a new place with a man she hardly knew to begin with.

A second theme linking many of the stories—marriage—became apparent to me only after the collection was assembled. In this case, my choices weren't consciously affected by the notion of this as a possible theme. Everyone's life inevitably bears some relationship to the institution of marriage. Every adult, after all, is either married, divorced, widowed, or single. So I didn't think about this much as I read. Only later did I find that marriage is crucial to many of the stories, even some of the more unusual ones. Take Jonathan Nolan's "Memento Mori," in which a man who has lost his short-term memory is obsessed with finding his wife's killer. The marriage was dissolved by her death before the story begins, but the relationship is still of crucial importance to the narrative. As it happens, this theme extends even to the titles of three of the stories in this collection: "The Butcher's Wife" by Louise Erdrich, "The Hunter's Wife" by Anthony Doerr, and "The Possible Husband" by Don Lee—though the Erdrich story is less about marriage than the title suggests and the Lee story only brings the title character to the cusp of such a relationship. Marriage is an essential aspect of several other stories, including Kevin Brockmeier's "The Ceiling," in which difficulties in a marriage parallel the ominous descent of the sky over a town, and Mary Yukari Waters's "Egg-Face," which concerns an attempt to arrange a match for a Japanese woman who has lived at home with her parents for too long.

Another theme I was conscious of in assembling this collection was that of the relationship between the writer and his or her subjects. In Alice Munro's "Family Furnishings," for instance, a woman publishes a story she has written about an eccentric aunt and learns about the impact of this only years later. In "Anthropology" by Andrea Lee a magazine piece about the narrator's aunts and uncles in North Carolina manages to offend the community as a result of the way she refers to their race. An anecdote related by a character in David Leavitt's "Speonk" is played out in variations in the imagination of another character who wasn't there to witness the actual events. And in David Foster Wallace's "Good Old Neon," the first-person narration morphs into the voice of the author when the story pushes beyond the limitations of the initial point of view.

The themes I've identified—travel, marriage, and writing—provide what I hope are some interesting connections, but they don't necessarily sweep up all of the stories in the collection. While one or the other could be stretched to fit almost any of the stories, my choices weren't made solely on this basis. For instance, in the David Gates story, "George Lassos Moon," the main character travels from Manhattan to his childhood home in upstate New York, and he does so on the heels of a failed marriage, but neither of these elements is central to the story. The protagonist of Heidi Jon Schmidt's "Blood Poison" also takes a trip, to visit her father in New York City, but her troubled relationship with him, rather than the fact of her traveling to visit him, is of greater significance. A theme can enliven a collection, and some connections are bound to emerge whether you choose stories on such a basis or not, but I wouldn't want to invest in particular themes to the point that they strangled off other possibilities. In editing this collection, I have always sought to strike a balance between looking for certain kinds of stories while remaining open to anything. The true theme of the O. Henry Awards is good fiction.

Beyond being an introduction to the work collected here, this is also, sadly, a good-bye. This is my sixth and final year as series editor. Starting with the 2003 volume, Laura Furman will assume this role. I've been reading stories for the O. Henry Awards since September 1995. Since then, nearly 20,000 short stories have crossed my desk, published in multiple issues of more than 300 different magazines and written by a number of authors it would be difficult to estimate with any accuracy. I've had the privilege of collecting 117 of these stories, written by 96 writers, and first published in 41 different magazines. In addition, I've had the good fortune of working with the 18 authors who have served as prize jurors. I also feel lucky to have encountered—in person, over the telephone, by letter, by e-mail, and online—many exceptional writers, magazine editors, book editors, agents, and readers. The prize jury and juror intros to the top-prize winners, the award for magazines, the shortlist of fifty stories accompanied by brief synopses, the inclusion of Canadian authors and publications, and the expanded magazines consulted listings that include Web site addresses are among the changes I brought to the O. Henry Awards. I'm most proud, however, of the editorial contribution I've been able to make to the eighty-two-volume history of this series through the stories collected since 1997. Several, I expect, will be read for many years to come. In some respects, it is liberating to no longer have to read six or seven stories a day. But knowing that any story in any magazine could be great, that I could bring such work to a larger audience, help launch or amplify or cap off a career, connect writers and readers—that's a thrill I will greatly miss. For all the hours and attention this job required, for all of its many demands, it was something I truly loved doing.

LARRY DARK, 2002

The Ceiling

By Kevin Brockmeier

INTRODUCED BY JOYCE CAROL OATES

It's rare that a tale of dark fantasy makes its way into a mainstream publication, and still more rare to discover such a tale in the distinguished O. Henry Awards anthology where, through the decades, that category of prose fiction we call "realism" has always predominated. Rarer still is a story like Kevin Brockmeier's "The Ceiling," which so powerfully conjoins the parable and the realistic short story, the horrific with the domestic. Though "The Ceiling" was written before September 11, 2001, it can now be read as a poetic meditation upon that tragic and unfathomable event in our history: an acknowledgment of our common humanity in the face of terror, and an eloquent if heartrending testimony to the resilience of the human spirit in extremis. In Brockmeier's small-town American setting, as finally claustrophobic as a checkerboard, there is no salvation beyond the ever-shrinking, ever more desperate stratagems of the doomed as they live out their final days. How like all of us, they are eager to accept what would have been, only just recently, unacceptable:

> *The plane of the ceiling was stretched across the firmament, covering my town from end to end, and I could see the lights of a thousand streetlamps caught like constellations in its smooth black polish. It occurred to me that if nothing were to change, if the ceiling were simply to hover where it was forever, we might come to forget that it was even there, charting for ourselves a new map of the night sky.*

Remarkably, "The Ceiling" remains a story of domestic life. A husband must come to terms with the mysterious estrangement of his wife and the diminishment of his marriage even as the world itself is diminished, irrevocably.

In the fairy-tale simplicity of its narration and its ever-accelerating momentum, "The Ceiling" may remind some readers of certain of the beautiful classic parables of Ray Bradbury, in particular "There Will Come Soft Rains." In Bradbury's masterpiece of elliptical narration following a nuclear holocaust in which silhouette-shadows of human beings baked on walls replace "characters," the collapse of civilization is suggested in the slow, then rapid, collapse of a house. In "The Ceiling," disaster similarly descends from the sky, but there is something even more terrifying about this fate, which seems not to have sprung from a human, political agent. As the narrator's wife observes, "It's a kind of sudden dread."

—JOYCE CAROL OATES

Kevin Brockmeier

The Ceiling

from *McSweeney's*

THERE WAS a sky that day, sun-rich and open and blue. A raft of silver clouds was floating along the horizon, and robins and sparrows were calling from the trees. It was my son Joshua's seventh birthday and we were celebrating in our back yard. He and the children were playing on the swing set, and Melissa and I were sitting on the deck with the parents. Earlier that afternoon, a balloon and gondola had risen from the field at the end of our block, sailing past us with an exhalation of fire. Joshua told his friends that he knew the pilot. "His name is Mister Clifton," he said, as they tilted their heads back and slowly revolved in place. "I met him at the park last year. He took me into the air with him and let me drop a soccer ball into a swimming pool. We almost hit a helicopter. He told me he'd come by on my birthday." Joshua shielded his eyes against the sun. "Did you see him wave?" he asked. "He just waved at me."

This was a story.

The balloon drifted lazily away, turning to expose each delta and crease of its fabric, and we listened to the children resuming their play. Mitch Nauman slipped his sunglasses into his shirt pocket. "Ever notice how kids their age will handle a toy?" he said. Mitch was our next-door neighbor. He was the single father of Bobby Nauman, Joshua's strange best friend. His other best friend, Chris Boschetti, came from a family of cosmetics executives. My wife had taken to calling them "Rich and Strange."

Mitch pinched the front of his shirt between his fingers and fanned himself with it. "The actual function of the toy is like some sort of obstacle," he said. "They'll dream up a new use for everything in the world."

I looked across the yard at the swing set: Joshua was trying to shinny up one of the A-poles; Taylor Tugwell and Sam Yoo were standing on the teeter swing; Adam Smithee was tossing fistfuls of pebbles onto the slide and watching them rattle to the ground.

My wife tipped one of her sandals onto the grass with the ball of her foot. "Playing as you should isn't Fun," she said: "it's Design." She parted her toes around the front leg of Mitch's lawn chair. He leaned back into the sunlight, and her calf muscles tautened.

My son was something of a disciple of flying things. On his bedroom wall were posters of fighter planes and wild birds. A model of a helicopter was chandeliered to his ceiling. His birthday cake, which sat before me on the picnic table, was decorated with a picture of a rocket ship—a silver white missile with discharging thrusters. I had been hoping that the baker would place a few stars in the frosting as well (the cake in the catalog was dotted with yellow candy sequins), but when I opened the box I found that they were missing. So this is what I did: as Joshua stood beneath the swing set, fishing for something in his pocket, I planted his birthday candles deep in the cake. I pushed them in until each wick was surrounded by only a shallow bracelet of wax. Then I called the children over from the swing set. They came tearing up divots in the grass.

We sang happy birthday as I held a match to the candles.

Joshua closed his eyes.

"Blow out the stars," I said, and his cheeks rounded with air.

That night, after the last of the children had gone home, my wife and I sat outside drinking, each of us wrapped in a separate silence. The city lights were burning, and Joshua was sleeping in his room. A nightjar gave one long trill after another from somewhere above us.

Melissa added an ice cube to her glass, shaking it against the others until it whistled and cracked. I watched a strand of cloud break apart in the sky. The moon that night was bright and full, but after a while it began to seem damaged to me, marked by some small inaccuracy. It took me a moment to realize why this was: against its blank white surface was a square of perfect darkness. The square was without blemish or flaw, no larger than a child's tooth, and I could not tell whether it rested on the moon itself or hovered above it like a cloud. It looked as if a window had been opened clean through the floor of the rock, presenting to view a stretch of empty space. I had never seen such a thing before.

"What is that?" I said.

Melissa made a sudden noise, a deep, defeated little oh.

"My life is a mess," she said.

Within a week, the object in the night sky had grown perceptibly larger. It would appear at sunset, when the air was dimming to purple, as a faint granular blur, a certain filminess at the high point of the sky, and would remain there through the night. It blotted out the light of passing stars and seemed to travel across the face of the moon, but it did not move. The people of my town were uncertain as to whether the object was spreading or approaching—we could see only that it was getting bigger—and this matter gave rise to much speculation. Gleason the butcher insisted that it wasn't there at all, that it was only an illusion. "It all has to do with the satellites," he said. "They're bending the light from that place like a lens. It just looks like something's there." But though his manner was relaxed and he spoke with conviction, he would not look up from his cutting board.

The object was not yet visible during the day, but we could feel it above us as we woke to the sunlight each morning: there was a tension and strain to the air, a shift in its customary balance. When we stepped from our houses to go to work, it was as if we were walking through a new sort of gravity, harder and stronger, not so yielding.

As for Melissa, she spent several weeks pacing the house from room to room. I watched her fall into a deep abstraction. She had cried into her pillow the night of Joshua's birthday, shrinking away from me beneath the blankets. "I just need to sleep," she said, as I sat above her and rested my hand on her side. "Please. Lie down. Stop hovering." I soaked a washcloth for her in the cold water of the bathroom sink, folding it into quarters and leaving it on her nightstand in a porcelain bowl.

The next morning, when I found her in the kitchen, she was gathering a coffee filter into a little wet sachet. "Are you feeling better?" I asked.

"I'm fine." She pressed the foot lever of the trash can, and its lid popped open with a rustle of plastic.

"Is it Joshua?"

Melissa stopped short, holding the pouch of coffee in her outstretched hand. "What's wrong with Joshua?" she said. There was a note of concern in her voice.

"He's seven now," I told her. When she didn't respond, I continued with, "You don't look a day older than when we met, honey. You know that, don't you?"

She gave a puff of air through her nose—this was a laugh, but I couldn't tell what she meant to express by it, bitterness or judgment or some kind of easy cheer. "It's not Joshua," she said, and dumped the coffee into the trash can. "But thanks all the same."

It was the beginning of July before she began to ease back into the life of our family. By this time, the object in the sky was large enough to eclipse the full moon. Our friends insisted that they had never been able to see any change in my wife at all, that she had the same style of speaking, the same habits and twists and eccentricities as ever. This was, in a certain sense, true. I noticed the difference chiefly when we were alone together. After we had put Joshua to bed, we would sit with one another in the living room, and when I asked her a question, or when the telephone rang, there was always a certain brittleness to her, a hesitancy of manner that suggested she was hearing the world from across a divide. It was clear to me at such times that she had taken herself elsewhere, that she had constructed a shelter from the wood and clay and stone of her most intimate thoughts and stepped inside, shutting the door. The only question was whether the person I saw tinkering at the window was opening the latches or sealing the cracks.

One Saturday morning, Joshua asked me to take him to the library for a story reading. It was almost noon, and the sun was just beginning to darken at its zenith. Each day, the shadows of our bodies would shrink toward us from the west, vanish briefly in the midday soot, and stretch away into the east, falling off the edge of the world. I wondered sometimes if I would ever see my reflection pooled at my feet again. "Can Bobby come, too?" Joshua asked as I tightened my shoes.

I nodded, pulling the laces up in a series of butterfly loops. "Why don't you run over and get him," I said, and he sprinted off down the hallway.

Melissa was sitting on the front porch steps, and I knelt down beside her as I left. "I'm taking the boys into town," I said. I kissed her cheek and rubbed the base of her neck, felt the cirrus curls of hair there moving back and forth through my fingers.

"Shh." She held a hand out to silence me. "Listen."

The insects had begun to sing, the birds to fall quiet. The air gradually became filled with a peaceful chirring noise.

"What are we listening for?" I whispered.

Melissa bowed her head for a moment, as if she were trying to keep count of something. Then she looked up at me. In answer, and with a sort of weariness about her, she spread her arms open to the world.

Before I stood to leave, she asked me a question; "We're not all that much alike, are we?" she said.

The plaza outside the library was paved with red brick. Dogwood trees were planted in hollows along the perimeter, and benches of distressed metal stood here and there on concrete pads. A member of a local guerrilla theater troupe was delivering a recitation from beneath a streetlamp; she sat behind a wooden desk, her hands folded one atop the other, and spoke as if into a camera. "Where did this object come from?" she said. "What is it, and when will it stop its descent? How did we find ourselves in this place? Where do we go from here? Scientists are baffled. In an interview with this station, Dr. Stephen Mandruzzato, head of the prestigious Horton Institute of Astronomical Studies, had this to say: 'We don't know. We don't know. We just don't know.'" I led Joshua and Bobby Nauman through the heavy dark glass doors of the library, and we took our seats in the Children's Reading Room. The tables were set low to the ground so that my legs pressed flat against the underside, and the air carried that peculiar, sweetened-milk smell of public libraries and elementary schools. Bobby Nauman began to play the Where Am I? game with Joshua. "Where am I?" he would ask, and then he'd warm-and-cold Joshua around the room until Joshua had found him. First he was in a potted plant, then on my shirt collar, then beneath the baffles of an air vent.

After a time, the man who was to read to us moved into place. He said hello to the children, coughed his throat clear, and opened his book to the title page: "Chicken Little," he began.

As he read, the sky grew bright with afternoon. The sun came through the windows in a sheet of fire.

Joshua started the second grade in September. His new teacher mailed us a list of necessary school supplies, which we purchased the week before classes began—pencils and a utility box, glue and facial tissues, a ruler and a notebook and a tray of watercolor paints. On his first day, Melissa shot a photograph of Joshua waving to her from the front door, his backpack wreathed over his shoulder and a lunch sack in his right hand. He stood in the flash of hard white light, then kissed her good-bye and joined Rich and Strange in the car pool.

Autumn passed in its slow, sheltering way, and toward the end of November, Joshua's teacher asked the class to write a short essay describing a community of local animals. The paragraph Joshua wrote was captioned "What Happened to the Birds." We fastened it to the refrigerator with magnets.

There were many birds here before, but now there gone. Nobody knows where they went. I used to see them in the trees. I fed one at the zoo when I was litle. It was big. The birds went away when no one was looking. The trees are quiet now. They do not move.

All of this was true. As the object in the sky became visible during the daylight—and as, in the tide of several months, it descended over our town—the birds and migrating insects disappeared. I did not notice they were gone, though, nor the muteness with which the sun rose in the morning, nor the stillness of the grass and trees, until I read Joshua's essay.

The world at this time was full of confusion and misgiving and unforeseen changes of heart. One incident that I recall clearly took place in the Main Street Barber Shop on a cold winter Tuesday. I was sitting in a pneumatic chair while Wesson the barber trimmed my hair. A nylon gown was draped over my body to catch the cuttings, and I could smell the peppermint of Wesson's chewing gum. "So how 'bout this weather?" he chuckled, working away at my crown.

Weather gags had been circulating through our offices and barrooms ever since the object—which was as smooth and reflective as obsidian glass, and which the newspapers had designated "the ceiling"—had descended to the level of the cloud base. I gave my usual response, "A little overcast today, wouldn't you say?" and Wesson barked an appreciative laugh.

Wesson was one of those men who had passed his days waiting for the rest of his life to come about. He busied himself with his work, never marrying, and doted on the children of his customers. "Something's bound to happen soon," he would often say at the end of a conversation, and there was a quickness to his eyes that demonstrated his implicit faith in the proposition. When his mother died, this faith seemed to abandon him. He went home each evening to the small house that they had shared, shuffling cards or paging through a magazine until he fell asleep. Though he never failed to laugh when a customer was at hand, the eyes he wore became empty and white, as if some essential fire in them had been spent. His enthusiasm began to seem like desperation. It was only a matter of time.

"How's the pretty lady?" he asked me.

I was watching him in the mirror, which was both parallel to and coextensive with a mirror on the opposite wall. "She hasn't been feeling too well," I said. "But I think she's coming out of it."

"Glad to hear it. Glad to hear it," he said. "And business at the hardware store?"

I told him that business was fine. I was on my lunch break.

The bell on the door handle gave a tink, and a current of cold air sent a little eddy of cuttings across the floor. A man we had never seen before leaned into the room. "Have you seen my umbrella?" he said. "I can't find my umbrella, have you seen it?" His voice was too loud—high and sharp, fluttery with worry—and his hands shook with a distinct tremor.

"Can't say that I have," said Wesson. He smiled emptily, showing his teeth, and his fingers tensed around the back of my chair.

There was a sudden feeling of weightlessness to the room.

"You wouldn't tell me anyway, would you?" said the man. "Jesus," he said. "You people."

Then he took up the ashtray stand and slammed it against the window.

A cloud of gray cinders shot out around him, but the window merely shuddered in its frame. He let the stand fall to the floor and it rolled into a magazine rack. Ash drizzled to the ground. The man brushed a cigarette butt from his jacket. "You people," he said again, and he left through the open glass door.

As I walked home later that afternoon, the scent of barbershop talcum blew from my skin in the winter wind. The plane of the ceiling was stretched across the firmament, covering my town from end to end, and I could see the lights of a thousand streetlamps caught like constellations in its smooth black polish. It occurred to me that if nothing were to change, if the ceiling were simply to hover where it was forever, we might come to forget that it was even there, charting for ourselves a new map of the night sky.

Mitch Nauman was leaving my house when I arrived. We passed on the lawn, and he held up Bobby's knapsack. "He leaves this thing every-where," he said. "Buses. Your house. The schoolroom. Sometimes I think I should tie it to his belt." Then he cleared his throat. "New haircut? I like it."

"Yeah, it was getting a bit shaggy."

He nodded and made a clicking noise with his tongue. "See you next time," he said, and he vanished through his front door, calling to Bobby to climb down from something.

By the time the object had fallen as low as the tree spires, we had noticed the acceleration in the wind. In the thin strip of space between the ceiling and the pavement, it narrowed and kindled and collected speed. We could hear it buffeting the walls of our houses at night, and it produced a con-stant low sigh in the darkness of movie halls. People emerging from their doorways could be seen to brace themselves against the charge and pres-sure of it. It was as if our entire town were an alley between tall buildings.

I decided one Sunday morning to visit my parents' gravesite: the ceme-tery in which they were buried would spread with knotgrass every spring, and it was necessary to tend their plot before the weeds grew too thick. The house was still peaceful as I showered and dressed, and I stepped as quietly as I could across the bath mat and the tile floor. I watched the water in the toilet bowl rise and fall as gusts of wind channeled their way through the pipes. Joshua and Melissa were asleep, and the morning sun flashed at the horizon and disappeared.

At the graveyard, a small boy was tossing a tennis ball into the air as his mother swept the dirt from a memorial tablet. He was trying to touch the ceiling with it, and with each successive throw he drew a bit closer, until, at the height of its climb, the ball jarred to one side before it dropped. The cemetery was otherwise empty, its monuments and trees the only material presence.

My parents' graves were clean and spare. With such scarce sunlight, the knotgrass had failed to blossom, and there was little tending for me to do. I combed the plot for leaves and stones and pulled the rose stems from the flower wells. I kneeled at the headstone they shared and unfastened a zip-per of moss from it. Sitting there, I imagined for a moment that my par-ents were living together atop the ceiling: they were walking through a field of high yellow grass, beneath the sun and the sky and the tousled white clouds, and she was bending in her dress to examine a flower, and he was bending beside her, his hand on her waist, and they were unaware that the world beneath them was settling to the ground.

When I got home, Joshua was watching television on the living room sofa, eating a plump yellow doughnut from a paper towel. A dollop of jelly had fallen onto the back of his hand. "Mom left to run an errand," he said.

The television picture fluttered and curved for a moment, sending spits of rain across the screen, then it recrystallized. An aerial transmission tower had collapsed earlier that week—the first of many such fallings in our town—and the quality of our reception had been diminishing ever since.

"I had a dream last night," Joshua said. "I dreamed that I dropped my bear through one of the grates on the sidewalk." He owned a worn-down cotton teddy bear, its seams looped with clear plastic stitches, that he had been given as a toddler. "I tried to catch him, but I missed. Then I lay down on the ground and stretched out my arm for him. I was reaching through the grate, and when I looked beneath the sidewalk, l could see another part of the city. There were people moving around down there. There were cars and streets and bushes and lights. The sidewalk was some sort of bridge, and in my dream I thought, 'Oh yeah. Now why didn't I remember that?' Then I tried to climb through to get my bear, but I couldn't lift the grate up."

The morning weather forecaster was weeping on the television.

"Do you remember where this place was?" I asked.

"Yeah."

"Maybe down by the bakery?" I had noticed Melissa's car parked there a few times, and I remembered a kid tossing pebbles into the grate.

"That's probably it."

"Want to see if we can find it?"

Joshua pulled at the lobe of his ear for a second, staring into the middle distance. Then he shrugged his shoulders. "Okay," he decided.

I don't know what we expected to discover there. Perhaps I was simply seized by a whim—the desire to be spoken to, the wish to be instructed by a dream. When I was Joshua's age, I dreamed one night that I found a new door in my house, one that opened from my cellar onto the bright, aseptic aisles of a drugstore: I walked through it, and saw a flash of light, and found myself sitting up in bed. For several days after, I felt a quickening of possibility, like the touch of some other geography, whenever I passed by the cellar door. It was as if I'd opened my eyes to the true inward map of the world, projected according to our own beliefs and understandings.

On our way through the town center, Joshua and I waded past a cluster of people squinting into the horizon. There was a place between the post office and the library where the view to the west was occluded by neither hills nor buildings, and crowds often gathered there to watch the distant blue belt of the sky. We shouldered our way through and continued into town.

Joshua stopped outside the Kornblum Bakery, beside a trash basket and a newspaper carrel, where the light from two streetlamps lensed together on the ground. "This is it," he said, and made a gesture indicating the iron grate at our feet. Beneath it we could see the shallow basin of a drainage culvert. It was even and dry, and a few brittle leaves rested inside it.

"Well," I said. There was nothing there. "That's disappointing."

"Life's disappointing," said Joshua.

He was borrowing a phrase of his mother's, one that she had taken to using these last few months. Then, as if on cue, he glanced up and a light came into his eyes. "Hey," he said. "There's Mom."

Melissa was sitting behind the plate glass window of a restaurant on the opposite side of the street. I could see Mitch Nauman talking to her from across the table, his face soft and casual. Their hands were cupped together beside the pepper crib, and his shoes stood empty on the carpet. He was stroking her left leg with his right foot, its pad and arch curved around her calf. The image was as clear and exact as a melody.

I took Joshua by the shoulders. "What I want you to do," I said, "is knock on Mom's window. When she looks up, I want you to wave."

And he did exactly that—trotting across the asphalt, tapping a few times on the glass, and waving when Melissa started in her chair. Mitch Nauman let his foot fall to the carpet. Melissa found Joshua through the window. She crooked her head and gave him a tentative little flutter of her fingers. Then she met my eyes. Her hand stilled in the air. Her face seemed to fill suddenly with movement, then just as suddenly to empty—it reminded me of nothing so much as a flock of birds scattering from a lawn. I felt a kick of pain in my chest and called to Joshua from across the street. "Come on, sport," I said. "Let's go home."

It was not long after—early the next morning, before we awoke—that the town water tower collapsed, blasting a river of fresh water down our empty streets. Hankins the grocer, who had witnessed the event, gathered an audience that day to his lunch booth in the coffee shop: "I was driving past the tower when it happened," he said. "Heading in early to work. First I heard a creaking noise, and then I saw the leg posts buckling. Wham!"—he smacked the table with his palms—"So much water! It surged into the side of my car, and I lost control of the wheel. The stream carried me right down the road. I felt like a tiny paper boat." He smiled and held up a finger, then pressed it to the side of a half-empty soda can, tipping it gingerly onto its side. Coca-Cola washed across the table with a hiss of carbonation. We hopped from our seats to avoid the spill.

The rest of the town seemed to follow in a matter of days, falling to the ground beneath the weight of the ceiling. Billboards and streetlamps, chimneys and statues. Church steeples, derricks, and telephone poles. Klaxon rods and restaurant signs. Apartment buildings and energy pylons. Trees released a steady sprinkle of leaves and pine cones, then came timbering to the earth—those that were broad and healthy cleaving straight down the heartwood, those that were thin and pliant bending until they cracked. Maintenance workers installed panels of light along the sidewalk, routing the electricity through underground cables. The ceiling itself proved unassailable. It bruised fists and knuckles. It stripped the teeth from power saws. It broke drill bits. It extinguished flames. One afternoon the television antenna tumbled from my rooftop, landing on the hedges in a zigzag of wire. A chunk of plaster fell across the kitchen table as I was eating dinner that night. I heard a board split in the living room wall the next morning, and then another in the hallway, and then another in the bedroom. It sounded like gunshots detonating in a closed room. Melissa and Joshua were already waiting on the front lawn when I got there. A boy was standing on a heap of rubble across the street playing Atlas, his upraked shoulders supporting the world. A man on a stepladder was pasting a sign to the ceiling: SHOP AT CARSON's. Melissa pulled her jacket tighter. Joshua took my sleeve. A trough spread open beneath the shingles of our roof, and we watched our house collapse into a mass of brick and mortar.

I was lying on the ground, a tree root pressing into the small of my back, and I shifted slightly to the side. Melissa was lying beside me, and Mitch Nauman beside her. Joshua and Bobby, who had spent much of the day crawling aimlessly about the yard, were asleep now at our feet. The ceiling was no higher than a coffee table, and I could see each pore of my skin reflected in its surface. Above the keening of the wind there was a tiny edge of sound—the hum of the sidewalk lights, steady, electric, and warm.

"Do you ever get the feeling that you're supposed to be someplace else?" said Melissa. She paused for a moment, perfectly still. "It's a kind of sudden dread," she said.

Her voice seemed to hover in the air for a moment.

I had been observing my breath for the last few hours on the polished undersurface of the ceiling: every time I exhaled, a mushroom-shaped fog would cover my reflection, and I found that I could control the size of this fog by adjusting the force and the speed of my breathing. When Melissa asked her question, the first I had heard from her in many days, I gave a sudden puff of air through my nose and two icicle-shaped blossoms appeared. Mitch Nauman whispered something into her ear, but his voice was no more than a murmur, and I could not make out the words. In a surge of emotion that I barely recognized, some strange combination of rivalry and adoration, I took her hand in my own and squeezed it. When nothing happened, I squeezed it again. I brought it to my chest, and I brought it to my mouth, and I kissed it and kneaded it and held it tight.

I was waiting to feel her return my touch, and I felt at that moment, felt with all my heart, that I could wait the whole life of the world for such a thing, until the earth and the sky met and locked and the distance between them closed forever.

SECOND PRIZE

Scordatura

By Mark Ray Lewis

INTRODUCED BY DAVE EGGERS

First there's the speed of it. The story takes off in a sprint, in a roaring lyrical sentence that travels sixteen lines without a period. On the first page there are maybe three periods. In the entire story, about eleven. And the characters, every one of them, are instantly human and distinct, and, even when the father of a Baptist minister is a pot-smoking beekeeper, completely logical. The story moves at a gallop all the way through, and the ending, even on the third reading, jerks us back and forth twice, drops us, throws us in the air like a baby, and leaves us panting.

It would be easy to make this a story about a sensitive, organ-playing gay man raised by an overbearing and bigoted Baptist minister, and how awful the Baptists are, how intolerant, with a litany of injustices the protagonist, named Oral—utterly perfect—suffers at their hands and his family's. But "Scordatura" is more nuanced. Oral loves his family. His father is funny, his mother is, well, his mother, and his sister, who has had her wilder days, has found God but has not lost her taste for black leather jackets and tight jeans. And then there's the grandfather.

We meet Oral after his lover has died and he's left New York City for Dallas. He spends a month or so at home, playing in his father's church, to his father's congregation, and does so because he loves his father, loves, in varying ways, the members of his father's flock, and loves to play the grand organ at the center of the church, filling it with his unceasing program of Bach, Bach, Bach.

(Scordatura, by the way, refers to a kind of musical fingering, invented centuries ago when the Bavarians needed notation for Scottish stringed instruments. What this has to do with the story I do not know.)

This is a story of a kind of conflict with one's past, but a human and real conflict, many layered and not easy to summarize or solve. Oral does want to rattle the cage he sees around his father and his fellow Baptists, and he has inherent and unfixable problems with his church, with any Christian church, but how to reconcile that with the glory of the music composed in its name? The gay man from New York City who would not find ready acceptance if the congregation knew his orientation fills the church with the cathedral sounds composed as tribute to His greatness.

Finally this is about how those closely surrounding a man who speaks for God—in particular Oral and his grandfather—live while hearing only echoes, and how these who hear dimly ask for, or don't ask for, or resist asking for, forgiveness.

—DAVE EGGERS

Mark Ray Lewis

Scordatura

from *Ontario Review*

WHEN YOU'RE seventeen and you're the gay son of a Baptist preacher from Dallas Texas and you have a lisp and a drawl and a musical gift and you were named Oral because an angel told your daddy to do so in a dream, then New York City can seem like it's saving your life. But when you're twenty-four and an epidemic has claimed all your friends and all your friends' friends including your one-true-love who you abandoned after a final ultimatum seven months before he died because he was drinking two bottles of red wine a day and *not communicating* and only finding out later that he had been HIV positive, and being shunned at the funeral by his hip political activist mom as well as the very last of the mutual friends in favor of his new lover who was only there at the end, and your tests keep coming up negative and your ruddy good health looks back at you from the mirror like a screaming miracle, then, when that happens, New York City can seem small and exhausted.

So after finding the keys and the title left stealthily/anonymously in your mail slot and sitting in his Volvo P-1800 and leaning over and slobbering on the soft vinyl case of the cello in the passenger seat and driving all over New Jersey feeling the vibrations of his beloved Webber fuel injectors, looking for a good cliff to sail off but feeling sure that God would find a way to fuck with you, like He'd catch you halfway down and make you say that you love Him, and returning to your neighborhood and searching for parking and finally you double-park, slosh through the blackened snow, stuff a suitcase full of sheet music and a pair of organ shoes and head for home. It's what anybody might do, including you.

You arrive in the morning feeling long-dead and ready for scraps.

Your house has been converted into a Discipleship House. You knew this but it surprises you again. There are four Christian young men living on bunk beds in your old room and six Christian young women living in the remodeled basement and everyone is assigned a night to make dinner and another night to do the dishes and they smile at you and say sweet simple things and no one in your family asks about Micah, especially not your sister. There's a soundtrack running in your head as usual but this one is especially repetitive, a Philip Glass tape you found in the glove compartment and let loop all the way down the belly of North America. When people talk you smile and nod and treat them like they're speaking in the middle of a concert, or if they start to push it you exit to the piano or go for a walk among the lava rock lawns and naked oaks and blooming Judas trees; it is the most beautiful time of year in Texas. Afternoons you join your mother in the backyard where she is landscaping more ground than ever, as if in response to losing control of the house. She has always preferred to garden in silence. You refuse gloves or tools and go to a corner and dig in the dirt with your soft white fingers, accomplishing little.

You sleep on the long couch in your dad's study where Micah slept when he used to come down with you, before you realized that he enjoyed it all too much—the traditional family and the role of playing your buddy—he treated it all like a big joke, and in response they fell in love with him. Your head is three feet from the computer where your dad files his sermons and behind that a picture of him carrying a football in the same preseason exhibition game that brought him off the bench and clipped his career in the knees, and a black-and-white picture of him standing like Samson between two pillars of the portico of First Baptist and your mom a step below, three months pregnant with your sister Rose, and at the bottom of the picture is JFK and the others in the spotless convertible about to enter a dark canyon formed by Cahill Manufacturing and the Lone Star Bank.

You brought no clothes and it would take two of you to wear your dad's, so you pilfer the closet of dead-guy clothes donated by widows and you imagine you're them, both before and after embalming. You remember that weird Sunday morning scene of walking in on your dad holding a suit coat for Micah to put his arms through and slapping his shoulders, "Perfect fit!" You go to your dad's barber and ask for the same, "the medium cut." You shower two or three times a day and use up to ten Q-tips and trim your nostril hairs and keep the nails at the quick. You sleep for ten-hour stretches. Your cock doesn't wake up at dawn and you don't think you miss it.

Your sister and her husband come over from Southwestern Seminary for dinner on Fridays. She still has her vintage Mustang and long legs and timeless style—the tight jeans and boots and Western shirts and black leather jacket—but the glint of rebellion that was growing in her eyes is completely gone now, as you knew it would be. You remember when she came to visit in New York during spring break of her senior year at Wheaton. You put her up with your friend Exene and she stayed coked to the gills the whole week and one afternoon she walked in on you and Micah—or somebody opened and shut that door—and on the way to the airport Sunday morning you made the mistake of stopping by the Cathedral of St. John the Divine where she started crying and within six months she had rededicated her life.

Before the second Sunday your dad asks you to play a solo and you say yes and get the key to the church and the organ and practice in the crimson-and-white auditorium full of empty wooden pews and curtained on three sides by stained glass. You close your eyes and imagine you're the young J.S. Bach, ten years old, parents both dead, trudging through the dark forest, across meadows and wet marshes, trying not to destroy your leather shoes, miles and miles of silence except for the chattering people, then finally making it to the cathedral at Ohrdruf, and walking through the tall doors and into the huge bright ornate house of God, the music blasting from the tall pipes, the ultimate holiness overpowering you, dropping you to your knees.

Your mother tells you that your grandfather called but you don't call him back, then he leaves a message that he wants you to record what you play in the services. He's been trying to be grandfatherly since you and Micah flew down to play at his wedding when he married Edna Pearl. She was your grandma's best friend and they married less than a year after your grandmother died. Your dad didn't attend the ceremony.

Sunday your dad puts your name in the bulletin and below his own on the marquee out front in bold red letters, big enough that even JFK couldn't have missed them. After the service the old ladies with penciled eyebrows come through the reception line and fall all over you. One says, what about that nice cello player? Another duet sometime?

The next three weeks you stay at the organ through the whole service and your dad asks you to organize the music for the upcoming Easter Sunday. "You love Easter," he says.

"What about Bob Sullivan?" you say.

"He's still the hymn leader," he says. "Unless you can warble and sing out of the side of your mouth like that." He's a joker.

You relish the opportunity to pick only your favorite hymns and organize a total Bach-fest, nothing but Bach for the musically challenged. They'll think they stumbled into Notre Dame.

You ponder the poetry of it: the Crucifixion, the Resurrection, and the Ascension, plus a nod to the Second Coming and the Rapture of the Elect before the Great Tribulation.

Easter Sunday you wake to your dad playing boogie-woogie piano in the living room: *woke up this morning feeling fine, woke up with heaven on my mind.* You vacate the study and you find a bright blue tuxedo coat among the dead men's clothes. It's gotta be forty years old. You match it with some black pants and walking out the door your dad stops you, carrying a bowl of cereal in one hand. Two Christian young women watch him from the table. "You know who that belonged to don't you? Deacon Whiteside. He wore it every Easter too."

"The Bubble Gum Man?" you say, just like a kid.

"Yup. You're asking for it, wearing that."

You stop by a station and spend money for the first time since you've been home. Gas and bubble gum. Standing at the pump you cringe at the clash between the coat and the car's forest green. You stuff the coat pockets with individually wrapped pieces and feel happy, or interested at least, driving the freeways downtown to church. It's sunny and beautiful just like it has been every goddamn Easter Sunday your whole life. Your pockets and your cheeks are full of gum and staying on the right side of the road is no problem, it requires no special concentration. You pull past the marquee bearing the family name twice, as well as a quote from your dad: Jesus Is King, Not Elvis.

You park in a staff-only spot up front and let yourself into the auditorium and practice for a while then you go to the old choir rehearsal room and lock the door until it's time to start playing the intro. On your way back into the auditorium Deacon Meinhart pulls you aside. "Schroeder" he calls you. He says the boss told him to give you the list of announcements and you pick up a bulletin and see that your name is there next to the announcements and you sit down at the organ and read over them. It's a small list of birthdays and hospitalizations, but you should've been asked first. You know exactly what he's doing and he's been doing it your whole life, since even before you were born. The weird thing is that now you don't seem to mind. *So what happened to Oral?* you hear one queer say to another queer at Cafe Pergolesi. *He went back to Dallas to become a preacher.*

You hate public speaking. Besides the speech impediment—which you forget about and some people actually like—you have a fear of losing control of yourself when addressing groups of people larger than, say, five. You like to attribute it to the time you were seven and you performed "We Three Kings" with your best friend Sean and his older brother for a Christmas concert. You and Sean had been covertly wearing panty hose every day for over a month since one Sunday playing at his house between services, he asked if you had ever worn them. No, you said, but you did not laugh at the idea. He pulled up his pant leg to show that he was indeed wearing a pair and he celebrated their warmth and comfortableness. Back at home you stole a pair from your mom's closet and it was December and they were warm, and comfortable, and it was all fine, until the middle of that song when you looked at him and his eyes said, *We're standing here in front of everyone in baggy purple robes and gold painted crowns and underneath it all we're wearing panty hose.* Then you had to stop singing and put your tongue into your lower lip to arrest the laugh and he looked up toward the ceiling lights and let out a painful sort of yelp and you pulled your crown down over your eyes and disintegrated, while his big brother plowed ahead—"field and fountain, moor and mountain, following yonder star."

You push the record button on the cassette player and begin with *Jesu meine Freude* a piece that you memorized a long time ago and you close your eyes and lean into the keys and skip tap on the foot pedals with your soft-soled shoes. Toward the end you hear a voice behind you and you glance back and there's a kid saying "Hey, do you have any gum?" You shift your hips so that your coat pocket slides off the edge of the bench and you nod your head to the side. "Can I have a piece?" the kid asks. "In the pocket," you say. The song is supposed to end but you improvise a coda so the kid will be able to make it back to his seat in time. "Hurry up," you say and you feel the pull of his hand rifling around. The kid is greedy. His hand gets stuck and you have to stop playing and slide off the bench to keep the coat from ripping in half. Pieces of gum fly all over the stairs which causes a riot of children to the front of the auditorium. You empty your other pocket onto the stairs and turn the pockets out to show that you have no more. An adult emerges, gives you a look, and pinches the first kid who approached between the shoulder and neck, leading him out a side door. "Be sure to check for panty hose," you want to call after them, as Micah could've and would've, but not you.

Now it's time for the opening announcements that you never agreed to give and you're not up for it, so you go to your dad, Pastor Paul, sitting in a wooden throne chair to the left of the pulpit and say, "I can't do the announcements. I'll start laughing."

He raises an eyebrow. "Laughter is a good place to start," he says. He holds his hand over his lapel mike. His voice is rich with reverb, like there's a reed in his throat. He's incapable of whispering and as a kid you enjoyed making him try. "Believe it or not, these people enjoy laughter," he says.

Over his shoulder you can see your sister Rose in a choir gown, in the front row, shoulders back, posture perfect. Behind her is the beautiful white alcove where your dad baptized you when you were six. Above the baptismal font hangs a set of the thickest bass pipes, copper tinged with streaks of red-brown and green.

"No, I mean I'll really lose it," you say. "It'll be just like 'We Three Kings.'"

You used the Three Kings excuse once before when you were sixteen and already headed back east and you went to your dad's study less than an hour before the annual all-Youth-led service was to begin in order to tell him you would not be able to preach the sermon. That time it was a lie, but a merciful one.

"I'll take over if that happens," he says.

"No, sir," you say. "You should've asked me first. Maybe next week."

He doesn't say anything but takes the list from you.

You go back to the organ. He approaches the pulpit and sniffs the microphone then sniffs his lapel mike and bends over and sniffs the carpet around the base of the pulpit. A few people in the audience laugh. "What's that smell?" he says. "Oral, do you smell that?"

You ignore him and frown down at the keyboard. You recall a time he took the pulpit after you and Micah played and he said, "Wouldn't that cello player make a fine son-in-law?" The congregation giggled, embarrassed for your sister, who turned red but not as red as you.

He takes a deep whiff and says, "Oh, oh. I'm sorry. I know what that is. Never mind. Deacon Fuller, could you close that door. I can't concentrate with the smell of my daddy's smoker wafting in here." Ha ha ha! Everyone laughs. "Yes that's Graydon tending his brisket, sending his regards down to the house of God. He says he has his calling and I have mine and last week when he invited me over for Easter I just couldn't refuse. The Bible says honor your parents that your days may be long on the earth and this afternoon I plan to do just that. Yes, a second and perhaps a third time, too.

"Wasn't that a fine piece of music Oral played? Purrrr-dee. Uh! I was especially surprised by that ending, that last note in particular. Who would've thought? Those old composers are something else. I mean Mozart and Chopin and whatnot . . . full of surprises." He holds his hand up to his brow and looks out at the congregation. "Are all the little munchkins back in their seats? Yes? We'll give them that one for free. Chalk it up to the Easter Bunny and sensory overload from all the colorful hats you lovely ladies are wearing. Plus Billy should probably get a prize. I don't know if you all made the connection but the legacy of the Bubble Gum Man lives on at First Baptist Dallas. Isn't that right Oral? I believe he's in it for good now. I don't think the munchkins are going to let him back down from his responsibilities hereafter." He holds up the list. "And do we have some birthdays to announce?"

Hymn #481, "Just a Closer Walk with Thee"

Instrumental, "Der Tag der ist so freudenreich" (The Day Which Is So Rich with Cheer) J.S. Bach

Hymn #334, "Blessed Assurance, Jesus Is Mine"

Instrumental, "Wachet Auf, ruft uns die Stimme" (Wake, The Voice Calleth) J.S. Bach

Pastor's Message, "Fourth and One on Your Own Thirty-five"
Scripture, John 16:2

It's not until near the end, actually into the altar call—you're already meandering around the keys to the melody of "Softly and Tenderly"—that he mentions AIDS. It sounds almost like an accident. He's in the middle of an inventory of the obvious signs that the world is coming to an end—war, earthquakes, famine, disease . . . He doesn't say explicitly that it was sent to earth by God as a punishment to homosexuals, though perhaps he's emphasized that enough already. They know what it means—the wages of sin, judgment. You know what he means. But there's a hesitation, an almost-embarrassment in his voice, like he has lost his train of thought for a moment or is uncertain of his pronunciation.

After lunch Edna Pearl and your mom start clearing plates and your grandpa says, "I gotta go take my medicine and check on the bees. Oral? You up for a ride?"

"Sure."

"Bring the tape," he says.

"Well don't take too much of your medicine," Edna Pearl says from the kitchen. "He gets weird when he takes too much of his medicine." No one responds to her, ever.

In the mud room your grandpa stops and says, "Have you had sex recently?"

"No sir," you say.

"That's what I thought," he says. "Me neither. Bees don't like the smell. Too much like bear."

You approach an old blue Dodge. "Four hundred dollars," he says, squaring his body to a side panel and banging it with a hard uppercut. "Army surplus. I think they shot missiles at it, but by God they missed."

There's a wire hat rack with a thick hinge attached to the middle of the ceiling with two dirty cowboy hats in it. "I need one of these for my Volvo," you say.

"That's illegal in Texas," he says. "You have to go to Sweden if you want to do shit like that."

As he drives down a gravel road, he pulls out a pipe and a Baggie of what looks like pot though it couldn't possibly be.

"Smoke a bowl?" he says.

"Good God," you say. "I didn't know you smoked pot."

"I suspect there's a lot you don't know about me," he says. "It's good for the eyes. I try not to enjoy the side effects. My acupuncturist gets it for me."

"Acupuncture?" you say. "What about Shacklee? The vitamins?"

He pulls a bottle of multivitamins out of a pocket in the seat cover. "To keep the wheels from falling off I like a multileveled approach. Smoke?" he says.

"No," you say. By the time you felt ready to allow mind-altering substances into your life, marijuana had become the drug of the dying, a smell linked to the Perry Street Hospice. "I've probably had a contact high."

"Contact high?" he says. "That sounds like an urban myth. Like cows asleep standing up. Maybe narcoleptic cows. Maybe in Oklahoma."

He takes a hit and hands the pipe to you. It's the first time you've ever inhaled smoke, any smoke, directly into your lungs. You remember as a kid taunting the cigarette smokers who'd bolt outside after the church service—you'd brush by them and then cough and gag and fall down dead on the lawn.

"So what's up with your boyfriend?" he says.

You feel a searing in your lungs as you inhale too quickly and begin a coughing fit that lasts a good two minutes.

He pats you on the back with his free hand. "I've awoken a sleeping monster," he says.

You get momentary control and say, "I guess there's a lot you know about me that I didn't know."

"Sure," he says. "I'm your grandpappy. I knew before you were ten years old. And I knew you were in for a hard ride."

"That's impossible," you say. "I didn't know until I was fourteen."

"You think so?" he says. "Different theories, I guess. So it's over with him . . ." He lifts a cassette out of the seat cover and reads it. "Micah."

"Over," you say.

"I'm sorry," he says.

You drive along in silence for a while.

"So," he says. "What is it you are doing now, may I ask? Is this a temporary thing, this living with your parents and devoting yourself to the First Baptist Dallas?"

You shrug.

"Seems kinda strange to me. I mean, from one P.K. to another. You never had the fortune of meeting your great-grandfather. Wonderful man. Used to like to grab me by the hair at the supper table. Sweet. A revivalist. Churches would call him when they wanted to be kicked in the ass. It was all about fire and brimstone, fear. When he visited a church it smoldered for weeks afterward. He could jump-start a dead horse. Shit. Your dad is different. A good guy, all in all. I suspect that makes it more difficult for you in some ways." He turns onto a dirt road. "It's been interesting watching you grow up, Oral. That is until you were fourteen and you stopped talking to me. Typical enough, though I could've done without the 'Meat Is Murder' T-shirts and calling me a butcher and all."

"Morrissey," you say, as an excuse.

"But I don't remember you seeming too happy last time you were living at home and going to church three times a week, that is, right before you went to school up north. You were one wound up little fucker as I recall. But hell, I guess things change . . . people change . . . I don't know . . . Tell me, has the Southern Baptist Convention recently passed a resolution to embrace tolerance? Last time I heard they were packing gay Christians off to sexual reorientation camp. *Re-orientation*," he says again. "Sounds pretty backward ass doesn't it? Pretty sick, actually. But what the hell do I know?"

"I'm like Bach," you say and you let that sink in.

"I don't follow," he says.

"I'm bringing spiritual sustenance to the dark forest." Your voice sounds trite but you go on, "I mean who really knows how Bach felt? What Bach wanted to fuck? No one."

"In other words you enjoy being a song and dance man for bigots, since after all there might be some historical precedent . . ."

"It's a great organ," you say.

"Yeah?" he says.

"In New York I played a 1901 Murray Harris, but only in a tiny sound-proof room. I was limited to two hours. Organs are meant to be played at high volume in large spaces. Preferably a sanctuary."

"Are you sure there's not some sort of charge you're getting out of it? Some sort of, I dunno, like it's a big charade? It seems to me it could only end in disaster for everyone concerned. Especially you."

"I don't have anything better to do right now," you say.

"No?" he says. "Can't think of anything? Bet I could make you a list."

"I'm resting," you say. "Taking a Sabbath."

"Good for you," he says. "But don't fall asleep. I remember how you'd cry as a kid and tell me you didn't want me to burn in hell. You'd get out your little Children's Bible. You could barely read but you'd open it up and point. Jesus Christ, it was unbearable! I mean, just don't forget where you come from." He slows to cross an abandoned railroad track. "Back by the pond near the house there's a certain fence post, a thick irregular one, covered in orange and green lichen, it's nice—I'll show you when we get back. Anyway, I walk out to that post every morning, first thing, before coffee. What do I do there? I don't know but I like to call it 'prayer.' I like the word. Although I'd never use it with your dad or any other Christian—they think they've got the patent. And I pray for you every day," he says.

"Really Grandpa?" you say, and you feel like you're about eight and inside a black-and-white television set. *A boy is drowning Lassie? Ruff! How far away? Ruff, Ruff, Ruff. Three miles? Ruff!* "Good God, I'm stoned," you say. "Good God." It's way too bright in Texas. You open the glove compartment and grab a pair of sunglasses and pull the smaller, inside hat (Edna Pearl's?) out of the hat rack. It's too big for you, but it rests on the top of the sunglasses. A black cow watches the approach of the truck with big mellow eyes and it occurs to you that the son of man never had a grandpa.

You pull past a row of salt licks, white and scooped out like decaying teeth. He backs up to a wooden water tower and cuts the engine but leaves the battery running. "Do you have the tape?" he says.

"Yes."

"Put it in," he says. "I'm going to tell you about the birds and the bees. I need a soundtrack."

"Listen for a funny part at the end of the first chorale prelude," you say.

"Okay," he says. "So. In the hive there are three different castes or groups or what have you. There's the queen—always only one unless there's a big problem going on. There's the worker-bees of which there are lots of subsets: home builders, field workers, nurse bees. They do everything including defending the hive and curing my arthritis with their venomous little kamikaze attacks. Then there's the drones. The drones do almost nothing, the bare minimum, the very least that they can get away with. They consider themselves the proud stewards of the royal jelly and if the hive needs to create a new queen, they have the power to do so. Their whole lives they dream of one day, that is, the day of the mating flight with the queen. Around here it happens in late fall but further north it happens in late summer. I try to wait until after to do my biggest extraction because the bees are most submissive then. It's when there's plenty of honey stored up for winter and things seem pretty calm and stable and the cracks are all caulked with propolis to keep out the weather and basically the workers are tired of taking care of the drones and they don't see the need to do it for another day. So the queen stops laying eggs and puts on something sexy and saunters out to the entrance of the hive and takes flight. Watching this the drones get horny as hell and go scurrying after. The queen flies up and around and around and she lets the drones mount her in midair, one at a time. One would hope that it's the best sex ever because when the drones go to pull out, the queen rips their dicks off with the super strong muscles of her vagina and calmly says, Next. And the next drone in line hops right up. The drone who just lost his dick tries to fly back to the hive—you can imagine it must be a terrible flight—but if he makes it he finds the worker bees are guarding the entrance, Sorry, no admittance. If he is insistent then they will bounce him off the landing board. The queen meanwhile keeps each of these dicks inside her and flies home and somehow catalogs them inside her so that later when she's fertilizing eggs she can actually pick the dick she wants to use."

You've doubled over on the bench seat, "Oh, that's the worst story I've ever heard," you say. "You got me high to tell me that?"

"Think about it. It's a good story. But don't go making a parable out of it. It's just weird, that's all," he says. "Now let's go get some honey."

He leaves the tape playing and the doors open. He opens the tailgate and hands you a safari-looking hat with a net and a pair of long suede gloves. You button the cuffs on your white shirt and tuck your pants into your socks. He takes out a tin cylinder with a spout at the top and bellows attached to the back side. He lights a piece of burlap and stuffs it in. He has you stand aside with your arms in the air and he runs it over your body like a metal detection wand. It makes you feel young and cooperative and a little giddy. He does the same to himself. You hear the end of the prelude and your dad sniffing the mike and joking about the brisket and you look at each other and laugh. You edited out the general announcements and a hymn so the tape goes immediately into the next chorale prelude. He takes a small pry bar out of the truck and holds it up. "The wonder bar," he says. He walks ahead of you past the wooden water tower and past a slimy green pipe dripping water into an old antique clawfoot bathtub.

"You could sell that tub for a lot of money in New York," you say.

"I'm kinda hoping it doesn't come to that," he says.

You go up a muddy cow-churned path and through a small grove of oaks. You can see the hives across a field about a hundred yards away, like stacks of unwrapped presents.

As you cross the field he says, "It's been the warmest winter on record. That means nectar."

He approaches the hives from behind. He takes the tin bellows and smokes the entrance and smokes all around the hives. You don't know why he's doing this but it seems perfect and holy and that association will dominate even later when you have your own hives in San Diego and neighbors call you to get swarms out of trees and you know that the smoke is meant to simulate forest fire. He pulls you to the front of the hive and points out a big odd looking bee. A drone, he mouths through his veil. He takes the wonder bar and pries off the lid of the top super and the air becomes thick and frenetic with loud bees. He leans over and looks in to make sure all the bees have exited through the one-way excluder. He lifts a rack of comb out and it drips with honey. Bees fly all around your head, some land on his bare hands and crawl up his arm. He puts the rack back into the super and points down at a detached abdomen and stinger pumping venom into the underside of his arm. It looks sad and painful but he smiles. Arthritis medicine. He lifts the whole super and hands it to you and it is very heavy with honey. You can feel it in the muscles that line your spine to create the small of your thin back. He puts the lid back onto the top of the hive and points to the truck and asks you with his arms and face if you can carry it okay. No problem, you nod and turn in that direction. He goes along beside you and smokes you with the bellows again, then he turns back to the other hive. After the smoke clears a throng of angry and confused bees begins circling your head and crawling on the net in front of your eyes and your back is aching and your arms are quivering and before you're halfway across the field you know it was a mistake, that you've overestimated your strength, but then you begin to hear the tape playing the faint organ music and you concentrate on the different voices of the melody. *O Mensch bewein deine Sünde gross.* What does that mean? You try to forget about the pain in your arms and back. It's the end of the service. The altar call. The mike is mostly overpowered by the organ but you can hear your dad's voice in the background, tinny and small, not unlike your own voice. You step forward careful on the dry, uneven ground and the sermon that you spent so much time preparing for that youth service begins to play back to you.

Always start with a joke. What joke? The hardest part. Buy a joke book. Find something with a sort of built-in irony to the end, like a boycott of Disney. Make them laugh and slowly hypnotize them and finally make them cringe, that's the idea. Use the *Cruden's Concordance* with the King James. Build a foundation on scripture. Revelations 3:15–16. Red letters: *I would thou wert cold or hot. So then because thou art lukewarm, and neither cold nor hot, I will spew thee out of my mouth.* That's the message to the church at Laodicea. The Lukewarm Church. And that's the message to you. You are the Lukewarm Church, make that clear. *We* are the Laodiceans, the Lukewarm Church. Then a sort of state of the sinful nation, bring in all sorts of random statistics, anything and everything, the decline of our great country through drugs and gangs, the Occult, New Age and prostitution, abortion, infanticide, evolution, uppity women, prayer in schools, whatever. All the favorites. Throw some barbs that indicate the complicity of the church, the middle class, the status quo, backed up with more red ink—Mark 10:25: Easier for a camel to pass through the eye of a needle than a rich fucker . . . etc. But don't dwell on economics too much. Just get the general feeling of culpability. Then back to the decline of the nation. The liberal media, sex on TV, the movies, bad language, the Lord's name in vain, etc. A culture of heathens, turning away from God. Sodom and Gomorrah. Then the big move. Pull the screen down and tell Jeremy (acting as associate pastor) to hit the projector and show the slides of them homosexuals in San Francisco, the Folsom Street Fair, dragging each other around on leashes and chains, the hollow of a butt cheek stark against black leather chaps. And infiltrating the Boy Scouts of America! Sanctioned pedophilia, the Green Party in Germany, etc. Whip them into a frenzy and return again to the Church of Laodicea and the killer Sword Quote which you totally shout: Peace? Peace? No! Not Peace! But a Sword! I came to bring a Sword!

Then when they're really frothing at the mouth the big shocker: And guess what? There's an avowed ho-mo-sexual right here in our midst! Yes. Right here among us, people. Who? Who? Me. I am. That's right. I'm a faggot. Yes, you heard me. Now quick, come forward and kill me. I hate you mediocre fuckers. Your sex is so boring! It's as basic as plumbing! You idiots could never master queer sex, don't try it, you can't even clap through a hymn. So c'mon, stone me! Yes! Kill me!

And those that hadn't fainted already would rise up against you? Slay you?

No.

At first they would probably cheer, thinking you were acting out some live drama. They would chuckle at your squeaky, impeded voice. Then everyone would become embarrassed and ashamed. Silence. A few might laugh uncomfortably. A lone, sincere voice, "God help him." Then another, "Help him, Jesus." A pained, constipated look on the faces of those who thought they knew you, who thought they loved you. Most would stand and turn to go. Yes, the Lukewarm Church. Your dad would be the first to walk out the back door without turning to salt. Deacons would come forward, shaking their heads, disappointed and shy. They'd gently escort you off stage as Bob Sullivan led the remaining members of the congregation in some quiet hymn of mercy, something whiny like "There Is a Fountain."

Later everyone would smile with a wince and treat you like a misfortunate stranger, like a cripple. Someone would hand you the testimony of an ex-gay. Then they'd wait it out until you buckled and the orderlies came to take you away. Only a matter of time.

You are almost to the grove of oaks and the pickup is just below the embankment but you feel exactly like you did the time in eighth grade when you tried out for wrestling and they stuck everyone in a small padded room and cranked the heat up to suck out salt water and you pushed and pulled and pinned and stayed strong until the end and you were standing there listening to the closing remarks of the thick squat coach and next thing you were lying on your back on the mat with everyone in a semicircle above you and the coach was holding your feet off the ground and asking if you remembered your name. Your name? Would that be Oral?

But maybe you could've tapped into that vicious hateful side of them, that current of fear that saturates all of their politics and most of their beliefs . . . pricked the vein of their animalistic nature . . . because they are animals, Jesus came to earth as a man among animals, this you know. You close your eyes and plunge forward and concentrate on your dad's distant voice prophesying the end of time and the chorale prelude from *Das Orgelbuchlein* which means the little organ book and suddenly you see the congregation steaming and boiling and seething hot, rising up in a fury and grabbing anything they can—Bibles, hymnals, keys, lipstick, money clips, shoes, pencils, anything, and they let it all fly as you grip your white pulpit full of honey. Yes! Yes! Finally! Stone me already! Yes! And you fall forward to the ground and roll over onto your back and throw off the veil and laugh and let the Texas sky shine on your hot face as everything flies through the air. You feel the venom pumping into your neck and your cheeks, then a figure stands between you and the sun. Your sister? Finally unable to bear it, rushing forward from the choir loft, awkward in her gown, gesturing with her hands, screaming Enough, No More.

Then you're being lifted out of murky water by big hairy-knuckled hands and strong Texas arms, water in your nose and your ears, and a windy wheezing voice and you know what your name is and your grandfather is saying it, *goddamn, crazy fucking preacher's kid.*

Two years later you get a call with the bad news about your granddad, the heart attack, the hospitalization.

Your friends from the ad department of the free weekly put you on a plane to DFW. At the hospital your dad spots you coming out of the elevator and he breaks from the family and crosses to you with a red, wet face. He pins you in a bear hug and speaks hoarsely into your ear. "It's wonderful. It's so wonderful. God is so *good,* son. My father, your grandfather, he confessed and repented and asked the Lord into his heart only moments before he passed away."

You exit down some stairs and out among the vents on the roof between two wings of the building. You hold your fist up to the blue sky and fast-moving white clouds and the stupid little birds and you say, "I'm so sick of You and Your Fucking Tricks." You see your sister watching you from a room window—serene, expressionless. You crouch at the edge and study the small brown pebbles. "That's it," you say. "I give up."

But it's not true, not for Oral. He gets sixty years of learning how to love this world before the moment he has to leave it.

The Butcher's Wife

By Louise Erdrich

INTRODUCED BY COLSON WHITEHEAD

Why do I like this story? "It's all in the goddam suet." This is the best sentence I've read all year. If I had a side gig in merchandizing, I'd have that slogan on T-shirts and mugs from Venice Beach to St. Marks Place. If I sold suet in a less pious country than this one, I'd fork over the money for the rights and use it in advertising campaigns. That suet would move off the shelves.

I could never be a food critic. I don't have the right adjectives, for one thing. Let's say that the larder is empty except for this sucks, *tastes good, and* yummy. *And then there is the problem of my poor palate, of my inability to understand the complete effects of cumin and thyme. Surely there is a time and place for tarragon, but I have never learned it. The interplay of individual ingredients is beyond me. All I know is that things taste great or things taste terrible. Is "The Butcher's Wife" a rich and satisfying read because of the "antlered and feeble" slugs, or "the Everclear in the gooseberry bush"? Is it the image of Fidelis hoisting the town Sheriff by his teeth and his "deranged eye, straining out of its socket"? Certainly there is a great villain in Tante, and that always spices things up. Maybe it is the capacity of people to surprise you by being unlikely, or the miracle of finding heroism in a pharmacy. Maybe it's all in the goddam suet.*

Every writer has a store of secret ingredients and secret recipes they hold dear. The paradox is that they probably don't even know why their stories end up working out the way they do. Was it the pinch of this or the sprinkling of that? Or just the proper marinating time? It's hard to know why things work out in the end, after all that scribbling and revision. Once the meal is over, all that is certain is that if you've pulled it off, the guests have been well entertained, and well fed. Why do I like this story? Umm, it tastes great. Sometimes when it comes to stories and food, it's best to let your companions try it for themselves.

—COLSON WHITEHEAD

Louise Erdrich

The Butcher's Wife

from *The New Yorker*

Here's an odd and paradoxical truth: a man's experience of happiness can later kill him. Though he appeared to be no more than an everyday drunk, Delphine Watzka's father, Roy, was more. He was a dangerous romantic. In his life, he had loved deeply, even selflessly, with all the profound gratitude of a surprised Pole. But the woman he had loved and married, Minnie Watzka, née Kust, now existed only in the person of her daughter, Delphine, and in photographs. Minnie had died when Delphine was very young, and afterward Roy indulged in a worship of those photographs. Some nights, he lit a line of votive candles on the dresser and drank steadily and spoke to Minnie until, from deep in his cups, she answered.

During the first years after Minnie's death, Roy bounced in and out of drink with the resilience of a man with a healthy liver. He remained remarkably sloshed even through Prohibition by becoming ecumenical. Hair tonic, orange-flower water, cough syrups of all types, even women's monthly elixirs fuelled his grieving rituals. Gradually, he destroyed the organ he'd mistaken for his heart. By the time Delphine reached her twelfth year, her father's need to drink was produced less by her mother's memory than by the drink itself. After that, she knew her father mainly as a pickled wreck. Home was chaos. Now Delphine was a grown woman and he was completely failing. In the spring of 1936, she quit secretarial school and moved back from the Twin Cities to their Minnesota farm to care for him.

As Delphine walked into town for supplies, she thought of her mother. She possessed only one tiny locket photo of Minnie, and while she was away she had found herself missing the other photographs. It was in that fit of longing to see her mother's face that Delphine entered Waldvogel's Meats, and met Eva Waldvogel.

The first true meeting of their minds was over lard.

"I'll take half a pound," Delphine said. She was mentally worn out by her father's insistence that since he was dying anyway he might as well kill himself more pleasurably with schnapps. All day long he'd been drunk underneath the mulberry trees, laughing to himself and trying to catch the fruit in his mouth. He was now stained purple with the juice.

"There's lard and there is lard." Eva reached into the glass case that was cooled by an electric fan. "My husband was trained back in Germany as a master butcher, and he uses a secret process to render his fat. Taste," she commanded, holding out a small pan. Delphine swiped a bit with the tip of her finger.

"Pure as butter!"'

"We don't salt it much," Eva whispered, as though this were not for just anyone to overhear. "But it won't keep unless you have an icebox."

"I don't have one," Delphine admitted. "Well, I did, but my dad sold it while I was away."

"Who is he, may I ask?"

Delphine liked Eva's direct but polite manners and admired her thick bun of bronze-red hair stuck through with two yellow lead pencils. Eva's eyes were a very pale, washed-out blue with flecks of green. There was, in one eye, an odd golden streak that would turn black when the life finally left her body, like a light going out behind the crack in a door.

"Roy Watzka," Delphine said slowly.

Eva nodded. The name seemed to tell her all that she needed to know. "Come back here." Eva swept her arm around the counter. "I'll teach you to make a mincemeat pie better than you've ever eaten. It's all in the goddam suet."

Delphine went behind the counter, past an office cascading with papers and bills, past little cupboards full of clean aprons and rags, and a knickknack shelf displaying figures made of German porcelain. She and Eva entered the kitchen, which was full of light from big windows set into the thick walls. Here, for Delphine, all time stopped. As she took in the room, she experienced a profound and fabulous expansion of being.

There was a shelf for big clay bread bowls and a pull-out bin containing flour. Wooden cupboards painted an astounding green matched the floor's linoleum. A heavy, polished meat grinder was bolted to the counter. The round table was covered with a piece of oilcloth with squares. In each red-trimmed square was printed a bunch of blue grapes or a fat pink-gold peach, an apple or a delicate green pear. On the windowsills, pots of geraniums bloomed, scarlet and ferociously cheerful.

Suddenly extremely happy, Delphine sat in a solid, square-backed chair while Eva spooned roasted coffee beans into a grinder and then began to grind them. A wonderful fragrance emerged. Delphine took a huge breath. Eva, her hands quick and certain, dumped the thin wooden drawer full of fresh grounds into a pale-blue speckled enamel coffeepot. She got water from a faucet in her sink, instead of from a pump, and then she put the coffee on the stove and lit the burner of a stunning white gas range with chrome trim swirled into the words "Magic Chef."

"My God," Delphine breathed. She couldn't speak. But that was fine, for Eva had already whipped one of the pencils out of her hair and taken up a pad of paper to set down the mincemeat recipe. Eva spoke English very well but her writing was of the old, ornate German style, and she wasn't a good speller. Delphine was grateful for this tiny flaw, for Eva appeared so fantastically skilled a being, so assured—she was also the mother of two sturdy and intelligent sons—that she would have been an unapproachable paragon to Delphine otherwise. Delphine—who had never really had a mother, much less a sister, who cleaned up shameful things in her father's house, who had been toughened by cold and hunger and was regarded as beneath notice by the town's best society, and yet could spell—stole confidence from the misspelled recipe.

The next time Delphine visited the Waldvogels' store, she noted the jangle of a cheerful shop bell. She imagined that it was only the first of many times that she would ring the bell as she entered the shop. This did not prove to be the case. By the next time Delphine came to the shop, she had already attained a status so familiar that she entered by the back door.

Delphine placed her order, as before, and, as before, Eva asked her to come in and sit down for a coffee. There was no cleanser on Eva's shelf that would be strong enough for the work Delphine had to do to make Roy's place habitable again, and Eva wanted to concoct something of her own.

"First off, a good vinegar-and-water washdown. Then I should order the industrial-strength ammonia for you, only be careful with the fumes. Maybe, if that doesn't work, a very raw lye."

Delphine shook her head. She was smitten with shame, and could not tell Eva that she was afraid her father might try to drink the stuff. Eva sipped her coffee. Today, her hair was bound back in a singular knot, in the shape of a figure eight, which Delphine knew was the ancient sign for eternity. Eva rose and turned away, walked across the green squares of linoleum to punch down the risen dough. As Delphine watched, a strange notion popped into her head, the idea that perhaps the most strongly experienced moments—such as this one, when Eva turned, and the sun met her hair, and for that one instant the symbol blazed out—those particular moments were eternal. They actually went somewhere—into a file of moments that existed beyond time's range and could not be pilfered by God.

Well, it *was* God, wasn't it, Delphine went on stubbornly, who had made time and thereby created the end of everything? Tell me this, Delphine wanted to say to her new friend, why are we given the curse of imagining eternity when we can't experience it, when we ourselves are so finite? She wanted to say it, but suddenly grew shy, and it was in that state of concentrated inattention that she first met Eva's husband, Fidelis Waldvogel, Master Butcher.

Before she actually met him, she sensed him, like a surge of electric power in the air when the clouds are low. Then she felt a heaviness. A field of gravity moved through her body. She was trying to rise, to shake the feeling, when he suddenly filled the doorway.

It was not his size. He was not extraordinarily tall or broad. But he shed power, as though there were a bigger man crammed into him. One thick hand hung down at his side like a hook; the other balanced on his shoulder a slab of meat. That cow's haunch weighed perhaps a hundred pounds or double that. He held it lightly, although the veins in his neck throbbed, heavy-blooded as a bull's. He looked at Delphine, and his eyes were white-blue. Their stares locked. Delphine's cheeks went fever red, and she looked down first. Clouds moved across the sun, and the red mouths of the geraniums on the windowsill yawned. The shock of his gaze caused her to pick up one of Eva's cigarettes. To light it. He looked away from her and conversed with his wife. Then he left without asking to be introduced.

That abruptness, though rude, was more than fine with Delphine. Already, she didn't want to know him. She hoped that she could avoid him. It didn't matter, so long as she could still be friends with Eva, and hold the job that she soon was offered, waiting on customers.

So it was. From then on, Delphine used the back door, which led past the furnace and the washtubs, the shelves of tools, the bleached aprons slowly drying on racks and hooks. She walked down the hallway cluttered with papers and equipment and lifted from a hook by the shop door the apron Eva had given her, blue with tiny white flowers. From then on, she heard the customer bell ring from the other side of the counter.

Within a week, Delphine had met most of the regular customers. Then she met Tante Marie-Christine, who was not a customer but Fidelis's sister. One afternoon, Tante swept in with just one clang of the bell, as though the bell itself had been muted by her elegance. She went right around to the case that held the sausage, wrenched it open, fished out a ring of the best bologna, and put it in her purse. Delphine stood back and watched—actually, she stood back and envied the woman's shoes. They were made of a thin, flexible Italian leather and were cleverly buttoned. They fit Tante's rather long, narrow feet with a winsome precision. She might not have had a captivating face—for she resembled her brother, replicated his powerful neck and too stern chin, and the eyes that on him were commanding on her were a ghostly blue that gave Delphine the shivers—but her feet were slim and pretty. She was vain about them, and all her shoes were made of the most expensive leather.

"Who are you?" Tante asked, rearing her head back and then swirling off in her fur coat without deigning to accept an answer. The question hung in the air long after Tante had gone back to invade Eva's kitchen. "Who are you?" is a question with a long answer or a short answer. When Tante dropped it in the air like that, Delphine was left to consider its larger meaning as she scrubbed down the meat counters and prepared to mop the floor.

Who are you, Delphine Watzka, you drunkard's child, you dropout secretary, you creature with a belly of steel and a heart that longs for a mother? Who are you, *what* are you—born a dirty Pole in a Polack's dirt? You with a cellar full of empty bottles and a stewed father lying on the floor? What makes you think you belong anywhere near this house, this shop, and especially my brother Fidelis, who is the master of all that he does?

When Tante swept back out with a loaf of her sister-in-law's fresh bread under her arm, and grabbed a bottle of milk, Delphine wrote it all down on a slip: "Tante took a bottle of milk, a ring of number-one bologna, and a loaf of bread." And she left it at that. When Tante found out that Delphine had written the items down, she was furious. Tante didn't take things. By her reckoning, she was owed things. She had once given her brother five hundred dollars to purchase equipment, and although he had paid her back she continued to take the interest out in ways that were intended to remind him of her dutiful generosity.

Eva's two boys, Franz and Louis, did not like Tante. Delphine could see that. Not that she knew all that much about children. She had not been around them often. But, as these boys belonged to Eva, she was interested in who they were.

At fourteen, Franz was strong and athletic, with one of those proud, easygoing American temperaments that are simultaneously transparent and opaque. His inner thoughts and feelings were either nonevident or nonexistent; she couldn't tell which. He always smiled at her and said hello, with only the faintest of German accents. He played football and was, in fact, a local hero. The second boy was more reclusive. Louis had a philosophical bent and a monkish nature, though he'd play with tough abandon when he could. His grades were perfect for one year, and abysmal the next, according to his interests. He had inherited his mother's long hands, her floss of red-gold hair, her thin cheeks, and eyes that looked out sometimes with a sad curiosity and amusement, as if to say, What an idiotic spectacle. Louis was polite, though more restrained than his brother. He anxiously accomplished errands for his father, but he clearly doted on his mother. Eva often stroked his hair, so like her own, with its curls clipped. When she held him close and kissed him, he pulled away, as boys had to, but did it gently, to show that he didn't want to hurt her feelings.

Nineteen thirty-six was a year of extremes. That winter, Minnesota had endured a bout of intense cold. Now it sucked in its breath and wilted in a brutal heat. As the heat wave wore on, cleaning became more difficult. Eva

Waldvogel, who prided herself on triumphing over anything that circumstance brought her way, could not keep the shop functioning with the efficiency she usually demanded. Now that Delphine was around Eva from the early morning on, she could see how her friend suffered. Eva's face was pale with the daily effort and sometimes she announced that she had to lie down, just for a minute, and rest. When Delphine checked on her, she often found Eva in such a sunken dead shock of slumber that she didn't have the heart to wake her. After an hour or two, Eva woke anyway, in a frenzy of energy, and pushed herself again.

They mopped down the floors of the slaughter room with bleach every single day. The meat cases were run on full cold, yet they were lukewarm and the meat within had to be checked constantly for rot. They bought only the smallest amount of milk to sell because it often soured during the drive to the store. They kept little butter or lard. The heat kept getting worse. The boys slept outside on the roof in just their undershorts. Eva dragged a mattress and sheets up there, too, and slept with them while Fidelis stayed downstairs, near his gun, for fear of a break-in.

When Delphine walked to work, just an hour after sunrise, the air was already stiff and metallic. If it broke, it would break violently, Fidelis said, to no one in particular. As he systematically sharpened the blades of his knives and saws, his back turned, he started singing, and Delphine realized, with a strange shock, that his voice was very beautiful. The heat made her flustered, and his voice dismayed her, so pure in a room that was slippery with blood. Sharply, she banged a ham down on the metal counter, and he went silent. It was a relief not to have to listen.

The sky went dark, the leaves turned brown, and nothing happened. Rain hung painfully nearby in an iron-gray sheet that stretched across the sky, but nothing moved. No breeze. No air. Delphine washed her face and donned the limp apron by the door. Late in the day, she stripped the wax off the linoleum in order to apply a new coat. The floor was already dry when she flipped the cardboard sign in the entry window from "Open" to "Closed." Now, in a special bucket, she mixed the wax and with a long brush painted the floor, back to front, in perfect swipes. She painted herself right up to the counter, put a box in the doorway so that the boys would not ruin the drying surface. She retreated. Hung up her apron, said a quick goodbye, and went home to swelter. Early the next morning, before the store opened, she'd return and apply another coat. Let it dry while she drank her morning coffee with Eva. Then, between customers, she'd polish that linoleum to a mighty finish with a buffing rag and elbow grease. That's what she had planned, anyway, and all that she had planned did occur, but over weeks and under radically different circumstances.

The next morning, while Delphine sat in the kitchen, the heat pushed at the walls. The strong black coffee sent her into a sweat. She drank from a pitcher of water that Eva had set on the table.

"Listen." Eva had been awake most of the night, doing her weekly baking in the thread of cool air. "I don't feel so good."

She said this in such an offhand way that Delphine hardly registered the words, but then she repeated herself as though she did not remember having said it. "I don't feel so good," Eva whispered. She put her elbows on the table and her hands curled around her china cup.

"What do you mean you don't feel so good?"

"It's my stomach. I get pains. I'm all lumped up." Beads of sweat trembled on her upper lip. "They come and go." Eva drew a deep breath and held it, then let it out. *There.* She pressed a dish towel to her face, blotted away the sweat. "Like a cramp, but I'm never quite over the monthly . . . That comes and goes, too."

"Maybe you're just stopping early?"

"I think so," Eva said. "My mother . . ." But then she shook her head and smiled, spoke in a high, thin voice. "Don't you hate a whiner?"

She jumped up awkwardly, banging herself against the counter, but then she bustled to the oven, moved swiftly through the kitchen, as though motion would cure whatever it was that had gripped her. Within moments, she seemed to have turned back into the unworried, capable Eva.

"I'm going out front to start polishing the floor," Delphine said. "By now, in this heat, it's surely dry."

"That's good," Eva said, but as Delphine passed her to put her coffee cup in the gray soapstone sink, the butcher's wife took one of Delphine's hands in hers. Lightly, her voice a shade too careless, she said the words that even in the heat chilled her friend.

"Take me to the doctor."

Then she smiled as though this were a great joke, lay down on the floor, closed her eyes, and did not move.

Fidelis had left early on a delivery, and he could not be found. He wasn't home, either, when Delphine returned from the doctor's. By then, she had

Eva drugged with morphine in the back seat, and a sheaf of instructions telling her whom to seek. What could possibly be done. Old Dr. Heech was telephoning the clinic to tell a surgeon he knew there to prepare for a patient named Eva Waldvogel.

Delphine found Louis and gave him a note for Fidelis. Louis dropped it, picked it up, his lithe boy's fingers for once clumsy with fright. He ran straight out to the car and climbed into the back seat, which was where Delphine found him, holding Eva as she sighed in the fervent relief of the drug. She was so serene that Louis was reassured and Delphine was able to lead him carefully away, terrified that Eva would suddenly wake, in front of the boy, and recognize her pain. From what Delphine had gathered so far, Eva must have been suffering for many months now. Her illness was remarkably advanced, and Heech in his alarm, as well as his fondness for Eva, scolded her with the violent despair of a doctor who knows he is helpless.

As Delphine led Louis back to the house, she tried to stroke his hair. He jerked away in terror at the unfamiliar tenderness. It was, of course, a sign to him that something was really wrong with Eva.

"Fidelis," Delphine had written in the note, "I have taken Eva to the clinic to the south called the Mayo, where Heech says emergency help will be found. She passed out this morning. It is a cancer. You can talk to Heech."

It was on the drive down to the Mayo Clinic that Delphine first really listened to the butcher's singing; only this time it was in her mind. She replayed it like a comforting record on a phonograph as she kept her foot calmly on the gas pedal of Dr. Heech's DeSoto and the speedometer hovered near eighty miles an hour. The world blurred. Fields turned like spoked wheels. She caught the flash of houses, cows, horses, barns. Then there was the long stop-and-go of the city. All through the drive, she replayed the song that Fidelis had sung just the morning before, in the concrete of the slaughter room, when she had been too crushed by the heat to marvel at the buoyant mildness of his tenor. "*Die Gedanken sind frei,*" he had sung, and the walls had spun each note higher, as if he were singing beneath the dome of a beautiful church. Who would think that a slaughterhouse would have the acoustics of a cathedral?

The song wheeled in her thoughts as she drove, and using what ragtag German she knew, Delphine made out the words: "*Die Gedanken sind frei, / Wer kann sie erraten, / Sie fliehen vorbei, / Wie nächtliche Schatten*"—

"Thoughts are free . . . they fly around like shadows of the night." The dead crops turned, row by row, in the fields, the vent blew the hot air hotter, and the wind boomed into the open windows. Even when it finally started to rain, Delphine did not roll the windows back up. The car was moving so fast that the drops stung like BBs on the side of her face and kept her alert. Occasionally, behind her, Eva made sounds. Perhaps the morphine, as well as dulling her pain, had loosened her self-control, for in the wet crackle of the wind Delphine heard a moan that could have come from Eva. A growling, as though her pain were an animal she had wrestled to earth.

The first treatment after Eva's surgery consisted of inserting into her uterus several hollow metal bombs, cast of German silver, containing radium. During the weeks that Eva spent in the hospital, the tubes were taken out, refilled, and reinserted several times. By the time she was sent home, she smelled like a blackened pot roast.

"I smell burned," she said, "like bad cooking. Get some lilac at the drugstore." Delphine bought a great purple bottle of flower water to wash her with, but it didn't help. For weeks, Eva passed charcoal and blood, and the smell lingered. The cancer spread. Next, Dr. Heech gave her monthly treatments of radium via long twenty-four-karat-gold needles, tipped with iridium, that he pushed into the new tumor with forceps so as not to burn his fingers. She took those treatments in his office, strapped to a table, dosed with ether for the insertion, then, after she woke, with a hypodermic of morphine. Delphine sat with her, for the needles had to stay in place for six hours.

"I'm a damn pincushion now," Eva said once, rousing slightly. Then she dropped back into her restless dream. Delphine tried to read, but shooting pains stabbed her own stomach when the needles went in; she even had a sympathetic morphine sweat. But she kept on going, and as she approached the house each day she said the prayer to God that she'd selected as the most appropriate to the situation: "Spit in your eye." The curse wasn't much, it didn't register the depth of her feeling, but at least she was not a hypocrite. Why should she even pretend to pray? That was Tante's field.

Tante had mustered a host of pious Lutheran ladies, and they came around every few afternoons to try to convert Eva, who was Catholic.

Once Eva became too weak to chase them off, Delphine did whatever she could think of to keep them from crowding around the bed like a flock of turkey vultures in a gloating prayer circle. Feeding them was her best strategy, for they filed out quickly enough when they knew that there was grub in the kitchen. After they'd gorged on Eva's pain and her signature Linzer torte, the recipe for which she'd given to Delphine, Tante would lead them away one small step at a time.

Delphine bleached the bloody aprons. She scrubbed the grimy socks. The boys' stained drawers and their one-strap overalls. She took their good suits out of mothballs and aired and pressed them. She sprinkled Fidelis's thick white cotton shirts with starch and every morning she ironed one for him, just as Eva had done. She took on the sheets, the sweat, the shit, and the blood, always blood. The towels and the tablecloths. Doing this laundry was a kind of good-bye gift. For once Eva left, Delphine would be leaving, too. Fidelis had others to help him. Tante, Delphine was sure, would find stepping in to care for the boys and her brother a perfect showcase for her pieties.

For all that he was a truly unbearable souse, no one in town disliked Roy Watzka. There were several reasons for this. First, his gross slide into abandon had been triggered by loss. That he had loved to the point of self-destruction fed a certain reflex feature in many a female heart, and he got handouts easily when strapped. Women made him sandwiches of pork or cold beans, and wrapped them carefully for him to eat when coming off a binge. Another reason was that Roy Watzka, during those short, rare times when he was sober, had a capacity for intense bouts of hard labor. He could work phenomenally. Plus, he told a good tale. He was not a mean drunk or a rampager, and it was well known that, although she certainly put up with more than a daughter should ever have to, he did love Delphine.

Eva liked him, or felt sorry for him, anyway, and she was one of those who had always given him a meal. Now that she was in trouble, Roy showed up for a different purpose. He came to the shop almost every afternoon, sometimes stinking of schnapps. But, once there, he'd do anything. He'd move the outhouse, shovel guts. Before he left, he'd sit with Eva and tell her crazy stories about the things that had happened to him as a young man: the pet hog he'd trained to read, how to extract the venom from a rattlesnake, the actual wolf-man he'd once known who taught him words in the Lycanthropian language, or the Latin names of flowers and where they came from. Listening sometimes, Delphine was both glad of Roy's adept distractions and resentful. Where had he learned these things? In bars, he said. She'd cleaned up after him all her life and never had he talked to her like this.

Delphine and Eva sat together on broken chairs in Eva's garden, each with a bottle of Fidelis's earth-dark, home-brewed beer held tight between their feet. They were protected from the mosquitos by citronella burning in a bucket, and sprigs of basil which Eva snapped off and thrust into their hair. Delphine wore a wash dress and an apron and a pair of low green pumps. Eva wore a nightgown and a light woollen shawl, with her feet bare in Japanese thongs. The slugs were naked. Antlered and feeble, they lived in the thickness of hay and the shredded newspapers that Eva had put down for mulch. They had already eaten many of the new seedlings from the topmost leaves down to the ground, and Eva had vowed to destroy them.

"Their last feast," she said, gesturing at her bean plants as she poured a little beer into a pie plate. "Now, they are doomed."

The beer was chilled from the glass refrigerator case in the store, newly installed. It seemed a shame to waste it on slugs. The two women sipped it slowly as the sun slanted through the margins of the stock pens.

"Maybe we should simply have shrivelled them with salt," Delphine said. But then she had a thought: We are close to Eva's own death, and can afford to make death easy on the helpless. She said nothing.

Eva's garden, Delphine had decided, reflected the dark underside of her organizational genius. It was everything raw and wild that Eva was not. It had grown rich on junk. Pot scrapings, tea leaves, and cucumber peelings all went into the dirt, buried haphazardly, sometimes just piled. Everything rotted down beneath the blistering Minnesota sun. Eva's method was to have no method. Give nature its head. She had apple trees that grew from cores. Rosebushes, bristling near the runner that collected steer's blood, were covered with blooms so fat and hearty that they looked sinister. The boys' dog dug up old bones that some former dog had buried and refused to rebury them. It would be awful in the spring, Delphine thought, when the snow melted away, to see the litter of femurs and clavicles, the knobs and knuckles. As if the scattered dead, rising to meet the Judgment, had had to change and swap their parts to fit.

Delphine had always had a tendency to think about fate, but she did so more often now that Eva's sickness put her constantly in mind of mortality, and also made her marvel at how anyone managed to live at all. Life was a precious feat of daring, she saw, improbable, as strange as a feast of slugs.

Eva bent over, flipped out a small pocket of earth with her trowel, and tamped in her quarter-full beer bottle as a trap. "Die happy," she encouraged. Delphine handed over her own three-quarters-drunk bottle, too. This one Eva planted by a hill of squash that would overpower the rest of the garden by fall, though she would not be there to see it. She settled back against the crisscrossed canvas webbing of her chair and forked open another bottle. It was a good day, a very good day for her.

"I'm going," Delphine said, but she continued to sit with Eva through sunset and on into the rising dark. It was as if they knew that no moment of the weeks to come would be this peaceful and that they would both, in fearful nights, remember these hours. How the air turned blue around them and the moths came out, invisible and sightless, flapping against the shuttered lamp at the other end of the yard.

Delphine shut her eyes, and her mind grew alert. All around her, she felt how quickly things formed and were consumed. It was going on beyond the wall of her sight, out of her control. She felt as though she could drift away like a boat of skin, never to return, leaving only her crumpled dress and worn green shoes.

She heard Eva's voice.

"I wish it were true, what I read—that the mind stays intact. The brain. The eyes to read with."

Delphine had sometimes thought that her friend didn't care if she became an animal or a plant, if all this thinking and figuring and selling of pork and blood meal were wasted effort. She treated her death with scorn or ridicule. But with that statement Eva revealed a certain fear she'd never shown before. Or a wistfulness.

"Your mind stays itself," Delphine said, as lightly as she could. "There you'll be, strumming on your harp, looking down on all the foolish crap people do."

"I could never play the harp," Eva said. "I think they'll give me a kazoo."

"Save me a cloud and I'll play a tune with you," Delphine said.

It wasn't very funny, so they laughed all the harder, laughed until tears started in their eyes, then they gasped and fell utterly silent.

"The boys are playing in the orchard. The men are already half lit," Delphine reported. It was the first weekend in September, a holiday. Eva struggled and Delphine helped her to sit up and look out the window of the little room off the kitchen where Fidelis had set up her bed. Eva smiled faintly, then fell back, nodding at the sight.

"Men are such fools," she whispered. "They think they're so smart hiding the Everclear in the gooseberry bush."

There was no saving her. They were well beyond that now. But even though the last few days were nightmarish Eva refused to die in a morbid way. She sometimes laughed freakishly at pain and made fun of her condition, more so now when the end was close.

They'd closed the shop at noon. Now everyone in town was celebrating. Fidelis had the old chairs and table out in the yard and on the table he had a summer sausage and a beer sausage, a watermelon, bowls of crackers, and beer in a tub of ice underneath the tomato plants, to wash down the high-proof alcohol that Eva knew he was hiding. Over and over the men sneaked their arms into the gooseberry fronds. With a furtive look at the house, they'd tip the bottle to their lips. Even Fidelis, normally so powerful and purposeful, acted like a guilty boy.

The men's voices rose and fell, rumbling with laughter at the tall tales they told, stern with argument at the outrages committed by the government, and sometimes they even fell silent and gazed stuporously into the tangled foliage. Roy was out there, trying to nurse along a beer, not gulp. As always, Fidelis was at the center of the gathering, prodding ever bolder stories out of the men or challenging them to feats of strength.

In the kitchen, Delphine cut cold butter into flour for a pastry. She had decided to make pies for the holiday supper—the men would need them to counteract the booze. The potatoes were boiling now, and she had a crock of beans laced with hot mustard, brown sugar, and blackstrap molasses. There were, of course, sausages. Delphine added a pinch of salt, rolled her dough in waxed paper, and set it in the icebox. Then she started on the fruit, slicing thin moons from the crate of peaches, peeling out the brownest bits of rosy flesh. It's nearly time, she thought, nearly time. She was thinking of Eva's pain. Delphine's sense of time passing had to do only with the duration of a dose of opium wine, flavored with cloves and cinnamon, or of the morphine that Dr. Heech had taught her to administer, though he warned her not to give too much, lest by the end even the morphine lose its effect.

Hearing Eva stir, Delphine set aside her pie makings. She put some water on to boil, to sterilize the hypodermic needle. Last night, she'd prepared a vial and set it in the icebox, the 1:30 solution, which Heech had told her she was better than any nurse at giving to Eva. Delphine was proud of this. The more so because she secretly hated needles, abhorred them, grew sickly hollow when she filled the syringe, and felt the prick in her own flesh when she gave the dose to Eva.

Now she knew, when she checked on Eva, not so much by the time elapsed as by the lucid shock of agony in Eva's stare, her mouth half open, her brows clenched, that she would need the relief very soon, as soon as the water had boiled. Delphine thought to divert her friend by massaging her sore hands.

Eva groaned as Delphine worked the dips between her knuckles, and then her forehead smoothed, her translucent eyelids closed over, she began to breathe more peacefully and said, softly, "How are the damn fools?"

Delphine glanced out the window and observed that they were in an uproar. Sheriff Hock had now joined them, and Fidelis was standing, gesturing, laughing at the big man's belly. Then they were all comparing their bellies. In the lengthening afternoon light, Fidelis's face was slightly fuzzy with the unaccustomed drink, and with the fellowship of other men, too, for lately he had been isolated in Eva's struggle to die.

"They're showing off their big guts to each other," Delphine said.

"At least not the thing below," Eva croaked.

"Oh, for shame!" Delphine laughed. "No, they've kept their peckers in. But something's going on. Here, I'm going to prop you up. They're better than burlesque."

She took down extra pillows from the shelves, shoved the bed up to the window, and propped Eva where she would see the doings in the yard. Now it looked like they were making and taking bets. Bills were waved. The men weren't stumbling drunk, but loud drunk. Roaring with jokes. All of a sudden, with a clatter, the men cleared the glasses and bottles, the crackers and the sticks of sausage, the bits of cheddar and the plates off the table. And then the Sheriff, a former actor who'd played large characters in local productions, lay down upon it on his back. He was longer than the table, and he balanced there, like a boat in dry dock, his booted feet sticking absurdly straight up and his head extended off the other end. His stomach made a mound. Now on the other side of the table, directly beneath Eva's window, stood Fidelis. He'd unbuttoned the top buttons of his white shirt and rolled his sleeves up over his solid forearms.

Suddenly, Fidelis bent over Sheriff Hock in a weightlifter's crouch and threw his arms fiercely out to either side. Delicately, firmly, he grasped in his jaws a loop that the women now saw had been specially created for this purpose in Sheriff Hock's thick belt.

There was a moment in which everything went still. Nothing happened. Then, a huge thing happened. Fidelis gathered his power. It was as if the ground itself flowed up through him, and flexed. His jaws flared bone-white around the belt loop, his arms tightened in the air, his neck and shoulders swelled impossibly, and he lifted Sheriff Hock off the table. With the belt loop in his teeth, he moved the town's Falstaff. Just a fraction of an inch. Then Fidelis paused. His whole being surged with a blind, suffusing ease. He jerked the Sheriff higher, balancing now, half out of the crouch.

In that moment of tremendous effort, Delphine saw the butcher's true face—his animal face, his ears flaming with heat, his neck cords popping—and then his deranged eye, straining out of its socket, rolled up to the window to see if Eva was watching. That's when Delphine felt a thud of awful sympathy. He was doing this for Eva. He was trying to distract her, and Delphine suddenly understood that Fidelis loved Eva with a helpless and fierce canine devotion, which made him do things that seemed foolish. Lift a grown man by the belt with his teeth. A stupid thing. Showing clearly that all his strength was nothing. Against her sickness, he was weak as a child.

Once Fidelis had dropped the Sheriff, to roars of laughter, Delphine went back into the kitchen to fetch the medicine. She opened the door of the icebox. Looked once, then rummaged with a searching hand. The morphine that Fidelis had labored with vicious self-disregard to pay for and which Delphine had guarded jealously was gone. The vial, the powder, the other syringe. She couldn't believe it. Searched once again, and then again. It wasn't there, and already Eva was restless in the next room.

Delphine rushed out and beckoned Fidelis away from the men. He was wiping down his face and neck, the sweat still pouring off him.

"Eva's medicine is gone."

"Gone?"

He was not as drunk as she'd imagined, or maybe the effort of lifting the Sheriff had sobered him.

"Gone. Nowhere. I've looked. Someone stole it."

"*Heiliges Kreuz Donnerwetter . . .*" he began, whirling around. That was just the beginning of what he had to say, but Delphine left before he got any further. She went back to Eva and gave her the rest of the opium wine. Spoon by spoon it went down; in a flash it came back up. "What a mess," Eva said. "I'm worse than a puking baby." She tried to laugh, but it came out a surprised, hushed groan. And then she was gasping, taking the shallow panting breaths she used to keep herself from shrieking.

"*Bitte . . .*" Her eyes rolled back and she arched off the bed. She gestured for a rolled-up washcloth to set between her teeth. It was coming. It was coming like a mighty storm in her. No one could stop it from breaking. It would take hours for Delphine to get another prescription from Dr. Heech, wherever he happened to be celebrating the holiday, and then to find the pharmacist. Delphine yelled out the garden door to Fidelis, and then sped out the other way. As she ran, a thought came into her mind. She decided to act on it. Instead of steering straight for Heech she gunned the shop's truck and stopped short at Tante's little closet of a house, two blocks from the Lutheran church, where Tante prayed every Sunday that the deplorable Catholic her brother had married desist from idolatry— saint worship—before her two nephews were confirmed.

"*Was wollen Sie?*"

When Tante opened the door to Delphine, her face had all the knowledge in it, and Delphine knew she'd guessed right. Delphine had remembered her clucking over the dose of the drug with her prayer friends in whispered consultation as they pressed up crumbs of lemon pound cake with their fingers.

"*Wo ist die Medizin?*" Delphine said, first in a normal tone of voice.

Tante affected Hochdeutsch around Delphine and made great pretense of having trouble understanding her. When Tante gave only a cold twist of a smile, Delphine screamed: "Where is Eva's medicine?" Delphine stepped in the door, shoved past Tante, and dashed to the refrigerator. On the way there, with an outraged Tante trailing, she passed a table with a long slim object wrapped in a handkerchief. Delphine grabbed for it on instinct, unrolled it, and nearly dropped the missing hypodermic.

"Where is it?" Delphine's voice was deadly. She turned, jabbing the needle at Tante, and then found herself as in a stage play advancing with an air of threat. The feeling of being in a dramatic production gave her leave to speak the lines she wished had been written for the moment.

"Come on, you rough old bitch, you don't fool me. So you're a habitual fiend on the sly!"

Delphine didn't really think that, but she wanted to make Tante so indignant that she would tell her where the morphine was. But when Tante gaped and couldn't rally her wits to answer, Delphine, disgusted, went to the little icebox, rooted frantically through it. With a savage permission, she tossed out all of Tante's food, even the eggs, and then she turned and confronted Tante. Her brain was swimming with desperation.

"Please, you've got to tell me. Where is it?"

Now Tante had gained control. She even spoke English.

"You will owe me for those eggs."

"All right," Delphine said. "Just tell me."

But Tante, with the upper hand, enjoyed her moment.

"They are saying that she is addicted. This cannot be. The wife of my brother? This cannot. It is a great shame on us."

Delphine now saw that she had been stupid to antagonize the only person who could provide morphine quickly. She'd blown her cover and now she regretted her self-indulgence, grew meek.

"Oh, Tante," she sighed, "you know the truth, don't you? Tante, our Eva will probably not make it, and she is suffering terribly. You see her only when she's comfortable, so of course how can you possibly know how the agony builds? Tante, have mercy on your brother's wife. There is no shame in keeping her comfortable—the doctor has said so."

"I think," Tante said, her black figure precise, "the doctor doesn't really know. He feels too sorry for her, and she is addicted, that is for sure, my good friend Mrs. Orlen Sorven can tell this."

"Tante, Tante, for the love of God . . ." Delphine begged from her heart. She thought of falling on her knees. Tante's frozen little mouth twitched.

"It doesn't matter, anyway. I have thrown it down the sinkhole."

Delphine turned and saw that on the edge of Tante's porcelain sink a clean-washed vial and the bottle that had held the powder were drying in the glow of sun. And when she saw this, she lost all control and didn't quite know what she was doing. She was strong, suddenly phenomenally strong, and when she grabbed Tante by the bodice, jerked her forward, and said, into her face, "O.K. You come and nurse her through this. You'll see," Tante found herself unable to resist, her struggles feeble against Delphine's surging force as she dragged her to the car, stuffed her inside, then roared off and dumped her at the house.

"I don't have time to go in there. You help her. You stay with her. You," she shrieked, roaring the engine. Then she was gone and Tante, with the smug grimness of a woman who has at last been allowed to take charge, entered the back door.

It did take hours, and in those hours, Delphine did pray. She prayed as though she meant what she said. She prayed her heart out, cussed and swore, implored the devil, made bargains, came to tears at the thwarted junctures where she was directed to one place and ended up at another. It proved impossible to track down either Heech or the pharmacist. She was returning empty-handed, driving back to the house, weeping angrily, when she saw her father tumbling along the road, his pants sagging, his loose shirt flopping off his hunched, skinny shoulders. As she drew near, she looked around to see if anyone else was watching, for an all-seeing rage had boiled up in her and she suddenly wanted to run him over. She put the truck in low gear and followed him, thinking how simple it would be. He was drunk again and wouldn't even notice. Then her life would be that much easier. But as she drew alongside him, she was surprised to meet his eyes and see that they were clear. He shuffled anxiously around to the side door, she saw that he had a purpose: out snaking himself booze at a time like this. Only the bottle in his hand was not the usual schnapps but a brown square-shouldered medicine bottle labelled "Sulphate of Morphia," for which he'd broken into the drugstore and sawed through the lock of the cabinet where the pharmacist kept the drugs he had to secure by law.

As Delphine slammed on the brakes, jumped from the truck, and ran to the house, she heard it from outside, the high-pitched keen of advanced agony, a white-silver whine. She rushed in, skidded across a litter of canning smashed down off the shelves, and entered the kitchen. There was

Tante, white and sick with shock, slumped useless in the corner of the kitchen, on the floor. Louis and Franz, weeping and holding on to their mother as she rummaged in the drawer for a knife. The whole of her being was concentrated on the necessity. Even young, strong Franz couldn't hold her back.

"Yes, yes," Delphine said, entering the scene. She'd come upon so many scenes of mayhem in her own house that now a cold flood of competence descended on her. With a swift step, she stood before Eva. "My friend," she said, plucking the knife away, "not now. Soon enough. I've got the medicine. Don't leave your boys like this."

Then Eva, still swooning and grunting as the waves of pain hit and twisted in her, allowed herself to be lowered to the floor.

"Get a blanket and a pillow," Delphine said, kindly, to Franz. "And you," she said to Louis, "hold her hand while I make this up and keep saying to her, 'Mama, she's making the medicine now. It will be soon. It will be soon.'"

A.M. Homes

Do Not Disturb

from *McSweeney's*

M Y WIFE, the doctor, is not well. In the end she could be dead. It started suddenly, on a country weekend, a movie with friends, a pizza, and then pain.

"I liked the part where he lunged at the woman with a knife," Eric says.

"She deserved it," Enid says.

"Excuse me," my wife says getting up from the table.

A few minutes later I find her doubled over on the sidewalk. "Something is ripping me from the inside out."

"Should I get the check?" She looks at me like I am an idiot.

"My wife is not well," I announce, returning to the table. "We have to go."

"What do you mean—is she all right?"

Eric and Enid hurry out while I wait for the check. They drive us home. As I open the front door, my wife pushes past me and goes running for the bathroom. Eric, Enid, and I stand in the living room, waiting.

"Are you all right in there?" I call out.

"No," she says.

"Maybe she should go to the hospital," Enid says.

"Doctors don't go to the hospital," I say.

She is a specialist in emergency medicine. All day she is at the hospital putting the pieces back together and then she comes home to me. I am not the one who takes care. I am the one who is always on the verge.

"Call us if you need us," Eric and Enid say, leaving.

She lies on the bathroom floor, her cheek against the white tile. "I keep thinking it will pass."

I tuck the bath mat under her head and sneak away. From the kitchen I call a doctor friend. I stand in the dark, whispering, "She's just lying there on the floor, what do I do?"

"Don't do anything," the doctor says, half-insulted by the thought that there is something to do. "Observe her. Either it will go away, or something more will happen. You watch and you wait."

Watch and wait. I'm thinking about our relationship. We haven't been getting along. The situation has become oxygenless and addictive, a suffocating annihilation, each staying to see how far it will go.

I sit on the edge of the tub, looking at her. "I'm worried."

"Don't worry," she says. "And don't just sit there staring."

Earlier in the afternoon we were fighting, I don't remember about what. I only know—I called her a bitch.

"I was a bitch before I met you and I'll be a bitch long after you're gone. Surprise me," she said, "tell me something new."

I wanted to say, I'm leaving. I wanted to say, I know you think I never will and that's why you treat me like you do. But I'm going. I wanted to get in the car, drive off and call it a day.

The fight ended with the clock. She glanced at it. "It's six-thirty, we're meeting Eric and Enid at seven; put on a clean shirt."

She is lying on the bathroom floor, the print of the bath mat making an impression on her cheek. "Are you comfortable?" I ask.

She looks surprised, as though she's just realized she's on the floor.

"Help me," she says, struggling to get up.

Her lips are white and thin.

"Bring me a trash can, a plastic bag, a thermometer, some Tylenol, and a glass of water."

"Are you going to throw up?"

"I want to be prepared," she says.

We are always prepared. The ongoing potential for things to go wrong is our bond, a fascination with crisis, with control. We have flare guns and fire extinguishers, walkie-talkies, a rubber raft, a small generator, a hundred batteries in assorted shapes and sizes, a thousand bucks in dollar bills, enough toilet paper and bottled water to get us through six months. When we travel we have smoke hoods in our carry-on bags, protein bars, water purification tablets, and a king-sized bag of M&M's.

She slips the digital thermometer under her tongue; the numbers move up the scale—each beep is a tenth of a degree.

"A hundred and one point four," I announce.

"I have a fever?" she says in disbelief.

"I wish things between us weren't so bad."

"It's not as bad as you think," she says. "Expect less and you won't be disappointed."

We try to sleep; she is hot, she is cold, she is mumbling something about having "a surgical belly," something about "guarding and rebound." I don't know if she's talking about herself or the NBA.

"This is incredible," she sits bolt upright and folds over again, writhing. "Something is struggling inside me. It's like one of those alien movies, like I'm going to burst open and something is going to spew out, like I'm erupting." She pauses, takes a breath. "And then it stops. Who would ever have thought this would happen to me—and on a Saturday night?"

"Is it your appendix?"

"That's the one thought I have, but I'm not sure. I don't have the classic symptoms. I don't have anorexia or diarrhea. When I was eating that pizza, I was hungry."

"Is it an ovary? Women have lots of ovaries."

"Women have two ovaries," she says. "It did occur to me that it could be Mittelschmertz."

"Mittelschmertz?"

"The launching of the egg, the middle of the cycle."

At five in the morning her temperature is 103. She is alternately sweating and shivering.

"Should I drive you back to the city or to the hospital out here?"

"I don't want to be the doctor who goes to the ER with gas."

"Fine."

I'm dressing myself, packing, thinking of what I'll need: cell phone, notebook, pen, something to read, something to eat, wallet, insurance card.

We are in the car, hurrying. There's an urgency to the situation, the unmistakable sense that something bad is happening. I am driving seventy miles an hour.

"I think I'm dying," she says.

I pull up to the emergency entrance and half-carry her in, leaving the car doors open, the engine running; I have the impulse to drop her off and walk away.

The emergency room is empty. There is a bell on the check-in desk. I ring it twice.

A woman appears. "Can I help you?"

"My wife is not well," I say. "She's a doctor."

The woman sits at her computer. She takes my wife's name and number. She takes her insurance card and then her temperature and blood pressure. "Are you in a lot of pain?"

"Yes," my wife says.

Within minutes a doctor is there, pressing on my wife. "It's got to come out," he says.

"What?" I ask.

"Appendix. Do you want some Demerol?"

She shakes her head. "I'm working tomorrow and I'm on call."

"What kind of doctor are you?"

"Emergency medicine."

In the cubicle next to her, someone vomits.

The nurse comes to take blood. "They called Barry Manilow, he's a very good surgeon." She ties off my wife's arm. "We call him Barry Manilow because he looks like Barry Manilow."

"I want to do right by you," Barry Manilow says, as he's feeling my wife's belly. "I'm not sure it's your appendix, not sure it's your gallbladder either. I'm going to call the radiologist and let him scan it. How's that sound?"

She nods.

I take the surgeon aside. "Should she be staying here? Is this the place to do this?"

"It's not a kidney transplant," he says.

The nurse brings me a cold drink. She offers me a chair. I sit close to the gurney where my wife lies. "Do you want me to get you out of here? I could hire a car and have us driven to the city. I could have you medevaced home."

"I don't want to go anywhere," she says.

Back in the cubicle, Barry Manilow is talking to her. "It's not your appendix. It's your ovary. It's a hemorrhagic cyst; you're bleeding and your hematocrit is failing. We have to operate. I've called a gynecologist and the anesthesiologist—I'm just waiting for them to arrive. We're going to take you upstairs very soon."

"Just do it," she says.

I stop Barry Manilow in the hall. "Can you try and save the ovary? She very much wants to have children. It's just something she hasn't gotten around to yet—first she had her career, then me, and now this."

"We'll do everything we can," he says, disappearing through the door marked Authorized Personnel Only.

I am the only one in the surgical waiting room, flipping through copies of *Field & Stream, Highlights for Children,* a pamphlet on colon cancer. Less than an hour later, Barry Manilow comes to find me. "We saved the ovary. We took out something the size of a lemon."

"The size of a lemon?"

He makes a fist and holds it up. "A lemon," he says. "It looked a little funny. We sent it to Pathology." He shrugs.

A lemon, a bleeding lemon, like a blood orange, a lemon souring in her. Why is fruit used as the universal medical measurement?

"She should be upstairs in about an hour."

When I get to her room she is asleep. A tube poking out from under the covers drains urine into a bag. She is hooked up to oxygen and an IV.

I put my hand on her forehead. Her eyes open.

"A little fresh air," she says, pulling at the oxygen tube. "I always wondered what all this felt like."

She has a morphine drip, the kind she can control herself. She keeps the clicker in hand. She never pushes the button.

I feed her ice chips and climb into the bed next to her. In the middle of the night I go home. In the morning she calls, waking me up.

"Flowers have been arriving like crazy," she says, "from the hospital, from the ER, from the clinic."

Doctors are like firemen; when one of their own is down they go crazy.

"They took the catheter out, I'm sitting up in a chair. I already had some juice and took myself to the bathroom," she says, proudly. "They couldn't be nicer. But of course, I'm a very good patient."

I interrupt her, "Do you want anything from the house?"

"Clean socks, a pair of sweatpants, my hairbrush, some toothpaste, my face soap, a radio, maybe a can of Diet Coke."

"You're only going to be there a couple of days."

"You asked if I needed anything. Don't forget to feed the dog."

Five minutes later she calls back—crying. "Guess what, I have ovarian cancer."

I run out the door. When I get there the room is empty. I'm expecting a big romantic crying scene, expecting her to cling to me, to tell me how much she loves me, how she's sorry we've been having such a hard time, how much she needs me, wants me, now more than ever. The bed is empty. For a moment I think she's died, jumped out the window, escaped.

In the bathroom, the toilet flushes. "I want to go home," she says, stepping out, fully dressed.

"Do you want to take the flowers?"

"They're mine, aren't they? Do you think all the nurses know I have cancer? I don't want anyone to know."

The nurse comes with a wheelchair; she takes us down to the lobby. "Good luck," she says, loading the flowers into the car.

"She knows," my wife says.

We're on the Long Island Expressway. I am dialing and driving. I call my wife's doctor in New York.

"She has to see Kibbowitz immediately," the doctor says.

"Do you think I'll lose my ovary?"

She will lose everything. Instinctively I know that.

We are home. She is on the bed with the dog on her lap. She peeks beneath the gauze; her incision is crooked, the lack of precision an incredible insult. "Do you think they can fix it?" she asks.

In the morning we go to Kibbowitz. She is again on a table, her feet in the stirrups, in launch position, waiting. Before the doctor arrives she is interviewed and examined by seven medical students. I hate them. I hate them for talking to her, for touching her, for wasting her time. I hate Kibbowitz for keeping her on the table for more than an hour, waiting.

She is angry with me for being annoyed. "They're just doing their job."

Kibbowitz arrives. He is enormous, like a hockey player, a brute and a bully. I can tell immediately that she likes him. She will do anything he says.

"Scootch down a little closer to me," he says settling himself on a stool between her legs. She lifts her ass and slides down. He examines her. He peeks under the gauze. "Crooked," he says. "Get dressed and meet me in my office."

"I want a number," she says. "A survival rate."

"I don't deal in numbers," he says.

"I need a number."

He shrugs. "How's seventy percent."

"Seventy percent what?"

"Seventy percent live five years."

"And then what?" I ask.

"And then some don't," he says.

"What has to come out?" she asks.

"What do you want to keep?"

"I wanted to have a child."

This is a delicate negotiation; they talk parts. "I could take just the one ovary," he says. "And then after the chemo you could try and get pregnant and then after you had a child we could go in and get the rest."

"Can you really get pregnant after chemo?" I ask.

The doctor shrugs. "Miracles happen all the time," he says. "The problem is you can't raise a child if you're dead. You don't have to decide now, let me know in a day or two. Meanwhile I'm going to book the operating room for Friday morning. Nice meeting you," he says, shaking my hand.

"I want to have a baby," she says.

"I want to have you," I say.

Beyond that I say nothing. Whatever I say she will do the opposite. We are at that point—spite, blame, and fault. I don't want to be held responsible.

She opens the door of the consulting room. "Doctor," she shouts, hurrying down the hall after him, clutching her belly, her incision, her wound. "Take it," she screams. "Take it all the hell out."

He is standing outside another examining room, chart in hand.

He nods. "We'll take it though your vagina. We'll take the ovaries, the uterus, cervix, omentum and your appendix if they didn't already get it in Southampton. And then we'll put a port in your neck and sign you up for chemotherapy, eight rounds should do it."

She nods.

"See you Friday."

We leave. I'm holding her hand, holding her pocketbook on my shoulder trying to be as good as anyone can be. She is growling and scratching; it's like taking a cat to the vet.

"Why don't they just say eviscerate? Why don't they just come out and say on Friday at nine we're going to eviscerate you—be ready."

"Do you want a little lunch?" I ask as we are walking down the street. "Some soup? There's a lovely restaurant near here."

She looks flushed. I put my hand to her forehead. She's burning up. "You have a fever. Did you mention that to the doctor?"

"It's not relevant."

Later when we are home, I ask, " Do you remember our third date? Do you remember asking me—how would you kill yourself if you had to do it with bare hands? I said I would break my nose and shove it up into my brain and you said you would reach up with your bare hands and rip your uterus out through your vagina and throw it across the room."

"What's your point?"

"No point, I just suddenly remembered it. Isn't Kibbowitz taking your uterus out through your vagina?"

"I doubt he's going to throw it across the room," she says. There is a pause. "You don't have to stay with me now that I have cancer. I don't need you. I don't need anyone. I don't need anything."

"If I left, I wouldn't be leaving because you have cancer. But I would look like an ass, everyone would think I couldn't take it."

"I would make sure they knew it was me, that I was a monster, a cold steely monster, that I drove you away."

"They wouldn't believe you."

She suddenly farts and runs embarrassed into the bathroom—as though this is the first time she's farted in her life. "My life is ruined," she yells, slamming the door.

"Farting is the least of it," I say.

When she comes out she is calmer. She crawls into bed next to me, wrung out, shivering.

I hold her. "Do you want to make love?"

"You mean one last time before I'm not a woman, before I'm a dried old husk?"

Instead of fucking we fight. It's the same sort of thing, dramatic, draining. When we're done, I roll over and sleep in a tight knot on my side of the bed.

"Surgical menopause," she says. "That sounds so final."

I turn toward her. She runs her hand over her pubic hair. "Do you think they'll shave me?"

I'm not going to be able to leave the woman with cancer. I'm not the kind of person who leaves the woman with cancer, but I don't know what you do when the woman with cancer is a bitch. Do you hope that the cancer prompts the woman to reevaluate herself, to take it as an opportunity, a signal for change? As far as she's concerned there is no such thing as the mind/body connection, there is science and there is law. There is fact and everything else is bullshit.

Friday morning, while she's in the hospital registration area waiting for her number to be called, she makes another list out loud: "My will is in the top left drawer of the dresser. If anything goes wrong pull the plug. No heroic measures. I want to be cremated. Donate my organs. Give it away, all of it, every last drop." She stops. "I guess no one will want me now that I'm contaminated." She says the word contaminated, filled with disgust, disappointment, as though she has soiled herself.

It is nearly eight P.M. when Kibbowitz comes out to tell me he's done. "Everything was stuck together like macaroni and cheese. It took longer than I expected. I found some in the fallopian tube and some on the wall of her abdomen. We cleaned everything out."

She is wheeled back to her room, sad, agitated, angry.

"Why didn't you come and see me?" she asks, accusitorily.

"I was right there the whole time, on the other side of the door waiting for word."

She acts as though she doesn't believe me, as though I went off and screwed a secretary from the patient services office while she was on the table.

"How're you feeling?"

"As though I've taken a trip to another country and my suitcases are lost."

She is writhing. I adjust her pillow, the position of the bed.

"What hurts?"

"What doesn't hurt? Everything hurts. Breathing hurts."

Because she is a doctor, because she did her residency at this hospital, they give me a small folding cot to set up in the corner of the room. Bending to unfold it, something happens in my back, a hot searing pain spreads across and down. I lower myself to the floor, grabbing the blanket as I go.

Luckily, she is sleeping.

The nurse coming in to check her vital signs sees me. "Are you in trouble?" she asks.

"It's happened before," I say. "I'll just lie here and see what happens."

She brings me a pillow and covers me with the blanket.

Eric and Enid arrive. My wife is asleep and I am still on the floor. Eric stands over me.

"We're sorry," Eric whispers. "We didn't get your message until today. We were at Enid's parents'—upstate."

"It's shocking, it's sudden, it's so out of the blue." Enid moves to look at my wife. "She looks like she's in a really bad mood, her brow is furrowed. Is she in pain?"

"I assume so."

"If there's anything we can do, let us know," Eric says.

"Actually, could you walk the dog?" I pull the keys out of my pocket and hold them in the air. "He's been home alone all day and all night."

"Walk the dog, I think we can do that," Eric says, looking at Enid for confirmation.

"We'll check on you in the morning," Enid says.

"Before you go; there's a bottle of Percocet in her purse—give me two."

During the night she wakes up. "Where are you?" she asks.

"I'm right here."

She is sufficiently drugged that she doesn't ask for details. At around six she opens her eyes and sees me on the floor.

"Your back?"

"Yep."

"Cancer beats back," she says and falls back to sleep.

When the cleaning man comes with the damp mop, I pry myself off the floor. I'm fine as long as I'm standing.

"You're walking like you have a rod up your ass," my wife says.

"Is there anything I can do for you?" I ask, trying to be solicitous.

"Can you have cancer for me?"

The pain management team arrives to check on my wife's level of comfort.

"On a scale of one to ten how do you feel?" the pain fellow asks.

"Five," my wife says,

"She lies," I say.

"Are you lying?"

"How can you tell?"

The specialist arrives, "I know you," he says, seeing my wife in the bed. "We went to school together."

My wife tries to smile.

"You were the smartest one in the class and now look," he reads my wife's chart. "Ovarian cancer and you, that's horrible."

My wife is sitting up high in her hospital bed, puking her guts into a metal bucket, like a poisoned pet monkey. She is throwing up bright green like an alien, like nothing anyone has seen before. Ted, her boss, stares at her, mesmerized.

The room is filled with people—people I don't know, medical people, people she went to school with, people she did her residency with, a man whose fingers she sewed back on, relatives I've not met. I don't understand why they don't excuse themselves, why they don't step out of the room. They're all watching her like they've never seen anyone throw up before—riveted.

She is not sleeping. She is not eating. She is not getting up and walking around. She is afraid to leave her bed, afraid to leave her bucket.

I make a sign for the door. I borrow a black Magic Marker from the charge nurse and print in large black letters: Do Not Disturb.

They push the door open. They come bearing gifts, flowers, food, books. "I saw the sign, I assumed it was for someone else."

I am wiping green spittle from her lips.

"Do you want me to get rid of everyone?" I ask.

I want to get rid of everyone. The idea that these people have some claim to her, some right to entertain, distract, bother her more than me, drives me up the wall. "Should I tell them to go?"

She shakes her head. "Just the flowers, the flowers nauseate me."

An hour later, I empty the bucket again. The room remains over-crowded. I am on my knees by the side of her hospital bed, whispering "I'm leaving."

"Are you coming back?" she whispers.

"No."

She looks at me strangely. "Where are you going?"

"Away."

"Bring me a Diet Coke."

She has missed the point.

It is heartbreaking seeing her in a stained gown, in the middle of a bed, unable to tell everyone to go home, unable to turn it off. Her pager is clipped to her hospital gown, several times it goes off. She returns the calls.

She always returns the calls. I imagine her saying, "What the hell are you bothering me for—I'm busy, I'm having cancer."

Later, I'm on the edge of the bed, looking at her. She is increasingly beautiful, more vulnerable, female.

"Honey?"

"What?" Her intonation is like a pissy caged bird—cawww. "What? What are you looking at? What do you want?" Cawww.

"Nothing."

I am washing her with a cool washcloth.

"You're tickling me," she complains.

"Make sure you tell her you still find her attractive," a man in the hall tells me. "Husbands of women who have mastectomies need to keep reminding their wives that they are beautiful."

"She had a hysterectomy," I say.

"Same thing."

Two days later, they remove the packing. I am in the room when the resident comes with long tweezers like tongs and pulls yards of material from her vagina, wads of cotton, gauze, stained battlefield red. It's like a magic trick gone awry, one of those jokes about how many people you can fit in a telephone booth; more and more keeps coming out.

"Is there anything left in there?" she asks.

The resident shakes his head. "Your vagina now just comes to a stop, it's a stump, an unconnected sleeve. Don't be surprised if you bleed, if you pop a stitch or two." He checks her chart and signs her out. "Kibbowitz has you on pelvic rest for six weeks."

"Pelvic rest?" I ask.

"No fucking," she says.

Not a problem.

Home. She watches forty-eight hours of Holocaust films an cable TV. Although she claims to compartmentalize everything, suddenly she identifies with the bald, starving, prisoners of war. She sees herself as a victim. She points to the naked corpse of a woman, "That's me," she says. "That's exactly how I feel."

"She's dead," I say.

"Exactly."

Her notorious vigilance is gone. As I'm fluffing her pillows, her billy club rolls out from under the bed. "Put it in the closet," she says.

"Why?" I ask, rolling it back under the bed.

"Why sleep with a billy club under the bed? Why do anything when you have cancer?"

During a break between *Schindler's List, Shoah,* and *The Sorrow and the Pity* she taps me, "I'm missing my parts," she says. "Maybe one of those lost eggs was someone special, someone who would have cured something, someone who would have invented something wonderful. You never know who was in there. They're my lost children."

"I'm sorry."

"For what?" She looks at me accusingly.

"Everything."

"Thirty-eight-year-olds don't get cancer, they get Lyme disease, maybe they have appendicitis, on rare occasions in some other parts of the world they have Siamese twins, but that's it."

In the middle of the night she wakes up, throws the covers off, "I can't breathe, I'm burning up. Open the window, I'm hot, I'm so hot."

"Do you know what's happening to you?"

"What are you talking about?"

"You're having hot flashes."

"I am not," she says as though I've insulted her. "They don't start so soon."

They do.

"Get away from me, get away," she yells. "Just being near you makes me uncomfortable, it makes my temperature unstable."

On Monday she starts chemotherapy.

"Will I go bald?" she asks the nurse.

"Most women buy a wig before it happens," the nurse says, plugging her into the magic potion.

I am afraid that when she's bald I won't love her anymore. I cannot imagine my wife bald.

One of the other women, her head wrapped in a red turban, leans over and whispers, "My husband says I look like a porno star." She winks. She has no eyebrows, no eyelashes, nothing.

We shop for a wig. She tries on every style, every shape and color. She looks like a man in drag, like it's all a horrible joke.

"Maybe my hair won't fall out?" she says.

"It's okay," the woman in the wig shop says. "Insurance covers it. Ask your doctor to write a prescription for a cranial prosthesis."

"I'm a doctor," my wife says.

The wig woman looks confused. "It's okay," she says, putting another wig on my wife's head.

She buys a wig. I never see it. She brings it home and immediately puts it in the closet. "It looks like Linda Evans, like someone on *Dynasty*. I just can't do it," she says.

Her scalp begins to tingle. Her hair hurts. "It's like someone grabbed my hair and is pulling as hard as they can."

"It's getting ready to go. It's like a time bomb. It ticks and then it blows."

"What are you, a doctor? Suddenly you know everything about cancer, about menopause, about everything?"

In the morning her hair is falling out. It's all over the pillow, all over the shower floor.

"Your hair's not really falling out," Enid says when we meet them for dinner. Enid reaches and touches her hair, sweeps her hand through it, as if to be comforting. She ends up with a hand full of hair; she has pulled my wife's hair out. She tries to put it back, she furiously pats it back in place.

"Forget that I was worried about them shaving my pubic hair, how 'bout it all just went down the drain."

She looks like a rat, like something that's been chewed on and spit out, like something that someone tried to electrocute and failed. In four days she is eighty percent bald.

She stands before me naked. "Document me."

I take pictures. I take the film to one of those special stores that has a sign in the window—we don't censor.

I give her a baseball cap to wear to work. Every day she goes to work; she will not miss a day, no matter what.

I, on the other hand, can't work. Since this happened, my work has been nonexistent. I spend my day as the holder of the feelings, the keeper of sensation.

"It's not my fault," she says. "What the hell do you do all day while I'm at the hospital?"

Recuperate.

She wears the baseball cap for a week and then takes a razor, shaves the few scraggly hairs that remain and goes to work bald, without a hat, without a wig—starkers.

There's something aggressive about her baldness.

"How do you feel?" I ask at night when she comes home from the hospital.

"I feel nothing."

"How can you feel nothing? What are you made of?"

"I am made of steel and wood," she says, happily.

As we're falling asleep she tells me a story, "It's true, it happened as I was walking into the hospital. I accidentally bumped into someone on the sidewalk. 'Excuse me,' I said and continued on. He ran after me, 'Excuse me, Excuse me. You knocked my comb out of my hand and I want you to go back and pick it up.' 'What? We bumped into each other, I said excuse me, that will have to suffice.' 'You knocked it out of my hand on purpose. You're just a bald bitch. A fucking bald bitch.' I wheeled around and chased him. 'You fucking crazy ass,' I screamed. 'You fucking crazy ass,' I screamed it about four times. He's lucky I didn't fucking kill him," she says.

I am thinking she's lost her mind. I'm thinking she's lucky he didn't kill her.

She gets up and stands on the bed—naked. She strikes a pose like a bodybuilder. "Cancer Man," she says, flexing her muscles, creating a new superhero. "'Cancer Man!"

Luckily she has good insurance. The bill for the surgery comes—it's itemized. They charge per part removed. Ovary $7,000, appendix $5,000 the total is $72,000. "It's all in a day's work," she says.

We are lying in bed. I am lying next to her, reading the paper.

"I want to go to a desert island, alone. I don't want to come back until this is finished," she says and then looks at me. "It will never be finished—do you know that? I'm not going to have children and I'm going to die."

"Do you really think you're going to die?"

"Yes."

I reach for her.

"Don't," she says. "Don't go looking for trouble."

"I wasn't. I was trying to be loving."

"I don't feel loving," she says. "I don't feel physically bonded to anyone right now, including myself."

"Will we ever again?"

"I don't know."

"You're pushing me away."

"I'm recovering," she says.

"It's been eighteen weeks."

Her blood counts are low. Every night for five nights, I inject her with Nupagen to increase the white blood cells. She teaches me how to prepare the injection, how to push the needle into the muscle of her leg. Every time I inject her, I apologize.

"For what?" she asks.

"Hurting you."

"Forget it," she says, disposing of the needle.

She rolls far away from me in her sleep. She dreams of strange things.

"I dreamed I was with my former boyfriend and he turned into a black woman slave and she was on top of me, between my legs, a lesbian slave fantasy."

"Could I have a hug?" I ask.

She glares at me. "Why do you persist? Why do you keep asking me for things I can't do, things I can't give?"

"A hug?"

"I can't give you one."

"Anyone can give a hug. I can get a hug from the doorman."

"Then do," she says. "I need to be married to someone who is like a potted plant, someone who needs nothing."

"Water?"

"Very little, someone who's like a cactus or an orchid."

"It's like you're refusing to be human," I tell her.

"I have no interest in being human."

This is information I should be paying attention to. She is telling me something and I'm not listening. I don't believe what she is saying.

I go to dinner with Eric and Enid alone.

"It's strange," they say. "You'd think the cancer would soften her, make her more appreciative. You'd think it would make her stop and think about what she wants to do with the rest of her life. When you ask her what does she say?" Eric and Enid want to know.

"Nothing. She says she wants nothing, she has no needs or desires. She says she has nothing to give."

Eric and Enid shake their heads. "What are you going to do?"

I shrug. None of this is new, none of this is just because she has cancer—that's important to keep in mind, this is exactly the way she always was, only more so.

A few days later a woman calls; she and her husband are people we see occasionally.

"Hi, how are you, how's Tom?" I ask.

"He's a fucking asshole," she says. "Haven't you heard? He left me."

"When?"

"About two weeks ago. I thought you would have known."

"I'm a little out of it."

"Anyway, I'm calling to see if you'd like to have lunch."

"Lunch, sure. Lunch would be good."

At lunch she is a little flirty, which is fine, it's nice actually, it's been a long time since someone flirted with me. In the end, when we're having coffee, she spills the beans, "So I guess, you're wondering why I called you?"

"I guess," I say, although I'm perfectly pleased to be having lunch, to be listening to someone else's troubles.

"I heard your wife was sick, I figured you're not getting a lot of sex and I thought we could have an affair."

I don't know which part is worse, the complete lack of seduction, the fact that she mentions my wife not being well, the idea that my wife's illness would make me want to sleep with her, her stun-gun bluntness—it's all too much.

"What do you think? Am I repulsive? Thoroughly disgusting? Is it the craziest thing you ever heard?"

"I'm very busy," I say, not knowing what to say, not wanting to be offensive, or seem to have taken offense. "I'm just very busy."

My wife comes home from work. "Someone came in today—he reminded me of you."

"What was his problem?"

"He jumped out the window."

"Dead?"

"Yes," she says, washing her hands in the kitchen sink.

"Was he dead when he got to you?" There's something in her tone that makes me wonder, did she kill him?

"Pretty much."

"What part reminded you of me?"

"He was having an argument with his wife."

"Oh?"

"Imagine her standing in the living room, in the middle of a sentence and out the window he goes. Imagine her not having a chance to finish her thought?"

"Yes, imagine, not being able to have the last word. Did she try and stop him?" I ask.

"I don't know," my wife says. "I didn't get to read the police report. I just thought you'd find it interesting."

"What do you want for dinner?"

"Nothing," she says. "I'm not hungry."

"You have to eat something."

"Why? I have cancer. I can do whatever I want."

Something has to happen.

I buy tickets to Paris, "We have to go." I invoke the magic word, "It's an emergency."

"It's not like I get a day off. It's not like I come home at the end of the day and I don't have cancer. It goes everywhere with me. It doesn't matter where I am, it's still me—it's me with cancer. In Paris I'll have cancer."

I dig out the maps, the guidebooks, everything we did on our last trip is marked with fluorescent highlighter. I am acting as though I believe that if we retrace our steps, if we return to a place where things were good, there will be an automatic correction, a psychic chiropractic event, which will put everything into alignment.

I gather provisions for the plane: smoke hoods, fresh water, fruit, M&M's, magazines.

"What's the point," she says, throwing a few things into a suitcase. "You can do everything and think you're prepared, but you don't know what's going to happen. You don't see what's coming until it hits you in the face."

She points at someone outside. "See that idiot crossing the street in front of the truck, why doesn't he have cancer? He deserves to die."

She lifts her suitcase—too heavy. She takes things out. She leaves her smoke hood on the bed. "If the plane fills with smoke, I'm going to be so happy," she says. "I'm going to breathe deeply, I'm going to be the first to die."

I stuff the smoke hood into my suitcase, along with her raincoat, her extra shoes, Ace bandages for her bad ankle, reusable ice packs just in case, vitamin C drops. I lift the suitcases, feeling like a pack animal, a sherpa.

In France, the customs people are not used to seeing bald women. They call her, "Sir."

"Sir, you're next, Sir. Sir, please step over here, Sir."

My wife is my husband. She loves it. She smiles. She catches my eye and strikes a subdued version of the superhero/bodybuilder pose, flexing. "Cancer Man," she says.

"And what is the purpose of your visit to France?" the inspector asks. "Business or pleasure?"

"Reconciliation," I say, watching her—Cancer Man.

"Business or pleasure?"

"Pleasure."

Paris is my fantasy, my last-ditch effort to reclaim my marriage, myself, my wife.

As we're checking in to the hotel, I remind her of our previous visit—the chef cut himself, his hand was severed, she saved it and they were able to reattach it. "You made medical history. Remember the beautiful dinner they threw in your honor?"

"It was supposed to be a vacation," she says.

The bellman takes us to our room—there's a big basket of fruit, bottles of Champagne and Evian with a note from the concierge welcoming us.

"It's not as nice as it used to be," she says, already disappointed. She opens the Evian and drinks. Her lips curl. "Even the water tastes bad."

"Maybe it's you. Maybe the water is fine. Is it possible you're wrong?"

"We see things differently," she says, meaning she's right, I'm wrong.

"Are you in an especially bad mood, or is it just the cancer?" I ask.

"Maybe it's you?" she says.

We go for a walk, across the river and down by the Louvre. There could be nothing better, nothing more perfect and yet I am suddenly hating Paris, hating it more than anything, the beauty, the fineness of it is dwarfed by her foul humor. I realize there is no saving it, no moment of reconciliation, redemption. Everything sucks. It is irredeemably awful and getting worse.

"If you're so unhappy, why don't you leave?" I ask her.

"I keep thinking you'll change."

"If I changed any more I can't imagine who I'd be."

"Well if I'm such a bitch, why do you stay?"

"It's my job, it's my calling to stay with you, to soften you."

"I absolutely do not want to be softer, I don't want to give another inch."

"Well, I am not a leaver, I worked hard to get here, to be able to stay."

She trips on a cobblestone, I reach for her elbow, to steady her and instead unbalance myself. She fails to catch me. I fall and recover quickly.

"Imagine how I feel," she says. "I'm a doctor and I can't fix it. I can't fix me, I can't fix you—what a lousy doctor."

"I'm losing you," I say.

"I've lost myself. Look at me—do I look like me?"

"You act like yourself."

"I act like myself because I have to, because people are counting on me."

"I'm counting on you."

"Stop counting."

All along the Tuileries there are Ferris wheels, the world's largest Ferris wheel is set up in the middle.

"Let's go," I say, taking her hand, pulling her toward them.

"I don't like rides."

"It's not much of a ride. It's like a carousel, only vertical. Live a little."

She gets on. There are no seat belts, no safety bars. I say nothing. I am hoping she won't notice.

"How is it going to end?" I ask while we're waiting for the wheel to spin.

"I die in the end."

The ride takes off, climbing, pulling us up and over. We are flying, soaring; the city unfolds. It is breathtaking and higher than I thought. And faster. There is always a moment on any ride where you think it is too fast, too high, too far, too wide, and that you will not survive.

"I have never been so unhappy in my life," my wife says when we're near the top. "'It's not just the cancer, I was unhappy before the cancer. We were having a very hard time. We don't get along, we're a bad match. Do you believe me?"

"Yes," I say, "We're a really bad match. We're such a good bad match it seems impossible to let it go."

"We're stuck," she says.

"You bet," I say.

"No. I mean the ride, the ride isn't moving."

"It's not stuck, it's just stopped. It stops along the way."

She begins to cry. "It's all your fault. I hate you. And I still have to deal with you. Every day I have to look at you."

"No, you don't. You don't have to deal with me if you don't want to."

She stops crying and looks at me. "What are you going to do, jump?"

"The rest of your life, or my life, however long or short, should not be miserable. It can't go on this way."

"We could both kill ourselves," she says.

"How about we separate?"

I am being more grown up than I am capable of being. I am terrified of being without her but either way, it's death. The ride lurches forward.

I came to Paris wanting to pull things together and suddenly I am desperate to be away from her, to never have this conversation again. She will be dying and we will still be fighting. I begin to panic, to feel I can't breathe. I have to get away.

"Where does it end?"

"How about we say good-bye."

"And then what? We have opera tickets."

I can't tell her I'm going. I have to sneak away, to tiptoe out backwards. I have to make my own arrangements.

We stop talking. We're hanging in midair, suspended. We have run out of things to say. When the ride circles down, the silence becomes more definitive.

I begin to make my plan. In truth, I have no idea what I am doing. All afternoon, everywhere we go, I cash traveler's checks, I get cash advances, I have about five thousand dollars' worth of francs stuffed in my pocket. I want to be able to leave without a trace, I want to be able to buy myself out of whatever trouble I get into. I am hysterical and giddy all at once.

We are having an early dinner on our way to the opera.

I time my break for just after the coffee comes. "Oops," I say, feeling my pockets, "I forgot my opera glasses."

"Really?" she says, "I thought you had them when we went out."

"They must be at the hotel. You go on ahead, I'll run back. You know I hate not being able to see."

She takes her ticket. "Hurry," she says. "I hate it when you're late."

This is the bravest thing I have ever done. I go back to the hotel and pack my bag. I'm going to get out. I'm going to fly away. I may never come back. I will begin again, as someone else, someone who wants to live, I will be unrecognizable.

I move to lift the bag off the bed, I pull it up and my knee goes out. I start to fall but catch myself. I pull at the bag and take a step—too heavy. I'll have to go without it. I'll have to leave everything behind. I drop the bag, but still I am falling, folding, collapsing. There is pain, spreading, pouring, hot and cold, like water down my back, down my legs.

I am lying on the floor, thinking that if I stay calm, if I can just find my breath, and follow my breath, it will pass. I lie there waiting for the paralysis to recede.

I am afraid of it being over and yet she has given me no choice, she has systematically withdrawn life support: sex and conversation. The problem is that despite this, she is the one I want.

There is a knock at the door. I know it is not her, it is too soon for it to be her.

"Entrez," I call out.

The maid opens the door, she holds the Do Not Disturb sign in her hand.

"Oooff," she says, seeing me on the floor. "Do you need the doctor?"

I am not sure if she means my wife or a doctor, a doctor other than my wife.

"No."

She takes a towel from her cart and props it under my head, she takes a spare blanket from the closet and covers me with it. She opens the Champagne and pours me a glass, tilting my head up so I can sip. She goes to her cart and gets a stack of night chocolates and sits beside me, feeding me Champagne and chocolate, stroking my forehead.

The phone in the room rings; we ignore it. She refills my glass. She takes my socks off and rubs my feet. She unbuttons my shirt and rubs my chest. I am getting a little drunk. I am just beginning to relax and then there is another knock, a knock my body recognizes before I am fully awake. Everything tightens. My back pulls tighter still, any sensation below my knees drops off.

"I thought something horrible happened to you. I've been calling and calling the room, why haven't you answered? I thought you'd killed yourself."

The maid excuses herself. She goes into the bathroom and refreshes my cool washcloth.

"What are you doing?" my wife asks.

There is nothing I can say.

"Knock off the mummy routine. What exactly are you doing? Were you trying to run away and then you chickened out? Say something."

To talk would be to continue; for the moment I am silenced. I am a potted plant and still that is not good enough for her.

"He is paralyzed," the maid says.

"He is not paralyzed, I am his wife, I am a doctor. I would know if there was something really wrong."

Jonathan Nolan

Memento Mori

"What like a bullet can undeceive!"
—HERMAN MELVILLE

from *Esquire*

YOUR WIFE *always used to say you'd be late for your own funeral. Remember that? Her little joke because you were such a slob—always late, always forgetting stuff, even before the incident.*

Right about now you're probably wondering if you were late for hers.

You were there, you can be sure of that. That's what the picture's for—the one tacked to the wall by the door. It's not customary to take pictures at a funeral, but somebody, your doctors, I guess, knew you wouldn't remember. They had it blown up nice and big and stuck it right there, next to the door, so you couldn't help but see it every time you got up to find out where she was.

The guy in the picture, the one with the flowers? That's you. And what are you doing? You're reading the headstone, trying to figure out whose funeral you're at, same as you're reading it now, trying to figure why someone stuck that picture next to your door. But why bother reading something that you won't remember?

She's gone, gone for good, and you must be hurting right now, hearing the news. Believe me, I know how you feel. You're probably a wreck. But give it five minutes, maybe ten. Maybe you can even go a whole half hour before you forget.

But you will forget—I guarantee it. A few more minutes and you'll be heading for the door, looking for her all over again, breaking down when you find the picture. How many times do you have to hear the news before some other part of your body, other than that busted brain of yours, starts to remember?

Never-ending grief, never-ending anger. Useless without direction. Maybe you can't understand what's happened. Can't say I really understand, either. Backwards amnesia. That's what the sign says. CRS disease. Your guess is as good as mine.

Maybe you can't understand what happened to you. But you do remember what happened to HER, don't you? The doctors don't want to talk about it. They won't answer my questions. They don't think it's right for a man in your condition to hear about those things. But you remember enough, don't you? You remember his face.

This is why I'm writing to you. Futile, maybe. I don't know how many times you'll have to read this before you listen to me. I don't even know how long you've been locked up in this room already. Neither do you. But your advantage in forgetting is that you'll forget to write yourself off as a lost cause.

Sooner or later you'll want to do something about it. And when you do, you'll just have to trust me, because I'm the only one who can help you.

Earl opens one eye after another to a stretch of white ceiling tiles interrupted by a hand-printed sign taped right above his head, large enough for him to read from the bed. An alarm clock is ringing somewhere. He reads the sign, blinks, reads it again, then takes a look at the room.

It's a white room, overwhelmingly white, from the walls and the curtains to the institutional furniture and the bedspread.

The alarm clock is ringing from the white desk under the window with the white curtains. At this point Earl probably notices that he is lying on top of his white comforter. He is already wearing a dressing gown and slippers.

He lies back and reads the sign taped to the ceiling again. It says, in crude block capitals, THIS IS YOUR ROOM. THIS IS A ROOM IN A HOSPITAL. THIS IS WHERE YOU LIVE NOW.

Earl rises and takes a look around. The room is large for a hospital— empty linoleum stretches out from the bed in three directions. Two doors and a window. The view isn't very helpful, either—a close of trees in the center of a carefully manicured piece of turf that terminates in a sliver of two-lane blacktop. The trees, except for the evergreens, are bare—early spring or late fall, one or the other.

Every inch of the desk is covered with Post-it notes, legal pads, neatly printed lists, psychology textbooks, framed pictures. On top of the mess is a half-completed crossword puzzle. The alarm clock is riding a pile of folded newspapers. Earl slaps the snooze button and takes a cigarette from the pack taped to the sleeve of his dressing gown. He pats the empty pockets of his pajamas for a light. He rifles the papers on the desk, looks quickly through the drawers. Eventually he finds a box of kitchen matches taped to the wall next to the window. Another sign is taped just above the box. It says in loud yellow letters, CIGARETTE? CHECK FOR LIT ONES FIRST, STUPID.

Earl laughs at the sign, lights his cigarette, and takes a long draw. Taped to the window in front of him is another piece of loose-leaf paper headed YOUR SCHEDULE.

It charts off the hours, every hour, in blocks: 10:00 P.M. to 8:00 A.M. is labeled GO BACK TO SLEEP. Earl consults the alarm clock; 8:15. Given the light outside, it must be morning. He checks his watch: 10:30. He presses the watch to his ear and listens. He gives the watch a wind or two and sets it to match the alarm clock.

According to the schedule, the entire block from 8:00 to 8:30 has been labeled BRUSH YOUR TEETH. Earl laughs again and walks over to the bathroom.

The bathroom window is open. As he flaps his arms to keep warm, he notices the ashtray on the windowsill. A cigarette is perched on the ashtray, burning steadily through a long finger of ash. He frowns, extinguishes the old butt, and replaces it with the new one.

The toothbrush has already been treated to a smudge of white paste. The tap is of the push-button variety—a dose of water with each nudge. Earl pushes the brush into his cheek and fiddles it back and forth while he opens the medicine cabinet. The shelves are stocked with single-serving packages of vitamins, aspirin, antidiuretics. The mouthwash is also single-serving, about a shot-glass-worth of blue liquid in a sealed plastic bottle. Only the toothpaste is regular-sized. Earl spits the paste out of his mouth and replaces it with the mouthwash. As he lays the toothbrush next to the toothpaste, he notices a tiny wedge of paper pinched between the glass shelf and the steel backing of the medicine cabinet. He spits the frothy blue fluid into the sink and nudges for some more water to rinse it down. He closes the medicine cabinet and smiles at his reflection in the mirror.

"Who needs half an hour to brush their teeth?"

The paper has been folded down to a minuscule size with all the precision of a sixth-grader's love note. Earl unfolds it and smooths it against the mirror. It reads—

IF YOU CAN STILL READ THIS, THEN YOU'RE A FUCKING COWARD.

Earl stares blankly at the paper, then reads it again. He turns it over. On the back it reads—

P.S.: AFTER YOU'VE READ THIS, HIDE IT AGAIN.

Earl reads both sides again, then folds the note back down to its original size and tucks it underneath the toothpaste.

Maybe then he notices the scar. It begins just beneath the ear, jagged and thick, and disappears abruptly into his hairline. Earl turns his head and stares out of the corner of his eye to follow the scar's progress. He traces it with a fingertip, then looks back down at the cigarette burning in the ashtray. A thought seizes him and he spins out of the bathroom.

He is caught at the door to his room, one hand on the knob. Two pictures are taped to the wall by the door. Earl's attention is caught first by the MRI, a shiny black frame for four windows into someone's skull. In marker, the picture is labeled YOUR BRAIN. Earl stares at it. Concentric circles in different colors. He can make out the big orbs of his eyes and, behind these, the twin lobes of his brain. Smooth wrinkles, circles, semicircles. But right there in the middle of his head, circled in marker, tunneled in from the back of his neck like a maggot into an apricot, is something different. Deformed, broken, but unmistakable. A dark smudge, the shape of a flower, right there in the middle of his brain.

He bends to look at the other picture. It is a photograph of a man holding flowers, standing over a fresh grave. The man is bent over, reading the headstone. For a moment this looks like a hall of mirrors or the beginnings of a sketch of infinity: the one man bent over, looking at the smaller man, bent over, reading the headstone. Earl looks at the picture for a long time. Maybe he begins to cry. Maybe he just stares silently at the picture. Eventually, he makes his way back to the bed, flops down, seals his eyes shut, tries to sleep.

The cigarette burns steadily away in the bathroom. A circuit in the alarm clock counts down from ten, and it starts ringing again.

Earl opens one eye after another to a stretch of white ceiling tiles, interrupted by a hand-printed sign taped right above his head, large enough for him to read from the bed.

You can't have a normal life anymore. You must know that. How can you have a girlfriend if you can't remember her name? Can't have kids, not unless you want them to grow up with a dad who doesn't recognize them. Sure as hell can't hold down a job. Not too many professions out there that value forgetfulness. Prostitution, maybe. Politics, of course.

No. Your life is over. You're a dead man. The only thing the doctors are hoping to do is teach you to be less of a burden to the orderlies. And they'll probably never let you go home, wherever that would be.

So the question is not "to be or not to be," because you aren't. The question is whether you want to do something about it. Whether revenge matters to you.

It does to most people. For a few weeks, they plot, they scheme, they take measures to get even. But the passage of time is all it takes to erode that initial impulse. Time is theft, isn't that what they say? And time eventually convinces most of us that forgiveness is a virtue. Conveniently, cowardice and forgiveness look identical at a certain distance. Time steals your nerve.

If time and fear aren't enough to dissuade people from their revenge, then there's always authority, softly shaking its head and saying, We understand, but you're the better man for letting it go. For rising above it. For not sinking to their level. And besides, says authority, if you try anything stupid, we'll lock you up in a little room.

But they already put you in a little room, didn't they? Only they don't really lock it or even guard it too carefully because you're a cripple. A corpse. A vegetable who probably wouldn't remember to eat or take a shit if someone wasn't there to remind you.

And as for the passage of time, well, that doesn't really apply to you anymore, does it? Just the same ten minutes, over and over again. So how can you forgive if you can't remember to forget?

You probably were the type to let it go, weren't you? Before. But you're not the man you used to be. Not even half. You're a fraction; you're the ten-minute man.

Of course, weakness is strong. It's the primary impulse. You'd probably prefer to sit in your little room and cry. Live in your finite collection of memories, carefully polishing each one. Half a life set behind glass and pinned to cardboard like a collection of exotic insects. You'd like to live behind that glass, wouldn't you? Preserved in aspic.

You'd like to but you can't, can you? You can't because of the last addition to your collection. The last thing you remember. His face. His face and your wife, looking to you for help.

And maybe this is where you can retire to when it's over. Your little collection. They can lock you back up in another little room and you can live the rest *of your life in the past. But only if you've got a little piece of paper in your hand that says you got him.*

You know I'm right. You know there's a lot of work to do. It may seem impossible, but I'm sure if we all do our part, we'll figure something out. But you don't have much time. You've only got about ten minutes, in fact. Then it starts all over again. So do something with the time you've got.

Earl opens his eyes and blinks into the darkness. The alarm clock is ringing. It says 3:20, and the moonlight streaming through the window means it must be the early morning. Earl fumbles for the lamp, almost knocking it over in the process. Incandescent light fills the room, painting the metal furniture yellow, the walls yellow, the bedspread, too. He lies back and looks up at the stretch of yellow ceiling tiles above him, interrupted by a handwritten sign taped to the ceiling. He reads the sign two, maybe three times, then blinks at the room around him.

It is a bare room. Institutional, maybe. There is a desk over by the window. The desk is bare except for the blaring alarm clock. Earl probably notices, at this point, that he is fully clothed. He even has his shoes on under the sheets. He extracts himself from the bed and crosses to the desk. Nothing in the room would suggest that anyone lived there, or ever had, except for the odd scrap of tape stuck here and there to the wall. No pictures, no books, nothing. Through the window, he can see a full moon shining on carefully manicured grass.

Earl slaps the snooze button on the alarm clock and stares a moment at the two keys taped to the back of his hand. He picks at the tape while he searches through the empty drawers. In the left pocket of his jacket, he finds a roll of hundred-dollar bills and a letter sealed in an envelope. He checks the rest of the main room and the bathroom. Bits of tape, cigarette butts. Nothing else.

Earl absentmindedly plays with the lump of scar tissue on his neck and moves back toward the bed. He lies back down and stares up at the ceiling and the sign taped to it The sign reads, GET UP, GET OUT RIGHT NOW. THESE PEOPLE ARE TRYING TO KILL YOU.

Earl closes his eyes.

They tried to teach you to make lists in grade school, remember? Back when your day planner was the back of your hand. And if your assignments came off in the shower, well, then they didn't get done. No direction, they said. No discipline. So they tried to get you to write it all down somewhere more permanent.

Of course, your grade-school teachers would be laughing their pants wet if they could see you now. Because you've become the exact product of their organizational lessons. Because you can't even take a piss without consulting one of your lists.

They were right. Lists are the only way out of this mess.

Here's the truth: People, even regular people, are never just any one person with one set of attributes. It's not that simple. We're all at the mercy of the limbic system, clouds of electricity drifting through the brain. Every man is broken into twenty-four-hour fractions, and then again within those twenty-four hours. It's a daily pantomime, one man yielding control to the next: a backstage crowded with old hacks clamoring for their turn in the spotlight. Every week, every day. The angry man hands the baton over to the sulking man, and in turn to the sex addict, the introvert, the conversationalist. Every man is a mob, a chain gang of idiots.

This is the tragedy of life. Because for a few minutes of every day, every man becomes a genius. Moments of clarity, insight, whatever you want to call them. The clouds part, the planets get in a neat little line, and everything becomes obvious. I should quit smoking, maybe, or here's how I could make a fast million, or such and such is the key to eternal happiness. That's the miserable truth. For a few moments, the secrets of the universe are opened to us. Life is a cheap parlor trick.

But then the genius, the savant, has to hand over the controls to the next guy down the pike, most likely the guy who just wants to eat potato chips, and insight and brilliance and salvation are all entrusted to a moron or a hedonist or a narcoleptic.

The only way out of this mess, of course, is to take steps to ensure that you control the idiots that you become. To take your chain gang, hand in hand, and lead them. The best way to do this is with a list.

It's like a letter you write to yourself. A master plan, drafted by the guy who can see the light, made with steps simple enough for the rest of the idiots to understand. Follow steps one through one hundred. Repeat as necessary.

Your problem is a little more acute, maybe, but fundamentally the same thing.

It's like that computer thing, the Chinese room. You remember that? One guy sits in a little room, laying down cards with letters written on them in a language he doesn't understand, laying them down one letter at a time in a sequence according to someone else's instructions. The cards are supposed to spell out a joke in Chinese. The guy doesn't speak Chinese, of course. He just follows his instructions.

There are some obvious differences in your situation, of course: You broke out of the room they had you in, so the whole enterprise has to be portable. And the guy giving the instructions—that's you, too, just an earlier version of you. And the joke you're telling, well, it's got a punch line. I just don't think anyone's going to find it very funny.

So that's the idea. All you have to do is follow your instructions. Like climbing a ladder or descending a staircase. One step at a time. Right down the list. Simple.

And the secret, of course, to any list is to keep it in a place where you're bound to see it.

He can hear the buzzing through his eyelids. Insistent. He reaches out for the alarm clock, but he can't move his arm.

Earl opens his eyes to see a large man bent double over him. The man looks up at him, annoyed, then resumes his work. Earl looks around him. Too dark for a doctor's office.

Then the pain floods his brain, blocking out the other questions. He squirms again, tying to yank his forearm away, the one that feels like it's burning. The arm doesn't move, but the man shoots him another scowl. Earl adjusts himself in the chair to see over the top of the man's head.

The noise and the pain are both coming from a gun in the man's hand—a gun with a needle where the barrel should be. The needle is digging into the fleshy underside of Earl's forearm, leaving a trail of puffy letters behind it.

Earl tries to rearrange himself to get a better view, to read the letters on his arm, but he can't. He lies back and stares at the ceiling.

Eventually the tattoo artist turns off the noise, wipes Earl's forearm with a piece of gauze, and wanders over to the back to dig up a pamphlet describing how to deal with a possible infection. Maybe later he'll tell his wife about this guy and his little note. Maybe his wife will convince him to call the police.

Earl looks down at the arm. The letters are rising up from the skin, weeping a little. They run from just behind the strap of Earl's watch all the way to the inside of his elbow. Earl blinks at the message and reads it again. It says, in careful little capitals, I RAPED AND KILLED YOUR WIFE.

It's your birthday today, so I got you a little present. I would have just bought you a beer, but who knows where that would have ended?

So instead, I got you a bell. I think I may have had to pawn your watch to buy it, but what the hell did you need a watch for, anyway?

You're probably asking yourself, Why a bell? In fact, I'm guessing you're going to be asking yourself that question every time you find it in your pocket. Too many of these letters now. Too many for you to dig back into every time you want to know the answer to some little question.

It's a joke, actually. A practical joke. But think of it this way: I'm not really laughing at you so much as with you.

I'd like to think that every time you take it out of your pocket and wonder, Why do I have this bell? a little part of you, a little piece of your broken brain, will remember and laugh, like I'm laughing now.

Besides, you do know the answer. It was something you learned before. So if you think about it, you'll know.

Back in the old days, people were obsessed with the fear of being buried alive. You remember now? Medical science not being quite what it is today, it wasn't uncommon for people to suddenly wake up in a casket. So rich folks had their coffins outfitted with breathing tubes. Little tubes running up to the mud above so that if someone woke up when they weren't supposed to, they wouldn't run out of oxygen. Now, they must have tested this out and realized that you could shout yourself hoarse through the tube, but it was too narrow to carry much noise. Not enough to attract attention, at least. So a string was run up the tube to a little bell attached to the headstone. If a dead person came back to life, all he had to do was ring his little bell till someone came and dug him up again.

I'm laughing now, picturing you on a bus or maybe in a fast-food restaurant, reaching into your pocket and finding your little bell and wondering to yourself where it came from, why you have it. Maybe you'll even ring it.

Happy birthday, buddy.

I don't know who figured out the solution to our mutual problem, so I don't know whether to congratulate you or me. A bit of a lifestyle change, admittedly, but an elegant solution, nonetheless.

Look to yourself for the answer.

That sounds like something out of a Hallmark card. I don't know when you thought it up, but my hat's off to you. Not that you know what the hell I'm talking about. But, honestly, a real brainstorm. After all, everybody else needs mirrors to remind themselves who they are. You're no different.

The little mechanical voice pauses, then repeats itself. It says, "The time is 8:00 A.M. This is a courtesy call." Earl opens his eyes and replaces the receiver. The phone is perched on a cheap veneer headboard that stretches behind the bed, curves to meet the corner, and ends at the minibar. The TV is still on, blobs of flesh color nattering away at each other. Earl lies back down and is surprised to see himself, older now, tanned, the hair pulling away from his head like solar flares. The mirror on the ceiling is cracked, the silver fading in creases. Earl continues to stare at himself, astonished by what he sees. He is fully dressed, but the clothes are old, threadbare in places.

Earl feels the familiar spot on his left wrist for his watch, but it's gone. He looks down from the mirror to his arm. It is bare and the skin has changed to an even tan, as if he never owned a watch in the first place. The skin is even in color except for the solid black arrow on the inside of Earl's wrist, pointing up his shirtsleeve. He stares at the arrow for a moment. Perhaps he doesn't try to rub it off anymore. He rolls up his sleeve.

The arrow points to a sentence tattooed along Earl's inner arm. Earl reads the sentence once, maybe twice. Another arrow picks up at the beginning of the sentence, points farther up Earl's arm, disappearing under the rolled-up shirtsleeve. He unbuttons his shirt.

Looking down on his chest, he can make out the shapes but cannot bring them into focus, so he looks up at the mirror above him.

The arrow leads up Earl's arm, crosses at the shoulder, and descends onto his upper torso, terminating at a picture of a man's face that occupies most of his chest. The face is that of a large man, balding, with a mustache and a goatee. It is a particular face, but like a police sketch it has a certain unreal quality.

The rest of his upper torso is covered in words, phrases, bits of information, and instructions, all of them written backward on Earl, forward in the mirror.

Eventually Earl sits up, buttons his shirt, and crosses to the desk. He takes out a pen and a piece of notepaper from the desk drawer, sits, and begins to write.

• • •

I don't know where you'll be when you read this. I'm not even sure if you'll bother to read this. I guess you don't need to.

It's a shame, really, that you and I will never meet. But, like the song says, "By the time you read this note, I'll be gone."

We're so close now. That's the way it feels. So many pieces put together, spelled out. I guess it's just a matter of time until you find him.

Who knows what we've done to get here? Must be a hell of a story, if only you could remember any of it. I guess it's better that you can't.

I had a thought just now. Maybe you'll find it useful.

Everybody is waiting for the end to come, but what if it already passed us by? What if the final joke of Judgment Day was that it had already come and gone and we were none the wiser? Apocalypse arrives quietly; the chosen are herded off to heaven, and the rest of us, the ones who failed the test, just keep on going, oblivious. Dead already, wandering around long after the gods have stopped keeping score, still optimistic about the future.

I guess if that's true, then it doesn't matter what you do. No expectations. If you can't find him, then it doesn't matter, because nothing matters. And if you do find him, then you can kill him without worrying about the consequences. Because there are no consequences.

That's what I'm thinking about right now, in this scrappy little room. Framed pictures of ships on the wall. I don't know, obviously, but if I had to guess, I'd say we're somewhere up the coast. If you're wondering why your left arm is five shades browner than your right, I don't know what to tell you. I guess we must have been driving for a while. And, no, I don't know what happened to your watch.

And all these keys: I have no idea. Not a one that I recognize. Car keys and house keys and the little fiddly keys for padlocks. What have we been up to?

I wonder if he'll feel stupid when you find him. Tracked down by the ten-minute man. Assassinated by a vegetable.

I'll be gone in a moment. I'll put down the pen, close my eyes, and then you can read this through if you want.

I just wanted you to know that I'm proud of you. No one who matters is left to say it. No one left is going to want to.

Earl's eyes are wide open, staring through the window of the car. Smiling eyes. Smiling through the window at the crowd gathering across the street. The crowd gathering around the body in the doorway. The blood emptying slowly across the sidewalk and into the storm drain.

A stocky guy, facedown, eyes open. Balding head, goatee. In death, as in police sketches, faces tend to look the same. This is definitely somebody in particular. But really, it could be anybody.

Earl is still smiling at the body as the car pulls away from the curb. The car? Who's to say? Maybe it's a police cruiser. Maybe it's just a taxi.

As the car is swallowed into traffic, Earl's eyes continue to shine out into the night, watching the body until it disappears into a circle of concerned pedestrians. He chuckles to himself as the car continues to make distance between him and the growing crowd.

Earl's smile fades a little. Something has occurred to him. He begins to pat down his pockets; leisurely at first, like a man looking for his keys, then a little more desperately. Maybe his progress is impeded by a set of handcuffs. He begins to empty the contents of his pockets out onto the seat next to him. Some money. A bunch of keys. Scraps of paper.

A round metal lump rolls out of his pocket and slides across the vinyl seat. Earl is frantic now. He hammers at the plastic divider between him and the driver, begging the man for a pen. Perhaps the cabbie doesn't speak much English. Perhaps the cop isn't in the habit of talking to suspects. Either way, the divider between the man in front and the man behind remains closed. A pen is not forthcoming.

The car hits a pothole, and Earl blinks at his reflection in the rearview mirror. He is calm now. The driver makes another corner, and the metal lump slides back over to rest against Earl's leg with a little jingle. He picks it up and looks at it, curious now. It is a little bell. A little metal bell. Inscribed on it are his name and a set of dates. He recognizes the first one: the year in which he was born. But the second date means nothing to him. Nothing at all.

As he turns the bell over in his hands, he notices the empty space on his wrist where his watch used to sit. There is a little arrow there, pointing up his arm. Earl looks at the arrow, then begins to roll up his sleeve.

"You'd be late for your own funeral," she'd say. Remember? The more I think about it, the more trite that seems. What kind of idiot, after all, is in any kind of rush to get to the end of his own story?

And how would I know if I were late, anyway? I don't have a watch anymore. I don't know what we did with it.

What the hell do you need a watch for, anyway? It was an antique. Deadweight tugging at your wrist. Symbol of the old you. The you that believed in time.

No. Scratch that. It's not so much that you've lost your faith in time as that time has lost its faith in you. And who needs it, anyway? Who wants to be one of those saps living in the safety of the future, in the safety of the moment after the moment in which they felt something powerful? Living in the next moment, in which they feel nothing. Crawling down the hands of the clock, away from the people who did unspeakable things to them. Believing the lie that time will heal all wounds—which is just a nice way of saying that time deadens us.

But you're different. You're more perfect. Time is three things for most people, but for you, for us, just one. A singularity. One moment. This moment. Like you're the center of the clock, the axis on which the hands turn. Time moves about you but never moves you. It has lost its ability to affect you. What is it they say? That time is theft? But not for you. Close your eyes and you can start all over again. Conjure up that necessary emotion, fresh as roses.

Time is an absurdity. An abstraction. The only thing that matters is this moment. This moment a million times over. You have to trust me. If this moment is repeated enough, if you keep trying—and you have to keep trying—eventually you will come across the next item on your list.

Edwidge Danticat

Seven

from *The New Yorker*

NEXT MONTH would make it seven years since he'd last seen his wife. Seven, a number he despised but had discovered was a useful marker. There were seven days between paychecks, seven hours, not counting lunch, spent each day at his day job, seven at his night job. Seven was the last number in his age—thirty-seven. And now there were seven hours left before his wife was due to arrive. Maybe it would be more, with her having to wait for her luggage and then make it through the long immigration line and past customs to look for him in the crowd of welcoming faces on the other side of the sliding doors at JFK. That is, if the flight from Port-au-Prince wasn't delayed, as it often was, or cancelled altogether.

He shared an apartment in the basement of a house in East Flatbush, Brooklyn, with two other men. To prepare for the reunion, he had cleaned his room. He had thrown out some cherry-red rayon shirts that he knew she would hate. And then he had climbed the splintered steps to the first floor to tell the landlady that his wife was coming. His landlady was also Haitian, a self-employed accountant.

"I don't have a problem with your wife coming," she had told him. She was microwaving a frozen dessert. "I just hope she is clean."

"She is clean," he said.

The kitchen was the only room in the main part of the house that he'd ever seen. It was spotless, and the dishes were neatly organized in glass cabinets. It smelled of pine-scented air freshener.

"Did you tell the men?" she asked. She opened the microwave and removed two small plastic plates of something that vaguely resembled strawberry cheesecake.

"I told them," he said.

He was waiting for her to announce that she would have to charge him extra. She had agreed to rent the room to one person, not two—a man she'd probably taken for a bachelor.

"I don't know if I can keep this arrangement if everyone's wife starts coming," she said.

He could not speak for the two other men. Michel and Dany had wives, too, but he had no idea if or when those wives would be joining them.

"A woman living down there with three men," the landlady said. "Maybe your wife will be uncomfortable."

He wanted to tell her that it was not up to her to decide whether or not his wife would be comfortable. But he had been prepared for this, too, for some unpleasant remark about his wife. Actually, he was up there as much to give notice that he was looking for an apartment as to announce that his wife was coming. As soon as he found one, he would be moving.

"O.K., then," she said, opening her silverware drawer. "Just remember, you start the month, you pay the whole thing."

"Thank you very much, Madame," he said.

As he walked back downstairs, he scolded himself for calling her Madame. Why had he acted like a servant who had been dismissed? It was one of those class things from home that he couldn't shake. On the other hand, if he had addressed the woman respectfully, it wasn't because she was so-called upper class, or because she spoke French (though never to him), or even because after five years in the same room he was still paying only $350 a month. If he had addressed the woman politely that day, it was because he was making a sacrifice for his wife.

After his conversation with the landlady, he decided to have a more thorough one with the men who occupied the other two rooms in the basement. The day before his wife was to arrive, he went into the kitchen to see them. The fact that they were wearing only white, rather sheer, loose boxers, as they stumbled about bleary-eyed, concerned him.

"You understand, she's a woman," he told them. He wasn't worried that she'd be tempted—they were skin and bones—but if she was still as sensitive as he remembered, their near-nakedness might embarrass her.

The men understood.

"If it were my wife," Michel said, "I would feel the same."

Dany simply nodded.

They had robes, Michel declared after a while. They would wear them.

They didn't have robes—all three men knew this—but Michel would buy some, out of respect for the wife. Michel, at forty, the oldest of the three, had advised him to pretty up his room—to buy some silk roses, some decorative prints for the walls (no naked girls), and some vanilla incense, which would be more pleasing than the air fresheners the woman upstairs liked so much.

Dany told him that he would miss their evenings out together. In the old days, they had often gone dancing at the Rendez-Vous, which was now the Cenegal night club. But they hadn't gone much since the place had become famous—Abner Louima was arrested there, then beaten and sodomized at a nearby police station.

He told Dany not to mention those nights out again. His wife wasn't to know that he had ever done anything but work his jobs—as a day janitor at Medgar Evers College and as a night janitor at King's County Hospital. And he wasn't going to tell her about those women who had occasionally come home with him in the early-morning hours. Those women, most of whom had husbands, boyfriends, fiancés, and lovers in other parts of the world, had never meant much to him anyway.

Michel, who had become a lay minister at a small Baptist church near the Rendez-Vous and never danced there, laughed as he listened. "The cock can no longer crow," he said. "You might as well give the rest to Jesus."

"Jesus wouldn't know what to do with what's left of this man," Dany said.

Gone were the late-night domino games. Gone was the phone number he'd had for the past five years, ever since he'd had a phone. (He didn't need other women calling him now.) And it was only as he stood in the crowd of people waiting to meet the flights arriving simultaneously from Kingston, Santo Domingo, and Port-au-Prince that he stopped worrying that he might not see any delight or recognition in his wife's face. There, he began to feel some actual joy, even exhilaration, which made him want to leap forward and grab every woman who vaguely resembled the latest pictures she had sent him, all of which he had neatly framed and hung on the walls of his room.

They were searching her suitcase. Why were they searching her suitcase? One meagre bag, which, aside from some gifts for her husband, contained the few things she'd been unable to part with, the things her relatives hadn't nabbed from her, telling her that she could get more, and better, where she was going. She had kept only her undergarments, a nightgown, and two outfits: the green princess dress she was wearing and a red jumper that she'd gift wrapped before packing so that no one would take it. People in her neighborhood who had travelled before had told her to gift wrap everything so that it wouldn't be opened at the airport in New York. Now the customs man was tearing her careful wrapping to shreds as he barked questions at her in mangled Creole.

"*Ki sa l ye?*" He held a package out in front of her before opening it.

What was it? She didn't know anymore. She could only guess by the shapes and sizes.

He unwrapped all her gifts—the mangoes, sugarcane, avocados, the orange- and grapefruit-peel preserves, the peanut, cashew, and coconut confections, the coffee beans, which he threw into a green bin decorated with drawings of fruits and vegetables with red lines across them. The only thing that seemed as though it might escape disposal was a small packet of trimmed chicken feathers, which her husband used to enjoy twirling in his ear cavity. In the early days, soon after he'd left, she had spun the tips of the feathers inside her ears, too, and discovered that from them she could get *jwisans,* pleasure, an orgasm. She had thought to herself then that maybe the foreign television programs were right: sex was mostly between the ears.

When the customs man came across the small package of feathers, he stared down at it, then looked up at her, letting his eyes linger on her face, mostly, it seemed to her, on her ears. Obviously, he had seen feathers like these before. Into the trash they went, along with the rest of her offerings.

By the time he was done with her luggage, she had little left. The suitcase was so light now that she could walk very quickly as she carried it in her left hand. She followed a man pushing a cart, which tipped and swerved under the weight of three large boxes. And suddenly she found herself before a door that slid open by itself, parting like a glass sea, and as she was standing there the door closed again, and when she moved a few steps forward it opened, and then she saw him. He charged at her and wrapped both his arms around her. And as he held her she felt her feet leave the ground. It was when he put her back down that she finally believed she was really somewhere else, on another soil, in another country.

He could tell she was happy that so many of her pictures were displayed on the wall facing his bed. During the ride home, he had nearly crashed the car twice. He wasn't sure why he was driving so fast. They dashed through the small talk, the inventory of friends and family members and the state of their health. She had no detailed anecdotes about anyone in particular. Some had died and some were still living; he couldn't even remember which. She was bigger than she had been when he left her, what people here might call chubby. It was obvious that she had been to a professional hairdresser, because she was elegantly coiffed with her short hair gelled down to her scalp and a fake bun bulging in the back. She smelled good—a mixture of lavender and lime. He had simply wanted to get her home, if home it was, to that room, and to reduce the space between them until there was no air for her to breathe that he wasn't breathing, too.

The drive had reminded him of the one they had taken to their one-night honeymoon at the Ifé Hotel, when he had begged the uncle who was driving them to go faster, because the next morning he would be on a plane for New York. That night, he'd had no idea that it would be seven years before he would see her again. He'd had it all planned. He knew that he couldn't send for her right away, since he would be overstaying a tourist visa. But he was going to work hard, to find a lawyer and get himself a green card, and then send for his wife. The green card had taken six years and nine months. But now she was here with him, staring at the pictures on his wall as though they were of someone else.

"Do you remember that one?" he asked, to reassure her. He was pointing at a framed eight-by-twelve of her lying on a red mat by a tiny Christmas tree in a photographer's studio. "You sent it last Noël?"

She remembered, she said. It was just that she looked so desperate, as if she were trying to force *him* to remember *her.*

"I never forgot you for an instant," he said.

She said that she was thirsty.

"What do you want to drink?" He listed the juices he had purchased from the Cuban grocer down the street, the combinations he was sure she'd be craving, papaya and mango, guava and pineapple, cherimoya and passion fruit.

"Just a little water," she said. "Cold."

He didn't want to leave her alone while he went to the kitchen. He would have called through the walls for one of the men to get some water, if they were not doing such a good job of hiding behind the closed doors of their rooms to give him some privacy.

When he came back with the glass, she examined it, as if for dirt, and then gulped it down. It was as though she hadn't drunk anything since the morning he'd got on the plane and left her behind.

"Do you want more?" he asked.

She shook her head.

It's too bad, he thought, that in Creole the word for love, *renmen*, is also the word for like, so that as he told her he loved her he had to embellish it with phrases that illustrated the degree of that love. He loved her more than there were seconds in the years they'd been apart, he babbled. He loved her more than the size of the ocean she had just crossed. To keep himself from saying more insipid things, he jumped on top of her and pinned her down on the bed. She was not as timid as she had been on their wedding night. She tugged at his black tie so fiercely that he was sure his neck was bruised. He yanked a few buttons off her dress and threw them aside as she unbuttoned his starched and ironed white shirt, and though in the rehearsals in past daydreams he had gently placed a cupped hand over her mouth, he didn't think to do it now. He didn't care that the other men could hear her, or him. Only for a moment did he think to feel sorry that it might be years before the others could experience the same thing.

He was exhausted when she grabbed the top sheet from the bed, wrapped it around her, and announced that she was going to the bathroom.

"Let me take you," he said.

"*Non non*," she said, "I can find it."

He couldn't stand to watch her turn away and disappear.

He heard voices in the kitchen, her talking to the men, introducing herself. He bolted right up from the bed when he remembered that all she had on was the sheet. As he raced to the door, he collided with her coming back.

There were two men playing dominoes in the kitchen, she told him, dressed in identical pink satin robes.

He left early for work the next day, along with the other men, but not before handing her a set of keys and instructing her not to let anyone in. He showed her how to work the stove and how to find all the Haitian stations on the AM/FM dial of his night-table radio. She slept late, reliving the night, their laughter after she'd seen the men, who, he explained, had hurried to buy those robes for her benefit. They had made love again and again, forcing themselves to do so more quietly each time. Seven times, by his count—once for each year they'd been apart—but fewer by hers. He had assured her that there was no need to be embarrassed. They were married, before God and a priest. This was crucial for her to remember. That's why he had seen to it on the night before he left. So that something more judicial and committing than a mere promise would bind them. So that even if their union had become a victim of distance and time, it could not have been easily dissolved. They would have had to sign papers to come apart, write letters, speak on the phone about it. He told her that he didn't want to leave her again, not for one second. But he had asked for the day off and his boss had refused. At least they would have the weekends, Saturdays and Sundays, to do with as they wished—to go dancing, sightseeing, shopping, and apartment hunting. Wouldn't she like to have her own apartment? To make love as much as they wanted and not worry that some men in women's robes had heard them?

At noon, the phone rang. It was him. He asked her what she was doing. She lied and told him that she was cooking, making herself something to eat. He asked what. She said eggs, guessing that there must be eggs in the refrigerator. He asked if she was bored. She said no. She was going to listen to the radio and write letters home.

When she hung up, she turned on the radio. She scrolled between the stations he had pointed out to her and was glad to hear people speaking Creole. There was music playing, too—*konpa* by a group named Top Vice. She switched to a station with a talk show. She sat up to listen as some callers talked about a Haitian-American named Patrick Dorismond who had been killed. He had been shot by a policeman in a place called Manhattan. She wanted to call her husband back, but he hadn't left a number. Lying back, she raised the sheet over her head and through it listened to the callers, each one angrier than the last.

• • •

When he came home, he saw that she had used what she had found in the refrigerator and the kitchen cabinets to cook a large meal for all four of them. She insisted that they wait for the other men to drift in before they ate, even though he had only a few hours before he had to leave for his night job.

The men complimented her enthusiastically on her cooking, and he could tell that this meal made them feel as though they were part of a family, something they had not experienced in years. They seemed to be happy, eating for pleasure as well as sustenance, chewing more slowly than they ever had before. Usually they ate standing up, Chinese or Jamaican takeout from places down the street. Tonight there was little conversation, beyond praise for the food. The men offered to clean the pots and dishes once they were done, and he suspected that they wanted to lick them before washing them.

He and his wife went to the room and lay on their backs on the bed. He explained why he had two jobs. It had been partly to fill the hours away from her, but also partly because he had needed to support both himself here and her in Port-au-Prince. And now he was saving up for an apartment and, ultimately, a house. She said that she, too, wanted to work. She had finished a secretarial course; perhaps that would be helpful here. He warned her that, because she didn't speak English, she might have to start as a cook in a restaurant or as a seamstress in a factory. He fell asleep mid-thought. She woke him up at nine o'clock, when he was supposed to start work. He rushed to the bathroom to wash his face, came back, and changed his overalls, all the while cursing himself. He was stupid to have overslept, and now he was late. He kissed her good-bye and ran out. He hated being late, being lectured by the night manager, whose favorite reprimand was "There's tons of people like you in this city. Half of them need a job."

She spent the whole week inside, worried that she'd get lost if she ventured out alone, that she might not be able to retrace her steps. Her days fell into a routine. She'd wake up and listen to the radio for news of what was happening both here and back home. Somewhere, not far from where she was, people were in the streets, marching, protesting Dorismond's death, their outrage made even greater by the fact that the Dorismond boy was the American-born son of a well-known singer, whose voice they had heard on the radio back in Haiti. "No justice, no peace!" she chanted while stewing chicken and frying fish. In the afternoons, she wrote letters home. She wrote of the meals that she had made, of the pictures of her on the wall, of the songs and protest chants on the radio. She wrote to family members, and to childhood girlfriends who had been so happy that she was finally going to be with her husband, and to newer acquaintances from the secretarial school who had been jealous. She also wrote to a male friend, a neighbor who had come to her house three days after her husband had left to see why she had locked herself inside.

He had knocked for so long that she'd had no choice but to open the door. She was still wearing the dress she'd worn to see her husband off. When she collapsed in his arms, he had put a cold compress on her forehead and offered her some water. She had swallowed so much water so quickly that she'd vomited. That night, he had lain down next to her, and in the dark had told her that this was love, if love there was—having the courage to abandon the present for a future that one could only imagine. He had assured her that her husband loved her.

In the afternoons, while she was writing her letters, she would hear someone walking back and forth on the floor above. She took to pacing as well, as she waited for the men to come home. She wanted to tell her husband about that neighbor who had slept next to her for those days after he'd left and in whose bed she had spent many nights after that. Only then would she feel that their future would be true. Someone had said that people lie only at the beginning of relationships. The middle is where the truth resides. But there had been no middle for her husband and herself, just a beginning and many dream-rehearsed endings.

He had first met his wife during carnival in the mountains in Jacmel. His favorite part of the festivities was the finale, on the day before Ash Wednesday, when a crowd of tired revellers would gather on the beach to burn their carnival masks and costumes and feign weeping, symbolically purging themselves of the carousing of the preceding days and nights. She had volunteered to be one of the official weepers—one of those who wailed convincingly as the carnival relics turned to ashes in the bonfire.

"*Papa Kanaval ou ale?*" "Where have you gone, Father Carnival?" she had howled, with real tears running down her face.

If she could grieve so passionately on demand, he thought, perhaps she could love even more. After the other weepers had left, she stayed behind until the last embers of the bonfire had dimmed. It was impossible to distract her, to make her laugh. She could never fake weeping, she told him. Every time she cried for anything, she cried for everything else that had ever hurt her.

He had travelled between Jacmel and Port-au-Prince while he was waiting for his visa to come through. And when he finally had a travel date he had asked her to marry him.

One afternoon, when he came home from work, he found her sitting on the edge of the bed in that small room, staring at the pictures of herself on the opposite wall. She did not move as he kissed the top of her head. He said nothing, simply slipped out of his clothes and lay down on the bed, pressing his face against her back. He did not want to trespass on her secrets. He simply wanted to extinguish the carnivals burning in her head.

She was happy when the weekend finally came. Though he slept until noon, she woke up at dawn, rushed to the bathroom before the men could, put on her red jumper and one of his T-shirts, then sat staring down at him on the bed, waiting for his eyes to open.

"What plan do we have for today?" she asked when they finally did.

The plan, he said, was whatever she wanted.

She wanted to walk down a street with him and see faces. She wanted to eat something, an apple or a chicken leg, out in the open with the sun beating down on her face.

As they were leaving the house, they ran into the woman whose footsteps she had been hearing all week long above her head. The woman smiled coyly and said, *"Bienvenue."* She nodded politely, then pulled her husband away by the hand.

They walked down a street filled with people doing their Saturday food shopping at outside stalls stacked with fruits and vegetables.

He asked if she wanted to take the bus.

"Where to?"

"Anywhere," he said.

From the bus, she counted the frame and row houses, beauty-shop signs, church steeples, and gas stations. She pressed her face against the window, and her breath occasionally blocked her view of the streets speeding by. She turned back now and then to look at him, sitting next to her. There was still a trace of sleepiness in his eyes. He watched her as though he were trying to put himself in her place, to see it all as if for the first time, but could not.

He took her to a park in the middle of Brooklyn, Prospect Park, a vast stretch of land, trees, and trails. They strolled deep into the park, until they could see only a few of the surrounding buildings, which towered like mountains above the landscape. In all her daydreams, she had never imagined that there would be a place like this here. This immense garden, he told her, was where he came to ponder the passing seasons, lost time, and interminable distances.

It was past seven o'clock when they emerged from the park and headed down Parkside Avenue. She had reached for his hand at 5:10 P.M., he had noted, and had not released it since. And now, as they were walking down a dimly lit side street, she kept her eyes upward, looking into the windows of apartments lit by the indigo glow of television screens. When she said she was hungry, they turned onto Flatbush Avenue in search of something to eat.

Walking hand in hand with her through crowds of strangers made him long for his other favorite piece of carnival theatre. A bride and groom, in their most lavish wedding clothing, would wander the streets. Scanning a crowd of revellers, they would pick the most stony-faced person and ask, "Would you marry us?" Over the course of several days, for variety, they would modify this request. "Would you couple us?" "Would you make us one?" "Would you tie the noose of love around our necks?" The joke was that when the person took the bait and looked closely, he or she might discover that the bride was a man and the groom a woman. The couple's makeup was so skillfully applied that only the most observant could detect this.

On the nearly empty bus on the way home, he sat across the aisle from her, not next to her as he had that morning. She pretended to keep her eyes on the night racing past the window behind him. He was watching her again. This time he seemed to be trying to see *her* as if for the first time, but could not.

She, too, was thinking of carnival, and of how, the year after they'd met, they had dressed as a bride and groom looking for someone to marry them. She had disguised herself as the bride and he as the groom, forgoing the traditional puzzle.

At the end of the celebrations, she had burned her wedding dress in the bonfire and he had burned his suit. She wished now that they had kept them. They could have walked these foreign streets in them, performing their own carnival. Since she didn't know the language, they wouldn't have to speak or ask any questions of the stony-faced people around them. They could perform their public wedding march in silence, a silence like the one that had come over them now.

Anthony Doerr

The Hunter's Wife

from *The Atlantic Monthly*

I T WAS the hunter's first time outside Montana. He woke, stricken still with the hours-old vision of ascending through rose-lit cumulus, of houses and barns like specks deep in the snowed-in valleys, all the scrolling country below looking December—brown and black hills streaked with snow, flashes of iced-over lakes, the long braids of a river gleaming at the bottom of a canyon. Above the wing the sky had deepened to a blue so pure he knew it would bring tears to his eyes if he looked long enough.

Now it was dark. The airplane descended over Chicago, its galaxy of electric lights, the vast neighborhoods coming clearer as the plane glided toward the airport—streetlights, headlights, stacks of buildings, ice rinks, a truck turning at a stoplight, scraps of snow atop a warehouse and winking antennae on faraway hills, finally the long converging parallels of blue runway lights, and they were down.

He walked into the airport, past the banks of monitors. Already he felt as if he'd lost something, some beautiful perspective, some lovely dream fallen away. He had come to Chicago to see his wife, whom he had not seen in twenty years. She was there to perform her magic for a higher-up at the state university. Even universities, apparently, were interested in what she could do. Outside the terminal the sky was thick and gray and hurried by wind. Snow was coming. A woman from the university met him and escorted him to her Jeep. He kept his gaze out the window.

They were in the car for forty-five minutes, passing first the tall, lighted architecture of downtown, then naked suburban oaks, heaps of ploughed snow, gas stations, power towers, and telephone wires. The woman said, "So you regularly attend your wife's performances?"

"No," he said. "Never before."

She parked in the driveway of an elaborate modern mansion, with square balconies suspended over two garages, huge triangular windows in the façade, sleek columns, domed lights, a steep shale roof.

Inside the front door about thirty nametags were laid out on a table. His wife was not there yet. No one, apparently, was there yet. He found his tag and pinned it to his sweater. A silent girl in a tuxedo appeared and disappeared with his coat.

The granite foyer was backed with a grand staircase, which spread wide at the bottom and tapered at the top. A woman came down. She stopped four or five steps from the bottom and said, "Hello, Anne" to the woman who had driven him there and "You must be Mr. Dumas" to him. He took her hand, a pale, bony thing, weightless, like a featherless bird.

Her husband, the university's chancellor, was just knotting his bow tie, she said, and she laughed sadly to herself, as if bow ties were something she disapproved of. The hunter moved to a window, shifted aside the curtain, and peered out.

In the poor light he could see a wooden deck the length of the house, angled and stepped, its width ever changing, with a low rail. Beyond it, in the blue shadows, a small pond lay encircled by hedges, with a marble birdbath at its center. Behind the pond stood leafless trees—oaks, maples, a sycamore as white as bone. A helicopter shuttled past, its green light winking.

"It's snowing," he said.

"Is it?" the hostess asked, with an air of concern, perhaps false. It was impossible to tell what was sincere and what was not. The woman who had driven him there had moved to the bar, where she cradled a drink and stared into the carpet.

He let the curtain fall back. The chancellor came down the staircase. Other guests fluttered in. A man in gray corduroy, with "Bruce Maples" on his nametag, approached him. "Mr. Dumas," he said, "your wife isn't here yet?"

"You know her?" the hunter asked. "Oh, no," Maples said, and shook his head. "No, I don't." He spread his legs and swiveled his hips as if stretching before a footrace. "But I've read about her."

The hunter watched as a tall, remarkably thin man stepped through the front door. Hollows behind his jaw and beneath his eyes made him appear ancient and skeletal—as if he were visiting from some other, leaner world. The chancellor approached the thin man, embraced him and held him for a moment.

"That's President O'Brien," Maples said. "A famous man, actually, to people who follow those sorts of things. So terrible, what happened to his family." Maples stabbed the ice in his drink with his straw.

For the first time the hunter began to think he should not have come.

"Have you read your wife's books?" Maples asked.

The hunter nodded.

"In her poems her husband is a hunter."

"I guide hunters." He was looking out the window to where snow was settling on the hedges.

"Does that ever bother you?"

"What?

"Killing animals. For a living, I mean."

The hunter watched snowflakes disappear as they touched the window. Was that what hunting meant to people? Killing animals? He put his fingers to the glass. "No," he said. "It doesn't bother me."

The hunter met his wife in Great Falls, Montana, in the winter of 1972. That winter arrived all at once—you could watch it come. Twin curtains of white appeared in the north, white all the way to the sky, driving south like the end of all things. Cattle galloped the fencelines, bawling. Trees toppled; a barn roof tumbled over the highway. The river changed directions. The wind flung thrushes screaming into the gorse and impaled them on the thorns in grotesque attitudes.

She was a magician's assistant, beautiful, fifteen years old, an orphan. It was not a new story: a glittery red dress, long legs, a traveling magic show performing in the meeting hall at the Central Christian Church. The hunter had been walking past with an armful of groceries when the wind stopped him in his tracks and drove him into the alley behind the church. He had never felt such wind; it had him pinned. His face was pressed against a low window, and through it he could see the show. The magician

was a small man in a dirty blue cape. Above him a sagging banner read
THE GREAT VESPUCCI. But the hunter watched only the girl; she was
graceful, young, smiling. Like a wrestler, the wind held him against the
window.

The magician was buckling the girl into a plywood coffin, which was
painted garishly with red and blue bolts of lightning. Her neck and head
stuck out at one end, her ankle and feet at the other. She beamed; no one
had ever before smiled so broadly at being locked into a coffin. The magician started up an electric saw and brought it noisily down through the
center of the box, sawing her in half. Then he wheeled her apart, her legs
going one way, her torso another. Her neck fell back, her smile faded, her
eyes showed only white. The lights dimmed. A child screamed. Wiggle
your toes, the magician ordered, flourishing his magic wand, and she did;
her disembodied toes wiggled in glittery high-heeled pumps. The audience squealed with delight.

The hunter watched her pink, fine-boned face, her hanging hair, her
outstretched throat. Her eyes caught the spotlight. Was she looking at
him? Did she see his face pressed against the window, the wind slashing at
his neck, the groceries—onions, a sack of flour—tumbled to the ground
around his feet?

She was beautiful to him in a way that nothing else had ever been beautiful. Snow blew down his collar and drifted around his boots. After some
time the magician rejoined the severed box halves, unfastened the buckles,
and fluttered his wand, and she was whole again. She climbed out of the
box and curtsied in her glittering dress. She smiled as if it were the
Resurrection itself.

Then the storm brought down a pine tree in front of the courthouse,
and the power winked out, streetlight by streetlight. Before she could
move, before the ushers could begin escorting the crowd out with flash-
lights, the hunter was slinking into the hall, making for the stage, calling
for her.

He was thirty years old, twice her age. She smiled at him, leaned over
from the dais in the red glow of the emergency exit lights, and shook her
head. "Show's over," she said. In his pickup he trailed the magician's van
through the blizzard to her next show, a library fundraiser in Butte. The
next night he followed her to Missoula. He rushed to the stage after each
performance. "Just eat dinner with me," he'd plead. "Just tell me your

name." It was hunting by persistence. She said yes in Bozeman. Her name was plain, Mary Roberts. They had rhubarb pie in a hotel restaurant.

"I know how you do it," he said. "The feet in the box are dummies. You hold your legs against your chest and wiggle the dummy feet with a string."

She laughed. "Is that what you do? Follow a girl from town to town to tell her her magic isn't real?"

"No," he said. "I hunt."

"And when you're not hunting?"

"I dream about hunting."

She laughed again. "It's not funny," he said.

"You're right," she said, and smiled. "It's not funny. I'm that way with magic. I dream about it. Even when I'm not asleep."

He looked into his plate, thrilled. He searched for something he might say. They ate.

"But I dream bigger dreams, you know," she said afterward, after she had eaten two pieces of pie, carefully, with a spoon. Her voice was quiet and serious. "I have magic inside of me. I'm not going to get sawed in half by Tony Vespucci all my life."

"I don't doubt it," the hunter said.

"I knew you'd believe me," she said.

But the next winter Vespucci brought her back to Great Falls and sawed her in half in the same plywood coffin. And the winter after that. Both times, after the performance, the hunter took her to the Bitterroot Diner, where he watched her eat two pieces of pie. The watching was his favorite part: a hitch in her throat as she swallowed, the way the spoon slid cleanly out from her lips, the way her hair fell over her ear.

Then she was eighteen, and after pie she let him drive her to his cabin, forty miles from Great Falls, up the Missouri and then east into the Smith River valley. She brought only a small vinyl purse. The truck skidded and sheered as he steered it over the unploughed roads, fishtailing in the deep snow, but she didn't seem afraid or worried about where he might be taking her, about the possibility that the truck might sink in a drift, that she might freeze to death in her pea coat and glittery magician's-assistant dress. Her breath plumed out in front of her. It was twenty degrees below zero. Soon the roads would be snowed over, impassable until spring.

At his one-room cabin, with furs and old rifles on the walls, he unbolted the door to the crawl space and showed her his winter hoard: a hundred smoked trout, plucked pheasants and venison quarters hanging frozen from hooks. "Enough for two of me," he said. She scanned his books over the fireplace—a monograph on grouse habits, a series of journals on upland game birds, a thick tome titled simply *Bear.* "Are you tired?" he asked. "Would you like to see something?" He gave her a snowsuit, strapped her boots into a pair of leather snowshoes, and took her to hear the grizzly. She wasn't bad on snowshoes, a little clumsy. They went creaking over wind-scalloped snow in the nearly unbearable cold.

The bear denned every winter in the same hollow cedar, the top of which had been shorn off by a storm. Black, three-fingered, and huge, in the starlight it resembled a skeletal hand thrust up from the ground, a ghoulish visitor scrabbling its way out of the underworld. They knelt. Above them the stars were knife points, hard and white. "Put your ear here," he whispered. The breath that carried his words crystallized and blew away. They listened, face-to-face, their ears over woodpecker holes in the trunk. She heard it after a minute, tuning her ears in to something like a drowsy sigh, a long exhalation of slumber. Her eyes widened. A full minute passed. She heard it again.

"We can see him," he whispered, "but we have to be dead quiet. Grizzlies are light hibernators. Sometimes all you do is step on twigs outside their dens and they're up."

He began to dig at the snow. She stood back, her mouth open, eyes wide. Bent at the waist, the hunter bailed the snow back through his legs. He dug down three feet and then encountered a smooth, icy crust covering a large hole in the base of the tree. Gently he dislodged plates of ice and lifted them aside. From the hole the smell of bear came to her, like wet dog, like wild mushrooms. The hunter removed some leaves. Beneath was a shaggy flank, a patch of brown fur.

"He's on his back," the hunter whispered. "This is his belly. His forelegs must be up here somewhere." He pointed to a place higher on the trunk.

She put one hand on his shoulder and knelt in the snow beside the den. Her eyes were wide and unblinking. Her jaw hung open. Above her shoulder a star separated itself from a galaxy and melted through the sky. "I want to touch him," she said. Her voice sounded loud and out of place in that wood, under the naked cedars.

"Hush," he whispered. He shook his head no.

"Just for a minute."

"No," he hissed. "You're crazy." He tugged at her arm. She removed the mitten from her other hand with her teeth and reached down. He pulled at her again but lost his footing and fell back, clutching an empty mitten. As he watched, horrified, she turned and placed both hands, spread-fingered, in the thick shag of the bear's chest. Then she lowered her face, as if drinking from the snowy hollow, and pressed her lips to the bear's chest. Her entire head was inside the tree. She felt the soft silver tips of fur brush her cheeks. Against her nose one huge rib flexed slightly. She heard the lungs fill and then empty. She heard blood slug through veins.

"Want to know what he dreams?" she asked. Her voice echoed up through the tree and poured from the shorn ends of its hollowed branches. The hunter took his knife from his coat. "Summer," her voice echoed. "Blackberries. Trout. Dredging his flanks across river pebbles."

"I'd have liked," she said later, back in the cabin as he built up the fire, "to crawl all the way down there with him. Get into his arms. I'd grab him by the ears and kiss him on the eyes."

The hunter watched the fire, the flames cutting and sawing, each log a burning bridge. Three years he had waited for this. Three years he had dreamed this girl by his fire. But somehow it had ended up different from what he had imagined. He had thought it would be like a hunt—like waiting hours beside a wallow with his rifle barrel on his pack to see the huge antlered head of a bull elk loom up against the sky, to hear the whole herd behind him inhale and then scatter down the hill. If you had your opening you shot and walked the animal down and that was it. But this felt different. It was exactly as if he were still three years younger, stopped outside the Central Christian Church and driven against a low window by the wind or some other, greater force.

"Stay with me," he whispered to her, to the fire. "Stay the winter."

Bruce Maples stood beside him, jabbing the ice in his drink with his straw. "I'm in athletics," he offered. "I run the athletic department here."

"You mentioned that."

"Did I? I don't remember. I used to coach track. Hurdles."

The hunter was watching the thin, stricken man, President O'Brien, as he stood in the corner of the reception room. Every few minutes a couple of guests made their way to him and took O'Brien's hands in their own.

"You probably know," the hunter told Maples, "that wolves are hurdlers. Sometimes the people who track them will come to a snag and the prints will disappear. As if the entire pack just leaped into a tree and vanished. Eventually they'll find the tracks again, thirty or forty feet away. People used to think it was magic—flying wolves. But all they did was jump. One great coordinated leap."

Maples was looking around the room. "Huh," he said. "I wouldn't know about that."

She stayed. The first time they made love, she shouted so loudly that coyotes climbed onto the roof and howled down the chimney. He rolled off her, sweating. The coyotes coughed and chuckled all night, like children chattering in the yard, and he had nightmares. "Last night you had three dreams, and you dreamed you were a wolf each time," she whispered. "You were mad with hunger and running under the moon."

Had he dreamed that? He couldn't remember. Maybe he talked in his sleep.

In December it never got warmer than fifteen below. The river froze—something he'd never seen. On Christmas Eve he drove all the way to Helena to buy her figure skates. In the morning they wrapped themselves head-to-toe in furs and went out to skate the river. She held him by the hips and they glided through the blue dawn, skating up the frozen coils and shoals, beneath the leafless alders and cottonwoods, only the bare tips of creek willows showing above the snow. Ahead of them vast white stretches of river faded into darkness.

In a wind-polished bend they came upon a dead heron, frozen by its ankles into the ice. It had tried to hack itself out, hammering with its beak first at the ice entombing its feet and then at its own thin and scaly legs. When it finally died, it died upright, wings folded back, beak parted in some final, desperate cry, legs like twin reeds rooted in the ice.

She fell to her knees beside the bird. In its eye she saw her face flatly reflected. "It's dead," the hunter said. "Come on. You'll freeze too."

"No," she said. She slipped off her mitten and closed the heron's beak in her fist. Almost immediately her eyes rolled back in her head. "Oh, wow," she moaned. "I can *feel* her." She stayed like that for whole minutes, the hunter standing over her, feeling the cold come up his legs, afraid to touch her as she knelt before the bird. Her hand turned white and then blue in the wind. Finally she stood. "We have to bury it," she said.

That night she lay stiff and would not sleep. "It was just a bird," he said, unsure of what was bothering her but bothered by it himself. "We can't do anything for a dead bird. It was good that we buried it, but tomorrow something will find it and dig it out."

She turned to him. Her eyes were wide. He remembered how they had looked when she put her hands on the bear. "When I touched her," she said, "I saw where she went."

"'What?"

"I saw where she went when she died. She was on the shore of a lake with other herons, a hundred others, all facing the same direction, and they were wading among stones. It was dawn, and they watched the sun come up over the trees on the other side of the lake. I saw it as clearly as if I were there."

He rolled onto his back and watched shadows shift across the ceiling. "Winter is getting to you," he said. He resolved to make sure she went out every day. It was something he'd long believed: go out every day in winter, or your mind will slip. Every winter the paper was full of stories about ranchers' wives, snowed in and crazed with cabin fever, who had dispatched their husbands with cleavers or awls.

Winter threw itself at the cabin. He took her out every day. He showed her a thousand ladybugs hibernating in an orange ball hung in a riverbank hollow; a pair of dormant frogs buried in frozen mud, their blood crystallized until spring. He pried a globe of honeybees from its hive, slow-buzzing, stunned from the sudden exposure, tightly packed around the queen, each bee shimmying for warmth. When he placed the globe in her hands, she fainted, her eyes rolled back. Lying there, she saw all their dreams at once, the winter reveries of scores of worker bees, each one fiercely vivid: bright trails through thorns to a clutch of wild roses, honey tidily brimming a hundred combs.

With each day she learned more about what she could do. She felt a foreign and keen sensitivity bubbling in her blood, as if a seed planted long ago were just now sprouting. The larger the animal, the more powerfully it could shake her. The recently dead were virtual mines of visions, casting them off with a slow-fading strength as if cutting a long series of tethers one by one. She pulled off her mittens and touched everything she could: bats, salamanders, a cardinal chick tumbled from its nest, still warm. Ten hibernating garter snakes coiled beneath a rock, eyelids sealed, tongues stilled. Each time she touched a frozen insect, a slumbering amphibian, anything just dead, her eyes rolled back and its visions, its heaven, went shivering through her body.

Their first winter passed like that. When he looked out the cabin window, he saw wolf tracks crossing the river, owls hunting from the trees, six feet of snow like a quilt ready to be thrown off. She saw burrowed dreamers nestled under roots against the long twilight, their dreams rippling into the sky like auroras.

With love still lodged in his heart like a splinter, he married her in the first muds of spring.

Bruce Maples gasped when the hunter's wife finally arrived. She moved through the door like a show horse, demure in the way she kept her eyes down, but assured in her step; she brought each tapered heel down and struck it against the granite. The hunter had not seen his wife for twenty years, and she had changed—become refined, less wild, and somehow, to the hunter, worse for it. Her face had wrinkled around the eyes, and she moved as if avoiding contact with anything near her, as if the hall table or the closet door might suddenly lunge forward to snatch at her lapels. She wore no jewelry, no wedding ring, only a plain black suit, double-breasted.

She found her nametag on the table and pinned it to her lapel. Everyone in the reception room looked at her and then looked away. The hunter realized that she, not President O'Brien, was the guest of honor. In a sense they were courting her. This was their way, the chancellor's way—a silent bartender, tuxedoed coat girls, big icy drinks. Give her pie, the hunter thought. Rhubarb pie. Show her a sleeping grizzly.

They sat for dinner at a narrow and very long table, fifteen or so high-backed chairs down each side and one at each end. The hunter was seated several places away from his wife. She looked over at him finally, a look of recognition, of warmth, and then looked away again. He must have seemed old to her—he must always have seemed old to her. She did not look at him again.

The kitchen staff, in starched whites, brought onion soup, scampi, poached salmon. Around the hunter guests spoke in half whispers about people he did not know. He kept his eyes on the windows and the blowing snow beyond.

The river thawed and drove huge saucers of ice toward the Missouri. The hunter felt that old stirring, that quickening in his soul, and would rise in the wide pink dawns, grab his fly rod, and hurry down to the river. Already trout were rising through the chill brown water to take the first insects of spring. Soon the telephone in the cabin was ringing with calls from clients, and his guiding season was on.

In April an occasional client wanted a mountain lion or a trip with dogs for birds, but late spring and summer were for trout. He was out every morning before dawn, driving with a thermos of coffee to pick up a lawyer, a widower, a politician with a penchant for wild cutthroat. He came home stinking of fish guts and woke her with eager stories—native trout leaping fifteen-foot cataracts, a stubborn rainbow wedged under a snag.

By June she was bored and lonely. She wandered through the forest, but never very far. The summer woods were dense and busy, not like the quiet graveyard feel of winter. Nothing slept for very long; everything was emerging from cocoons, winging about, buzzing, multiplying, having litters, gaining weight. Bear cubs splashed in the river. Chicks screamed for worms. She longed for the stillness of winter, the long slumber, the bare sky, the bone-on-bone sound of bull elk knocking their antlers against trees.

In September the big-game hunters came. Each client wanted something different: elk, antelope, a bull moose, a doe. They wanted to see grizzlies, track a wolverine, shoot sandhill cranes. They wanted the heads of seven-by-seven royal bulls for their dens. Every few days he came home smelling of blood, with stories of stupid clients, of the Texan who sat, wheezing, too out of shape to get to the top of a hill for his shot. A blood-thirsty New Yorker claimed he wanted only to photograph black bears; then he pulled a pistol from his boot and fired wildly at two cubs and their mother. Nightly she scrubbed blood out of the hunter's coveralls, watched it fade from rust to red to rose in a basin filled with river water.

She began to sleep, taking long afternoon naps, three hours or more. Sleep, she learned, was a skill like any other, like getting sawed in half and reassembled, or like divining visions from a dead robin. She taught herself to sleep despite heat, despite noise. Insects flung themselves at the screens, hornets sped down the chimney, the sun angled hot and urgent through the southern windows; still she slept. When he came home each autumn night, exhausted, forearms stained with blood, she was hours into sleep. Outside, the wind was already stripping leaves from the cottonwoods— too soon, he thought. He'd take her sleeping hand. Both of them lived in the grip of forces they had no control over—the October wind, the revolutions of the earth.

That winter was the worst he could remember: from Thanksgiving on they were snowed in, the truck buried under six-foot drifts. The phone line went down in December and stayed down until April. January began with a chinook followed by a terrible freeze. The next morning a three-inch crust of ice covered the snow. On the ranches to the south cattle crashed through and bled to death kicking their way out. Deer punched through with their tiny hooves and suffocated in the deep snow beneath. Trails of blood veined the hills.

In the mornings he would find coyote tracks written in the snow around the door to the crawl space, two inches of hardwood between them and all his winter hoard hanging frozen beneath the floorboards. He reinforced the door with baking sheets, nailing them up against the wood and over the hinges. Twice he woke to the sound of claws scrabbling against the metal and charged outside to shout the coyotes away.

Everywhere he looked something was dying: an elk keeling over, an emaciated doe clattering onto ice like a drunken skeleton. The radio reported huge cattle losses on the southern ranches. Each night he dreamt of wolves, of running with them, soaring over fences and tearing into the steaming carcasses of cattle.

In February he woke to coyotes under the cabin. He grabbed his bow and knife and dashed out into the snow barefoot, his feet going numb. They had gone in under the door, chewing and digging the frozen earth under the foundation. He unbolted what was left of the door and swung it free.

Elk arrows were all he had, aluminum shafts tipped with broadheads. He squatted in the dark entrance—their only exit—with his bow at full draw and an arrow nocked. Above him he could hear his wife's feet pad quietly over the floorboards. A coyote made a coughing sound. Others shifted and panted. Maybe there were ten. He began to fire arrows steadily into the dark. He heard some bite into the foundation blocks at the back of the crawl space, others sink into flesh. He spent his whole quiver: a dozen arrows. The yelps of speared coyotes went up. A few charged him, and he lashed at them with his knife. He felt teeth go to the bone of his arm, felt hot breath on his cheeks. He lashed with his knife at ribs, tails, skulls. His muscles screamed. The coyotes were in a frenzy. Blood bloomed from his wrist, his thigh.

She heard the otherworldly screams of wounded coyotes come up through the floorboards, his grunts and curses as he fought. It sounded as if an exit had been tunneled all the way from hell to open under their house, and what was now pouring out was the worst violence that place could send up. She knelt in front of the fireplace and felt the souls of coyotes as they came through the boards on their way skyward.

He was blood-soaked and hungry, and his thigh had been badly bitten, but he worked all day digging out the truck. If he did not get food, they would starve, and he tried to hold the thought of the truck in his mind. He lugged slate and tree bark to wedge under the tires, excavated a mountain of snow from the truck bed. Finally, after dark, he got the engine turned over and ramped the truck up onto the frozen, wind-crusted snow. For a brief, wonderful moment he had it careening over the icy crust, starlight washing through the windows, tires spinning, pistons churning, what looked to be the road unspooling in the headlights. Then he crashed through. Slowly, painfully, he began digging it out again.

It was hopeless. He would get it up, and then it would break through a few miles later. Hardly anywhere was the sheet of ice atop the snow thick enough to support the truck's weight. For twenty hours he dug and then revved and slid the truck over eight-foot drifts. Three more times it crashed through and sank to the windows. Finally he left it. He was ten miles from home, thirty miles from town.

He made a weak and smoky fire with cut boughs and lay beside it and tried to sleep, but he couldn't. The heat from the fire melted snow, and trickles ran slowly toward him but froze solid before they reached him. The stars twisting in their constellations above had never seemed farther or colder. In a state that was neither fully sleep nor fully waking, he watched wolves lope around his fire, just outside the reaches of light, slavering and lean. He thought for the first time that he might die if he did not get warmer. He managed to kneel and turn and crawl for home. Around him he could feel the wolves, smell blood on them, hear their nailed feet scrape across the ice.

He traveled all that night and all the next day, near catatonia, sometimes on his feet, more often on his elbows and knees. At times he thought he was a wolf, and at times he thought he was dead. When he finally made it to the cabin, there were no tracks on the porch, no sign that she had gone out. The crawl-space door was still flung open, and shreds of the siding and the doorframe lay scattered about.

She was kneeling on the floor, ice in her hair, lost in some kind of hypothermic torpor. With his last dregs of energy he constructed a fire and poured a mug of hot water down her throat. As he fell into sleep, he watched himself as from a distance, weeping and clutching his near-frozen wife.

They had only flour and a few crackers in the cupboards. When she could speak, her voice was quiet and far away. "I have dreamt the most amazing things," she murmured. "I have seen the places where coyotes go when they are gone. I know where spiders go, and geese . . ."

Snow fell incessantly. Night was abiding; daylight passed in a breath. The hunter was beyond hungry. Whenever he stood up, his eyesight fled in slow, nauseating streaks of color. He went out with lanterns to fish, shoveled down to the river ice, chopped through it with a maul, and shivered over the hole jigging a ball of dough on a hook. Sometimes he brought back a trout; other times they ate a squirrel, a hare, once a famished deer whose bones he cracked and boiled, or only a few handfuls of rose hips. In the worst parts of March he dug out cattails to peel and steam the tubers.

She hardly ate, sleeping eighteen, twenty hours a day. When she woke, it was to scribble on notebook paper before plummeting back into sleep, clutching at the blankets as if they gave her sustenance. There was, she was learning, strength hidden at the center of weakness, ground at the bottom of the deepest pit. With her stomach empty and her body quieted, without the daily demands of living, she felt she was making important discoveries. She was only nineteen and had lost twenty pounds since marrying him. Naked, she was all rib cage and pelvis.

He read her scribbled dreams, but they seemed to be senseless poems and gave him no clues to her.

· · ·

Snail: sleds down stones in the rain.
Owl: fixes his eyes on hare, drops as if from the moon.
Horse: rides across the plains with his brothers . . .

In April the temperature rose above zero and then above twenty. He strapped an extra battery to his pack and went to dig out the truck. Its excavation took all day. He drove it slowly back up the slushy road in the moonlight and asked if she'd like to go to town the next morning. To his surprise, she said yes. They heated water for baths and dressed in clothes they hadn't worn in six months. She threaded twine through her belt loops to keep her trousers up.

Behind the wheel his chest filled to have her with him, to be moving out into the country, to see the sun above the trees. Spring was coming; the valley was dressing up. Look there, he wanted to say, those geese streaming over the road. The valley lives. Even after a winter like that.

She asked him to drop her off at the library. He bought food—a dozen frozen pizzas, potatoes, eggs, carrots. He nearly wept at seeing bananas. In the parking lot he drank a half gallon of milk. When he picked her up at the library, she had applied for a library card and borrowed twenty books. They stopped at the Bitterroot for hamburgers and rhubarb pie. She ate three pieces. He watched her eat, the spoon sliding out of her mouth. This was better. This was more like his dreams.

"Well, Mary," he said, "I think we made it."

"I love pie," she said.

As soon as the line was repaired, the phone began to ring. He took his fishing clients down the river. She sat on the porch, reading, reading.

Soon her sudden and ravenous appetite for books could not be met by the Great Falls Public Library. She wanted other books—essays about sorcery, primers on magic-working and conjury that had to be mail-ordered from New Hampshire, New Orleans, even Italy. Once a week the hunter drove to town to collect a parcel of books from the post office: *Arcana Mundi, The Seer's Dictionary, Paragon of Wizardry, Occult Science Among the Ancients.* He opened one to a random page and read "Bring water, tie a soft fillet around your altar, burn it on fresh twigs and frankincense . . ."

She regained her health, took on energy, no longer lay under furs dreaming all day. She was out of bed before he was, brewing coffee, her nose already between pages. With a steady diet of meat and vegetables her body bloomed, her hair shone, her eyes and cheeks glowed. How beautiful she seemed to him in those few hours he was home. After supper he would watch her read in the firelight, blackbird feathers tied all through her hair, a heron's beak hanging between her breasts.

In November he took a Sunday off and they cross-country skied. They came across a bull elk frozen to death in a draw. Ravens shrieked at them as they skied to it. She knelt and put her palm on the leathered skull. "There," she moaned. "I feel him."

"What do you feel?" he asked, standing behind her. "What is it?"

She stood, trembling. "I feel his life flowing out," she said. "I see where he goes, what he sees."

"But that's impossible," he said. "It's like saying you know what I dream."

"I do," she said. "You dream about wolves."

"But that elk's been dead at least a day. It doesn't go anywhere. It goes into the crops of those ravens."

How could she tell him? How could she ask him to understand such a thing? How could anyone understand? More clearly than ever she could see that there was a fine line between dreams and wakefulness, between living and dying, a line so tenuous it sometimes didn't exist. It was always clearest for her in winter. In winter, in that valley, life and death were not so different. The heart of a hibernating newt was frozen solid, but she could warm and wake it in her palm. For the newt there was no line at all, no fence, no River Styx, only an area between living and dying, like a snowfield between two lakes: a place where dreams and wakefulness met, where death was only a possibility and visions rose shimmering to the stars like smoke. All that was needed was a hand, the heat of a palm, the touch of fingers.

That February the sun shone during the days and ice formed at night— slick sheets glazing the wheat fields, the roofs and roads. One day he dropped her off at the library, the chains on the tires rattling as he pulled away, heading back up the Missouri toward Fort Benton.

Around noon Marlin Spokes, a snowplough driver the hunter knew from grade school, slid off the Sun River Bridge in his plough and dropped forty feet into the river. He was dead before they could get him out of the truck. She was reading in the library, a block away, and heard the plough crash into the riverbed like a thousand dropped girders. When she got to the bridge, sprinting in her jeans and T-shirt, men were already in the water—a telephone man from Helena, a jeweler, a butcher in his apron, all of them had scrambled down the banks and were wading in the rapids, prying the door open. The men lifted Marlin from the cab, stumbling as they carried him. Steam rose from their shoulders and from the crushed hood of the plough. She careened down the snow-covered slope and splashed to them. Her hand on the jeweler's arm, her leg against the butcher's leg, she reached for Marlin's ankle.

When her finger touched Marlin's body, her eyes rolled back and a single vision leaped to her: Marlin Spokes pedaling a bicycle, a child's seat mounted over the rear tire with a helmeted boy—Marlin's own son—strapped into it. Spangles of light drifted over the riders as they rolled down a lane beneath giant, sprawling maples. The boy reached for Marlin's hair with one small fist. In the glass of a storefront window their reflection flashed past. Fallen leaves turned over in their wake. This quiet vision—like a ribbon of rich silk—ran out slowly and fluidly, with great power, and she shook beneath it. It was she who pedaled the bike. The boy's fingers pulled through her hair.

The men who were touching her or touching Marlin saw what she saw, felt what she felt. At first they spoke of it only in their basements, at night, but Great Falls was not a big town, and this was not something one could keep locked in a basement. Soon they discussed it everywhere—in the supermarket, at the gasoline pumps. People who didn't know Marlin Spokes or his son or the hunter's wife or any of the men in the river that morning soon spoke of the event like experts. "All you had to do was *touch* her," a barber said, "and you saw it too." "The most beautiful lane you've ever dreamed," a deli owner raved. "You didn't just pedal his son around," movie ushers whispered, "you *loved* him."

He could have heard anywhere. In the cabin he built up the fire, flipped idly through a stack of her books. He couldn't understand them—one of them wasn't even in English.

After dinner she took the plates to the sink.

"You read Spanish now?" he asked.

Her hands in the sink stilled. "It's Portuguese," she said. "I understand only a little."

He turned his fork in his hands. "Were you there when Marlin Spokes was killed?"

"I helped pull him out of the truck. I don't think I was much good."

He looked at the back of her head. He felt like driving his fork through the table. "What tricks did you play? Did you hypnotize people?"

Her shoulders tightened. Her voice came out furious. "Why can't you—" she began, but her voice fell off. "It wasn't tricks," she muttered. "I helped carry him."

When she started to get phone calls, he hung up on the callers. But they were relentless: a grieving widow, an orphan's lawyer, a reporter from the *Great Falls Tribune*. A blubbering father drove all the way to the cabin to beg her to come to the funeral parlor, and finally she went. The hunter insisted on driving her. It wasn't right, he declared, for her to go alone. He waited in the truck in the parking lot, engine rattling, radio moaning.

"I feel so alive," she said afterward, as he helped her into the cab. Her clothes were soaked through with sweat. "Like my blood is fizzing through my body." At home she lay awake, far away, all night.

She got called back and called back, and each time he drove her. He would take her after a whole day of duck hunting and pass out from exhaustion while he waited in the truck. When he woke, she would be beside him, holding his hand, her hair damp, her eyes wild. "You dreamt you were with the wolves and eating salmon," she said. "They were washed up and dying on the shoals."

He drove them home over the dark fields. He tried to soften his voice. "What do you do in there? What really?"

"I give them solace. I let them say good-bye to their loved ones. I help them know something they'd never otherwise know."

"No," he said. "I mean what kind of tricks? How do you do it?"

She turned her hands palms up. "As long as they're touching me, they see what I see. Come in with me next time. Go in there and hold hands. Then you'll know."

He said nothing. The stars above the windshield seemed fixed in their places.

Families wanted to pay her; most wouldn't let her leave until they did. She would come out to the truck with fifty, a hundred—once four hundred—dollars folded into her pocket. She began to go off for weekends, disappearing in the truck before he was up, a fearless driver. She knelt by roadkill—a crumpled porcupine, a shattered deer. She pressed her palm to the truck's grille, where the husks of insects smoked. Seasons came and went. She was gone half the winter. Each of them was alone. They never spoke. On longer drives she was sometimes tempted to keep the truck pointed away and never return.

In the first thaws he would go out to the river and try to lose himself in the rhythm of casting, in the sound of pebbles driven downstream, clacking together. But even fishing had become lonely for him. Everything, it seemed, was out of his hands—his truck, his wife, the course of his own life.

As hunting season came on, his mind wandered. He was botching kills—getting upwind of elk, or telling a client to unload and call it quits thirty seconds before a pheasant burst from cover. When a client missed his mark and pegged an antelope in the neck, the hunter berated him for being careless, knelt over its tracks, and clutched at the bloody snow. "Do you understand what you've done?" he shouted. "How the arrow shaft will knock against the trees, how the animal will run and run, how the wolves will trot behind it to keep it from resting?"

The client was red-faced, huffing. "Wolves don't hunt here," the client said. "There haven't been wolves here for twenty years."

She was in Butte or Missoula when he discovered her money in a boot: six thousand dollars and change. He canceled his trips and stewed for two days, pacing the porch, sifting through her things, rehearsing his arguments. When she saw him, the sheaf of bills jutting from his shirt pocket, she stopped halfway to the door, her bag over her shoulder, her hair pulled back.

"It's not right," he said.

She walked past him into the cabin. "I'm helping people. I'm doing what I love. Can't you see how good I feel afterward?"

"You take advantage of them. They're grieving, and you take their money."

"They *want* to pay me," she shrieked. "I help them see something they desperately want to see."

"It's a grift. A con."

She came back out on the porch. "No," she said. Her voice was quiet and strong. "This is real. As real as anything: the valley, the river, your trout hanging in the crawl space. I have a talent. A gift."

He snorted. "A gift for hocus-pocus. For swindling widows out of their savings." He lobbed the money into the yard. The wind caught the bills and scattered them over the snow.

She hit him, once, hard across the mouth. "How dare you?" she cried. "You, of all people, should understand. You who dreams of wolves every night."

In the months that followed, she left the cabin more frequently and for longer durations, visiting homes, accident sites, and funeral parlors all over central Montana. Finally she pointed the truck south and didn't turn back. They had been married five years.

Twenty years later, in the Bitterroot Diner, he looked up at the ceiling-mounted television and there she was, being interviewed. She lived in Manhattan, had traveled the world, had written two books. She was in demand all over the country.

"Do you commune with the dead?" the interviewer asked.

"No," she said, "I help people. I commune with the living. I give people peace."

"Well," the interviewer said, turning to speak into the camera, "I believe it."

The hunter bought her books at the bookstore and read them in one night. She had written poems about the valley, written them to the animals: you rampant coyote, you glorious buck. She had traveled to Sudan to touch the backbone of a fossilized stegosaur, and wrote of her frustration when she divined nothing from it. A TV network flew her to Kamchatka to embrace the huge, shaggy neck of a mammoth as it was airlifted from a glacier. She'd had better luck with that one, describing an entire herd slogging big-footed through a slushy tide, tearing at sea grass and flaring their ears to catch the sun. In a handful of poems there were even vague allusions to him—a brooding, blood-soaked presence that hovered outside the margins like a storm on its way, like a killer hiding in the basement.

The hunter was fifty-eight years old. Twenty years was a long time. The valley had diminished slowly but perceptibly: roads came in, and the grizzlies left, seeking higher country. Loggers had thinned nearly every accessible stand of trees. Every spring runoff from logging roads turned the river chocolate-brown, and the soil from the old forests was being washed into the Missouri. In his cabin, bent over the table, he set aside her books, took a pencil, and wrote her a letter.

A week later a Federal Express truck drove all the way to the cabin. Inside the envelope was her response, on embossed stationery. The handwriting was hurried and efficient. *I will be in Chicago,* it said, *day after tomorrow. Enclosed is a plane ticket. Feel free to come. Thank you for writing.*

After sherbet the chancellor called his guests into the reception room. Burning candles had been distributed around the room: on the sills, the banister, the mantel, the bookshelves. The bar had been taken down; in its place three caskets had been set on the carpet. A bit of snow that had fallen on the lids—they must have been kept outside—was melting, and drops ran onto the carpet, where they left dark circles. Around the caskets cushions had been placed on the floor. The hunter leaned against the entryway and watched guests drift uncomfortably into the room, some cradling coffee cups, others gulping at gin or vodka in deep tumblers. Eventually everyone settled on the floor in a circle.

The hunter's wife came in then, elegant in her dark suit. She knelt and motioned for O'Brien to sit beside her. His face was pinched and inscrutable. Again the hunter had the impression that he was not of this world but of a slightly leaner one.

"President O'Brien," his wife said, "I know this is difficult for you. Death can seem so final, like a blade dropped through the neck. But the nature of death is not at all final. It is not some dark cliff off which we leap. I hope to show you it is merely a fog, something we can peer into and out of, something we can know and face and not necessarily fear. By each life taken from our collective lives we are diminished. But even in death we have much to celebrate. It is only a transition, like so many others."

She moved into the circle and unfastened the lids of the caskets. From where he sat the hunter could not see inside. His wife's hands fluttered around her waist like birds. "Think," she said. "Think hard about something you would like resolved, some matter, gone now, in the grips of the past, which you wish you could take back—perhaps with your daughters, a moment, a lost feeling, a desperate wish."

The hunter closed his eyes. "Think now," his wife was saying, "of some wonderful moment, some fine and sunny minute you shared, your wife and daughters, all of you together." Her voice was lulling. Behind his eyelids the glow of the candles made an even orange wash. He knew her hands were reaching for whatever—whoever—lay in those caskets. Somewhere inside him he felt her extend across the room.

His wife said more about beauty and loss being the same thing, about how they ordered the world, and he felt something happening—a strange warmth, a flirting presence, something dim and unsettling, like a feather brushed across the back of his neck. Hands on both sides of him reached for his hands. Fingers locked around his fingers. He wondered if she was hypnotizing him, but it didn't matter. He had nothing to fight off or snap out of. She was inside him now; she had reached across and was poking about.

Her voice faded, and he felt himself swept up as if rising toward the ceiling. Air washed lightly in and out of his lungs; warmth pulsed in the hands that held his. In his mind he saw a sea emerging from fog. The water was broad and flat and glittered like polished metal. He could feel dune grass moving against his shins, and wind coming over his shoulders. All around him bees shuttled over the dunes. Far out a shorebird was diving for crabs. He knew that a few hundred yards away two girls were building castles in the sand; he could hear their song, soft and lilting. Their mother was with them, reclining under an umbrella, one leg bent, the other straight. She was drinking iced tea, and he could taste it in his mouth, sweet and bitter with a trace of mint. Each cell in his body seemed to breathe. He became the girls, the diving bird, the shuttling bees; he was the mother of the girls and the father; he could feel himself flowing outward, richly dissolving, paddling into the world like the very first cell into the great blue sea . . .

When he opened his eyes, he saw linen curtains, women in gowns kneeling. Tears were visible on many people's cheeks—O'Brien's and the chancellor's and Bruce Maples's. His wife's head was bowed. The hunter gently released the hands that held his, stood, and walked out into the kitchen, past the sudsy sinks, the stacks of dishes. He let himself out a side door and found himself on the wooden deck that ran the length of the house, a couple of inches of snow already settled on it.

He felt drawn toward the pond, the birdbath, the hedges. He walked to the pond and stood at its rim. The snow fell steadily, and the undersides of the clouds glowed with reflected light from the city.

Before long his wife stepped onto the deck and came down to join him.

There were things he had been preparing to say: something about a final belief, an expression of gratitude for providing a reason to leave the valley, if only for a night. He wanted to tell her that although the wolves were gone, may always have been gone, they still came to him in dreams. That they could run there, fierce and unfettered, was surely enough. She would understand. She had understood long before he did.

But he was afraid to speak. He could see that speaking would be like dashing some very fragile bond to pieces, like kicking a dandelion gone to seed; the wispy, tenuous sphere of its body would scatter in the wind. So instead they stood together, the snow fluttering down from the clouds to melt into the water, where their reflected images trembled like two people trapped against the glass of a parallel world, and he reached, finally, to take her hand.

Mary Yukari Waters

Egg-Face

from *Zoetrope: All-Story*

KEIKO NAKAJIMA was thirty years old, and she had never been on a date. In addition, she had never held a job. The latter might have been acceptable; even in these modern times, many middle-class women in the Kin-nanji district did not work outside the home. But such women were usually married.

"Anything new with that Nakajima girl, the middle one?" some housewife might say while shelling peas with her children on the veranda, or gossiping with neighbors in one of the narrow alleyways leading to the open-air market. There never was. Keiko was spotted strolling in the dusk or running the occasional errand at the market; in the mornings, children on their way to school saw her feeding the caged canary on the upstairs balcony. Like some retired person, neighbors said. Like Buddha in a lotus garden.

Wasn't she depressed? Wasn't she desperate? They waylaid her in the alleys: the young housewives applying subtle pressure; the old women probing bluntly, secure in the respect due their age. Keiko met their questions (Do you want children someday? What do you do in your free time?) with an indecisive "Saaa . . . ," a cocked head, and an expression suggesting that such a puzzle had never even crossed her mind before. Comments and advice alike were absorbed with a "Haaa . . ." of humble illumination.

"There's no give-and-take," declared old Mrs. Wakame. She was a formidable busybody who ambushed passersby from the comfort of her front stoop, where she lingered on the pretext of watering her dozens of tiny potted flowers. "Talking to that girl is like—" old Mrs. Wakame said, then shook her head and quoted an old saying about a sumo wrestler charging through squares of cotton hung from doorways.

But Keiko was not stupid. She was too retiring, even for a girl, but her schoolwork had always been good. Her business degree from Ninjo College would have guaranteed her a job if only this recession, now in its ninth year, had not hit the country just as her class was graduating. Managers had begun to be laid off despite decades of service; quotas for college recruits were slashed below half. Keiko, like many in her class, was rejected repeatedly at interviews the summer before March graduation.

Like her classmates, she had waited for the next interviewing season. Up to that point, she did not attract undue attention. But the following summer, when neighbors made polite inquiries of Mrs. Nakajima as to why her daughter was not interviewing—or at least making do with part-time work—they were told that Keiko would marry directly from home, bypassing the typical three or four years of pre-marriage employment. Nine years went by, however, and nothing happened.

Perhaps there was an inheritance? There was the house, which was all paid off, according to the Tatsumi woman, whose husband worked at Mitsui Bank. But split among three daughters it wasn't much. Moreover, Mr. Nakajima drew but a modest salary at some little export company in Shibuken. How much savings could they possibly have after private-college tuition for three daughters, not to mention wedding expenses for the eldest? Old Mrs. Wakame had noticed Mrs. Nakajima buying bargain mackerel caught off American shores, as well as low-grade rice from Indonesia and Thailand.

There was little to be gleaned from the other two daughters. The Nakajima sisters, apparently, were not close; Sachiko and Tomoko showed little insight into Keiko's mind and even less interest. They at any rate were leading normal lives. Sachiko, the eldest, had recently married a confectioner's son and was now living in Gion. Twenty-five-year-old Tomoko, unmarried and therefore still living at home, had been dating her current boyfriend for five months. She had landed a bank-teller job after two years of interviewing; each day she rode the No. 72 bus to and from work, looking like a stewardess in Shinwa Bank's official navy jumper.

"They should have *forced* her to work, for her own good." "Life's just passing her by." "That father should bring home company underlings for dinner. Isn't that how the Fujiwaras met?" Ecstatic approval followed each comment, fanning a glow of well-being that lingered as the housewives went their separate ways. Their ruminations moved in endless circles, like a merry-go-round from which they could disembark at any moment if a better topic came along.

It was out of genuine kindness—as well as curiosity, the kind that drives children to poke sleeping animals—that old Mrs. Wakame phoned Keiko's mother. She felt justified in using the telephone, because this time, unlike other outdoor occasions when Mrs. Nakajima had managed to slip away, she had a legitimate favor to bestow. This sense of the upper hand made old Mrs. Wakame's voice expansive. A young man, she told Mrs. Nakajima, a former student of her retired husband, was interested in marriage. Should she act as matchmaker and set up a meeting?

There was a brief silence.

"That is very kind," Mrs. Nakajima said with dignity. "We accept."

Mrs. Nakajima herself had married through a matchmaker, but that was decades ago; nowadays, love marriages were prevalent. As a result, Keiko had received only one other matchmaking offer, five years ago, involving an elementary-school principal with forty-three years to Keiko's twenty-five. Trusting in future offers, Mrs. Nakajima had declined without even setting up a meeting. "A middle-aged man! How could I do that to a young girl?" she had said. "It would just crush her spirit."

"What spirit?" said her youngest daughter, Tomoko. That scornful remark had hurt Mrs. Nakajima deeply, for of her three daughters Keiko resembled her mother the most.

Today, Mrs. Nakajima and Keiko sat at the kitchen table in the awkward aftermath of old Mrs. Wakame's phone call. It was about four o'clock, and Mr. Nakajima and Tomoko were still at work. Granny was home—she sat upstairs all day, coming down only for meals—but by unspoken assent, they made no move to go to her with the news.

A breeze wafted in through the open window, bringing with it the aggressive smell of fresh grass. Since the last rain, weeds had invaded the neighborhood, appearing overnight, in startling hues of neon, through cracks in the asphalt, from under ceramic roof tiles, even within the stone lanterns in the garden. The garden itself, cut off from the western sun by a high bamboo fence, now lay in deepening shadow.

Also drifting in on the breeze, from the direction of Asahi Middle School, came the synchronized shouts—"Fight! Fight! Fight!"—of the baseball team running laps. It was April again, the start of another new school year.

Instinctively Mrs. Nakajima, considered closing the window, turning on the little radio that was permanently set, at cozy low volume, to the easy-listening station. For the shouts were a disturbing reminder that for the past nine years, while Keiko's life ground to a halt, mindless toddlers had been transforming into young adults whose voices now rose with strength and promise. Aaa, each new spring came so quickly! . . . as if the rest of the world followed a different clock.

But the phone call changed things. Suddenly the air in the kitchen, which still smelled faintly of this morning's prayer incense, altered—attuning itself to that elusive forward momentum of the outside world. For the first time, Mrs. Nakajima dared to hope her daughter's destiny could be saved, like a pan snatched from a stove in the nick of time.

With a sharp, anxious sigh, Mrs. Nakajima pushed herself up from the low table. Keiko, idly prying off the label from a jar of salted plums, glanced up in mild puzzlement.

"That jar's so low already," Mrs. Nakajima said by way of explanation.

"I can buy another jar," Keiko offered. "I'll take my bicycle." She ran errands for everyone in the family, which was only fair since she wasn't working. That had been Mrs. Nakajima's job for many years. She had not minded it for herself, but it smote her to see the same affable subservience in her daughter.

According to the résumé, Toshi Funaba was twenty-eight years old—Keiko's junior by two years. He had a business degree from Noraku University, where old Mr. Wakame had taught (hardly an elite school, but a good one), and he held a position as assistant manager at a merchandising company called Sabin Kogyo. Two photographs were enclosed with the résumé, casual outdoor shots: Toshi in a wet suit, sitting on the beach and gazing pensively out over the waters of Kobe Bay; Toshi in a Nike T-shirt, triumphantly holding aloft a small mackerel on a line.

"His hobbies," Mr. Nakajima read over the gentle clacking of chopsticks at the dinner table, "are scuba diving, sailing, dirt biking, and deep-sea fishing."

"Hehhh! . . ." Around the table, there was an exhaling of exaggerated awe.

"Expensive hobbies," remarked Granny. She held out the photographs at arm's length, gripping the rim of her eyeglasses with a free hand as if it were a telescope. She noted with a quickening of interest—nothing much, after all, ever happened upstairs—that this boy was better-looking than Keiko.

The entire discussion had an air of unreality. Over the years, it had been an unspoken rule to spare Keiko any reminder of her situation; tonight, however, the practical necessities of Mrs. Wakame's offer unleashed in the family a heady tingle.

Tomoko, born in the year of the tiger, had just had an exhausting day at the bank. This was not the life she had envisioned for herself. Her feet ached. One of these days her ankles would swell up like some old matron's. And tomorrow would be no better, nor the day after that. Oh, what was the point of struggling and coming home spent, only to see Big Sister smiling and doing nothing, not a single thing, and getting everyone's sympathy besides? Granny actually gave her spending money out of her pension because "the poor girl has no income of her own." And now a prospective husband was dropped into her lap, a better catch than Tomoko's own boyfriend at the office. It was not to be borne.

"Let's hope you can keep up with him," she said to her big sister.

Keiko cocked her head in her usual evasive way, but said nothing.

Mrs. Nakajima waved away Tomoko's remark with an airy gesture that was at odds with the fierce, helpless glance she shot in her youngest daughter's direction. "Men don't care about that kind of thing, do they, Papa?" she said. Mr. Nakajima grunted, still staring at the résumé. Tomoko chewed stonily. Her red fingernail polish gleamed under the electric light.

"Well, well," Granny said heartily, "that Wakame woman has once again outdone herself."

There had been a time, several years ago, when Tomoko had insisted on knowing all the details of her mother's courtship. "Saa," Mrs. Nakajima had told her, "we dated for three months. He used to visit me once a week on his way home from work. I remember we took lovely walks in the dusk."

"Did you flirt with each other?" Tomoko asked. It had caught her mother off guard. Neither of her other daughters had asked such a bald question.

"Of course not!" Mrs. Nakajima said. "It was nothing like that." The impact of her words, now beyond retrieval, spread out in slow motion to fill the moment.

"He never even took you downtown?" Tomoko was referring to those chic tea rooms where, since before the war, young men in love were known to take their dates.

"I don't recall," Mrs. Nakajima had said shortly. She met Tomoko's level gaze and felt, for a brief instant, a stab of dislike. "We preferred eating pork buns or fried noodles at one of the local places."

Tonight at the dinner table, Mr. Nakajima expounded on Toshi Funaba's workplace. He had heard good things about Sabin Kogyo. Despite this long recession plaguing the country, Sabin Kogyo had remained stable: its asset-liability ratio was excellent, and the yearly decline of its annual gross revenue was milder than most of its counterparts in the industry. The family fell silent before these indisputable statistics.

"It might really happen, ne!" Mrs. Nakajima whispered to her husband later that night, as they lay down to sleep on their separate futons.

"Nnn, it might!" he replied.

"Kobe's not far," Mrs. Nakajima said. "She can come visit us on the train." They stared up into the dark, thinking.

Mrs. Nakajima had never had a boyfriend before her marriage. Mr. Nakajima had dated sporadically, his crowning achievement being a one-night sexual encounter with a barmaid at the establishment he and his coworkers frequented after work. They had no advice to pass on to Keiko. They did not fully comprehend how they themselves had become linked together; they merely hoped Keiko would grow into marriage as they had—in the same mysterious way she had learned to crawl, then later to walk.

Old Mrs. Wakame was feeling the first stirrings of doubt. Just this afternoon she had met Toshi Funaba and his parents for the first time—something she should have done before approaching the Nakajimas, but at the time she had not been able to wait. A silent young man, she reported to the housewives standing about her front stoop. But not shy. Just silent . . .

What old Mrs. Wakame did not mention was how much this young man reminded her of her own teenage grandson, who had declared, when he was six, "Granny, I love you better than anybody else." That moment still burned in her chest but with pain now. For lately, whenever his parents brought him to visit, he sat before the television, distant and bored. Every so often, he would condescend to utter a strained little "Hohhh . . ." at her best offerings of gossip. Only when he talked to his own friends—Mrs. Wakame had overheard him using her hallway phone—did his voice take on the animated and confidential tones he had once used with her. This young man Toshi Funaba exuded the same air as her grandson.

"Sohh—" said one woman, nodding deeply. "Parents are pressuring him."

He'll liven up, Mrs. Wakame assured them, once he meets Keiko.

The problem, according to one of the housewives, was that matchmaking was not what it had once been. Men who used it these days no longer understood the subtle difference between evaluating an arranged marriage prospect versus a love-match prospect. This boy Toshi, with his fancy hobbies (neighbors had seen photos; old Mrs. Wakame had made copies), seemed typical of a new breed that confused matchmakers with dating services.

"Soh soh," someone else said, "they grow up watching actresses on television."

A Mrs. Konishi, whose own daughter had just gotten engaged (a love match), made a pretty moue of concern. Poor Keiko, she said. In the old days she would have been just fine. Keiko had the qualities of an ideal wife: gentleness, deference, domesticity. Plus a college degree.

Eighty-two-year-old Mrs. Tori, bowed over a trembling cane, lifted her head. Even in our day, she said querulously, men liked women who could at least hold up their own end of a conversation.

Sachiko, Mrs. Nakajima's eldest daughter, came over from Gion on the local bus. It was Thursday. Keiko's date was set for Saturday afternoon.

"I don't understand," Sachiko said to her mother, who had been waiting for her outside in the alley. "Tomoko knows makeup as well as I do. Plus she *lives* here."

"It isn't fitting," Mrs. Nakajima whispered, glancing toward the house, "for younger sisters to be teaching older sisters. Besides . . ." She lifted her head, its home-permed waves webbed with white hairs, and looked up at her tall daughter. "Besides, Tomoko has the wrong attitude." Her haggard expression gave Sachiko, who had seen little of her family since her own recent wedding, an eerie glimpse of her mother in old age.

In the dining room, which boasted the best natural light, Sachiko now spread out the contents of her plastic makeup pouch onto the large low table. "We'll just do one side of your face," she told her little sister, "so you can see the difference."

"Haaa . . ." Keiko agreed, nodding but not venturing to touch anything. Mrs. Nakajima retired to the kitchen in high spirits, humming a Strauss waltz.

As children, Sachiko and Keiko had played together at this table when Sachiko's more lively neighborhood friends were unavailable, for the sisters were close in age whereas Tomoko was five years behind. Today Sachiko recalled an early memory: a silent house, rain making pinpricks of sound on the broad hydrangea leaves in the garden. In the bracken-filtered light, she and Keiko had drawn pictures or gazed out the window. *Jikkuri-gata,* their mother had teased: characters of contemplation. Time passed. They were—in her memory—silent: mindless, timeless, knowing they were provided for, vaguely registering the faint clatter of the outside world. Dinner noises in the kitchen . . . an ambulance siren in the distance . . .

Keiko had managed to remain in that world. Sachiko thought of what awaited her back at home: laundry, cooking, wrapping tea sweets for tomorrow's customers, the already faded romance with her husband, the perpetual polite tension of living among in-laws. She sat on an unfamiliar red floor cushion that must have been purchased after she moved away, and she thought how quickly she had become a visitor in her own home.

Keiko, with self-conscious care, was dabbing her face with a damp foundation sponge. "Egg-face," some boy had once called her in fourth grade, and the name had stuck for the remainder of her elementary-school years. Her mother would pacify her ("An oval face is a sign of beauty! White skin is better than dark!"), while Granny, skilled at self-promotion, remarked, "At least she takes after me in the skin area." In truth there was a certain quality to Keiko's cheekbones, packed high like an Eskimo's, which lent to her face the suggestion of a blank shell. Her other features, overshadowed by this denseness of bone, appeared shrunken in contrast. The children in their unwitting astuteness had caught her essence: that bland surface of her personality which allowed, with minimal effort, deflection of any attack.

"Now some blush." Sachiko handed Keiko the oversized brush. "Put on as much as you're comfortable with. No, right here. The round part of your cheek." Keiko touched the tip of the brush to her skin: once, then twice.

"More than *that*!" Sachiko's voice rose in exasperation. She flicked her own wrist rapidly, suggesting many, many more strokes.

"Ara!" Keiko breathed as a soft stain of pink, barely visible, bloomed on her cheek. "It's pretty." Then, apparently embarrassed by this outburst, she lowered her gaze to the blush compact in her lap. She shut it with a tiny click.

Their mother came in to view the result: a job worthy of the Shiseido ads, in subtle tones of grey and peach. Mrs. Nakajima examined it with a look of wonder; she herself had never gone beyond liquid foundation, adding red lipstick only when she went out. "Lovely," she said, "just lovely. Aren't you glad, Keiko-chan?" Keiko, with an obliging laugh, nodded. "Look at yourself in the mirror!" her mother said, steering her around to face the mirror and looking over her shoulder.

Mrs. Nakajima, peering at Keiko's flushed face in the mirror, understood that a change had taken place. In her daughter's eyes was a look she had seen in alley cats, when they warily approached a proffered treat. It was a look terrible and bottomless in its hope. Mrs. Nakajima's belly shifted in unease, as if her body knew something she did not.

Unsure what to make of this, Mrs. Nakajima put it from her mind. The three of them went upstairs to show Granny. She was hunched over on a floor cushion, watching sumo on television. "There—which side of her face looks better?" Sachiko demanded, pushing Keiko forward.

"Maaa, what an improvement!" cried the old lady, looking up and clapping her hands. "That side, definitely. Look how dewy and white the skin is!"

No one spoke.

"Granny!" said Sachiko. Her voice became loud and slow even though there was nothing wrong with Granny's hearing. "We didn't even do that side. We did the other side." She exchanged a wry glance with her mother. Even Keiko gave a little smile, tucking her hair behind one ear.

After they had gone, Granny turned back to her television set. She could no longer concentrate on the sumo match; she still seemed to hear Sachiko's muffled laughter drifting up the stairs. Maa, so what if her eyesight was no longer perfect? In her own day, at least, she had been a great beauty. Upslanted eyes ("exquisite, like bamboo leaves," someone had said), a face compared with the one in that famous Tondai lithograph, a long shapely neck that was the envy of her village. She had held sway over a dozen eligible suitors, eventually marrying into a professor's family despite her own lack of education. How dare they forget it! Her daughter-in-law, her granddaughters—for all their pitiful fuss over face paint—had nothing to work with. Ridiculous bumpkins! Oh, youth and insolence would leave them soon enough. A nervous tic began throbbing under her left eye.

"How did it go, do you think?" Mrs. Nakajima whispered for the second time to old Mrs. Wakame, who was sitting beside her on the homebound train. "Did he like her, do you think? Will he ask to meet her again?" Keiko was sitting three seats ahead, out of earshot.

The lunch date had taken place at a restaurant called Miyagi whose sushi turned out to be, befitting its seaside location, of uncommonly good quality. Old Mrs. Wakame loved sushi, especially the *kampachi,* which she and her husband could now rarely afford on his pension. But her match-making duties came first, so for the first half of the date she delayed eating, chatting instead about everything from weather to chrysanthemums. The auspicious cuisine, as well as the pleasant conversation (mostly among the four parents, although this was to be expected), erased the uneasiness of her earlier meeting with Toshi.

It was further into the lunch, after they had covered jobs and hobbies (Keiko's hobbies were walking and reading) and the table's energy was flagging from the generous portions of salmon and *hamachi* and eel and squid, that Toshi began amusing himself with questions of his own. "Keiko-san, what is your favorite color?" he asked, tapping his cigarette over an ashtray. "Keiko-san, what is your favorite animal?"

Old Mrs. Wakame threw him an uncertain glance but his handsome face looked reassuring, full of the grave manly concern that was so attractive in samurai dramas. And Keiko was holding her own so well, answering each question correctly after a long thoughtful pause, although at times she did present her answers with unnecessary bows that were quick and clumsy, like a child's. So Mrs. Wakame paid them little heed. Hunching over her lacquered box, she applied herself single-mindedly to the sushi she had been waiting for, narrowing her eyes in pleasure as the freshly ground wasabi warmed her sinuses.

She suddenly came to. Toshi's question was ringing in her ears: "Keiko-san, what do you want most in life?" The table was silent, save for the steady clinks of ice in the men's whiskey glasses. Toshi's mother, a fashionably dressed woman, glanced at her watch.

"Saaa—" With all eyes upon her, Keiko cocked her head.

"We all want the same thing, don't we," Mrs. Nakajima broke in, nodding at her daughter as if in agreement. "A long healthy life, happiness . . ."

With a small predatory smile, Toshi Funaba exhaled cigarette smoke toward the ceiling.

Recalling this now, old Mrs. Wakame sighed and shifted position on her train seat. "Saaa, it went well enough, don't you think?" she said to Keiko's mother. "Who can predict?" she added.

They both fell silent, sipping Morinaga Orange Drink from slender cans around which they had wrapped their handkerchiefs.

The train rattled along the tracks and the city spread out below them: modern high-rises crowding out old buildings of wood and tile, balconies and verandas bedecked with futons hung out to air. The spring air was translucent with smog. All the soot expelled during the day—all the soot expelled during this long depression—was falling back down to earth, the sediment floating in the busy streets. Late-afternoon sunlight slanted through it, creating an amber viscosity in which the traffic below would eventually still.

Old Mrs. Wakame stood up to roll down the shade, and her eye fell upon a travel poster displayed above the window: a promotion for some resort showing, in brilliant colors, a lone crane flying over snowfields. It brought to mind the television program she had seen last night, an NHK dramatization of the Crane Maiden legend: a crane, rescued from a trap by an old weaver, returns to him disguised as a beautiful maiden. This role was played by the lovely Junji Mariko in a rare appearance. The credits said so, at any rate, but who could really tell? Her face was averted from the camera, shielded by a fall of glossy hair. She would weave him wondrous silks free of charge, she murmured, as long as he promised never to watch her in the process. "You mustn't peek," she implored. "I couldn't bear for you to learn the secret of my weaving."

Something about that graceful turning away of the head—so old-fashioned, and now extinct—had touched old Mrs. Wakame deeply. And when the weaver, overcome by curiosity, finally peeked through a crack in the shoji screen ("Is that actor Mori Daiji?" asked her husband, exhaling a cloud of cigarette smoke. "Maaa, he's certainly aged."), Mrs. Wakame had uttered a shrill cry of awful nameless regret. She had felt silly afterward. For everyone knew what he would see: a crane, half-plucked and grotesque, feeding its own feathers into the loom . . .

What this had to do with anything, Mrs. Wakame did not know. Again, she shifted position on the plush seat. Images flashed into her mind of Keiko at the lunch table: lipstick smeared on her front tooth, trembling hands with red-painted fingernails bitten to the quick. "I would like children," she had said, as smoke from Toshi's ashtray rose up between them. "I have always wanted children." Remorse hit old Mrs. Wakame like a wave, and she lowered her Morinaga Orange Drink onto the windowsill.

Don Lee

The Possible Husband

from *Bamboo Ridge*

WINTER

Somewhere approaching a hundred. Not an outrageous number, really. Duncan Roh had started at fourteen, and he was forty-one now, so a rather modest average of four a year. Some of them had been *haoles*—whites—but most had been Asian amazons like Sunny Foo, his current lover, who tended to walk with her pelvis a little ahead of her, long, lazy steps seeming to drift too wide.

Sunny Foo was his restaurant designer. For unknown and regrettable reasons, Duncan—recently retired, with enough cash to pursue the sole thing he'd ever been committed to, big-wave surfing, full-time—had decided to open a sushi restaurant in Rosarita Bay. He wanted to name it Banzai Pipeline, after the famous break on the North Shore of Oahu, where he had grown up. His idea for decor had been a couple of surf-boards on the walls and a big-screen TV playing surf videos. But Sunny had other ideas, very expensive, outlandish ideas, like double-molded Plexiglas canopied over the length of the sushi bar, pumped with rushing water, sculpted to resemble a perfect, hollow Pipeline barrel just before it tubed.

Sunny argued that diners wanted restaurants to be *theater*, to be an *event*, but Duncan said no, absolutely not. The restaurant was supposed to take six months to build and cost a quarter of a million dollars. Now it was eight months and pushing 400K. They got into screaming rows, obscenity-laden tirades. Then, naturally, they started fucking. And, naturally, Duncan found himself relenting: well, if we really have to have those tiny scallop-shaped sconces, and they're two hundred bucks apiece, okay. With Sunny, sex and manipulation seemed conjoined. Whenever a new section was installed or finished in the restaurant, she wanted to fuck there, as if to christen her conquest.

This Friday, it was the patinaed copper walls, rippling with water that cascaded from ceiling to floor—a compromise on the original wave concept. Lit by recessed lamps, the walls reflected a flickering amber and green warmth, reminding Duncan of mornings of his youth, sitting on his surfboard, lifted up and down by rills as the sun broke over the horizon. He had to admit that the walls were beautiful.

"You see?" Sunny said. "I *do* know what I'm doing." She kicked a curled shard of copper sheet that was lying on the still-unfinished floor. The work crew had left quickly for the weekend, dropping tools and materials on the spot, and Duncan navigated around nail guns and circular saws and tubs of joint compound as he followed Sunny to the far wall, against which she stood, palms flush on the slick metal, as if waiting to be frisked, miniskirt scooched over her bum.

At Duncan's house on Skyview Ridge Road, they put Sunny's clothes in the dryer and took a hot bath together. "Are you ever going to get some furniture for this place?" she asked. Most of the house—bought three years ago, a three-story cedar-and-glass behemoth with wraparound decks—was empty.

"One of these days."

"You could let me decorate it for you."

"Thanks, but you're bankrupting me enough," Duncan said. "Besides, I don't trust your tastes. Everything has to be a theme park."

Her own high-rise condo in San Francisco looked like an industrial machine shop, an amalgam of sleek steel and chrome. Her bed was the centerpiece—a frightening apparatus with iron-beam posts extending upward to intersect at a hulking block and tackle, thick chains dangling over the sheets. Duncan couldn't imagine sleeping underneath the contraption—not that he would ever be invited. Sunny had imposed strict ground rules: they didn't spend the night, they didn't go on "dates," they didn't chat on the phone, they just fucked. They got together on Tuesday and Friday nights, and had no ownership over the rest of the week.

In the tub, Sunny drew her knees apart and grasped his penis between the arches of her feet.

"That's not going to do anything," Duncan told her.

"No?" she said. "Come on, giddyup."

"I'm not nineteen," he said. "I need a little more time to reload."

"I thought Korean men were so virile. The view alone deserves a salute."

The view was pretty good: she was especially tall and long-limbed for a Chinese woman, and she had candied proportions, large areolas on her breasts, hairless and pink down there, too. "Sunny, how many people have you slept with?"

"Men or women?"

"*Ho brah,*" Duncan said. At his parents' house in Haleiwa, they had spoken a mix of English, Korean, and Hawaiian Pidgin.

"I've kind of lost count, if you want to know the truth," Sunny said. "But I can tell you exactly how many animals."

She was kidding, wasn't she? Although there was that block and tackle above her bed, and her dog, a big, muscular Rhodesian Ridgeback named Foo Man Stud, seemed unusually attached to her, snarling and lunging at Duncan whenever he saw him, restrained from tearing him apart only by his choke chain, which Sunny would yank mercilessly, laughing. Sunny used to like choking Duncan, too, sliding her hand from his chest to his throat as they made love, until he asked her to stop.

He looked at Sunny, who was scooping bathwater over her breasts. She smiled at him, then slipped the tip of her tongue out and set it aflutter in a reptilian blur.

"You're a piece of work, aren't you?" he said.

"You don't know the half of it."

Maybe she was into asphyxiophilia, a host of other depravities. He didn't want to know. Sex at this point in his life was more interesting in theory than in practice, and, more and more, this arrangement with Sunny was becoming too weird, too impersonal for him, as if he were there purely to service and amuse her.

"Sunny," he said, "I don't think we should see each other anymore."

She raised an eyebrow. "No?"

"No. If you want, you can keep working on the restaurant."

"Well, *duh,*" she said. "Otherwise I'd sue your ass for sexual harassment."

She got out of the tub and slowly toweled herself dry and began combing her hair.

"You don't want to know why?" he asked.

"Why you're dumping me?"

He nodded.

"Oh, it's probably I'm too independent for you, I can't give you a commitment, I'm not subservient enough, I just want you for sex, I'm a ballbuster, a bitch, a slut, what do you know, just like a man. Nothing I haven't heard before. It's pathetic how easily intimidated Asian men are."

SPRING

Esther Miyabe didn't like sex much, which, after Sunny, didn't really bother Duncan. They met at the grand opening of Banzai Pipeline, introduced to each other by a former colleague of Duncan's from Summit Strategy, the venture capital firm on Sand Hill Road where he had made his killing.

Esther, a fourth-generation Japanese American, was impressed with Duncan's restaurant, and with his money, and with his house, which he allowed her to furnish and decorate in tasteful country casual. Esther owned a nice Victorian herself in Pacific Heights, where he was supposed to be at four o'clock. She had invited over a group of scientists from her biotech lab, Genetein, to watch the semifinals of the NCAA basketball tournament. All week, though, Duncan had been tracking satellite images, wave models, and buoy reports, and he knew a good-sized swell would be arriving at Rummy Creek with the outgoing tide.

"It might be the last swell of the season," he told Esther on the phone in the morning.

"Fine," she said.

"I'll be there by six, in plenty of time for the second game."

"You do what you have to do. You think surfing's more important, you go ahead," she said.

"Come on, Esther. It's just the Final Four. You don't even like basketball."

"You don't understand anything, do you?" she said.

He had tried, but he couldn't explain Rummy Creek to her. It was an aberration, a freak of nature. There weren't supposed to be any big-wave breaks in Rosarita Bay, where the main stretch of shoreline, Pismo Beach, offered only mushy, waist-high dribblers. Rummy Creek? It was way off the highway, hidden behind the Air Force radar station. Some windsurfers knew about it, launching off an occasional ramp on the inside break, but on the outside, even during a fat ten-foot swell, it barely capped over. No one ever thought to surf Rummy Creek until Duncan Roh twelve years ago.

He lived in San Francisco then, still working as an investment analyst. On a January day, his regular spot, Ocean Beach, had been blown out by an onshore gale, and he drove down the coast to explore, glimpsed the radar dish, and hiked down to it. His father, an Army civilian, supervised radar installations in Hawaii, and Duncan thought he'd be curious about what was there. Before he crested the headlands, he could hear and feel it—the concussive detonation of an enormous wave breaking. As he came over the rise, he was stunned to see that the reef was at least half a mile out. Sets of waves smoked in and humped up into towering gray-green peaks, pitched out, boomed, and peeled left and right, foam roiling.

Over the next week, Duncan figured out the topography of the outer reef. It sat twenty-five feet below the surface, shoaling abruptly out of deep water, which explained why it usually lay inert. About thirty days each winter, however, groundswells generated by Aleutian storms pumped unimpeded across open ocean, and the first thing they hit after two thousand miles was Rummy Creek, causing waves to jack up into grinding, monster barrels big enough to enclose a horse.

It took Duncan a month to work up the nerve to attempt a ride. He chose a smallish fifteen-footer, stroking hard to get up to speed, hopping on his feet. He thought he had taken off safely on the shoulder, but the wave surged upward, forcing him to drop steeply down its face. He landed, wobbled, regained his balance, and leaned hard to carve back up the wall, then screamed down the line, shooting across two hundred yards before the whitewater caught up to him and blasted him off his board— the ride of his life.

He became obsessed with Rummy Creek, and surfed it alone for the next seven years. At first he had wanted to keep the place to himself, but when he finally told a few surfers about it, no one would paddle out with him. It was too scary, too dangerous. The water was fifty degrees, and even with a neoprene wet suit, hood, gloves, and booties, hypothermia could quickly set in, making you too disoriented to survive a hold-down, which was unavoidable at Rummy Creek. The waves were so big, so fast, so heavy, they created their own wind. When they broke, they registered on seismographs at Berkeley. As you skittered across the ambient chop on the face, the waves were relentless, chasing after you like an avalanche, an imploding building, a malevolent Niagara, and if you fell and got sucked over the falls, they would drive you deep to the bottom, which was rutted with sharp crevices and caves. Down there, the turbulence aerated the water, not dense enough to swim. For half a minute, you were stuck in a punishing, mauling spin cycle, your eardrums close to rupturing from the pressure, and if you were lucky enough to claw to the surface, you were still in the impact zone, another wave about to dump on you, or, almost as unpleasantly, you were pulled by the current and pummeled against the jagged rocks on the inside, which would cut you up nicely for the great white sharks that prowled the shore and sometimes left carcasses of sea lions on the beach, cartilage and intestines and bone hanging out of missing bellies.

Yet, gradually, Tank, JuJu, and Skunk B. joined Duncan at Rummy Creek (they called him DooRow). They were young turks from Santa Cruz with bleached cornrows and tattoos and pierced tongues, all soul surfers, purists who shunned contests and fame. They did everything they could to keep this gnarly, mysto spot secret, vibing out any Barneys who came over the hill, Tank keying cars and snapping antennas. Even the townspeople cooperated. They all knew about the place, but if a stranger slunk into Rosarita Bay and asked about the location of a big-wave break, they'd deny its existence.

Word would leak out eventually, Duncan knew. Some photographer from a surf magazine would capture Rummy Creek on a good day, and instantly it'd be all over, world-famous overnight, just like the North Shore. Then there'd be a hundred punks on the water, six yahoos vying for each wave, and Duncan would be crowded off this reef he'd discovered, this primeval place that inspired and terrorized his every waking moment.

Everywhere else, he was merely an average surfer, not close to being a professional. Particularly on small waves, while prepubescent kids were ripping out aerials and snapbacks, Duncan looked like a novice. But on big waves, he excelled, and he was at his best at Rummy Creek. It was where Duncan felt the most alive. He didn't have time to think about anything except the pitch and shape of each wave. He wasn't obliged to anyone who could get in his way or disappoint him. He was attuned to every dip and yaw of his board, sentient to a world ablaze in iridescent color: the bottle-green of the water, the spindrift floating across the air, the magenta sky underneath black storm clouds, the patches of mustard bursting on the hills. He was out there on the terrible sea, and it was pointless and deadly, what he was doing, and it was beautiful.

He got to Esther's house at eight-thirty.

"Why didn't you at least change?" Esther said. "And what the hell happened to your leg?"

"Just a scratch," he said.

His hair was stiff with salt, and he was wearing his usual après-surf apparel: fleece vest, T-shirt, shorts, and sheepskin Ugg boots. The swell hadn't quite lived up to billing, a little lumpy and small, but he had managed to snag some decent rides, not falling until the end of the day, when he got careless taking off on a wave and was crunched, hitting the bottom and gashing his shin through his wet suit.

The cut was simple to fix—seventeen stitches and several feet of gauze—but the doctor at the clinic had been concerned about his shoulder, which she thought he might have separated, and had made him wait for an x-ray.

"The second game still on?" he asked Esther. He caught the last few minutes of the blowout, ate some of the sushi he'd had delivered from Banzai, and tried to chitchat with Esther's coworkers from Genetein. Most, like her, were crystallographers, an occupation in the pharmaceutical industry that Duncan didn't fully understand, no matter how often Esther tried to educate him. Something to do with growing protein crystals and studying the three-dimensional molecular structures of potential drugs, hopefully billion-dollar drugs.

The conversation at these parties always excluded Duncan, the talk revolving around science (cytosolic phospholipase A_2?), research publications, conferences, and political maneuvers for promotions. The only topic he could have participated in didn't interest him much anymore: money. These Genetein scientists were cash-rich from a merger with Pfizer a few years back, and they all wanted to discuss stocks and IPOs with Duncan, but, insisting he was retired, he politely recused himself.

"You couldn't give them a nibble?" Esther said as they undressed for bed.

"I wasn't being evasive. I'm totally out of the loop since I quit."

"People think you're weird," she said.

"Why?"

"Because you don't do anything but surf."

"I have the restaurant."

"You have a manager running it. You're not even there most nights."

"I like my life," Duncan said, lying on the bed. "I worked very hard to get this life."

"So you could regress into a postadolescent slacker?" She flashed him a *shaka* with her hand, thumb and pinkie extended out. "Aloha, dude," she said mockingly.

Duncan laughed. She was cute. "You know there's more to me than that," he said.

"Is there? What are you going to do when you're too old to surf?" Esther wiped a tissue over her Mary Janes, then went to the closet and placed the shoes on her tiered rack, nudging them until they were straight and equidistant from the other pairs. When she came back to the bed, she was crying a little.

"Hey," Duncan said softly. "What's wrong?"

"I've put so much into this relationship," Esther said, "and I'm beginning to think it's not going to work."

SUMMER

He met Ariel Belieu, Rosarita Bay's reference librarian, in a meditation class, which he joined sensing Esther might have been prophetic: perhaps his surfing days were numbered. He had herniated a disk in his final session at Rummy Creek in the spring, to add to his collection of four broken ribs, a lung contusion, a fractured forearm, and a dislocated knee. He was logging more hours at the chiropractor's, and his doctor had told him he was showing signs of osteoporosis.

Duncan hoped meditation would help him focus, keep him sharp enough to avoid bad falls. In the class, he developed a visualization ritual—a succession of images that arose unbidden. He saw himself in a clearing of a tropical forest, standing underneath an outdoor shower, and he inhaled as he lifted the shower's pump lever, exhaled as he pushed it down, water streaming down his hair, his back, lifted and pushed the lever twice more, inhaling, exhaling. Then he walked down a path through the trees, his feet suctioning off the wet, gray clay, until he broke through the lush leafage to a wide mesa of brilliant yellow, dry grass that sloped down to the ocean, where rows of flawless A-frame peaks were breaking, crests feathering in the wind. At the cliff's edge was a swimming pool, and he dove into it, gliding down and parking himself peacefully on the bottom, looking up at the wavering surface, and then he emerged and sat in a white Adirondack chair, everything now irradiated in a kaleidoscope of colors, a wonderful phantasmagoria that eventually contracted into a sphere of glowing orange amid darkness, a warm, hovering spot of light.

It was elusive, that transcendent spot of light. He couldn't get there very often. His meditation teacher told him it was called a *thigle* in Tibetan and a *bindhu* in Sanskrit, and she was amazed that he had seen it at all, particularly in the first week of class. It was a stage reserved for advanced practitioners.

Ariel never saw the *thigle,* and soon she quit meditating altogether. She had signed up for the class to combat stress, a common and severe affliction among reference librarians, Duncan was surprised to learn. Too many stupid questions from stupid patrons who turned abusive when an answer wasn't forthcoming.

He made up a goofy routine—Funk & Wagnalls. Whenever he picked her up, as he did this Thursday for dinner, he asked, "What the Funk?" The dumbest request of the day.

"A high school girl wanted photographs of the Underground Railroad."

Duncan was slow on the take, but then laughed uproariously. "Okay," he said, "Wagnalls?" An intriguing nugget of referential miscellany.

"Sharks are the only intrauterine cannibals in the world," Ariel said. "The fetuses prey on each other in the womb until just one remains."

"Ugh," Duncan said. "Sharks. I hate even thinking about them."

They decided to go to Clothilde's Bistro, both a little tired of sushi and teriyaki by this point. Clothilde's was a relatively new restaurant on Main Street, modeled after a French country bistro with dark paneling and chairs upholstered in red velvet, and it was one of Ariel's favorite places to eat. "Food from the homeland," she said, though she was from Indiana. Still, she was ethnically French-Jewish, with brooding Gallic features, and she was an epicurean snob. She had been aghast when she'd discovered Duncan making a fried Spam sandwich for lunch one day. Spam was beloved in Hawaii. Locals bought Spam by the case. "Gross," Ariel had said.

"When you grow up with it, it's kind of comforting," he had told her.

His childhood was of intense interest to Ariel, because hers had been miserable, and he claimed that his had been anything but. He couldn't recall, in fact, being depressed at any time in his life. She was appalled. She didn't believe him. Denial, she declared. There had to be some reason he had never married, never lived with anyone, never lasted more than ten months in any relationship. So she began an inquisition, questioning him about his family in Hawaii, subjecting him to hours of probing, like coerced psychodynamic therapy sessions, that left him exhausted and demoralized.

A couple of nights ago, though, Ariel thought she had stumbled onto a clue, a tantalizing glimmer of bleakness, a *thigle* of pain deep within his oppressive aura of beatitude. She had asked him when he had cried last, and, after pondering, he remembered crying—quite a bit, actually—when he was twelve. For a year his father had been assigned to Yongsan Eighth Army Base in Seoul, Korea. It was the only time in Duncan's life since he was a six-year-old grommet that he would not surf at least twice a week.

"Tell me what you remember about Korea," Ariel said.

As they ate in Clothilde's, he told her what he could remember.

He remembered meeting Korean relatives he couldn't communicate with, and their poverty. He remembered traditional Han-bok clothes, so colorful, and trekking through muddy hills to visit the graves of nameless ancestors. He remembered Quonset huts painted in uniform pastels of blue, green, and yellow on the base, and GIs with M-16s, and military parades on Knight Field with howitzers firing off twenty-one-gun salutes.

"Go on," Ariel said to him, excited. "What else?"

He remembered an air show, the Blue Angels in their Phantom F-4s flying acrobatic stunts over Collier Field House. For the finale, they had buzzed the Han River—dry at the time, and a stone's throw from the base—and dropped napalm onto the sandbars, terrific billows of flames rising into the air. He had been thrilled by the show, but also disturbed, not understanding why until later: the arrogance of the demonstration, dropping live bombs during peacetime into the river of a foreign capital, merely to entertain the troops.

He remembered, too, going to the barber shop on Main Post, and his father ordering "the works" for him: shampoo, haircut, facial, massage.

After a man trimmed his hair, a young Korean woman, one of a gaggle standing by in extremely tight, extremely short blue dresses, reclined the chair so he was lying flat, and slathered a green mineral mask on him. She returned a few minutes later to wipe it off, then wrapped a hot towel over his face and discreetly laid a thicker, larger towel over his hips. The woman took a seat on the side of the barber chair and squeezed her ass against his arm and bumped her breasts against his chest as she reached across him. From this stationary, awkward position, she massaged Duncan for ten minutes, and he got an erection, despite the shame he felt for himself and the woman, despite the eddy of rage that had swirled in him all year. He had hated not being able to surf, but more than that he had hated the *haole* Army culture.

"Is that why you go out with Asian women more than whites?" Ariel asked.

"I don't know. Maybe. I haven't really given it much thought."

"Is it what made you obsessed with making money?"

"I don't know about that," he said.

"Have you ever thought surfing might be a form of escapism for you? Maybe even a death wish?"

"Ariel," Duncan said, "everything doesn't have to have meaning."

"Not everything, but some things do. What worries me is you've done so little work on yourself. You won't even acknowledge you've got issues. Those stories about Korea—they're textbook. You don't think they have something to do with the way you describe surfing as 'soaring' and waves as 'bombs'? With your objectification of women? Duncan, don't you realize? You're a basket case."

"Ariel," Duncan said, laughing, "sometimes the past is just the past."

She raked the tines of her fork across her crème brûlée. "You know, Duncan," she said, "unless you can develop some self-awareness, we're definitely not going to make it."

FALL

"You're late," Lily Kim told him at Beryl's Bookstore & Café. "You're always late. Why is that, when you have no responsibilities?"

This was the cantankerous Korean woman he was beginning to fall for, but who would not have him—yet. Lily Kim and Duncan were not "dating," though they had seen each other a dozen times in the last few months. They were "friends," meaning they chatted on the phone, they went out for coffee, they saw movies, they took walks, they swam laps together at the YMCA pool, they hung out at each other's homes, but they didn't sleep over, and they didn't touch, much less kiss.

"Traffic's terrible on 71," he told her.

"We never had traffic on weekends before all you high-tech yuppies moved in with your SUVs."

"Nice to see you, too," he said. She was standing in the travel section, thumbing through a guidebook, swaddled in a corduroy skirt, woolen leggings, clodhopper shoes, and a barn jacket over a crewneck over a turtleneck (she got cold easily). "What are you reading?"

She flipped the guidebook around so he could see.

"Ah, Bali," he said.

Lily frowned. "You've been there, haven't you?"

"Twice. There's a break in Uluwatu that can get double-overhead."

She shoved the guidebook back into its slot on the shelf, annoyed. It seemed that whenever she showed Duncan a photograph of a beach, he had surfed it. During the summer, when Rummy Creek was flat, he was frequently on planes, chasing waves, hopping from Tahiti and Indonesia to Chile and Costa Rica.

Lily couldn't afford to travel. She was an artist who generated a lot of critical acclaim but few sales. To pay the rent, she taught painting and drawing at San Vicente University and three other colleges. As a youth, she had taken a trip to Korea on a roots pilgrimage, and she had gone on the requisite European backpack tour and a few initial-infatuation Mexican holidays with boyfriends, but for the most part she hadn't gotten beyond driving distance of Rosarita Bay, her hometown, in years. She yearned to go someplace warm and exotic. The walls of her house were tacked with calendars and posters and photographs torn from magazines of tropical islands—quotidian tourist images of beaches and sunsets that she appropriated for her current series, *The Far & Away*. She rephotographed the seascapes and in the darkroom enlarged them into disjointed panels—square mounted grids jarringly scaled and off-focus and saturated in a lurid hue. In an interview in the local paper, Lily had explained that her technique was an extension of Impressionism—the fragmented brushstrokes and intense palette of colors used to capture light and movement more immediately. But the impetus for her work, she said, was largely political, a protest against the commodification of nature—banal travelogue images now more familiar, and therefore more real, to people than the actual experience of being in nature.

Duncan missed the message entirely. Lily's work didn't have an ironic effect on him at all. It viscerally and exactly conveyed his experience in the natural world. Walking by a gallery on Main Street, he saw one of her pieces—a purplish exposure of a choppy sea lapping against a pebbled beach (Java, a left point break he had surfed a couple of years back, it turned out)—and he quickly bought it, his first art purchase.

He met Lily when she came to install the piece in his house. After she finished, he had asked her out for coffee. She had fired back, "Are you married?" then "Are you involved with someone?" then "Are you gay but don't know it?" He answered no to each question, but Lily wasn't convinced of his trustworthiness, and on their get-togethers—she was adamant about not having them described as dates—she interrogated him about his romantic proclivities, wary of his less-than-stellar track record. He tried to persuade her that, yes, he had gone out with his share of women, but he was not a womanizer. He didn't have any sort of deep-seated, oedipally induced Peter Pan complex that prevented him from engaging in a healthy, long-term commitment.

Lily was difficult to sway. She was a serial cohabitator. Thirty-nine now, she had lived with four different men since college, mostly older artists who had ended up cheating on her. She didn't have a great opinion of artists—or men. She was sick of men. All her life she had been hemmed in and held back and pushed down by them.

They sat down in the bookstore's café section and ordered cappuccinos. While Lily talked about next week's pumpkin festival on Main Street—strictly cornball, but she couldn't resist going year after year—Duncan stared at her face. He was fascinated by the light and shadows on her face in the café, the lines of her cheekbones drawn by crescent umbras, her brown-tinted hair glinting as if by static. In her studio, he had seen some of Lily's old paintings—her medium before photography—and one in particular, a self-portrait, had floored him. It was composed of blacks and dark blues and grays, but somehow had seemed luminous, dripping with color, and he had wondered how she'd done it. Now, looking at her face, he had a revelation, a *thigle* visitation. Suddenly he saw what she saw.

"Lily," he said, "I have something very important to ask you."

"What?" she asked, looking terrified, as if he were about to propose.

"Teach me how to paint."

She appeared relieved, then confused, then peeved. "Take a class. Only, not one of my classes. Someone else's class."

"Give me private lessons. I'll pay you."

She grimaced. "I wish you'd stop trying to bribe me. Like wanting to buy that painting when you know it's crap."

"I love that painting."

"I don't like the implications: cash for some goods rendered, untold services implied."

"You know I'm not like that," he said. She allowed Duncan so little. "You don't think this will pan out, do you?"

"Why would I think that?" she said. "You're the epitome of middle-aged, male-ego wish fulfillment, enamored with this image of yourself as a lone-wolf maverick. You're perpetually looking for the perfect woman, just like you're looking for the perfect wave. You're one of those guys who bail at the first sign of intimacy with the three-week jitters or the three-month willies. Basically, you're every woman's nightmare."

Duncan was used to these outbursts, no longer scared off by them. "Secretly you find me irresistible," he said. "Otherwise you wouldn't keep hanging out with me."

"Did I mention deluded? Megalomaniacal?"

Duncan's pager began beeping. He pulled it out, glanced at the numbers, then stowed it back in his pocket.

"What was that?" Lily asked.

"Nothing," he said. Buoy reports. Significant wave height twenty-one feet at nineteen-second intervals. A huge swell by tomorrow. The pager automatically alerted him when a buoy topped twenty. "Lily," he said, "I'm such a nice guy. I really am."

"Would the fifty women you've slept with agree?"

He had fudged a bit on the tally, which didn't seem like that much of a lie, since often he felt as if he were dating the same woman over and over again, varying only in the texture of their complaints about him. "I really tried to make every single one of those relationships work," he told Lily.

"I see," she said. "So it's not always your fault."

"Not always."

"You're a victim yourself."

"Well, kind of."

"Of circumstance."

"Sometimes, yes."

"You're never going to get it," Lily said. "Subconsciously you're doing everything you can to end up alone."

It seemed a terrible fate to Duncan. He realized that was why he had opened the restaurant. To rescue himself from one-pot meals and nights alone with videos and errands invented to get out of the house.

"There are all these women out there," Lily said, "reduced to babbling idiots because they can't find a decent man. Then they get sold into this self-indulgent therapy bullshit on the premise that there's something wrong with *them*. It's so unnecessary, because it's really quite simple. Men are pigs. Everything you say and do, it's like you're missing some higher brain functions and you're operating purely on the stem. All I hear is oink."

"So the reason you're afraid of getting involved with me," Duncan said, "it's not that I'm a surfer, or a sexist, or that I'm emotionally unavailable, or not ambitious enough, or that I'm repressed or too shallow or not Korean enough—it's got nothing to do with any of that. It's just that I'm a *man*?"

Lily smiled. "Exactly."

When he reached the headlands in the morning, he saw Skunk B. pulling into an exquisite twenty-five-foot barrel. Duncan strapped on his ankle leash, waded into the shorebreak, and flopped onto the ebb of some backwash, paddling the rip into the channel. Fifteen minutes later, he reached the lineup, and Tank, JuJu, and Skunk B. yelled to him in elation. The sky was an adamantine blue, cirrus clouds fanned across the northern horizon. The tide was going out, and there wasn't a whiff of wind. The water was green and glassy, clean, and for four hours they took turns shredding wave after wave, the boys hooting when Duncan nailed a drop, carved the bottom for a higher line, and then flew, gliding sweet S-turns from peak to trough to peak, speeding across the bowls. It was heaven. If only he could find a way to share this sort of elemental joy with Lily.

And then Duncan got drilled. By now, there were no more lulls between sets, just one bomb after another, and it was getting truly immense. As he teetered down the crest of a beast, his board hit a bump and wheelied, and he was thrown into freefall. He hit the water, was sucked back up the face, and catapulted. Then he was at the bottom, churning, flesh feeling like it was being peeled. His board had splintered into four pieces—somehow he had seen that, as well as a photographer on a Jet Ski in the channel—but Duncan was intact and conscious, and he waited for the turbulence to subside so he could surface. Just as he was being released, just as he sensed himself lifting, the pressure slackening, the rush and roar quieting, he felt something clamp around his leg. His leash—a fifteen-foot line of polyurethane that tied his ankle to the broken-off tail of his board—had snagged on something underwater. A second wave was about to unload on him, and he couldn't reach the Velcro strap to unfasten the leash.

Later, JuJu told him, "Dude, we were going to get the pine *box* for you," and Duncan thought that, too, as he yanked his leg up, and yanked, and yanked, trying to get free, trying not to panic. But then he found himself noticing—delirious?—how beautiful it was down there, shafts of light refracting off the boiling icy water. He could hear boulders clacking and rolling on the ocean floor, water sucking off the reef, howling, and he was thinking how much he wanted to talk to Lily right then, describe the movement of colors to her, the shifting contours and shadows, and bedazzled, he kept staring at the cyclones of water whirling in phosphorescent blurs—like a photograph taken with the shutter open—as he ran out of air.

Bill Roorbach

Big Bend

from *The Atlantic Monthly*

T HAT NIGHT Mr. Hunter (the crew all called him Mr. Hunter) lay
quietly awake two hours before the line of his thoughts finally
made the twitching conversion to mirage and hallucination that heralded
ease and melting sleep.

Primarily what had kept him up was a worry that he was being too
much the imperious old businessman, the self he thought he'd conquered,
even killed in retirement, the part of himself poor Betty had least admired
(though this was the part that brought home the bacon). This area of
worry he packaged and put in its box with a resolution to ask only questions for at least one day of work, no statements or commands or observa-
tions or commentary no matter what, to Stubby or anyone else, no matter
what, questions only.

Secondarily, Stubby, who was now asleep and snorting in the next
bunk of their rather nice but rustic staff accommodations here at Big Bend
National Park. Stubby was not hard to compartmentalize, particularly: Mr.
Hunter would simply stop laughing with or smiling at or even acknowledging Stubby's stupid jokes and jibes, would not rise to bait (politics primarily), would not pretend to believe Stubby's stories, especially those
about his exploits with women. Scott was Stubby's actual name, his age
fifty-three, an old hippie who'd never cut his ponytail or jettisoned the
idea that corporations were ruining the world and who called the unlikely

women of his tall tales "chicks" and "chiquitas." Strange bedfellows, Stubby and Mr. Hunter, having gotten the only two-bed room in the workers' dorm by dint of advanced age.

Thirdly, Martha Kolodny of Chicago, here in blazing, gorgeous, blooming, desolate Big Bend on an amateur ornithological quest. Stubby called her Mothra, which at first was funny, given Ms. Kolodny's size and thorough, squawking presence, but which was funny no longer, certainly, given the startling fact of Mr. Hunter's crush on her, which had arrived unannounced after his long conversation with her just this evening and in the middle of a huge laugh from the heart of Ms. Kolodny's heart, a huge and happy hilarious laugh from the heart of her very handsome heart. The Kolodny compartment in his businesslike brain he closed and latched with a simple instruction to himself: *Do not have crushes, Mr. Hunter.* He was too old for crushes (sneakers, he'd called them in high school, class of 1945). And Ms. Kolodny not the proper recipient of a crush in any case, possibly under forty and certainly over 150 pounds, Mr. Hunter's own lifelong adult weight, and married, completely married, a stack of two large rings on the proper finger, large gemstones blazing.

Fourthly, fifthly, sixthly, seventhly, eighthly, up to numbers uncountable, many concerns, placed by Mr. Hunter carefully one by one in their nighttime lockers: the house in Atlanta (Arnie would take care of the yard and the gardens, and Miss Feather would clean the many rooms as always in his absence); the neglect of his retirement portfolio (Fairchild Ltd. had always needed prodding, but had always gotten the job done, and in the last several years spectacularly); the coming Texas summer (he'd lived through hot summers in more humid climes); his knee (but his knee hadn't acted up at all—he was predicting, and predicting was always a mistake and a manufactured basis for worry and to be abolished except when proceeding from reasonable evidence, of which there was none in this case, his knee having been perfect for nearly thirty years since surgery after hyperextension in tennis).

Many concerns, more and less easily dismissed, and overshadowed all of them by Bitty (he always called her): Betty, his wife, his girl, his one and only love, his lover, his helpmate, his best friend, mother of their three (thoroughly adult) children, dead of stroke three years. They'd planned all they'd do when he retired, and when he did retire she died. So he was mourning not only her loss but the loss of his long-held vision of the future, the thought that one distant day she would bury him. No compartment big enough to compartmentalize Bitty, but a kind of soft peace like sleep when he thought of her now and no longer the sharp pains and gouged holes everywhere in him and the tears every night. Count your blessings, Mr. Hunter, he had thought wryly, and had melted a little at one broad edge of his consciousness, and had soon fallen asleep in the West Texas night.

The United States Forest Service hired old people—senior citizens—as part of their policy of nondiscrimination based on age and so forth, pleasant jobs at above minimum wage. And because they didn't accept volunteers for the real, honest work that Mr. Hunter had decided to escape into for a salutary year, he signed on for pay, though he certainly didn't need the money. And here in Texas Mr. Hunter found himself, rich as Croesus and older, shoveling sand up into the back of the smallest dump truck he'd ever seen, half shovels so as not to hurt his back, and no one minded how little he did: he was old in the eyes of his fellows on the work crew, a seventy-something, as Stubby razzed him, $6.13 an hour.

The crew was motley, all right: Mr. Hunter, assumed to be the widower he was, assumed to be needy, which of course he was not. In fact, the more he compared himself to his new colleagues the wealthier he knew himself to be: Dylan Briscoe, painfully polite, adrift after college, had wanted to go to Yellowstone to follow his Ranger girlfriend, was assigned here last summer, lost girl, met new girl, spent winter in Texas with Juanita from Lajitas, a plain-spoken Mexican-American woman of no beauty, hovered near Mr. Hunter on every job, and gave him his crew name because constitutionally unable to associate the word Dennis with such an old geezer; Freddy, a brainy, obnoxious jock taking a semester off from the University of Alabama, fond of beer, leery of Mr. Hunter, disdainful of Stubby, horrible on the subject of women ("gash," he called them collectively), resentful of work, smelling of beer from the start of the day, yet despite all well-read and decently educated; Luis Marichal, the crew boss, about whom much was assumed by the others (jail, knife fights, mayhem) but of whom little was actually known, who was liked awfully well by all, despite his otherness, for saying "Quit complaining" in a scary voice to Freddy more than once and who for Mr. Hunter had a gentle smile always; finally, Stubby, short and fat and truly good humored. Nothing had needed to be assumed about Stubby, for Stubby told all: he'd recently beat a drug habit, was once a roadie for the Rolling Stones, had been married thrice, had a child from each marriage, had worked many tech jobs in the early days of computers, had fallen into drink after the last divorce or before it, then cocaine, then heroin, had ended up in the hospital four months in profound depression, had recovered, had "blown out the toxins," had found that work with his hands and back made him sane, and sane he was, he said. This work crew in Texas had made him so.

$6.13 an hour all of them, excepting Dylan, hired on some student-intern program with a lower payscale, too shy to ask for parity, and of course excepting Luis, who'd been crew here many years though he wasn't thirty, and was foreman—Luis made probably nine bucks an hour, with four young kids to support. And in a way excepting Mr. Hunter, who in addition to his $6.13 an hour from the Seniors-in-the-Parks Program was watching his retirement lump sum grow into a mountain in *eight figures*. His $6.13 and a great deal more he was feeding purposefully back to Luis in deals on genuinely exquisite paintings by Luis's tubsome wife, improbably named Cleopatra, religious tablitas of the sort Bitty had loved so well, and so Dennis Hunter.

And Dennis shoveled sand with the rest of them, a wash of sand from the last big rain that had made nearly a dune in the shoulder of the road for a hundred yards, a dune dangerous to bicyclists and this a national park, so the crew shoveling into the small dump truck, Luis driving, if rolling the truck ahead a few feet at a time could be called driving. Dennis Hunter in comfortable and expensive relaxed-fit jeans, shoveling, which he preferred to the jobs the other Senior Program folks got: cashier at the postcard stand, official greeter, filing associate, inventory specialist, cushiony nonsense along those lines.

"Fucking say-and," Freddy said. "Endless fucking say-and. Why don't they drive down the backloader?"

"Then only one person would have a job," Stubby told him with elaborate superciliosity. "Five of us are cheaper than the machine to run. Even ten would be. Don't you wish your only job away, Homecoming King."

"Fucking endless fucking desert of fucking say-and," Freddy said.

"Quit that bitching," Luis said.

"Spic," Freddy said, under his breath such that Mr. Hunter heard. No excuse, an educated boy like that.

"It is nice and cool today," said Dylan, peacemaker.

"What kind of work would you most prefer, Frederick?" said Mr. Hunter slyly.

"Love slaaaave to Sharon Stone," Freddy said unwryly.

"She's like, my age," Stubby said.

"She wouldn't like no Freddy," Luis said.

They shoveled a while and Dylan was right; it was a good day for it, cool under high cloud cover, a rare day of breezes in the desert. Around them here in April after a wet winter all was in bloom: prickly pear, cholla, century plants, scores of others, colors picked from the sunset and the sandstone cliffs and the backs of birds.

"Lovely here indeed," Mr. Hunter said.

"I'd fuck her so fie-est," Freddy said.

"I'm not so sure women like it fast," Stubby said slowly.

"From Freddy, fast is the only way woman gonna like it," Luis said. "The faster the better, and gone."

Freddy grew redder, but didn't say it. He'd said it once early on and Luis had scared him, just a look in his eyes that Freddy was not going to forget. Alabama football: tough. Texas border town: tougher.

Stubby put a cheek on the handle of his shovel, grew dreamy in a way familiar to all of them: "Sticky Fingers tour one time I swear I was crating the JBL's when this little spacey chick comes up under the tower and squeaks, like, Where's Mick? and she was so sincere and I go, Mick's already in the Concorde flying home, baby, and she goes, You *know* him? And I did know him a little, of course. I go, He's a nice man, a little vain. And I look down and realize she's got her shirt off and she's got these goofy little boobs and she's dancing and taking her pants down. If Mick's not around, she's thinking I'm good enough!"

"Yeah, right," Freddy said.

"And she goes, The show got me so hot. And we go back behind the speakers and I swear her goofy little bush is trimmed off shape of a heart and she's sopping as the bog end of a beaver pond and I take her behind those crates and . . ."

"Penthouse Letter," Dylan said, risking all, and Mr. Hunter laughed for him, and Luis, though Mr. Hunter and probably Luis had no idea what the referent of the joke actually was. Dylan needed the laughs badly, soaked them up.

The Stones groupie turned out to be a long story, her twin sister and all, and everyone teased Stubby and threw shovelsful of sand up into the bed of the small dump truck, none of them working hard, but together making progress down the road, exposing its shoulder wetly.

"Oh Lord, I gotta dip this thang," Freddy said.

"You take off the gas cap," Luis said.

"Fuck a truck," Stubby said, and everyone laughed and laughed, as if this were the wittiest crack ever made.

Such an inefficient team! The likes of which would in the past have made Mr. Hunter smolder. But he shoveled as lightly as anybody and did not laugh at Stubby's stories and thought of Martha Kolodny for no reason he could make sense of, her laugh from the center of her heart and soul and her large frame that oughtn't to be alluring to him at all but was indeed. And her braininess—intelligence always was sexy to him. She was smart as Bitty and as quick, though Bitty would have called her noisy.

Luis said, "Dylan, what about you? Who is your perfect *mujer*?"

And Dylan blushed and said, "Juanita," with evident pride and huge love for her.

And everyone at once said, "Juanita from Lajitas," which was fun to say and which had become a chant and which they knew Dylan liked a lot to hear. Not even Freddy from Alabama would say anything that might harm Dylan-boy's spirit at all.

"You are like me," Luis said. "A steady heart and a solid love."

And Stubby, damn him, said, "Mr. Hunter, what about you?"

"Have you noticed that I'm only asking questions today?" said Mr. Hunter.

"But I saw you stalking Mothra. Mothra, Queen of the Birdwatchers' Bus. She's a cute one, she is. Tall drink of water, she is. I'll bet she was one athlete in her day! Iron Woman! Anchor in the Freestyle Relay! Bench press two hundred pounds, easy. What do you say, Mr. Hunter? You were gabbing with her nearly three hours yesterday in the parking lot there. You were! No, no, sir, you were! You're a better man than I! More power to ya! She won't give me the time of day, you she's laughing and shouting and joking! And she was scratching her nose the whole time, which Keith Richards once told me is the sure sign you're going to get a little wiggle in."

And all work (such as it was) ceased. Mr. Hunter made a game smile and smiled some more and enjoyed the breeze and the attention, really. He asked a question: "Do you know that right at the beginning of Plato's *Republic* there's a discussion of just this subject, of love and sex? And do you know that one of the fellows sitting around Socrates says something like, *I saw Sophocles*—the old poet, he calls him—*I saw the old poet down in town the other day, three score and ten, and I asked him: At your age, Sophocles, what of love?* And do you know what Sophocles told that man? Sophocles told that man: *I feel I have been released by a mad and furious beast!*"

The crew stood with eyebrows raised a long time, absorbing this tale from the mysterious void of time that was Mr. Hunter's life.

After a long silence, Stubby said, "Oh, fuck you."

Mr. Hunter knew what Stubby meant: the implied analogy was faulty. And Stubby was right. Martha Kolodny was certainly on Mr. Hunter's mind, Martha Kolodny of all women, and the mad and furious beast had hold of Mr. Hunter certainly. And though it wasn't like he'd had no erections in the past affectionless three years, the one he'd had this morning had caught his attention surely. And it wasn't all about erections, either, it was that laugh from the heart and the bright conversation and something more: Martha Kolodny could *see* Mr. Hunter, and he hadn't been seen clearly in three years nor had his particular brand of jokes been laughed at nor had his ideas been praised, nor had someone noticed his hair like that (still full it was, and shiny, and bone-in-the-desert white), nor looked at his hands so, nor gazed in his eyes.

At the Thursday Evening Ranger's Program a very bright young scientist lectured about Mexican fruit bats with passion, somewhat mollifying Dennis Hunter's disappointment. Oh, in the growing night the assembled travelers and Rangers and tourists and campers and workers (including Stubby) did see bats as promised. And among the assembled listeners there were a number of birders from Martha Kolodny's bus. But Martha was not among them.

Dennis Hunter lurked on a back bench in clean clothes—Hong Kong tailored white shirt, khaki pants, Birkenstocks (ah, retirement), eight-needle silken socks—trying to remember how long Martha had said her birding group would be here. Till April 17, was the date he remembered, almost his second daughter's birthday, his second daughter who was, yes, about Martha's age. Five more days, only five. That bats don't get in your hair, that they have sonar, that they are rodents—all this was old news.

Then there was a sweeping presence and a suppressed laugh from deep inside the heart of someone's capacious heart and Martha stood just beside him. "May I sit?" she said. This was a whisper, but still louder in Dennis's ear than the Ranger's lecture. She sat on his bench and slid to his side like an old friend, got herself settled, deep and quiet, perfume expansile, put her chin in the air and raised her eyebrows, seemed to try to find her place in the stream of words as the passionate Ranger introduced a film.

The heavy narration covered the same ground the lecture had, with less fervor and erudition, but the pictures of bats were pleasing to watch, all sorts of camera tricks and lighting tricks and slow-motion tricks and freeze-frames and animation. Bats streaming out of Carlsbad Caverns, not eight hours from here. "Always wanted to see that," Martha said, leaning into Dennis. "Always, always."

"I thought for you it was birds," Dennis said.

Martha put a hand to her nose, scratched. "Whatever has wings," she said. Her other hand was on the bench close between them, and she leaned on it so her head was not a breath away from Dennis's. He smelled her shampoo, coconut and vanilla. Her henna-red hair, braided back into a thick lariat, her strong chin, the strong slope of her nose, her deep tan, her wrinkles from laughing from the heart of her, her wide shoulders, loose white shirt—all of it, all of her, was in his peripheral vision as he watched the film, which was more truly peripheral though he stared at it, her many scents in his nostrils, inside him.

Last night they'd taken care of the small talk: Martha Kolodny was an arts administrator, which title Dennis pretended not to understand, though he knew well enough what it meant: she was the kind of person he'd disdained in his years as marketing wizard at Pfizer (years he then told her about). He'd felt the truth talking to Martha of something Bitty had said once: he had really grown up after sixty-five. Martha had patiently explained that she ran a grantswriting office that helped provide funding—not such huge figures as Martha seemed to think—for several arts organizations, the Chicago Lyric Opera among them. Dennis Hunter could surely appreciate the Lyric Opera if not so much the private foundations that made individual grants to artists smearing excrement on flags and Bibles.

Martha herself had once danced—modern dance—with high hopes. She was too *big,* she had said daintily, "My teachers always said I was too *big.*" And she had laughed that laugh that came from the heart of her heart and smote Dennis.

Her husband was a medical scientist at Northwestern, both a Ph.D. and an M.D. His first name was Wences. He was first-generation Polish. He was working on neuroreceptors, about which Dennis knew a thing or two, from years with the drug company. The couple had no kids, for they'd married rather late, after (at her age) kids were impossible. Wences and she barely saw each other. For them, the passion had fled. "I'm caught," she had said. "I'm caught in an *economic arrangement.*" Her eyes had been significant, Dennis thought.

The film ended abruptly. The Ranger-scientist took the podium in the dark that followed. A spotlight hit his face. Martha sat up, looked at Dennis fondly; that was the only word for how she looked at him, like an old friend. She whispered, "One Batman joke from this boy and we're out of here!"

And in a television voice the Ranger said, "That's the Bat Signal, Robin."

"That's it," Martha said, feigning great shock. She rose and took Dennis's hand and pulled him ungently to his feet and the two of them left the natural amphitheater and were soon striding along a rough path that led into the Chisos Mountains night.

"I knew you'd be at the talk!" Martha said.

"I'm not there now," Dennis said.

She said, "I can't get you out of my head!" She was breathless from the walk. They pulled up at the end of a looping path that looked out over the great basin of the Rio Grande under brilliant stars, under coruscating stars.

"I shoveled sand all day with the boys. Thinking of you."

"I love when you grin just like that," said Martha hotly.

But you are married, Dennis thought to say. He held the words back forcibly: what if she didn't mean anything romantic at all? What an awful gaffe that would be!

They looked out into the blackness of the valley and up into the depths of space and were quiet a long ten minutes. "Mexico over there," Dennis said.

"You know you can rent a canoe and paddle across the Rio Grande to Mexico for lunch? No customs inspection necessary."

He said, "Someone did say that. And at the hot springs, apparently, you can swim across pretty easily. But no lunch."

"Unless you brought your own," Martha said.

"And the hot springs are very nice, too, I hear. Nice to soak in, even in the heat, I hear." He'd heard all this from Freddy in the grossest terms, Freddy who said it was the place he'd bring a *bitch,* if there were anything but *stanking* javelinas around here.

"Do you hear that snorting?" Martha said, as if in league with his thoughts.

"Javelina," said Dennis. He couldn't help the grin. Javelina was the Spanish for what Americans called banded peccaries, Dennis knew, like little pigs, partially tame, sturdy little wild pigs that patrolled the parking lots and restaurant Dumpsters around here for scraps. They were more cute than threatening, though there were stories of mayhem among tourists as scary as the bear stories in Glacier Park.

"There's worse in Chicago," said Martha, meaning just that she wasn't afraid.

"In Atlanta we have bombers and disgruntled office workers," said Dennis.

"Somehow I knew you'd be here," said Martha softly.

"I would like to kiss you," Dennis said. He'd forgotten entirely how this sort of thing was done, knowing just that now—this he'd read—now in the twenty-first century, one got permission for everything, each step, before proceeding.

"I told my husband I wouldn't mess around with anyone while I was in Texas," Martha said. Then, less lightly: "That's the shambles our marriage is in."

"Well, Martha, darling, a kiss is certainly not necessary to a good friendship," Dennis said, glad he'd asked and not just acted to a rebuff and embarrassment, though he was embarrassed enough.

But Martha kissed him, full on the lips, and he was glad for the Listerine he'd swilled and glad life hadn't ended and glad to remember all the electrical connections and brightened cells and glowing nerves he indeed was remembering from the bottom of his feet to the tip of his tongue as he kissed her and was kissed.

They talked and necked—no better expression for it—for an hour under the stars.

"Well," Dennis said, "I'm afraid, despite best intentions, you have kissed in Texas." He felt badly for Wences Kolodny.

"But I have not messed around," breathed Martha.

"On technicalities are the great cases won."

She said, "Do you want to take a little swim to Mexico tomorrow?"

"I'll unpack my swimming trunks."

"I said nothing to Wences about messing around in Mexico."

"That isn't funny to me," Dennis said.

But they kissed till near eleven, when the Chicago birders' bus loaded quickly and headed back to the birders' hotel on the outskirts of the enormous national park.

Dennis walked back to the workers' dorm with feelings he hadn't had in fifty years, pain both physical and metaphysical, elation sublime, ambivalence scratching and snarling like some enraged animal under his squeaky cot.

Mr. Hunter no longer had the physical strength of his estimable colleagues on the work detail, but they had not his old man's stamina. With his steady work all day he outperformed the college boys, though Stubby could do more than the whole crew did all of most days in a single hour when he got inspired, which he did just before lunch this day, Friday. Stubby worked like a dog and demon and an ox, worked as if possessed: every cliché applied. He said, "We don't want Luis in trouble if this sand ain't up and off the road, boys!" They'd got about a quarter of it up the day previous, and already by noon this day two quarters more.

And this day, my God, it was hot. Plain, blazing sun. Mr. Hunter wore $400 chinos and a Gramicci T-shirt. His enormous Mexican straw hat (two hours pay at the tourist store in Terlingua) bobbed about his head to general hilarity, a foolish hat, but it kept him from falling over with heatstroke. The rest of the boys wore shorts and baseball caps, no shirts, and roasted in the sun, all of them except Dylan, who covered himself well against skin cancer years hence and advised the same for all, daily. Freddy the Homecoming King was going to be one spotted and speckled and scarred old geezer if he ever got past forty running his car dealership or his insurance agency: already he was burned crimson and sweating angrily. Stubby's Herculean flinging of sand into the little dump truck seemed to have caught the corner of Freddy's competitive instinct, and Freddy's competitive instinct trumped his more general laggardly nature every time. The kid *worked*, he actually *worked*. He said, "Fucking say-and!"

Luis shoveled too: that sand really did need to be up today, for Monday they started trail maintenance, and no excuses. Mr. Hunter got to sit in the truck and roll it forward down the slight hill in tiny and perfect increments, pumping the heavy clutch, worrying about his knee, then sitting there in the dry heat, no breeze, drinking from the great cooler of water, dispensing water to the other men when they came to his door.

At lunchtime the younger crew climbed on top of the damp load of sand for the ride back up into the mountain. Mr. Hunter slid over so Luis could drive. And the wind was pleasant, if hot, and the view was spectacular: otherworldly landscape, baked sand, a plane of cactus, bright cliffs of sandstone and limestone, old reefs in yellows and purples and blues and reds.

Mr. Hunter said, "Before I leave here, Luis, I would like to commission Cleopatra to do a large painting along the lines of the one you showed me in the Boquillas chapel. With that hunched angel hovering over Mary, do you know? And the little bald man."

"Santo Sebastiano," said Luis, crossing himself. "I will suggest it to her."

"I mean truly, the same size as the one you showed me in the chapel."

"That is large, Mr. Hunter. Where in your room could it go? And this would be a hard work for Cleopatra, weeks of time. For the chapel it was a gift, but you are not Jesus." He smiled like the only visitor to a hospital bedside: pity and sorrow and self-satisfaction.

"I am only a man, it's true. But I will pay five thousand for the painting, and extra to pack it and arrange for shipping to Atlanta."

"Did you rob a bank?" Luis loved to probe Mr. Hunter's wealth. He alone among the crew had noted the cut of the clothing, the whiter skin where an embarrassingly rich watch had lain, the quality of even the work shoes Mr. Hunter wore on detail, the gold covering all his back teeth, the tidy precision of his knee scars, this mystery of a rich man at common labor.

Mr. Hunter smiled with Luis: "Your wife's paintings are worth no less."

The crew dumped the small truck's twelve yards of sand at the head of the Gorge Trail, where next week they'd make use of it repairing a season of washouts and collapses and violated switchbacks. And one hundred yards up the trail, in the shade of a juniper tree, sitting each upon his own rock and looking out over the long gorge to a sliver of the Rio Grande and thence into Mexico, the crew ate lunch, each in his style: Stubby a huge sandwich of cheeses and sprouts and peppers and who knew what vegetarian excesses on thick bread he'd baked himself; Dylan a plain tortilla wrapped around beans; Luis a small feast packed in a series of paper bundles by Cleopatra, tortillas and three kinds of beans and slivers of meat and roasted peppers and whole tiny avocados and an orange and several whole tomatoes and tamales in cornhusks and more, always more; Freddy, poor bigoted kid, a single enormous bag of barbecue potato chips from the PX and his usual ungrateful snacking from Luis's bounty. Mr. Hunter didn't eat lunch, not anymore, but had a few samples of Cleopatra's cooking, marvelous.

As the crew settled down into what should normally have been something like a siesta, Stubby turned to Mr. Hunter. He said, "Where did you and the bird lady go last night when you left the lecture so early?"

"Why is it you ask?" Mr. Hunter said wryly, as the attention of the crew fell pleasingly upon him.

"I was only worried, is all," said Stubby, even more wryly.

After a long silence Luis grinned and said, "Tell us, Sophocles, old poet, what of love?"

"Love!" Stubby said. "You should have smelled our room in the night! What perfume! And perfume, my brothers, does not rub off without some rubbing!"

Still wryly—there was no other safe tack to take—Mr. Hunter said, "Do you imply that it is wrong for an old man to seek romance?"

"Not s'long as it's with an old lady," Freddy said.

"She's not as old as all that," said Stubby. "She's not yet my age, and I'm a youth, as you can see."

"Is she over forty?" Dylan said helpfully. He got embarrassed, bit into his burrito, looked out over the dry valley of the Rio Grande.

"Ah, forty!" Stubby said. "Forty is the youth of old age and the old age of youth!"

Freddy said equably, "How old are y'all, anyway, Mr. Hunter?" He leaned a long way, gave a short smile, reached and took another of Luis's tortillas.

"Three score and fourteen," Mr. Hunter said. "Seventy-four. The youth of death, I would say, if pressed."

"Y'all? No way. You don't fucking look it!" Freddy said.

And Dylan, too: "You don't even look sixty!"

And Stubby: "You do to me! You look sixty as hell, and that's a compliment!"

"What of love, Sophocles?" Luis said again.

Mr. Hunter could not help himself. He beamed. He said, "Do any of you really believe my private hours are any of your business?"

Stubby: "Do we not have the right to learn from those older than us and do you, Mr. Hunter, not have the duty to teach us?"

"Tay-ake her to Viagra Falls," Freddy said.

"Mr. Hunter has twice the cactus you have, hombre," said Luis.

"It's not all about sex," Dylan said.

"Thank you, Dylan," said Stubby. "And do tell us: What is it all about?"

"Blow jobs," Freddy said animatedly.

Dylan shrugged Freddy's coarseness off. He thought of Juanita (this you could see in his reverent face). He said slowly, "Closeness. Is what it's about."

But Mr. Hunter didn't mind that some part of this was indeed about sex, and that sex was certainly perhaps some of the closeness he was missing, and further, had the enlivening notion that sex and he might be in the same place this evening if he got off work early enough. But then there was the trouble, the trouble that had awakened him so early this morning and that would not be shut off in its compartment: "Gentlemen, let me state the problem: Martha is married. And my conscience tells me not to proceed, even as my heart says go."

"And what of thy pecker?" said Stubby, triply wry.

"My pecker says go," said Mr. Hunter, which made everyone laugh. He had never spoken like this to them and indeed not in his life.

"Then listen, brainiac," said Freddy: "Go for it!"

No laughter at this. Just an expectant turning to Mr. Hunter, who said nothing, sagging a little.

"Listen to your conscience," said Luis. "Listen well. If you spoke this way of Cleopatra, I would kill you just for speaking. For the doing I'd kill her, as well."

"Then y'all'd be single again, at least," Freddy said.

"Hey, I don't know," Stubby said. "This woman, this bird-watcher, Mothra, obviously she's looking for something her marriage isn't giving her. She's taking power here. She's taking care of her needs. She's unfulfilled. Who's to say she should honor this husband, who apparently does not honor her?"

Dylan said, "But she made a promise."

"What is the nature of the promise we make in marriage?" Mr. Hunter said. He tried to sound wry, playing Socrates, but this was too close to the heart of his worry, even under a tree in hot shade.

Dylan said, "That we should love, honor, and obey."

"The flesh is weak," Luis said opprobriously.

"The flesh has a job to do," Stubby said.

"I say, go for it," Freddy said.

A long silence in the windless day, punctuated erratically by the squawks of Mexican jays.

"I don't see how," said Mr. Hunter.

Freddy: "Well, the boy kisses the girl . . ."

And the crew, except for Luis, laughed. He said, "And what of your wife in heaven? What will happen when you see her there?"

"You're not really saying that," Stubby said, incredulous. "It's till death do you part. Man, come on."

"I agree with Stubby," Dylan said. "But still, the woman you're talking about is married!"

"Y'all should just go up to Juarez," Freddy said helpfully. "Soak that nut."

"It's not sex he's after," Dylan said bravely.

"Sure it is," Stubby said. He picked up a stone, weighed it, then flung it with an elegant arm into the chasm below them. "Get real. A man alone, a woman who likes him. I'm with Freddy: go for it."

"I notice that you say 'it,'" Dylan said. "But what of the woman, who is not an 'it'?"

"Go for *her*," Stubby said, conceding Dylan's point.

"I don't see how I really can," Mr. Hunter said.

"There are many women in the world," Luis said. "You do not need to break God's law."

The others, except Mr. Hunter, hadn't seen Luis as religious till now. The air grew more serious. Everyone stared off, each in his own thoughts.

Until this from Stubby: "Actually, there's probably more here than the moral question. You've really fallen for this chick, you know? How are you going to feel if it goes further and then—boom—she's off to Chicago and back to her husband? Leaves you alone! That's going to be a blow, Dennis!"

"When Tina broke up with me . . ." Freddy said. The others waited, but that was all he managed. Freddy looked off into the sky, and for the first time you could see his heart in his face and think of him as tender.

"There might be that kind of price," Stubby said.

"This is good advice," said Mr. Hunter. "I don't know if I could stand the aftermath of any one-night stand."

Stubby slid off his rock, leaned back against it, closed his eyes. Dylan lay down, chewing a twig. Luis stood, stretched, patted Mr. Hunter's shoulder, walked up the path to be alone. Luis prayed after lunch, Mr. Hunter knew. Freddy you might think was softly weeping if you didn't know what a tough customer he was.

Mr. Hunter had made up his mind: no married woman for him.

Martha an athlete, Stubby had joked, and so she was: forty-seven years old, Dennis Hunter's height and weight, and walked with the physical confidence of an athlete, looked in her shorts and stretch top as if she might jump up and fly at any moment. But in Dennis's little rental car her folded legs seemed delicate and soft. Her skin was beautiful to him, and her smell, and her voice. "I couldn't sleep all last night," she said.

"I could barely work today," he said.

The other talk on the hour's drive to Hot Springs Canyon was about the landscape of the park, and they didn't need to say much for looking at that landscape, the great buttes and cliffs and mesas miles away and unmoving. Martha read from her guidebook: "The park is 708,221 acres."

Dennis Hunter hadn't known that.

She read: "The Rio Grande was known to the Spanish conquistadors as the Great River of the North, and to the early pioneers as the River of Ghosts."

"I'm told this was Comanche territory," Dennis said. Luis had said so.

Martha nodded her head, then shook it, then nodded it. "Comanche country," she repeated, saying it from the heart of her heart, where her laughter came from.

Oh God, and Dennis felt his heart flowing out to her entirely, yet not leaving his rib cage at all. They drove slowly through the great basin of the River of Ghosts, past the Chisos Mountains. A pickup truck zoomed up from behind, passed easily, zoomed out of sight, New Mexico plates. Dennis thought about how easily he could declare his love and ask dear Martha her intentions. Perhaps Wences was out. Perhaps a split was imminent. How to ask? Dennis said, "Chisos means something like ghostly in the Apache language." Luis had told him that, too.

Just quietly driving along, looking at the landscape. "Yes, it is," Martha said. "Ghostly, all right." She put her hands up in a gesture of amazement. She'd taken off her rings. "Living things don't belong here. Not people certainly."

Dennis felt himself and the car almost lifting off the pavement. Not that he was faint, not at all; he felt more present if anything, floating car and all, with warm blood in his air-conditioned face and something humming in him, thighs to lungs. She'd taken off her rings. Dennis had never taken his ring off, not once for any reason, not since the night it went on his finger, June 11, 1947.

He said, "I've seen javelina, mule deer, pronghorn antelope, and a gray fox since I've been here. Also, Luis showed me the droppings of a bobcat and a raccoon and owls."

And just then a roadrunner zipped diagonally across the road in front of them, stiff posture a little comical, even somehow portentous, even to pragmatic Dennis.

Martha Kolodny shifted a little toward him, really interested in what he'd seen and what he knew. She said, "I've seen a lot, too: roadrunner, elf owl, Harris's hawk (I saw a pair), Inca dove, ladderback and golden-fronted woodpeckers, verdin, a hooded oriole maybe, pyrrhuloxia, vermilion flycatcher, a varied bunting (I think, I hope, my prize of the trip), an ash-throated flycatcher, canyon wrens (I heard them only), other wrens, a curved-billed thrasher, sage thrashers, many sparrows, a great-tailed grackle."

"You've got the list by heart," Dennis said, afloat in adoration.

She smiled, plainly pleased with his fascination and infatuation. She said, "All new additions to my life list and not one of which is found in Chicago, or much of anywhere but here."

In the small canyon where the hot springs lay they walked in the hot sun along sea-bed cliffs, striated layers of the ages thrown up by earth forces at odd angles. Martha heard immediately a great horned owl, and got it calling to her by hooting saucily. Dennis Hunter floated, he floated along the dry path and felt that Martha floated, too.

Together they inspected the abandoned ruins of the old hotel and store there, the hotel and store Martha had read aloud about from her booklet.

Together they found the petroglyphs she'd read about, and walked along the path, a Comanche path that had become a commercial enterprise's trail to the hot springs, now but a park path for tourists. Martha took Dennis's hand. He wanted to declare his love. How old-fashioned he knew he was! She'd laugh at him, he thought, and this laugh would come from her teeth and not her heart.

The path descended between thick reeds and willows and the canyon wall. Soon Martha stopped, put a finger in the air. "Hear the river?"

Yes, Dennis heard it, a rushing sound ahead. Martha's hand in his, dry hands casually clasped, pressure of fingers in a small rhythm, a pulse of recognition: something profound between them.

A group of four British-sounding tourists with wet hair and mussed clothing came up the path. Their presence explained the one other car back at the end of the dusty and eroded canyon road. Dennis let go Martha's hand, oh, casually.

Approaching, a tall man with wire glasses said, "There's an owl up in the cliff." He pointed high in the sandstone bluff. "Just there."

Martha saw the big bird immediately, and pointed to it for Dennis's sake. When he saw it he was amazed at its size. He'd been seeking something smaller.

"Bloke's calling a mate," said the tall Britisher. His friends nodded.

A pretty young woman said, "We've heard her response."

And the owl, on cue, hooted spookily. Across the river came another bird's hoot.

Martha took Dennis's hand and pulled him along. "River of British Ghosts," she said.

Dennis couldn't get the words as the Rio Grande came into view: "Doesn't it . . . isn't it . . . doesn't this just . . . *tickle* you?" That was pathetic. He thought and tried again: "This little sprite of a muddy river, this ancient flow, this reed-bound oasis? That this is the famous border?"

"Dennis, I don't know what to do."

"That that is Mexico over there?"

"May I see you in Atlanta?"

They stopped there on the plain and dusty rock—flat, polished sandstone, solidified mud really—they stopped and held hands and looked at the river and could not look at each other.

She said, "What is this between us?"

Dennis could think of a word for what was between them. It was passion, nothing less, on the one hand, and her husband, nothing less, on the other, both between them and no way to say a word at this moment about either. He let a long squeeze of her hand say what it could, then pulled her along. Brightly, he said, "I expected gun turrets and chain-link fence and border stations."

"Well, there's nothing but desert for hundreds of miles. They just don't watch much here."

Pleasingly, no other soul occupied the hot springs, a steady gush of very hot water rising up out of a deteriorated square culvert built a century past. The buildings were gone, swept away by floods, they must have been. But one foundation remained, and formed a sort of large bathtub, well, enormous, maybe the size of a patio. In the hot air of the day the water didn't steam at all. A kind of soft moss grew in there.

Martha sat on a rock and took her shoes off. Dennis liked her feet. He wondered if Wences liked her feet. He liked her knees very much. He liked that she was so strong and big, he did very much, so unlike Bitty, who was a bone. He liked the fatty dimpling of Martha's thighs in her black shorts. She dipped her feet in. "Wow, hot," she said.

"Maybe too hot for today?" Dennis said.

"No, no, it's wonderful! And then the river will feel cold," she said. "A blessing," she said. Then: "Well, no one's around." And she pulled off her shirt, just like that, and clicked something between her breasts to make her bra come loose, and shed it, then stepped out of her shorts and then her lacy panties (worn for him, he was startled to realize) and slipped into the hot water in a fluid motion, Dennis more or less looking away, looking more or less upward at the cliff (cliff swallows up there).

"I'm not sitting here alone," Martha said.

So Dennis tried a fluid kind of stripping like hers, but ended up hopping on one foot, trying to get his pants past his ankles, but stripped and hopped, and slid into the hot water, self-conscious about his old body, the way his skin had got loose, the spots of him.

"It's love between us," he said, which was not the same as declaring love. "And that you are married," he said.

"No touching in Texas," said Martha, far too lightly.

The water was shallow and she sat up to her waist and bare-breasted in the hot water and not exactly young herself. The hot water was gentle and very hot and melted them both, turned them red like lobsters.

"Swim," said Martha. And she climbed out of the pool down old steps into the river and dropped herself into the current. Stroke stroke out of the current and she was standing on the bottom again, waist deep. She was forty-seven and married and standing waist deep and naked in the Rio Grande River not twenty feet from Mexico. Dennis felt her gaze, thought of his knee, considered Wences, heard Luis's stern voice, heard Freddy's (*Go for it*), heard Bitty's funny laugh, thought of his three children, heard his daughter Candy (*Daddy, I know mother would* want *you to date*) and followed Martha, climbed in the river after her, enjoying the cold of it after the scalding spring. Stroke, stroke, stroke, he was being swept away in the current, pictured himself washed up on a flat rock dead and naked miles downstream. But Martha got hold of his hand laughing and they stood waist deep together in the stream rushing past, silty, sweetly warm water.

"I'll get our stuff," Martha said.

She swam back and bundled everything—large towels, clothes, binoculars, bottle of wine—and easily swam with one arm in the air till she was back by Dennis Hunter's side, holding the bundle all in front of her chest, dry, and if not absolutely dry, what difference? It would dry in seconds in the sun and parched air.

Suddenly she said, "The American Association of Arts Administrators conference is in Atlanta this June." They stood in the flow of the river. "I could stay a week with you," she said. "Maybe more. It's June. Two months from now, only."

"After that?" Dennis said.

Solemnly: "We shall see what we shall see." Then she laughed from the heart of the heart of her and Dennis laughed and stumbled and they made their way through the water to Mexico.

"I hope no one shoots us going back," Dennis said.

They made the rocky shore in Mexico and walked, not far, walked in Mexico until they were out of sight of the hot springs across the river, and right there under the late sun she spread the blanket and right there hugged him naked and the two older Americans in Mexico kissed and Dennis Hunter was a young man again—no, really—a boy in love, a tanned and buff shoveler of sand, a repairer of trails, a knower of animals, a listener to birds, anything but a widower alone in Atlanta the rest of his miserable days, miserable days alone.

Richard Ford

Charity

from *Tin House*

O N THE FIRST day of their Maine vacation, they drove up to
    Harrisburg after work, flew to Philadelphia, then flew to Portland,
where they rented a Ford Explorer at the airport, ate dinner at a Friendly's
then drove up 95 as far as Freeport—it was long after dark—where they
found a B & B directly across from L. L. Bean, which surprisingly was
open all night.

Before getting into the rickety canopy bed and passing out from
exhaustion, Nancy Marshall stood at the dark window naked and looked
across the shadowy street at the big, lighted Bean's building, shining like a
new opera house. At 1 A.M., customers were streaming in and out toting
packages, pulling garden implements, pushing trail bikes, and disappearing into the dark in high spirits. Two large Conant tourist buses from
Canada sat idling at the curb, their uniformed drivers sharing a quiet
smoke on the sidewalk while their Japanese passengers were inside buying
up things. The street was busy here, though farther down the block the
other expensive franchise outlets were shut.

Tom Marshall turned off the light in the tiny bathroom and came and
stood just behind her, wearing blue pajama bottoms. He touched her
shoulders, stood closer to her until she could feel him aroused.

"I know why the store's open till one o'clock," Nancy said, "but I don't
know why all the people come." Something about his conspicuous warm

presence made her feel a chill. She covered her breasts, which were near the window glass. She imagined he was smiling.

"I guess they love it," Tom said. She could feel him properly—very stiff now. "This is what Maine means. A visit to Bean's after midnight. It's the global culture. They're probably on their way to Atlantic City."

"Okay," Nancy said. Because she was cold, she let herself be pulled to him. This was all right. She was exhausted. His cock fit between her legs— just there. She liked it. It felt familiar. "I asked the wrong question." There was no reflection in the glass of her or him behind her, inching into her. She stood perfectly still.

"What would the right question be?" Tom pushed flush against her, bending his knees just a fraction to find her. He was smiling.

"I don't know," she said. "Maybe the question is, what do they know that we don't? What are we doing over here on this side of the street? Clearly the action's over there."

She heard him exhale, then he moved away. She had been about to open her legs, lean forward a little. "Not that." She looked around for him. "I don't mean that." She put her hand between her legs just to touch, her fingers covering herself. She looked back at the street. The two bus drivers she believed could not see through the shadowy trees were both looking right at her. She didn't move. "I didn't mean that," she said to Tom faintly.

"Tomorrow we'll see some things we'll like," he said cheerfully. He was already in bed. That fast.

"Good." She didn't care if two creeps saw her naked; it was exactly the same as her seeing them clothed. She was forty-five. Not so slender, but tall, willowy. Let them look. "That's good," she said again. "I'm glad we came."

"I'm sorry?" Tom said sleepily. He was almost gone, the cop's blessed gift to be asleep the moment his head touched the pillow.

"Nothing," she said, at the window, being watched. "I didn't say anything."

He was silent, breathing. The two drivers began shaking their heads, looking down now. One flipped a cigarette into the street. They both looked up again, then stepped out of sight behind their idling buses.

Tom Marshall had been a policeman for twenty-two years. They had lived in Harlingen, Maryland, the entire time. He had worked robberies and made detective before anyone. Nancy was an attorney in the Potomac County public defender's office and did women's cases, family defense, disabled rights, children at risk. They had met in college at Macalaster in Minnesota. Tom had hoped to be a lawyer, expected to do environmental or civil rights, but had interviewed for the police job because they'd suddenly produced a child. He, however, found that he liked police work. Liked robberies. They were biblical (though he wasn't religious), but not as bad as murders. Nancy had started law school before their son, Anthony, graduated. She hadn't wanted to get trapped with too little to do when the house suddenly became empty. The reversal in their careers seemed ironic but insignificant.

In his twenty-first year, though, two and a half years ago, Tom Marshall had been involved in a shooting inside a Herman's sporting goods, where he'd gone to question a man. The officer he partnered with had been killed, and Tom had been shot in the leg. The thief was never caught. When his medical leave was over, he went back to work with a medal for valor and a new assignment as an inspector of detectives, but that had proved unsatisfying. And over the course of six months he became first bored by his office routine, then alienated, then had experienced "emotional issues"—mostly moodiness—which engendered bad morale consequences for the men he was expected to lead. So that by Christmas he retired, took his pension at forty-three, and began a period of at-home retooling, which after a lot of reading led him to the idea of inventing children's toys and actually making them himself in a small work-space he rented in an old wire factory converted to an artists' co-op in the nearby town of Brunswick, on the Potomac.

Tom Marshall, as Nancy observed, had never been truly "cop-ish." He was not silent or cynical or unbending or self-justifying or given to explosive terrifying violence. He was instead, a tall, beanpoley, smilingly handsome man with long arms, big bony hands and feet, a shock of coarse black hair, and a generally happy disposition. He was more like a high school science teacher, which Nancy thought he should've been, though he was happy to have been a cop once he was gone from the job. He liked to read Victorian novels, hike in the woods, watch birds, study the stars. And he could fix and build anything—food processors, lamps, locks—could fashion bird and boat replicas, invent ingenious furniture items. He had the disposition of a true artisan, and Nancy had never figured out why he'd stayed a cop so long except that he'd never thought his life was his own when he was young, but rather that he was a married man with responsibilities. Her most pleasing vision of her married self was standing someplace, *anyplace,* alongside some typical Saturday-morning project of Tom's—building a teak inlaid dictionary stand, fine-tuning a home-built go-cart for Anthony, rigging a timed sprinkling system for the yard—and simply *watching* him admiringly, raptly, almost mystically, as if to say "how marvelous and strange and lucky to be married to such a man." Marrying Tom Marshall, she believed, had allowed her to learn the ordinary acts of devotion, love, attentiveness, and the acceptance of another—acts she'd never practiced when she was younger because, she felt, she'd been too selfish. A daddy's girl.

Tom had gotten immediately and enthusiastically behind the prospect of Nancy's earning a law degree. He came home on flex time to be with Anthony during his last year of high school. He postponed vacations so she could study, and never talked about his own law school aspirations. He'd rented a hall, staged a graduation party, and driven her to her bar exam in the back of a police car, then staged another party when she passed. He applauded her decision to become a public defender, and didn't gripe about the low pay and long hours, which he said were the costs of important satisfactions and of making a contribution.

For a brief period then, after Tom took his retirement and began work at the co-op, and Anthony had been accepted at Goucher and was interning for the summer in D.C., and Nancy had gotten on her feet with the county, their life on earth seemed as perfect as ever could be imagined. Nancy began to win more cases than she lost. Anthony was offered a job for whenever he graduated. And Tom dreamed up and actually fabricated two toy sculptures for four-year-olds, which he surprisingly sold to France, Finland, and to Neiman Marcus.

One of these toys was a ludicrously simple dog shape that Tom cut out on a jigsaw, dyed yellow, red, and green, and drew on dog features. But he cut the shape in a way to effectively make *six* dogs that fitted together, one on the other, so that the sculpture could be taken apart and reassembled endlessly by its child owner. Tom called it Wagner-the-Dog, and made twenty thousand dollars off of it, and had French interest for any new ideas. The other sculpture was a lighthouse made of balsam, which also fitted together in a way you could dismantle but was, he felt, too intricate. It sold only in Finland and didn't make any money. Maine Lighthouse, he called it, and didn't think it was very original. He was planning a Web site.

The other thing Tom Marshall did once everything was wonderful was have an affair with a silk-screen artist who also rented space in the artists' co-op—a woman much younger than Nancy, named Crystal Blue, whose silk-screen operation was called "Crystal Blue's Creations," and who Nancy had been nice to on the occasions she visited Tom's space to view his new project.

Crystal was a pretty little airhead with no personality of any sort, who printed Maxfield Parrish–like female profiles in diaphanous dresses, using garish, metallic colors. These she peddled out of an electric-blue van with her likeness on the side, usually to bikers and amphetamine addicts at fourth-rate craft fairs in West Virginia and southern Pennsylvania. Nancy realized Crystal would naturally be drawn to Tom, who was a stand-up, handsome, wide-eyed guy—the opposite of Crystal. And Tom might be naturally attracted to Crystal's cheapness, which posed as a lack of inhibition. Though only up to a point, she assumed—the point being when Tom stopped to notice there was nothing there to be interested in. Another encounter, of course. But along with that would quickly come boredom, the annoyance of managing small-change deceptions, and the silly look Crystal kept on her large, too-Italian mouth which would inevitably become irritating. Plus the more weighty issues of betrayal and the risk of doing irreparable damage to something valuable in his—and Nancy's—life.

Tom, however, managed to look beyond these impediments, and to fuck Crystal in her silk-screen studio on an almost daily basis for months, until her boyfriend figured it out and called Nancy at her office and blew Tom's cover by saying in a nasal, West Virginia accent, "Well, what're we gonna do with our two artistic lovebirds?"

When Nancy confronted Tom—at dinner in an Asian restaurant down the street from the public defender's office—with a recounting of the boyfriend's phone conversation, he became very grave and fixed his gaze on the tablecloth and laced his large bony fingers around a salad fork.

It was true, he admitted, and he was sorry. He said he thought fucking Crystal was a "reaction" to suddenly being off the force after half his life, and being depressed about his line-of-duty injury, which still caused him discomfort when it rained. But it was also a result of pure exhilaration about his new life, something he needed to celebrate on his own and in his own way—a "universe feeling" he called it, wherein acts took place outside the boundaries of convention, obligation, the past, and even good sense (just as events occurred in the universe). This new life, he said, he wanted to spend entirely with Nancy, who'd sat composed and said little, though she wasn't thinking about Crystal, or Tom, or Crystal's boyfriend, or even about herself. While Tom was talking (he seemed to go on and on and on), she was actually experiencing a peculiar sense of weightlessness and near disembodiment, as though she could see herself listening to Tom from a comfortable but slightly dizzying position high up around the red, scrolly, Chinese-looking crown molding. The more Tom talked, the less present, the less substantial, the less *anything* she felt. If Tom could've gone on talking—recounting his problems, his anxieties, his age-related feelings of underachievement, his dwindling sense of self-esteem since he quit chasing robbers with a gun, Nancy realized she might just have disappeared entirely. So that the problem (if that's what all this was—a problem) might simply be solved: no more Crystal Blue; no more morbid, regretful Tom; no more humiliating, dismal disclosures implying your life was even more like every other life than you were prepared to concede—all of it gone in the breath of her own dematerialization.

She heard Tom say—his long, hairy-topped fingers turning the ugly, institutional salad fork over and over like a prayer totem, his solemn gaze fastened on it—that it was absolutely over with Crystal now. Her hillbilly boyfriend had apparently set the phone down from talking to Nancy, driven to Crystal's studio and kicked it to pieces, then knocked her around a little, after which the two of them got in his Corvette and drove to Myrtle Beach to patch things up. Tom said he would find another space for his work, that Crystal would be out of his life as of today (not that she'd ever really been *in* his life), and that he was sorry and ashamed. But if Nancy would forgive him and not leave him, he could promise her that things such as this would never happen again.

Tom brought his large blue cop's eyes up off the table and sought hers. His face—always to Nancy a craggy, handsome face, a face with large cheekbones, deep eye sockets, a thick chin, and overlarge white teeth—looked at that moment more like a skull, a death's-head. Not really, of course; she didn't see an actual death's-head like on a pirate flag. But it was the thought she experienced, and the words: "Tom's face is a death's-head."

And though she was sure she wasn't obsessive or compulsive or a believer in omens or symbols as sources of illumination, she had thought the words—Tom's face is a death's-head—and pictured them as a motto on the lintel of a door to a mythical courtroom that was something out of Dante. One way or another, this, the idea of a death's-head, had to be somewhere in what she believed.

When Tom was finished apologizing, Nancy told him without anger that changing studios shouldn't be necessary if he could stay away from Crystal when she came back from Myrtle Beach. She said she had perhaps misjudged some things, and that trouble in a marriage, especially a long marriage, always came about at the instigation of both partners, and that trouble like this was just a symptom and not terribly important per se. And that while she didn't care for what he'd done, and had thought that very afternoon about divorcing him simply so she wouldn't have to think about it anymore, she actually didn't believe his acts were directed at her, for the obvious reason that she hadn't done anything to deserve them. She believed, she said, that what he'd done was related to the issues he'd just been talking about, and that her intention was to forgive him and try to see if the two of them couldn't weather adversity with a greater-than-ever intimacy.

"Why don't you just fuck *me* tonight?" she said to him, right at the table. The word *fuck* was provocative, but also, she realized, slightly pathetic as an address to your husband. "We haven't done that in a while." *Though of course you've been doing it every day with your retarded girlfriend* were the words she'd thought but didn't like thinking.

"Yes," Tom said, too gravely. Then, "No."

His large hands were clasped, forkless, on the white tablecloth not far from hers. Neither moved as though to effect a touch.

"I'm so sorry," Tom said for the third or fourth time, and she knew he was. Tom wasn't a man distanced from what he felt. He didn't say something and then start thinking what it could mean now that he'd said it, finally concluding it didn't mean anything. He was a good, sincere man, qualities that had made him an exemplary robbery detective, a superb interrogator of felons. Tom meant things. "I hope I haven't ruined our life," he added sadly.

"I hope not, too," Nancy said. She didn't want to think about ruining her life, which seemed ridiculous. She wanted to concentrate on what an honest, decent man he was. Not a death's-head. "You probably haven't," she said.

"Then let's go home now," he said, folding his napkin after dabbing his mouth. "I'm ready."

Home meant he would fuck her, and no doubt do it with ardor and tenderness and take it all the way. He was very good at that. Crystal hadn't been crazy to want to fuck Tom instead of her nasal, crybaby boyfriend. Nancy wondered, though, why she herself expected that now; why *fuck me*? Probably it was *fuck me* instead of *fuck you*. Since she didn't much want that now, though it would surely happen. It made her regretful; because she was, she realized, the very sort of person she'd determined Tom was not, even though she was not an adulterer and he was: she was a person who said things, then looked around and wondered why she'd said them and what their consequences could be, and (often) how she could get out of doing the very things she said she desired. She'd never exactly recognized this about herself, and now considered the possibility that it had just become true, or been made true by Tom's betrayal. But what was it, she wondered, as they left the restaurant headed for home and bed? What was that thing she was? Surely it was a thing anyone should be able to say. There would be a word for it. She simply couldn't bring that word to mind.

The next morning, Friday—after the night in Freeport—they ate breakfast in Wiscasset, in a shiny little diner that sat beside a large greenish river, over which a low concrete bridge moved traffic briskly north and south. The gilt-edged sign outside Wiscasset said it was *The Prettiest Village in Maine,* which seemed to mean there were few houses, and those few were big and white and expensive looking, with manicured yards and plaques by the front doors telling everyone when the house was built. Across the river, which was called the Sheepscot, white summer cottages speckled out through forested riverbank. This was Maine—small in scale, profusely scenic, annoyingly remote, exclusive, and crowded. She knew they were close to the ocean, but she hadn't seen it yet, even from the plane last night. The Sheepscot was clearly an estuary; gulls were flying upriver in the clear morning air, crisp little lobster craft, a few sailboats sat at anchor.

When they'd parked and hiked down toward the diner, Tom had stopped to bend over, peering into several windows full of house-for-sale pictures, all in color, all small white structures with crisp green roofs situated "minutes" from some body of water imprecisely seen in the background. All the locales had Maine-ish names. Pemaquid Point. Passamaquoddy something. Stickney Corner. The houses looked like the renter cabins across the river—places you'd get sick of after one season then have to put back on the market. She couldn't gauge if prices were high or low, though Tom thought they were too high. It didn't matter. She didn't live here.

When he'd looked in at two or three realty windows, Tom stood up and stared down at the river beyond the diner. Water glistened in the light September air. He seemed wistful, but also to be contemplating. The salt-smelling breeze blew his hair against the part, revealing where it was thinning.

"Are you considering something 'only steps from the ocean'?" she said, to be congenial. She put her arm in under his. Tom was an enthusiast, and when a subject he wanted to be enthusiastic about proved beyond him, it often turned him gloomy, as though the world were a hopeless place.

"I was just thinking that everything's been discovered in this town," he said. "You needed to be here twenty years ago."

"Would you like to live in Wiscasset, or Pissamaquoddy or whatever?" She looked down the sloping main street—a block of glass-fronted antique shops, a chic deli, a fancy furniture store above which were lawyers' and CPA offices. These buildings, too, had plaques telling their construction dates. 1880s. Not really so old. Harlingen had plenty of buildings that were older.

"I wish I'd considered it *that* long ago," Tom said. He was wearing tan shorts, wool socks, a red Bean's canvas shirt, and running shoes. They were dressed almost alike, though she had a blue anorak and khaki trousers. Tom looked like a tourist not an ex-cop, which, she guessed, was the idea. Tom liked the idea of transforming yourself.

"A vacation is *not* to regret things, or even to think about things permanently." She tugged his arm. She felt herself being herself on his behalf. The street through town—Route 1—was already getting crowded, the bridge traffic slowing to a creep. "The idea of a vacation is to let your spirits rise on the breeze and feel unmoored and free."

Tom looked at her as though she'd become the object of his longing. "Right," he said. "You'd make somebody a great wife." He looked startled for saying that and began walking away as if embarrassed.

"I *am* somebody's wife," she said, coming along, trying to make it a joke, since he'd meant something sweet, and nothing was harmed. It was just that whatever was wrong between them caused unexpected events to point it out but not identify it. They loved each other. They knew each other very well. They were married people of good will. Everything was finally forgivable—a slip of the tongue, a botched attempt at lovemaking, a conversation that led nowhere or to the wrong place. The question was: What did all these reserves of tender feeling and kind regard actually come to? And not *come to*? Walking down the hill behind her husband, she felt the peculiar force of having been through life only once. These three days were to determine, she understood, if anything more than just this minimum made sense. It was an important mystery.

Inside the Miss Wiscasset Diner, Nancy perused *The Down East Penny-saver*, which had a dating exchange on the back. *Men seeking women. Women seeking men.* Nothing else was apparently permissible. No *Men seeking men.* Tom studied the map they'd picked up in the B & B, and which contained a listing of useful "Maine Facts" in which everything occasioned an unfunny variation on the state name: Maine Events. Mainely Antiques. Mainiac Markdowns. Maine-line Drugs. Roof Maine-tenance. No one seemed able to get over what a neat name the place had.

Out on the river, a black metal barge was shoving a floating dredger straight up the current. The dredger carried an immense bucket suspended on a cable at the end of an articulated boom. The whole enterprise was so large as to seem ridiculous.

"What do you suppose that's for?" Nancy said. The diner was noisy with morning customers and contained a teeming greasy-bacon and buttery-toast smell.

Tom looked up from his map out at the dredger. It would not get past the bridge where Highway 1 crossed the river. It was too tall. He looked at her and smiled as though she hadn't said anything, then went back to his "Maine Facts."

"If you're interested, all the women seeking men are either 'full-figure gals over fifty,'" she said, forgetting her question, "or else they're sixteen-year-olds seeking mature 'father figures.' The same men get all the women in Maine."

Tom took a sip of his coffee and knitted his brows. They had until

Sunday, when they were flying out of Bangor. They knew nothing about Maine, but had discussed a drive to Bar Harbor and Mount Katahdin, which they'd heard were pretty. Nancy had proposed to visit the national park, a bracing hike, then maybe a swim in the late-lasting-summer ocean if it wasn't too frigid. They'd imagined leaves would be turning, but they weren't yet because of all the summer rain.

They were also not able to tell exactly how far anything was from anything else. The map was complicated by quirky peninsulas extending back south and the road having to go up and around and back down again. The morning's drive from Freeport had seemed long, but not much distance was covered. It made you feel foreign in your own country. Though they'd always found happiness inside an automobile—as far back as when Tom played drums in a college rock band and she'd gone along on the road trips, sleeping in the car and in ten-dollar motels. In the car, who they really were became available to the other. Guards went down. They felt free.

"There's a town called Belfast," Tom said, back to his map. "It's not far up. At least I don't think it is." He looked back at where the floating dredger was making its slow turn in the river, beginning to ease back toward the ocean. "Did you see that thing?"

"I don't get what 'down east' means," Nancy said. Everything in the *Pennysaver* that wasn't a play on "Maine" had "down east" somehow attached to it. The dating exchange was called "Down East in Search of." "Does it mean that if you follow one of the peninsulas as far as you can go south, you get east?"

This was a thing Tom should know. It was his idea to come here instead of the Eastern Shore place they liked. Maine had all of a sudden "made sense" to him—something hazy about the country having started here and the ocean being "primary" among experiences, and his having grown up near Lake Michigan and that never seeming remotely primary.

"That's what I thought it meant," Tom said.

"So what does Maine mean? Maine what?" she asked. Nothing was in the *Pennysaver* to explain anything.

"That I do know," Tom said, watching the barge turning and starting back downstream. "It means main *land.* As opposed to an island."

She looked around the crowded diner for their waitress. She was ready for greasy bacon and buttery toast and had wedged the *Pennysaver* behind the napkin dispenser. "They have a high opinion of themselves here," she said. "They seem to admire virtues you only understand by suffering difficulty and confusion. It's the New England spirit I guess." Tom's virtues, of course, were that kind. He was perfect if you were dying or being robbed or swindled—a policeman's character traits, and useful in many more ways than policing. "Isn't Maine the state where the woman was shot by a hunter while she was pinning up clothes on the line? Wearing white gloves or something, and the guy thought she was a deer? You don't have to defend that, of course."

He gave her his policeman's regulation blank stare across the tabletop. It was an expression his face could change into, leaving his real face—normally open and enthusiastic—back somewhere forgotten. He took injustice personally.

She blinked, expecting him to say something else.

"Places that aren't strange aren't usually interesting," he said solemnly.

"It's just my first morning here." She smiled at him.

"I want us to see this town Belfast." He re-consulted the map. "The write-up makes it seem interesting."

"Belfast. Like the one where they fight?"

"This one's in Maine, though."

"I'm sure it's wonderful."

"You know me," he said, and unexpectedly smiled back, "ever hopeful." He was an enthusiast again. He wanted to make their trip be worthwhile. And he was absolutely right: it was too soon to fall into disagreement. That could come later.

Early in the past winter Tom had moved out of their house and into his own apartment, a grim little scramble of white, drywalled rectangles which were part of a new complex situated across a wide boulevard from a factory-outlet mall and adjacent to the parking lot of a large veterinary clinic where dogs could be heard barking and crying day and night.

Tom's departure was calculatedly not dramatic. He himself had seemed reluctant, and once he was out, she was very sorry not to see him, not to sleep next to him, have him there to talk to. Some days she would come home from her office and Tom would be in the kitchen, drinking a beer or watching CNN while he heated something in the microwave—as though this was fine to live elsewhere and then turn up like a memory. Sometimes she would discover the bathroom door closed, or find him coming up from the basement or just standing in the backyard staring at the hydrangea beds as if he was considering weeding them.

"Oh, *you're* here," she'd say. "Yeah," he'd answer, sounding not entirely sure how he'd come to be present. "It's me." He would sometimes sit down in the kitchen and talk about what he was doing in his studio. Sometimes he'd bring her a new toy he'd made—a colorful shooting star on a pedestal, or a new Wagner in brighter colors. They talked about Anthony, at Goucher. Usually, when he came, Nancy asked if he'd like to stay for dinner. And Tom would suggest they go out, and that he "pop" for it. But that was never what she wanted to do. She wanted him to stay. She missed him in bed. They had never talked about being apart, really. He was doing things for his own reasons. His departure had seemed almost natural.

Each time he was there, though, she would look at Tom Marshall in what she tried to make be a new way, see him as a stranger; tried to decide anew if he was in fact so handsome, or if he looked different from how she'd gotten used to him looking in twenty years; tried to search to see if he was as goodwilled or even as large and rangy as she'd grown accustomed to thinking. If he truly had an artisan's temperament and a gentle manner, or if he was just a creep or a jerk she had unwisely married then gradually gotten used to. She considered the possibility of having an affair—a colleague or a delivery boy. But that seemed too mechanical, too much trouble, the outcome so predictable. Tom's punishment would have to be that she *considered* an affair and expressed her freedom of choice without telling him. In a magazine she picked up at the dentist's, she read that most women radically changed their opinions of their husbands once they spent time away from them. Except women were natural conciliators and forgivers and therefore preferred not to be apart. In fact, they found it easy, even desirable, to delude themselves about many things, but especially about men. According to the writer, a psychologist, women were hopeless.

Yet following each reassessment, she decided again that Tom Marshall was all the things she'd always thought him to be, and that the reasons she'd have given to explain why she loved him were each valid. Tom was good; and being apart from him was not good, even if he seemed able to adjust to being alone and even to thrive on it. She would simply have to make whatever she could of it. Because what Nancy knew was, and she supposed Tom understood this, too, they were in an odd place together; were standing upon uncertain emotional territory that might put to the test exactly who they were as humans, might require that new facets of the diamond be examined.

This was a *very* different situation from the ones she confronted at the public defender's every day, and that Tom had encountered with the police—the cut-and-dried, overdramatic, and beyond-repair problems, where things went out of control fast, and people found themselves in court or in the rough hands of the law as a last-ditch way of resolving life's difficulties. If people wouldn't overdramatize so much, Nancy believed, if they remained pliable, did their own thinking, restrained themselves, then things could work out for the better. Though for some people that must be hard.

She had been quite impressed by how she'd dealt with things after Tom had admitted fucking Crystal d'Amato (her real name). Once Tom made it clear he didn't intend to persist with Crystal, she'd begun to feel all right about it almost immediately. For instance, she noticed she hadn't experienced awful stress about envisioning Tom bare-assed on top of Crystal wherever it was they'd done it (she envisioned a big paint-stained sheet of white canvas). Neither did the idea of Tom's betrayal seem important. It wasn't really a betrayal—Tom was a good man; she was an adult; betrayal had to mean something worse that hadn't really happened. In a sense, when she looked at Tom now with her benign, inquiring gaze, fucking Crystal was one of the most explicable new things she knew about him.

And yet, she realized, as spring came on and Tom remained in the Larchmere Apartments—cooking his miserly meals, watching his tiny TV, doing his laundry in the basement, going to his studio in the co-op—the entire edifice of their life was beginning to take on clearer shape and to grow smaller. Like a valuable box lost overboard into the smooth wake of an ocean liner. Possibly it was a crisis. Possibly they loved each other well enough, perhaps completely. Yet the strongest force keeping them together wasn't that love, she thought, but a matching curiosity about what the character of their situation was, and the novelty that neither of them knew for sure.

But as Tom had stayed away longer, seemingly affable and well-adjusted, she indeed had begun to feel an *ebbing,* something going out of her, like water seeping from a cracked beaker, restoring it to its original vacant state. This, admittedly, did not seem altogether good. And yet it might be the natural course of life. She felt isolated, it was true, but isolated in a grand sort of way, as if by being alone and getting on with things, she was achieving something. Unassailable and strong was how she felt—not that anyone wanted to assail her, though the question remained: what was the character of this strength, and what in the world would you do with it alone?

"Where's Nova Scotia?" Nancy said, staring at the sea. Since leaving Rockland, an hour back on Route 1, they'd begun glimpsing ocean, its surface calm, dense, almost unpersuasively blue, encircling large, distinct, forested islands Tom declared were reachable only by ferries and were the strongholds of wealthy people who were only there in the summer and didn't have heat.

"It's a parallel universe out there," he said as his way of expressing that he didn't approve of life like that. Tom had an affinity for styles of living he considered authentic. It was his one conventional-cop attitude. He thought highly of the Mainers for renting their seaside houses for two months in the summer and collecting fantastic sums that paid their bills for the year. This was authentic to Tom.

Nova Scotia was in her head now, because she felt it would be truly exotic to go there, far beyond the green, clean-boundaried islands. Though she couldn't exactly tell what direction she faced out the car window. If you were on the east coast, looking at the ocean, you should be facing east. But her feeling was this rule didn't apply in Maine, which had something to do with distances being farther than they looked on the map, with how remote it felt here, and with whatever "down east" meant. Perhaps she was looking south.

"You can't see it. It's way out there," Tom said, referring to Nova Scotia, driving and taking quick glances at the water. They had driven through Camden, choked with tourists sauntering along sunny streets, wearing bright, expensive clothing, trooping in and out of the same expensive outlet stores they'd seen in Freeport. They had thought tourists would be gone after Labor Day, but then their own presence disproved that.

"I just have a feeling we'd be happier visiting there," she said. "Canada's less crowded."

A large block of forested land lay solidly beyond a wide channel of blue water Tom had pronounced to be the Penobscot Bay. The block of land was Islesboro, and it too, he said, was an island, and rich people also lived there in the summer and had no heat. John Travolta had his own airport there. She mused out at the long undifferentiated island coast. Odd to think John Travolta was there right now. Doing what? It was nice to think of *it* as Nova Scotia, like standing in a meadow watching cloud shapes imitate mountains until you feel you're *in* the mountains. Maine, a lawyer in her office said, possessed a beautiful coast, but the rest was like Michigan.

"Nova Scotia's 150 miles across the Bay of Fundy," Tom said, upbeat for some new reason.

"I once did a report about it in high school," Nancy said. "They still speak French, and a lot of it's backward, and they don't much care for Americans."

"Like the rest of Canada," Tom said.

Route 1 followed the coast along the curvature of high tree-covered hills that occasionally sponsored long, breathtaking views toward the bay below. A few white sails were visible on the pure blue surface, though the late morning seemed to have furnished little breeze.

"It wouldn't be bad to live up here," Tom said. He hadn't shaved, and rubbed his palm across his dark stubble. He seemed happier by the minute.

She looked at him curiously "Where?"

"Here."

"Live in Maine? But it's mortifyingly cold except for today." She and Tom had grown up in the suburbs of Chicago—she in Glen Ellyn, Tom in a less expensive part of Evanston. Their very first agreement had been that they hated the cold. They'd chosen Maryland for Tom to be a policeman because it was unrelentingly mild. Her feelings hadn't changed. "Where would you go for the two months when you were renting the house to the Kennedy cousins just so you could afford to freeze here all winter?"

"I'd buy a boat. Sail it around." Tom extended his estimable arms and flexed his grip on the steering wheel. Tom was in dauntingly good health. He played playground basketball with black kids, mountain-biked to his studio, did push-ups in his apartment every night before climbing into bed alone. And since he'd been away, he seemed healthier, calmer, more hopeful, though the story was somehow that he'd moved a mile away to a shitty apartment to make *her* happier. Nancy looked down disapprovingly at the pure white pinpoint sails backed by blue water in front of the fault-lessly green-bonneted island where summer people sat on long white porches and watched the impoverished world through expensive tele-scopes. It wasn't that attractive. In the public defender's office she had, in the last month, defended a murderer; two pretty adolescent sisters accused of sodomizing their brother; a nice secretary who, because she was obese, had become the object of taunts in her office full of gay men; and an elderly Japanese woman whose house contained ninety-six cats she was feeding, and who her neighbors considered, reasonably enough, deranged and a health hazard. Eventually the obese secretary, who was from the Philippines, had stabbed one of the gay men to death. How could you give all that up and move to Maine with a man who appeared not to want to live with you, then be trapped on a boat for the two months it wasn't snowing? These were odd times of interesting choices.

"Maybe you could talk Anthony into doing it with you," she said, thinking peacefully again that Islesboro was Nova Scotia and everyone there was talking French and speaking ill of Americans. She had almost said, "Maybe you can persuade Crystal to drive up and fuck you on your yacht." But that wasn't what she felt. Poisoning perfectly harmless conver-sation with something nasty you didn't even mean was what the people she defended did and made their lives impossible. She wasn't even sure he'd heard her mention Anthony. It was possible she was whispering.

"Keep an open mind," Tom said, and smiled an inspiriting smile.

"Can't," Nancy said. "I'm a lawyer. I'm forty-five. I believe the rich already stole the best things before I was born, not just twenty years ago in Wiscasset."

"You're tough," Tom said, "but you have to let me win you."

"I already told you, you already did that," she said. "I'm your wife. That's what that means. Or used to. You win."

This was Tom's standard view, of course, the lifelong robbery-detective *slash* enthusiast's view: someone was always needing to be won over so as to a better view of things; someone's spirit being critically lower or higher than someone else's; someone forever acting the part of the holdout. But she wasn't a holdout. *He'd* fucked Crystal. *He'd* picked up and moved out. *That* didn't make *her* not an enthusiast. Though none of it converted Tom Marshall into a bad person in need of punishment. They merely didn't share a point of view—his being to sentimentalize loss by feeling sorry for himself; hers being to not seek extremes even when it meant ignoring the obvious. She wondered if he'd even heard her say he'd ever won her. He was thinking about something else now, something that pleased him. You couldn't blame him.

When she looked at him Tom was just past looking at her, as if *he'd* spoken something and *she* hadn't responded. "What?" she said, and pulled a strand of hair past her eyes and to the side. She looked at him straight on. "Do you see something you don't like?"

"I was just thinking about that old line we used to say when I was first being a policeman. 'Interesting drama is when the villain says something that's true.' It was in some class you took. I don't remember."

"Did I just say something true?"

He smiled. "I was thinking that in all those years my villains never said much that was true or even interesting."

"Do you miss having new villains every day?" It was the marquee question, of course, the one she'd never actually thought to ask a year ago, during the Crystal difficulties. The question of the epic loss of vocation. A wife could only hope to fill in for the lost villains.

"No way," he said. "It's great now."

"It's better living by yourself?"

"That's not really how I think about it."

"How do you really think about it?"

"That we're waiting," Tom said earnestly. "For a long moment to pass. Then we'll go on."

"What would we call that moment?" she asked.

"I don't know. A moment of readjustment, maybe."

"Readjustment to exactly what?"

"Each other?" Tom said, his voice going absurdly up at the end of his sentence.

They were nearing a town. *Belfast, Maine.* Black-and-white corporate-limits sign slid past. *Established 1790. A Maine Enterprise Center.* Settlement was commencing. The highway had gradually come nearer sea level. Traffic slowed as the roadside began to repopulate with motels, shoe outlets, pottery barns, small boatyards selling posh wooden dinghies—the signs of enterprise.

"I wasn't conscious I needed readjustment," Nancy said. "I thought I was happy just to go along. I wasn't mad at you. I'm still not. Though your view makes me feel a little ridiculous."

"I thought you wanted one," Tom said.

"One what? A chance to feel ridiculous? Or a period of *readjustment*?" She made the word sound idiotic. "Are you a complete stupe?"

"I thought you needed time to reconnoiter." Tom looked deviled at being called a stupe. It was old Chicago code to them. An ancient language of disgust.

"Jesus, why are you talking like this?" Nancy said. "Though I suppose I should know why, shouldn't I?"

"Why?" Tom said.

"Because it's bullshit, which is why it sounds so much like bullshit. What's true is that *you* wanted out of the house for your own reasons, and now you're trying to decide if you're tired of it. And me. But you want *me* to somehow take the blame." She smiled at him in feigned amazement. "Do you realize you're a grown man?"

He looked briefly down, then raised his eyes to hers with contempt. They were still moving, though Route 1 took the newly paved bypass to the left, and Tom angled off into Belfast proper, which in a split second turned into a nice, snug neighborhood of large Victorian, colonial, Federal, and Greek Revival residences established on large lots along an old bumpy street beneath tall surviving elms, with a couple of church steeples anchored starkly to the still-summery sky.

"I do realize that. I certainly do," Tom said, as if these words had more impact than she could feel.

Nancy shook her head and faced the tree-lined street, on the right side of which a new colonial-looking two-story brick hospital addition was under construction. New parking lot. New oncology wing. A helipad. Jobs all around. Beyond the hospital was a modern, many-windowed school named for Margaret Chase Smith, where the teams, the sign indicated, were called the *Solons*. Someone, to be amusing, had substituted "colons" in dripping blood-red paint. "There's a nice new school named for Margaret Chase Smith," Nancy said, to change the subject away from periods of readjustment and a general failure of candor. "She was one of my early heroes. She made a brave speech against McCarthyism and championed civic engagement and conscience. Unfortunately she was a Republican."

Tom spoke no more. He disliked arguing more than he hated being caught bullshitting. It was a rare quality. She admired him for it. Only, he was possibly now *becoming* a bullshitter. How had that happened?

They arrived to the inconspicuous middle of Belfast, where the brick streets sloped past handsome elderly red-brick commercial edifices. Most of the business fronts had not been modernized; some were shut, though the diagonal parking places were all taken. A small harbor with a town dock and a few dainty sailboats on their low-tide moorings lay at the bottom of the hill. A town in transition. From what to what, she wasn't sure.

"I'd like to eat something," Tom said stiffly, steering toward the water.

A chowder house, she already knew, would appear at the bottom of the street, offering pleasant but not spectacular water views through shuttered screens, terrible food served with white plasticware, and paper placemats depicting a lighthouse or a puffin. To know this was the literacy of one's very own culture. "Please don't stay mad," she said wearily. "I just had a moment. I'm sorry."

"I was trying to say the right things," he said irritably.

"I know you were," she said. She considered reaching for the steering wheel and taking his hand. But they were almost to the front of the restaurant she'd predicted—green beaverboard with screens and a big red-and-white MAINELY CHOWDAH sign facing the Penobscot, which was so picturesque and clear and pristine as to be painful.

They ate lunch at a long, smudged-oil-cloth picnic table overlooking little Belfast harbor. They each chose lobster stew. Nancy had a beer to make herself feel better. Warm, fishy ocean breezes shifted through the screens and blew their paper mats and napkins off the table. Few people were eating. Most of the place—which was like a large screened porch—had its tables and green plastic chairs stacked, and a hand-lettered sign by the register said that in a week the whole place would close for the winter.

Tom maintained a moodiness after their car argument, and only reluctantly came around to mentioning that Belfast was one of the last "undiscovered" towns up the coast. In Camden, and farther east toward Bar Harbor, the rich already had everything bought up. Any property that sold did so within families, using law firms in Philadelphia and Boston. Realtors were never part of it. He mentioned the Rockefellers, the Harrimans, and the Fisks. Here in Belfast, though, he said, development had been held back by certain environmental problems—a poultry factory that had corrupted the bay for decades so that the expensive sailing set hadn't come around. Once, he said, the now attractive harbor had been polluted with chicken feathers. It all seemed improbable. Tom looked out through the dusty screen at a bare waterside park across the sloping street from the chowder house. An asphalt basketball court had been built, and a couple of chubby white kids were shooting two-hand jumpers and dribbling a ball clumsily. There was a new jungle gym at the far end where no one was playing.

"Over there," Tom said, his plastic spoon between his thumb and index finger, pointing at the empty grassy park that looked like something large had been present there once. "That's where the chicken plant was—smack against the harbor. The state shut it down finally." Tom furrowed his thick brow as if the events were grave.

An asphalt walking path circled the grassy sward. A man in a silver wheelchair was just entering the track from a van parked up the hill. He began patiently pushing himself around the track while a little girl began frolicking on the infield grass, and a young woman—no doubt her mother—stood watching beside the van.

"How do you know about all that?" Nancy said, watching the man foisting his wheelchair forward.

"A guy, Mick, at the co-op's from Bangor. He told me. He said now was the moment to snap up property here. In six months it'll be too pricey. It's sort of a last outpost."

For some reason the wheelchair rider she was watching seemed like a young man, though even at a distance he was clearly large and bulky. He was arming himself along in no particular hurry, just making the circle under his own power. She assumed the little girl and the woman were his family, making up something to do in the empty, unpretty park while he took his exercise. They were no doubt tourists, too.

"Does that seem awful to you? Things getting expensive?" She breathed in the strong fish aroma off the little harbor's muddy recesses. The sun had moved so that she put her hand up to shield her face. "You're not against progress, are you?"

"I like the idea of transition," Tom said confidently. "It creates a sense of possibility."

"I'm sure that's how the Rockefellers and the Fisks felt," she said, realizing this was argumentative, and wishing not to be. "Buy low, sell high, leave a beautiful corpse. That's not the way that goes, is it?" She smiled, she hoped infectiously.

"Why don't we take a walk?" Tom pushed his plastic chowder bowl away from in front of him the way a policeman would who was used to eating in greasy spoons. When they were college kids, he hadn't eaten that way. Years ago, he'd possessed lovely table manners, eaten unhurriedly and enjoyed everything. It had been his Irish mother's influence. Now he was itchy, interested elsewhere, and his mother was dead. Though this habit was as much his nature as the other. It wasn't that he didn't seem like himself. He did.

"A walk would be good," she said, happy to leave, taking a long last look at the harbor and the park with the man in the wheelchair slowly making his journey around. "Trips are made in search of things, right?" She looked for Tom, who was already off to the cashier's, his back going away from her. "Right," she said, answering her own question and coming along.

They walked the early-September afternoon streets of Belfast—up the brick-paved hill from the chowder house, through the tidy business section past a hardware store, a closed movie theater, a credit union, a bank, a biker bar, a pair of older Realtors, several lawyers' offices, and a one-chair barbershop, its window cluttered with high school pictures of young-boy clients from years gone by. A slender young man with a ponytail and his hippie girlfriend were moving large cardboard boxes from a beater panel truck into one of the glass storefronts. Something new was happening there. Next door a shoe-store space had been turned into an organic bakery whose sign was a big loaf of bread that looked real. An art gallery was beside it. It wasn't an unpleasant-feeling town, waiting quietly for what would soon surely arrive. She could see why Tom would like it.

From up the town hill, more of the harbor was visible below, as was the mouth of another estuary that trickled along an embankment of deep green woods into the Penobscot. A high, thirties-vintage steel bridge crossed the river the way the bridge had in Wiscasset, though everything was smaller here, less going on, less up-and-coming—the great bay blue and wide and inert, just another park, sterile, fishless, ready for profitable alternative uses. It was, Nancy felt, the way all things became. The presence of an awful-smelling factory or a poisonous tannery or a cement factory could almost seem like something to wish for, remember fondly. Tom was not thinking that way.

"It's nice here, isn't it?" she said to make good company of herself. She'd taken off her anorak and tied it around her waist vacationer-style. The beer made her feel loose-limbed, satisfied. "Are we down east yet?"

They were stopped in front of another Realtor's window. Tom was again bent over studying the rows of snapshots. The walk had also made her warm, but with her sweater off, the bay breeze produced a nice sunny chill.

Another Conant tour bus arrived at the stoplight in the tiny central intersection, red and white like the ones that had let off Japanese consumers last night at Bean's. All the bus windows were tinted, and as it turned and began heaving up the hill back toward Route 1, she couldn't tell if the passengers were Asians, though she assumed so. She remembered thinking these people knew something she didn't. What had it been? "Do you ever think about what the people in buses think when they look out their window and see you?" she said, watching the bus shudder through its gears up the hill toward a blue Ford agency sign.

"No," Tom said, still peering in at the pictures of houses for sale.

"I just always want to say, 'Hey, whatever you're thinking about me, you're wrong. I'm just as out of place as you are.'" She set her hands on her hips, enjoying the sensation of talking with no one listening. She felt isolated again, unapprehended—as if for this tiny second she had achieved yet another moment of getting on with things. It was a grand feeling insofar as it arose from no apparent stimulus, and no doubt would not last long. Though here it was. This beleaguered little town had provided one pleasant occasion. The great mistake would be to try to seize such a feeling and keep it forever. It was good just to know it was available at all. "Isn't it odd," she said, facing back toward the Penobscot, "to be seen, but to understand you're being seen wrong. Does that mean . . ." She looked around at her husband.

"Does it mean what?" Tom had stood up and was watching her, as if she'd come under a spell. He put his hand on her shoulder and gently sought her.

"Does it mean you're not inhabiting your real life?" She was just embroidering a mute sensation, doing what married people do.

"Not you," Tom said. "Nobody would say that about you."

Too bad, she thought, the tourist bus couldn't come by when his arm was around her, a true married couple out for a summery walk on a sunny street. Most of that would be accurate.

"I'd like to inhabit mine more," Tom said as though the thought made him sad.

"Well, you're trying." She patted his hand on her shoulder and smelled him warm and slightly sweaty. Familiar. Welcome.

"Let's view the housing stock," he said, looking over her head up the hill, where the residential streets led away under an old canopy of elms and maples, and the house fronts were white and substantial in the afternoon sun.

On the walk along the narrow, slant, leaf-shaded streets, Tom suddenly seemed to have things on his mind. He took long surveyor's strides over the broken sidewalk slabs, as though organizing principles he'd formulated before today. His calves, which she admired, were hard and tanned, but the limp from being shot was more noticeable with his hands clasped behind him.

She liked the houses, most of them prettier and better appointed than she'd expected—prettier than her and Tom's nice blue cape, the one she still lived in. Most were pleasant variations on standard Greek Revival concepts, but with green shutters and dressy, curved, two-step porches, an occasional widow's walk, and sloping lawns featuring shagbark hickories, older maples, thick rhododendrons and manicured pachysandra beds. Not very different from the nice neighborhoods of eastern Maryland. She felt happy being on foot where normally you'd be in the car, preferred it now to arriving and leaving, which now seemed to promote misunder-standings and fractiousness of the sort they'd already experienced. She could appreciate these parts of a trip when you were *there,* and everything stopped moving and changing. She'd continued to feel flickers of the pleasing isolation she'd felt downtown. Though it wasn't pure lonely isola-tion, since Tom was here; instead it was being alone *with* someone you knew and loved. That was ideal. That's what marriage was.

Tom had now begun talking about "life-by-forecast," the manner of leading life, he was saying, that made you pay attention to mistakes you'd made that hadn't seemed like they *were* going to be mistakes before you made them, but that clearly were mistakes when viewed later. Sometimes very bad mistakes. "Life-by-forecast" meant that you tried very hard to feel in advance how you'd feel afterward. "You avoid the big calamities," Tom said soberly. "It's what you're supposed to learn. It's adulthood, I guess."

He was talking, she understood, indirectly but not very subtly about Crystal-whatever-her-name-had-been. Too bad, she thought, that he worried about all that so much.

"But wouldn't you miss some things you might like, doing it that way?" She was, of course, arguing *in behalf* of Tom fucking Crystal, in behalf of big calamities. Except it didn't matter so much. She was at that moment more interested in imagining what this street, Noyes Street, would look like full in the teeth of winter. Everything white, a gale howling in off the bay, a deep freeze paralyzing all activity. Unthinkable in the late summer's idyll. Now, though, was the time when people bought houses. Then was the time they regretted it.

"But when you think about other peoples' lives," Tom said as they walked, "don't you always assume they're making fewer mistakes than you are? Other people always seem to have a firmer grasp of things."

"That's an odd thing for a policeman to think. Aren't you supposed to have a good grasp on rectitude?" This was quite a silly conversation, she thought, peering down Noyes Street in the direction of where she calculated *she* herself lived, hundreds of miles to the south, where she represented the law, defended the poor and friendless.

"I was never a very good policeman," Tom said, stopping to stare up at a small, pristine Federalist mansion with Greek ornamental urns on both sides of its high white front door. The lawn, mowed that morning, smelled sweet. Lawnmower tracks still dented its carpet. A lone male homeowner was standing inside watching them through a mullioned front window. Somewhere, on another street, a chain saw started then stopped, and then there was the sound of more than one metal hammer striking nails, and men's voices in laughing conversation at rooftop level. Preparations were in full swing for a long winter.

"You just weren't like all the other policemen," Nancy said. "You were kinder. But I do *not* assume other people make fewer mistakes. The back of everybody's sampler is always messier than the front. I accept both sides."

The air smelled warm and rich, as if wood and grass and slate walls exuded a sweet, lazy-hours ether-mist. She wondered if Tom was getting around in his laborious way to some new divulgence, a new Crystal, or some unique unpleasantness that required the ruin of an almost perfect afternoon to perform its dire duty. She hoped for better. Though once you'd experienced such a divulgence, you didn't fail to expect it again. But thinking about something was not the same as caring about it. That was one useful lesson she'd learned from practicing the law, one that allowed you to go home at night and sleep.

Tom suddenly started up walking again, having apparently decided not to continue the subject of other people's better grip on the alternate sides of the sampler, which was fine.

"I was just thinking about Pat La Blonde while we were down at the chowder house," he said, staying his course ahead of her in long studious strides as though she was beside him.

Pat La Blonde was Tom's partner who'd been killed when Tom had been wounded. Tom had never seemed very interested in talking about Pat before. She lengthened her steps to be beside him, give evidence of a visible listener. "I'm here," she said, and pinched a fold of his sweaty shirt.

"I just realized," Tom went on, "all the life that Pat missed out on. I think about it all the time. And when I do, everything seems so damned congested. When Pat got killed, everything started getting in everything else's way for me. Like I couldn't have a life because there was so much confusion. I know you don't think that's crazy."

"No, I don't," Nancy said. She thought she remembered Tom saying these very things once. Though it was also possible she had thought these things *about* him. Marriage was that way. Possibly they had both felt the same thing as a form of mourning. "It's why you quit the force, isn't it?"

"Probably." Tom stopped, put his hands on his hips and took in an estimable yellow Dutch colonial sitting far back among ginkgos and sugar maples, and reachable by a curving flagstone path from a stone front wall to its bright red, perfectly centered, boxwood-banked front door. "That's a nice house," he said. A large black Labrador had been lying in the front yard, but when Tom spoke it struggled up and trotted out of sight around the house's corner.

"It's lovely." Nancy touched the back of his shirt again, down low where it was damp and warm. The muscles were ropy here. She was sorry not to have touched his back recently. In Freeport, last night.

"I think," Tom said and seemed reluctant, "since that time when Pat was killed, I've been disappointed about life. You know it?" He was still looking at the yellow house, as if that was all he could stand. "Or I've been afraid of being disappointed. Life was just fine, then all at once I couldn't figure out a way to keep anything simple. So I just made it more complicated." He shook his head and looked at her.

Nancy carefully removed her hand from the warm small of his back and put both her hands behind her in a protective way. Something about Tom's declaration had just then begun to feel like a prologue to something that might, in fact, spoil a lovely day, and refashion everything. Possibly he had planned it this way.

"Can you see a way now to make it *less* complicated?" she said, looking down at her leather shoe toes on the grainy concrete sidewalk. A square had been stamped into the soft mortar, and into the middle of it was incised PENOBSCOT CONCRETE—1938. She was purposefully not making eye contact.

"I do," Tom said. He breathed in and then out importantly.

"So can *I* hear about it?" It annoyed her to be here now, to have something sprung on her.

"Well," Tom said, "I think I *could* find some space in a town like this to put my workshop. If I concentrated, I could probably dream up some new toy shapes, maybe hire somebody. Expand my output. Go ahead with the Web site idea. I think I could make a go of it with things changing here. And if I didn't, I'd still be in Maine, and I could find something else. I could be a cop if it came to that." He had his blue, black-flecked eyes trained on her, though Nancy had chosen to listen with her head lowered, hands behind her. She looked up at him now and created a smile for her lips. The sun was in her face. Her temples felt wonderfully warm. A man in khaki shorts was just exiting the yellow house, carrying a golf bag, headed around to where the black Labrador had disappeared. He noticed the two of them and waved as if they were neighbors. Nancy waved back and redirected her smile out at him.

"Where do *I* go?" she said, still smiling. A brown-and-white Belfast police cruiser idled past, its uniformed driver paying them no mind.

"My thought is, you come with me," Tom said. "It can be our big adventure." His solemn expression, the one he'd had when he was talking about Pat La Blonde, stayed on his handsome face. Not a death's face at all, but one that wanted to signify something different. An invitation.

"You want me to move to Maine?"

"I do." Tom achieved a small, hopeful smile and nodded.

What a very peculiar thing, she thought. Here they were on a street in a town they'd been in fewer than two hours, and her estranged husband was suggesting they leave their life, where they were both reasonably if not impossibly happy, and *move* here.

"And why again?" she said, realizing she'd begun shaking her head though she was also still smiling. The roof workers were once more laughing at something in the clear, serene afternoon. The chain saw was still silent. Hammering commenced again. The man with the golf bag came backing down his driveway in a Volvo stationwagon the same bright red color as his front door. He was talking on a cell phone. The Labrador was trotting along behind, but stopped as the car swung into the street.

"Because it's still not ruined up here," Tom said. "And because I know too much about myself where I am, and I'd like to find out something new before I get too old. And because I think if I—or if we—do it now, we won't live long enough to see everything get all fucked up around here. And because I think we'll be happy." Tom suddenly glanced upward as if something had flashed past his eyes. He looked puzzled for an instant, then looked at her again as if he wasn't sure she would be there.

"It isn't exactly life-by-forecast, is it?"

"No," Tom said, still looking befuddled. "I guess not." He could be like an extremely earnest, extremely attractive boy. It made her feel old to notice it.

"So, am I supposed to agree or not agree while we're standing here on the sidewalk?" She thought of the woman pinning clothes to a line, wearing white gloves. No need to reintroduce that, or the withering cold that would arrive in a month.

"No, no," Tom said haltingly. He seemed almost ready to take it all back, upset now that he'd said what he wanted to say. "No. You don't. It's important, I realize."

"Did you plan all this?" she asked, "This week? This whole town? This moment? Is this a scheme?" She was ready to laugh about it and ignore it.

"No." Tom ran his hand through his hair, where there were scatterings of assorted grays. "It just happened."

"And if I said I didn't believe you, what then?" She realized her lips were ever-so-slightly disapprovingly everted. It had become a habit in the year since Crystal.

"You'd be wrong." Tom nodded.

"Well." Nancy smiled and looked around her at the pretty, serious houses, the demure, scenically shaded street, the sloped lawns that set it all off just right for everybody. If you seek a well-tended ambience, look around you. It was not the Michigan-of-the-East. Why wouldn't one move here? she thought. It was a certain kind of boy's fabulous dream. In a way, the whole world dreamed it, waited for it to materialize. Odd that she never had.

"I'm getting tired now." She gave Tom a light finger pat on his chest. She felt in fact heavy-bodied, older even than she'd felt before. Done in. "Let's find someplace to stay here." She smiled more winningly and turned back the way they'd come, back down the hill toward the middle of Belfast.

In the motel—a crisp, new Maineliner Inn beyond the bridge they'd seen at lunch, where the room offered a long, unimpeded back-window view of the wide and sparkling bay—Tom seemed the more bushed of the two of them. In the car he'd exhibited an unearned but beleaguered stoicism which had no words to accompany its vulnerable-seeming moodiness. And once they were checked in, had their suitcases opened, and the curtains on the small cool spiritless room, he'd turned on the TV with no sound, stretched out on the bed in his shoes and clothes, and gone to sleep without saying more than that he'd like to have a lobster for dinner. Sleep, for Tom, was always profound, congestion or no congestion.

For a while Nancy sat in the stiff Naugahyde chair beside a table lamp and leafed through the magazines previous guests had left in the night-stand drawer: a *Sailing* with an article on the London-to-Cape Town race; a *Marie Claire* with several bar graphs about ovarian cancer's relation to alcohol use; a *Hustler* in which an amateur artist-guest had drawn inky mustaches on the girls and little arrows toward their crotches with bubble messages that said *Evil lurks here,* and *Members Only,* and *Stay with your unit.* Naughty nautical types with fibroids, she thought, pushing the magazines back in the drawer.

There was another copy of the same *Pennysaver* they'd read at breakfast. She looked at more of the *Down East In Search Ofs. Come North to meet mature Presque Isle, cuddly n/s, sjf, cutie pie. Likes contradancing and midnight boat rides, skinny dipping in the cold, clean ocean. Possibilities unlimited for the right sjm, n/s between 45 and 55 with clean med record. Only serious responses desired. No flip-flops or Canucks plz. English only.* Touching, she thought, this generalized sense of the possible, of what lay out there waiting. What, though, was a lonely *sjf* doing in Maine? And what could a flip-flop be that made them so unlikable? Cuddly, she assumed, meant fat.

She wished to think about very few things for a while now. On the drive across from Belfast she'd become angry and acted angry. Said little. Then, when Tom was in the office paying for the room while she waited in the car, she'd suddenly become completely *un*angry, though Tom hadn't noticed when he came back with the key. Which was why he'd gone to sleep—as if his sleep were her sleep, and when he woke up everything would be fixed. Peaceful moments, of course, were never unwelcome. And it was good not to complicate life before you absolutely had to. All Tom's questing may simply have to do with a post facto fear of retirement— another "reaction"—and in a while, if she didn't exacerbate matters, he'd forget it. Life was full of serious but meaningless conversations.

On the silent TV a golf match was underway; elsewhere a movie featuring a young, smooth-cheeked Clark Gable; elsewhere an African documentary with tawny, emaciated lions sprawled in long brown grass, dozing after an off-stage kill. The television cast pleasant watery light on Tom. Soon oceans of wildebeests began vigorously drowning in a muddy, swollen river. It was peaceful in the silence—even with all the drownings—as if what one heard rather than what one saw caused all the problems.

Just outside the window she could hear a child's laughing voice and a man's patient, deeper one attempting to speak some form of encouragement. She inched back the heavy plastic curtain and against the sharp rays of daylight looked out at the motel lawn, where a large, thick-bodied young man in a silver wheelchair, wearing a red athletic singlet and white cotton shorts—his legs thick, strong, tanned and hairy as his back—was attempting to hoist into flight a festive orange-paper kite using a small fishing rod and line, while a laughing little blond girl held the kite above her head. Breeze gently rattled the kite's paper, on which had been painted a smiling oriental face. The man in the wheelchair kept saying, "Okay, run now, run," so that the little girl, who seemed perfectly seven, jumped suddenly, playfully one way and then another, the kite held high, until she had leaped and boosted it up and off her fingers, while the man jerked the rod and tried to winch the smiling face into the wind. Each time, though, the kite drooped, and lightly settled back onto the grass that grew all the way down to the shore. And each time the man said, his voice rising at the end of his phrases, "Okay now. Up she goes again. We can do this. Pick it up and try it again." The little girl kept laughing. She wore tiny pink shorts and a bright-green top, and was barefoot and brown-legged. She seemed ecstatic.

He was the man from the park in town, Nancy thought, letting the curtain close. A coincidence of no importance. She looked at Tom asleep in his clothes, breathing noiselessly, hands clasped on his chest like a dead man's, his bare, brown legs crossed at the ankles in an absurdly casual attitude, his blue running shoes resting one against the other. In peaceful sleep his handsome, unshaved features seemed ordinary.

She changed the channel and watched a ball game. The Cubs versus a team whose aqua uniforms she didn't recognize. Her father had been a Cubs fan. They considered themselves northsiders. They'd traveled to Wrigley on warm autumn afternoons like this one. He would remove her from school on a trumped-up excuse, buy seats on the first baseline and let her keep score with a stubby blue pencil. The sixties, those were. She made an effort to remember the players' names, using their blue-and-white uniforms and the viny outfield wall as fillips to memory thirty years on. She could think of smiling Ernie Banks, and a white man named Ron something, and a tall sad-faced high-waisted black man from Canada who pitched well but later got into some kind of police trouble and cried about it on TV. It was too little to remember.

Though the attempt at memory made her feel better—more settled in the same singular, getting-on-with-it way that standing on the sunny street corner being misidentified by a busload of Japanese tourists had made her feel: as if she was especially credible when seen without the benefit of circumstance and the encumbrances of love, residues of decisions made long, long ago. More credible, certainly, than she was here now, trapped in East Whatever, Maine, with a wayward husband on his way down the road, and suffering spiritual congestion no amount of life-by-forecast or authentic marriage could cure.

This whole trip—in which Tom championed some preposterous idea for the sole purpose of having her reject it so he could then do what he wanted to anyway—made her feel unkind toward her husband. Made *him* seem stupid and childish. Made him seem inauthentic. Not a grownup. It was a bad sign, she thought, to find *yourself* the adult, whereas your lifelong love interest was suddenly an overexuberant child passing himself off as an enthusiast whose great enthusiasm you just can't share. Since what it meant was that in all probability life with Tom Marshall was over. And not in the way her clients at the public defender's saw things to their conclusions—using as their messenger-agents whiskey bottles, broom handles, car bumpers, firearms, sharp instruments, flammables, the meaty portion of a fist. There, news broke vividly, suddenly, the lights always harsh and grainy, the volume turned up, doors flung open for all to see. (Her job was to bring their affairs back into quieter, more sensible orbits so all could be understood, felt, suffered more exquisitely.)

For her and for Tom, basically decent people, the course would be different. Her impulse was to help. His was to try and then try harder. His perfidy was enthusiasm. Her indifference was patience. But eventually all the enthusiasm would be used up, all the patience. Possibilities would diminish. Life would cease to be an open, flat plain upon which you walked with a chosen other, and become instead cluttered, impassable. Tom had said it: life became a confinement in which everything got in everything else's way. And what you finally sought became not a new, clearer path, but a way out. Their own son no doubt foresaw life that way, as something that should be easy. Though it seemed peculiar—now that he was away—to think they even *had* a son. She and Tom seemed more like each other's parents.

But, best just to advance now toward what she wanted, even if it didn't include Tom, even if she didn't know how to want what didn't include Tom. And even if it meant she *was* the kind of person who did things, said things, then rethought, even regretted their consequences later. Tom wasn't, after all, trying to improve life for her, no matter what he thought. Only his. And there was no use talking people out of things that improved their lives. He had wishes. He had fears. He was a good enough man. Life shouldn't be always trying, trying, trying. You should live most of it without trying so hard. He would agree *that* was authentic.

Inside the enclosed room a strange, otherworldly golden glow seemed to fall on everything now. On Tom. On her own hands and arms. On the bed. All through the static air, like a fog. It was beautiful, and for a moment she wanted to speak to Tom, to wake him, to tell him that something or other would be all right, just as he'd hoped; to be enthusiastic in some hopeful and time-proven way. But she didn't, and then the golden fog disappeared, and for an instant she seemed to understand *slightly* better the person she was—though she lacked a proper word for it, and knew only that the time for saying so many things was over.

Outside, the child's voice was shouting. "Oh, I love it. I love it so much." When Nancy pulled back the curtain, the softer light fell across the chair back, and she could see that the wheelchair man had his kite up and flying, the fiberglass fishing rod upward in one hand while he urged his chair down the sloping lawn. The bare-legged child was hopping from one bare foot to the other, a smashing smile on her long, adult's face, which was turned up toward the sky.

Nancy stood and snapped on the desk lamp beside Tom's open suitcase. One bright, intact, shrink-wrapped Wagner dog and one white Maine Lighthouse were tucked among his shirts and shaving kit and socks. Here was also his medal for valor in a blue cloth case, and the small automatic pistol he habitually carried in case of attack. She plucked up only the Wagner dog, returned the room to its shadows, and stepped out the back door onto the lawn.

Here, on the outside, the air was fresh and cool and only slightly breezy, the sky now full of quilty clouds as though rain were expected. A miniature concrete patio with blue plastic-strand chairs was attached to each room. The kite, its slant-eyed face smiling down, was dancing and tricking and had gained altitude as the wheelchair man rolled farther away down the lawn toward the bay.

"Look at our kite," the little girl shouted, shading her eyes toward Nancy and pointing delightedly at the diminishing kite face.

"It's sensational," Nancy said shading her own eyes to gaze upward. The kite made her smile.

The wheelchair man turned his head to view her. He *was* large, with thick shoulders and smooth rounded arms she could see under his red singlet. His head was round, his thick hair buzzed short, his eyes small and dark and fierce and unfriendly. She smiled at him and for no reason shook her head as though the kite amazed her. An ex-jock, she thought. A shallow-end diving accident, or some football collision that left him flying his kite from a metal chair. A pity.

The man said nothing, just looked at her without gesture, his expression so intent he seemed unwilling to be bothered. She, though, felt the pleasure to be had from only watching, of having to make no comment.

The cool breeze, the nice expansive water view to Islesboro, a kite standing aloft were quite enough.

Then her mind flooded with predictable things. The crippled man's shoes. You always thought of them. His were black and sockless, like bowling shoes, shoes that would never wear out. He would merely grow weary of seeing them, give them away to someone more unfortunate than himself. Was this infuriating to him? Did he speak about it? Was the wife, wherever she might be, terribly tired all the time? Did she get up at night and stand at the window staring out, wishing some quite specific things, then return to bed unmissed? Was pain involved? Did phantom pains even exist? Did he have dreams of painlessness? Of rising out of his chair and walking around laughing, of never knowing a chair? She thought about a dog with its hind parts attached to a little wheeled coaster, trotting along as if all was well. Did *anything* work down below, she wondered? Were there understandings, allowances? Did he think his predicament "interesting"? Had being crippled opened up new and important realms of awareness? What did *he* know that she didn't?

Maybe being married to him, she thought, would be better than many other lives. Though you'd fast get to the bottom of things, begin to notice too much, start to regret it all. Perhaps while he was here flying a kite, the wife was in the hotel bar having a drink and a long talk with the bartender, speaking about her past, her father, her hometown, how she'd thought about things earlier in life, what had once made her laugh, who she'd voted for, what music she'd preferred, how she liked Maine, how authentic it seemed, when they thought they might head home again. How they wished they could stay and stay and stay. The thing she—Nancy—would not do.

"Do you want to fly our kite?" the man was saying to her, his voice trailing up at the end, almost like Tom's. He was, for some reason, smiling now, his eyes bright, looking back over his hairy round shoulder with a new attitude. She noticed he was wearing glasses—surprising to miss that. The kite, its silky monofilament bellying upward in a long sweep, danced on the wind almost out of sight, a fleck upon the eye.

"Oh do, do," the little girl called out. "It'll be so good." She had her arms spread wide and up over her head, as if measuring some huge and inconceivable wish. She was permanently smiling.

"Yes," Nancy said, walking toward them. "Of course."

"You can feel it pulling you," the girl said. "It's like you're going to fly up to the stars." She began to spin around and around in the grass then like a little dervish. The wheelchair man looked to his daughter, smiling.

Nancy felt embarrassed. Seen. It was shocking. The spacious blue bay spread away from her down the hill, and off of it arose a freshened breeze. It was far from clear that she could hold the kite. It *could* take her up, pull her away, far and out of sight. It was unnerving. She held the toy Wagner to give to the child. That would have its fine effect. And then, she thought, coming to the two of them, smiling out of flattery, that she would take the kite—the rod, the string—yes, of course, and fly it, take the chance, be strong, unassailable, do everything she could to hold on.

Deborah Eisenberg

Like It or Not

from *The Threepenny Review*

K ATE WOULD have a little tour of the coast, Giovanna would have the satisfaction of having provided an excursion for her American houseguest without having to interrupt her own work, and the man whom everyone called Harry would have the pleasure, as Giovanna put it, of Kate's company: demonstrably, a good thing for all.

"I wish this weren't happening," Kate said. "I'll be inconveniencing him. And besides—"

"No." Giovanna waved a finger. "This is the point. He goes every few months to check on this place of his. He loves to show people about, he loves to poke around the little shops. So, why not? You'll go with him as far as one of the towns, you'll give him a chance to shop, you'll give him a chance to shine, you'll spend the night at some pleasant hotel, then he'll go on and you'll find your way back here by taxi and train."

So, yes—it was hard to say just who was doing whom a favor.

"The coast is very beautiful," Giovanna added. "You don't feel like enjoying such things right now, I know, but right now is when your chance arrives."

The whole thing had twisted itself into shape a week or so earlier at a party—a noisy roomful of Giovanna's friends. Harry had been speaking to Kate in English, but his unplaceable accent and the wedges of other languages flashing around Kate chopped up her concentration. She tried to follow his voice—he was obliged to go frequently to the coast . . .

Had she left enough in the freezer? Brice and Blair were hardly children, but whenever they came back home they reverted to sheer incompetence. Besides, they'd be so busy dealing with their father.

And was Kate fond of it? the person, Harry, was asking.

"Fond of . . ." She searched his face. "Oh. Well, actually I've never . . ." and then both she and he were silenced, rounding this corner of the conversation and seeing its direction.

Giovanna had simply stood there, smiling a bright, vague smile, as though she couldn't hear a thing. And Harry had been polite—technically, at least; Kate gave him every opportunity to weasel out of an invitation to her, but he'd shouldered the burden manfully. And so there it was, the thing that was going to happen, like it or not. Still, Giovanna was right. And perhaps the very fact that Kate was in no mood to do anything proved, in fact, that she should submit gracefully to whatever . . . *opportunity* came her way.

Over and over, now that she was visiting Giovanna, she'd recall—the phone ringing, herself answering . . . as if, listening hard enough this time, she might hear something different. Sitting on the sofa, shoes off . . . She'd almost knocked over her cup of tea, answering the phone with her hands full of the quizzes she was grading. "Has Baker talked to you about what's going on with him?" Norman had asked.

It was the gentleness of Norman's voice that stayed with her, the date—December 19th—on the quizzes she held, the tea swaying in her cup. What practical difference did Baker's illness make to her life? Almost none. It was a good fifteen years since she and Baker had gotten divorced.

She'd sent out her annual Christmas letter: *Sorry to be late this year, everyone, (as usual!) but school seems to get more and more time-consuming. Always more administrative annoyances, more student crises. This year we had to learn a new drill, in addition to the fire drill and the cyclone drill—a drive-by shooting drill! You can tell how old each of the teachers here is by what we do when we hear that bell. Anyone else remember the atomic bomb drill? Whenever the alarm rings, I'm the one who dives under the desk. Blair is surviving her first year of law school. Brice swears he'll never . . .* and so on. She looked at what she'd written—apparently a description of her life.

To Giovanna's copy she appended a note: "I'm fine, really, but Baker's sick. Very. And Blair and Brice are here this week spending days with him and Norman, nights with me. Blair's fiancé calls every few hours, frantically apologizing. He pleads, she storms. Grand opera! Will she just please tell him why she's angry? She's not angry, she insists—it's just all this apologizing . . . I guess the diva gene skipped a generation. Speaking of which, Mother asks after you. She still talks about how that boring friend of Baker's followed you back to Europe after the wedding. She's weirdly sweet sometimes these days. Think that means she's dying? It scares me out of my wits, actually . . ."

Giovanna faxed Kate at school: Come stay over spring break. No excuses.

It had been so many years since they'd seen each other, letters were so rarely exchanged, that Giovanna had come to seem abstract; Kate hadn't even been aware of confiding. She stared at the fax as she went into her classroom. The map was still rolled down over the blackboard from the previous class. In fact, Giovanna was not only capable, evidently, of reading the note, she was also less than fifteen inches away.

They had met almost thirty years earlier at a college to which Kate had been entrusted on the basis of its patrician reputation and its august location, and to which Giovanna had been exiled on the basis of its puritanical reputation and backwater location, far removed from her own country and her customary amusements. Kate had first encountered the famous Giovanna in the hall outside her room, passed out on the floor, had dragged her inside, revived her, and from then on had joyfully assisted her in and out windows on extralegal forays, after hours, to destinations unequivocally off-limits, with scandalously older men—the more distinguished of the professors, local politicians, visiting lecturers and entertainers . . .

The two girls found one another's characteristics, both national and personal, hilarious and illuminating. They scrutinized each other—the one stolid, socially awkward, midwestern, and oblique; the other polished, European, and satirical—as if each were looking into a transforming mirror, which reflected now certain qualities, now certain others. So many possibilities had floated in that mirror!

While Giovanna worked long hours at her firm, Kate walked dutifully through the city, staring at churches, paintings, and fountains. What had she seen? She couldn't have said. She drew the line absolutely, she'd told

Blair, at taking photographs. "But, Mother," Blair had said. "You'd get so much more out of your trip!" Poor Brice—how would he be faring at home with his sister? From the time they were small Blair had been trying to turn him upside down and shake him, as if she could dislodge hidden problems from his pockets like loose change.

At night, Kate and Giovanna ate in local trattorias, then sat in Giovanna's huge apartment, sipping wine and talking lazily. How pleasant it must be to live like Giovanna, surrounded by beauty, by beautiful objects, so many of which had been in her family for generations. The years slid through their conversation, looping around, forming a fragile, shifting lace. "Is it possible?" Giovanna said. "We're older than your mother was when we met."

"Too strange," Kate said. "Too scary." When she dropped by every week or so now to check on her mother, Kate would often find her asleep in a chair, her head drooping sideways, her mouth slightly open. "Most of the time she's still fairly true to form, thank heavens. She's attached the one available old gent around and she's running him ragged. He simply beams. All the sweet local widows are still standing at his door, clutching their pies and pot roasts. They don't know what hit them. You know, all those years, when Baker and I were having so much trouble and neither of us quite understood what was happening and the kids were frantic and the house was pandemonium all the time—just as we'd all start screaming at each other, the phone would ring and there she'd be, saying, 'So, how is everyone enjoying this beautiful Sunday afternoon?' Now the phone rings and there she is, saying, 'Kate! What are you doing at home on a Saturday night?'"

"Ah, well." Giovanna lit a cigarette, kindling its forbidden fragrance. "She's having an adventure. And what about you?"

"Me!" Kate said. "Me?"

"What about that guy you wrote me about a year or two ago—Rover, Rower."

"Rowan. Oh, lord. Blair was very enthusiastic about that one. One day she said to me, 'Mother, where's this going, this thing with Rowan?' I said, '*Going?* I'm almost fifty!'"

Giovanna exhaled a curtain of smoke. From behind it, her steady gaze rested on Kate. "You broke it off?"

"Give me a drag, please. Of course not. Though to tell you the truth, I just don't feel the need to put myself through all that again. I really don't. Anyhow, the day came, naturally, when he said he wasn't, guess what, ready for *commitment*—he actually used the word—so soon after his divorce. And then naturally the *next* day came, when I heard he'd married a twenty-three-year-old."

"You should live here." Giovanna yawned. "Here in Europe, you still have the chance to lose your lovers to someone your own age."

Much nicer, they'd agreed, clinking glasses.

There was no stone, arch, column, pediment, square inch of painting in the vicinity that Harry couldn't expound upon. He knew what pirates had lived in which of the caves below them, the Latin names of the trees, all twisted by wind, the composition of the rocks . . . Did Kate see the dome way off there? They didn't have time to stop, unfortunately, but it was a very important church, as no doubt she knew, built by X in the twelfth century, rebuilt by Y in the thirteenth, then built again on the orders of the Archbishop of Z . . . Inside there was a wonderful Annunciation by A, a wonderful Pietà by B, and of course she'd seen reproductions, hadn't she, of the altarpiece.

It wasn't fair. He expected everyone to be as yielding to beautiful objects as he was, as easily transported. Her expression, she hoped, as the avalanche of information rained down, was not the one she saw daily on the faces of her students. Her poor, exasperating students, so resentful, so uncomprehending . . . The truth was that most of them had so many problems in their personal lives that each precious, clarifying fragment Kate struggled to hand over to them was just one more intrusion. Yet there she stood, day after day, talking, talking, talking . . . And every once in a while—she could see it—it was as if a door opened in a high stone wall.

". . . but I'm boring you," Harry was saying. "You're a serious person! And my life, I'm afraid, has been devoted, frivolously, to beauty."

True, true, she was a grunting barbarian, he was a rarified esthete. She was a high school biology teacher, he was a—well, he was a what, exactly? As far as she could gather, whatever it was he did seemed to involve finding art or rarities, oddities, for collectors and billionaires and grotesquely expensive hotels. He'd traveled all over, there'd been a wife or two, his family had come from everywhere—Central Asia, all around the Mediterranean . . .

"Mendelssohn or salsa?" He waved a handful of CDs. "To—what is it? To soothe our savage . . . Ack!" He honked and swerved as a giant tour bus in front of them braked shudderingly on the precipitous incline. "They have no idea how to drive! Simply not a clue!"

For miles before and behind them, caravans of tour buses clogged the road, winding along the cliffs. "Is there always this much traffic?" Kate asked.

"From now through October it will be sheer hell," Harry announced with satisfaction, as though he'd only been waiting for an opening. "And why do they come here? For what? We'll see them later, shuffling around in the churches while the guides shout and flap their arms. Blinking, loading their cameras . . . They'd much prefer to be at Disney World. They are at Disney World. Little ducks and mice frolic at their side along the road of life. So why come to bother us here, on this road? Ah, we'll never know, we'll never know. And neither will they."

"Americans, I suppose," Kate said meekly.

"Not necessarily, my dear." Harry reached over and patted her hand. "Imbeciles pour in from all over."

One was supposed to get used to things, Kate thought, not find them increasingly annoying; that was the point of getting older. And how old was he, anyhow? It stood to reason that he was at least her age. Probably older.

Though actually, he looked no age in particular. He was wildly vigorous and agile, and an urgent, clocklike energy pulsed off him. He'd ordered wine when they'd stopped for lunch, in a restaurant overhanging the cliffs where they'd soon be driving again, and her heart had dropped along with the level of alcohol in the bottle, to the very bottom. Harry, however, showed no sign of having consumed a thing. "Don't worry," he'd said as they left—whether noting some expression she'd failed to inhibit, or engaging in a private dialogue—"I'm not drunk." And indeed, though the coastline waved back and forth beneath them like streamers and the racy little car flew out over the heartstopping curves, it snapped back onto the road as if it were attached by elastic. Way below them, the water sparkled and ruffled, on and on and on.

It was late in the afternoon by the time they reached their destination. Majestic and serene, the hotel rose up in front of them with the terraced cliffs, the clouds, the trees, as if it had sprung from a magic seed. Harry chivalrously swung her suitcase from the trunk and carried it into the lobby. "What on earth do you have in here?" Rowan would have asked, smiling to illustrate that he wasn't criticizing her.

Harry, of course, was completely indifferent. Or perhaps he knew perfectly well what weighed those hundreds of pounds—all the jars of things she'd taken, humiliatingly, to smearing on her skin or swallowing.

And what about Harry's elegant little accoutrement, hardly bigger than a briefcase? What could he have fitted into that? A set of tiny tools, no doubt—wrenches, screwdrivers, brushes—with which to disassemble himself and clean his parts . . .

The hotel, vast as it was, had apparently been a private villa at some time. The cool sound of bells and leaf-scented air pooled here and there in the lobby. Afternoon sunlight, yellow as wildflowers, drowsed on the floors. Marble, stone, wood seemed to breathe faintly.

Splendid in uniform, the men at the desk opened their arms at the sight of Harry, tilting their heads to the side and exclaiming softly with delight. As they came forward, he clasped their hands, speaking a few words to each, like the true king returning. They were now referring to her, Kate realized at a certain point. One of the men caught her look of slight confusion and addressed her in English. "We were discussing, Signora, which room would be most suitable for you. It would be possible to give you the Rose Room, which has a fireplace and a magnificent four-poster bed. Or the room at the easternmost end of the hotel is also available, with a balcony overlooking the water."

She glanced at Harry. "It doesn't matter," he said expansively. "They're both lovely rooms." He turned to the desk clerk. "Perhaps the East Room—" He gave her a brief, inquiring smile. "—Yes. The Signora might enjoy breakfasting on her balcony."

Oh, right—she'd been meant to speak, but never mind. How wonderful, just to go upstairs now, to sink back against giant, feather pillows . . . A man in a red and gold jacket stood slightly behind her, with her suitcase. Well, yes, of course—*Harry* wasn't going to show her to her room.

"Well—" she turned toward him and held out her hand "—you must be exhausted."

"Not at all," he said, taking her hand absently and glancing around as if for a place to put it, "I never get tired."

Just as she'd feared. And it seemed that there were several churches, several villas, a little museum, and an ex-convent that were absolutely obligatory.

"And would you care to wash up?" he said, instructively. "We'll find one another in the bar." As she trotted after the bellman, she glimpsed, from the corner of her eye, Harry bending to kiss the beringed claw of an ancient lady in black, almost hidden within the wings of an enormous brocaded chair.

Kate followed, up a flowing staircase and along silent corridors. The bellman opened the massive wooden door to her room, and then the french doors onto her balcony. Lordy! No wonder no one else in the lobby looked much like a schoolteacher. Water gleams fleeted in, rocking the room gently; the high ceiling curved above her, and the stone floors floated underfoot.

Though she took as little time as possible, only slipping her few things onto the satiny hangers and splashing at her face, when she reached the bar Harry had almost emptied a glass of something. "Ah!" he said, leaping to his feet as though she'd been dawdling for an hour. "Oh. But forgive me—will you have something to drink before we set off, or would you prefer a look around before the light goes completely?"

He led her rapidly through the churches, the ex-convent, the now-public villas, bounding up and down the steep town steps and cobbled streets, providing scholarly commentary. She was *worse,* she thought, than her students—than the tourists from the buses! Who were indeed standing around town in bewildered-looking herds, uneasily gripping their cameras as though they were passports.

"Good—" Harry said, striding through the garden leading to the little museum. "—still open!" His gesture, which swept the paintings, the small mounted sculptures, was proprietary.

He was looking at a lump of stone in a glass case. No, a head; a stone coronet sat on heavy twists of stone hair over a dreaming stone face. A real girl must have modeled for it, Kate thought—an actual princess, or a young queen.

Or possibly some girl right off the streets for whom the artist had conceived a passion. Had she lived to be old? It was hard to imagine this girl old. Trouble, she looked like; pure trouble. A provocative reserve emanated from the faint stone smile, sending a hiss of fire through the stone-cooled air. Trouble even now, Kate thought. This girl had seen to it that the sculptor's obsession would be inflicted on whoever saw her for all time to come.

Kate glanced at Harry for a translation of the bit of text on the glass case, but he had turned away, to an elaborate marble, whose racing lines were taking a moment to resolve in front of her. A faun, or possibly a satyr, something with furry haunches and little hooves and horns had seized a young woman from behind. Her head was arched way back against him and her long hair whipped around her face, which was slightly contorted. Her eyes were almost closed. One of the creature's hands was splayed out between the girl's sharp pelvic bones, and the other pinned her own hand to one of her adolescent breasts. Her free arm reached out, with what intent it was impossible to guess—it had broken off at the elbow. Kate stumbled slightly on an uneven stone underfoot. "Goodness me—" she said.

"Yes, marvelous—" Harry glanced at his watch. "Second century after Christ, probably a copy of a Greek piece. Are we through here? The church I particularly want you to see closes in minutes."

In the lobby, the delicate afternoon had given way to a rich, deep twinkling. More people had arrived; the bellboys, in their red and gold, were loading huge leather cases onto trolleys. The tapping of high heels echoed faintly from the corridors. "Dinner at 8:30?" Harry said. "By the way, how did you find your room—satisfactory?"

"Glorious," Kate said. "It's . . . *glorious* . . ."

"Glorious." He smiled at her and briefly her arms and legs seemed to need rearrangement; what did one generally do with them? "Well, very good then. We'll have a bit of a rest, yes? And meet in the bar."

Dinner at 8:30. Once again, they'd be sitting at a table together. But what had she imagined was going to happen? They could hardly have dinner separately.

She found her room waiting; the crisp linen had been turned down, mysteriously, the heavy shutters drawn. She was being attended to, as if she—of all people, she thought—had come upon the palace where the poor Beast waited for his release. She sat for a while on the balcony, watching ribbons of mist twine below her through the trees and listening to distant bells from hidden fields and towns. Grass, petal, wave, stone turned to velvet—indistinct glowing patches—as veil on veil of twilight dropped over them.

A jar of aromatic bath salts had been provided. She poured them like a libation under the faucet—why not? they represented her salary—and took a long soak, moving from time to time to solicit the water's musical response.

One assumed there was such a thing as chance; when one was young, one assumed that the way one's life was to express itself was one of many possible ways, and later, one assumed that this had been true.

Of course, even if she hadn't married Baker, she'd never have been living like this. She'd never have been living like Giovanna, casually surrounded by silk-covered furniture and lovely old pieces of glass and silver, entertaining herself in her spare time with one admirer or another. Those things were probably not within the compass of her particular possibilities.

But surely it was within that compass, surely with one degree's alteration in direction here or there it could have happened, that she and Baker would not have gotten married. And if they had not, if they hadn't had children, one thing was certain—that Baker would now mean no more to her than any young man she might have met in the course of her school duties; she'd have a harmless memory of a nice young man.

And from all the years with him? You couldn't feel love once it was gone. What you could feel for a long time was the sorrow of its fading, like the burning afterimage of a setting sun. And then that was gone, too. What she would remember for the rest of her life was the fact, at least, of the shocking pain they'd been forced to inflict on one another. Eventually when they'd touched, it was like touching a wound.

When both the children had left for school, she'd expected a long period of lonely freedom, an expansion. But now that Baker was sick, Blair and Brice hovered closely, as if it were she who needed consolation, not they. Blair asked questions continuously. *Why did you and Dad . . . How did you feel when . . .*

They'd been over and over it all from the children's adolescence on. "I've told you what I can," Kate said. "I'm sorry. It was moving very fast back then."

But at the time it hadn't felt fast. There were long days of paralysis, sleepless nights. How could so much anguish have been expended on something that now seemed so remote?

"What can I say to you?" she told Blair. "I had a reasonably civil relationship with my parents, but I never understood them. I don't suppose their life together was entirely without chaos and misery, but I have no idea what went on between them. Or with either of them, actually. Of course you don't understand us. No one has ever understood their parents. And what, for that matter, do I know about you?"

Blair stared at Kate, tears spilling up into her eyes. "You knew it was me from the *back* that time, going by in Jeffrey's car at about *eighty*, even though I was supposedly at *Jennifer's*!"

Kate sighed. "That's different," she'd said.

She wrapped herself in a vast, soft towel and contemplated her clothing. A faint breeze came through the french doors, and the black dress swayed slightly on its hanger.

It was a dress that she'd recklessly allowed Blair to talk her into buying from a terrifying shop in Chicago. That same evening she'd thought of its cost and actually covered her face in embarrassment; of course she'd return it. But then, the sight of it swathed in its tissue paper . . .

It was a little daring, that dress. Nonetheless, she'd gone out in it several times, before Rowan came to his senses and married an infant.

She reached over to the hanger. It was now or never. She slipped the dress over her head, and breathed in; the zipper climbed, cinching her tightly. She turned to challenge the mirror: now or never.

All right, then—never, the mirror said, coolly. And what did she think this was—a *date*?

The bar was almost filled. The tender glimmer from candles and lamps embraced the encampments of guests; bright little clusters of laughter bloomed here and there amid clinking glass and conversation. Harry was sitting at the far end of the room, his back to her.

Kate's hands went cold. He was with people. A family, it seemed. A pretty girl, just a little older, Kate judged, than her students, was stretched out on a recamier, in a display of intense boredom. The father was a great, blocky affair, wearing a blazer with gold buttons, and a little boy in an identical blazer perched stiffly on a settee.

The woman next to the boy leaned towards Harry, her red-nailed fingers playing with a large solitaire at her throat. "Really!" Kate heard her exclaim, and she laughed gaily. Her toenails were the fevered red of her fingernails and her lipstick. Her little white suit was as tense as an origami construction, but a snippet of lace peeked out aggressively from under the jacket.

Harry was gesticulating; his voice came into focus: ". . . insisted, but *insisted,*" he was saying, "that I jump on the Concorde. What could I do? A call from Dubzhinski. In New York I literally had to scamper to make my connection. I fell off the plane in Los Angeles, and was at the Polo Lounge in seconds. I took her out of my case, unwrapped her, and set her down in front of us on the bar. There she was, with her little chin thrust forward and her hands clasped behind her back, and those astonishing legs. Dubzhinski was trembling. I could actually hear that tiny, hard heart of his. It was hammering away like a cash register at Christmas time. He was paralyzed, he stared, and then he reached out and upended her to look under her tutu. 'Go ahead,' I said, 'we can authenticate her right here.' And the next—"

The wife was glancing sidelong at Kate with slight alarm, as though Kate might be hoping to sell them pencils. Harry swiveled in his chair, looked at her blankly, then sprang to his feet. "My dear!" he said. "Ah, we're a chair short! What shall, what shall, what shall we do, eh?"

For a moment everyone except the girl was standing and bobbing about and pushing one another towards seats. "Oh," Kate began. "Well, I could just—" Just what? But then a murmuring waiter in a white coat was there with a smile of compassion for her that pierced her like a bayonet.

Harry and the Reitzes had met several years before, in Paris, it was explained, at the home of a mutual friend, about whom they'd just been reminiscing.

"Oh, Franz and I couldn't really claim that M. Dubzhinski is a *friend.* We just happened to be with the LaRues. But you know—" Mrs. Reitz addressed Kate "—that house is even more gorgeous than in the pictures." She turned back to Harry, but her perfume continued to loiter thuggishly around Kate. "I know there are people who say M. Dubzhinsky is . . . Well. But he was charming to me that time. Simply charming."

"'Charming . . .'" Mr. Reitz tried out the word and smiled pityingly. "I wouldn't entirely agree. But harmless enough at bottom. Colorful, as the expression goes. I believe it was one of your countrymen—" he nodded at Kate "—who put it so well: *I've never met a man I didn't like.*"

The girl sat up slowly, fluffing her long hair back. "Really?" she said. "I have."

Mrs. Reitz's eyes were not quite closed. Her face was more unresponsive than if she hadn't heard at all. But Mr. Reitz was speaking to Kate. "My wife, too, is American."

Was the girl's arrogance affected, or was it entirely real? As cocky as Kate's students could be, as irritating, they were actually, for all their show, quite humble. Of course, Kate had never encountered a child as privileged as this girl, with this hard candy gloss . . . "Texas," Mrs. Reitz was saying, leaning over to touch Kate's wrist, her own flashing and clanging with jewelry. "But I guess you heard that, right off! I wouldn't change Zurich for anything, but I get homesick. I miss Los Angeles. I miss Dallas. I miss New York."

"I'm from Cincinnati," Kate said.

"Oh." Mrs. Reitz's smile was puzzled. "I see."

"I'm really just visiting," Kate said.

"Ah," Mrs. Reitz said, archly.

"No," Kate said. "A friend in Rome."

"A mutual friend," Harry said, fussily, as he snagged a waiter. "Champagne? Champagne, my dear?" he asked Kate and then the girl, who had been drinking nothing. "Good. And another round for the rest of us, thank you. Yes, this kind lady has been good enough to accompany me thus far and have a little look at the area. Tomorrow she returns, I believe, do you not?"

"How nice," Mrs. Reitz said. Her gaze swept Kate's flowered dress, her face, her cardigan, and lapsed from Kate like a cat's.

"We're going up to Rome ourselves tomorrow or Sunday," Mr. Reitz said.

"We're doing the palaces on the kids' spring break," Mrs. Reitz explained.

"The question is," Mr. Reitz said, "which day exactly will we travel? We're told that the traffic is quite terrible on Saturday. But also we're told that the traffic is quite terrible on Sunday."

"That is true," Harry said. He looked at one child, then the other. "Are you glad to be on holiday?"

The boy nodded vigorously. "Yes, thank you."

"And you?" Harry asked.

The girl, who was reclining again, opened her eyes and looked steadily at him. "Not madly." She closed her eyes again and crossed her arms over her chest, as though she were sunbathing, or dying.

"Sit up, sweetheart," Mrs. Reitz murmured. "Well!" She cast a misty look at the room in general. "At least we've been lucky with the weather.

They said it's been raining and raining and raining," she explained to Kate. "I was afraid it was going to rain today."

"But it didn't," Mr. Reitz said.

"No," Mrs. Reitz agreed. "It didn't."

"We have good luck with the weather," Mr. Reitz said, "but bad luck with the traffic. It took us all day to get here. We expected to arrive at three o'clock. But we arrived almost at seven."

The girl emitted a small sigh, which floated down among them like a feather.

"Now, *you've* determined it's best to drive up tomorrow . . ." Mrs. Reitz furrowed deferentially at Kate.

"I'll be taking the train," Kate said.

"The train!" Mrs. Reitz said. "What a *marvelous*—"

"I want to take the train," the little boy said mournfully. "I wanted to take the train," he explained to Kate. "But we can't because of the Porsche."

"That's the problem, sweetie," Mrs. Reitz said absently, reaching over to a small silver bowl of mixed nuts, which Harry was nervously plundering. "Excuse me!" he said, retracting his hand as though it had been bitten.

"I am so sorry!" Mrs. Reitz exclaimed. "Oh, I am simply starving."

"I can imagine," Harry said distractedly.

"And I suppose spring holidays are the reason for all this damned, if you'll pardon me, traffic," Mr. Reitz said. "Yes, the only occasions on which one has the opportunity to travel with one's family, others are traveling with theirs. What a paradox!"

The boy's straw slurped among the ice at the bottom of his drink.

"Darling," Mrs. Reitz said. "Your father was merely making an observation."

The boy blushed red. "My baby," Mrs. Reitz said. She drew him to her and stroked his silky hair, smiling first at her husband, then at Harry. "You know, I absolutely adore this place. It's so romantic. Don't you just keep imagining all the things that must have gone on in these rooms? Oh, my. For hundreds of years!" The boy sat stock still until his mother released him, recrossing her legs and primly readjusting the hem of her little skirt.

"Good heavens—" Harry glanced at his watch "—they'll have been waiting with our table! I do wish we could ask you to join us, but, that is, they're very strict. Please excuse us."

"What an ordeal!" he said to Kate as they were seated. "How horrible!

Was I terribly rude? I suppose I should have invited them to dine with us. And why not? Would it be possible for them to bore us any more than they already have? But yes, on reflection, yes. I feel I might still recover."

The dining room was an aerie, a bower, hung with a playful lattice of garlands. Its tile floors were adorned with painted baskets of fruit, and there were real ones scattered here and there on stands. But even as the waiters glided by with trays of glossy roasted vegetables and platters of fish, even while Harry took it upon himself to order for her, knowledgeably and solicitously, Kate felt tainted. Despite the room's conceit that eating was a pastime for elves and fairies, Mrs. Reitz's carnality had disclosed the truth: this aggregation of hairy vertebrates, scrubbed, scented, prancing about on hind legs, was ruthlessly bent on physical gratifications—tactile, visual, gustatory, genital . . . The candies! The flowers! A trough providing mass feedings for naked guests would be less pornographic.

The Reitzes were being led to their own table. Mrs. Reitz waggled one set of fingers in their direction, holding her jacket closed beneath her collarbones with the other, as if an enormous wind were about to whip it open, exposing her.

"One encounters these terrible people wherever one goes," Harry said. "They all know me—it's the unfortunate side of my work, if I can use such an elevated term for, actually, my little hobby . . . They're all clients, or friends of clients. Clients of clients . . ."

Despite Mrs. Reitz's speedy (and uncalled for!) assessment of Kate as out of the running, Kate thought, Mrs. Reitz was probably not much younger, really. The bouncing gold hair, the vivacity, the strained skin suggested it.

All those years ago, when she'd finally confessed to her mother about Baker and Norman, Kate had waited quietly through her mother's initial monologue. "Don't worry," her mother said grimly. "I won't say I told you so."

In fact, she never had told Kate so. On the contrary, she'd been elated by Baker's family, his appearance, his education, his law firm. "I can't say I'm overly surprised about . . . this other person, but does he have to move *out*? Why can't people of your generation set aside your personal appetites for one instant? The children are going to be confused enough as it is! Oh, I simply can't believe he's leaving you for—for—for *an electrician*! Well, but I'm sure he'll continue to support you."

Kate had smiled faintly. "You are? He's going into public interest law."

"My God, my God!" her mother cried. "Oh, I suppose I should feel compassion for him. He was always so weak, so lost. But why did he have to marry you? Why did he feel he had the right to ruin your life while he was working things out for himself? Well, and yet I can understand it. I suppose he thought you could help him. You were always such a sweet girl. And not, if you don't mind my saying so, very threatening, sexually."

"And the worst thing," Harry was saying, "is that they all seem to want something from me. I don't know what! Perhaps they imagine I'll be able to pick up some piece for a song, something to transform a salon from the ordinarily to the spectacularly vulgar. Some great, blowsy, romping nymph with an enormous behind . . ."

Kate contemplated him as he talked decoratively on. One had to acknowledge, even admire, such vitality, so strong a will to enjoy, to entertain, even if, as was clearly the case, it was only to enjoy and entertain himself.

"Giovanna tells me you're a teacher," he said unexpectedly, laying down his fork and knife as if her response required his full attention.

"Nothing very exalted, I'm afraid," Kate said. "Just high school biology."

"It sounds rather exalted to me," he said. "I should think it would be rather a beautiful subject."

Kate glanced at him. "It is, actually." She put down her own fork and noted the sudden haloed clarity of her thought, the detailed vibrancy of her awareness, and concluded she was drunk. Natural enough—she'd certainly been drinking. "I have to admit that I do find it beautiful. Of course, what I teach is very rudimentary—basic evolutionary theory, simple genetic principles, taxonomies, a lot of structural stuff. Pretty much what I learned myself in school. You know, an oak tree, a tadpole, the shape of its growth, the way the organism works . . ."

"I understand nothing about biology," he said. "Nothing, nothing, nothing at all . . ."

"Oh, well. Neither do I, really." Kate found she was laughing loudly. She composed herself. "I mean, not what's going on now, all the fantastic molecular frontiers, the borders with chemistry, physics . . . the real mysteries . . ."

He rested his chin on the backs of his clasped hands, and gazed at her. "What seems so simple to you—a tree, a tadpole—those things are completely mysterious to me!"

"Actually, I'm not being at all—" Was he, in fact, interested? Well, it wasn't her place to judge. At least he was pretending to be. At least he was—Stop that, she told herself; a conversation was something that humans quite routinely went about having. "I mean, I'm not being . . . Because actually it's all hugely . . . It brings you to your knees, really, doesn't it? You know, it's really quite funny—there are my students, rows of little humans, staring at me. And there I am, a human, staring right back. And I'm holding up pictures! Charts! Of what's inside us. And the students write things down in their notebooks. Our hearts are pumping, the blood is going round and round, our lungs are bringing air in and out . . . *Class, look at the pictures. These are our lungs, our kidneys, our stomachs, our veins and arteries, our spleens, our brains, our hearts* . . . There we are, having to look at pictures of what's going on every instant inside our very own bodies!"

"I don't even yet have it straight. Where any of those things are," Harry said ruefully. "My kidneys, my spleen, my heart . . ."

Kate shook her head. "It's a wonder we can understand anything at all about ourselves . . . We can't even see our own kidneys . . ."

"Ah!" Harry grunted. "So I have recovered, after all." He summoned the waiter to order for Kate a little chalice of raspberries and scented froth, then sat back to observe as she took the first spoonful. "Extraordinary, no?" he said. "It's up to you. I'm not allowed." He smiled briefly and shallowly, then rubbed his forehead. "To tell you the truth, it's a rather stressful trip for me, always—going back to this little farmhouse of mine. I spent summers there in my childhood . . . Really, I'm very glad to have had a pretext for stopping here overnight . . ."

Harsh tears shot up to Kate's eyes. Fatigue, she thought. "Tell me . . ."
"Yes?"
"Tell me . . . Oh—well, tell me, then . . . Have you known Giovanna long?"

"For many centuries. Our families are vaguely intertwined, though I never met her until I was a young man. There was a party, very grand, and in all the enormous crowd, women in spectacular gowns, I caught a glimpse of a young girl. I remember every detail of that glimpse—the exact posture, the smile, every button on the dress. She was scarcely thirteen. There were eight years between us."

His hand was resting on the table, three, maybe four inches from hers.

"There were?" The cuff on his shirt was very white. She raised her eyes from it to smile at him. "Aren't there still?"

He sat back and studied her, amusement and sorrow competing in his own smile. "Well, now it's a different eight years." He sighed, and signaled for the check.

"Oh, please, let me—You did lunch, and drinks. You've taken all this time . . ."

"Madam," he said gently. "You will put your purse away for this one evening, please. But will you join me for a last drink in the bar? A digestif. And I will have, if you won't find it too disgusting, a cigar."

But the Reitzes were already ensconced again in the bar, and waved them over. Kate glanced at Harry, but he had gone completely unreadable; he had simply disappeared.

Mrs. Reitz slid to one side of her settee and parted the space next to her. Again, there was a scuffle. Harry won, and Kate found herself sitting with Mrs. Reitz, suffocating under the dome of her perfume like a dying bug, while he went off to commandeer a chair.

And a very good thing it was, actually, that Norman was an electrician! He'd completely rewired her little house. And that at a time when she was barely getting by, even with the money Baker managed to scrape up for the kids.

The waiter was already prepared with a cigar for Harry, undoubtedly in accord with ancient custom. "Here, please," Mr. Reitz said. "One of those for me, too."

"Oh, dear—" Mrs. Reitz fluttered towards Kate. "I know men have to have them, but I never get used to them, do you?"

"I never get used to anything—" Kate was startled by her own slightly swaggering tone. "—I mean, except for the things that aren't happening any longer."

"That's an interesting way of putting it . . . ," Mrs. Reitz said cautiously. Good. Kate had frightened her.

The girl was slung out sullenly upon a curvy white and gold chair, far above the juvenile sniping of her elders. "Ooch," Mr. Reitz said, patting the prairie-like region of his stomach. "It's impossible to speak after such a meal. But really, have you no good advice for us? Saturday, or Sunday, to Rome."

"Whichever you choose," Harry exhaled with pleasure, "you will wish you had chosen the other."

"Let us be prudent," Mr. Reitz said. "We will play the early bird. Let us be ready to make our final decision at breakfast. If," he turned to the girl, "we think we can get up in good time, for a change."

The girl lifted a long, shining hair from her dress and considered it. "We'll do our best," she said.

"I surely do envy you," Mrs. Reitz said. "This little girl of mine has a talent for sleep. But I can never sleep near the sea at all. It makes me so *rest*less . . ."

"The sea?" Mr. Reitz said. "Restless? How very original. One is always learning the most surprising new things about one's spouse! But it's a good thing then about our room. I must say, I was quite annoyed earlier with the staff. I had my secretary specifically request the view. They swore she never did, but a people which is known for its charm is not often known also for its honesty."

"I have a terrible time sleeping in hotels, myself," Harry said. "Unfortunately, I'm always in hotels these days . . . How did it happen, how did it happen? Oh, it's hard to believe, isn't it, that it's the same person who has lived each bit of one's life. Yes, an hour or two of sleep, and then I'm up again, wandering around all night. In fact, I'd best go up now and try to get some sleep before I lose my chance."

Kate attempted to smile pleasantly. "I think I'll go up now, too."

"And how is your room, my dear?" Harry asked.

Kate looked at him. Why hadn't she just gone directly up after dinner?

"Good heavens, yes, where is my brain!" he said. "Glorious. Of course, you said—glorious."

He did in fact lie in his room for an hour or so, letting images of the girl play over his nerves. Her throat, the curve of her cheek . . . the clear, poreless skin, so close in color to the brows, the lashes, the light, long hair . . . her startling greenish blue eyes. She was clever about clothes, obviously— that mother surely hadn't chosen the dress, simple, and stylishly long, stopping just at narrow shins. On her feet she wore elegant straw sandals.

When the buzzing of the girl in his head grew unbearable, he would convert it into thoughts of the astonishing Russian sleigh bed he had come across in an antique store that he would pass by again on his way to the farmhouse tomorrow. Things, things—at his age! But it seemed that age only increased his appetite to acquire.

The shop was one of several in the area he returned to often, ostensibly to pick up an item for one client or another. These places sometimes came into possession of surprisingly good pieces—occasionally an object which perhaps would have been consigned to a museum had it not, fortunately, fallen into ignorant hands, to be rescued then by him.

He had bought the most fetching little madonna at one of them on his last trip. He noted the bed at the time, but the madonna had simply absorbed all his attention, until he got her settled into the right spot. Only then did he begin to remember the bed—its fluent maple curves, its allusion to careless pleasure . . . This time he would buy it for certain. Assuming it was still there! Oh, why hadn't he called weeks ago, when he realized how badly he wanted it?

But the problem remained: Where to put it—Rome? Paris? Both places were small, and he already had exquisite beds in each.

He could move one of them out here, to the farmhouse. But that was the point. He always meant to be emptying the place out so he could sell it. And yet, each time he saw it . . . Those summers, when he was ten, eleven, twelve . . . Those were happy years, insofar as years could be said to be happy. Years filled with sensations so potent they seemed like clues to a riddle.

The place wouldn't bring much of anything, once the money was divided between himself and his surviving brother. It was a nuisance; it would simply eat cash if it were to be kept from falling to bits. His brother, and his own sons, one in Istanbul, one in London, showed no particular interest in it. Only he, only he was enslaved by the memory of the sun on the leaves around the door, the way the fruit tasted in the morning.

It was dark when you entered. As you opened the shutters, grand, churchly prisms turned everything in their path to phantoms. The cool aroma of the waxed stone floors blended with the smell of sun-warmed herbs. First the big room, then the room they'd used informally as a library, then the huge kitchen . . . At the long wooden table, almost transparent in the light falling from the high window, sat the girl. Water dripped slowly somewhere, onto crockery or stone. He turned, readjusting his pillow. Perhaps he had slept for some minutes.

The bar was now empty except for a sprawling group of five or six men and a woman, which was scaling peaks of drunken happiness—a TV crew, the waiter told him, which had filmed a commercial nearby that day. One of them was pounding away on a small piano in a corner, and the others sang along, loudly and terribly, arms around shoulders. Harry sipped a cognac and regarded them with melancholy affection. They were still young, almost young. For an instant he could see, as if it were incandescently mapped, the path of years that lay ahead of each of them, its particular sorrows, joys, terrors . . . He'd have one drink, and return to his room.

When the girl appeared in the doorway, he restrained himself from jumping to his feet. For a moment he hadn't understood that she was real.

She approached; he stood and bent over her hand.

"I thought I might find Mother down here," she said vaguely.

Wordlessly, he pulled out a chair for her.

"Huh. Well, I guess Franz has learned to sleep with his eyes open," she said. "May I have a drink, please?"

He was glad for the excuse to walk over to the bar and stand there for some moments while glasses were warmed and cognacs were poured; his brains were in such a clamor that he'd hardly been able to hear what she said, let alone make sense of it. The TV crew was now singing an American popular song, stumbling over the words and filling in with la la las. Harry had read somewhere recently about the woman who'd written the song and recorded it. She'd grown up in a ghetto, he recalled, impoverished; the song was the story of her life.

The girl stared down at the little candle on the table, in an aureole of her own silence, impervious to the racket of the TV crew. After a few minutes he dared to speak. "Do you go to school in Zurich?"

She lifted an eyebrow. "Fortunately not. I'm at a boarding school in the States. One more year and I'm free."

Tears kept coming to his eyes, as if he had been broken open; impressions, almost visible, were floating up around him, released from the hidden world by an enchanted touch: damp leaves and earth, a dappled meadow—treasure no doubt collected by his yielding and ravenous childhood senses, and stored. Every once in a while, some magic girl could unlock it. Then how to keep aloft in the radiant ether?

"Actually, I've hardly lived in Zurich at all," she said. "Mother married Franz when I was eleven, and they shipped me off to school when I was thirteen. I spent summers with my father, anyhow."

"And where does he live, my dear?"

"Oh, he's still near Dallas. Bossing a bunch of cows around. He's got some new kids . . ." She propped herself up at the table on her elbows, her long, delicate forearms together, her chin in her palms. "Mother and Franz! What a joke."

He smiled gently. "It's quite mysterious, what attracts one human being to another . . ."

"Not in this case," she said. "I mean, did you notice the size of his bank account?" She frowned, studying the small flame in front of her. "So . . . Mother said you have places all over."

"Really," he said. "All over?"

"But—I mean, where do you live?"

"Here and there. Like you."

Her green-blue gaze lingered on him, then withdrew. "She said you've got a title, too."

"Oh, lying around in a drawer somewhere."

She poked at the soft wax of the candle for a few moments, allowing him to watch her. "So, why don't you use it?" she asked.

"Evidently it's not necessary!"

She glanced at him quizzically, then smiled to herself, and poked again at the candle. "Okay . . . Well, your turn . . ."

"My turn . . . All right . . . Well, why off to school at such a tender age?"

"Want to guess? Or want me to tell you."

He was sorry he'd raised the question. Any number of scenarios, all of them sordid, sprang to mind.

"I bet you can guess."

"No," he said. "You needn't—"

"Because Mother thought I was having an affair. With my piano teacher."

How many more years was his heart going to stand the sort of strain to which he was subjecting it now? "And were you?" he asked, against his will.

"Not exactly. You know. I'd go over to his apartment after school with my school books and my sheet music and my little uniform. Mother loved it that I had to wear a uniform, obviously. She'd still have me in anklets and hair ribbons if she could. And one day Mr. Schulte sort of wrestled me off the piano bench onto the floor. I mean, he left my uniform on. I guess he liked it, too. And then we'd work on Brahms. So that's sort of how it went every Tuesday. He hardly ever spoke to me, except for, you know, you should practice more, watch the tempo here, don't hold your wrists like that, this is legato . . ." She glanced at Harry speculatively, then sat back demurely with her drink.

How pitiable she was. Her bravado, her coarseness, her self-involvement—completely innocent. Perhaps never again would she be so dazzled by the primacy of her own life. "Was he—"

"The first, uh huh. Not Franz, if that's what you were thinking. No slummy boys in an alley . . ."

It was not what he'd intended to ask. No matter. He closed his eyes and listened to her clear voice; behind the shining veil, she continued to talk.

". . . The sad fact is that Mother had this humongous crush on Schulte, it was totally obvious. He was always sort of kissing her hand and, you know, gazing at her with big, soulful eyes . . ." The girl sighed languorously. "Actually, I have to admit he was kind of attractive, in a creepy kind of way . . ."

One of the drunken singers had toppled off her heights of joy and was now crying; a few of the others were embracing her, mussing her hair, singing into her ear, and attempting to rock her to the music, such as it was. The girl directed an abstracted stare of distaste in their direction, then looked away, obliterating them. The word "kidney," throbbing on a flat, stylized shape, hung for an instant in Harry's mind. Then the girl dangled her empty glass by the stem and Harry caught his breath, seeing her in her flouncy bedroom, dangling a pen, with which she was about to record her most intimate feelings. A gilt-edged diary, a heart-shaped lock . . .

"Are you happy enough, my dear?" The question leapt urgently from him.

"Enough for what? Oh, well. It lies ahead, right?"

"It does," he said passionately, tears coming again to his eyes. "It does . . ."

An expression of pure derision passed quickly across her face.

"Ahead or behind," he amended, and the candle between them received a tiny smile. "Ahead or behind. That you can count on . . ."

Just beyond the cordial room, the world was whispering. Harry—it had been a long time since he had thought of himself as anything other than Harry, though what offhand joke or misunderstanding had landed him with the name he no longer quite remembered—closed his eyes to let the shimmering air, the faint ruffling of the sea from outside the open windows reach him, embrace him. "It's a remarkable night," he said. "Shall we walk for just a bit?"

She sighed, and sat herself up in her chair, throwing her hair back over her shoulders again.

No, he must send his afflicted princess up to sleep. He would lie down, himself, drifting along on whatever currents her inebriating presence had conjured up.

"I don't know," she said, dreamily. "I was thinking. We could go upstairs. Don't you think? I mean, you could authenticate me."

It seemed to him that she blushed faintly, though more likely it was only the flames that had roared up in front of his eyes. "I guess my room would be better," she continued. "When and if Franz ever starts to snore, Mother is sure to be out prowling for you."

They had put her in what they called the Rose Room, though except for the faint pinkish tone of the walls and the splendid four-poster, it was deliciously austere.

He perched on the chaise, in the muted light of the small lamp next to it, his lovely dark farmhouse floating near him, the night just beyond the room's closed shutters . . . Perhaps the nervous American schoolteacher was sitting on her balcony like a sentinel at the prow of a ship keeping them from harm . . . How many wonders there used to be for him! The miraculous human landscapes! Long, brilliant nights . . . Was there never to be one of those again? Whatever role he'd been assigned in the girl's drama—her drama of triumph, her drama of degradation—it was certain to be a despicable or ridiculous one. There was no chance—at least almost no chance—that she would receive from him what he so longed to provide: even a tiny portion of pleasure or solace. And when she remembered him, no doubt she would remember him with contempt.

Briefly he closed his eyes, luxuriating in the purity of her face and body, the glowing skein of sensation she was causing the air to spin out around him, his sharp thrill of longing—everything, in short, he was waiting (like a bride!) to lose. Lazily, as though moving into a trance, she dropped one piece of clothing, then another, on the floor.

When Kate awoke, it was already late. She opened her shutters and brightness was everywhere.

The night before, she'd sat for a long while on her balcony. The sky was extraordinary—terrifying, really, with great, flaring starbursts. How long had all those blades of cold light traveled in order to cross here and pass on through this one night's heart? she wondered. Trillions and trillions of years.

She would have liked to be able to return to the cozy bar for the comfort of voices around her and a glass of something soothing. But for all she knew, the Reitzes were still there.

And the fact is, women of her age were conspicuous on their own. People tended to pity, even fear you. In any case, she was hardly the sort of person who could sit alone in such a room at this hour, exposed; one more drink could be a disaster. Oh, and worst of all—the kindness of the waiters!

So she listened to the sea altering the rocks below her, the wind around her shaping the trees, as the starlight shot past. Time itself made no sound at all.

Baker had told her about Norman—he was desperately sorry, he said, his beautiful, dark eyes imploring her not to turn away; but there was nothing to be done. And there she was at the edge of a cliff. She'd been walking along, and just where she was about to take her next step, in that instant there was nothing.

So she went back to school to get a teaching degree, and then there was far too much to do to brood about Baker. Only sometimes at night she'd awaken as if falling from a ledge, crying out—landing hard against what her life had turned out to be, her bedclothes limp with sweat and tears.

After Baker had been living with Norman for a while, it was as if he'd always lived with Norman. There was only a residue of feeling when she and Baker met, exchanging the children or going about their separate lives—a sort of cold ash that faintly recorded their footsteps.

She had been luckier than a lot of her friends, as she learned bit by bit; Norman was wonderful with the children—so forthcoming, so understanding . . . and often when he came by to drop them off he'd sit in the kitchen with her, chatting over a leisurely beer. Through the years, in fact, they'd become truly close.

Terrible, the body's yearning, terrible. But you could always outwait it. First, there had been nothing in front of her, then—however ineptly— she, the children, Baker, and Norman wove together a swaying bridge, crossing step by cautious step over the awful chasm. And here, on the other side, Baker was dying.

· · ·

The morning lobby was bright and busy. Harry was waiting to say good-bye to her, evidently, and the Reitzes were there, too. Harry put down the newspaper he seemed to have been trying to read, and stood to greet her, his arms open. "My dear! We've only just finished breakfast. We kept hoping you'd deign to join us."

"Yes, I slept and slept," she said.

"The sleep of the just!" Mr. Reitz said. "Like me!"

"And will we meet again?" Harry said to Kate. "Ah, who can say, who can say . . ."

In the bright light Mrs. Reitz's skin looked dry and fragile, as she lingered near Harry. "Now, promise me," she was saying to him, "the next time you're in Zurich—"

"Can we go now?" The girl, who had been standing at the door watching the cars pull up and depart, turned. "I'm sorry," she said to Kate, "but they always say I'm holding them up. And I've been waiting for hours!"

Kate smiled at the childish intensity of the girl's distress, and just caught herself before smoothing back the girl's hair as she used to Blair's when Blair would get herself into a state over some passing trifle. "Be patient," she used to say. "Be patient. It will be over soon, it will be better tomorrow, next week you won't even remember . . ."

Chitra Banerjee Divakaruni

The Lives of Strangers

from *Agni*

THE SEEPAGE of rainwater has formed a tapestry against the peeling walls of the Nataraj Yatri House dining hall, but no one except Leela notices this. The other members of the pilgrimage party jostle around the fire that sputters in a corner and shout at the pahari boy to hurry with the tea. Aunt Seema sits at one of the scratched wooden tables with a group of women, all of them swaddled in the bright shawls they bought for this trip. From time to time they look down at their laps with a startled expression, like sparrows who have awakened to find themselves plumaged in cockatoo feathers.

Aunt beckons to Leela to come sit by her. "Baap re," she says, "I can't believe how cold it is here in Kashmir. It's quite delightful, actually. Just think, in Calcutta right now people are bathing in sweat, even with the fans on full speed!"

The women smile, pleased at having had the foresight to leave sweaty Calcutta behind at the height of summer for a journey which is going to earn them comfort on earth and goodwill in heaven. They hold their chins high and elongate their necks as classical dancers might. Plump, middle-aged women who sleepily read love stories in *Desh* magazine through the interminable train journey from Howrah Station, already they are metamorphosed into handmaidens of Shiva, adventure-bound toward his holy shrine in Amarnath. Their eyes sparkle with zeal as they discuss how remote the shrine is. How they will have to walk across treacherous glaciers for three whole days to reach it. Contemplating them, Leela wonders if this is the true lure of travel, this hope of a transformed self. Will her own journey, begun when she left America a month ago, bring her this coveted change?

Tea arrives, sweet and steaming in huge aluminum kettles, along with dinner: buttery wheat parathas, fatly stuffed with spicy potatoes. When they have eaten, the guide advises them to get their rest. This is no touristy excursion, he reminds them sternly. It is a serious and sacred yatra, and dangerous, too. He talks awhile of the laws to be observed while on pilgrimage: no non-vegetarian food, no sex. Any menstruating women should not proceed beyond this point. There is a lot more, but his Bengali is full of long, formal words that Leela does not know, and her attention wanders. He ends by saying something about sin and expiation, which seems to her terribly complex and thus very Indian.

Later in bed, Leela will think of Mrs. Das. At dinner Mrs. Das sat by herself at a table that was more rickety than the others. In a room filled with nervous laughter (for the headman had frightened them all a bit, though no one would admit it) she held herself with an absorbed stillness, her elbows pulled close as though she had been taught early in life not to take up too much space in the world. She did not speak to anyone. Under her frizzy pepper-colored hair, her face was angular and ascetic.

Leela has not met Mrs. Das, but she knows a great deal about her because Aunt Seema's friends discuss her frequently. Mostly they marvel at her bad luck.

"Can you imagine!" the doctor's wife says, "her husband died just two years after her marriage, and right away her in-laws, who hated her because it had been a love match, claimed that the marriage wasn't legal. They were filthy rich—the Dases of Tollygunge, you understand—they hired the shrewdest lawyers. She lost everything—the money, the house, even the wedding jewelry."

"No justice in this world," Aunt says, clicking her tongue sympathetically.

"She had to go to work in an office," someone else adds. "Think of it, a woman of good family, forced to work with low-caste peons and clerks! That's how she put her son through college and got him married."

"And now the daughter-in-law refuses to live with her," Aunt says. "So she's had to move into a women's hostel. A women's hostel! At her age!"

The doctor's wife shakes her head mournfully. "Some people are like that, born under an unlucky star. They bring bad luck to themselves and everyone close to them."

Leela studies the kaleidoscope of emotions flitting across the women's faces. Excitement, pity, cheerful outrage. Can it be true, that part about an unlucky star? In America she would have dealt with such superstition with fluent, dismissive ease, but India is complicated. Like entering a murky, primal lake, in India she has to watch her step.

Leela's happiest childhood memories were of aloneness: reading in her room with the door closed, playing chess on the computer, embarking on long bike rides through the city, going to the movies by herself. You saw more that way, she explained to her parents. You didn't miss crucial bits of dialogue because your companion was busy making inane remarks. Her parents, themselves solitary individuals, didn't object. People—except for a select handful—were noisy and messy. They knew that. Which was why, early in their lives, they had escaped India to take up research positions in America. Ever since Leela could remember, they had encouraged her taste for privacy. When Leela became a computer programmer, they applauded the fact that she could do most of her work from home. When she became involved with Dexter, another programmer she had met at one of the rare conferences she attended, they applauded that too, though more cautiously.

Her relationship with Dexter was a brief affair, perhaps inevitably so. Looking back in search of incidents to remember it by, Leela would only be able to recall a general feeling, something like being wound tightly in a blanket on a cold day, comforting yet restrictive. Even when things were at their best, they never moved in together. Leela preferred it that way. She preferred, too, to sleep alone, and often moved after lovemaking to the spare bed in her apartment. When you slept, you were too vulnerable. Another person's essence could invade you. She had explained it once to Dexter. He had stroked her hair with fingers she thought of as sensitive and artistic, and had seemed to understand. But apparently he hadn't. It was one of the facts he dwelt on at some bitter length before he left.

"You're like one of those spiny creatures that live at the bottom of the ocean," he said. "Everything just slides off of that watertight shell of yours. You don't need me—you don't need *anyone*."

He wasn't totally right about that. A week after he left, Leela ended up in the emergency ward, having swallowed a bottle of sleeping pills.

An encounter with death—even an aborted one (Leela had called 911 as soon as she finished taking the pills)—alters one in unaccountable ways. After having to deal with the hospital, the police, and the mandatory counselor assigned to her, Leela should have heaved a sigh of relief when she returned to her quiet, tidy apartment. Instead, for the first time, she found her own company inadequate. Alone, there seemed no point in opening the drapes or cleaning up the TV dinner containers stacked up on the coffee table. The place took on a green, underwater dimness. Her computer gathered dust as she wandered from room to room, sometimes with her eyes closed, trailing her fingers as though they were fins across the furniture, testing the truth of Dexter's accusation.

She didn't know when it was that she started thinking about India, which she had never visited. The idea attached itself to the underneath of her mind and grew like a barnacle. In her imagination the country was vast and vague. Talismanic. For some reason she associated it with rain, scavenger crows, the clanging of orange trams and the purplish green of elephant ears. Were these items from some story her parents had told in her childhood? No. Though her parents' stories had spanned many topics—from the lives of famous scientists to the legends of Greece and Rome—they never discussed their homeland, a country they seemed to have shed as easily and completely as a lizard drops its tail.

When she called her parents to inform them she was going, she did not tell them why. Perhaps she herself did not know. Nor did she speak of the suicide attempt, which filled her with a rush of mortification whenever it intruded on her thoughts. As always with her decisions, they did not venture advice, though she thought she heard her mother suppress a sigh. They waited to see if she had more to say, and when she didn't, they told her how to contact Aunt Seema, who was her mother's cousin.

"Try to stay away from the crowds," her father said.

"That's impossible," said her mother. "Just be sure to take your shots before you go, drink boiled water at all times, and don't get involved in the lives of strangers."

What did Leela expect from India? The banalities of heat and dust, poverty and squalor, yes. The elated confusion of city streets where the beetle-black Ambassador cars of the rich inched their way, honking, between sweating rickshaw pullers and cows who stood unmoving, as dignified as dowagers. But she had not thought Calcutta would vanquish her so easily with its melancholy poetry of old cotton saris hung out to dry on rooftops. With low-ceilinged groceries filled with odors she did not recognize but knew to be indispensable. In the evenings, the shopkeeper waved a lamp in front of a vividly colored calendar depicting Rama's coronation. His waiting customers did not seem to mind. Sometimes at dawn she stood at her bedroom window and heard, cutting through the roar of buses, the cool, astonishing voice of a young man in a neighboring house practicing a morning raag.

At the airport, Aunt Seema had been large, untidy, and moist—the exact opposite of Leela's mother. She launched herself at Leela with a delighted cry, kissing her on both cheeks, pulling her into her ample, talcum-powder-scented bosom, exclaiming how overjoyed she was to meet her. In America Leela would have been repelled by such effusion, especially from a woman she had never seen in her life. Here it seemed as right—and as welcome—as the too-sweet glass of orange squash the maid brought her as soon as she reached the house.

Aunt dressed Leela in her starched cotton saris, put matching bindis on her forehead, and lined her eyes with kajal. She forced her to increase her rudimentary Bengali vocabulary by refusing to speak to her in English. She cooked her rui fish sautéed with black jeera, and moglai parathas stuffed with eggs and onions, which had to be flipped over deftly at a crucial moment—food Leela loved though it gave her heartburn. She took her to the Kalighat temple for a blessing, to night-long music concerts, and to the homes of her friends, all of whom wanted to arrange a marriage for her. Leela went unprotestingly. Like a child acting in her first play, she was thrilled by the vibrant unreality of the life she was living. At night she lay in the big bed beside Aunt (Uncle having been banished to a cot downstairs) and watched the soft white swaying of the mosquito net in the breeze from the ceiling fan. She pondered the unexpected pleasure she took in every disorganized aspect of the day. India was a Mardi Gras that never ended. Who would have thought she'd feel so at home here?

So when Aunt Seema said, "You want to see the real India, the spiritual India? Let's go on a pilgrimage," she agreed without hesitation.

The talk starts at the end of the first day's trek. In one of the women's tents, where Leela lies among pilgrims who huddle in blankets and nurse aching muscles, a voice rises from the dark.

"Do you know, Mrs. Das's bedroll didn't get to the camp. They can't figure out what happened—the guides swear they tied it onto a mule this morning—"

"That's right," responds another voice. "I heard them complaining because they had to scrounge around in their own packs to find her some blankets."

In the anonymous darkness, the voices take on cruel, choric tones. They release suspicion into the close air like bacteria, ready to multiply wherever they touch down.

"It's like that time on the train, remember, when she was the only one who got food poisoning—"

"Yes, yes—"

"I wonder what will happen next—"

"As long as it doesn't affect us—"

"How can you be sure? Maybe next time it will—"

"I hate to be selfish, but I wish she wasn't here with us at all—"

"Me, too—"

Leela wonders about the tent in which Mrs. Das is spending her night. She wonders what people are saying in there. What they are thinking. An image comes to her with a brief, harsh clarity: the older woman's body curled into a lean comma under her borrowed blankets. In the whispery dark, her thin, veined lids squeezed shut in a semblance of sleep.

Struggling up the trail through the morning mist, the line of pilgrims in gay woolen clothes looks like a bright garland. Soon the light will grow brutal and blinding, but at this hour it is sleepy, diffuse. A woman pauses to chant. Om Namah Shivaya, Salutations to the Auspicious One. The notes tremble in the air, Leela thinks, like silver bubbles. The pilgrims are quiet—there's something about the snowy crags that discourages gossip. The head guide has suggested that walking time be utilized for reflection and repentance. Leela finds herself thinking, instead, of accidents.

She remembers the first one most clearly. It must have been a special occasion, maybe a birthday or an out-of-town visitor, because her mother was cooking. She rarely made Indian food from scratch, and Leela remembers that she was snappish and distracted. Wanting to help, the four-year-old Leela had pulled at a pot and seen the steaming dal come at her in a yellow rush. It struck her arm with a slapping sound. She screamed and raced around the kitchen—as though agony could be outrun. Long after her mother immersed her arm in ice water and gave her Tylenol to reduce the pain, she continued to sob—tears of rage at being tricked, Leela realizes now. She'd had no intimations, until then, that good intentions were no match for the forces of the physical world.

More accidents followed, in spite of the fact that she was not a particularly physical child. They blur together in Leela's memory like the landscape outside the window of a speeding car. She fell from her bike in front of a moving car—luckily the driver had good reflexes, and she only needed a few stitches on her chin. She sat in the passenger seat of her mother's van, and a stone—from who knows where—shattered the windshield, filling Leela's lap with jagged silver. A defective electrical wire caught fire at night in her bedroom while she slept. Her mother, up for a drink of water, smelled the smoke and ran to the bedroom to discover the carpet smoldering around the sleeping Leela's bed. Do all these close escapes mean that Leela is lucky? Or is her unlucky star, thwarted all this time by some imbalance in the stratosphere, waiting for its opportunity?

She thinks finally of the suicide attempt, which, since arriving in India, she has quarantined in a part of her mind she seldom visits. Can it be classified as an accident, an accident she did to herself? She remembers the magnetic red gleam of the round pills in the hollow of her palm, how unexpectedly solid they had felt, like metal pellets. The shriek of the ambulance outside her window. The old man who lived across the hall peering from a crack in his door, grim and unsurprised. The acidic ache in her throat when they pumped her stomach. Leela had kept her eyes on the wall of the emergency room afterwards, too ashamed to look at the paramedic who was telling her something. Something cautionary and crucial which might help her now, as she steps warily along this beautiful glacial trail, watching for crevasses. But for the life of her she cannot recall what it was.

Each night the pilgrims are assigned to different tents by the head guide, according to some complicated logic Leela has failed to decipher. But tonight, when she finds herself in Mrs. Das's tent, her bedroll set down next to the older woman's makeshift one, she wonders if it is destiny that has brought her here.

All her life, like her parents, Leela has been a believer in individual responsibility. But lately she finds herself wondering. When she asked Aunt Seema yesterday, she touched Leela's cheek in a gesture of amused affection. "Ah, my dear—to believe that you control everything in your life! How absurdly American!"

Destiny is a seductive concept. Ruminating on it, Leela feels the events of her life turn weightless and pass through her like clouds. The simplistic, sublunary words she assigned to them—pride, shame, guilt, folly—no longer seem to apply.

"Please," Mrs. Das whispers in Bengali, startling Leela from thought. She sits on the tarpaulin floor of the tent, propped against her bedroll, her legs splayed out crookedly from under her sari. "Could you ask one of the attendants to bring some warm water? My feet hurt a lot."

"Of course," Leela says, jumping up. An odd gladness fills her as she performs this small service. Aunt, who was less than happy about Leela's tent assignment tonight, had whispered to her to be sure to stay away from Mrs. Das. But Aunt is at the other end of the camp, while destiny has placed Leela here.

When the water comes in a bucket, Mrs. Das surreptitiously removes her shoes. They are made of rough leather, cheap and unlovely. They make Leela feel guilty about her fleece-lined American boots, even though the fleece is fake. Then she sucks in a horrified breath.

Freed of shoes and socks, Mrs. Das's feet are in bad shape, swollen all the way to the calves. The toes are blistered and bluish with frostbite. The heels weep yellowish pus. Mrs. Das looks concerned but not surprised—this has obviously been going on for a couple of days. She grits her teeth, lurches to her feet, and tries to lift the bucket. Leela takes it from her and follows her to the opening of the tent, and when Mrs. Das has difficulty bending over to wash her feet, she kneels and does it for her. She feels no disgust as she cleans off the odorous pus. This intrigues her. Usually she doesn't like touching people. Even with her parents, she seldom went beyond the light press of lips to cheek, the hurried pat on the shoulder. In her Dexter days, if he put his arm around her, she'd find an excuse to move away after a few minutes. Yet here she is, tearing strips from an old sari and bandaging Mrs. Das's feet, her fingers moving with a deft intelligence she did not suspect they possessed, brown against the matching brown of Mrs. Das's skin. This is the first time, she thinks, that she has known such intimacy. How amazing that it should be a stranger who has opened her like a dictionary and brought to light this word whose definition had escaped her until now.

• • •

Someone in the tent must have talked, for here through the night comes the party's doctor, his flashlight making a ragged circle of brightness on the tent floor as he enters. "Now what's the problem?" he asks Mrs. Das, who attempts a look of innocence. What problem could he be referring to? The doctor sighs, hands Leela his torch, removes the sari strips, and clicks his tongue gravely as he examines Mrs. Das's feet. There's evidence of infection, he says. She needs a tetanus shot immediately, and even then the blisters might get septic. How could she have been so foolish as to keep this a secret from him? He pulls a thick syringe from his bag and administers an injection. "But you still have to get down to the hospital at Pahelgaon as soon as possible," he ends. "I'll ask the guide to find some way of sending you back tomorrow."

Mrs. Das clutches the doctor's arm. In the flashlight's erratic beam, her eyes, magnified behind thick glasses, glint desperately. She doesn't care about her feet, she says. It's more important for her to complete the pilgrimage—she's waited so long to do it. They're only a day or so away from Shiva's shrine. If she had to turn back now, it would kill her much more surely than a septic blister.

The doctor's walrus mustache droops unhappily. He takes a deep breath and says that two extra days of hard walking could cause gangrene to set in, though a brief uncertainty flits over his face as he speaks. He repeats that Mrs. Das must go back tomorrow, then hurries off before she can plead further.

The darkness left behind is streaked with faint cobwebs of moonlight. Leela glances at the body prone on the bedding next to her. Mrs. Das is completely quiet, and this frightens Leela more than any fit of hysterics. She hears shufflings from the other end of the tent, whispered comments sibilant with relief. Angrily, she thinks that had the patient been anyone else, the doctor would not have been so adamant about sending her back. The moon goes behind a cloud; around her, darkness packs itself tightly, like black wool. She pushes her hand through it to where she thinks Mrs. Das's arm might be. Against her fingers Mrs. Das's skin feels brittle and stiff, like cheap waterproof fabric. Leela holds Mrs. Das's wrist awkwardly, not knowing what to do. In the context of Indian etiquette, would patting be considered a condescending gesture? She regrets her impetuosity.

Then Mrs. Das turns her wrist—it is the swift movement of a night animal who knows its survival depends on mastering such economies of action—and clasps Leela's fingers tightly in her own.

Late that night Mrs. Das tries to continue up the trail on her own, is spotted by the lookout guide, apprehended and brought back. It happens quickly and quietly, and Leela sleeps through it all.

By the time she wakes, the tent is washed in calm mountain light and abuzz with women and gossip.

"There she was, in the dark on her own, without any supplies, not even an electric torch, can you imagine?"

"Luckily the guide saw her before she went beyond the bend in the mountain. Otherwise she'd be in a ravine by now—"

"Or frozen to death—"

"Crazy woman! They say when they caught her, she fought them tooth and nail—I'm telling you, she actually drew blood! Like someone possessed by an evil spirit—"

Leela stares at Mrs. Das's bedroll, two dark, hairy blankets topped by a sheet. It looks like the peeled skin of an animal turned inside out. The women's excitement crackles through the air, sends little shocks up her arms. Are people in India harder to understand because they've had so many extra centuries to formulate their beliefs? She recalls the expression on Dexter's face before he slammed the door, the simple incandescence of his anger. In some way, she had expected it all along. But Mrs. Das—? She curls her fingers, remembering the way the older woman had clasped them in her dry, birdlike grip.

"Did she really think she could get to the shrine all by herself!" someone exclaims.

Leela spots Aunt Seema and tugs at her sari. "Where is Mrs. Das now?"

"The guides have put her in a separate tent where they can keep an eye on her until they can send her back," Aunt says, shaking her head sadly. "Poor thing—I really feel sorry for her. Still, I must confess I'm glad she's leaving." Then a suspicious frown takes over her face. "Why do you want to know? Did you talk to her last night? Leela, stop, where are you going?"

Mrs. Das, whom Leela finds in a small tent outside of which a guide keeps watch, does not look like a woman who has recently battled several men tooth and nail. Cowled in a faded green shawl, she dozes peacefully against the tent pole, though this could be due to the Calmpose tablets the doctor has made her take. Or perhaps there's not much outside her head that she's interested in at this point. She has lost her glasses in her night's adventuring, and when Leela touches her shoulder, she looks up, blinking with dignity.

Leela opens her mouth to say she is sorry about how Mrs. Das has been treated. But she hears herself saying, "I'm going back with you." The dazed expression on Mrs. Das's face mirrors her own inner state. When after a moment Mrs. Das warily asks her why, all she can do is shrug her shoulders. She is uncertain of her motives. Is it her desire to prove (but to whom?) that she is somehow superior to the others? Is it pity, an emotion she has always distrusted? Is it some inchoate affinity she feels toward this stranger? But if you believe in destiny, no one can be a stranger, can they? There's always a connection, a reason because of which people enter your orbit, bristling with dark energy like a meteor intent on collision.

Traveling down a mountain trail fringed by thick, seeded grasses the same gray as the sky, Leela wants to ask Mrs. Das about destiny. Whether she believes in it, what she understands it to encompass. But Mrs. Das grips the saddle of the mule she is sitting on, her body rigid with a single-minded terror of a person who has never ridden an animal. Ahead, the guide's young, scraggly bearded son whistles a movie tune Leela remembers having heard in another world, during an excursion with Aunt Seema to some Calcutta market.

Aunt Seema was terribly upset with Leela's decision to accompany Mrs. Das—no, even with that intense adverb, upset is too simple a word to describe the change in her urbane aunt, who had taken such gay control of Leela's life in the city. The new Aunt Seema wrung her hands and lamented, "But what would your mother say if she knew that I let you go off alone with some stranger?" (Did she really believe Leela's mother would hold her responsible? The thought made Leela smile.) Aunt's face was full of awful conviction as she begged Leela to reconsider. Breaking off a pilgrimage like this, for no good reason, would rouse the wrath of Shiva. When Leela said that the occurrences of her life were surely of no interest to a deity, Aunt gripped her shoulders with trembling hands.

"Stop!" she cried, her nostrils flaring. "You don't know what you're saying! That bad-luck woman, she's bewitched you!"

How many unguessed layers there were to people, skins that came loose at an unexpected tug, revealing raw, fearful flesh. Amazing, that folks could love one another in the face of such unreliability! It made Leela at once sad and hopeful.

Walking downhill, Leela has drifted into a fantasy. In it, she lives in a small rooftop flat on the outskirts of Calcutta. Mrs. Das, whom she has rescued from the women's hostel, lives with her. They have a maid who shops and runs their errands, so the women rarely need to leave the flat. Each evening they sit on the terrace beside the potted roses and chrysanthemums (Mrs. Das has turned out to be a skillful gardener) and listen to music—a tape of Bengali folk songs (Mrs. Das looks like a person who would enjoy that), or maybe one of Leela's jazz CDs, to which Mrs. Das listens with bemused attention. When they wish each other good night, she touches Leela's arm. "Thank you," she says, her eyes deep as a forest.

They have come to a riverbed. There isn't much water, but the boulders on which they step are slippery with moss. It's starting to rain, and the guide eyes the sky nervously. He pulls at the balking mule, which stumbles. Mrs. Das gives a harsh, crowlike cry and flings out her hand. Leela grasps it and holds on until they reach the other side.

"Thank you," says Mrs. Das. It is the first time she has smiled, and Leela sees that her eyes are, indeed, deep as a forest.

"But Madam!" the proprietor at the Nataraja Inn cries to Leela in an English made shaky by distress. "You people are not to be coming back for two more days! Already I am giving your rooms to other pilgrim party. Whole hotel is full. This is middle of pilgrim season—other hotels are also being full." He gives Leela and Mrs. Das, who are shivering in their wet clothes, an accusing look. "How is it you two are returned so soon?"

The guide, who has brought in the bedrolls, says something in a rapid pahari dialect that Leela cannot follow. The clerk pulls back his head in a swift, turtlelike motion and gives Mrs. Das a glance full of misgiving.

"Please," Leela says. "We're very tired, and it's raining. Can't you find us something?"

"Sorry, Madams. Maybe Mughal Gardens in marketplace is having space—"

Leela can feel Mrs. Das's placid eyes on her. It is obvious that she trusts the younger woman to handle the situation. Leela sighs. Being a savior in real life has drawbacks she never imagined in her rooftop fantasy.

Recalling something Aunt Seema said earlier, she digs in the waistband of her sari and comes up with a handful of rupee notes which she lays on the counter.

The clerk rocks back on his heels, torn between avarice and superstition. Then his hand darts out and covers the notes. "We are having a small small storeroom on top of hotel. Big enough for one person only." He parts his lips in an ingenuous smile. "Maybe older madam can try Mughal Gardens?"

Leela gives the clerk a reprimanding look. "We'll manage" she says.

The clerk has not exaggerated. The room, filled with discarded furniture, is about as big as Leela's queen-size bed in America. Even after the sweeper carries all the junk out into the corridor, there isn't enough space to open the two bedrolls without their edges overlapping. Leela tries to hide her dismay. It strikes her that since she arrived in India, she has not been alone even once. With sudden homesickness, she longs for her wide, flat bedroom, its uncomplicated vanilla walls, its window from which she had looked out onto nothing more demanding than a clump of geraniums.

"I've caused you a lot of inconvenience."

Mrs. Das's voice is small but not apologetic. (Leela rather likes this.) "You shouldn't have come back with me," she adds matter-of-factly. "What if I *am* bad luck, like people believe?"

"Do you believe that?" Leela asks. She strains to hear Mrs. Das's answer above the crash of thunder.

"Belief, disbelief," Mrs. Das shrugs. "So many things I believed to be one way turned out otherwise. I believed my son's marriage wouldn't change things between us. I believed I would get to Shiva's shrine, and all my problems would disappear. Last night on the mountain I believed the best thing for me would be to fall into a crevasse and die." She smiles with unexpected sweetness as she says this. "But now—here we are together."

Together. When Mrs. Das says it in Bengali, eksangay, the word opens inside Leela with a faint, ringing sound, like a distant temple bell.

"I have something I want to give you," Mrs. Das says.

"No, no," says Leela, embarrassed. "Please, I'd rather you didn't."

"He who gives," says Mrs. Das, "must be prepared to receive." Is this an ancient Indian saying, or one that she has made up herself? And what exactly does it mean? Is giving then a privilege, in return for which you must allow others the opportunity to do the same? Mrs. Das unclasps a thin gold chain she is wearing. She leans forward and Leela feels her fingers fumbling for a moment on the nape of her neck. She wants to protest, to explain to Mrs. Das that she has always hated jewelry, all that metal clamped around you. But she is caught in a web of unfamiliar ideas. Is giving the touchstone by which the lives of strangers become your own? The expression on Mrs. Das's face is secretive, prayerful. And then the skin-warm, almost weightless chain is around Leela's throat.

Mrs. Das switches off the naked bulb that hangs on a bit of wire from the ceiling. The two of them lie down, each on her blanket, and listen to the wind, which moans and rattles the shutters like a madwoman wanting to be let in. Leela hopes Aunt Seema is safe, that the storm has not hit the mountain the way it has Pahelgaon. But the world outside this square, contained room has receded so far that she is unable to feel anxiety. Rain falls all around her, insulating as a lullaby. If she were to stretch out her arm, she would touch Mrs. Das's face.

She says, softly, "Once I tried to kill myself."

Mrs. Das says nothing. Perhaps she is asleep.

Leela finds herself speaking of the pills, the ambulance, the scraped-out space inside her afterwards. Perhaps it had always been there, and she had not known? She talks about her father and mother, their unbearable courtesy, which she sees only this moment as having been unbearable. She asks questions about togetherness, about being alone. What the value of each might be. She sends her words into the night, and does not need a reply.

She has never spoken so much in her life. In the middle of a sentence, she falls asleep.

Leela is dreaming. In the dream, the glacial trails have been washed away by rain. She takes a false step, sinks into slush. Ice presses against her chest. She opens her mouth to cry for help, and it too fills with ice. With a thunderous crack, blackness opens above her, a brilliant and brutal absence of light. She knows it has found her finally, her unlucky star.

Leela wakes, her heart clenched painfully like an arthritic fist. How real the dream was. Even now she feels the freezing weight on her chest, hears the ricochet of the cracked-open sky. But no, it is not just a dream. Her blanket is soaked through, and the floor is awash with water. She scrambles for the light switch and sees, in the dim glare, a corner of the roof hanging down, swinging drunkenly. In the midst of all this, Mrs. Das sleeps on, covers pulled over her head. Leela is visited by a crazy wish to lie down beside her.

"Quick, quick!" she cries, shaking her. "We have to get out of here before that roof comes down."

Mrs. Das doesn't seem to understand what Leela wants from her. Another gust of wind hits the roof, which gives an ominous creak. Her eyes widen, but she makes no move to sit up.

"Come on," shouts Leela. She starts to drag her to the door. Mrs. Das offers neither resistance nor help. A long time back Leela had taken a CPR course, she has forgotten why. Mrs. Das's body, slack and rubbery, reminds her of the dummy on whose chest she had pounded with earnest energy. The thought depresses her, and this depression is the last emotion she registers before something hits her head.

Leela lies on a lumpy mattress. Even with her eyes closed, she knows that the clothes she is wearing—a baggy blouse, a limp cotton sari which swathes her loosely—are not hers. Her head feels stuffed with steel shavings. Is she in heaven, having died a heroic death? But surely celestial bedding would be more comfortable, celestial clothing more elegant—even in India? She is ashamed of having thought that last phrase. She moves her head a little. The jab of pain is like disappointed lightning.

"Doctor, doctor, she's waking up," Aunt Seema says from somewhere, her voice damp and wobbly like a biscuit that's been dunked in tea. But why is Leela thinking like this? She knows she should appreciate her aunt's loving concern and say something to reassure her. But it is so private, so comfortable, behind her closed eyes.

"Finally," says the doctor's voice. "I was getting worried." Leela can smell his breath—it's cigarettes, a brand she does not know. It smells of cloves. When she has forgotten everything else, she thinks, she will remember the odors of this journey.

"Can you hear me, Leela?" the doctor asks. "Can you open your eyes?" He taps on her cheek with maddening persistence until she gives up and glares at him.

"You're lucky, young lady," he says as he changes the bandage around her head. "You should be thankful you were hit by a piece of wood. Now if that had been a sheet of rusted metal—"

Lucky. Thankful. Leela doesn't trust such words. They change their meaning as they swoop, sharp-clawed, about her head. The room is full of women; they wring their hands in gestures that echo her aunt's. She closes her eyes again. There's a question she must ask, an important one—but when she tries to catch it in a net of words, it dissolves into red fog.

"It's all my fault," Aunt Seema says in a broken voice that baffles Leela. Why should Aunt feel so much distress at problems which are, after all, hers alone? "Leela doesn't understand these things—how can she?—but I should have made her stay away from that accursed woman—"

"Do try to be quiet." The doctor's voice is testy, as though he has heard this lament many times already. "Give her the medicine and let her rest."

Someone holds Leela's head, brings a cup to her lips. The medicine is thick and vile. She forces it down her throat with harsh satisfaction. Aunt sobs softly, in deference to the doctor's orders. Her friends murmur consolations. From time to time, phrases rise like a refrain from their crooning: *the poor girl, Shiva have mercy, that bad-luck woman, oh, what will I tell your mother.*

A commotion at the door.

"I've got to see her, just for a minute, just to make sure she's all right—"

There's a heaving inside Leela.

"No," says one of the women. "Daktar-babu said no excitement."

"Please, I won't talk to her—I'll just take a look."

"Over my dead body you will," Aunt Seema bursts out. "Haven't you done her enough harm already? Go away. Leela, you tell her yourself—"

Leela doesn't want to tell anyone anything. She wants only to sleep. Is that too much to ask for? A line comes to her from a poem, *Death's second self which seals up all in rest.* She imagines snow, great fluffy quilts of it, packed around her. But the voices scrape at her, *Leela, Leela, Leela . . .*

The room is full of evening. Leela sees Mrs. Das at the door, trying to push her way past the determined bulk of the doctor's wife. Her disheveled hair radiates from her head like crinkly white wires, giving her, for a moment, the look of an alien in a *Star Trek* movie. When she sees that Leela's eyes are open, she stops struggling and reaches out toward her.

Why does Leela do what she does next? Is it the medication, which makes her lightheaded? The pain, which won't let her think? Or is it some dark, genetic strain which, unknown to her, has pierced her pragmatic, American upbringing with its sharp, knotted root? At times, later, she will tell herself, *I didn't know what I was doing.* At other times, she'll say, *liar.* For doesn't her response to Mrs. Das come from the intrinsic and fearful depths of who she is? The part of her that knows she is no savior?

Leela sits up in bed. "Aunt's right," she says. Her teeth chatter as though she is fevered. "All of them are right. You *are* cursed. Go away. Leave me alone."

"No," says Mrs. Das. But it is a pale sound, without conviction.

"Yes!" says Leela. "Yes!" She grasps the chain Mrs. Das has given her and yanks at it. The worn gold gives easily. Falling, it makes a small, skittery sound on the wood floor.

Darkness is bursting open around Seema like black chrysanthemums.

Mrs. Das stares at the chain, then turns and stumbles from the room. Her shadow, long and misshapen, touches Leela once. Then it, too, is gone.

The pilgrimage party makes much of Leela as she lies recovering. The women bring her little gifts from their forays into town—an embroidered purse, a bunch of Kashmiri grapes, a lacquered jewelry box. When they hold out the presents, Leela burrows her hands into her blanket. But the women merely nod to each other. They whisper words like *shock* and *been through so much*. They hand the gifts to Aunt, who promises to keep them safely until Leela is better. When they leave, she feels like a petulant child.

From the doorway, the men ask Aunt Seema how Leela is coming along. Their voices are gruff and hushed, their eyes furtive with awe—as though she were a martyr-saint who took upon herself the bad luck that would have otherwise fallen on them. Is it cynical to think this? There is no one anymore whom Leela can ask.

On the way back to Srinagar, where the party will catch the train to Calcutta, by unspoken consent Leela is given the best seat on the bus, up front near the big double windows.

"It's a fine view, and it won't joggle you so much," says one of the women, plumping up a pillow for her. Another places a footrest near her legs. Aunt Seema unscrews a thermos and pours her a glass of pomegranate juice—to replace all the blood Leela lost, she says. The juice is the color of blood. Its thin tartness makes Leela's mouth pucker up, and Aunt says, in a disappointed voice, "Oh dear, is it not so sweet then? Why, that Bahadur at the hotel swore to me—"

Leela feels ungracious, boorish. She feels angry for feeling this way. "I have a headache," she says and turns to the window where, hidden behind her sunglasses, she watches the rest of the party get on the bus. Amid shouts and laughter, the bus begins to move.

She waits until the bus has lurched its way around three hairpin bends. Then she says, "Aunt—?" She tries to make her voice casual, but the words come out in a croak.

"Yes, dear? A little more juice?" Aunt asks hopefully.

"Where is Mrs. Das? Why didn't she get on the bus?"

Aunt fiddles with the catch of her purse. Her face indicates her discomfort at the baldness of Leela's questions. A real Indian woman would have known to approach the matter delicately, sideways.

But the doctor's wife, who is sitting behind them, leans forward to say, "Oh, her! She went off somewhere on her own, when was it, three, no, four nights ago, right after she created that ruckus in your sickroom. She didn't take her bedroll with her, or even her suitcase. Strange, no? Personally, I think she's a little bit touched up here." She taps her head emphatically.

Misery swirls, acidic, through Leela's insides. She raises her hand with great effort to cover her mouth, so it will not spill out.

"Are you okay, dear?" Aunt asks.

"She looks terribly pale," the doctor's wife says. "It's all these winding roads—enough to make anyone vomity."

"I might have some lemon drops," says Aunt, rummaging in her handbag.

Leela accepts the sour candy and turns again to the window. Behind her she hears the doctor's wife's carrying whisper, "If I were you, I'd get a puja done for your niece once you get to Calcutta. You know, to avert the evil eye—"

Outside the bus, mountains and waterfalls are speeding past Leela. Sunlight slides like opportunity from the narrow green leaves of debdaru trees and is lost in the underbrush. What had the guide said, at the start of the trip, about expiation? Leela cannot remember. And even if she did, would she be capable of executing those gestures, delicate and filled with power, like the movements of a Bharatnatyam dancer, which connect humans to the gods and to each other? Back in America, her life waits to claim her, unchanged, impervious, smelling like floor polish. In the dusty window, her reflection is a blank oval. She takes off her dark glasses to see better, but the features which peer back at her are unfamiliar, as though they belong to someone she has never met.

Ann Beattie

That Last Odd Day in L.A.

from *The New Yorker*

K ELLER WENT back and forth about going into Cambridge to see
Lynn, his daughter, for Thanksgiving. If he went in November, he'd
miss his niece and nephew, who made the trip back East only in
December, for Christmas. They probably could have got away from their
jobs and returned for both holidays, but they never did. The family had
gathered for Thanksgiving at his daughter's ever since she moved into her
own apartment, which was going on six years now; Christmas dinner was
at Keller's sister's house, in Arlington. His daughter's apartment was near
Porter Square. She had once lived there with Ray Ceruto, before she
decided she was too good for a car mechanic. A nice man, a hard worker, a
gentleman—so naturally she chose instead to live in serial monogamy
with men Keller found it almost impossible to get along with. Oh, but
they had white-collar jobs and white-collar aspirations: with her current
boyfriend, she had recently flown to England for all of three days in order
to see the white cliffs of Dover. If there had been bluebirds, they had gone
unmentioned.

Years ago, Keller's wife, Sue Anne, had moved back to Roanoke,
Virginia, where she now rented a "mother-in-law apartment" from a
woman she had gone to school with back in the days when she and Keller
were courting. Sue Anne joked that she herself had become a sort of ideal
mother-in-law, gardening and taking care of the pets when her friends

went away. She was happy to have returned to gardening. During the almost twenty years that she and Keller had been together, their little house in the Boston suburbs, shaded by trees, had allowed for the growth of almost nothing but springtime bulbs, and even those had to be planted in raised beds because the soil was of such poor quality. Eventually, the squirrels discovered the beds. Sue Anne's breakdown had had to do with the squirrels.

So: call his daughter, or do the more important thing and call his neighbor and travel agent, Sigrid, at Pleasure Travel, to apologize for their recent, rather uneventful dinner at the local Chinese restaurant, which had been interrupted by a thunderstorm grand enough to announce the presence of Charlton Heston, which had reminded Keller that he'd left his windows open. He probably should not have refused to have the food packed to go. But when he'd thought of having her to his house to eat the dinner—his house was a complete mess—or of going to her house and having to deal with her son's sour disdain, it had seemed easier just to bolt down his food.

A few days after the ill-fated dinner, he had bought six raffle tickets and sent them to her, in the hope that a winning number would provide a bicycle for her son, though he obviously hadn't given her a winning ticket, or she would have called. Her son's expensive bicycle had been taken at knifepoint, in a neighborhood he had promised his mother he would not ride through.

Two or three weeks before, Sigrid and Keller had driven into Boston to see a show at the MFA and afterward had gone to a coffee shop where he had clumsily, stupidly, splashed a cup of tea onto her when he was jostled by a mother with a stroller the size of an infantry vehicle. He had brought dishtowels to the door of the ladies' room for Sigrid to dry herself off with, and he had even—rather gallantly, some might have said—thought to bite the end off his daily vitamin-E capsule from the little packet of multivitamins he carried in his shirt pocket and urged her to scrape the goop from the tip of his finger and spread it on the burn. She maintained that she had not been burned. Later, on the way to the car, they had got into a tiff when he said that it wasn't necessary for her to pretend that everything was fine, that he liked women who spoke honestly. "It could not have been all right that I scalded you, Sigrid," he'd told her.

"Well, I just don't see the need to criticize you over an *accident*, Keller," she had replied. Everyone called him by his last name. He had been born Joseph Francis, but neither Joe nor Joseph nor Frank nor Francis fit.

"It was clumsy of me, and I wasn't quick enough to help," he said.

"You were fine," she said. "It would have brought you more pleasure if I'd cried, or if I'd become irrational, wouldn't it? There's some part of you that's always on guard, because the other person is sure to become *irrational.*"

"You know a little something about my wife's personality," he said.

Sigrid had lived next door before, during, and after Sue Anne's departure. "So everyone's your wife?" she said. "Is that what you think?"

"No," he said. "I'm apologizing. I didn't do enough for my wife, either. Apparently I didn't act soon enough or effectively enough or—"

"You're always looking for forgiveness!" she said. "I don't forgive you or not forgive you. How about that? I don't know enough about the situation, but I doubt that you're entirely to blame for the way things turned out."

"I'm sorry," he said. "Some people say I'm too closemouthed and I don't give anyone a chance to know me, and others—such as you or my daughter—maintain that I'm self-critical as a ploy to keep their attention focussed on me."

"I didn't say any such thing! Don't put words in my mouth. I said that my getting tea dumped on my back by accident and the no doubt very complicated relationship you had with your wife really don't—"

"It was certainly too complicated for me," Keller said quietly.

"Stop whispering. If we're going to have a discussion, at least let me hear what you're saying."

"I wasn't whispering," Keller said. "That was just the wheezing of an old man out of steam."

"Now it's your age! I should pity you for your advanced age! What age are you, exactly, since you refer to it so often?"

"You're too young to count that high," he smiled. "You're a young, attractive, successful woman. People are happy to see you walk into the room. When they look up and see me, they see an old man, and they avert their eyes. When I walk into the travel agency, they all but duck into the kneeholes of their desks. That's how we got acquainted, as you recall, since calling on one's neighbors is not the American Way. Only your radiant face met mine with a smile. Everybody else was pretending I wasn't there."

"Listen: are you sure this is where we parked the car?"

"I'm not sure of anything. That's why I had you drive."

"I drove because your optometrist put drops in to dilate your pupils shortly before we left," she said.

"But I'm fine now. At least, my usual imperfect vision has returned. I can drive back," he said, pointing to her silver Avalon. "Too noble a vehicle for me, to be sure, but driving would be the least I could do, after ruining your day."

"Why are you saying that?" she said. "Because you're pleased to think that some little problem has the ability to ruin my day? You are being *impossible*, Keller. And don't whisper that that's exactly what your wife would say. Except that she's a fellow human being occupying planet Earth, I don't *care* about your wife."

She took her key ring out of her pocket and tossed the keys to him.

He was glad he caught them, because she sent them higher into the air than necessary. But he did catch them, and he did remember to step in front of her to hold open her door as he pushed the button to unlock the car. Coming around the back, he saw the PETA bumper sticker her husband had adorned the car with shortly before leaving her for a years-younger Buddhist vegan animal-rights activist.

At least he had worked his way into his craziness slowly, subscribing first to *Smithsonian* magazine and only later to newsletters with pictures of starved, manacled horses and pawless animals with startled eyes—material she was embarrassed to have delivered to the house. In the year before he left, he had worked at the animal-rescue league on weekends. When she told him he was becoming obsessed with the plight of animals at the expense of their marriage and their son, he'd rolled up one of his publications and slapped his palm with it over and over, protesting vehemently, like someone scolding a bad dog. As she recalled, he had somehow turned the conversation to the continued illegal importation of elephant tusks into Asia.

"You always want to get into a fight," she said, when she finally spoke again, as Keller wound his way out of Boston. "It makes it difficult to be with you."

"I know it's difficult. I'm sorry."

"Come over and we can watch some *Perry Mason* reruns," she said. "It's on every night at eleven."

"I don't stay up that late," he said. "I'm an old man."

• • •

Keller spoke to his daughter on the phone—the first time the phone had rung in days—and listened patiently while she set forth her conditions, living her life in the imperative. In advance of their speaking, she wanted him to know that she would hang up if he asked when she intended to break up with Addison (Addison!) Page. Also, as he well knew, she did not want to be questioned about her mother, even though, yes, they were in phone contact. She also did not want to hear any criticism of her glamorous life, based on her recently having spent three days in England with her spendthrift boyfriend, and also, yes, she had got her flu shot.

"This being November, would it be possible to ask who you're going to vote for?"

"No," she said. "Even if you were voting for the same candidate, you'd find some way to make fun of me."

"What if I said, 'Close your eyes and imagine either an elephant or a donkey'?"

"If I close my eyes, I see . . . I see a horse's ass, and it's you," she said. "May I continue?"

He snorted. She had a quick wit, his daughter. She had got that from him, not from his wife, who neither made jokes nor understood them. In the distant past, his wife had found an entirely humorless psychiatrist who had summoned Keller and urged him to speak to Sue Anne directly, not in figurative language or through allusions or—God forbid—with humor. "What should I do if I'm just chomping at the bit to tell a racist joke?" he had asked. The idea was of course ludicrous; he had never made a racist joke in his life. But of course the psychiatrist missed his tone. "You anticipate the necessity of telling racist jokes to your wife?" he had said, pausing to scribble something on his pad. "Only if one came up in a dream or something," Keller had deadpanned.

"I thought you were going to continue, Lynn," he said. "Which I mean as an observation, not as a reproach," he hurried to add.

"Keller," she said (since her teenage years, she had called him Keller), "I need to know whether you're coming to Thanksgiving."

"Because you would get a turkey weighing six or seven ounces more?"

"In fact, I thought about cooking a ham this year, because Addison prefers ham. It's just a simple request, Keller: that you let me know whether or not you plan to come. Thanksgiving is three weeks away."

"I've come up against Amy Vanderbilt's timetable for accepting a social invitation at Thanksgiving?" he said.

She sighed deeply. "I would like you to come, whether you believe that or not, but since the twins aren't coming from L.A., and since Addison's sister invited us to her house, I thought I might not cook this year, if you didn't intend to come."

"Oh, by all means don't cook for me. I'll mind my manners and call fifty-one weeks from today and we'll set this up for next year," he said. "A turkey potpie from the grocery store is good enough for me."

"And the next night you could be your usual frugal self and eat the left-over packaging," she said.

"Horses don't eat cardboard. You're thinking of mice," he said.

"I stand corrected," she said, echoing the sentence he often said to her. "But let me ask you another thing. Addison's sister lives in Portsmouth, New Hampshire, and she issued a personal invitation for you to join us at her house for dinner. Would you like to have Thanksgiving there?"

"How could she issue a personal invitation if she's never met me?" he said.

"Stop it," his daughter said. "Just answer."

He thought about it. Not about whether he would go but about the holiday itself. The revisionist thinking on Thanksgiving was that it commemorated the subjugation of the Native Americans (formerly the Indians). Not as bad a holiday as Columbus Day, but still.

"I take it your silence means that you prefer to be far from the maddening crowd," she said.

"That title is much misquoted," he said. "Hardy's novel is *Far from the Madding Crowd,* which has an entirely different connotation, 'madding' meaning frenzied. There's quite a difference between 'frenzied' and 'annoying.' Consider, for instance, your mother's personality versus mine."

"You are *incredibly* annoying," Lynn said. "If I didn't know that you cared for me, I couldn't bring myself to pick up the phone and let myself in for your mockery, over and over."

"I thought it was because you pitied me."

He heard the click, and there was silence. He replaced the phone in its cradle, which made him think of another cradle—Lynn's—with the decal of the cow jumping over the moon on the headboard and blue and pink beads (the cradle manufacturer having hedged his bets) on the rails. He could remember spinning the beads and watching Lynn sleep. The cradle was now in the downstairs hallway, used to store papers and magazines for recycling. Over the years, some of the decal had peeled away, so that on last inspection only a torso with two legs was successfully making the jump over the brightly smiling moon.

He bought a frozen turkey potpie and, as a treat to himself (it was not true that he constantly denied himself happiness, as Lynn said—one could not deny what was rarely to be found), a new radio whose FM quality was excellent—though what did he know, with his imperfect hearing? As he ate Thanksgiving dinner (two nights before Thanksgiving, but why stand on formality?—a choice of Dinty Moore beef stew or Lean Cuisine vegetable lasagna remained for the day of thanks itself), he listened with pleasure to Respighi's "Pini di Roma." He and Sue Anne had almost gone to Rome on their honeymoon, but instead they had gone to Paris. His wife had just finished her second semester of college, where she had declared herself an art-history major. They had gone to the Louvre and to the Jeu de Paume and on the last day of the trip he had bought her a little watercolor of Venice she kept admiring, in a rather elaborate frame that probably accounted for the gouache's high price—it was a gouache, not a watercolor, as she always corrected him. They both wanted three children, preferably a son followed by either another son or a daughter, though if their second child was a son, then of course they would devoutly wish their last to be a daughter. He remembered with bemusement the way they had prattled on, strolling by the Seine, earnestly discussing those things that were most out of their control: Life's Important Matters.

Sue Anne conceived only once, and although they (she, to be honest) had vaguely considered adoption, Lynn remained their only child. Lacking brothers and sisters, she had been fortunate to grow up among relatives, because Keller's sister had given birth to twins a year or so after Lynn was born, and in those days the two families lived only half an hour apart and saw each other almost every weekend. Now Sue Anne and his sister Carolynne (now merely Carol), who lived in Arlington with her doctor husband (or who lived apart from him—he was forbidden to inquire about the status of their union), had not spoken for months, and the twins, Richard and Rita, who worked as stockbrokers and had never married—smart!—and shared a house in the Hollywood Hills, were more at ease with him than his own daughter was. For years Keller had promised to visit the twins, and the previous summer, Richard had called his bluff and sent him a ticket to Los Angeles. Richard and Rita had picked Keller up at LAX in a BMW convertible and taken him to a sushi restaurant where at periodic intervals laser images on the wall blinked on and off like sexually animated hieroglyphics dry-humping to a recording of "Walk Like an Egyptian." The next morning, the twins had taken him to a museum that had been created as a satire of museums, with descriptions of the bizarre exhibits which were so tongue-in-cheek he was sure the majority of people there thought that they were touring an actual museum. That night, they turned on the lights in their pool and provided him with bathing trunks (how could he have thought to pack such a thing?—he never thought of a visit to sprawling Los Angeles as a visit to a *beach*), and on Sunday they had eaten their lunch of fresh pineapple and prosciutto poolside, drinking prosecco instead of mineral water (the only beverages in the house, except for extraordinarily good red wine, as far as he could tell), and in the late afternoon they had been joined by a beautiful blond woman who had apparently been, or might still be, Jack Nicholson's lover. Then he went with Rita and Richard to a screening (a shoot-'em-up none of them wanted to see, though the twins felt they must, because the cinematographer was their longtime client), and on Monday they had sent a car to the house so Keller wouldn't get lost trying to find his way around the freeways. It transported him to a lunch with the twins at a restaurant built around a beautiful terraced garden, after which he'd been dropped off to take the MGM tour and then picked up by the same driver—a dropout from Hollywood High who was working on a screenplay.

It was good they had bought him a ticket for only a brief visit, because if he'd stayed longer he might never have gone home. Though who would have cared if he hadn't? His wife didn't care where he lived, as long as she lived in the opposite direction. His daughter might be relieved that he had moved away. He lived where he lived for no apparent reason—at least, no reason apparent to him. He had no friends, unless you called Don Kim a friend—Don, with whom he played handball on Mondays and Thursdays. And his accountant, Ralph Bazzorocco. He supposed Bazzorocco was his friend, though with the exception of a couple of golf games each spring and the annual buffet dinner he and Bazzorocco's other clients were invited to every April 16th—and except for Bazzorocco's calling to wish him a happy birthday, and "Famiglia Bazzorocco" (as the gift card always read) sending him an enormous box of biscotti and Baci at Christmas . . . oh, he didn't know. Probably that was what friendship was, he thought, a little ashamed of himself. He had gone to the hospital to visit Bazzorocco's son after the boy injured his pelvis and lost his spleen playing football. He'd driven Bazzorocco's weeping wife home in the rain so she could shower and change her clothes, then driven her, still weeping, back to the hospital. OK: he had friends. But would any of them care if he lived in Los Angeles? Don Kim could easily find another partner (perhaps a younger man more worthy as a competitor); Bazzorocco could remain his accountant via the miracle of modern technology. In any case, Keller had returned to the North Shore.

Though not before that last odd day in L.A. He had said, though he hadn't planned to say it (Lynn was not correct in believing that everything that escaped his lips was premeditated), that he'd like to spend his last day lounging around the house. So they wouldn't feel too sorry for him, he even asked if he could open a bottle of Merlot—whatever they recommended, of course—and raid their refrigerator for lunch. After all, the refrigerator contained a tub of mascarpone instead of cottage cheese, and the fruit drawer was stocked with organic plums rather than puckered supermarket grapes. Richard wasn't so keen on the idea, but Rita said that of course that was fine. It was *Keller's* vacation, she stressed. They'd make a reservation at a restaurant out at the beach that night, and if he felt rested enough to eat out, fine; if not, they'd cancel the reservation and Richard would cook his famous chicken breasts marinated in Vidalia-onion sauce.

When Keller woke up, the house was empty. He made coffee (at home, he drank instant) and wandered out through the open doors to the patio as it brewed. He surveyed the hillside, admired the lantana growing from Mexican pottery urns flanking one side of the pool. Some magazine had been rained on—it must have rained during the night; he hadn't heard it, but then, he'd fallen asleep with earphones on, listening to Brahms. He walked toward the magazine—as offensive as litter along the highway, this copy of *Vogue* deteriorating on the green tiles—then drew back, startled. There was a small possum: a baby possum, all snout and pale narrow body, clawing the water, trying futilely to scramble up the edge of the pool. He looked around quickly for the pool net. The night before, it had been leaning against the sliding glass door, but it was no longer there. He went quickly to the side of the house, then ran to the opposite side, all the while acutely aware that the drowning possum was in desperate need of rescue. No pool net. He went into the kitchen, which was now suffused with the odor of coffee, and threw open door after door looking for a pot. He finally found a bucket containing cleaning supplies, quickly removed them, then ran back to the pool, where he dipped the bucket in, missing, frightening the poor creature and adding to its problems by making it go under. He recoiled in fear, then realized that the emotion he felt was not fear but self-loathing. Introspection was not his favorite mode, but no matter: he dipped again, leaning farther over this time, accepting the ludi-crous prospect of his falling in, though the second time he managed to scoop up the possum—it was only a tiny thing—and lift it out of the water. The bucket was full, because he had dipped deep, and much to his dismay, when he saw the possum curled up at the bottom, he knew imme-diately that it was already dead. The possum had drowned. He set the bucket down and crouched on the tile beside it before he had a second, most welcome epiphany and realized almost with a laugh that it wasn't dead: it was playing possum. Though if he didn't get it out of the bucket, it really would drown. He jumped up, turned the bucket on its side, and stood back as water and possum flowed out. The water dispersed. The pos-sum lay still. That must be because he was watching it, he decided, although he once more considered the grim possibility that it was dead.

He stood still. Then he thought to walk back into the house, far away from it. It was dead; it wasn't. Time passed. Then, finally, as he stood unmoving, the possum twitched and waddled off—the flicker of life in its body resonated in Keller's own heart—and then the event was over. He continued to stand there, cognizant of how much he had loathed himself just moments before. Then he went out to retrieve the bucket. As he grasped the handle, tears welled up in his eyes. What the hell! He cried at the sink as he rinsed the bucket.

He dried his eyes on the crook of his arm and washed the bucket thor-oughly, much longer than necessary, then dried it with a towel. He put the Comet, the Windex, and the rag and the brush back inside and returned the bucket to its place under the sink and tried to remember what he had planned to do that day, and again he was overwhelmed. The image that popped into his mind was of Jack Nicholson's girlfriend, the blonde in the bikini with the denim shirt thrown over it. He thought . . . what? That he was going to get together with Jack Nicholson's girlfriend? Whose last name he didn't even know?

But that *had* been what he was thinking. No way to act on it, but yes—that was what he had been thinking, all along.

The water had run off, though the tiles still glistened. No sign, of course, of the possum. It was doubtless off assimilating its important life lesson. On a little redwood table was a waterproof radio that he turned on, finding the classical station, adjusting the volume. Then he unbuckled his belt and unzipped his fly, stepped out of his pants and underpants, and took off his shirt. Carrying the radio, he walked to the deep end of the pool, placed the radio on the rim and dove in. He swam underwater for a while, and then, as his head broke the surface, he had the distinct feeling that he was being watched. He looked back at the house, then looked slowly around the pool area. The fence that walled it off from the neighbors was at least ten feet high. Behind the pool, the terrace was filled with bushes and fruit trees and pink and white irises—Keller was crazy: he was alone in a private compound; no one was there. He went under the water again, refreshed by its silky coolness, and breaststroked to the far end, where he came up for air, then used his feet to push off the side of the pool so he could float on his back. When he reached the end, he pulled himself out, then saw, in the corner of his eye, who was watching him. High up on the terrace, a deer was looking down. The second their eyes met, the deer was gone, but in that second it had come clear to him—on this day of endless revelations—that the deer had been casting a beneficent look, as if in thanks. He had felt that: that a deer was acknowledging and thanking him. He was flabbergasted at the odd workings of his brain. How could a grown man—a grown man without any religious beliefs, a father who, in what now seemed like a different lifetime, had accompanied his little daughter to "Bambi" and whispered, as every parent does, "It's only a movie," when Bambi's mother was killed . . . how could a man with such knowledge of the world, whose most meaningful accomplishment in as long as he could remember had been to fish an animal out of a swimming pool—how could such a man feel unequivocally that a deer had appeared to bless him?

But he knew it had.

As it turned out, the blessing hadn't exactly changed his life, though why should one expect so much of blessings, just because they were blessings?

Something that *had* profoundly changed his life had been Richard's urging him, several years before, to take a chance, take a gamble, trust him, because the word he was about to speak was going to change his life. "Plastics?" he'd said, but Richard was too young: he hadn't seen the movie. No, the word had been "Microsoft." Keller had been in a strange frame of mind that day (one month earlier, to the day, his father had killed himself). At that point, he had hated his job so much, had stopped telling half-truths and finally admitted to Sue Anne that their marriage had become a dead end, that he assumed he was indulging the self-destructiveness his wife and daughter always maintained was the core of his being when he turned over almost everything he had to his nephew to invest in a company whose very name suggested smallness and insubstantiality. But, as it turned out, Richard had blessed him, as had the deer, now. The blonde had not, but then, very few men, very few indeed, would ever be lucky enough to have such a woman give them her benediction.

"You're *fun*!" Rita laughed, dropping him off at LAX. On the way, he had taken off his white T-shirt and raised it in the air, saying, "I hereby surrender to the madness that is the City of Angels." It had long been Rita's opinion that no one in the family understood her uncle; that all of them were so defensive that they were intimidated by his erudition and willfully misunderstood his sense of humor. Richard was working late, but he had sent, by way of his sister (she ran back to the car, having almost forgotten the treat in the glove compartment), a tin of white-chocolate brownies to eat on the plane, along with a note Keller would later read that thanked him for having set an example when he and Rita were kids, for not unthinkingly going with the flow, and for his wry pronouncements in a family where, Richard said, everyone else was "afraid of his own shadow." "Come back soon," Richard had written. "We miss you."

Back home, on the telephone, his daughter had greeted him with a warning: "I don't want to hear about my cousins who are happy and successful, which are synonymous, in your mind, with being rich. Spare me details of their life and just tell me what you did. I'd like to hear about your trip without feeling diminished by my insignificance in the face of my cousins' perfection."

"I can leave them out of it entirely," he said. "I can say, quite honestly, that the most significant moment of my trip happened not in their company but in the meeting of my eyes with the eyes of a deer that looked at me with indescribable kindness and understanding."

Lynn snorted. "This was on the freeway, I suppose? It was on its way to be an extra in a remake of *The Deer Hunter*?"

He had understood, then, the urge she so often felt when speaking to him—the urge to hang up on a person who had not even tried to understand one word you had said.

"How was your Thanksgiving?" Sigrid asked. Keller was sitting across from her at the travel agency, arranging to buy Don Kim's stepdaughter a ticket to Germany so she could pay a final visit to her dying friend. The girl was dying of A.L.S. The details were too terrible to think about. Jennifer had known her for eleven of her seventeen years, and now the girl was dying. Don Kim barely made it from paycheck to paycheck. It had been necessary to tell Don that he had what he called "a considerable windfall from the eighties stock market" in order to persuade him that in offering to buy Jennifer a ticket, he was not making a gesture he could not afford. He had had to work hard to persuade him. He had to insist on it several times, and swear that in no way had he thought Don had been hinting (which was true). The only worry was how Jennifer would handle such a trip, but they had both agreed she was a very mature girl.

"Very nice," Keller replied. In fact, that day he had eaten canned stew and listened to Albinoni (probably some depressed DJ who hadn't wanted to work Thanksgiving night). He had made a fire in the fireplace and caught up on his reading of *The Economist*. He felt a great distance between himself and Sigrid. He said, trying not to sound too perfunctorily polite, "And yours?"

"I was actually . . ." She dropped her eyes. "You know, my ex-husband has Brad for a week at Thanksgiving and I have him for Christmas. He's such a big boy now, I don't know why he doesn't put his foot down, but he doesn't. If I knew then what I know now, I'd never have let him go, no matter what rights the court gave that lunatic. You know what he did before Thanksgiving? I guess you must not have read the paper. They recruited Brad to liberate turkeys. They got arrested. His father thinks that's fine: traumatizing Brad, letting him get hauled into custody. And the worst of it is, Brad's scared to death, but he doesn't dare *not* go along, and then he has to pretend to me that he thinks it was a great idea, that I'm an indifferent—" She searched for the word. "That I'm subhuman because I eat dead animals."

Keller had no idea what to say. Lately, things didn't seem funny enough to play off of. Everything just seemed weird and sad. Sigrid's ex-husband had taken their son to liberate turkeys. How could you extemporize about that?

"She could go Boston, London, Frankfurt on British Air," Sigrid said, as if she hadn't expected him to reply. "It would be somewhere around 750." She hit the keyboard again. "789 plus taxes," she said. "She'd be flying out at 6 P.M. Eastern Standard, she'd get there midmorning." Her fingers stopped moving on the keyboard. She looked at him.

"Can I use your phone to make sure that's a schedule that's good for her?" he said. He knew that Sigrid wondered who Jennifer Kim was. He had spoken of her as "my friend, Jennifer Kim."

"Of course," she said. She pushed a button and handed him the phone. He had written the Kims' telephone number on a little piece of paper and slipped it in his shirt pocket. He was aware that she was staring at him as he dialled. The phone rang three times, and then he got the answering machine. "Keller here," he said. "We've got the itinerary but I want to check it with Jennifer. I'm going to put my travel agent on," he said. "She'll give you the times, and maybe you can call her to confirm it. O.K.?" He handed the phone to Sigrid. She took it, all business. "Sigrid Crane of Pleasure Travel, Ms. Kim," she said. "I have a British Airways flight that departs Logan at six zero zero P.M., arrival into Frankfurt by way of London nine five five A.M. My direct line is—"

He looked at the poster of Bali framed on the wall. A view of water. Two people entwined in a hammock. Pink flowers in the foreground.

"Well," she said, hanging up. "I'll expect to hear from her. I assume I should let you know if anything changes?"

He cocked his head. "What doesn't?" he said. "You'd be busy every second of the day if you did that."

She looked at him, expressionless. "The ticket price," she said. "Or shall I issue it regardless?"

"Regardless." (Now, there was a word he didn't use often!) "Thanks." He stood.

"Say hello to my colleagues hiding under their desks on your way out," she said.

In the doorway, he stopped. "What did they do with the turkeys?" he said.

"They took them by truck to a farm in Vermont where they thought they wouldn't be killed," she said. "You can read about it in yesterday's paper. Everybody's out on bail. Since it's a first offense, my son might be able to avoid having a record. I've hired a lawyer."

"I'm sorry," he said.

"Thank you," she said.

He nodded. Unless she had two such garments, she was wearing the same gray sweater he had spilled tea on. It occurred to him that, outside his family, she was the only woman he spoke to. The woman at the post office, women he encountered when running errands, the UPS delivery person, who he personally thought might be a hermaphrodite, but in terms of real female acquaintances, Sigrid was the only one. He should have said more to her about the situation with her ex-husband and son, though he could not imagine what he would have said. He also could not get a mental picture, humorous or otherwise, of liberated turkeys, walking around some frozen field in—where had she said? Vermont.

She took an incoming call. He glanced back at the poster, at Sigrid sitting there in her gray sweater, noticing for the first time that she wore a necklace dangling a silver cross. Her high cheekbones, accentuated by her head tipped forward, were her best feature; her worst feature was her eyes, a bit too close together, so that she always seemed slightly perplexed. He raised his hand to indicate good-bye, in case she might be looking, then realized from what he heard Sigrid saying that the person on the other end must be Don Kim's stepdaughter; Sigrid was reciting the Boston to Frankfurt schedule, tapping her pen as she spoke. He hesitated, then went back and sat down, though Sigrid had not invited him back. He sat there while Jennifer Kim told Sigrid the whole sad story—what else could the girl have been saying to her for so long? Sigrid's eyes were almost crossed when she finally glanced up at him, then put her fingers on the keyboard and began to enter information. "I might stop by tonight," he said quietly, rising. She nodded, talking into the telephone headset while typing quickly.

Exiting, he thought of a song Groucho Marx had sung in some movie which had the lyrics "Did you ever have the feeling that you wanted to go, and still you had the feeling that you wanted to stay?" He had a sudden mental image of Groucho with his cigar clamped in his teeth (or perhaps it had been Jimmy Durante who sang the song?), and then Groucho's face evaporated and only the cigar remained, like a moment in "Alice in Wonderland." And then—although Keller had quit smoking years before when his father died—he stopped at a convenience store and bought a pack of cigarettes and smoked one, driving home, listening to some odd space-age music. He drove through Dunkin' Donuts and got two plain doughnuts to have with coffee as he watched the evening news, remembering the many times Sue Anne had criticized him for eating food without a plate, as if dropped crumbs were proof that your life was about to go out of control.

In his driveway, he saw that his trash can had been knocked over, the plastic bag inside split open, the lid halfway across the yard. He looked out the car window at the rind of a melon, then at the bloody Kleenex he'd held to his chin when he'd nicked himself shaving—he had taken to shaving before turning in, to save time in the morning, now that his beard no longer grew so heavily—as well as issues of *The Economist* that a better citizen would have bundled together for recycling. He turned off the ignition and stepped out of the car, into the wind, to deal with the mess.

As he gathered it up, he felt as if someone were watching him. He looked up at the house. Soon after Sue Anne left, he had taken down not only the curtains but the blinds as well, liking clear, empty windows that people could go ahead and stare into, if such ordinary life was what they found fascinating. A car passed by—a blue van new to this road, though in the past few weeks he'd seen it often—as he was picking up a mealy apple. Maybe a private detective stalking him, he thought. Someone his wife had hired, to see whether another woman was living in the house. He snatched up the last of the garbage and stuffed it in the can, intending to come out later to rebag it. He wanted to get out of the wind. He planned to eat one of the doughnuts before the six-o'clock news.

Sigrid's son was sitting with his back against the storm door, his knees drawn in tight to his chest, smoking a cigarette. Keller was startled to see him, but did his best to appear unfazed, stopping on the walkway to extract a cigarette of his own from the pack in his pocket. "Can I trouble you for a light?" he said to the boy.

It seemed to work. Brad looked taken aback that Keller wasn't more taken aback. So much so that he held out the lighter with a trembling hand. Keller towered above him. The boy was thin and short (time would take care of one, if not the other); Keller was just over six feet, with broad shoulders and fifteen or twenty pounds more than he should have been carrying, which happened to him every winter. He said to the boy, "Is this a social call, or did I miss a business appointment?"

The boy hesitated. He missed the humor. He mumbled, "Social."

Keller hid his smile. "Allow me," he said, stepping forward. The boy scrambled up and stepped aside so Keller could open the door. Keller sensed a second's hesitation, though Brad followed him in.

It was cold inside. Keller turned the heat down to fifty-five when he left the house. The boy wrapped his arms around his shoulders. The stub of the cigarette was clasped between his second and third fingers. There was a leather bracelet on his wrist, as well as the spike of some tattoo.

"To what do I owe the pleasure?" Keller said.

"Do you . . ." The boy was preoccupied, looking around the room.

"Have an ashtray? I use cups for that," Keller said, handing him the mug from which he'd drunk his morning coffee. He had run out of milk, so he'd had it black. And damn—he had yet again forgotten to get milk. The boy stubbed out his cigarette in the mug without taking it in his hands. Keller set it back on the table, tapping off the ash from his own cigarette. He gestured to a chair, which the boy walked to and sat down.

"Do you, like, work or anything?" the boy blurted out.

"I'm the idle rich," Keller said. "In fact, I just paid a visit to your mother, to get a ticket to Germany. For a friend, not for me," he added. "That being the only thing on my agenda today, besides reading the *Wall Street Journal*"—he had not heard about the boy's arrest because he never read the local paper, but he'd hesitated to say that to Sigrid—"and once again forgetting to bring home milk."

Keller sat on the sofa.

"Would you not tell my mother I came here?" the boy said.

"O.K.," Keller said. He waited.

"Were you ever friends with my dad?" the boy asked.

"No, though once we both donated blood on the same day, some years ago, and sat in adjacent chairs." It was true. For some reason, he had never told Sigrid about it. Not that there was very much to say.

The boy looked puzzled, as if he didn't understand the words Keller had spoken.

"My dad said you worked together," the boy said.

"Why would I lie?" Keller said, leaving open the question: Why would your father?

Again, the boy looked puzzled. Keller said, "I taught at the college."

"I was at my dad's over Thanksgiving, and he said you worked the same territory."

In spite of himself, Keller smiled. "That's an expression," Keller said. "Like 'I cover the waterfront.'"

"Cover what?" the boy said.

"If he said we 'worked the same territory,' he must have meant that we were up to the same thing. A notion I don't understand, though I do suppose it's what he meant."

The boy looked at his feet. "Why did you buy me the raffle tickets?" he said.

What was Keller supposed to tell him? That he'd done it as an oblique form of apology to his mother for something that hadn't happened, and that he therefore didn't really need to apologize for? The world had changed: here sat someone who'd never heard the expression "worked the same territory." But what, exactly, had been Brad's father's context? He supposed he could ask, though he knew in advance Brad would have no idea what he meant by context.

"I understand Thanksgiving was a pretty bad time for you," Keller said. He added, unnecessarily (though he had no tolerance for people who added things unnecessarily), "Your mother told me."

"Yeah," the boy said.

They sat in silence.

"Why is it you came to see me?" Keller asked.

"Because I thought you were a friend," the boy surprised him by answering.

Keller's eyes betrayed him. He felt his eyebrows rise slightly.

"Because you gave me *six* raffle tickets," the boy said.

Clearly, the boy had no concept of one's being emphatic by varying the expected numbers: one rose instead of a dozen; six chances instead of just one.

Keller got up and retrieved the bag of doughnuts from the hall table. The grease had seeped through and left a glistening smudge on the wood, which he wiped with the ball of his hand. He carried the bag to Brad and lowered it so he could see in. Close up, the boy smelled slightly sour. His hair was dirty. He was sitting with his shoulders hunched. Keller moved the bag forward an inch. The boy shook his head no. Keller folded the top, set the bag on the rug. He walked back to where he'd been sitting.

"If you'd buy me a bike, I'd work next summer and pay you back," Brad blurted out. "I need another bike to get to some places I got to go."

Keller decided against unscrambling the syntax and regarded him. The tattoo seemed to depict a spike with something bulbous at the tip. A small skull, he decided, for no good reason except that these days skulls seemed to be a popular image. There was a pimple on Brad's chin. Miraculously, even to a person who did not believe in miracles, Keller had gone through his own adolescence without ever having a pimple. His daughter had not had similar good luck. She had once refused to go to school because of her bad complexion, and he had made her cry when he'd tried to tease her out of being self-conscious. "Come on," he'd said to her. "You're not Dr. Johnson, with scrofula." His wife, as well as his daughter, had then burst into tears. The following day, Sue Anne had made an appointment for Lynn with a dermatologist.

"Would this be kept secret from your mother?"

"Yeah," the boy said. He wasn't emphatic, though; he narrowed his eyes to see if Keller would agree.

He asked, "Where will you tell her you got the bike?"

"I'll say from my dad."

Keller nodded. "That's not something she might ask him about?" he said.

The boy put his thumb to his mouth and bit the cuticle. "I don't know," he said.

"You wouldn't want to tell her it was in exchange for doing yard work for me next summer?"

"Yeah," the boy said, sitting up straighter. "Yeah, sure, I can do that. I *will*."

It occurred to Keller that Molly Bloom couldn't have pronounced the word *will* more emphatically. "We might even say that I ran into you and suggested it," Keller said.

"Say you ran into me at Scotty's," the boy said. It was an ice-cream store. If that was what the boy wanted him to say, he would. He looked at the bag of doughnuts, expecting that in his newfound happiness the boy would soon reach in. He smiled. He waited for Brad to move toward the bag.

"I threw your trash can over," Brad said.

Keller's smile faded. "What?" he said.

"I was mad when I came here. I thought you were some nutcase friend of my dad's. I know you've been dating my mom."

Keller cocked his head. "So you knocked over my trash can, in preparation for asking me to give you money for a bike?"

"My dad said you were a sleazebag who was dating Mom. You and Mom went to Boston."

Keller had been called many things. Many, many things. But sleazebag had not been among them. It was unexpected, but it stopped just short of amusing him. "And if I *had been* dating Sigrid?" he said. "That would mean you should come over and dump out my trash?"

"I never thought you'd lend me money," Brad mumbled. His thumb was at his mouth again. "I didn't . . . why would I think you'd give me that kind of money, just because you bought twelve bucks' worth of raffle tickets?"

"I'm not following the logic here," Keller said. "If I'm the enemy, why, exactly, did you come to see me?"

"Because I didn't know. I don't know what my father's getting at half the time. My dad's a major nutcase, in case you don't know that. Somebody ought to round him up in one of his burlap bags and let him loose far away from here so he can go live with his precious turkeys."

"I can understand your frustration," Keller said. "I'm afraid that with all the world's problems, setting turkeys free doesn't seem an important priority to me."

"Why? Because you had a dad that was a nutcase?"

"I'm not understanding," Keller said.

"You said you understood the way I feel. Is it because you had a dad that was nuts, too?"

Keller thought about it. In retrospect, it was clear that his father's withdrawal, the year preceding his death, had been because of depression, not old age. He said, "He was quite a nice man. Hardworking. Religious. Very generous, even though he didn't have much money. He and my mother had a happy marriage." To his surprise, that sounded right: for years, in revising his father's history, he had assumed that everything had been a façade, but now that he, himself, was older, he tended to think that people's unhappiness was rarely caused by anyone else, or alleviated by anyone else.

"I came here and threw over your trash and ripped up a bush you just planted," Brad said.

The boy was full of surprises.

"I'll replant it," Brad said. He seemed, suddenly, to be on the verge of tears. "The bush by the side of the house," he said tremulously. "There was new dirt around it."

Indeed. Just the bush Keller thought. On a recent morning, after a rain, he had dug up the azalea and replanted it where it would get more sun. It was the first thing he could remember moving in years. He did almost nothing in the yard—had not worked in it, really, since Sue Anne left.

"Yes, I think you'll need to do that," he said.

"What if I don't?" the boy said shrilly. His voice had changed entirely.

Keller frowned, taken aback at the sudden turnaround.

"What if I do like I came to do?" the boy said.

Suddenly there was a gun pointed at Keller. A pistol. Pointed right at him, in his living room. And, as suddenly, he was flying through the air before his mind even named the object. It went off as he tackled the boy, wrestling the gun from his hand. "You're both fucking nutcases, and you were, too, dating that bitch!" Brad screamed. In that way, because of so much screaming, Keller knew that he had not killed the boy.

The bullet had passed through Keller's forearm. A "clean wound," as the doctor in the emergency room would later say, his expression betraying no awareness of the irony inherent in such a description. With an amazing surge of strength, Keller had pinned the boy to the rug with his good arm as the other bled onto the doughnut bag, and then the struggle was over and Keller did not know what to do. It had seemed they might stay that way forever, with him pinning the boy down, one or the other of them—both of them?—screaming. He somehow used his wounded arm as well as his good arm to pull Brad up and clench him to his side as he dragged the suddenly deadweight, sobbing boy to the telephone and dialled 911. Later, he would learn that he had broken two of the boy's ribs, and that the bullet had missed hitting the bone in his own forearm by fractions of an inch, though the wound required half a dozen surprisingly painful sutures to close.

Keller awaited Sigrid's arrival in the emergency room with dread. His world had already been stood on its head long ago, and he'd developed some fancy acrobatics to stay upright, but Sigrid was just a beginner. He remembered that he had thought about going to her house that very night. It might have been the night he stayed. Everything might have been very different, but it was not. And this thought: if his wife held him accountable for misjudging the importance of their daughter's blemishes, might Sigrid think that, somehow, the violent way things had turned out had been his fault? Among the many things he had been called had been provocative. It was his daughter's favorite word for him. She no longer even tried to find original words to express his shortcomings: he was *provocative.* Even she would not buy the sleazebag epithet. No: he was *provocative.*

In the brightly lit room, they insisted he remain on a gurney. Fluid from a bag was dripping into his arm. Sigrid—there was Sigrid!—wept and wept. Her lawyer accompanied her: a young man with bright-blue eyes and a brow too wrinkled for his years, who seemed too rattled to be in charge of anything. Did he hover the way he did because he was kind, or was there a little something more between him and Sigrid? Keller's not having got involved with Sigrid hadn't spared her any pain, he saw. Once again, he had been instrumental in a woman's abject misery.

Trauma was a strange thing, because you could be unaware of its presence, like diseased cells lurking in your body (a natural enough thought in a hospital) or like bulbs that would break the soil's surface only when stirred in their depths by the penetrating warmth of the sun.

Keller remembered the sun—no, the moon—of Lynn's cradle. The cradle meant to hold three babies that held only one. He had suggested that Sue Anne, depressed after the birth, return to school, get her degree in art history, teach. He had had a notion of her having colleagues. Friends. Because he was not a very good friend to have. Oh, *sometimes,* sure. It had been a nice gesture to buy a plane ticket for someone who needed to visit a dying friend. How ironic it was, his arranging for that ticket the same day he, himself, might have died.

Sigrid was wearing the gray sweater, the necklace with the cross. Her son had blown apart her world. And Keller was not going to be any help: he would not even consider trying to help her put it together again. All the king's horses, and all the king's men . . . even Robert Penn Warren couldn't put Sigrid together again.

Keller had tried that before: good intentions; good suggestions; and his wife had screamed that whatever she did, it was *never enough, never enough,* well, maybe it would be enough if she showed him what strength she possessed—what strength he hadn't depleted with his sarcasm and his comic asides and his endless equivocating—by throwing the lamp on the floor, his typewriter against the wall (the dent was still there), the TV out the window. These thoughts were explained to him later, because he had not been home when she exhibited her significant strength. The squirrels had eaten every bulb. There was not going to be one tulip that would bloom that spring. He suspected otherwise—of course the squirrels had not dug up *every* bulb—but she was in no state of mind to argue with. Besides, there were rules, and his role in the marriage was not to be moderate, it was to be *provocative*. His daughter had said so.

And there she was, his daughter, rushing to his side, accompanied by a nurse: the same person who had once been shown to him swaddled in a pink blanket, now grown almost as tall as he, her face wrinkled then, her face wrinkled now.

"Don't squint," he said. "Put your glasses on. You'll still be pretty."

He stood quickly to show her he was fine, which made the nurse and a doctor who rushed to his side very angry. He said, "I don't have health insurance. I demand to be discharged. The gun got discharged, so it's only fair that I be discharged also."

The nurse said something he couldn't hear. The effort of standing had left him light-headed. Across the room, Sigrid appeared in duplicate and went out of focus. Lynn was negating what he'd just said, informing everyone in a strident voice that of course he had health insurance. The doctor had quite firmly moved him back to his gurney, and now many hands were buckling straps over his chest and legs.

"Mr. Keller," the nurse said, "you lost quite a bit of blood before you got here, and we need you to lie down."

"As opposed to up?" he said.

The doctor, who was walking away, turned. "Keller," he said, "this isn't *ER*, where we'd do anything for you, and the nurse isn't your straight man."

"Clearly not," he said quickly. "She's a woman, we assume."

The doctor's expression did not change. "I knew a wiseass like you in med school," he said. "He couldn't do the work, so he developed a comedy routine and made a big joke of flunking out. In the end, I became a doctor and he's still talking to himself." He walked away.

Keller was ready with a quick retort, heard it inside his head, but his lips couldn't form the words. What his nearest and dearest had always wished for was now coming true: his terrible talent with words was for the moment suspended. Truly, he was too tired to speak.

The phrase "nearest and dearest" carried him back in time and reminded him of the deer. The deer that had disappeared in the Hollywood Hills. His own guardian angel, appropriately enough a little mangy, with hooves rooting it to the ground, instead of gossamer wings to carry it aloft. And his eyes closed.

When he opened them, Keller saw that his daughter was looking down at him, and nodding slowly, a tentative smile quivering like a parenthesis at the sides of her mouth, a parenthesis he thought might contain the information that, yes, once he had been able to reassure her easily, as she, in believing, had reassured him.

In appreciation, he attempted his best Jack Nicholson smile.

David Gates

George Lassos Moon

from *GQ*

AUNT LISSA's saying something very serious, and bad Carl's playing with the metal creamer thing. He thumbs the lid up, lets it drop. Tiny clank. Aunt Lissa says, "Are you following?"

"Absolutely."

"Give me strength." Big sigh. "All right, enough said. What'll it be? I don't imagine you've been eating."

"Coffee," he says, which makes him sound blown away (like he's *not*) because he's got a cup right in front of him. He just means he's fine.

"You've got to eat a *little* something."

"Let me look in the Book of Life." He lifts the menu from the metal rack. "Pray *Jee*-zus that mah name be written thar." Inside they've got a color picture of a hot dog with gleaming highlights. "This is incredible," he says.

"Why am I doing this?" Aunt Lissa says.

"You're an enabler," he says. "That's a joke." He'd better start marking them as such.

"Carl. You do understand what's going on, yes? Could you look at me?"

He sees in Aunt Lissa's eyeglasses a tiny thing of his own face. Boy he is *never* taking drugs again, except down drugs. "You mean do I know I got arrested?" he says. He rubs his fingers back and forth across the stubble on his jaw, and it sounds exactly, *exactly*, like sawing wood. He's even going to get off the Paxil, which makes like an empty space underneath your consciousness. Gives the other shit a boost, too.

"Thank heaven for little mercies." She looks at her watch. Man's watch. "I still don't quite—you were visiting somebody here?"

"Long story." He thumbs up the lid of the creamer thing again. Lets it down without a sound.

"I don't want to know, do I?" She checks the watch again. "Now what about your job? Do you need to call them? I assume this is a working day."

"Hey, it works for me," he says. "Joke."

"All right. I've done my duty," she says. "I guess I should tell you, I called Elaine. I had no idea you were . . ."

"Right," he says. "Actually, you know what I actually want? I actually want waffles." He holds his palms six inches apart to show her the squareness.

"Is there anything you *would* like to talk about?"

He picks up his fork and drags the tines across the paper napkin. "Okay, what movie?"

"What movie *what*?"

He nods. "Think about it."

Sigh. "You know, since your thing isn't until Friday? Why don't we go down to the farm for a couple of days. I'm sure Henry would like to see you."

"What, are you on the pipe?" Actually, he wouldn't mind just staying right here. He looks down at his feet under the table: wet running shoes in a puddle of snowmelt. He'd patched them with Shoe Goo where the soles were separating from the uppers: so much for this, what's the word, this *canard* that he doesn't take care of himself. This duck.

"He *is* your brother," Aunt Lissa says.

The waffles arrive, and Carl mooshes the ball of butter with his fork. "You never guessed my movie."

"I'm afraid I'm not following," she says.

He sucks the fork clean, drags the tines across his napkin again and holds it up so she can see the marks.

"Wait," she says. "This *is* ringing a bell."

"Should." He puts the napkin in his lap. "You took me to see it. Film series they used to have?"

She claps her hands. "Of course." Shakes her head. "What could I have been thinking of? You were all of what?" She watches him pour syrup. "If I could have just a bite," she says, "I'd be your friend for life."

When they get to the car, Aunt Lissa paws in her purse, then looks in the window. "I *knew* I left the keys in the switch," she says. "Is your side locked?"

"You don't have a spare?"

"Actually, I—oh. *Damn it.* It's under the hood, and of course you can't—oh. This is *so* exasperating. Well, there's a gas station." He looks where she's looking. Sunoco: sky blue, sun yellow. "Maybe they have a slim jim."

He looks at her. "How do you know about slim jims?"

"I've done this before," she says. "Don't ever get old."

"Yeah, I wouldn't worry."

"Oh pooh. Just because—oh, I don't know. We don't have time for this discussion now."

"Thank heaven for little mercies," he says. "You want me to go over?"

She looks at him. "It's nice of you, dear. But I think I'd better."

Aunt Lissa's driving him down the Thruway into the snow country. It's the pea-soup Volvo Uncle Martin bought the year he died, and she still steers strong-handed, chin jutting. She'd looked older when she showed up at the jail, but now she's settled back into Aunt Lissa. Drunk driving. Which is the most incredible joke in the world because he was just drinking to try to ease down off the other shit.

In fact, wasn't it right along here somewhere, near the exit for Coxsackie? He had Hot Country Radio going because the Best of the Sixties Seventies and Eighties started playing *Here come old flattop,* which was *not* a helpful song when you just wanted words that hooked up to something. Once he caught himself watching for the place where the Big Bang happened, except that was actually on the Connecticut Turnpike, near exit 63. Meanwhile he was working on a theory that if he could make it as far as Kingston he'd be okay. He had a bottle of Old Crow between his thighs, sticking up like a peepee, or a tepee—you know, as in "sticking up like a tent pole"—which he put there precisely *because* it was a joke. Here, he'll spell it out: being drunk fucks up your sexual performance. When the cop pulled him over, he turned the radio off but decided that hiding the bottle would look furtive. The cop said, *And do you know how fast you were going, Carl?* And Carl said, *I think I got carried away by the radio,* which was *not* a surreal saying but just the very, very traditional association of up tempos with driving fast. He pointed at the radio as evidence. The cop said, *You were going thirty miles an hour.*

Black trees stick up out of the white hillsides. Sky seems white, too. He closes one eye and looks from hills to sky, then back again. Maybe what it is, the sky is a darker white? Aunt Lissa's telling him, again, the story of how she and Uncle Martin came to buy the place in Germantown. The house just *spoke to her,* that's her formulation, so they stopped and an old woman came to the door. *We were admiring your house and just decided to stop and tell you so.* And the old woman said, *Well, it happens to be for sale, and my son is coming tomorrow to put a sign up.* They bought the house, Henry bought the hill.

Carl thinks Aunt Lissa might actually have turned *into* that old woman, but actually that might be just to scare himself. As a kid, he used to scare himself thinking that his mother, to keep from dying, had quick turned herself into Aunt Lissa when she saw that his father was steering them across the divider. Since his mother and Aunt Lissa were sisters, it looked believable. He used to watch Aunt Lissa's face and see his mother in there, coming and going.

They take the exit for Catskill and Cairo and pass an abandoned cinder-block store with plywood in the windows and a Henry Craig Realty sign. "Hammerin' Hank," Carl says. "Now, that has to make you proud." Zero reaction.

Aunt Lissa stops at Price Chopper, then takes him into Ames, where he picks out a three-pack of Fruit of the Loom briefs, three black Fruit of the Loom pocket tees, a gray hooded sweatshirt, 90–10 cotton-polyester, which is incredible for just some mystery brand, a package of white socks and a pair of Wrangler blue jeans. The darker blue to last him longer. Aunt Lissa says she'll treat him but he says No, no, he has money, like flipping away his cigarette before the firing squad.

Coming around the last corner, he tries to see if he can tell independently what it was about the house that *spoke to her.* It'll be a way to test his—let's say this exactly—his *congruence.* He squints and says in his mind, *Okay now what exactly is the charming thing here?* Like, *There are x number of bunnies hidden in this picture, can you find them?* Could it be the wooden gingerbread along the porch? No, because "form follows function" is a major thing in world esthetics, and Aunt Lissa takes the train down for shows at the Modern. Yet olden fanciness is also a thing; she gardens with heirloom varieties. See, this is the kind of shit he needs to be able to sort out again.

She parks by the kitchen door, then reaches under and yanks the hood release. "Fool me twice, shame on me. Could you get the groceries?" She lifts the hood and pulls a magnetic hide-a-key box off the engine block. "Voilà." Closes the hood and tucks the hide-a-key up under the front bumper. "There. You don't think anybody would look there, do you?"

"*I* wouldn't," he says.

Up the hill behind Aunt Lissa's house, Henry's lights are on and white smoke snake-charms out of his metal chimney. Can you actually own a *hill*? Half a hill, really, but it's like the moon in that no one sees the side that's turned away. Down low in the sky, there's a thing of orange that tints the whole snow. He takes the grocery bags, follows Aunt Lissa onto the screened-in porch and stands shivering while she rattles a key in the storm door. "We never used to lock up," she says. If this were a movie scene, you'd cut right here.

He closes the door behind him and rubs his feet on the hairy brown mat. That old-refrigerator smell of an empty house in winter. Aunt Lissa clomps in her flopping rubber boots to the thermostat and the house goes bump; then she clomps into the kitchen. Carl hears water running. The *foomp* of a lighted burner.

She comes back in, rubbing the knuckles of one hand, then the other. "It should warm up soon," she says. "I keep the downstairs at fifty." She pulls a chair over to the register. "I put water on for tea."

"You have coffee?"

"Instant."

He makes a cross with his index fingers.

"It's terrible for you anyway." She sits down, still wearing her coat. "Supposed to be a full moon tonight. I hope it doesn't cloud over again."

"*When the moon is in the sky, tell me what am I,*" he sings, "*to do?*"

"Wait, I *know* that song," she says.

"So what movie?" He thinks he hears a car, gets up and goes to the window. A Grand Cherokee's pulling up behind the Volvo, headlights beaming, grille a toothy smile. "Huh. Looks like a small businessman."

"Be nice."

The headlights go out, the car door opens. "Yep," he says. "Big as life and twice as natural."

Aunt Lissa turns on the porch light. There's Henry wiping his feet.

"I saw you drive in, so I thought I'd stop down," Henry says. "Carl?" Quick look at Carl.

"Yo, mah buvva," Carl says. "You keepin' it real, yo?" Henry cocks his head. "You know," Carl says. "Like real estate."

"I'm not up on my jive talk." Henry turns to Aunt Lissa. "Why don't you come on up to the house while it's getting warm in here? Connie's making soup."

"Yum," Aunt Lissa says. "We might stop up later. How about some tea? I just put water on."

Henry twists the sleeve of his leather jacket. "So how'd it go?"

"Well, I suppose it was fine," Aunt Lissa says. "I don't have a lot in my experience to compare it to."

"Hell, I should have done this."

"But you had your closing. It was perfectly fine."

Henry looks at Carl. "So what were *you* doing up this way?"

Carl looks at the tabletop. Honey oak with flamelike grain. "I don't know, long story."

"Aren't they all. Hell happened to your face?"

Carl shakes his head.

"Christ," Henry says. "Shouldn't he be back in detox?"

"I hate to do it," Aunt Lissa says.

"He goes up in front of a judge in this kind of shape, they'll do it *for* you."

"I think what Carl needs most is just to get some rest," she says.

"*I* think what Carl needs most," Carl says, "is a good old pop of Demerol. Speaking as Carl."

The way he knows Henry heard this, something jumps in that fat throat. "Well they're probably going to want him in some kind of a program."

"Hey, *Teletubbies,*" Carl says. "That's actually an incredibly cool show."

Now Henry looks at him. "I'm glad this amuses you, Carl."

Aunt Lissa gets up, so the thing that's been going on for a while now must be the whistling teakettle. Good that it's *something*. "Now what's anybody's pleasure?" she says. "We have Earl Grey, plain old Lipton's, chamomile . . . green tea?" Sad: back when she used to read him *The Tale of Peter Rabbit,* she said camo-*myle*.

"Actually, I better hit it back up the hill." Henry looks out the window. "Looks like it's starting again."

"Sorry, this is kind of getting to me," Carl says and goes into the kitchen, where steam's whistling out of the little pisshole. He takes the kettle off the burner and the noise stops.

"Lissa," he hears Henry say, "are you sure you're up to this?" Or maybe he said "listen."

"Oh for heaven's sake," she says.

He hears the door close, and Aunt Lissa comes into the kitchen. "You had to show off for him."

"He's a dick. Pardon the expression." Carl hears the Cherokee start up, and he looks out the window: snowflakes fluttering through headlight beams.

"I know the expression," she says. "Now help me put this stuff away."

"Is that a denial?" he says.

"You," she says, "are wicked."

The way all this current shit started, he'd gotten involved with a person who was also from Albany—actually Schenectady—and when they'd been together a couple of days, she'd thought up this idea. Rent a car, both get as much cash as possible from their cash machines (this was like a Saturday night), buy whatever they could buy, drive up to her parents' house, her parents being in Florida, and sell it at a major markup to all these people she still knew. This was a very young person: cigarette smoker, chopped-off hair bleached white. Tiny stud in her left nostril that looked like a blackhead and seven gold rings around her left ear; nothing in her right. So when she went on modeling jobs she could give them two different looks.

She was temping, filling in for somebody's assistant. Carl at this point was sort of not living at home anymore, staying with people, carrying his laptop and a duffel bag with clothes and DVDs: *42nd Street, Spellbound, The Maltese Falcon, It's a Wonderful Life*—you know, the Western Canon. What was weird, he didn't feel weird. This was thanks to the Paxil, which he was now getting through two doctors at two drugstores, because the Oxford doctor had said forty milligrams was "rather a lot." And he was using again on top of it, but not big-time, and mostly to help him write: he'd been posting stuff about *42nd Street* on this actually really very serious Web site.

> any dickhead can see that dorothy brock (bebe daniels) is the same person as peggy sawyer (ruby keeler), but the scrim of gender may prevent said dickhead from discerning that julian marsh (warner baxter) is also mutatis mutandis a projection of the "sweet" sawyer's nut-cutting inner self, the very name suggesting she'd "saw off" your "peg" to get "a leg up," it being no accident that brock's "broken" (note further pun) leg is sawyer's big "break."

He told the temp with the things in her ear that there were all too few outlaws on the seventeenth floor, and he said Albany was their shared shame. Then she was bold enough to show up at the Christmas party when she'd only worked there a week. He said could he get her a drink—he was on like number three—and she said, "So how much of an outlaw *are* you?" He held up his left hand, worked his ring off and said, "Observe me closely." He pinched the ring between thumb and forefinger, showed her both sides, put it in his mouth and swallowed. It scraped going down, but no worse than swallowing, say, a hard candy. And it would, in theory, be recoverable. He chased it with a last swallow, put his glass down and pulled his cheeks open with his forefingers. She ignored this, looked in his glass, then looked at him. "How did you do that? Let me see your hands."

Anyhow, you'll never guess what happened: they ended up using most of the shit themselves. They pretty much stayed in her parents' bed, watching cable, DVDs on Carl's laptop and a video called *Barely 18* that her father kept duct-taped up inside his radial saw. And *Monday Night Football*, which is how they figured out it was now Monday, or had been Monday. Carl called his supervisor's voice mail and said he had the flu. This Kerri—he'd briefly thought the *i* was a turn-on—called whoever's voice mail it was and said she had food poisoning. Carl pointed out how stupid this was: she'd have to come up with something else tomorrow. And she said, Well, it would've been nice if he'd said that before.

They'd gotten like two of their eight hundred dollars back when they had this fight—*literally* a fight, where she was hitting him and he hurt her wrists trying to hold her and she told him, *Get the fuck out, just get the fuck out.* She'd dug it that it took him forever to come—the Paxil plus the other shit made an orgasm just too high to climb up to—and then she stopped digging it. *I don't like you, I don't know you.* She hit first, remember that. He grabbed her wrists with both hands, found he didn't have a third hand to hit her with, then tried to get both her wrists in one hand so he'd have a hand free, and she broke loose and hit again, *Get out get out,* in the middle of the night, middle of the afternoon, actually.

So he got in his car and made it onto the main drag, just barely, where he pulled into some non-Dunkin' donut place, like an indie donut place, guided the car between yellow lines and closed his eyes: it looked like when they score a touchdown and the flash cameras go off. No way he could drive all the way back to New York like this. Had to get something to take the edge off, and he had no idea where you went in Albany anymore. Actually, Aunt Lissa would put up, but he was in no shape to deal with her: she was in the sort of space where she'd be "hurt" if he'd "come to town and didn't call." He had an incredibly scary thought that it was actually her in the car next to him, but he nerved himself to look and it was just one of those Winnie-the-Pooh things.

He went in and bought a fat old sugar donut, which he thought might weight him down, take him earthward, but the shit he'd been snorting made it taste nasty, and he spit the mouthful into a napkin. Though in all fairness, maybe it really did taste nasty. At least there must be a liquor store open, unless it was already Sunday again.

Morning sun on snow. Clean blue sky.

Carl's sitting at the kitchen table looking out the window. Aunt Lissa's gone to town for the paper and left him with what she biblically called "tea with milk and honey," though it's hard to trust its dimensionality: it appears to be a flat khaki disc fitted into the cup. Halfway up the hill, Henry's house hangs off like the house in *North by Northwest.* Snow clings along the tops of the tree branches in simplified versions of their shapes, and dead apples, like dog-toy balls, hang from the leafless apple tree. Some have a curve of snow on top, like a phase of the moon.

When he hears Aunt Lissa's car, he gets up and turns her radio back on. The *diddle-diddle-dum* morning Baroque had been sounding too much like thoughts racing. What we've got now is some sprightly guitar piece. Almost certainly not a harp.

She sets the *Times* before him, like the dainty dish before the king. "Voilà," she says. "Glorious morning out." She drapes her coat over the back of a chair. "Now what would you like? I can fix pancakes, we have oatmeal . . ."

He shakes his head, holds up a hand.

"Toast? You can't not eat."

"Let me guess. Is breakfast the most important meal, do you think?"

"Stop."

"What about the importance of dietary fiber?" That was when he remembered about the ring. Long gone. Must be.

"You're welcome to sit here and make witticisms to yourself," she says. "I've got to work on my presentation." Aunt Lissa's reading group is doing *To the Lighthouse* next week.

"Don't we all," he says.

He manages to hold back from retching until he hears her on the stairs, then gags up nothing and feels sweat popping out of his face. After a while, he stands up and sees how that feels. He scrunches up a slice of bread in his fist to make a bolus and eats it just for something solid. Then pops his Paxil and puts his mouth under the faucet. The cops got a hard-on when they found the Paxil, of course—*And what's this, Carl?*—but they had to give it back. Actually, he really needs just to get off absolutely every-thing and just purify, purify, purify. On the other hand, don't the laws of physics suggest that all this not-unhappiness will have to be paid for by an equal and opposite period of negative happiness, an equal distance below the baseline? Lately he's big on that thing about being nice to the right people on the way up because you're going to meet them again on the way down, "people" meaning entities in your mind.

He goes back up to the guest room to lie down again. For a nightstand, she's put a lamp on a small mission bookshelf that she's stocked with light reading. He picks out *Try and Stop Me*, by Bennett Cerf, and stacks the two pillows against the headboard. The idea is what, that Bennett Cerf has so many stories you better not try to stop him? Carl's studying a cartoon of Dorothy Parker hurling a giant pen like a javelin when Aunt Lissa knocks on his open door.

"I was going through some pictures the last time I came down here." She holds up an envelope. "I pulled these out to have them copied for you, and then of course I forgot all about them. Don't ever get old."

"Yeah, you warned me about that." He claps hands, then holds them out, meaning *throw it*. She comes over and hands it to him.

He flips through with Aunt Lissa in his peripheral vision. The one of him as a baby, held by his mother wearing a black dress and pearl necklace, his father in a tuxedo, grinning a Mr. Skeleton grin, his fingers making a V behind her head. The one of Uncle Martin pitching to him in the back-yard in Albany, when he was like eleven and had Henry's old Hank Aaron bat, with *Hank* in quotes. The one of him at six, in that red flannel cow-boy shirt with the white pinstripes and slant pockets. Chubby cheeks. Little heartbreaker.

"*These* cover the waterfront," he says, still looking at that last one. "Incredible."

"Now you can't have them until I make copies."

"I don't know where I'd even keep them at this point."

"Well, they'll be here. You know, it's *such* a glorious day. You really should go out and get some fresh air."

Outside, the cold makes his face sting, but he can feel no difference to his body thanks to Uncle Martin's old Eddie Bauer coat. Maybe she'll give it to him: that thing where you have a hooded sweatshirt under a denim jacket doesn't really cut it. He walks as far as the corner, to the house with the sign on the lawn that says STOP THE DREDGING. It's about the Hudson River.

Walking back to Aunt Lissa's he now sees something else that could have spoken to her: that vine that—losing the word here—*ornates?* that ornates the porch in summertime and is now this brown wirelike arrange-ment clinging to the chalky posts. Does green somehow seep back up into it, or could a whole new vine grow quickly enough to replace it every year? Both seem impossible, yet one must be true. But he remembers the name: Dutchman's-pipe. Now that's something that hangs together: when he was a kid, Uncle Martin used to have this expression for a hopeful patch of blue among the clouds, *enough to make a Dutchman a pair of britches*. It gave you the idea of big people living in the sky.

When the phone rings, he's back looking at *Try and Stop Me*. He can't really follow the anecdotes, but he's into the cartoons. In one, captioned "Mankiewicz en riposte," a smirking man removes a cigarette from his mouth and blows a cloud of smoke with an arrow in it at a quailing man.

The anecdote presumably would make clear whether we're talking Joe or Herman. See? Carl cold knows this shit.

Aunt Lissa calls, "Carl? For you." He gets up off the bed, pads out into the hall with socks sliding on the glossy floor and looks down the stairs at her looking up. "Elaine."

The wall phone in the kitchen in still the only phone in the house. Aunt Lissa's going to break her neck some night coming down those stairs. Because of the socks, he's extra careful himself.

"Carl. Hi. I just wanted to make sure you were okay."

"Oh yeah. You know, thanks."

"Lissa called me yesterday. Apparently she didn't know that, you know . . ."

"Right," he says.

"I hope you didn't mind that I told her."

"No, no. God no." He picks up Aunt Lissa's egg timer. Such an amazing touch, giving the Wicked Witch red sand. "So," he says. Like, *To what do we owe the pleasure?*

"I really didn't call because I want anything," she says.

"Right." He sees something move out the side window and puts the egg timer down. Just a gray squirrel across the snow.

"So are you using again? Or just drinking?"

"Neither one. You know, to any degree." He picks it up again.

"Well, so how come they busted you?"

"Oh, you know. Just a stupid thing. Open container."

"I heard it was a little more than that."

"Well, you know. They throw in the kitchen sink to make it sound really dire."

"Right," she says. He would actually like to steal this egg timer. Whip it out at parties. "Did I tell you somebody called about the guitar?"

"And?"

"He wanted to know if you'd take less."

"Like how much?" He puts the egg timer back, sand side down, like a good boy.

"He didn't really say. I've got his number here."

"Look, why don't you just call him, get whatever you can get and keep the money, you know? I mean, I owe you for this month and last month, plus the—"

"Okay, look," she says, "let's not worry about the money for now."

"Right." But Carl heard that *for now*, don't think he didn't.

When he wakes up, out of a dream involving King Tut's tomb, he smells something yummy. It's like a famous smell, but he can't come up with the name. Not coriander—much more household. He goes down to the kitchen.

"You must have needed that nap," Aunt Lissa says. Something's hissing in the skillet. Onion! She gets under with the spatula. Hiss louder. "I thought I'd make a quiche to take up."

"Oh. So."

"Connie asked us for around seven."

"Cool."

"I know it's not the most comfortable thing for you."

"You figured that out," he says.

"I must say, they *have* been wonderful."

"In all fairness," he says.

She pokes a fingernail through the plastic that covers—like a bouquet—the parsley on a styrofoam tray and plows it open. *Nosegay?* "You know, I've often thought we made a mistake keeping Henry at Mount Hermon after the accident. If we'd brought him back to Albany to finish high school, maybe you two would've had a better chance at . . ." She takes the parsley over to the sink.

"Bonding?" he says.

"It's easy to make light of it."

"Yeah, I guess I'm just a merry Andrew," he says. "Like a merry widow."

She turns the water on and begins washing the parsley.

"God, I'm sorry," he says. "I didn't mean anything by that."

"I do all right," she says.

He watches her dry the parsley in a dish towel.

"So when I get this in the oven," she says, "what do you say we try on that suit? You'll want to look as respectable as we both know you really are."

"Now that hurt," he says.

She laughs, a girl-laugh. "What are we going to do with you?"

Up in her bedroom, she opens the closet door and pushes jingling hangers to the side. "I gave his suits to Goodwill, but he kept this one down here just in case." She holds up a gray suit with fat lapels.

"I hear these are coming back," Carl says.

"Never you mind. Let's see the jacket on you."

Carl puts the jacket on. Tight in his armpits and across the shoulders, sleeves too short. She lifts the pants up to his front. "Well," she says.

"They've obviously mistaken me for a much shorter man," Carl says.

"Maybe I can let the cuffs down," she says. "We'll make this work."

By seven o'clock it's already down in the zeros, but Aunt Lissa insists they walk up the hill. Carl puts on the Eddie Bauer, Aunt Lissa hands him the quiche to carry, and they step out into the cold. She doesn't know he found that vodka under the kitchen sink, so he keeps his distance from her. Sky's so incredibly clear there looks to be nothing between you and the stars, as if "the atmosphere" were an exploded theory like phlogiston.

"Jim!" he says when Henry opens the door. "They didn't tell me *you* were here. It was *grand* of you to come."

Henry says, "Let's not let the cold in, shall we?"

"Where can I put this?" Carl says.

"What is it?"

"I thought I'd make a quiche," Aunt Lissa says.

"Christ, you didn't have to do that." Henry holds out his hands. "Should it go in the oven?"

"Wouldn't hurt just to warm it up," Aunt Lissa says.

Aunt Lissa takes one end of the couch, Carl takes the other. Over on the sideboard, glass decanters with silver tags like good doggies: SCOTCH, RYE, BRANDY. At different levels, but all the same amber.

Connie comes in from the kitchen, wearing black leggings as if she were a slim person, and a big sweater that comes way down. "Lissa, that was so nice of you. Carl? Good to see you too?" She bends down to give Lissa a kiss, and Carl can't help but see her movieolas swing forward.

"Now what can I get anybody? Tea? Hot chocolate?"

"I wouldn't mind just a touch of that port you had the other night," Aunt Lissa says. "But I bet Carl would take you up on the hot chocolate."

"Yeah, let's go crazy," Carl says. That vodka could use a booster, but he can bide his time. Shit, if he gets a second alone in here, he can tip up a decanter.

"Carl, you haven't changed a bit," Connie says.

"Me either," Carl says. She gets a look on her face like, *What?*

They eat while watching *Who Wants to Be a Millionaire;* Connie says she's *totally hooked on it.* It's a new one on Carl, but he likes the thing where the host guy and the person are sitting across from each other in the middle of space, and the damned-soul voices are going *Ah ah ah.* There's a question where, was Mata Hari a spy during *(a)* World War I, *(b)* World War II, *(c)* the Vietnam War or *(d)* the Gulf War? The person says, *(b)* World War II, and Aunt Lissa says it amazes her what people don't know. Henry says it amazes him what people *do* know, like when they get onto those questions about rock bands. Talking Heads, that was his last new band. And that's got to be how many years now? Connie wants to know, what exactly *is* trivia? Because to one person it may be trivial, but. When the show's over, Henry gets out the cards for gin rummy and asks what would anybody like. A touch more of that port for Aunt Lissa, Diet Coke for Connie, same for Carl. Henry gets himself a glassful of ice and pours in SCOTCH. Carl is absolutely fine with this. If nothing else, he'll eventually get another crack at that vodka. He fans his cards out and holds them up to his face for a sneaky smell of them.

At ten o'clock, Henry puts on the news. Big fire in Albany, hoses arching icy rooster tails in the dark and a young woman talking into a microphone and blowing out white breath. "The apparent cause?" she says. "A faulty heating unit."

"A faulty crack pipe," Henry says.

"Now you don't know that," Connie says.

"I know that part of *town.*"

She gets up. "I better put that stuff in the dishwasher."

Aunt Lissa gets up, too. "Let me give you a hand."

Now there's a thing about the dredging, people in parkas outside some building holding signs. "Those GE fuckers have got the yahoos stirred up," Henry says. "The money they spent buying ads, they could've cleaned *up* the fucking PCBs."

"Wait, so you think they *should* dig up the river?" Carl had assumed Henry was a Republican.

"What do you, just let sleeping dogs lie? That philosophy hasn't gotten *you* too far. Your thing is tomorrow, right?"

"10 A.M."

"Well, I guess if you manage not to lose your shit in front of the judge, they'll let you off with a fine. Yank your license, of course."

"I don't plan to lose my shit," Carl says.

"They're going to want cash probably. How much you have with you?"

"Couple hundred." That was before the clothes.

"Got to be more than that," Henry says. "So you were going to do what? To hit *her* up?" Tosses his head in the direction of the kitchen. "Look, call my office. Here." Lifts a hip as if to fart, digs out his wallet, hands Carl a card. "Or call my cell. I'll probably be out showing. That's got all my numbers. Let me know how much to bring, and I'll drive up myself."

"You're kidding. Well. Thanks." Carl looks at the card, then reaches up under his sweatshirt and puts it in his T-shirt pocket.

"Yeah. So I'm assuming that you don't need to be here past tomorrow. Correct?"

"I honestly haven't been thinking."

"Well, why don't you honestly get cracking and *do* a little thinking. I mean, I know you're the one damaged soul in God's green universe."

Carl gives him the finger, but Aunt Lissa's coming in from the kitchen and he converts it to scratching his nose. "We should think about getting down the hill," she says to Henry. "We need to be there by ten."

Henry gets up. "Well, let me run you down."

"The air'll do us good. Do *me* good, anyway. That last glass of port was the bridge too far."

"Then you should definitely let me drive you."

"Oh pooh," she says. She crooks her elbow at Carl. "I've got my protector here."

When they get outside, the moon's up: big, round, alarming. Carl says, "George Lassos Moon. You remember she draws the picture?"

Aunt Lissa stops walking. "This looks a little slippery through here," she says. "Could I have your arm till we get past this part?"

Carl raises his right elbow and feels her hands clamp around the puffy sleeve. He takes a couple of baby steps: now she's got *him* worried. "So what movie?" he says. "Easy one."

"Carl, I'm sorry," she says. "I've had enough for one night."

The sun's on their right as they head up to Albany. Carl's pulled the visor over, but he can't face too far left because he had a couple of pulls at that bottle of vodka when Aunt Lissa went up to brush her teeth; he's opened his window a crack to let out fumes. He also thought to pour his Paxils into an envelope and fill up the vial; only a shot, but it could come in handy. Another blinding-sunny day. Too warm to wear the Eddie Bauer; it's draped over his seat back. The pavement's wet and Aunt Lissa has to keep squirting fluid and using the wipers to clear salt spatter.

"I wonder," she says. "Do you remember much about when you first came to live with us?"

"Yeah, I remember thinking it was weird that all my stuff was there but it was the wrong room," he says, at the windshield. "And that incredible wallpaper. The bucking broncos."

"Now that," she says, "was Martin's idea," and he knows the whole rest word for word. *I remember he came* "I remember he came back from the store with the rolls under his arm, and he said," *Now this is what* "Now this is what a six-year-old boy would like."

"Right." Aunt Lissa's spin on the whole thing has always been that she and Martin just picked up where his parents left off, as if it deeply made no difference who anybody was.

She does another wiper thing.

"You know," Carl says, "I don't think in all these years I've ever even said I appreciated what you guys did?"

She takes her eyes off the road long enough to stare at him. "You can't be serious. I still have that lovely letter you wrote the day you graduated from high school."

"That," he says. "Yeah. Well, I guess the point is, here I am again."

"This too shall pass," she says. "I'm only glad that I'm still able to help."

"What, the son you never had?" He says this by way of experiment, to see how it would feel to go just the opposite way and be a total shit.

"I imagine there's something of that." Aunt Lissa smiles, shakes her head. "Do you want to *really* talk?"

"Probably not," he says.

Sign for the New Baltimore Service Area.

"I need to use the rest room," she says. "Shall we get you some coffee? They have a Starbucks now."

"I thought it was bad for you."

"You *told* me I was an enabler," she says. "You know, you still make the mistake of thinking you can see everyone and no one can ever see you. It was cute when you were six."

He shades his eyes and looks out his window below the visor. A farm-house with a cinder-block chimney goes by.

"Have you thought what you're going to do?" she says.

"I guess take a bus back to the city." Make some calls to see who he might be able to stay with.

"I mean in the longer term."

"Oh, that. Yeah, I thought I'd run for Congress. Mah fellameri-cans . . ."

"Give me strength," she says. "You and Elaine have been married what, two years?"

"Give or take."

"Well, isn't there a chance that . . . ? I don't know. I've hardly met Elaine." She swings left to pass an ass-dragging station wagon, black Lab pacing in the wayback behind a dog gate, then into the right lane again.

"Well, I *would* say, come up and stay with me until things get straight-ened out." Shakes her head no. "It's not that you're not welcome."

"But what would Henry say."

"Henry can say whatever he damn well pleases." She sighs. "He'd be right."

In the service area, she parks next to a Sidekick with four cross-country skis on the roof rack. A leg sticks out the driver's window: sheathed in metallic blue, foot wearing some robot sneaker. It's a pretty woman with iridescent blue sunglasses and big blond kinky hair, tipping a flat silver flask into her mouth. She sees him looking and lifts the flask by way of a toast. Carl can't read this. Outlaw recognition? Or to scandalize, mistaking him for what he must look like? Light blue oxford shirt, maroon tie, gray suit.

Aunt Lissa, getting out of the car, misses the whole transaction. "Aren't you coming in?"

"I'll just hang."

He watches her go inside, then gets out of the car. "Cheers," he says. He takes the pill vial out of his pocket, pries the cap off and drains the fucker. The woman draws in her leg, and up goes her window.

He goes around to the front of Aunt Lissa's car, squats, feels behind the bumper and plucks away the little metal box. Then walks over to the Side-kick and circles his fist counterclockwise. The woman puts the window halfway down.

"How about I race you to New York?" he says. "Loser buys the first round."

"I'm waiting for my friend," she says. "Plus, you're going the wrong way."

"So I'll race you to what? Lake Placid."

She puts up her window.

"Bitch," he says. But again just experimentally, like pretending to be somebody who'd hit on a woman and then call her bitch.

He gets into the driver's seat, his bottom warmed by leftover heat from Aunt Lissa's bottom, and sticks the key in the switch. If he really does this, all she actually needs to do is go back inside and call Henry. Henry of course will make her call the police, call the police himself, so you'd want to get off at the next exit and take back roads down. Be a good joe and leave her car at the train station in Poughkeepsie.

Experimentally, he backs out of the parking space. Puts it in drive, turns left, toward the entrance ramp, stops, puts it in park and races the engine, playing with how it would feel. Feels incredible.

Heidi Jon Schmidt

Blood Poison

from *Epoch*

"**Y**OU PROBABLY don't believe this is my daughter," my father said to the cabdriver. "You're wondering: Where did a broken-down old guy like him come up with a gal like that?"

It was only an hour since I'd gotten off the train and already my father had explained to two strangers that we weren't having an affair. The first was the bartender at the Oyster Bar, where Pop had pulled out my stool as if New York was his overcoat and he was spreading it over a puddle for me. The bartender looked as if he had long since stopped seeing individual faces or thinking of anything except whatever he himself was obsessed with—money or football or his prostate or maybe some kind of love or ideal. He nodded without listening, dealing out some packets of crackers like cards. The place was full—of men and women who looked busier and more purposeful than I'd ever been—and the chalkboard listed oysters named for all the places I'd have felt more at home: Cotuit, Wellfleet, Chincoteague—low-tide towns where the few people left behind through the winter huddled in the souvenir shop doorways, stamping their feet and swearing under the clouds of their breath.

To the bartender I'd given an apologetic smile, which went, of course, unnoticed. Ahmed Sineduy, license number 0017533, cried "Yes!" with wonderful enthusiasm, as if he had indeed been trying to imagine what would attract me to my father.

"In fact," Pop crowed, "I *created* her!"

I'd convinced him to have a drink at lunch—a mistake, but I wanted one myself. He makes me nervous—I don't know him very well. He and my mother married young, and after I was born he drifted away, taking long and longer visits to his mother in the city until finally we noticed that he was living with her and visiting us. I'd study the New York news every night, first thinking I might see him, later that if I came to understand the city, I'd get a sense of my father, too. Phrases like "truck rollover in the Midtown Tunnel" were invested with incalculable glamour for me, and when people spoke of the Queensboro Bridge or the East River they might as well have been talking about the Great Obelisk of Shalmanezar and the Red Sea.

Twice a year my mother put me on the train to the city so I could spend the weekend with him. In my grandmother's apartment it was still 1945, and I pushed the mother-of-pearl buttons on the radio set, expecting to hear FDR, while Pop made supper and Grammy offered me hoarded bits of chocolate and cake. We tried to act familiar, which meant we couldn't ask the kind of questions that might have helped us figure each other out, and year after year the distance grew. If Pop was doing well in the market he talked a mile a minute, spreading out maps and showing me pictures of the houses—sometimes whole islands—he meant to buy. When he was losing he was silent, and would start out of his trance every few minutes to ask how I was doing in school. As soon as I could I'd escape to the guest room, pull the velvet drapes, and fold myself into the heavy bed linens, where in my fantasies some man as commanding and enveloping as Zeus the swan held me in the tightest grip you can imagine, while all the lights of the city whirled over our heads.

So, yes, I was an overheated child, and so fervid an adolescent I became accustomed to seeing my teachers squirm and look away from me, praying I'd go elsewhere for the extra help next time. By college the pedagogical discomfort was happily transformed, and there was no end to the office hours available for a girl whose palpitating heart was quite nearly visible through her blouse. How I loved school!

With my father I keep my hair shaken down over my eyes like a dog, though I still come twice a year to visit. It pleases him to think of himself as a father, and God has damned me to try and please him. When my mother gave up her quest to draw him back to us and started the divorce, he sobbed like a lost little boy. And now that my grandmother's dead, I'm the only family he has.

This time I was even "on business"—I was flying to Cincinnati in the morning for a job interview—a Visiting Assistant Professor job of the sort that a person like me would be very lucky to have; a job I needed to escape a debilitating love: a professor, of course, my Louis—an authority on Balzac, about whom no one else gives a damn. When I first met him he was railing at some translator's disrespect for an original text, and I remember thinking that he was *really angry,* that a crime against meaning was no less brutal to him than a physical assault. Needless to say I threw myself at him, and at Balzac. I swam through *The Human Comedy* as if it were a river I had to cross to reach him, but when I reached the other shore he was gone. By then I'd studied long enough to see Louis had such feeling for literature because ordinary life seemed so empty to him. And I was the very emissary of the ordinary—eating, bleeding, laughing, et cetera—a constant reminder of how much better Balzac had done than God. Louis began to inflict little cruelties, insults and condescensions, like cigarette burns, wherever he knew I was tender, and I slowly found myself entirely absorbed in these wounds—with each I became sicker, but it seemed an ailment only Louis's gentle care could cure. In a minute of clarity I realized I'd have to tear myself out of his life by the roots, and taking a job in a distant city looked like the surest way.

The cab zipped uptown, switching lanes and skirting bike messengers and double-parked delivery trucks with an ease I should have found alarming, but I leaned back. I had faith in Ahmed. As long as he was talking to my father I was safe.

"Seventy-nine?" Ahmed asked.

"Fifty-six and a half!" my father replied. His age.

"Fifty-six?" Ahmed hit the brake. We were already somewhere in the Sixties.

"Seventy-ninth Street," I said. "Museum of Natural History." Natural History in springtime; in September, the Met. Once, when I was maybe ten, we tried something different, a piano concert at Lincoln Center. I had a velvet dress, and Pop kept whispering things about the music to me, pointing out the movements in a concerto, praising the pianist's fine technique. He had never said a word about music before, and certainly I'd never heard him speak with rapture—he was trying to impress me, I realized—he wanted my esteem. And I tried—I worked at admiring him the way a doubting priest works at faith.

"But you must see plenty of men out with girls who aren't their daughters," he was saying to Ahmed, thinking perhaps of Louis, who's fifty-three. "It happens all the time."

He made it sound like a horror: something too awful to think about, like a child crushed under a bus or chained in a basement, one of the travesties he absorbs out of the paper, and can't stop talking about, almost as if he'd suffered them himself. He keeps his eye trained on the pain in the newspaper; he can't bear to look at real life.

He quit his job during the divorce; he couldn't stand to give money to people who rejected him. After that he went into business for himself, borrowing office space from acquaintances, empty desks he could use for a few months or a year, in a cubicle on the eighteenth or twenty-fifth or forty-seventh floor where a couple of sour men smoked cigars and followed the ticker tape all day. Visiting, I'd stand at the window, watching the secretaries gather like pigeons on the pavement below, thinking that someday I'd become one of them and work silently all day among people who took no notice of me. Then we'd go home to Grammy, who still called him Skipper, his childhood name. They fought over trifles as if they were married, but she had no notion of money and was happy as long as he didn't waste food or throw away any reusable string. When she died she left him a pantry full of egg crates and plastic containers, but he had already spent her fortune.

In his new flat on Staten Island, he was perfectly content, he told me again and again. Yes, it faced north, but he wasn't one of these people who had to have sunlight, and what a relief just to cook for himself. It wasn't as if he were isolated—he had the *Times* and fifty-two channels. He would have been amazed to realize that the pretty morning news anchor he admired was younger than I was, that if he were to meet her by one of the fabulous accidents he imagined, he, too, would be "out with a girl" right now.

"Have any children yourself?" he asked Ahmed, with his salesman's hearty voice.

"Seventy-nine!" Ahmed declared.

"No English," I mouthed to Pop, twice before he understood.

"Aha!" he said. He cleared his throat. He had that tutelary gleam in his eye—he was going to show me how little distance there is between cultures, how much can be accomplished with a smile, a concerned tone. He thought, quite rightly, that I was an awkward, inward girl, in need of social training. Where did Ahmed come from, he asked—Syria? Lebanon? India, perhaps?

When Ahmed said Karachi, my father turned out to have a few words of Punjabi, and an enthusiastic accent, too.

Ahmed burst into speech.

"Whoa, whoa, you're way beyond me!" Pop said. "Slow down, wa-a-a-y down."

By Seventy-ninth Street Ahmed had taught him some basic insults, and the words for *father and daughter.*

"Nice guy," Pop said as the cab fishtailed away from us. "Wish I could have tipped him."

"What did you say to him?" I asked.

"Isn't it a beautiful evening," he told me. "The janitor at the office taught me. He has a wife and three kids back there. . . . He doesn't have much hope of getting them over, but he sends money. . . ."

He sighed so heavily, thinking of this family torn apart, that I was afraid he was going to cry. He's so tall, has such broad shoulders, that when he gets weepy it's like seeing a statue melt. Even now I'll be doing the dishes or walking the dog and I suddenly feel his sadness go through me. I think of him as a little boy, his own father dying—he'll say "when I died," by accident, when he speaks of it—I never know what to do to assuage it, any more than I did when I was ten. One morning back then he told me that my mother didn't want to make love to him anymore. I had only the vaguest idea of what he meant and I sat stupidly over my cinnamon toast searching for something helpful while his lip began to tremble, as if I was his last hope and had failed him.

By now he's so solitary he expects no consolation, and he walked along tightly for a minute, entirely constricted by sadness, and then threw it off with a quick little gesture, like breaking a chain.

"He taught me to say 'Wow, get the legs on that babe,' too," he laughed, holding the door to the automatic teller open for me. There was hardly room for two people in the booth. I edged into the corner while he fed his card to the machine.

"We'll have to see," he said, "Last week they credited me with fifty dollars by mistake. In fact, I'm overdrawn." He punched in his number: 1014, the date of his marriage to my mother.

"I've got money," I said. I was embarrassed how much—Louis never let me help with the rent, so my salary went straight into the bank.

"No, no, honey," he told me. "I think we'll be fine here. I've *been* making money. I started with five thousand and I was doing great all through March—I was up to twenty-five. Then I lost a few thousand last week, a few more Monday, and Friday another seventeen. . . ."

By my math this meant he was broke. I'd guessed it, seeing his posture from the train window as he waited on the platform, and when, over the whole course of lunch, he never spoke of buying any islands at all.

"As long as they didn't catch the error," he said, "we ought to be all right." We heard the rollers inside the machine as they shuffled the bills; then it spat three starched twenties at us through pursed rubber lips.

"The town's ours," said Pop, as if we'd drawn three cherries on a slot machine. His luck was turning, he could feel it. I could hardly keep up with him as he strode back toward the museum.

"Two adults," he said to the cashier, and "Can it really be, you're an adult?" to me, and then, to the cashier again, "She's my daughter. What do you think?"

Her badge read CYNTHIA POST, DOCENT. She had a kind of brisk official grace, and she glanced at me and gave him a perfunctory smile. As I accepted my museum pin from her, I thought that although she might have been unhappy in her life she did not look as if she'd often been confused. She would have spent her whole life here, walking to the museum past her grocery, her florist, her dry cleaner, the school she and her children had attended, the church she had been married in. I regarded her with both condescension and jealousy—I would never belong so squarely to anything. I'd put on a hat that morning because it seems to me that only very confident people wear hats—so that I'd appear to be self-assured—but I felt only foolish and ostentatious, like a child dressed up in her mother's clothes.

My father, of course, looked great. Age has given him the look of dignity, and he takes a professional pleasure in conversation. No one has ever sounded more reasonable, more calm and knowing. If he told you to buy something, you'd buy, or he'd explain it slower, with more stubborn patience, until you did. He solicited Cynthia Post's suggestion of the best exhibit, and as we took the direction she suggested (something interactive in the Rocks and Minerals) her smile was newly warm. Following him down the corridor, one hand on my hat as I tried to keep pace with his stride, I felt for a minute as I used to when I visited: happy and excited just to be in his company, sure that if I could only manage to keep my hand in his he'd pull me around the corner into a new world.

"Did she say the second right, or the third?" he asked me. The hallway ended in three closed doors. Two were locked, so we went through the third and down another long passage toward a sign that read ENTRANCE, which turned out to be one of a pile of ENTRANCE signs stored against another locked door. There was hardly any light and I felt terribly claustrophobic suddenly, as if we were locked here forever. After all the years of visiting museums I'm still never comfortable in one—even in a roomful of Renoirs I long for a window, and the Museum of Natural History, the final repository of moon rocks and extinct sparrows and other small, dun-colored things whose significance one would never believe if it weren't written out for you, always seemed to me the loneliest place in the world. To stand here now with my father was to guess what it might feel like in my grave.

Pop took a credit card out of his wallet and slid it down the doorjamb.

"Voilà!" he said, pushing the door open and ushering me through. "I'm way over the limit on that card anyway," he said.

We were in my favorite room—the dioramas of aboriginal life. It was empty except for us and a troop of black Girl Scouts whose noses were pressed to the glass to see Cro-Magnon man forage and the Vikings set to sea. I peered in over their heads; I love ant colonies, too, and model trains, quattrocento crucifixions—those representations of life where everyone takes part, whether sowing or winnowing, rowing or raising the sail. You never see anyone like me, loitering at the edge of the scene, too fearful to make an effort, wishing only to escape his little glassed-in world.

My father checked his watch. He had done the fatherly thing by bringing me: now what? He turned his attention to the scouts. He's friend to all little girls now, watching them on the street, in the library or the supermarket, befriending them in elevators, smiling down over them with an unbearable nostalgia. Nostalgia for me, I suppose, though, like most nostalgia this was not yearning for something lost but for something that had never been; an old wish so deeply etched into memory that finally it was clear as if real. Every one of these children was the child I might have been—a child who flew off the school bus into her father's arms and who was gentle and delicate, shy and kind. I had been most disappointing, talking too much, laughing too loudly, though "unnaturally" silent with him. He was still saving elephant jokes for me while I was soldiering my pompous twelve-year-old way through *The Feminine Mystique,* and I could tell from his face, when he walked in to find me reading it in the bathtub, that he was certain it must be filth. He stood there looking down at me with his characteristic puzzled, hurt expression, wondering what could be wrong, how I could have become the way I was. "Does your mother know you're reading that?" he asked finally, but he left before I could answer as if he had to get away from me. Even my body was becoming obscene.

Now he looked down over these little girls in their uniforms and berets as if he might find a new daughter among them. Two of them, whispering together, became gradually aware of him and grew silent.

"Why you staring?" one of them asked, sharp as her own mother, I supposed. The mother who had woven those hundred braids and fastened them with red and yellow beads.

"I was wondering which badges you have there," he told her.

She was maybe seven; pride quickly overwhelmed her suspicion. She lifted her sash and began, in a careful, earnest voice, to describe them, pressing a finger to each embroidered circle: there was one for reading, one for learning to swim, one for refusing drugs. He bent to look more closely, asking how she had earned them, expressing amazement that such a small girl could have accomplished such difficult tasks. The whole troop, wary at first, then eager, reconstellated around him.

"Girls?" Their leader fixed a level gaze on them—they had been taught not to take up with strangers, in fact there was a badge for that, too. They turned unwillingly from my father's attention and reformed their line of pairs, holding hands as they went on toward the Bird Room. The one with the red and yellow beads took a last quick glance over her shoulder at us as she left the room.

"It's terrific," he said, watching them. "They're from Paterson. You know what a sewer Paterson is? But that little girl, she looked me right in the eye when I spoke to her, she—"

He broke off. His eyes were brimming.

"If I could find the right woman," he said, "I'd start all over again, and this time it wouldn't be one child, I'd like to have four or five—or six! or seven! I suppose that surprises you . . ." he said with some kind of belligerence.

"Not at all," I said. I'd have been surprised if he didn't dream of such things, but it seems his penance for never having completely entered into marriage is that he can't get completely divorced. He never dated anyone after my mother. He told me once that as a young man he had assumed that husband and wife became, sexually, one being, so that if split, both halves must die. Adultery must then be physically appalling: when a colleague of his had casually mentioned a mistress, my father had begun to retch as if he'd heard of a bestial crime.

"I'm so glad we can *talk* to each other!" he said now. We had come to the Hall of Dinosaurs, and I made a show of studying a stegosaurus spine.

"People have such awful relations with their children these days," he went on. "But I feel there's nothing I wouldn't be comfortable telling you."

I was afraid this might be true, and indeed, a minute later he was feeling comfortable enough to tell me about a sore he had on his back, somewhere near the seventh vertebra—no, he hadn't been to the doctor—and here, with his arm twisted and groping in the back of his shirt, he stopped to ponder medical costs and the arrogance of the educated, and to remind me that he had treated his own athlete's foot for years with a simple formula of diluted sulfuric acid. But this thing was painful, and he couldn't see it, that was the real problem.

"It's there, there, a little up," he said, turning his back to me and trying to reach it with his thumb.

"A little *up,*" he said again, with irritation, because I was supposed, apparently, to examine it. I looked around in the vain hope that someone might come through, some white rabbit of a scientist carrying a large bone, the kind of man I always dream will save me.

"Up, up, *there,*" Pop said, giving a little moan as I touched the sore. "It hurts," he said, in the voice of a child.

"I'll look at it when we get back to the island," I promised, thinking he'd forget it by then.

The Hall of African Mammals opened before us, long, cool and dark like the nave of a cathedral, its polished marble walls glistening, its chapels dedicated not to saints but to species endangered or extinct. In the center was a stuffed woolly mammoth lifting its trumpeting head. A young waiter in a tuxedo shirt was arranging café tables around it.

"Hello!" my father called to him, across the room. "Is this a private party?"

No, it was a regular thing on Fridays, came the answer, though not until five.

It was a quarter past four. Could my father prevail upon him—? He'd been bringing me here since I was six—

The waiter interrupted him—sit anywhere, he said. It was easier to pour a couple of early drinks than listen to the story. He brought us two gin-and-tonics and a cup of Goldfish crackers and left us alone.

As I lifted my drink my father looked me up and down quickly, startled, as if he had just realized again that he was out with a woman. I was glad the waiter had gone—I didn't think I could bear to have myself explained again.

"So, what's this job in Columbus?" Pop asked, the way he used to ask me about school.

"Cincinnati," I said, but though he had asked the same question, with the same error, at lunch, I was relieved to hear it. It's the sort of thing fathers and daughters talk about, and I had, for once, a good answer.

"Assistant professor," I told him, "I mean, it's mainly teaching composition, but—"

"But it's a job," he said. "You won't be on the dole anymore."

"A teaching fellowship isn't quite the dole."

"It's all Greek to me, sweetie," he said with a laugh. "I'm sure it's very important. Nothing wrong with a little work, though."

If he saw the irony in this, it didn't show in his face. These were phrases he'd heard, "Greek to me," and "Nothing wrong with a little work." He repeated them just to have something to say. He hadn't gone to college—his mother thought it extravagant, so he'd never quite understood what I'd been doing studying all the time. To deal him a sharp reply would have been like striking a child.

"It'll be a lot of work," I said, careful to keep the eager, Horatio Alger note in my voice. "But it's great just to get an interview. You wouldn't believe it, but they said almost two hundred people applied. And now it's just between me and two others. And they've been so nice, you should have heard what they said about my articles. . . . Considering the market," I said, thinking now that in fact I hadn't done so terribly badly, had accomplished a little and had time to accomplish more, that I could really give him something to be proud of, that he might even see that if there was promise in my life, his, too, could be redeemed. "I'm doing pretty well."

"You can go pretty far with a nice set of tits these days," he said.

He was smiling as if he had just gotten off a wonderful mot, and I wanted to smile, too, because if I smiled we could go on as if he hadn't said this, and soon it would really seem he had not. I couldn't manage it, but I carefully avoided looking down to see if my sweater was too tight, or crossing my arms over my chest, or cringing or shrinking in any way. I looked past him for a minute, at a kudu, lithe and proud in its glass enclosure, looking out over a glittering lake.

You're all he's got, I said to myself. *Be kind.*

"Do you suppose that's real water?" I asked, hoping to lead him back to safety. He likes a mechanical question, and can spend hours explaining about pistons and spark plugs, how the keystone holds the arch and the moon pulls the tide. Now he began on the properties of chlorine, but a morose fog settled into his voice and he stared a long time into the scene.

"No," he said suddenly, rousing himself. "By God, I *wouldn't* mind marrying again, not one little bit." His voice rang against the marble walls. "I'd like to find a woman who loves to cook, and loves to talk, and loves to hike, and loves to fuck—"

He paused, darting a glance toward me, worrying I might be offended? Hoping so? Testing, to see if I might be the woman described?

"And then I'd like to buy a piece of property on the sunny side of a good, serious hill, and we'd start building a house there."

He drained his drink and looked around for the waiter.

"I was right," he told me, "I *knew* T-bills were going to turn around this week. If only I'd been able to get a solid position, we could be having this drink . . . on Antigua! Or, how would you like Positano? Looking out over the Bay of Naples? Bougainvillea cascading down the hillsides? What would you think about that?"

"I've *been* making money," he said again. "This time next year, who knows?" He lifted the empty glass to his lips again.

"*Where is* he?" I asked, but the waiter was gone.

Then came the Girl Scouts, two by two, swinging their clasped hands, unable to quite keep themselves from skipping until they stood before the woolly mammoth, whereupon a hush seized them as if they were in the presence of a god or a living dream. Daneesha, the one with the red and

yellow beads, greeted my father now as an old friend, shaking off her partner and running to him to show off a new gyroscope from the souvenir
shop.

He woke up. For a minute he was in the thrall not of the past or the
future but of Daneesha and her gyroscope, which he spun for her on his
fingertip, then along its string. Soon he was writing out his phone number, inviting her to dinner the next time she came into town.

"Your whole family," he told her. "Do you like spaghetti?"

It was just her mother and herself, she said, and they loved spaghetti.
She was hungry, as I'd been: she wanted to draw her hand along a man's
scratchy cheek, to be lifted in a pair of arms that could carry her anywhere.
As she took the business card with his number, her clear smile faded into
an expression of secret greed. She pocketed it quickly, and, as if afraid he
would snatch it back from her, ran back to the troop, whose leader turned
a hard warning glance at him. I remembered that the mother of a little girl
in his building had told him if she found her daughter at his place one
more time she'd call the police. Nobody gets it, I thought—it's not that he
wants sex with little girls, it's that he wants to live like they do, in a world
before all that.

"It's hard to believe that you used to be that age," he said, as the Scouts
went off toward the planetarium. He checked his watch.

"If we leave now," he began, "we can change at the World Trade Center
before the crush. . . ." Call Hunan Kitchen from the ferry terminal, catch
the 5:40 boat, be on the island by 6:15, and pick up dinner on the way
home. And he was off into the city with me only one step behind. The
subway station felt just like always, comforting in its clangor, the crowd of
preoccupied faces pressing onto the escalator, the couple of latecomers
running edgewise down the stairs. The doors of one train closed with
hydraulic authority and it slid smoothly off as another slammed in around
the bend. Pop put one token in the stile for me, waved me through and
strode ahead of me again toward the first car. From here we could easily
cross to the express at Grand Central. And it was waiting, already packed.
I folded myself between two men in suits and swayed with them all the
way downtown. *I do,* I thought, *I love it here.* At South Ferry we ran up the
ramp, and though the boat was boarding Pop dialed Hunan Kitchen: he
could see by the size of the crowd that there was plenty of time.

We were the last up the gangplank, and the first to disembark, running down the iron stairway down to the street, crossing with the light, turning up the street past the Hadassah Thrift Shop and Winnie's Bridal and Formal, and Island Cleaners, where suits and dresses moved in stately procession on their conveyor, and as we opened the door at Hunan Kitchen they were calling our number.

"Steaming!" Pop said, opening the little cartons and setting them in the center of the table, as proud as if we had ridden unscathed through the gears of a great machine.

"It's all in the timing," he told me, feeling paternal now, ready to share the wisdom of his lifetime with me. "It's an instinct—you have to have a sense of it. The crowd is going one direction, everyone's jumping on the bandwagon, and you have to be willing to stop and think, 'Maybe there's another way.' I'm always ready to take the risk, move against the prevailing winds, and it's paid off for me."

He gestured in the direction of the newspaper, still folded to the market tables. "What I would have done this week, if I'd had the money," he said, "nobody else even considered, but it would have been *very* profitable."

He shook his head. "But for a lack of cash, really, I'd be on top of the world today. I've just gotta get back in there, sweetie, and with this kind of opportunity, you know, by November, the clouds are closing in here, and I can be thinking where I'd like to retire to."

He popped the beer top as if it were champagne, but in another minute he was lost to his thoughts again. The lamp over the table, all four hundred watts of it (he had hated my mother's dinners by candle) shone pitilessly down on his face. Everything in his apartment, the bare bulbs, the month's worth of newspapers piled by the couch, the box of sugar he plunked down defiantly before me as if to say "I suppose you expected a bowl," still set itself against my mother. But on the wall facing his chair hung her engagement photograph, taken when she was twenty and secure in a luxuriant beauty. I had nothing of her in me, I thought—I was his daughter exactly and it made me want to rip at my skin.

"Curaçao is nice," Pop said suddenly. "Coves, inlets, nice private spots. I don't need a glittering night life, wide beaches, high-rise hotels. . . ." His voice swelled. "Some people have to have that, the glamour—it makes them feel like they are somebody, I guess. . . . I never felt that way. That's one thing I like about Beverly Dill [this was the news anchor he admired]—she's down to earth. She's smart, but not so smart you wouldn't trust her. She's not looking for fame or money, not the kind of gal who would turn up her nose at—"

"I have found you ridiculous since the time I was old enough to laugh." I could taste these words on my tongue, and they were delicious. To have nothing to be proud of but the fact that you didn't like high-rise hotels! To be cooped in your deathly apartment beneath a photograph of your former wife, sketching, sketching on the blueprints for the next one as if anyone at all could bear to love you!

But it was valor, almost, his relentless optimism, the way, though his life has eroded beneath him, he refused to feel the loss, counting his blessings, keeping his eye on the future even if by now he could see no more in the future than these worn old fantasies, the escape to the island, the beautiful woman's love. To despise him was to remember, suddenly, a time when I was twelve and he had driven me to the dentist for an extraction that went awry. An hour of bloody probing and wrenching ended in an operation with scant anesthesia, but the worst part was seeing Pop stand by helpless, one minute trying to make light of it, the next turning away, aghast. If I'd ever dreamed he could take care of me I had to admit myself wrong that day. On the way home we passed a Kmart and suddenly he was doubling back, determined to buy me a gift. Dazed and aching, I waded in behind him among racks of too-blue jeans and stacks of lawn furniture poised to fall. In the music department I grabbed the first thing on the rack, just to get it over with. It was *Yellow Submarine,* and I still can't hear it without thinking of everything I wanted that purchase to assuage: he was failing, at marriage, at work, at fatherhood, and he had one hope left, the hope that I was too young to see.

Now I continued to pretend. "—at the simpler things in life," I said. This was a phase of his, and to speak it was a way to say, covertly, "It's okay, it's only money you've lost, nothing important."

"The *simpler things in life.* Exactly," he said. "*Exactly.* There are so few people, sweetie, who really understand. . . ." He turned to me with a true smile, even a loving smile, and I felt, and despised myself for feeling, overjoyed. His discourse on simplicity carried us to bedtime, when he cleared the newspapers off the sofa, pulled it out for me, and gave me sheets, the same ones Grammy had ripped up their worn middles and restitched for him before she died. As I made up the bed I heard him brush his teeth while the bathroom radio gave the financial news. A cold rain pricked at the window, and under the marquee of the defunct movie house across the street a tired prostitute looked up and down the empty street. I went to pull the curtain, but of course there wasn't any.

"You know, the way you're standing, you could almost have been your mother for a minute there."

I jumped. I hadn't heard him come out of the bathroom.

"Sweetie," he said, coming toward me, "it's only me."

I was afraid for a minute he was going to put his arms around me, but instead he took off his shirt.

"Would you mind just looking at my back for me? This—boil, or whatever it is—I . . ." He trailed off—I could see he didn't like to ask.

"Oh, Pop, I don't know anything about boils," I said, but after all he was alone, while I had Louis to look at any boils of mine, so I sat him down to examine him. His skin was coarse and oily—I remembered all I knew about skin, how it's the body's largest organ and full of various glands. How heavy a skin is, like a wet suit: I pictured his folded over the back of a chair. The sore was a round raw center in a nimbus of pus, and I saw he'd been picking at it, like a child who can't leave a scab alone.

"Press it and see what's in it, sweetie," he said. "I thought something crawled out of it yesterday."

He looked up at me and some ancient, familiar shadow crossed his face. Was he cut so absolutely free of his moorings, so adrift in fantasy, that his night-terrors were as alive to him as his island dreams? I felt frightened myself, suddenly—he seemed a mire that might any minute pull me in, and I tried to remind myself that he was only a man, a lost, confused man who had no one to care for him but me.

I set my finger to the edge of the inflammation, and the pain pleased him. "It doesn't sting," he said, "more like a burn. . . ."

"It just needs to be disinfected," I said. "There's only a little swelling here, nothing to worry about." Truly, I thought it might want lancing, but I knew if I suggested that he'd ask me to do it, and dabbing it with a bit of cotton soaked in witch hazel was almost more than I could bear.

"That's good," he said with a little shudder. "That's so good."

"There," I said. Blood poison was unlikely, and no one could count me responsible if his blood was poisoned, or neglectful if he died. I probably wouldn't feel more than the occasional prick of guilt myself—nothing compared to the way I felt for hating him so. "I think it's going to heal up fine."

"It's wonderful to have family, isn't it, sweetie?" he said, standing up, relieved, it seemed, of every fear and sorrow by my little ministration. "So few people understand that, that it's family, not glamour, or money, or fame, that's the important thing."

He turned, glowing with good feeling, to hug me.

I knew it would be insane to scream. I leaned stiffly toward him, patting his back above the sore, concentrating on my breath so as not to panic, doubly gentle because I felt as if my fingers might sprout claws.

"Is there a sheet or something I could tack up over the window?" I asked when he released me.

He looked puzzled. "Nobody can see in here, sweetie," he said. "We're on the sixth floor."

He was right, of course. Still I felt exposed.

"If you're nervous," he said, "you can come in and sleep with me."

His voice was studiedly casual, but his eyes had the angry gleam of a man who has bet everything on a single number and is watching the wheel spin. It was a proposition, and I felt the room swinging around me like a nauseating carnival ride, in the center of which I—my heart, breath, mind, and most of all my eyes—must keep fixed absolutely still.

"I'm okay," I said. Very lightly, hoping I could somehow back away from him without moving. It was the first such suggestion I had ever declined. Professors were so magnificently arrogant, they'd leave the marks of their grip on my arm, asking me to bed as if they were challenging me to a duel—it would have been cowardice to refuse. And the others, the timid boys who tried a little ruse, like my father—I could never bear to turn down. Men—you can feel their sadness—but how to assuage it? You have to do it through sex, they can't take nourishment any other way. And I was always so grateful to be wanted, to feel them drinking their strength from my beauty, drinking and drinking until they seemed powerful as gods.

Pop shrugged. "We used to do it, when you were two years old," he said.

"So, Columbus tomorrow!" he said when I didn't answer. "Teaching, you say?"

I nodded.

"What would you teach?" he asked, sounding baffled.

"Comparative literature."

"You don't need some kind of certificate for that?"

"No," I said, knowing he didn't count the Ph.D.

"Amazing. Hey, you don't think there might be a something out there for me, do you? I've got a real soft spot for the Midwest. Good people, salt of the earth. Nothing keeping me here—you might say I'm footloose and fancy free. We could get a nicer place if there were two of us. I've *been* making money. . . ."

To invite him would be suicide. To say no was more of a homicide. I settled for silence; cowardice seemed a bloodless crime.

"Well, just something to think about . . ." he said. "It's just great to have you here, sweetie."

He spoke so sincerely that I was afraid he was going to hug me again, but no, he went into his bedroom and closed the door, and a few minutes later I saw the light blink out beneath.

I curled against the far arm of the couch, pulling my knees to my chest, keeping the blanket tight around me, the way I used to sleep as a child. I had a recurring dream then that some awful force had come to suck me out the window, and I'd hold my breath, playing dead until it went away. I was always looking for a charm, something to wrap myself in for safety, the image of Zeus or Louis or whoever—everyone needs something like that, something to grab hold of in the dark. Now I tried to think of Cincinnati—a sleepy river town, sun on the factories, the pleasure of getting to know a new city—but all I could feel was that I didn't dare leave Louis, I needed him to keep my father at bay. After a long time I fell not asleep but into a kind of purgatorial consciousness, full of specters but still at one remove from that room.

"There's no one else," a voice said, so clear it seemed to rouse me, "*you'll* have to marry him."

Then I heard my father's bedsprings and his feet as they touched the floor. Soon he would pad past me on his way to the bathroom. I held myself tighter, trying to take the deep, slow breaths of a sleeper. He might be only inches away from me, but he wouldn't guess I'd awakened, and I'd never let him know.

David Leavitt

Speonk

from *Double Take*

I'VE NEVER been to Speonk. To me it is just a stop on the train, a dot on a map. For all I know, it might be "Llanview," or "Pine Valley," or "Genoa City"—one of those imaginary towns that come to life for an hour a day on soap operas. Probably, however, Speonk isn't like any of those places. Probably it is a town full of satellite dishes.

This begins in traffic, on a summer Sunday evening on Long Island. After a comatose weekend spent in crowded houses on the wrong side of the Montauk Highway, three people are making their sleepy way back to New York. I am in the car with Naomi and her friend Jonathan, an actor who for the past two years has played Evan Malloy (dubbed "Evil Evan") on *The Light of Day*. Recently Jonathan decided he'd had enough of rape, blackmail, drug peddling, larceny, and the like and gave the producers of the show six weeks' notice: just enough time for Evan to commit murder, frame his good-as-gold brother, Julian, and at the eleventh hour get found out. Evan went to prison, and Jonathan, on the heels of his final taping, went to Penn Station, where he caught a train for Bridgehampton, relieved that their paths had finally diverged. He spent the weekend sleeping on the beach, and now, two days later, is sitting languid in the backseat of Naomi's car, still looking a bit like the tough guy he's become famous for playing, in a baseball cap and dirty white T-shirt.

"Even with this traffic, I think we should be back in the city by ten," Naomi says.

He laughs. "That'll still be less time than it took me to get out here."

"You came by train, didn't you?" I ask.

"Jonathan had a little trouble getting to Bridgehampton," Naomi says. "It took him—how long was it, Jonathan? Six, seven hours?"

"Seven and a half."

"What happened?"

He stretches his arms over his head, so that when I look over my shoulder, I catch a glimpse of the hair in his armpits. "Well, you know how in Jamaica you have to change trains," he says. "I got on the train across the platform and asked the conductor if it was going to Bridgehampton, and he said it was. So then I settled back and fell asleep, and when I woke up, a different conductor was shaking my shoulder and saying, 'Last stop, last stop.' Only we weren't in Montauk. We were in Speonk."

"Speonk?"

"The lousy conductor in Jamaica lied to me. He put me on the wrong train."

"I think," Naomi interjects, "the conductor must have recognized you from the show and decided this was a perfect opportunity to get back at you for all the rotten things you did. Or rather, the rotten things Evan did. A woman spat at him once."

"No."

"Yes. She walked right up to him in the middle of Lincoln Center and spat in his face. Isn't that right, Jonathan?"

He shrugs. "God knows why. The show is crap. God knows why people take it seriously."

"But go on with your story," I say. "So you were in Speonk. What did you do?"

"Well, I found a pay phone and called Ben Brandt, who I was supposed to be staying with. I had no idea where I was, and I wanted to ask how far Speonk was from Bridgehampton."

"You should have called me, Jonathan," Naomi says. "I would have picked you up."

"I know, but I didn't think to. So anyway, Ben answers the phone and he goes, 'Speonk! Where's that?' And I go, 'Nowhere.'"

"Can you believe Ben didn't offer to go get him? Some friend."

"It was, like 1:30 in the morning, and there weren't any trains. But I read in the schedule that there was a train I could catch at four from

Hampton Bays. Hampton Bays isn't that far from Speonk. So I called Ben back and said, 'What should I do?' and he goes, 'Hitchhike.' So I hitchhiked."

"And someone picked you up."

"A truck picked me up. Finally. This great big hulk of a guy, with tattoos, and this smaller guy. They were cousins. They recognized me from the show. They said they'd take me to Hampton Bays, provided I came home with them first so the big guy could show me to his wife."

"Get out."

"Can you believe it?"

Jonathan shrugs. "It was just stupid. It was the middle of the fucking night. The guy called his wife on his cell phone, he must have gotten her out of bed. She was in her bathrobe when we got there."

"So what happened then? What did she say?"

"She wanted to know what it was like behind the scenes, if any of the couples on the show were couples in real life. The usual. She seemed sort of confused. I don't think she quite understood that we were just actors, that it's just a lousy job. I told her what I could, and she made me some coffee, and then her husband and his cousin drove me to Hampton Bays, and I caught the train."

"It was five by the time he pulled into Bridgehampton," Naomi adds. "At least Ben had the decency to pick him up *then*."

In the backseat, Jonathan yawns, stretches his legs. "It was just stupid," he says. "A stupid waste of time."

The traffic grinds to a halt.

I don't know where we were then. We might have been anywhere. We might have been in Speonk.

For a while, when I was in high school, I used to watch *The Light of Day*. This was years before Jonathan played Evil Evan. In those days, I was much preoccupied with the fate of Sister Mary, a sweet young nun torn between Faith (in the person of Jesus Christ) and Passion (in the person of a severely smitten Jewish boy who was determined to lure her from the convent). What kept me watching was anxiety bled with a little bit of love: love for Sister Mary drew me in, while anxiety over her fate brought me back day after day, especially after she went off to war-torn "San Carlos" to do good works and ended up being kidnapped by the sadistic guerrilla leader Pedro Santos. For weeks, I lived in suspense, wondering whether Jeremy, her adoring suitor, would succeed in rescuing Mary before the malevolent Santos, with his Castro-like beard and cigar, gave in to lust and raped her. Every afternoon Santos's tobacco-scented breath puffed out over Mary's face; every afternoon, at the crucial instant, Chance stopped his hand on her breast. And then Chance took a day off: Jeremy saved Mary, but only after Santos had ravished her and vanished. Returning to "Montclair Heights," Mary left the convent and married Jeremy, whose child everyone took it for granted that she was carrying. Later, though, Santos turned up in Montclair Heights. Despite everything that had happened, the former nun found herself powerfully attracted to the ex-guerrilla—at which point I left for college. Years passed. By the time I tuned in again, Jeremy was dead, Santos was out of the picture, Mary was blowsy, much divorced, and played by a different actress. For Evil Evan had ushered in a new era: *he* was Mary's son by Pedro Santos.

Of course, if I'd been tuning in all along—as, presumably, the woman in Speonk had—then perhaps this chain of events wouldn't have surprised me so much. After all, a soap opera is something you live with every day. What keeps you watching isn't, as with movies or novels, the assurance that a hostage taken at the beginning will be a hostage freed at the end. Instead, stories verge into one another. New plots rise from the ashes of old ones. Suffering is a principle: too much happiness foretells imminent catastrophe, just as minor fatigue bodes terminal illness. Time is elastic. Generally speaking, it conforms to time in the world—that is to say, Christmas comes for them when it comes for us, their springs and summers are shaped like ours. Only sometimes time compresses, too, and a single afternoon will take weeks to unfold. And sometimes time accelerates perversely so that a boy (Evan) graduates from high school eight years after his birth. And sometimes time seems not to exist at all.

The Light of Day, of course, goes on without Jonathan. It has been going on for forty-six years. I think of it the way I think of my life, as narration without beginning or end. Oh, I know it began once, just as I know that someday it will have to end—all things do—yet this assurance is, finally, a haze for me, less a knowledge than a vagueness. The specificity of ending, that's what's so hard to get your mind around, the fact that one day, at some specific hour and in some specific place, this thing is going to happen. And it could happen anytime, anywhere. It could be tomorrow. It could be in Speonk.

Evil Evan took some people hostage, as I recall, in the last days of Jonathan's tenure. He took his lawyer and his lawyer's pregnant wife hostage. He paraded the wife around the courtroom, holding a gun to her abdomen.

This was just the sort of thing that Evil Evan did, and that Jonathan claimed he could no longer tolerate. It drove him crazy, he said, having to point a gun at a pregnant woman's abdomen, even if he knew that she wasn't really pregnant, that the gun was a prop, that the softness into which he was pressing its barrel was only a foam-rubber mold affixed to the inside of her dress.

"But isn't that just part of being an actor?" Naomi asked in the car, fishing in her purse for tollbooth tokens.

To which he replied: "It was a principle of my training that you have to become the character you play. And when you have to become Evil Evan five days a week, well, after a while it starts to make you nuts, you know what I'm saying? I mean, I would wake up in the morning and think, *Good, today I get to rape a fourteen-year-old. Cool.* Maybe some people can go, you know, 'This is just my job,' but not me."

We reached the city, and Naomi dropped Jonathan off at Second Avenue and Fifty-eighth Street; then we headed downtown together.

"Of course, there's more to that story than meets the eye," she said, once we were alone.

"Oh?"

She nodded. "One of those wasp-waisted space cadets he's always going for. Works for Revlon or something. For the first six months they were together, she never watched *The Light of Day,* she was always working. Then one week she was home sick and decided to tune in. Wouldn't you know it? *That* was the week Evil Evan raped the fourteen-year-old."

"And his girlfriend didn't like it?"

"Are you kidding? She practically had a seizure. She kept saying that when she looked into his eyes she saw the eyes of a rapist, or some nonsense like that. I told him I thought it was idiotic, he shouldn't take her seriously, but has Jonathan ever once listened to me where women are concerned? No. So he up and quits a perfectly decent job, gives up a great salary, just to prove to some bimbo that he's willing to make a sacrifice for her love."

"I had no idea being an actor could be so complicated," I said.

"It's not being an actor that's complicated," Naomi corrected. "It's

Jonathan who makes things complicated—especially where his girlfriends are concerned."

We arrived at my building. I kissed Naomi on the cheek and stepped out of the car onto the curb. She drove off in what seemed to me an irritated fashion. Not that I cared: the truth is, I hardly know Naomi—she was just a friend of one of the girls I was sharing a beach house with that summer, and Jonathan—well, I only met him that once, that time in the car. They were just acquaintances, people who offered me a ride one weekend. Beyond what I picked up on the Long Island Expressway, I couldn't tell you much about Jonathan's life. I don't know where he grew up or went to school. (Naomi works for an Internet start-up, I believe.)

And yet, as the summer progressed, the story stayed with me. Perhaps it was the trucker with the tattoos who kept it alive, or my own memories of coffee before dawn in college, or else just the very idea of Speonk at two in the morning—an invented Speonk, the streets so silent that you could hear the thunk of the traffic light as it changed from yellow to red. Sometimes, when I tried to imagine what really happened to Jonathan, I wondered if he'd been in some kind of danger. This is the soap opera watcher in me. The soap opera watcher in me envisions the house into which the trucker led him as painted in the most ominous colors—arterial purples, the pale blues of suffocation—and filled with padlocked doors, rolls of rusty wire, rags soaking in gasoline. In this scenario, the trucker and his wife cannot even begin to distinguish Jonathan from Evil Evan. When he walks into their kitchen, she cries, "How could you do it? And to a woman in her condition?"

"It wasn't me," Jonathan answers meekly. "I swear to you, *I* didn't do it." All in vain. His fate is sealed: his mouth will be stuffed with rags, his wrists bound with rusty wire. And then, in that basement to which the padlocked door leads, he will be imprisoned, tortured, punished for deeds not his own . . .

Admittedly, the soap opera watcher in me is inclined to exaggeration.

A more realistic scenario, then: zoom in on a small, tidy, rural kitchen, the floor a blue and white linoleum checkerboard, the countertops corn-yellow Formica. Dishes dry on a rubber rack. Tin canisters marked "Flour," "Sugar," and "Tea" are lined up next to the electric stove. There's a smell of pot roast and stale coffee. When the truck driver and his cousin bring Evan—Jonathan—inside, the wife stands from where she's been waiting at the breakfast table. Although she's still in her bathrobe, she's put on rouge, lipstick. She's wearing earrings. A Sara Lee pound cake defrosts on top of the refrigerator, where the cat can't get to it.

Jonathan sits down. He looks tired and tough and lost in his dirty white T-shirt. She stares at him, perhaps touches him, remarks how much smaller he appears offscreen (I noticed this, too): not a villain, just a boy, a tough boy, tired and lost. He rests his head on his palm, and his head is next to the television set, the very television set on which, every weekday for two years, she's watched him, as if he really had stepped through the screen and come to life. Yet the truth is, he's been here all along: in her kitchen, in her house. In Speonk.

She asks him what it's like playing Evil Evan. He tells her that as of today, he's quit.

"But how can that be?" she asks. "The murder trial's not over yet."

"We always tape a few weeks ahead."

Her eyes widen. "So you mean that in a few weeks, Evan will be gone?"

"An inside tip—don't tell your friends, I'm sworn to secrecy on this— he's going to the slammer. The hoosegow."

The trucker's cousin laughs—probably at the word "hoosegow."

"So now you're a little bit ahead of the game," Jonathan says.

The wife blushes. "Well, don't worry, your secret's safe with me. I won't tell a soul."

Jonathan would like to say that for all he cares, she can print the news in the *Speonk Gazette,* but he controls himself. Much better to give her the gratification of a secret.

She offers him a slice of pound cake; he says no, thank you. She offers him coffee; he accepts. It is late, the middle of the night; her husband and his cousin are shifting restlessly near the refrigerator, and Evil Evan is drinking coffee in her kitchen out of a mug that says LIFE'S A BEACH. He drinks it in three gulps, puts down the mug. The truck driver suggests they'd better scoot if they want to get to Hampton Bays in time for his train. Jonathan has fulfilled his part of the bargain, and now the truck driver intends to do the same.

Jonathan stands; the wife stands. They look at each other for a moment. Then they say good-bye. The three men leave her, as men always do, alone with the television and the kitchen. Outside, she hears the truck's engine turn over as it pulls away, toward Hampton Bays and sunlight and the train that will take Evan out of her life for good.

• • •

Well, that's one way things could have turned out. But though this might be an end to Jonathan's story, it isn't the end to mine.

One Saturday, a few weeks after Naomi drove us to New York, I ran into her on the beach in Bridgehampton.

"Guess what?" she said, leaping up from the sand. "The other day, I looked up Speonk on a map, and it's only an hour from here—less in the middle of the night, when there wouldn't be traffic."

"So?"

"Well, doesn't that make it seem a little improbable?"

"What?"

"That Ben wouldn't pick him up."

"Pick up Jonathan? Maybe Ben was busy."

She rolled her eyes. "Are you kidding? He's one of Jonathan's best friends. But even if he did say no—which I find hard to believe—then why didn't Jonathan just call a taxi to take him to Hampton Bays?"

"Well, maybe taxis don't run that late in Speonk." I sat down on the edge of her towel.

"Fine. So why didn't he call me? He *knows* I would have picked him up."

I didn't want to get into the thorny question of why he might not have wanted to call Naomi.

"What are you saying?" I asked. "That he made up the whole story?"

"Not the *whole* story, necessarily. It's just, when you think about it, it's full of holes. For instance, this idea that he had no other choice but to hitchhike. Of course he had other choices! I've just listed them. And then the larger inconsistency, which is, how likely is it that some truck driver, some guy who spends all his time on the road, is going to recognize an actor from a soap opera?"

"Don't they usually drive at night?"

"Sure. But would *The Light of Day* really be up the alley of your average trucker?"

"Who says he was your average trucker?"

Naomi threw sand at me then. "Oh, be quiet, you're just playing devil's advocate," she said. "I can hear it in your voice, you're as dubious as I am. You're wondering, Was Jonathan just making the whole thing up for the sake of giving a performance? You know, poor Jonathan, he couldn't bear playing the villain anymore, so he quits, and on his last day of work, look what happens. No matter where he travels, Evil Evan follows him. It's like something out of Stephen King."

"Or a soap opera."

"Exactly."

Making an excuse, I got up and walked farther down the beach. Somehow I couldn't stomach any more of Naomi's suspiciousness—not at that moment. And yet I have to say this for her: with the tenacity that distinguishes certain very relentless and untrusting natures, she had managed to root out from Jonathan's story every questionable detail, every immoderate coincidence, and had laid those trophies before me the way a cat will lay out the remnants of its prey. And faced with such evidence, how could I not revise my own imagined version of what took place?

So: third variation.

Let's agree, at the very least, that Jonathan did end up in Speonk that night. Let's also agree that, either from necessity or by choice, he decided to hitchhike to Hampton Bays. A truck picks him up, only this time the driver is alone. No cousin tags along for the ride. The driver is beer-bellied, hairy-shouldered, wears a New York Knicks baseball cap. He grips the wheel so tightly his knuckles whiten, and the contemplation of those knuckles—the knowledge that this man could crush his neck with his bare hands if he wanted—provokes a weird commingling of panic and arousal in Jonathan. His mouth waters. From the little green cardboard tree that dangles from the rearview mirror, there emanates a smell of men's rooms, of urinal cakes.

If the driver recognizes Jonathan, though, he doesn't let on. Instead he says, "Jerry," and holds his hand out sideways as he slows for a red light.

"Jonathan."

They shake. With an audible *thunk,* the light changes to green. The truck accelerates. "You know, if I take you straight to Hampton Bays, you'll just have to wait at the station," Jerry says. "Tell you what, why don't we go to my place? My wife will make us some coffee."

"Won't she be asleep?"

"Norma?" He laughs. "She never sleeps. Never goes to bed before three, and then she reads."

"Well, if you're sure—"

Without signaling, Jerry maneuvers the truck off the main drag and onto a narrow street lined with shingled houses. In most of them, the lights are off. A few more turns—left, right, left, Jonathan notes, in case he has to escape—and they pull into a graveled driveway bordered with lawn and geraniums. "Home, sweet home," Jerry says, switching off the ignition.

They climb out of the cab. The house is dark except for a yellowish light glimmering in one window. Taking a ring of keys from his belt, Jerry opens the door and shouts, "Norma!"

"In here."

They step through the front hall, where Jerry hangs his cap on a peg. A smell of pot roast and stale coffee lingers in the air. Pushing open a swing door, Jerry leads Jonathan into the kitchen, where a woman with long, badly dyed hair is sitting at the breakfast table, smoking and doing the *New York Times* crossword puzzle. Behind her is a padlocked door. In front of her sits a half-empty glass of orange juice and an ashtray in which a cigarette is smoldering. She is holding a pencil.

Lifting her eyes from the puzzle, she looks Jonathan over—not with surprise, exactly, though not with complacency, either; instead, her expression might best be described as one of slight botheration, enough to tell Jonathan that, though her husband may not be in the habit of bringing strangers home at two in the morning, neither is it unheard of for him to do so.

"Norma, this is Jonathan," Jerry says, and hoists himself up to sit on the corn-yellow countertop. "Jonathan, Norma."

"Hey."

"He was hitching near the station. Got the wrong train out of Jamaica. Has to get to Hampton Bays, but the next train don't leave for a couple of hours."

"Bummer."

"Make some coffee, will you?"

Obediently—but with evident impatience—Norma puts down her pencil, gets up out of her chair, and walks to the stove. She has a big behind. She's wearing an old-fashioned lacy pink bathrobe, buttoned to the neck. Her age is difficult to read. Forty? Forty-five? Although she has the long hair of a girl, and she's painted her nails with glittery pink polish, nonetheless the skin around her throat is pliant and loose. There are tiny, colorless hairs on her cheeks. She reminds Jonathan of an over-the-hill Grateful Dead groupie he once saw interviewed on television—"rode hard and put up wet" was how Ben Brandt described her—and for that very reason, he finds her powerfully attractive, much more attractive than, say,

Betsy, the pretty girlfriend for whose sake (at least in part) he has quit his job. It's that slight air of slaggishness—the dyed hair, the glittery nails, and then the odd touch of the grandmotherly bathrobe: it all contributes to a fantasy he's working up, has been working up ever since Jerry invited him home. After all, he's no innocent: he's seen the ads in the back of the *Village Voice,* on Internet bulletin boards: COUPLE SEEKS SINGLE . . . INSATIABLE MOM CAN'T GET ENOUGH . . . GIVE IT TO MY WIFE WHILE I WATCH. Is this the real story, then, the real reason Jerry brought him here? And if so, will she go along with it? (Probably; to avoid trouble with her husband, he suspects, she's no doubt gone along with far worse things. Even so, her lack of interest is vivid, and the knowledge that she would submit, if at all, reluctantly, only heightens his curiosity.)

And no one, not Betsy nor Naomi nor Ben, will ever know. For he goes unrecognized. That's the icing on the cake. Evil Evan is so far from here he might as well be dead.

Unless, of course, they *do* recognize him and are just pretending not to, so that they can spring something on him at a compromised moment.

The coffee is ready. Norma pours it into mugs and hands one to Jerry, the other to Jonathan. "Thanks," he says. "Oh, 'Life's a Beach.' You know, I never got that joke before."

Norma says nothing. She sits down, grinds out her cigarette, and takes up her pencil.

"Any milk?" Jerry asks.

"Went sour."

A sound of gulping from behind Jonathan. "Is that today's puzzle you're doing?"

Norma nods.

"I finished it on the train, so if you get stuck on anything, just let me know."

For the first time since his arrival, something akin to a smile passes over Norma's lips. "OK, smarty-pants, so long as you're offering. Twenty-six across: 'Monster's home.'"

He grins. "Loch," he says.

"Shit. Like Loch Ness." She erases. "I had 'lair.' So that means twenty-six down is—'Musical Lynn.' 'Loretta'!"

"I was born a coal miner's daughter," Jerry sings.

"Any others?"

She scans. "Thirty-seven down: 'Bygone queen.'"

"All right. How many letters have you got?"

"T-blank-blank-blank-I-N-A. At first I thought it might be 'Titania,' but that doesn't fit."

"'Tsarina.'"

"'Tsarina.'" She writes in the word. "Which means that fifty-two across—'Bleep'—is . . . *'Edit out'!*"

"Why do you waste your time with these stupid puzzles?" Jerry asks. "Up all night, and doing what? Working on your novel? Nope. Puzzles."

"You're writing a novel?"

"I don't like to talk about it," Norma says. "He knows that. He knows I don't like to talk about it."

She returns to the crossword. Behind where she and Jonathan are sitting, her husband chuckles a little. And how curious! Now the Grateful Dead groupie is, of all things, a novelist. She sits up at night doing crossword puzzles. Out of the lips of her jokey husband emerge the words "Butcher Holler . . ."

Soon it will be time to go. Jerry will drive him to Hampton Bays, where he will catch a train to Bridgehampton, where Ben Brandt will pick him up: his own life. And then, in that crowded summer rental on the wrong side of the Montauk Highway, maybe he will tell his friends the story of Jerry and Norma, or some variation on it, adding a twist to make it more interesting and less incriminating. Months will go by, and Betsy will or will not agree to marry him. Evil Evan will recede, and the best part is, he will recede far faster than Jerry and Norma. Far faster than Speonk.

Somewhere a bird starts singing. Only the song isn't coming from outside: it's the clock above the kitchen sink. Instead of numbers, each hour is marked by a different singing bird: great horned owl for twelve, northern mockingbird for one, black-capped chickadee . . .

Who's singing now? Northern cardinal. Three in the morning.

"We'd better scoot if you're going to make your train," Jerry says, alighting from the countertop.

"Fine, just one more clue," Norma says. "Thirty-one across: 'Arizona attraction.'"

"'Petrified forest,'" Jonathan says.

"'Petrified forest,' of course." Feverishly she erases. "Good, now I can finish the damn thing. Now, finally, I can finish the damn thing and go to bed."

Andrea Lee

Anthropology

from *The Oxford American*

(M Y COUSIN says: Didn't you think about what *they* would think,
that they were going to read it, too? Of course Aunt Noah and
her friends would read it, if it were about them, the more so because it was
in a fancy Northern magazine. They can read. You weren't dealing with a
tribe of Mbuti pygmies.)

It is bad enough and quite a novelty to be scolded by my cousin, who
lives in a dusty labyrinth of books in a West Village artists' building and
rarely abandons his Olympian bibliotaph's detachment to chide anyone
face to face. But his chance remark about pygmies also punishes me in an
idiosyncratic way. It makes me remember a girl I knew at Harvard, a girl
with the unlikely name of Undine Loving, whom everybody thought was
my sister, the way everybody always assumes that young black women
with light complexions and middle-class accents are close relations, as if
there could be only one possible family of us. Anyway, this Undine—who
was, I think, from Chicago and was prettier than I, with a pair of bright
hazel eyes in a round, merry face that under cropped hair suggested a boy
chorister, and an equally round, high-spirited backside in the tight Levi's
she always wore—this Undine was a grad student, the brilliant protégé of
a famous anthropologist, and she went off for a year to Zaire to live among
pygmies. They'll think she's a goddess, my boyfriend at the time annoyed
me by remarking. After that I was haunted by an irritating vision of

Undine: tall, fair, and callipygian among reverent little brown men with peppercorn hair: an African-American Snow White. I lost sight of her after that, but I'm certain that, in the Ituri Forest, Undine was as dedicated a professional who ever took notes—abandoning toothpaste and toilet paper and subjecting herself to the menstrual hut, clear and scientific about her motives. Never even fractionally disturbing the equilibrium of the Lilliputian society she had chosen to observe. Not like me.

Well, of course, I never had a science, never had a plan. (That's obvious, says my cousin.) Two years ago, the summer before I moved to Rome, I went to spend three weeks with my Great-Aunt Noah, in Ball County, North Carolina. It was a freak impulse: a last-minute addressing of my attention to the country I was leaving behind. I hadn't been there since I was a child. I was prompted by a writer's vague instinct that there was a thread to be grasped, a strand, initially finer than spider silk, that might grow firmer and more solid in my hands, might lead to something that for the want of a better term I call *of interest*. I never pretended—

(You wanted to investigate your *roots,* says my cousin flatly.) He extracts a cigarette from a red pack bearing the picture of a clove and the words *Kretek Jakarta* and lights it with the kind of ironic flourish that I imagine he uses to intimidate his students at NYU. The way he says *roots*—that spurious '70s term—is so shaming. It brings back all the jokes we used to make in college about fat black American tourists in polyester dashikis trundling around Senegal in Alex Haley tour buses. Black intellectuals are notorious for their snobbish reverence toward Africa—as if crass human nature didn't exist there, too. And, from his West Village aerie, my cousin regards with the same aggressive piety the patch of coastal North Carolina that, before the diaspora north and west, was home to five generations of our family.

We are sitting at his dining table, which is about the length and width of the Gutenberg Bible, covered with clove ash and Melitta filters and the corrected proofs of his latest article. The article is about the whitewashed "magic houses" of the Niger tribe and how the dense plaster arabesques that ornament their facades, gleaming like cake icing, are echoed faintly across the ocean in the designs of glorious, raucous Bahia. He is very good at what he does, my cousin. And he is the happiest of scholars, a minor celebrity in his field, paid royally by obscure foundations to rove from hemisphere to hemisphere, chasing artistic clues that point to a primeval tropical unity. Kerala, Cameroon, Honduras, the Phillipines. Ex-wife, children, a string of overeducated girlfriends left hovering wistfully in the dust behind him. He is always traveling, always alone, always vaguely belonging, always from somewhere else. Once he sent me a postcard from Cochin, signed, "Affectionately yours, The Wandering Negro."

Outside on Twelfth Street, sticky acid-green buds are bursting in a March heat wave. But no weather penetrates this studio, which is as close as a confessional and has two computer screens glowing balefully in the background. As he reprimands me I am observing with fascination that my cousin knows how to smoke like a European. I'm the one who lives in Rome, dammit, and yet it is he who smokes with one hand drifting almost incidentally up to his lips and then flowing bonelessly down to the table-top. And the half-sweet smell of those ridiculous clove cigarettes has per-meated every corner of his apartment, giving it a vague atmosphere of stale festivity as if a wassail bowl were tucked away on his overstuffed book-shelves.

I'd be more impressed by all this exotic intellectualism if I didn't remember him as a boy during the single summer we both spent with Aunt Noah down in Ball County. A sallow bookworm with a towering forehead that now in middle age has achieved a mandarin distinction but was then cartoonish. A greedy solitary boy who stole the crumbling syrupy crust off fruit cobblers and who spent the summer afternoons shut in Aunt Noah's unused living room fussily drawing ironclad ships of the Civil War. The two of us loathed each other, and all that summer we never willingly exchanged a word, except insults as I tore by him with my gang of scabby-kneed girlfriends from down the road.

The memory gives me courage to defend myself. All I did, after all, was write a magazine article.

(An article about quilts and superstitions! A fuzzy folkloristic excur-sion. You made Aunt Noah and the others look cute and rustic and back-ward like a mixture of *Amos 'n' Andy* and *The Beverly Hillbillies*. Talk about quilts—you embroidered your information. And you mortally offended them—you called them black.)

But they *are* black.

(They don't choose to define themselves that way, and if anybody knows that, you do. We're talking about a group of old people who don't look black and who have always called themselves, if anything, colored.

People whose blood has been mixed for so many generations that their lives have been constructed on the idea of being a separate caste. Like in Brazil, or other sensible countries where they accept nuances. Anyway, in ten years Aunt Noah and all those people you visited will be dead. What use was it to upset them by forcing your definitions on them? It's not your place to tell them who they are.)

I nearly burst out laughing at this last phrase, which I haven't heard for a long time. It's not your place to do this, to say that. My cousin used it primly and deliberately as an allusion to the entire structure of family and tradition he thinks I flouted. The phrase is a country heirloom, passed down from women like our grandmother and her sister Eleanora and already sounding archaic on the lips of our mothers in the suburbs of the North. It evokes those towns on the North Carolina–Virginia border, where our families still own land: villages marooned in the tobacco fields, where—as in every other rural community in the world—"place," identity, whether defined by pigmentation, occupation, economic rank, or family name, forms an invisible web that lends structure to daily life. In Ball County everyone knows everyone's place. There, the white-white people, the white-black people like Aunt Noah, and the black-black people all keep to their own niches, even though they may rub shoulders every day and even though they may share the same last names and the same ancestors. Aunt Eleanora became Aunt Noah—Noah as in *know*— because she is a phenomenal chronicler of place and can recite labyrinthine genealogies with the offhand fluency of a bard. When I was little I was convinced that she was called Noah because she had actually been aboard the Ark. And that she had stored in her head—perhaps on tiny pieces of parchment, like the papers in fortune cookies—the name of every child born since the waters receded from Ararat.

I was scared to death when I went down to Ball County after so many years. Am I thinking this or speaking aloud? Something of each. My cousin's face grows less bellicose as he listens. We actually like each other, my cousin and I. Our childhood hostility has been transmogrified into a bond that is nothing like the instinctive understanding that flows between brothers and sisters. It is more a deeply buried iron link of formal respect. When I was still living in Manhattan we rarely saw each other, but we knew we were snobs about the same occult things. That's why I allow him to scold me. That's why I have to try to explain things to him.

I was scared, I continue. The usual last-minute terrors you get when you're about to return to a place where you've been perfectly happy. I was convinced it would be awful: ruin and disillusion, not a blade of grass the way I remembered it. I was afraid above all that I wouldn't be able to sleep. That I would end up lying awake in a suffocating Southern night contemplating a wreath of moths around a lightbulb, and listening to an old woman thumping around in the next bedroom like a revenant in a coffin. I took medication with me. Strong stuff.

(Very practical, says my cousin.)

But the minute I got there I knew I wouldn't need it. You know I hate driving, so I took an overnight bus from the Port Authority. There isn't a plane or a train that goes near there. And when I got off the bus in front of Ball County Courthouse at dawn, the air was like milk. Five o'clock in the morning at the end of June and ninety percent humidity. White porches and green leaves swimming in mist. Aunt Noah picked me up and drove me down Route 14 in the Oldsmobile that Uncle Pershing left her. A car as long and slow as Cleopatra's barge. And I just lay back, waking up, and sank into the luxurious realization that you can go home again. From vertical New York, life had turned horizontal as a mattress: tobacco, corn, and soybeans spreading out on either side. And you know the first thing I remembered?

(What?)

What it was like to pee in the cornfields. You know I used to run races through the rows with those girls from down the road, and very often we used to stop and pee, not because we had to, but for the fun of it. I remembered the exact feeling of squatting down in that long corridor of leaves, our feet sinking into the sides of the furrow as we pulled down our Carter's cotton underpants, the heat from the ground blasting up onto our backsides as we pissed lakes into the black dirt.

The last time before my visit that I had seen Aunt Noah was two years earlier at my wedding in Massachusetts. There she elicited great curiosity from my husband's family, a studious clan of New England Brahmins who could not digest the fact that the interracial marriage to which they had agreed with such eager tolerance had allied them with a woman who appeared to be an elderly white Southern housewife. She looked the same as she had at the wedding and very much as she had when we were kids. Eighty-three years old, with smooth graying hair colored intermittently with Loving Care and styled in a precise 1950s helmet that suited her crisp pastel shirtwaist dresses and flat shoes. The same crumpled pale-skinned face of an aged belle, round and girlish from the front but the profile displaying a blunt leonine nose and calm predator's folds around the mouth—she was born, after all, in the magisterial solar month of July. The same blue-gray eyes, shrewd and humorous, sometimes alight with the intense love of a childless woman for her nieces and nephews but never sentimental, never suffering a fool. And, at odd moments, curiously remote.

Well, you look beautiful, she said, when she saw me get off the bus.

And the whole focus of my life seemed to shift around. At the close of my twenties, as I was beginning to feel unbearably adult, crushed by the responsibilities of a recently acquired husband, apartment, and job, here I was offered the brief chance to become a young girl again. Better than being a pampered visiting daughter in my mother's house: a pampered visiting niece.

Driving to her house through the sunrise, she said: I hear you made peace with those in-laws of yours.

Things are okay now, I said, feeling my face get hot. She was referring to a newlywed spat that had overflowed into the two families and brought out all the animosity that had been so dutifully concealed at the wedding.

They used excuses to make trouble between you and your husband. He's a nice boy, so I don't lay blame on your marrying white. But you have to watch out for white folks. No matter how friendly they act at first, you can't trust them.

As always it seemed funny to hear this from the lips of someone who looked like Aunt Noah. Who got teased up North by kids on the street when she walked through black neighborhoods. Until she stopped, as she always did, and told them what was what.

The sky was paling into tropical heat, the mist chased away by the brazen song of a million cicadas. The smell of fertilizer and drying earth flowed through the car windows, and I could feel my pores starting to pump out sweat, as if I'd parachuted into equatorial Africa.

Aunt Noah, I said, just to tweak her, you wouldn't have liked it if I'd married a black-black man.

Oh, Lord, honey, no, she said. She put on the blinker and turned off the highway into the gravel driveway. We passed beneath the fringes of the giant willow that shaded the brick ranch house Uncle Pershing built fifty years ago as a palace for his beautiful childless wife. The house designed to rival the houses of rich white people in Ball County. Built and air-conditioned with the rent of dark-skinned tenants who cultivated the acres of tobacco that have belonged to Noah and Pershing's families for two hundred years. They were cousins, Noah and Pershing, and they had married both for love and because marrying cousins was what one did among their people at that time. A nigger is just as bad as white trash, she said, turning off the engine. But honey, there were still plenty of boys you could have chosen from our own kind.

(You stayed two weeks, my cousin says, jealously.)

I was researching folkways, I tell him, keeping a straight face. I was hoping to find a mother lode of West African animism, pithy backwoods expressions, seventeenth-century English thieves' cant, poetic upwellings from the cyclic drama of agriculture, as played out on the Southeastern tidal plain. I wanted to be ravished by the dying tradition of the peasant South, like Jean Toomer.

(My cousin can't resist the reference. *Fecund Southern night, a pregnant Negress,* he declaims, in the orotund voice of a Baptist preacher.)

What I really did during my visit was laze around and let Aunt Noah spoil me. Every morning scrambled eggs, grits, country ham, and hot biscuits with homemade peach preserves. She was up for hours before me, working in her garden. A fructiferous Eden of giant pea vines, prodigious tomato plants, squash blossoms like Victrola horns. She wore a green sun hat that made her look like an elderly infant, blissfully happy. Breakfast over and the house tidy, we would set out on visits where she displayed me in the only way she knew how, as an ornamental young sprig on the family tree. I fell into the gratifying role of the cherished newlywed doll. Dressing in her frilly pink guest room, I put on charming outfits: long skirts, flowery blouses. I looked like a poster girl for *Southern Living.* Everyone we visited was enchanted. My husband, who telephoned me every night, began to seem very far away: a small white boy's voice sounding forlornly out of Manhattan.

The people we called on all seemed to be distant relatives of Aunt Noah's and mine, and more than once I nearly fell asleep in a stuffy front room listening to two old voices tracing the spiderweb of connections. I'd decided to write about quilts, and that gave us an excuse to go chasing around Ball County peering at old masterpieces dragged out of mothballs, and new ones stitched out of lurid polyester. Everybody had quilts, and everybody had some variation of the same four family names. Hopper, Osborne, Amiel, Mills. There was Gertie Osborne, a little freckled woman with the diction of a Victorian schoolmistress who contributed the "Rambling Reader" column to the *Ball County Chronicle*. The tobacco magnate and head deacon P.H. Mills, tall and rich and silent in his white linen suits. Mary Amiel, who lived up the road from Aunt Noah and wrote poetry privately printed in a volume entitled *The Flaming Depths*. Aunt Noah's brother-in-law Hopper Mills, who rode a decrepit Vespa over to check up on her every day at dawn.

I practiced pistol shooting in the woods and went to the tobacco auction and rode the rope-drawn ferry down at Crenshaw Crossing. And I attended the Mount Moriah Baptist church, where years before I had passed Sunday mornings in starched dresses and cotton gloves. The big church stood unchanged under the pines: an air-conditioned Williamsburg copy in brick as vauntingly prosperous as Aunt Noah's ranch house.

After the service, they were all together outside the church, chatting in the pine shade: the fabled White Negroes of Ball County. An enterprising *Ebony* magazine journalist had described them that way once, back in 1955. They were a group who defied conventional logic: Southern landowners of African descent who had pale skins and generations of free ancestors. Republicans to a man. People who'd fought to desegregate Greensboro and had marched on Washington yet still expected their poorer, blacker tenants to address them as Miss Nora or Mr. Fred. Most of them were over seventy: their sons and daughters had escaped years ago to Washington or Atlanta or Los Angeles or New York. To them I was the symbol of all those runaway children, and they loved me to pieces.

(But then you went and called them black. In print, which to people raised on the Bible and the *McGuffey Readers* is as definitive as a set of stone tablets. And you did it not in some academic journal but in a magazine that people buy on newsstands all over the country. To them it was the worst thing they could have read about themselves—)

I didn't—

(Except perhaps being called white.)

I didn't mean—

(It was the most presumptuous thing you could have done. They're old. They've survived, defining themselves in a certain way. We children and grandchildren can call ourselves Afro-American or African-American or black or whatever the week's fashion happens to be.)

You—

(And of course you knew this. We all grew up knowing it. You're a very smart woman, and the question is why you allowed yourself to be so careless. So breezy and destructive. Maybe to make sure you couldn't go back there.)

I say: That's enough. Stop it.

And my cousin, for a minute, does stop. I never noticed before how much he looks like Uncle Pershing. The same mountainous brow and reprobative eyes of a biblical patriarch that look out of framed photographs in Aunt Noah's living room. A memory reawakens of being similarly thundered at, in the course of that childhood summer, when I lied about borrowing Uncle Pershing's pocketknife.

We sit staring at each other across this little cluttered table in Greenwich Village. I am letting him tell me off as I would never allow my brother or my husband—especially my husband. But the buried link between my cousin and me makes the fact that I actually sit and take it inevitable. As I do, it occurs to me that fifty years ago, in the moribund world we are arguing about, it would have been an obvious choice for the two of us to get married. As Ball County cousins always did. And how far we have flown from it all, as if we were genuine emigrants, energetically forgetful of some small, dire old-world country plagued by dictators, drought, locusts, and pogroms. Years ago yet another of our cousins, a dentist in Atlanta, was approached by Aunt Noah about moving his family back to Ball County and taking over her house and land. I remember him grimacing with incredulity about it as we sat over drinks once in an airport bar. Why did the family select him for this honor? he asked, with a strained laugh. The last place anyone would ever want to be, he said.

I don't know what else to do but stumble on with my story.

Aunt Noah was having a good time showing me off. On one of the last days of my visit, she drove me clear across the county to the house where she grew up. I'd never been there, though I knew that was where it had all begun. It was on this land, in the 1740s, before North Carolina statutes about slavery and mixing of races had grown hard and fast, that a Scotch-Irish settler—a debtor or petty thief deported to the pitch-pine wilderness of the penal colony—allowed his handsome half-African, half-Indian bondservant to marry his only daughter. The handsomeness of the bondservant is part of the tradition, as is the pregnancy of the daughter. Their descendants took the land and joined the group of farmers and artisans who managed to carve out an independent station between the white planters and the black slaves until after the Civil War. Dissertations and books have been written about them. The name some scholars chose for them has a certain lyricism: Tidewater Free Negroes.

My daddy grew tobacco and was the best blacksmith in the county, Aunt Noah told me. There wasn't a man, black or white, who didn't respect him.

We had turned onto a dirt road that led through fields of tobacco and corn farmed by the two tenant families who divided the old house. It was a nineteenth-century farmhouse, white and green with a rambling porch and fretwork around the eaves. I saw with a pang that the paint was peeling and that the whole structure had achieved the undulating organic shape that signals imminent collapse.

I can't keep it up, and, honey, the tenants just do enough to keep the roof from falling in, she said. Good morning, Hattie, she called out, stopping the car and waving to a woman with cornrowed hair and skin the color of dark plums, who came out of the front door.

Good morning, Miss Nora, said Hattie.

Mama's flower garden was over there, Aunt Noah told me. You never saw such peonies. We had a fish pond and a greenhouse and an icehouse. Didn't have to buy anything except sugar and coffee and flour. And over there was a paddock for trotting horses. You know there was a fair every year where Papa and other of our kind of folks used to race their sulkies. Our own county fair.

She collected the rent, and we drove away. On the road, she stopped and showed me her mother's family graveyard, a mound covered with Amiel and Hopper tombstones rising in the middle of a tobacco field. She told me she paid a boy to clean off the brush.

You know it's hard to see the old place like that, she said. But I don't see any use in holding on to things just for the sake of holding on. You children are all off in the North, marrying your niggers or your white trash—honey, I'm just fooling, you know how I talk—and pretty soon we ugly old folks are going to go. Then there will just be some bones out in the fields and some money in the bank.

That was the night that my husband called from New York with the news we had hoped for: His assignment in Europe was for Rome.

(You really pissed them off, you know, says my cousin, continuing where he left off. You were already in Italy when the article was published, and your mother never told you, but it was quite an item for the rest of the family. There was that neighbor of Aunt Noah's, Dan Mills, who was threatening to sue. They said he was ranting: *I'm not African-American like they printed there! I'm not black!*)

Well, God knows I'm sorry about it now. But really—what could I have called them? The quaint colored folk of the Carolina lowlands? Mulattos and octoroons, like something out of *Mandingo*?

(You could have thought more about it, he says, his voice softening. You could have considered things before plunging into the quilts and the superstitions.)

You know, I tell him, I did talk to Aunt Noah just after the article came out. She said: Oh, honey, some of the folks around here got worked up about what you wrote, but they calmed right down when the TV truck came around and put them on the evening news.

My cousin drums his fingers thoughtfully on the table as I look on with a certain muted glee. I can tell that he isn't familiar with this twist in the story.

(Well— he says.) Rising to brew us another pot of coffee. Public scourging finished; case closed. By degrees he changes the subject to a much-discussed new book on W.E.B. Du Bois in Germany. Have I read about that sojourn in the early 1930s? Dubois's weirdly prescient musings on American segregation and the National Socialist racial laws?

We talk about this and about his ex-wife and his upcoming trip to Celebes and the recent flood of Nigerian Kok statues on the London art market. Then, irresistibly, we turn again to Ball County. I surprise my cousin by telling him that if I can get back to the States this fall, I may go down there for Thanksgiving. With my husband. Aunt Noah invited us. That's when they kill the pigs, and I want to taste some of that fall bar-beque. Why don't you come too? I say.

(Me? I'm not a barbeque fan, he says. Having the grace to flush slightly on the ears. Aren't you afraid that they're going to burn a cross in front of your window? he adds with a smile.)

I'll never write about that place again, I say. Just one thing, though—
(What?)
What would you have called them?

He takes his time lighting up another Kretek Jakarta. His eyes, through the foreign smoke, grow as remote as Aunt Noah's, receding in the distance like a highway in a rearview mirror. And I have a moment of false nostalgia. A quick glimpse of an image that never was: a boy racing me down a long corridor of July corn, his big flat feet churning up the dirt where we'd peed to mark our territory like two young dogs, his skinny figure tearing along ahead of me, both of us breaking our necks to get to the vanishing point where the green rows come together and geometry begins. Gone.

His cigarette lit, my cousin shakes his head and gives a short exasperated laugh. (In the end, it doesn't make a damn bit of difference, does it? he says.)

Alice Munro

Family Furnishings

from *The New Yorker*

Aᴌꜰʀɪᴅᴀ. Mʏ father called her Freddie. The two of them were first cousins and lived on adjoining farms and then for a while in the same house. One day they were out in the fields of stubble playing with my father's dog, whose name was Mack. That day the sun shone, but did not melt the ice in the furrows. They stomped on the ice and enjoyed its crackle underfoot.

How could she remember a thing like that? my father said. She made it up, he said.

"I did not," she said.

"You did so."

"I did not."

All of a sudden they heard bells pealing, whistles blowing. The town bell and the church bells were ringing. The factory whistles were blowing in the town three miles away. The world had burst its seams for joy, and Mack tore out to the road, because he was sure a parade was coming. It was the end of the First World War.

Three times a week, we could read Alfrida's name in the paper. Just her first name—Alfrida. It was printed as if written by hand, a flowing, fountain-pen signature. Round and About the Town, with Alfrida. The town mentioned was not the one close by, but the city to the south, where Alfrida lived, and which my family visited perhaps once every two or three years.

Now is the time for all you future June brides to start registering your preferences at the China Cabinet, and I must tell you that if I were a bride-to-be—which alas I am not—I might resist all the patterned dinner sets, exquisite as they are, and go for the pearly-white, the ultra-modern Rosenthal . . .

Beauty treatments may come and beauty treatments may go, but the masques they slather on you at Fantine's Salon are guaranteed—speaking of brides—to make your skin bloom like orange blossoms. And to make the bride's mom—and the bride's aunts and for all I know her grandmom—feel as if they'd just taken a dip in the Fountain of Youth . . .

You would never expect Alfrida to write in this style, from the way she talked.

She was also one of the people who wrote under the name of Flora Simpson, on the Flora Simpson Housewives' Page. Women from all over the countryside believed that they were writing their letters to the plump woman with the crimped gray hair and the forgiving smile who was pictured at the top of the page. But the truth—which I was not to tell—was that the notes that appeared at the bottom of each of their letters were produced by Alfrida and a man she called Horse Henry, who otherwise did the obituaries. The women gave themselves such names as Morning Star and Lily-of-the-Valley and Green Thumb and Little Annie Rooney and Dishmop Queen. Some names were so popular that numbers had to be assigned to them—Goldilocks 1, Goldilocks 2, Goldilocks 3.

Dear Morning Star, Alfrida or Horse Henry would write,

Eczema is a dreadful pest, especially in this hot weather we're having, and I hope the baking soda does some good. Home treatments certainly ought to be respected, but it never hurts to seek out your doctor's advice. It's splendid news to hear your hubby is up and about again. It can't have been any fun with both of you under the weather . . .

In all the small towns of that part of Ontario, housewives who belonged to the Flora Simpson Club would hold an annual summer picnic. Flora Simpson always sent her special greetings but explained that there were just too many events for her to show up at all of them and she did not like to make distinctions. Alfrida said that there had been talk of sending Horse Henry done up in a wig and pillow bosoms, or perhaps herself leering like the Witch of Babylon (not even she, at my parents' table, could quote the Bible accurately and say "Whore") with a ciggie-boo stuck to her lipstick. But, oh, she said, the paper would kill us. And anyway, it would be too mean.

She always called her cigarettes ciggie-boos. When I was fifteen or sixteen she leaned across the table and asked me, "How would you like a ciggie-boo, too?" The meal was finished, and my younger brother and sister had left the table. My father was shaking his head. He had started to roll his own.

I said thank you and let Alfrida light it and smoked for the first time in front of my parents.

They pretended that it was a great joke.

"Ah, will you look at your daughter?" said my mother to my father. She rolled her eyes and clapped her hands to her chest and spoke in an artificial, languishing voice. "I'm like to faint."

"Have to get the horsewhip out," my father said, half rising in his chair.

This moment was amazing, as if Alfrida had transformed us into new people. Ordinarily, my mother would say that she did not like to see a woman smoke. She did not say that it was indecent, or unladylike—just that she did not like it. And when she said in a certain tone that she did not like something it seemed that she was not making a confession of irrationality but drawing on a private source of wisdom, which was unassailable and almost sacred. It was when she reached for this tone, with its accompanying expression of listening to inner voices, that I particularly hated her.

As for my father, he had beaten me, in this very room, not with a horsewhip but his belt, for running afoul of my mother's rules and wounding my mother's feelings, and for answering back. Now it seemed that such beatings could occur only in another universe.

My parents had been put in a corner by Alfrida—and also by me—but they had responded so gamely and gracefully that it was really as if all three of us—my mother and my father and myself—had been lifted to a new level of ease and aplomb. In that instant I could see them—particularly my mother—as being capable of a kind of lightheartedness that was scarcely ever on view.

All due to Alfrida.

Alfrida was always referred to as a career girl. This made her seem to be younger than my parents, though she was known to be about the same age. It was also said that she was a city person. And the city, when it was spoken of in this way, meant the one she lived and worked in. But it meant something else as well—not just a distinct configuration of buildings and sidewalks and streetcar lines or even a crowding together of individual people. It meant something more abstract that could be repeated over and over, something like a hive of bees, stormy but organized, not useless or deluded exactly, but disturbing and sometimes dangerous. People went into such a place when they had to and were glad when they got out. Some, however, were attracted to it—as Alfrida must have been, long ago, and as I was now, puffing on my cigarette and trying to hold it in a non-chalant way, though it seemed to have grown to the size of a baseball bat between my fingers.

My family did not have a regular social life—people did not come to the house for dinner, let alone to parties. It was a matter of class, maybe. The parents of the boy I married, about five years after this scene at the dinner table, invited people who were not related to them to dinner, and they went to afternoon parties that they spoke of, unself-consciously, as cock-tail parties. It was a life such as I had read of in magazine stories, and it seemed to me to place my in-laws in a world of storybook privilege.

What our family did was put boards in the dining-room table two or three times a year to entertain my grandmother and my aunts—my father's older sisters—and their husbands. We did this at Christmas or Thanksgiving, when it was our turn, and perhaps also when a relative from another part of the province showed up on a visit. This visitor would always be a person rather like the aunts and their husbands and never the least bit like Alfrida.

My mother and I would start preparing for such dinners a couple of days ahead. We ironed the good tablecloth, which was as heavy as a bed quilt, and washed the good dishes, which had been sitting in the china cabinet collecting dust, and wiped the legs of the dining-room chairs, as well as making the jellied salads, the pies and cakes, that had to accom-pany the central roast turkey or baked ham and bowls of vegetables. There had to be far too much to eat, and most of the conversation at the table had to do with the food, with the company saying how good it was and being urged to have more, and saying that they couldn't, they were stuffed, and then the aunts' husbands relenting, taking more, and the aunts taking just a little more and saying that they shouldn't, they were ready to burst.

And dessert still to come.

There was hardly any idea of a general conversation, and in fact there was a feeling that conversation that passed beyond certain understood limits might be a disruption, a showing-off. My mother's understanding of the limits was not reliable, and she sometimes could not wait out the pauses or honor the aversion to follow-up. So when somebody said, "Seen Harley upstreet yesterday," she was liable to say, perhaps, "Do you think a man like Harley is a confirmed bachelor? Or he just hasn't met the right person?"

As if, when you mentioned seeing a person you were bound to have something further to say, something *interesting*.

Then there might be a silence, not because the people at the table meant to be rude but because they were flummoxed. Till my father would say with embarrassment, and oblique reproach, "He seems to get on all right by hisself."

If his relatives had not been present, he would more likely have said "himself."

And everybody went on cutting, spooning, swallowing, in the glare of the fresh tablecloth, with the bright light pouring in through the newly washed windows. These dinners were always in the middle of the day.

The people at that table were quite capable of talk. Washing and drying the dishes, in the kitchen, the aunts would talk about who had a tumor, a septic throat, a bad mess of boils. They would tell about how their own digestions, kidneys, nerves were functioning. Mention of intimate bodily matters seemed never to be so out of place, or suspect, as the mention of something read in a magazine, or an item in the news—it was improper somehow to pay attention to anything that was not close at hand. Meanwhile, resting on the porch, or during a brief walk out to look at the crops, the aunts' husbands might pass on the information that somebody was in a tight spot with the bank, or still owed money on an expensive piece of machinery, or had invested in a bull that was a disappointment on the job.

It could have been that they felt clamped down by the formality of the dining room, the presence of bread-and-butter plates and dessert spoons, when it was the custom, at other times, to put a piece of pie right onto a dinner plate that had been cleaned up with bread. (It would have been an offense, however, not to set things out in this proper way. In their own houses, on like occasions, they would put their guests through the same paces.) It may have been just that eating was one thing, and talking was something else.

When Alfrida came it was altogether another story. The good cloth would be spread and the good dishes would be out. My mother would have gone to a lot of trouble with the food and she would be nervous about the results—and probably she would have abandoned the usual turkey-and-stuffing-and-mashed-potatoes menu and made something like chicken salad surrounded by mounds of molded rice with cut-up pimientos, and this would be followed by a dessert involving gelatin and egg white and whipped cream, taking a long, nerve-racking time to set because we had no refrigerator and it had to be chilled on the cellar floor. But the constraint, the pall over the table, was quite absent. Alfrida not only accepted second helpings, she asked for them. And she did this almost absentmindedly, and tossed off her compliments in the same way, as if the food, the eating of the food, was a secondary though agreeable thing, and she was really there to talk, and make other people talk, and anything you wanted to talk about—almost anything—would be fine.

She always visited in summer, and usually she wore some sort of striped, silky sundress, with a halter top that left her back bare. Her back was not pretty, being sprinkled with little dark moles, and her shoulders were bony and her chest nearly flat. My father would always remark on how much she could eat and remain thin. Or he turned truth on its head by noting that her appetite was as picky as ever, but she still hadn't been prevented from larding on the fat. (It was not considered out of place in our family to comment about fatness or skinniness or pallor or ruddiness or baldness.)

Her dark hair was done up in rolls above her face and at the sides, in the style of the time. Her skin was brownish-looking, netted with fine wrinkles, and her mouth wide, the lower lip rather thick, almost drooping, painted with a hearty lipstick that left a smear on the teacup and water tumbler. When her mouth was opened wide—as it nearly always was, talking or laughing—you could see that some of her teeth had been pulled at the back. Nobody could say that she was good-looking—any woman over twenty-five seemed to me to have pretty well passed beyond the possibility of being good-looking, anyway, to have lost the right to be so, and perhaps even the desire—but she was fervent and dashing. My father said thoughtfully that she had zing.

Alfrida talked to my father about things that were happening in the world, about politics. My father read the paper, he listened to the radio, he had opinions about these things but rarely got a chance to talk about them. The aunts' husbands had opinions too, but theirs were brief and unvaried and expressed an everlasting distrust of all public figures and particularly all foreigners, so that most of the time all that could be gotten out of them were grunts of dismissal. My grandmother was deaf—nobody could tell how much she knew or what she thought about anything, and the aunts themselves seemed fairly proud of how much they didn't know or didn't have to pay attention to. My mother had been a schoolteacher, and she could readily have pointed out all the countries of Europe on the map, but she saw everything through a personal haze, with the British Empire and the royal family looming large and everything else diminished, thrown into a jumble-heap that it was easy for her to disregard.

Alfrida's views were not really so far away from those of the uncles. Or so it appeared. But instead of grunting and letting the subject go, she gave her hooting laugh, and told stories about prime ministers and the American president and John L. Lewis and the mayor of Montreal—stories in which they all came out badly. She told stories about the royal family too, but there she made a distinction between the good ones like the king and queen and the beautiful Duchess of Kent and the dreadful ones like the Windsors and old King Eddy, who—she said—had a certain disease and had marked his wife's neck by trying to strangle her, which was why she always had to wear her pearls. This distinction coincided pretty well with one my mother made but seldom spoke about, so she did not object—though the reference to syphilis made her wince.

I smiled at it, knowingly, with a foolhardy composure.

Alfrida called the Russians funny names, Mikoyan-sky, Uncle Joe-sky. She believe that they were pulling the wool over everybody's eyes, and that the United Nations was a farce that would never work and that Japan would rise again and should have been finished off when there was the chance. She didn't trust Quebec either. Or the pope. There was a problem for her with Senator McCarthy—she would have liked to be on his side, but his being a Catholic was a stumbling block. She called the pope the poop. She relished the thought of all the crooks and scoundrels to be found in the world.

Sometimes it seemed as if she was putting on a show—a display, maybe to tease my father. To rile him up, as he himself would have said, to get his goat. But not because she disliked him or even wanted to make him uncomfortable. Quite the opposite. She might have been tormenting him as young girls torment boys at school, when arguments are a peculiar delight to both sides and insults are taken as flattery. My father argued with her, always in a mild steady voice, and yet it was clear that he had the intention of goading her on. Sometimes he would do a turnaround, and say that maybe she was right—that with her work on the newspaper, she must have sources of information that he couldn't have. You've put me straight, he would say, if I had any sense I'd be obliged to you. And she would say, Don't give me that load of baloney.

"You two," said my mother, in mock despair and perhaps in real exhaustion, and Alfrida told her to go and have a lie-down, she deserved it after this splendiferous dinner, she and I would manage the dishes. My mother was subject to a tremor in her right arm, a stiffness in her fingers, that she believed came when she got overtired.

While we worked in the kitchen Alfrida talked to me about celebrities—actors, even minor movie stars, who had made stage appearances in the city where she lived. In a lowered voice still broken by wildly disrespectful laughter she told me stories of their bad behavior, the rumors of private scandals that had never made it into the magazines. She mentioned queers, man-made bosoms, household triangles—all things that I had found hints of in my reading but felt giddy to hear about, even at third or fourth hand, in real life.

Alfrida's teeth always got my attention, so that even in these confidential recitals I sometimes lost track of what was being said. Those teeth that were left, across the front, were each of a slightly different color, no two alike. Some with a fairly strong enamel tended towards shades of dark ivory, others were opalescent, shadowed with lilac, and giving out fish-flashes of silver rims, occasionally a gleam of gold. People's teeth in those days seldom made such a solid, handsome show as they do now, unless they were false. But these teeth of Alfrida's were unusual in their individuality, clear separation, and large size. When Alfrida let out some jibe that was especially, knowingly outrageous, they seemed to leap to the fore like a palace guard, like jolly spear-fighters.

"She always did have trouble with her teeth," the aunts said. "She had that abscess, remember, the poison went all through her system."

How like them, I thought, to toss aside Alfrida's wit and style and turn her teeth into a sorry problem.

"Why doesn't she just have them all out and be done with it?" they said.

"Likely she couldn't afford it," said my grandmother, surprising everybody as she sometimes did, by showing that she had been keeping up with the conversation all along.

And surprising me with the new, everyday sort of light this shed on Alfrida's life. I had believed that Alfrida was rich—rich at least in comparison with the rest of the family. She lived in an apartment—I had never seen it, but to me that fact conveyed at least the idea of a very civilized life—and she wore clothes that were not homemade, and her shoes were not Oxfords like the shoes of practically all the other grown-up women I knew—they were sandals made of bright strips of the new plastic. It was hard to know whether my grandmother was simply living in the past, when getting your false teeth was the solemn, crowning expense of a lifetime, or whether she really knew things about Alfrida's life that I never would have guessed.

The rest of the family was never present when Alfrida had dinner at our house. She did go to see my grandmother, who was her aunt, her mother's sister. My grandmother no longer lived at her own house but lived alternately with one or the other of the aunts, and Alfrida went to whichever house she was living at the time, but not to the other house, to see the other aunt who was as much her cousin as my father was. And the meal she took was never with any of them. Usually she came to our house first and visited awhile, and then gathered herself up, as if reluctantly, to make the other visit. When she came back later and we sat down to eat, nothing derogatory was said outright against the aunts and their husbands, and certainly nothing disrespectful about my grandmother. In fact, it was the way that my grandmother would be spoken of by Alfrida—a sudden sobriety and concern in her voice, even a touch of fear (what about her blood pressure, had she been to the doctor lately, what did he have to say?)—that made me aware of the difference, the coolness or possibly unfriendly restraint, with which she asked after the others. Then there would be a similar restraint in my mother's reply, and an extra gravity in my father's—a caricature of gravity, you might say—that showed how they all agreed about something they could not say.

On the day when I smoked the cigarette Alfrida decided to take this a bit further, and she said solemnly, "How about Asa, then? Is he still as much of a conversation grabber as ever?"

My father shook his head sadly, as if the thought of this uncle's garrulousness must weigh us all down.

"Indeed," he said. "He is indeed."

Then I took my chance.

"Looks like the roundworms have got into the hogs," I said. "Yup."

Except for the "yup," this was just what my uncle had said, and he had said it at this very table, being overcome by an uncharacteristic need to break the silence or to pass on something important that had just come to mind. And I said it with just his steady grunts, his innocent solemnity.

Alfrida gave a great, approving laugh, showing her festive teeth. "That's it, she's got him to a *T*."

My father bent over his plate, as if to hide how he was laughing too, but of course not really hiding it, and my mother shook her head, biting her lips, smiling. I felt a keen triumph. Nothing was said to put me in my place, no reproof for what was sometimes called my sarcasm, my being smart. The word "smart" when it was used about me, in the family, might mean intelligent, and then it was used rather grudgingly—"oh, she's smart enough some ways"—or it might be used to mean pushy, attention-seeking, obnoxious. *Don't be so smart.*

Sometimes my mother said sadly, "You have a cruel tongue."

Sometimes—and this was a great deal worse—my father was disgusted with me.

"What makes you think you have the right to run down decent people?"

This day nothing like that happened—I seemed to be as free as a visitor at the table, almost as free as Alfrida, and flourishing under the banner of my own personality.

But there was a gap about to open, and perhaps that was the last time, the very last time, that Alfrida sat at our table. Christmas cards continued to be exchanged, possibly even letters—as long as my mother could manage a pen—and we still read Alfrida's name in the paper, but I cannot recall any visits during the last couple of years I lived at home.

It may have been that Alfrida asked if she could bring her friend and had been told that she could not. If she was already living with him, that would have been one reason, and if he was the same man she had later, the fact that he was married would have been another. My parents would have been united in this. My mother had a horror of irregular sex or flaunted sex—of any sex, you might say, for the proper married kind was not acknowledged at all—and my father too judged these matters strictly at that time in his life. He might have had a special objection, also, to a man who could get a hold over Alfrida.

She would have made herself cheap in their eyes. I can imagine either one of them saying it. *She didn't need to go and make herself cheap.*

But she may not have asked at all, she may have known enough not to. During the time of those earlier, lively visits there may have been no man in her life, and then when there was one, her attention may have shifted entirely. She may have become a different person then, as she certainly was later on.

Or she may have been wary of the special atmosphere of a household where there is a sick person who will go on getting sicker and never get better. Which was the case with my mother, whose symptoms joined together, and turned a corner, and instead of a worry and an inconvenience became her whole destiny.

"The poor thing," the aunts said.

And as my mother was changed from a mother into a stricken presence around the house, these other, formerly so restricted females in the family seemed to gain some little liveliness and increased competence in the world. My grandmother got herself a hearing aid—something nobody would have suggested to her. One of the aunts' husbands—not Asa, but the one called Irvine—died, and the aunt who had been married to him learned to drive the car and got a job doing alterations in a clothing store and no longer wore a hairnet.

They called to see my mother, and saw always the same thing—that the one who had been better-looking, who had never quite let them forget she was a schoolteacher, was growing month by month more slow and stiff in the movements of her limbs and more thick and importunate in her speech, and that nothing was going to help her.

They told me to take good care of her.

"She's your mother," they reminded me.

"The poor thing."

Alfrida would not have been able to say those things, and she might not have been able to find anything to say in their place.

Her not coming to see us was all right with me. I didn't want people coming. I had no time for them, I had became a furious housekeeper—

waxing the floors and ironing even the dish towels, and this was all done to keep some sort of disgrace (my mother's deterioration seemed to be a unique disgrace that infected us all) at bay. It was done to make it seem as if I lived with my parents and my brother and my sister in a normal family in an ordinary house, but the moment somebody stepped in our door and saw my mother they saw that this was not so and they pitied us. A thing I could not stand.

I won a scholarship. I didn't stay home to take care of my mother or of anything else. I went off to college. The college was in the city where Alfrida lived. After a few months she asked me to come for supper, but I could not go, because I worked every evening of the week except on Sundays. I worked in the city library, downtown, and in the college library, both of which stayed open until nine o'clock. Some time later, during the winter, Alfrida asked me again, and this time the invitation was for a Sunday. I told her that I could not come because I was going to a concert.

"Oh—a date?" she said, and I said yes, but at the time it was not true. I would go to the free Sunday concerts in the college auditorium with another girl, or two or three other girls, for something to do and in the faint hope of meeting some boys there.

"Well you'll have to bring him around sometime," Alfrida said. "I'm dying to meet him."

Towards the end of the year I did have someone to bring, and I had actually met him at a concert. At least, he had seen me at a concert and had phoned me up and asked me to go out with him. But I would never have brought him to meet Alfrida. I would never have brought any of my new friends to meet her. My new friends were people who said, "Have you read *Look Homeward Angel*? Oh, you have to read that. Have you read *Buddenbrooks*?" They were people with whom I went to see *Forbidden Games* and *Les Enfants du Paradis* when the Film Society brought them in. The boy I went out with, and later became engaged to, had taken me to the Music Building, where you could listen to records at lunch hour. He introduced me to Gounod and because of Gounod I loved opera, and because of opera I loved Mozart.

When Alfrida left a message at my rooming house, asking me to call back, I never did. After that she didn't call again.

· · ·

She still wrote for the paper—occasionally I glanced at one of her rhapsodies about Royal Doulton figurines or imported ginger biscuits or honeymoon negligees. Very likely she was still answering the letters from the Flora Simpson housewives, and still laughing at them. Now that I was living in that city I seldom looked at the paper that had once seemed to me the center of city life—and even, in a way, the center of our life at home, sixty miles away. The jokes, the compulsive insincerity, of people like Alfrida and Horse Henry now struck me as tawdry and boring.

I did not worry about running into her, even in this city that was not, after all, so very large. I never went into the shops that she mentioned in her column. I had no reason ever to walk past the newspaper building, and she lived far away from my rooming house, somewhere on the south side of town.

Nor did I think that Alfrida was the kind of person to show up at the library. The very word, "library," would probably make her turn down her big mouth in a parody of consternation, as she used to do at the books in the bookcase in our home—those books not bought in my time, some of them won as school prizes by my teenaged parents (there was my mother's maiden name, in her beautiful lost handwriting), books that seemed to me not like things bought in a store at all, but like presences in the house just as the trees outside the window were not plants but presences rooted in the ground. *The Mill on the Floss, The Call of the Wild, The Heart of Midlothian*. "Lot of hotshot reading in there," Alfrida had said. "Bet you don't crack those very often." And my father had said no, he didn't, falling in with her comradely tone of dismissal or even contempt and to some extent telling a lie, because he did look into them, once in a long while, when he had the time.

That was the kind of lie that I hoped never to have to tell again, the contempt I hoped never to have to show, about the things that really mattered to me. And in order not to have to do that, I would pretty well have to stay clear of the people I used to know.

At the end of my second year I was leaving college—my scholarship had covered only two years there. It didn't matter—I was planning to be a writer anyway. And I was getting married.

Alfrida had heard about this, and she got in touch with me again.

"I guess you must've been too busy to call me, or maybe nobody ever gave you my messages," she said.

I said that maybe I had been, or maybe they hadn't.

This time I agreed to visit. A visit would not commit me to anything, since I was not going to be living in this city in the future. I picked a Sunday, just after my final exams were over, when my fiancé was going to be in Ottawa for a job interview. The day was bright and sunny—it was around the beginning of May. I decided to walk. I had hardly ever been south of Dundas Street or east of Adelaide, so there were parts of the city that were entirely strange to me. The shade trees along the northern streets had just come out in leaf, and the lilacs, the ornamental crab apple trees, the beds of tulips were all in flower, the lawns like fresh carpets. But after a while I found myself walking along streets where there were no shade trees, streets where the houses were hardly an arm's reach from the side-walk, and where such lilacs as there were—lilacs will grow anywhere—were pale, as if sun-bleached, and their fragrance did not carry. On these streets, as well as houses there were narrow apartment buildings, only two or three stories high—some with the utilitarian decoration of a rim of bricks around their doors, and some with raised windows and limp cur-tains falling out over their sills.

Alfrida lived in a house, not in an apartment building. She had the whole upstairs of a house. The downstairs, at least the front part of the downstairs, had been turned into a shop, which was closed, because of Sunday. It was a secondhand shop—I could see through the dirty front windows a lot of nondescript furniture with stacks of old dishes and uten-sils set everywhere. The only thing that caught my eye was a honey pail, exactly like the honey pail with a blue sky and a golden beehive in which I had carried my lunch to school when I was six or seven years old. I could remember reading over and over the words on its side.

All pure honey will granulate.

I had no idea then what "granulate" meant, but I liked the sound of it. It seemed ornate and delicious.

I had taken longer to get there than I had expected and I was very hot. I had not thought that Alfrida, inviting me to lunch, would present me with a meal like the Sunday dinners at home, but it was cooked meat and vegetables I smelled as I climbed the outdoor stairway.

"I thought you'd got lost," Alfrida called out above me. "I was about to get up a rescue party."

Instead of a sundress she was wearing a pink blouse with a floppy bow at the neck, tucked into a pleated brown skirt. Her hair was no longer done up in smooth rolls but cut short and frizzed around her face, its dark brown color now harshly touched with red. And her face, which I remembered as lean and summer-tanned, had got fuller and somewhat pouchy. Her makeup stood out on her skin like orange-pink paint in the noon light.

But the biggest difference was that she had gotten false teeth, of a uniform color, slightly overfilling her mouth and giving an anxious edge to her old expression of slapdash eagerness.

"Well—haven't you plumped out," she said. "You used to be so skinny."

This was true, but I did not like to hear it. Along with all the girls at the rooming house, I ate cheap food—copious meals of Kraft dinners and packages of jam-filled cookies. My fiancé, so sturdily and possessively in favor of everything about me, said that he liked full-bodied women and that I reminded him of Jane Russell. I did not mind his saying that, but usually I was affronted when people had anything to say about my appearance. Particularly when it was somebody like Alfrida—somebody who had lost all importance in my life. I believed that such people had no right to be looking at me, or forming any opinions about me, let alone stating them.

This house was narrow across the front, but long from front to back. There was a living room whose ceiling sloped at the sides and whose windows overlooked the street, a hall-like dining room with no windows at all because side bedrooms with dormers opened off it, a kitchen, a bathroom also without windows that got its daylight through a pebbled-glass pane in its door, and across the back of the house a glassed-in sunporch.

The sloping ceilings made the rooms look makeshift, as if they were only pretending to be anything but bedrooms. But they were crowded with serious furniture—dining-room table and chairs, kitchen table and chairs, living-room sofa and recliner—all meant for larger, proper rooms. Doilies on the tables, squares of embroidered white cloth protecting the backs and arms of sofa and chairs, sheer curtains across the windows and heavy flowered drapes at the sides—it was all more like the aunts' houses than I would have thought possible. And on the dining-room wall—not in the bathroom or bedroom but in the dining room—there hung a picture that was the silhouette of a girl in a hoopskirt, all constructed of pink satin ribbon.

A strip of tough linoleum was laid down on the dining-room floor, on the path from the kitchen to the living room.

Alfrida seemed to guess something of what I was thinking.

"I know I've got far too much stuff in here," she said. "But it's my parents' stuff. It's family furnishings, and I couldn't let them go."

I had never thought of her as having parents. Her mother had died long ago, and she had been brought up by my grandmother, who was her aunt.

"My dad and mother's," Alfrida said. "When Dad went off, your grandma kept it because she said it ought to be mine when I grew up, and so here it is. I couldn't turn it down, when she went to that trouble."

Now it came back to me—the part of Alfrida's life that I had forgotten about. Her father had married again. He had left the farm and got a job working for the railway. He had some other children, the family moved from one town to another, and sometimes Alfrida used to mention them, in a joking way that had something to do with how many children there had been and how close they came together and how much the family had to move around.

"Come and meet Bill," Alfrida said.

Bill was out on the sunporch. He sat, as if waiting to be summoned, on a low couch or daybed that was covered with a brown plaid blanket. The blanket was rumpled—he must have been lying on it recently—and the blinds on the windows were all pulled down to their sills. The light in the room—the hot sunlight coming through the rain-marked yellow blinds—and the rumpled rough blanket and faded, dented cushion, even the smell of the blanket, and of the masculine slippers, old scuffed slippers that had lost their shape and pattern, reminded me—just as much as the doilies and the heavy polished furniture in the inner rooms had done, and the ribbon-girl on the wall—of my aunts' houses. There, too, you could come upon a shabby male hideaway with its furtive yet insistent odors, its shamefaced but stubborn look of contradicting the female domain.

Bill stood up and shook my hand, however, as the uncles would never have done with a strange girl. Or with any girl. No specific rudeness would have held them back, just a dread of appearing ceremonious.

He was a tall man with wavy, glistening gray hair and a smooth but not young-looking face. A handsome man, with the force of his good looks somehow drained away—by indifferent health, or some bad luck, or lack of gumption. But he had still a worn courtesy, a way of bending towards a woman, that suggested the meeting would be a pleasure, for her and for himself.

Alfrida directed us into the windowless dining room where the lights were on in the middle of this bright day. I got the impression that the meal had been ready some time ago, and that my late arrival had delayed their usual schedule. Bill served the roast chicken and dressing, Alfrida the vegetables. Alfrida said to Bill, "Honey, what do you think that is beside your plate?" and then he remembered to pick up his napkin.

He had not much to say. He offered the gravy, he inquired as to whether I wanted mustard relish or salt and pepper, he followed the conversation by turning his head towards Alfrida or towards me. Every so often he made a little whistling sound between his teeth, a shivery sound that seemed meant to be genial and appreciative and that I thought at first might be a prelude to some remark. But it never was, and Alfrida never paused for it. I have since seen reformed drinkers who behaved somewhat as he did—chiming in agreeably but unable to carry things beyond that, helplessly preoccupied. I never knew whether that was true of Bill, but he did seem to carry around a history of defeat, of troubles borne and lessons learned. He had an air too of gallant accommodation towards whatever choices had gone wrong or chances hadn't panned out.

These were frozen peas and carrots, Alfrida said. Frozen vegetables were fairly new at the time.

"They beat the canned," she said. "They're practically as good as fresh."

Then Bill made a whole statement. He said they were better than fresh. The color, the flavor, everything was better than fresh. He said it was remarkable what they could do now and what would be done by way of freezing things in the future.

Alfrida leaned forward, smiling. She seemed almost to hold her breath, as if he was her child taking unsupported steps, or a first lone wobble on a bicycle.

There was a way they could inject something into a chicken, he told us, there was a new process that would have every chicken coming out the same, plump and tasty. No such thing as taking a risk on getting an inferior chicken anymore.

"Bill's field is chemistry," Alfrida said.

When I had nothing to say to this she added, "He worked for Gooderhams."

Still nothing.

"The distillers," she said. "Gooderhams Whisky."

The reason that I had nothing to say was not that I was rude or bored (or any more rude than I was naturally at that time, or more bored than I had expected to be) but that I did not understand that I should ask questions—almost any questions at all, to draw a shy male into conversation, to shake him out of his abstraction and set him up as a man of a certain authority, therefore the man of the house. I did not understand why Alfrida looked at him with such a fiercely encouraging smile. All of my experience of a woman with men, of a woman listening to her man, hoping and hoping that he will establish himself as somebody she can reasonably be proud of, was in the future. The only observation I had made of couples was of my aunts and uncles and of my mother and father, and those husbands and wives seemed to have remote and formalized connections and no obvious dependence on each other.

Bill continued eating as if he had not heard this mention of his profession and his employer, and Alfrida began to question me about my courses. She was still smiling, but her smile had changed. There was a little twitch of impatience and unpleasantness in it, as if she was just waiting for me to get to the end of my explanations so that she could say—as she did say—"You couldn't get me to read that stuff for a million dollars."

"Life's too short," she said. "You know, down at the paper we sometimes get somebody that's been through all that. Honors English. Honors Philosophy. You don't know what to do with them. They can't write worth a nickel. I've told you that, haven't I?" she said to Bill, and Bill looked up and gave her his dutiful smile.

She let this settle.

"So what do you do for fun?" she said.

A Streetcar Named Desire was being done in a theater in Toronto at that time, and I told her that I had gone down on the train with a couple of friends to see it.

Alfrida let the knife and fork clatter onto her plate.

"That filth," she cried. Her face leapt out at me, carved with disgust. Then she spoke more calmly but still with a virulent displeasure.

"You went *all the way to Toronto* to see that filth."

We had finished the dessert, and Bill picked that moment to ask if he might be excused. He asked Alfrida, then with the slightest bow he asked me. He went back to the sunporch and in a little while we could smell his pipe. Alfrida, watching him go, seemed to forget about me and the play. There was a look of such stricken tenderness on her face that when she stood up I thought she was going to follow him. But she was only going to get her cigarettes.

She held them out to me, and when I took one she said, with a deliberate effort at jollity, "I see you kept up the bad habit I got you started on." She might have remembered that I was not a child anymore and I did not have to be in her house and that there was no point in making an enemy of me. And I wasn't going to argue—I did not care what Alfrida thought about Tennessee Williams. Or what she thought about anything else.

"I guess it's your own business," Alfrida said. "You can go where you want to go." And she added, "After all—you'll pretty soon be a married woman."

By her tone, this could mean either "I have to allow that you're grown up now" or "Pretty soon you'll have to toe the line."

We got up and started to collect the dishes. Working close to each other in the small space between the kitchen table and counter and the refrigerator, we soon developed without speaking about it a certain order and harmony of scraping and stacking and putting the leftover food into smaller containers for storage and filling the sink with hot, soapy water and pouncing on any piece of cutlery that hadn't been touched and slipping it into the baize-lined drawer in the dining-room buffet. We brought the ashtray out to the kitchen and stopped every now and then to take a restorative, businesslike drag on our cigarettes. There are things women agree on or don't agree on when they work together in this way—whether it is all right to smoke, for instance, or preferable not to smoke because some migratory ash might find its way onto a clean dish, or whether every single thing that has been on the table has to be washed even if it has not been used—and it turned out that Alfrida and I agreed. Also, the thought that I could get away, once the dishes were done, made me feel more relaxed and generous. I had already said that I had to meet a friend that afternoon.

"These are pretty dishes," I said. They were creamy-colored, slightly yellowish, with a rim of blue flowers.

"Well—they were my mother's wedding dishes," Alfrida said. "That was one other good thing your grandma did for me. She packed up all my mother's dishes and put them away until the time came when I could use them. Jeanie never knew they existed. They wouldn't have lasted long, with that bunch."

Jeanie. That bunch. Her stepmother and the half brothers and sisters.

"You know about that, don't you?" Alfrida said. "You know what happened to my mother?"

Of course I knew. Alfrida's mother had died when a lamp exploded in her hands—that is, she died of burns she got when a lamp exploded in her hands—and my aunts and my mother had spoken of this regularly. Nothing could be said about Alfrida's mother or about Alfrida's father, and very little about Alfrida herself—without that death being dragged in and tacked onto it. It was the reason that Alfrida's father left the farm (always somewhat of a downward step morally if not financially). It was a reason to be desperately careful with coal oil, and a reason to be grateful for electricity, whatever the cost. And it was a dreadful thing for a child of Alfrida's age, whatever. (That is—whatever she had done with herself since.)

If it hadn't've been for the thunderstorm she wouldn't ever have been lighting a lamp in the middle of the afternoon.

She lived all that night and the next day and the next night and it would have been the best thing in the world for her if she hadn't've.

And just the year after that the Hydro came down their road, and they didn't have need of the lamps anymore.

The aunts and my mother seldom felt the same way about anything, but they shared a feeling about this story. The feeling was in their voices whenever they said Alfrida's mother's name. The story seemed to be a horrible treasure to them, something our family could claim that nobody else could, a distinction that would never be let go. To listen to them had always made me feel as if there was some obscene connivance going on, a fond fingering of whatever was grisly or disastrous. Their voices were like worms slithering around in my insides.

Men were not like this, in my experience. Men looked away from frightful happenings as soon as they could and behaved as if there was no use, once things were over with, in mentioning them or thinking about them ever again. They didn't want to stir themselves up, or stir other people up.

So if Alfrida was going to talk about it, I thought, it was a good thing that my fiancé had not come. A good thing that he didn't have to hear about Alfrida's mother, on top of finding out about my mother and my family's relative or maybe considerable poverty. He admired opera and Laurence Olivier's *Hamlet,* but he had no time for tragedy—for the squalor of tragedy—in ordinary life. His parents were healthy and good-looking and prosperous (though he said of course that they were dull), and it seemed he had not had to know anybody who did not live in fairly sunny circumstances. Failures in life—failures of luck, of health, or finances—all struck him as lapses, and his resolute approval of me did not extend to my ramshackle background.

"They wouldn't let me in to see her, at the hospital," Alfrida said, and at least she was saying this in her normal voice, not preparing the way with any special piety, or greasy excitement. "Well, I probably wouldn't have let me in either, if I'd been in their shoes. I've no idea what she looked like. Probably all bound up like a mummy. Or if she wasn't she should have been. I wasn't there when it happened, I was at school. It got very dark and the teacher turned the lights on—we had the lights, at school—and we all had to stay till the thunderstorm was over. Then my Aunt Lily—well, your grandmother—she came to meet me and took me to her place. And I never got to see my mother again."

I thought that was all she was going to say but in a moment she continued, in a voice that had actually brightened up a bit, as if she was preparing for a laugh.

"I yelled and yelled my fool head off that I wanted to see her. I carried on and carried on, and finally when they couldn't shut me up your grandmother said to me, 'You're just better off not to see her. You would not want to see her, if you knew what she looks like now. You wouldn't want to remember her this way.'

"But you know what I said? I remember saying it. I said, But she would want to see me. *She would want to see me.*"

Then she really did laugh, or make a snorting sound that was evasive and scornful.

"I must've thought I was a pretty big cheese, mustn't I? *She would want to see me.*"

This was a part of the story I had never heard.

And the minute that I heard it, something happened. It was as if a trap had snapped shut, to hold these words in my head. I did not exactly understand what use I would have for them. I only knew how they jolted me and released me, right away, to breathe a different kind of air, available only to myself.

She would want to see me.

The story I wrote, with this in it, would not be written till years later, not until it had become quite unimportant to think about who had put the idea into my head in the first place.

I thanked Alfrida and said that I had to go. Alfrida went to call Bill to say good-bye to me, but came back to report that he had fallen asleep.

"He'll be kicking himself when he wakes up," she said. "He enjoyed meeting you."

She took off her apron and accompanied me all the way down the outside steps. At the bottom of the steps was a gravel path leading around to the sidewalk. The gravel crunched under our feet and she stumbled in her thin-soled shoes.

She said, "Ouch! Goldarn it," and caught hold of my shoulder.

"How's your dad?" she said.

"He's all right."

"He works too hard."

I said, "He has to."

"Oh, I know. And how's your mother?"

"She's about the same."

She turned aside towards the shop window.

"Who do they think is ever going to buy this junk? Look at that honey pail. Your dad and I used to take our lunch to school in pails just like that."

"So did I," I said.

"Did you?" She squeezed me. "You tell your folks I'm thinking about them, will you do that?"

Alfrida did not come to my father's funeral. I wondered if that was because she did not want to meet me. As far as I knew she had never made public what she held against me; nobody else would know about it. But my father had known. When I was home visiting him and learned that Alfrida was living not far away—in my grandmother's house, in fact, which she had finally inherited—I had suggested that we go to see her. This was in the flurry between my two marriages, when I was in an expansive mood, newly released and able to make contact with anyone I chose.

My father said, "Well, you know, Alfrida was a bit upset."

He was calling her Alfrida now. When had that started?

I could not even think, at first, what Alfrida might be upset about. My father had to remind me of the story, published several years ago, and I was surprised, even impatient and a little angry, to think of Alfrida's objecting to something that seemed now to have so little to do with her.

"It wasn't Alfrida at all," I said to my father. "I changed it, I wasn't even thinking about her. It was a character. Anybody could see that."

But as a matter of fact there was still the exploding lamp, the mother in her charnel wrappings, the staunch, bereft child.

"Well," my father said. He was in general quite pleased that I had become a writer, but there were reservations he had about what might be called my character. About the fact that I had ended my marriage for personal—that is, wanton—reasons, and the way I went around justifying myself—or perhaps, as he would have said, weaseling out of things. He would not say so—it was not his business anymore.

I asked him how he knew that Alfrida felt this way.

He said, "A letter."

A letter, though they lived not far apart. I did feel sorry to think that he had had to bear the brunt of what could be taken as my thoughtlessness, or even my wrongdoing. Also that he and Alfrida seemed now to be on such formal terms. I wondered what he was leaving out. Had he felt compelled to defend me to Alfrida, as he had to defend my writing to other people? He would do that now, though it was never easy for him. In his uneasy defense he might have said something harsh.

Through me, peculiar difficulties had developed for him.

There was a danger whenever I was on home ground. It was the danger of seeing my life through other eyes than my own. Seeing it as an ever-increasing roll of words like barbed wire, intricate, bewildering, uncomforting—set against the rich productions, the food, flowers, and knitted garments, of other women's domesticity. It became harder to say that it was worth the trouble.

Worth my trouble, maybe, but what about anyone else's?

My father had said that Alfrida was living alone now. I asked him what had become of Bill. He said that all of that was outside of his jurisdiction. But he believed there had been a bit of a rescue operation.

"Of Bill? How come? Who by?"

"Well, I believe there was a wife."

"I met him at Alfrida's once. I liked him."

"People did. Women."

I had to consider that the rupture might have had nothing to do with me. My stepmother had urged my father into a new sort of life. They went bowling and curling and regularly joined other couples for coffee and doughnuts at Tim Horton's. She had been a widow for a long time before she married him, and she had many friends from those days who became new friends for him. What had happened with him and Alfrida might have been simply one of the changes, the wearing-out of old attachments, that I understood so well in my own life but did not expect to happen in the lives of older people—particularly, as I would have said, in the lives of people at home.

My stepmother died just a little while before my father. After their short, happy marriage they were sent to separate cemeteries to lie beside their first, more troublesome, partners. Before either of those deaths Alfrida had moved back to the city. She didn't sell the house, she just went away and left it. My father wrote to me, "That's a pretty funny way of doing things."

There were a lot of people at my father's funeral, a lot of people I didn't know. A woman came across the grass in the cemetery to speak to me—I thought at first she must be a friend of my stepmother's. Then I saw that the woman was only a few years past my own age. The stocky figure and crown of gray-blond curls and floral-patterned jacket made her look older.

"I recognize you by your picture," she said. "Alfrida used to always be bragging about you."

I said, "Alfrida's not dead?"

"Oh, no," the woman, said, and went on to tell me that Alfrida was in a nursing home in a town just north of Toronto.

"I moved her down there so's I could keep an eye on her."

Now it was easy to tell—even by her voice—that she was somebody of my own generation, and it came to me that she must be one of the other family, a half sister of Alfrida's, born when Alfrida was almost grown up.

She told me her name, and it was of course not the same as Alfrida's—she must have married. And I couldn't recall Alfrida's ever mentioning any of her half family by their first names.

I asked how Alfrida was, and the woman said her own eyesight was so bad that she was legally blind. And she had a serious kidney problem, which meant that she had to be on dialysis twice a week.

"Other than that—?" she said, and laughed. I thought, yes, a sister, because I could hear something of Alfrida in that reckless, tossed laugh.

"So she doesn't travel too good," she said. "Or else I would've brought her. She still gets the paper from here and I read it to her sometimes. That's where I saw about your dad."

I wondered out loud, impulsively, if I should go to visit, at the nursing home. The emotions of the funeral—all the warm and relieved and reconciled feelings opened up in me by the death of my father at a reasonable age—prompted this suggestion. It would have been hard to carry out. My husband—my second husband—and I had only two days here before we were flying to Europe on an already delayed holiday.

"I don't know if you'd get so much out of it," the woman said. "She has her good days. Then she has her bad days. You never know. Sometimes I think she's putting it on. Like, she'll sit there all day and whatever anybody says to her, she'll just say the same thing. *Fit as a fiddle and ready for love.* That's what she'll say all day long. *Fit-as-a-fiddle-and-ready-for-love.* She'll drive you crazy. Then other days she can answer all right."

Again, her voice and laugh—this time half submerged—reminded me of Alfrida, and I said, "You know I must have met you, I remember once when Alfrida's stepmother and her father dropped in, or maybe it was only her father and some of the children—"

"Oh, that's not who I am," the woman said. "You thought I was Alfrida's sister? Glory. I must be looking my age."

I started to say that I could not see her very well, and it was true. In October the afternoon sun was low, and it was coming straight into my eyes. The woman was standing against the light, so that it was hard to make out her features or her expression.

She twitched her shoulders nervously and importantly. She said, "Alfrida was my birth mom."

Mawm. Mother.

Then she told me, at not too great length, the story that she must have told often, because it was about an emphatic event in her life and an adventure she had embarked on alone. She had been adopted by a family in eastern Ontario; they were the only family she had ever known ("and I love them dearly"), and she had married and had her children, who were grown up before she got the urge to find out who her own mother was. It wasn't too easy, because of the way records used to be kept, and the secrecy ("It was kept one hundred percent secret that she had me"), but a few years ago she had tracked down Alfrida.

"Just in time too," she said. "I mean, it was time somebody came along to look after her. As much as I can."

I said, "I never knew."

"No. Those days, I don't suppose too many did. They warn you, when you start out to do this, it could be a shock when you show up. Older people, it's still heavy-duty. However. I don't think she minded. Earlier on, maybe she would have."

There was some sense of triumph about her, which wasn't hard to understand. If you have something to tell that will stagger someone, and you've told it, and it has done so, there has to be a balmy moment of power. In this case it was so complete that she felt a need to apologize.

"Excuse me talking all about myself and not saying how sorry I am about your dad."

I thanked her.

"You know Alfrida told me that your dad and her were walking home from school one day, this was in high school. They couldn't walk all the way together because, you know, in those days, a boy and a girl, they would just get teased something terrible. So if he got out first he'd wait just where their road went off the main road, outside of town, and if she got out first she would do the same, wait for him. And one day they were walking together and they heard all the bells starting to ring and you know what that was? It was the end of the First World War."

I said that I had heard that story too.

"Only I thought they were just children."

"Then how could they be coming home from high school, if they were just children?"

I said that I had thought they were out playing in the fields. "They had my father's dog with them. He was called Mack."

"Maybe they had the dog all right. Maybe he came to meet them. I wouldn't think she'd get mixed up on what she was telling me. She was pretty good on remembering anything involved your dad."

Now I was aware of two things. First, that my father was born in 1902, and that Alfrida was close to the same age. So it was much more likely that they were walking home from high school than that they were playing in the fields, and it was odd that I had never thought of that before. Maybe they had said they were in the fields, that is, walking home across the fields. Maybe they had never said "playing."

Also, that the feeling of apology or friendliness, the harmlessness that I had felt in this woman a little while before, was not there now.

I said, "Things get changed around."

"That's right," the woman said. "People change things around. You want to know what Alfrida said about you?"

Now. I knew it was coming now.

"What?"

"She said you were smart, but you weren't ever quite as smart as you thought you were."

I made myself keep looking into the dark face against the light.

Smart, too smart, not smart enough.

I said, "Is that all?"

"She said you were kind of a cold fish. That's her talking, not me. I haven't got anything against you."

That Sunday, after the noon dinner at Alfrida's, I set out to walk all the way back to my rooming house. If I walked both ways, I reckoned that I would have covered about ten miles, which ought to offset the effects of the meal I had eaten. I felt overfull, not just of food but of everything that I had seen and sensed in the apartment. The crowded, old-fashioned furnishings. Bill's silences. Alfrida's love, stubborn as sludge, and inappropriate, and hopeless—as far as I could see—on the grounds of age alone.

After I had walked for a while, my stomach did not feel so heavy. I made a vow not to eat anything for the next twenty-four hours. I walked north and west, north and west, on the streets of the tidily rectangular small city. On a Sunday afternoon there was hardly any traffic, except on the main thoroughfares. Sometimes my route coincided with a bus route for a few blocks. A bus might go by with only two or three people in it. People I did not know and who did not know me. What a blessing.

I had lied, I was not meeting any friends. My friends had mostly all gone home to wherever they lived. My fiancé would be away until the next day—he was visiting his parents, in Cobourg, on the way home from Ottawa. There would be nobody in the rooming house when I got there—nobody I had to bother talking to or listening to. I had nothing to do.

When I had walked for over an hour, I saw a drugstore that was open. I went in and had a cup of coffee. The coffee was reheated, black and bitter—its taste was medicinal, exactly what I needed. I was already feeling relieved, and now I began to feel happy. Such happiness, to be alone. To see the hot late-afternoon light on the sidewalk outside, the branches of a tree just out in leaf, throwing their skimpy shadows. To hear from the back of the shop the sounds of the ball game that the man who had served me was listening to on the radio. I did not think of the story I would make about Alfrida—not of that in particular—but of the work I wanted to do, which seemed more like grabbing something out of the air than constructing stories. The cries of the crowd came to me like big heartbeats, full of sorrows. Lovely formal-sounding waves, with their distant, almost inhuman assent and lamentation.

This was what I wanted, this was what I thought I had to pay attention to, this was how I wanted my life to be.

David Foster Wallace

Good Old Neon

Hay un concepto que es el corruptor y el desatinador de los otros.
—Borges, *Discusión*, 1932

from *Conjunctions*

M Y WHOLE life I've been a fraud. I'm not exaggerating. Pretty much all I've ever done all the time is try to create a certain impression of me in other people. Mostly to be liked or admired. It's a little more complicated than that, maybe. But when you come right down to it it's to be liked, loved. Admired, approved of, applauded, whatever. You get the idea. I did well in school, but deep down the whole thing's motive wasn't to learn or improve myself but just to do well, to get good grades and make sports teams and perform well. To have a good transcript or varsity letters to show people. I didn't enjoy it much because I was always scared I wouldn't do well enough. The fear made me work really hard, so I'd always do well and end up getting what I wanted. But then, once I got the best grade or made All City or got Angela Mead to let me put my hand on her breast, I wouldn't feel much of anything except fear that I wouldn't be able to get it again. The next time or next thing I wanted. I remember being down in the rec room in Angela Mead's basement on the couch and having her let me get my hand up under her blouse and not even really feeling the soft aliveness or whatever of her breast because all I was doing was thinking, 'Now I'm the guy that Mead let get to second with her.' Later that seemed so sad. This was in middle school. She was a very large-hearted, quiet, self-contained, thoughtful girl—she's a veterinarian now, with her own practice—and I never even really saw her, I couldn't see anything except who I might be in her eyes, this cheerleader and probably number two or three among the most desirable girls in middle school that year. She was much more than that, she was beyond all that adolescent ranking and popularity crap, but I never really let her be or saw her as more, although I put up a very good front as somebody who could have deep conversations and really wanted to know and understand who she was inside.

Later I was in analysis, I tried analysis like almost everybody else then in their late twenties who'd made some money or had a family or whatever they thought they wanted and still didn't feel that they were happy. A lot of people I knew tried it. It didn't really work although it did make everyone sound more aware of their own problems and added some useful vocabulary and concepts to the way we all had to talk to each other to fit in and sound a certain way. You know what I mean. I was in regional advertising at the time in Chicago, having made the jump from media buyer for a large consulting firm, and at only twenty-nine I'd made creative associate, and verily as they say I was a fair-haired boy and on the fast track but wasn't happy at all, whatever *happy* means, but of course I didn't say this to anybody because it was such a cliché—'Tears of a Clown,' 'Richard Cory,' etc.—and the circle of people who seemed important to me seemed much more dry, oblique and contemptuous of clichés than that, and so of course I spent all my time trying to get them to think I was dry and jaded as well, doing things like yawning and looking at my nails and saying things like, *'Am I happy?* is one of those questions that, if it has got to be asked, more or less dictates its own answer,' etc. Putting in all this time and energy to create a certain impression and get approval or acceptance that then I felt nothing about because it didn't have anything to do with who I really was inside, and I was disgusted with myself for always being such a fraud, but I couldn't seem to help it. Here are some of the various things I tried: EST, riding a ten-speed to Nova Scotia and back, hypnosis, cocaine, sacro-cervical chiropractic, joining a charismatic church, jogging, pro bono work for the Ad Council, meditation classes, the Masons, analysis, the Landmark Forum, the Course in Miracles, a right-brain drawing workshop, celibacy, collecting and restoring vintage Corvettes, and trying to sleep with a different girl every night for two straight months (I racked up a total of thirty-six for sixty-one and also got chlamydia, which I told friends about, acting like I was embarrassed but secretly expecting most of them to be impressed—which, under the cover of making a lot of jokes at my expense, I think they were—but for the most part the two months just made me feel shallow and predatory, plus I missed a great deal of sleep and was a wreck at work—that was also the period I tried cocaine). I know this part is boring and probably boring you, by the way, but it gets a lot more interesting when I get to the part where I kill myself and discover what happens immediately after a person dies. In terms of the list, analysis was pretty much the last thing I tried.

The analyst I saw was O.K., a big soft older guy with a big ginger mustache and a pleasant, sort of informal manner. I'm not sure I remember him alive too well. He was a fairly good listener, and seemed interested and sympathetic in a somewhat distant way. At first I suspected he didn't like me or was uneasy around me. I don't think he was used to patients who were already aware of what their real problem was. He was also a bit of a pill-pusher. I balked at trying antidepressants, I just couldn't see myself taking pills to try to be less of a fraud. I said that even if they worked, how would I know if it was me or just the pills? By that time I already knew I was a fraud. I knew what my problem was. I just couldn't seem to stop. I remember I spent maybe the first twenty times or so in analysis acting all open and candid but was in reality sort of fencing with him or leading him around by the nose, basically showing him that I wasn't just another one of those patients who stumbled in with no clue what their real problem was or were totally out of touch with the truth about themselves. When you come right down to it, I was trying to show him that I was at least as smart as he was and that there wasn't much of anything he was going to see about me that I hadn't already seen and figured out. And yet I wanted help and really was there to try to get help. I didn't even tell him how unhappy I was until five or six months into the analysis, mostly because I didn't want to seem like just another whining, self-absorbed yuppie, even though I think even then I was on some level conscious that that's all I really was, deep down.

Right from the start, what I liked best about the analyst was that his office was a mess. There were books and papers everyplace, and usually he had to clear things off the chair so I could sit down. There was no couch, I sat in an easy chair and he sat facing me in his beat-up old desk chair whose back part had one of those big rectangles or capes of back-massage beads attached to it the same way cabbies often have them on their seat in the cab. This was another thing I liked, the desk chair and the fact that it was a little too small for him (he was a large guy) so that he had to sit sort of almost hunched with his feet flat on the floor, or else sometimes put his hands behind his head and lean way back in the chair in a way that made the back portion squeak terribly when it leaned back. There always seems to be something patronizing or a little condescending about somebody crossing their legs when they talk to you, and the desk chair didn't allow him to do this, if he ever crossed his legs his knee would have been up around his chin. And yet he had apparently never gone out and gotten himself a bigger or nicer desk chair, or even bothered to oil the medial joint's springs to keep the back from squeaking, a noise that I know would have driven me up the wall if it had been my chair and I had to spend all day in it. I noticed all this almost right away. The little office also reeked of pipe tobacco, which is a pleasant smell, plus Dr. Gustafson never took notes or answered everything with a question or any of the cliché analyst things that would have made the whole thing too horrible to keep going back whether it even helped or not. The whole effect was of a sort of likable, disorganized, laid back guy, and things in there actually did get better after I realized that he probably wasn't going to do anything to make me quit fencing with him and trying to anticipate all his questions and show that I already knew the answer—he was going to get his $65 either way— and finally came out and told him about being a fraud and feeling alienated (I had to use the uptown word, of course, but it was still the truth) and starting to see myself ending up living this way my whole life and being totally unhappy. I told him I wasn't blaming anybody for my being a fraud. I had been adopted, but it was as a baby, and the stepparents who adopted me were better and nicer than most of the biological parents I knew anything about, and I was never yelled at or abused or pressured to hit .400 in Legion ball or anything, and they took out a second mortgage to send me to an elite college when I could have gone scholarship to UW–Eau Claire, etc. Nobody'd ever done anything bad to me, every problem I ever had I'd been the cause of. I was a fraud, and the fact that I was lonely was my own fault (of course his ears pricked up at *fault*, which is a loaded term) because I seemed to be so totally self-centered and fraudulent that I experienced everything in terms of how it affected people's view of me and what I needed to do to create the impression of me I wanted them to have. I said I knew what my problem was, what I couldn't do was stop it. I also admitted to Dr. Gustafson some of the ways I'd been jerking him around early on and trying to make sure he saw me as smart and self-aware, and said I'd known early on that playing around and showing off in analysis were a waste of time and money but that I couldn't seem to help myself, it just happened automatically. He smiled at all this, which was the first time I remember seeing him smile. I don't mean he was sour or humorless, he had a big red friendly face and a pleasant expression, but this was the first time he'd smiled like a human being having an actual conversation. And yet at the same time I already saw what I'd left myself open for—and sure enough he says it. 'If I understand you right,' he says, 'you're saying that you're basically a calculating, manipulative person who always says what you think will get somebody to approve of you or form some impression of you you think you want.' I told him that was maybe a little simplistic but basically accurate, and he said further that as he understood it I was saying that I felt as if I was trapped in this false way of being and unable ever to be totally open and tell the truth irregardless of whether it'd make me look good in others' eyes or not. And I somewhat resignedly said yes, and that I seemed always to have had this fraudulent, calculating part of my brain firing away all the time, as if I were constantly playing chess with everybody and figuring out that if I wanted them to move a certain way I had to move in such a way as to induce them to move that way. He asked if I ever played chess, and I told him I used to in middle school but quit because I couldn't be as good as I eventually wanted to be, how frustrating it was to get just good enough to know what getting really good at chess would be like but not being able to get that good, etc. I was laying it on sort of thick in hopes of distracting him from the big insight and question I realized I'd set myself up for. But it didn't work. He leaned back in his loud chair and paused as if he were thinking hard, for effect—he was thinking that he was going to get to feel like he'd really earned his $65 today. Part of the pause always involved stroking his mustache in an unconscious way. I was reasonably sure that he was going to say something like, 'So then how were you able to do what you just did a moment ago?,' in other words meaning how was I able to be honest about fraudulence if I was really a fraud, meaning he thought he'd caught me in a logical contradiction or paradox. And I went ahead and played a little dumb, probably, to get him to go ahead and say it, partly because I still held out some hope that what he'd say might be more discerning or incisive than I had predicted. But it was also partly because I liked him, and liked the way he seemed genuinely pleased and excited at the idea of being helpful but was trying to exercise professional control over his facial expression in order to make the excitement look more like simple pleasantness and clinical interest in my case or whatever. He was hard not to like, he had what is known as an engaging manner. By way of decor, the office wall behind his chair had two framed prints, one being that Wyeth one of the little girl in the wheat field crawling uphill toward the farmhouse, the other a still life of two apples in a bowl on a table by Cézanne. (To be honest, I only knew it was Cézanne because it was an Art Institute poster and had a banner with info on a Cézanne show underneath the painting, which was a still life, and which was weirdly discomfiting because there was something slightly off about the perspective or style that made the table look crooked and the apples almost square.) The prints were obviously there to give the analyst's patients something to look at, since many people like to look around or look at things on the wall while they talk. I didn't have any trouble looking right at him most of the time I was in there, though. He did have a talent for putting you at ease, there was no question about it. But I had no illusions that this was the same as having enough insight or firepower to find some way to really help me, though.

There was a basic logical paradox that I called the 'fraudulence paradox' that I had discovered more or less on my own while taking a mathematical logic course in school. I remember this as being a huge undergrad lecture course that met twice a week in an auditorium with the professor up on stage and on Fridays in smaller discussion sections led by a graduate assistant whose whole life seemed to be mathematical logic. (Plus all you had to do to ace the class was sit down with the textbook that the prof had edited and memorize the different modes of argument and normal forms and axioms of first-order quantification, meaning the course was as clean and mechanical as logic itself in that if you put in the time and effort, out popped the good grade at the other end. We only got to paradoxes like the Berry and Russell paradoxes and the incompleteness theorem at the very end of the term, they weren't on the final.) The fraudulence paradox was that the more time and effort you put into trying to appear impressive or attractive to other people, the less impressive or attractive you felt inside—you were a fraud. And the more of a fraud you felt like, the harder you tried to convey an impressive or likable image of yourself so that other people wouldn't find out what a hollow, fraudulent person you really were. Logically, you would think that the moment a supposedly intelligent nineteen-year-old became aware of this paradox, he'd stop being a fraud and just settle for being himself (whatever that was) because he'd figured out that being a fraud was a vicious infinite regress that ultimately resulted in being frightened, lonely, alienated, etc. But here was the other, higher-order paradox, which didn't even have a form or name—I didn't, I couldn't. Discovering the first paradox at age nineteen just brought home to me in spades what an empty, fraudulent person I'd basically been ever since I was four and lied to my stepdad because I'd realized somehow right in the middle of his asking me if I'd broken the bowl that if I said I did it but 'confessed' it in a sort of clumsy, implausible way, then he wouldn't believe me and would instead believe that my sister Fern, who's my step-parents' biological daughter, was the one who'd actually broken the antique Moser glass bowl that my stepmom had inherited from her biological grandmother and loved, plus it would lead or induce him to see me as a kind, good stepbrother who was so anxious to keep Fern (whom I really did like) from getting in trouble that I'd be willing to lie and take the punishment for it for her. I'm not explaining this very well. I was only four, for one thing, and the realization didn't hit me in words the way I just now put it, but rather more in terms of feelings and associations and certain mental flashes of my stepparents' faces with various expressions on them. But it happened that fast, at only four, that I figured out how to create a certain impression by knowing what effect I'd produce in my stepdad by implausibly 'confessing' that I'd punched Fern in the arm and stolen her Hula Hoop and had run all the way downstairs with it and started Hula Hooping in the dining room right by the sideboard with all my stepmom's antique glassware and figurines on it, while Fern, forgetting all about her arm, and hoop because of her concern over the bowl and other glassware, came running downstairs shouting after me, reminding me about how important the rule was that we weren't supposed to play in the dining room. . . . Meaning that by lying in such a deliberately unconvincing way I could actually get everything that a direct lie would supposedly get me, plus look noble and self-sacrificing, plus also make my stepparents feel good because they always tended to feel good when one of their kids did something that showed character, because it's the sort of thing they couldn't really help but see as reflecting favorably on them as shapers of their kids' character. I'm putting all this in such a long, rushing, clumsy way to try to convey the way I remember it suddenly hit me, looking up at my stepfather's big kindly face as he held two of the larger pieces of the Moser bowl and tried to look angrier than he really felt. (He had always thought the more expensive pieces ought to be kept secure in storage somewhere, whereas my stepmom's view was more like what was the point of having nice things if you didn't have them out where people could enjoy them.) How to appear a certain way and get him to think a certain thing hit me just that fast. Keep in mind I was only around four. And I can't pretend it felt bad, realizing it—the truth is it felt great. I felt powerful, smart. It felt a little like looking at part of a puzzle you're doing and you've got a piece in your hand and you can't see where in the larger puzzle it's supposed to go or how to make it fit, looking at all the holes, and then all of a sudden in a flash you see, for no reason right then you could point to or explain to anyone, that if you turn the piece this one certain way it will fit, and it does, and maybe the best way to put it is that in that one tiny instant you feel suddenly connected to something larger and much more of the complete picture the same way the piece is. The only element I'd forgotten to anticipate was Fern's reaction to getting blamed for the bowl, and punished, and then punished even worse when she continued to deny that she'd been the one playing around in the dining room, and my stepparents' position was that they were even more upset and disappointed about her lying than they were about the bowl, which they said was just a material object and not ultimately important in the larger scheme of things. (My stepparents spoke this way, they were people of high ideals and values, humanists. Their big ideal was total honesty in all the family's relationships, and lying was the worst, most disappointing infraction you could commit, in their view as parents. They tended to discipline Fern a little more firmly than they did me, by the way, but this too was an extension of their values. They were concerned about being fair and having me be able to feel that I was just as much their real child as Fern was, so that I'd feel maximally secure and loved, and sometimes this concern with fairness caused them to bend a little too far over backwards when it came to discipline.) So that Fern, then, got regarded as being a liar when she was not, and that must have hurt her way more than the actual punishment did. She was only five at the time. It's horrible to be regarded as a fraud or to believe that people think you're a fraud or liar. It's one of the worst feelings in the world. And even though I have had no real direct experience of it, I'm sure it must be doubly horrible when you were actually telling the truth and they didn't believe you. I don't think Fern ever quite got over that episode, although the two of us never talked about it afterward except for one sort of cryptic remark she made over her shoulder once when we were both in high school and having an argument about something and Fern was storming out of the house. She was sort of a classically troubled adolescent—smoking, makeup, mediocre grades, dating older guys, etc.—whereas I was the family's fair-haired boy and had a killer GPA and played varsity ball, etc. One way to put it is that I looked and acted much better on the surface then than Fern did, although she eventually settled down and ended up going on to college and is now doing O.K. She's also one of the funniest people on earth, with a very dry, subtle sense of humor—I like her a lot. The point being that that was the start of my being a fraud, although it's not as if the broken-bowl episode was somehow the origin or matrix of my fraudulence or some kind of childhood trauma that I'd never gotten over and had to go into analysis to work out. The fraud part of me was always there, just as the puzzle piece, objectively speaking, is a piece of the puzzle even before you see how it fits. For a while I thought that possibly one or the other of my biological parents had been frauds or had carried some type of fraud gene or something and that I had inherited it, but that was a dead end, there was no way to know. And even if I did, what difference would it make? I was still a fraud, it was still my own unhappiness that I had to deal with.

Once again, I'm aware that it's clumsy to put it all this way, but the point is that all of this and more was flashing through my head just in the time of the small, dramatic pause Dr. Gustafson allowed himself before delivering his big reductio ad absurdum argument that I couldn't be a total fraud if I had just come out and admitted my fraudulence to him just now. I know that you know just as well as I do how fast thoughts and associations can fly through your head. You can be in the middle of a creative meeting at your job or something, and enough material can rush through your head just in the little silences when people are looking over their notes and waiting for the next presentation that it would take exponentially longer than the whole meeting just to try to put a few seconds' silence's thoughts into words. This is another paradox, that many of the most important impressions and thoughts in a person's life are ones that flash through your head so fast that *fast* isn't even the right word, they seem totally different from or outside of the regular sequential clock time we all live by, and they have so little relation to the sort of linear, one-word-after-another-word English we communicate with each other with that it could easily take a whole lifetime just to spell out the contents of one split-second's flash of thoughts and connections, etc.—and yet we all seem to go around trying to use English (or whatever language our native country happens to use, it goes without saying) to try to convey to other people what we're thinking and to find out what they're thinking, when in fact deep down everybody knows it's a charade and they're just going through the motions. What goes on inside is just too fast and huge and all interconnected for words to do more than barely sketch the outlines of at most one tiny little part of it at any given instant. The internal head-speed of these ideas, memories, realizations, emotions, and so on is even faster, by the way—exponentially faster, unimaginably faster—when you're dying, meaning during that vanishingly tiny nanosecond between when you technically die and when the next thing happens, so that in reality the cliché about people's whole life flashing before their eyes as they're dying isn't all that far off—although the *whole life* here isn't really a sequential thing where first you're born and then you're in the crib and then you're up at the plate in Legion ball, etc., which it turns out that that's what people usually mean when they say 'my whole life,' meaning a discrete, chronological series of moments that they add up and call their lifetime. It's not really like that. The best way I can think of to try to say it is that it all happens at once, but that *at once* doesn't really mean a finite moment of sequential time the way we think of time while we're alive, plus that what turns out to be the meaning of the term *my life* isn't even close to what we think we're talking about when we say 'my life.' Words and chronological time create all these total misunderstandings of what's really going on at the most basic level. And yet at the same time English is all we have to try to understand it and try to form anything larger or more meaningful and true with anybody else, which is yet another paradox. Dr. Gustafson—whom I would meet again later and find out that he had almost nothing to do with the big doughy repressed guy sitting back against his chair's beads in his River Forest office with colon cancer in him already at that time and him knowing nothing yet except that he didn't feel quite right down there in the bathroom lately and if it kept on he'd make an appointment to go in and ask his internist about it—Dr. G. would later say that the whole *my life flashed* phenomenon at the end is more like being a whitecap on the surface of the ocean, meaning that it's only at the moment you subside and start sliding back in that you're really even aware there's an ocean at all. When you're up and out there as a whitecap you might talk and act as if you know you're just a whitecap on the ocean, but deep down you don't think there's really an ocean at all. It's almost impossible to. Or like a leaf that doesn't believe in the tree it's part of, etc. There are all sorts of ways to try to express it.

And of course all this time you've probably been noticing what seems like the really central, overarching paradox, which is that this whole thing where I'm saying words can't really do it and time doesn't really go in a straight line is something that you're hearing as words that you have to start listening to the first word and then each successive word after that in chronological time to understand, so if I'm saying that words and sequential time have nothing to do with it you're wondering why we're sitting here in this car using words and taking up your increasingly precious time, meaning aren't I sort of logically contradicting myself right at the start. Not to mention am I maybe full of BS about knowing what happens—if I really did kill myself, how can you even be hearing this? Meaning am I a fraud. That's O.K., it doesn't really matter what you think. I mean it probably matters to you, or you think it does—that isn't what I meant by *doesn't matter*. What I mean is that it doesn't really matter what you think about me, because despite appearances this isn't even really about me. All I'm trying to do is sketch out one little part of what it was like before I died and why I at least thought I did it, so that you'll have at least some idea of why what happened afterward happened and why it had the impact it did on who this is really about. Meaning it's like an abstract or sort of intro, meant to be very brief and sketchy . . . and yet of course look how much time and English it's seeming to take even to say it. It's interesting if you really think about it, how clumsy and laborious it seems to be to convey the smallest thing. How much time would you even say has passed, so far?

One reason why Dr. Gustafson would have made a terrible poker player or fraud is that whenever he thought it was a big moment in the analysis he would always make a production of leaning back in his desk chair, which made that loud sound as the back tilted back and his feet went back on their heels so the soles showed, although he was good at making the position look comfortable and very familiar to his body, like it felt good doing that when he had to think. The whole thing was both slightly overdramatic and yet still likable for some reason. Fern, by the way, has reddish hair and slightly asymmetrical green eyes—the kind of green people buy tinted contact lenses to get—and is attractive in a sort of witchy way. I think she's attractive, anyway. She's grown up to be a very poised, witty, self-sufficient person, with maybe just the slightest whiff of the perfume of loneliness that hangs around unmarried women at thirty. The fact is that we're all lonely, of course. Everyone knows this, it's almost a cliché. So another layer of my essential fraudulence is that I pretended to myself that my loneliness was special, that it was uniquely my fault because I was somehow especially fraudulent and hollow. It's not special at all, we've all got it. In spades. Dead or not, Dr. Gustafson knew more about all this than I, so that he spoke with what came off as genuine authority and pleasure when he said (maybe a little superciliously, given how obvious it was), 'But if you're constitutionally false and manipulative and unable to be honest about who you really are, Neal' (Neal being my given name, it was on my birth certificate when I got adopted), 'how is it that you were able to drop the sparring and manipulation and be honest with me a moment ago' (for that's all it had been, in spite of all the English that's been expended on just my head's partial contents in the tiny interval between then and now) 'about who you really are?' So it turned out I'd been right in predicting what his big logical insight was going to be. And although I played along with him for a while so as not to prick his bubble, inside I felt pretty bleak indeed, because now I knew that he was going to be just as pliable and credulous as everyone else, he didn't appear to have anything close to the firepower I'd need to give me any hope of getting helped out of the trap of fraudulence and unhappiness I'd constructed for myself. Because the real truth was that my 'confession' of being a fraud and of having wasted time sparring with him over the previous weeks in order to manipulate him into seeing me as exceptional and insightful had itself been kind of manipulative. It was pretty clear that Dr. Gustafson, in order to survive in private practice, could not be totally stupid or obtuse about people, so it seemed reasonable to assume that he'd noticed the massive amount of fencing and general showing off I'd been doing during the first weeks of the analysis, and thus had come to some conclusions about my apparently desperate need to make a certain kind of impression on him, and though it wasn't totally certain it was thus at least a decent possibility that he'd sized me up as a basically empty, insecure person whose whole life involved trying to impress people and manipulate their view of me in order to compensate for the inner emptiness. It's not as if this is an incredibly rare or obscure type of personality, after all. So the fact that I had chosen to be supposedly 'honest' and to diagnose myself aloud was in fact just one more move in my campaign to make sure Dr. Gustafson understood that as a patient I was uniquely acute and self-aware, and that there was very little chance that he was going to see or diagnose anything about me that I wasn't already aware of and able to turn to my own tactical advantage in terms of creating whatever image or impression of myself I wanted him to see at that moment. His big supposed insight, then— which had as its ostensible, first-order point that my fraudulence could not possibly be as thoroughgoing and hopeless as I claimed it was, since my ability to be honest with him about it logically contradicted my claim of being incapable of honesty—actually had as its larger, unspoken point the claim that he could discern things about my basic character that I myself could not see or interpret accurately, and thus that he could help me out of the trap by pointing out inconsistencies in my view of myself as totally fraudulent. The fact that this insight that he appeared so coyly pleased and excited about was not only obvious and superficial but also wrong—this was depressing, much the way discovering that somebody is easy to manipulate is always a little depressing. A sort of corollary to the fraudulence paradox is that you simultaneously want to fool everyone you meet and yet also somehow always hope that you'll come across someone who is your match or equal and can't be fooled. But this was sort of the last straw, I mentioned I'd tried a whole number of different things that hadn't helped already. So *depressing* is a gross understatement, actually. Plus of course the obvious fact that I was paying this guy for help in getting out of the trap and he'd now showed that he didn't have the mental firepower to do it. So I was now thinking about the prospect of spending time and money driving in to River Forest twice a week just to yank the analyst around in ways he couldn't see so that he'd think that I was actually less fraudulent than I thought I was and that analysis was gradually helping me see this. Meaning that he'd probably be getting more out of it than I would, for me it would just be fraudulence as usual.

However tedious and sketchy all this is, you're at least getting an idea, I think, of what it was like inside my head. If nothing else, you're seeing how exhausting and solipsistic it is to be like this. And I had been this way my whole life, at least from age four onward, as far as I could recall. Of course, it's also a really stupid and egotistical way to be, of course you can see that. This is why the ultimate and most deeply unspoken point of the analyst's insight—namely, that who and what I believed I was was not what I really was at all—which I thought was false, was in fact true, although not for the reasons Dr. Gustafson, who was leaning back in his chair and smoothing his big mustache with his thumb and forefinger while I played dumb and let him feel like he was explaining to me a contradiction I couldn't understand without his help, believed.

One of my other ways of playing dumb for the next several sessions after that was to protest his upbeat diagnosis (irrelevantly, since by this time I'd pretty much given up on Dr. Gustafson and was starting to think of various ways to kill myself without causing pain or making a mess that would disgust whoever found me) by means of listing the various ways I'd been fraudulent even in my pursuit of ways to achieve genuine and uncalculating integrity. I'll spare you giving you the whole list again. I basically went all the way back to childhood (which analysts always like you to do) and laid it on. Partly I was curious to see how much he'd put up with. For example, I told him about going from genuinely loving ball, loving the smell of the grass and distant sprinklers, or the feel of pounding my fist into the glove over and over and yelling, 'Hey batterbatter,' and the big low red tumid sun at the game's start versus the arc lights coming on with a clank in the glowing twilight of the late innings, and of the steam and clean burned smell of ironing my Legion uniform, or the feel of sliding and watching all the dust it raised settle around me, or all the parents in shorts and rubber flip-flops setting up lawn chairs with Styrofoam coolers, little kids hooking their fingers around the backstop fence or running off after fouls. The smell of the ump's aftershave and sweat, the little whisk broom he'd bend down and tidy the plate with. Mostly the feel of stepping up to the plate knowing anything was possible, a feeling like a sun flaring somewhere high up in my chest. And how by only maybe fourteen all that had disappeared and turned into worrying about averages and if I could make All City again or being so worried I'd screw up that I didn't even like ironing the uniform anymore before games because it gave me too much time to think, standing there so nerved up about doing well that night that I couldn't even notice the little chuckling sighs the iron made any-more or the singular smell of the steam when I hit the little button for steam. How I'd basically ruined all the best parts of everything like that. How sometimes it felt like I was actually asleep and none of it was even real and someday out of nowhere I was maybe going to suddenly wake up in mid-stride. That was part of the idea behind things like joining the charismatic church up in Naperville, to try to wake up spiritually instead of living in this fog of fraudulence. 'The truth shall set you free'—the Bible. This was what Beverly-Elizabeth Slane liked to call my Holy Roller phase. And the charismatic church really did seem to help a lot of the parishioners and congregants I met. They were humble and devoted and charitable, and gave tirelessly without thought of personal reward in active service to the church and in donating resources and time to the church's campaign to build a new altar with an enormous cross of thick glass whose crossbeam was lit up and filled with aerated water and was to have various kinds of beautiful fish swimming in it. (Fish being a prominent Christ symbol for charismatics. In fact, most of us who were the most devoted and active in the church had bumper stickers on our cars with no words or anything except a plain line drawing of the outline of a fish—this lack of ostentation impressed me as classy and genuine.) But with the real truth here being how quickly I went from being someone who was there because he wanted to wake up and stop being a fraud to being somebody who was so anxious to impress the congregation with how devoted and active I was that I volunteered to help take the collection, and never missed one study group the whole time, and was on two different committees for coordinat-ing fundraising for the new aquarial altar and deciding exactly what kind of equipment and fish would be used for the crossbeam. Plus often being the one in the front row whose voice in the responses was loudest and who waved both hands in the air the most enthusiastically to show that the Spirit had entered me, and speaking in tongues—mostly consisting of *d*'s and *g*'s—except not really, of course, because in fact I was really just pre-tending to speak in tongues because all the parishioners around me were speaking in tongues and had the Spirit, and so in a kind of fever of excite-ment I was able to hoodwink even myself into thinking that I really had the Spirit moving through me and was speaking in tongues when in reality I was just shouting, 'Dugga muggle ergle dergle' over and over. (In other words, so anxious to see myself as truly born-again that I actually convinced myself that the tongues' babble was real language and somehow less false or inadequate than plain English at expressing the feeling of the Holy Spirit rolling like a juggernaut right through me.) This went on for about four months. Not to mention falling over backward whenever Pastor Steve came down the row and popped me in the forehead with the heel of his hand, but falling over backward on purpose, not genuinely being struck down by the Spirit like the other people on either side of me (one of whom actually fainted and had to be brought around with salts). It was only when I was walking out to the parking lot one night after Wednesday Night Praise that I suddenly experienced a flash of self-awareness or clarity in which I suddenly stopped conning myself and realized that I'd been a fraud all these months in the church, too, and was really only saying and doing these things because all the real parishioners were doing them and I wanted everyone to think I was sincere. It just about knocked me over, that was how vividly I saw how I'd deceived myself. The revealed truth was that I was an even bigger fraud in church about being a newly reborn authentic person than I'd been before Deacon and Mrs. Halberstadt first rang my doorbell out of nowhere as part of their missionary service and talked me into giving it a shot. Because at least before the church thing I wasn't conning myself—I'd known that I was a fraud since at least age nineteen, but at least I'd been able to admit and face the fraudulence directly instead of BSing myself that I was something I wasn't.

All this was presented in the context of a very long pseudo-argument about fraudulence with Dr. Gustafson that would take way too much English to relate to you in any detail, so I'm just telling you about some of the more garish examples. With Dr. G. it was more in the form of a prolonged, multi-session back-and-forth on whether or not I was a total fraud, during which I got more and more disgusted with myself for even playing along. By this point in the analysis I'd pretty much decided he was an idiot, or at least very limited in his insights into what was really going on with people. (There was also the blatant issue of the mustache and of him always playing with it.) Essentially, he saw what he wanted to see, which was just the sort of person I could practically eat for lunch in terms of creating whatever ideas or impressions of me I wanted. For instance, I told him about the period of trying jogging, during which I seemed never to fail to have to increase my pace and pump my arms more vigorously whenever someone drove by or looked up from his yard, so that I ended up with bone spurs and eventually had to quit altogether. Or spending at least two or three sessions recounting the example of the introductory meditation class at the Downers Grove Community Center that Melissa Betts of Settleman, Shannon got me to take, at which through sheer force of will I'd always force myself to remain totally still with my legs crossed and back perfectly straight long after the other students had given up and fallen back on their mats shuddering and holding their heads. Right from the first class meeting, even though the small brown instructor had told us to shoot for only ten minutes of stillness at the outset because most Westerners' minds could not maintain more than a few minutes of still-ness and mindful concentration without feeling so restless and ill at ease that they couldn't stand it, I always remained absolutely still and focused on breathing my prana with the lower diaphragm longer than any of them, sometimes for up to thirty minutes, even though my knees and lower back were on fire and I had what felt like swarms of insects crawling over my arms and shooting out the top of my head—and Master Gurpreet, although he kept his facial expression inscrutable, gave me a deep and seemingly respectful bow and said that I sat almost like a living statue of mindful repose, and that he was impressed. The problem was that we were all also supposed to continue practicing our meditation on our own at home between classes, and when I tried to do it alone I couldn't seem to sit still and follow my breath for more than even a few minutes before I felt like crawling out of my skin and had to stop. I could only sit and appear quiet and mindful and withstand the unbelievably restless and horrible feelings when all of us were doing it together in the class—meaning only when there were other people to make an impression on. And even in class, the truth was that I was often concentrating not so much on follow-ing my prana as on keeping totally still and in the correct posture and hav-ing a deeply peaceful and meditative expression on my face in case anyone was cheating and had their eyes open and was looking around, plus also to ensure that Master Gurpreet would continue to see me as exceptional and keep addressing me by what became sort of his class nickname for me, which was 'the statue.'

In the final few class meetings, when Master Gurpreet told us to sit still and focused for only as long as we comfortably could and then waited almost an hour before finally hitting his small bell with the little silver thing to signal the period of meditation's end, only I and an extremely thin, pale girl who had her own meditation bench that she brought to class with her were able to sit still and focused for the whole hour, although at several different points I'd get so cramped and restless, with what felt like bright blue fire going up my spine and shooting invisibly out of the top of my head as blobs of color exploded over and over behind my eyelids, that I thought I was going to jump up screaming and take a header right out the window. And at the end of the course, when there was also an opportunity to sign up for the next session, which was called 'Deepening the Practice,' Master Gurpreet presented several of us with different honorary certificates, and mine had my name and the date and was inscribed in black calligraphy *Champion Meditator, Most Impressive Western Student, the Statue.* It was only after I fell asleep that night (I'd finally sort of compromised and told myself I was practicing the meditative discipline at home at night by lying down and focusing on following my breathing very closely as I fell asleep, and it did turn out to be a potent sleep aid) that while I was asleep I had the dream about the statue in the commons and realized that Master Gurpreet had actually in all likelihood seen right through me the whole time, and that the certificate was in reality a subtle rebuke or joke at my expense. Meaning he was letting me know that he knew I was a fraud and not even coming close to actually quieting my mind's ceaseless conniving about how to impress people in order to achieve mindfulness and honor my true inner self. (Of course, what he seemed not to have divined was that in reality I had no true inner self, and that the more I tried to be genuine the more empty and fraudulent I ended feeling inside, which I told nobody about until my stab at analysis with Dr. Gustafson.) In the dream, I was in the town commons in Aurora, over near the Pershing tank memorial by the clock tower, and what I'm doing in the dream is sculpting an enormous marble or granite statue of myself, using a huge iron chisel and a hammer the size of those ones they give you to try to hit the bell at the top of the big thermometer thing at carnivals, and when the statue's finally done I put it up on a big bandstand or platform and spend all my time polishing it and keeping birds from sitting on it or doing their business on it, and cleaning up litter and keeping the grass neat all around the bandstand. And in the dream my whole life flashes by like that, the sun and moon go back and forth across the sky like windshield wipers over and over, and I never seem to sleep or eat or take a shower (the dream takes place in dream time as opposed to waking, chronological time), meaning

I'm condemned to a whole life of being basically nothing but a custodian to this statue. I'm not saying it was subtle or hard to figure out. Everybody from Fern, Master Gurpreet, the anorexic girl with her own bench, and Ginger Manley, to people from the firm and some of the media reps we bought time from (I was still a media buyer at this time) all walk by, some several times—at one point Melissa Betts and her new fiancé even spread out a blanket and have a sort of little picnic in the shade of the statue—but none of them ever look over or say anything. It's obviously another dream about fraudulence, like the dream where I'm supposedly the big pop star on stage but really all I do is lip synch to one of my stepparents' old Mamas and Papas records that's on a record player just offstage, and some-body whose face I can't ever look over long enough to make out keeps putting his hand in the area of the record as if he's going to make it skip or scratch, and the whole dream makes my skin crawl. These dreams were obvious, they were warnings from my subconscious that I was hollow and a fraud and it was only a matter of time before the whole charade fell apart. Another of my stepmother's treasured antiques was a silver pocket watch of her maternal grandfather's with the Latin RESPICE FINEM inscribed on the inside of the case. It wasn't until after she passed away and my step-father said she'd wanted me to have it that I bothered to look up the term, after which I'd gotten the same sort of crawly feeling as with Master Gurpreet's certificate. Much of the nightmarish quality of the dream about the statue was due to the way the sun raced back and forth across the sky and the speed with which my whole life blew rapidly by like that in the commons. It was obviously also my subconscious enlightening me as to the meditation instructor's having seen through me the whole time, after which I was too embarrassed even to go try to get a refund for 'Deepening the Practice,' which there was now no way I felt like I could show up for, even though I also still had fantasies about Master Gurpreet becoming my mentor or guru and using all kinds of inscrutable Eastern techniques to show me the way to meditate myself into having a true self . . .

. . . Etc., etc. I'll spare you any more examples, for instance I'll spare you the literally countless examples of my fraudulence with girls—with the ladies, as they say—in just about every dating relationship I had, or the almost unbelievable amount of fraudulence and calculation involved in my career, not just in terms of manipulating the consumer and manipulat-ing the client into trusting that your agency's ideas are the best way to manipulate the consumer, but in the interoffice politics of the agency itself, like for example in sizing up what sorts of things your superiors want to believe (including the belief that they're smarter than you and that that's why they're your superior) and then in giving them what they want but doing it just subtly enough that they never get a chance to view you as a sycophant or yes-man—which they want to believe they do not want—but instead see you as a tough-minded independent thinker who from time to time bows to the weight of their superior intelligence and creative firepower, etc., etc. The whole agency was one big ballet of fraudulence and manipulating people's images of your ability to manipulate images, a virtual hall of mirrors. And I was good at it, I thrived there, remember.

It was the sheer amount of time Dr. Gustafson spent touching and smoothing his mustache that indicated that he wasn't aware of doing it and in fact was subconsciously reassuring himself that it was still there. Which is not an especially subtle habit, in terms of insecurity, since after all facial hair is known as a secondary sex characteristic, meaning what he was really doing was subconsciously reassuring himself that something *else* was still there, if you know what I mean. This was some of why it was no real surprise when it turned out that the overall direction he wanted the analysis to proceed in involved issues of masculinity and how I understood my masculinity (my 'manhood' in other words). This also helped explain everything from the lost-female-crawling and two-testicle-shaped-objects-that-looked-deformed prints on the wall, plus the little African or Indian drums and little figurines with (sometimes) exaggerated sex characteristics on the shelf over his desk, plus the pipe, the unnecessary size of his wedding band, even the somewhat overdone little-boy clutter of the office itself. It was pretty clear that there were some major sexual insecurities and maybe even homosexual-type ambiguities that Dr. Gustafson was subconsciously trying to hide from himself and reassure himself about, and one obvious way he did this was to sort of project his insecurities onto his patients and get them to believe that America's culture had a uniquely brutal and alienating way of brainwashing its males from an early age into all kinds of beliefs and superstitions about what being a 'real man' was, such as competitiveness instead of concert, winning at all costs, dominating others through intelligence or will, being strong, not showing your true emotions, depending on others seeing you as a real man in order to reassure yourself of your manhood, seeing your own value solely in terms of accomplishments, being obsessed with your career or income, feeling as if you were constantly being judged and on display, etc. This was later in the analysis, after the endless period where after every example of fraudulence I gave him he'd make a show of congratulating me on being able to reveal what I felt were shameful fraudulent examples, and said that this was proof that I had much more of an ability to be genuine than I (apparently because of my insecurities or male fears) seemed able to give myself credit for. Plus it didn't exactly seem like a coincidence that the cancer he was even then harboring was in his colon—that shameful, dirty, secret place right near the rectum—with the idea being that using your rectum or colon to secretly *harbor an alien growth* was a blatant symbol both of homosexuality and of the repressive belief that its open acknowledgment would equal disease and lethality. Dr. Gustafson and I both had a good laugh over this one after we'd both died and were outside linear time and in the process of dramatic change, you can bet on that. (*Outside time* is not just an expression or manner of speaking, by the way.) By this time in the analysis I was playing with him the way a cat does with a hurt bird. If I'd had an ounce of real self-respect I would have stopped and gone back to the Downers Grove Community Center and thrown myself on Master Gurpreet's mercy, since except for maybe one or two girls I'd dated he was the only one who'd appeared to see all the way through to the core of my fraudulence, plus his oblique, very dry way of indicating this to me betrayed a sort of serene indifference to whether I even understood that he saw right through me that I found incredibly impressive and genuine— here in Master Gurpreet was a man with, as they say, nothing to prove. But I didn't, instead I more or less conned myself into sticking with going in to see Dr. G. twice a week for almost nine months (toward the end it was only once a week because by then the cancer had been diagnosed and he was getting radiation treatments every Tuesday and Thursday), telling myself that at least I was trying to find some venue in which I could get help finding a way to be genuine and stop manipulating everybody around me to see 'the statue' as erect and impressive, etc.

Nor however is it strictly true that the analyst had nothing interesting to say or didn't sometimes provide helpful models or angles of looking at the basic problem. For instance, it turned out that one of his basic operating premises was the claim that there were really only two basic, fundamental orientations a person could have toward the world, (1) love and (2) fear, and that they couldn't coexist (or, in logical terms, that their domains were exhaustive and mutually exclusive, or that their two sets had no intersection but their union comprised all possible elements, or that

$$'(\forall x) ((Fx \rightarrow \sim (Lx)) \ \& \ (Lx \rightarrow \sim (Fx))),' \text{ or } ' \sim((\exists x) (Fx \ \& \ Lx))'),$$

meaning in other words that each day of your life was spent in service to one of these masters or the other, and 'One cannot serve two masters'— the Bible again—and that one of the worst things about the conception of competitive, achievement-oriented masculinity that America supposedly hard-wired into its males was that it caused a more or less constant state of fear that made genuine love next to impossible. That is, that what passed for love in American men was usually just the need to be regarded in a certain way, meaning that today's males were so constantly afraid of 'not measuring up' (Dr. G.'s phrase, with evidently no pun intended) that they had to spend all their time convincing others of their masculine 'validity' (which happens to also be a term from formal logic) in order to ease their own insecurity, making genuine love next to impossible. Although it seemed a bit simplistic to see this fear as just a male problem (try watching a girl stand on a scale sometime), it turns out that Dr. Gustafson was very nearly right in this concept of the two masters—though not in the way that he, when alive and confused about his own real identity, thought— and even while I played along by pretending to argue or not understand quite what he was driving at, the idea struck me that maybe the real root of my problem was not fraudulence but a basic inability to really love, even to genuinely love my stepparents, or Fern, or Melissa Betts, or Ginger Manley of Aurora West High in 1979, whom I'd often thought of as the only girl I'd ever truly loved, though Dr. G.'s bromide about men being brainwashed to equate love with accomplishment or conquest also applied here. The plain truth was that Ginger Manley was just the first girl I ever went all the way with, and most of my tender feelings about her were really just nostalgia for the feeling of immense cosmic validation I'd felt when she finally let me take her jeans all the way off and put my 'manhood' inside her, etc. There's really no bigger cliché than losing your virginity and later having all kinds of retrospective tenderness for the girl involved. Or what Beverly-Elizabeth Slane, a research technician I used to see outside of work when I was a media buyer, and had a lot of conflict with toward the end, said, which I don't think I ever told Dr. G. about, fraudulence-wise, probably because it hit too close to the bone. Toward the end she compared me to some piece of ultra-expensive new medical or diagnostic equipment that can discern more about you in one quick scan than you could ever know about yourself—but the equipment doesn't care about you, you're just a sequence of processes and codes. What the machine understands about you doesn't actually *mean* anything to it. Even though it's really good at what it does. Beverly had a bad temper combined with some serious firepower, she was not someone you wanted to have pissed off at you. She said she'd never felt the gaze of someone so penetrating, discerning, and yet empty of care, like she was a puzzle or problem I was figuring out. She said that it was thanks to me that she'd discovered the difference between being penetrated and really known versus penetrated and just violated—needless to say, these thanks were sarcastic. Some of this was just her emotional makeup. She found it impossible to really end a relationship unless all bridges were burned and things got said that were so devastating that there could be no possibility of a rapprochement to haunt her or prevent her moving on. Nevertheless it penetrated, I never did forget what she said in that letter.

Even if being fraudulent and being unable to love were in fact ultimately the same thing (a possibility that Dr. Gustafson never seemed to consider no matter how many times I tried to set him up to see it), being unable to really love was at least a different model or lens through which to see the problem, plus initially it seemed like a promising way of attacking the fraudulence paradox in terms of reducing the self-hatred part that reinforced the fear and the consequent drive to try to manipulate people into providing the approval I'd denied myself. This period was pretty much the zenith of my career in analysis, and for a few weeks (during a couple of which I actually didn't see Dr. Gustafson at all, because some sort of complication in his illness required him to go into the hospital, and when he came back he appeared to have lost not only weight but some kind of essential part of his total mass, and no longer seemed way too large for his old desk chair, which still squeaked but now not as loudly; plus a lot of the clutter and papers had been straightened up and put in several brown cardboard banker's boxes against the wall under the two sad prints, and when I came back in to see him the absence of mess was especially disturbing and sad, for some reason) it was true that I felt some of the first genuine hope I'd had since the early, self-deluded part of the experiment with Naperville's Church of the Flaming Sword of the Redeemer. And yet at the same time these weeks also led more or less directly to my decision to kill myself, although I'm going to have to simplify and linearize a great deal of interior stuff in order to convey to you what actually happened. Otherwise it would take an almost literal eternity to recount it, we already agreed about that. It's not that words or human language stop having any meaning or relevance after you die, by the way. It's more the specific, one-after-the-other temporal ordering of them that does. Or doesn't. It's hard to explain. In logical terms, something expressed in words will still have the same *cardinality* but no longer the same *ordinality*. All the different words are still there, in other words, but it's no longer a question of which one comes first. Or you could say it's no longer the series of words but now more like some limit toward which the series converges. It's hard not to want to put it in logical terms, since they're the most abstract and universal. Meaning they have no connotation, you don't feel anything about them. Or maybe imagine everything anybody on earth ever said or even thought to themselves all getting collapsed and exploding into one large, combined, instantaneous sound—although *instantaneous* is a little misleading, since it implies other instants before and after, and it isn't really like that. It's more like the sudden internal flash when you see or realize something—a sudden flash or whatever of epiphany or insight. It's not just that it happens way faster than you could break the process down and arrange it into English, but that it happens on a scale in which there isn't even time to be aware of any sort of time at all in which it's happening, the flash—all you know is that there's a before and an after, and afterward you're different. I don't know if that makes sense. I'm just trying to give it to you from several different angles, it's all the same thing. Or you could think of it as being more a certain configuration of light than a world-sum or series of sounds, too, afterward. Which is in fact true. Or as a theorem's proof—because if a proof is true it's true everywhere and all the time, not just when you happen to say it. The thing is that it turns out that logical symbolism really would be the best way to express it, because logic is totally abstract and universal and outside what we think of as time. It's the closest thing to what it's really like. That's why it's the logical paradoxes that really drive people nuts. A lot of history's great logicians have ended up killing themselves, this is a fact.

And keep in mind this flash can happen anywhere, at any time.

Here's the basic Berry paradox, by the way, if you might want an example of why logicians with incredible firepower can devote their whole lives to solving these things and still end up beating their heads against the wall. This one has to do with really big numbers—meaning really big, past a trillion, past ten to the trillion to the trillion, way up there. When you get way up there, it takes a while even to describe numbers this big in words. 'The quantity one trillion, four hundred and three billion to the trillionth power' takes twenty syllables to describe, for example. You get the idea. Now, even higher up there in these huge, cosmic-scale numbers, imagine the very smallest number that can't be described in under twenty-two syllables. The paradox is that *the very smallest number that can't be described in under twenty-two syllables,* which of course is itself a description of this number, only has twenty-one syllables in it. So now what are you supposed to do?

What actually led to it in casual terms, though, occurred during maybe the third or fourth week that Dr. G. was back seeing patients after his hospitalization, although I'm not going to pretend that the specific incident wouldn't strike most people as absurd or even sort of insipid, as causes go. The truth is just that late at night one night in August after Dr. G.'s return, when I couldn't sleep (which happened a lot ever since the cocaine period) and was sitting up drinking a glass of milk and watching television, flipping the remote almost at random between different cable stations the way you do when it's late, I happened on part of an old *Cheers* episode from late in the series' run where the analyst character, Frasier (who went on to have his own show), and Lilith, his fiancée and also an analyst, are just entering the stage set of the underground tavern, and Frasier is asking her how her workday at her office went, and Lilith says, 'If I have one more yuppie come in and start whining to me about how he can't love, I'm going to throw up.' This line got a huge laugh from the show's audience, which indicated that they—and so by demographic extension the whole national audience at home, as well—recognized what a cliché and melodramatic type of complaint the inability-to-love concept really was. And, sitting there, when I realized that once again I'd managed to con myself, this time into thinking that this was a truer or more promising way to conceive of the problem of fraudulence—and, by extension, that I'd also somehow deluded myself into almost believing that poor old Dr. Gustafson had anything in his mental arsenal that could actually help me, and that the real truth was more that I was continuing to see him partly out of pity and partly so that I could pretend to myself that I was taking steps to becoming more authentic when in fact all I was doing was jerking a gravely ill shell of a man around and feeling superior to him because I was able to analyze his own psychological makeup so much more accurately than he could analyze mine—the flash of realizing all this at the very same time that the huge audience laugh showed that nearly everyone in the United States had probably already seen through the complaint's inauthenticity as long ago as whenever the episode had originally run—all this flashed through my head in the tiny interval it took to realize what I was watching and to remember who the characters of Frasier and Lilith even were, maybe half a second at most, and it more or less destroyed me, that's the only way I can describe it, as if whatever hope of any way out of the trap I'd made for myself had been blasted out of mid-air or laughed off the stage, as if I were one of those stock comic characters who is always both the butt of the joke and the only person not to get the joke—and in sum I went to bed feeling as fraudulent, befogged, hopeless and full of self-contempt as I'd ever felt, and it was the next morning after that that I woke up having decided that I was going to kill myself and end the whole farce. (As you probably recall, *Cheers* was an enormously popular series, and even in syndication its metro numbers were so high that if a local advertiser wanted to buy time on it the slots cost so much that you pretty much had to build his whole local strategy around those slots.) I'm compressing a huge amount of what took place in my psyche that next-to-last night, all the different realizations and conclusions I reached as I lay there in bed unable to sleep or even move (no single series' line or audience laugh is in and of itself going to constitute a reason for suicide, of course)—although to you I imagine it probably doesn't seem all that compressed at all, you're thinking here's this guy going on and on and why doesn't he get to the part where he kills himself and explain or account for the fact that he's sitting here next to me in a piece of high-powered machinery telling me all this if he died in 1991. Which in fact I knew I would from the moment I woke up. It was over, I'd decided to end the charade. After breakfast, I called in sick to work and stayed home the whole day alone. I knew that if I was around anyone I'd automatically lapse into fraudulence. I had decided to take a whole lot of Benadryl and then just as I got really sleepy and relaxed I'd get the car up to top speed on a rural road way out in the extreme west suburbs and drive it head-on into a concrete bridge abutment. Benadryl makes me extremely foggy and sleepy, it always has. I spent most of the morning on letters to my lawyer and CPA, and brief notes to the creative head and managing partner who had originally brought me aboard at Samieti and Cheyne. Our creative group was in the middle of some very ticklish campaign preparations, and I wanted to apologize for leaving them in the lurch. Of course I didn't really feel all that sorry—Samieti and Cheyne was a ballet of fraudulence, and I was well out of it. The note was probably ultimately just so that the people who really mattered at S. & C. would be more apt to remember me as a decent, conscientious guy who it turned out was maybe just a little too sensitive and tormented by his personal demons—'Almost too good for this world' is what I seemed to be unable to keep from fantasizing a lot of them saying after news of it came through. I did not write Dr. Gustafson a note. He had his own share of problems, and I knew that in the note I'd spend a lot of time trying to seem as if I was being honest but really just dancing around the truth, which was that he was a deeply repressed homosexual or androgyne and had no real business charging patients to let him project his own masculinity conflicts onto them, and that the truth was that he'd be doing himself and everybody else a favor if he'd just go over to Garfield Park and fellate somebody in the bushes and try honestly to decide if he liked it or not, and that I was a total fraud for continuing to drive all the way in to River Forest to see him and bat him around like a catnip toy while telling myself there was some possible nonfraudulent point to it. (All of which, of course, even if they weren't dying of colon cancer right in front of you you still could never actually come out and say to somebody, since certain truths might well destroy them—and who has that right?)

I did spend almost two hours before taking the first of the Benadryl composing a handwritten note to my sister Fern. In the note I apologized for whatever pain my suicide and the fraudulence and/or inability to love that had precipitated it might cause her and my stepdad (who was still alive and well and now lived in Marin County, California, where he taught part-time, and did community outreach with Marin County's homeless). I also used the occasion of the letter and all the sort of last-testament urgency associated with it to license apologizing to Fern about manipulating my stepparents into believing that she'd lied about the antique glass bowl in 1967, as well as for half a dozen other incidents and spiteful or fraudulent actions that I knew had caused her pain and that I had felt bad about ever since, but had never really seen any way to broach with her or express my honest regret for. (It turns out there are things that you can discuss in a suicide note that would appear almost bizarre if expressed in any other kind of venue.) Just one example of such an incident was during a period in the mid '70s, when Fern, as part of puberty, underwent some physical changes that made her look chunky for a year or two—not fat, but wide-hipped and bosomy and much more broad than she'd been as a pre-teen—and of course she was very, very sensitive about it (puberty also being a time of terrible self-consciousness and sensitivity about one's body image, obviously), so much so that my stepparents took great pains not to say anything about Fern's new breadth or even ever to bring up any topics related to eating habits, diet and exercise, etc. And I for my own part never said anything about it either, not directly, but I had worked out all kinds of very subtle and indirect ways to torment Fern about her size in such a way that my stepparents never saw anything and I could never really be accused of anything that I couldn't look all around myself with a shocked, incredulous facial expression as if I had no idea what she was talking about, such as just a quick raise of my eyebrow when her eyes met mine as she was having a second helping at dinner, or a quick, quiet, 'Are you sure you can fit into that?' when she came home from the store with a new skirt. The one I still remembered the most vividly involved the second-floor hall of our house, which was in Aurora and was a three-story home (including the basement) but not all that spacious or large, a skinny three-decker such as many you always see all crammed together in Naperville and Aurora. The second-floor hallway, which ran between Fern's room and the top of the stairway on one end and my room and the second-floor bathroom on the other, was cramped and somewhat narrow, but not nearly as narrow as I would go out of my way to pretend that it was whenever Fern and I passed each other in it, with me squashing my back against the hallway wall and splaying my arms out and wincing as if there would barely be enough room for someone of her enormous breadth to squeeze past me, and she would never say anything or even look at me when I did it but would just go past me into the bathroom and close the door. But I knew it must have hurt her. A little while later, she entered an adolescent period where she hardly ate anything at all, and smoked cigarettes and chewed several packs of gum a day, and used a lot of makeup, and for a while she got so thin that she looked angular and a bit like an insect (although of course I never said that), and I once, through their bedroom's keyhole, overheard a brief conversation in which my step-mother said she was worried because she didn't think Fern was having her normal time of the month anymore because she had become so under-weight, and she and my stepfather discussed the possibility of taking her to see some kind of specialist. That period passed on its own, but in the letter I told Fern that I'd always remembered this and other periods when I'd been cruel or tried to make her feel bad, and that I regretted them very much, although I said I wouldn't want to seem so egotistical as to think that a simple apology could erase any of the hurt I'd caused her when we were growing up. On the other hand, I also assured her that it wasn't as if I had gone around for years carrying excessive guilt or blowing these various incidents out of proportion. They were not life-altering traumas or any-thing like that, and in many ways they were probably all too typical of the sorts of cruelties that kids tend to inflict on one another growing up. I also assured Fern that neither these incidents nor my remorse about them had anything to do with my killing myself. I simply said, without going into anything like the level of detail I've given you (because my purpose in the letter was of course very different), that I was killing myself because I was an essentially fraudulent person who seemed to lack either the character or the firepower to find a way to stop even after I'd realized my fraudulence and the terrible toll it exacted (I told her nothing about the different real-izations or paradoxes, what would be the point?). I also inserted that there was also a good possibility that, when all was said and done, I was nothing but just another yuppie who couldn't love, and that I found the banality of this unendurable, largely because I was evidently so hollow and insecure that I had a pathological need to see myself as somehow special or excep-tional at all times. Without going into much explanation or argument, I also told Fern that if her initial reaction to these reasons for my killing myself was to think that I was being much, much too hard on myself, then she should know that I was already aware that that was the most likely reaction my note would produce in her, and had probably deliberately constructed the note to at least in part prompt just that reaction, just the way my whole life I'd often said and done things designed to prompt cer-tain people to believe that I was a genuinely outstanding person whose personal standards were so high that he was far too hard on himself, which in turn made me appear attractively modest and unsmug, and was a big reason for my popularity with so many people in all different avenues of my life—what Beverly-Elizabeth Slane had termed my 'talent for ingratiation'—but was essentially calculated and fraudulent. I also told Fern that I loved her very much, and asked her to relay these same sentiments to Marin County for me.

Now we're getting to the part where I actually kill myself. This occurred at 9:17 P.M. on August 19, 1991, if you want the time fixed precisely. Plus I'll spare you most of the last couple hours' preparations and back-and-forth conflict and dithering, which there was a lot of. Suicide runs so counter to so many hardwired instincts and drives that nobody in his right mind goes through with it without going through a great deal of internal back-and-forth, intervals of almost changing your mind, etc. The German logician Kant was right in this respect, human beings are all pretty much identical in terms of our hard-wiring. Although we are seldom conscious of it, we are all basically just instruments or expressions of our evolutionary drives, which are themselves the expressions of forces that are way larger and more important than we are. (Although actually being conscious of this is a whole different matter.) So I won't really even try to describe the several different times that day when I sat in my living room and had a furious mental back-and-forth about whether to actually go through with it. For one thing, it was intensely mental and would take an enormous amount of time to put into words, plus it would come off as somewhat cliché or banal in the sense that many of the thoughts and associations are basically the same sorts of generic things that anyone who's confronting imminent death will end up thinking. As in, 'This is the last time I will ever tie my shoes,' 'This is the last time I will look at this rubber tree on top of the stereo cabinet,' 'How delicious this lungful of air right here tastes,' 'This is the last glass of milk I'll ever drink,' 'What a totally priceless gift this totally ordinary sight of the wind picking trees' branches up and moving them around and laying them back down is.' Or, 'I will never again hear the plaintive sound of the fridge going on in the kitchen' (the kitchen and breakfast nook are right off my living room), etc. Or, 'I won't see the sun come up tomorrow or watch the bedroom gradually undim and resolve' and at the same time trying to summon the memory of the exact way the sun comes up over the fog of the humid fields and the wet-looking I-55 ramp that lay due east of my bedroom's sliding glass door in the morning. It had been a hot, wet August, and if I went through with killing myself I wouldn't ever get to feel the incremental cooling and drying that starts here around mid-September, or see the leaves turn or hear them rustle along the edge of the courtyard outside S. & C.'s floor of the building on S. Dearborn, or see snow or put a shovel and bag of sand in the trunk, or bite into a perfectly ripe, ungrainy pear, or put a piece of toilet paper on a shaving cut. If I went in and went to the bathroom and brushed my teeth it would be the last time I did those things. I sat there and thought about that, looking at the rubber tree. Everything seemed to tremble a little, the way something reflected in water will tremble. I watched the sun begin to drop down over the townhouse developments going up south of Darien's corporation limit on Lily Cache Rd. and realized that I would never see the newest homes' construction and landscaping completed, or that the homes' white insulation wrap with the trade name TYVEK all over it flapping in the wind would one day have vinyl siding or plate brick and color-coordinated shutters over it and I wouldn't see this happen or be able to drive by and know what was actually written there under all the exteriors. Or the breakfast nook window's view of the big farm's fields next to my development, with the plowed furrows all parallel so that if I lean and line their lines up just right they seem to be rushing together toward the horizon as if shot out of something huge. You get the idea. Basically, I was in that state in which a man realizes that everything he sees will outlast him. As a verbal construction I know that's a cliché. As a state in which to actually be, though, it's something else, believe me. Where now every movement takes on a kind of ceremonial aspect. The very sacredness of the world as seen (the same kind of state Dr. G. will try to describe with analogies to oceans and whitecaps and trees, you might recall I mentioned this already). This is literally about one one-trillionth of the various thoughts and internal experiences I underwent in those last few hours, and I'll spare both of us recounting any more, since I'm aware it ends up seeming somewhat lame. Which in fact it wasn't, but I won't pretend it was fully authentic or genuine, either. A part of me was still calculating, performing—and this was part of the ceremonial quality of that last afternoon. Even as I wrote my note to Fern, for instance, expressing sentiments and regrets that were real, a part of me was noticing what a fine and sincere note it was, and anticipating the effect on Fern of this or that heartfelt phrase, while yet another part was observing the whole scene of a man in a dress shirt and no tie sitting at his breakfast nook writing a heartfelt note on his last afternoon alive, the blonde wood table's surface trembling with sunlight and the man's hand steady and face both haunted by regret and ennobled by resolve, this part of me sort of hovering above and just to the left of myself, evaluating the scene, and thinking what a fine and genuine-seeming performance in a drama it would make if only we all had not already been subject to countless scenes just like it in dramas ever since we first saw a movie or read a book, which somehow entailed that real scenes like the one of my suicide note were now compelling and genuine only to their participants and to anyone else would come off as banal and even somewhat cheesy or maudlin, which is somewhat paradoxical when you consider—as I did, sitting there at the breakfast nook—that the reason scenes like this will seem stale or manipulative to an audience is that we've already seen so many of them in dramas, and yet the reason we've seen so many of them in dramas is that the scenes really are dramatic and compelling and let us communicate very deep, complicated emotional realities that are almost impossible to articulate in any other way, and at the same time still another facet or part of me realizing that from this perspective my own basic problem was that at an early age I'd somehow chosen to cast my lot with my life's drama's supposed audience instead of with the drama itself, and that I even now was watching and gauging my supposed performance's quality and probable effects, and was in the final analysis the very same manipulative fraud writing the note to Fern that I had been throughout the life that had brought me to this climactic scene of writing and signing it and addressing the envelope and affixing postage and putting the envelope in my shirt pocket (totally conscious of the resonance of its resting there, next to my heart, in the scene), planning to drop it in a mailbox on the way out to Lily Cache Rd. and the bridge abutment into which I planned to drive my car at speeds sufficient to displace the whole front end and impale me on the steering wheel and kill me instantly. Self-loathing is not the same thing as being into pain or a lingering death. If I was going to do it, I wanted it instant.

On Lily Cache, the bridge abutments and sides' steep banks support State Route 4 (also known as the Braidwood Highway) as it crosses overhead on a cement overpass so covered with graffiti that most of it you can't even read. (This sort of defeats the purpose of graffiti, in my opinion.) The abutments themselves are just off the road and as wide as this car. Plus the intersection is isolated way out in the countryside around Romeoville, ten or so miles south of the southwest suburbs' limits. It is the true boonies. The only homes are farms set way back from the road and embellished with silos and barns, etc. At night in the summer the dew point is high and there's always fog. It's farm country. I've never once passed under 4 here without seeming to be the only thing on either road. The corn high and the fields like a green ocean all around, insects the only real noise. Driving alone under creamy stars and the little cocked scythe of moon, etc. The idea was to have the accident and whatever explosion and fire was involved occur someplace isolated enough that no one else would see it, so that there would be as little an aspect of performance to the thing as I could manage and no temptation to spend my last few seconds trying to imagine what impression the sight and sound of the impact might make on someone watching. I was partly concerned that it might be spectacular and dramatic and might look as if the driver was trying to go out in as dramatic a way as possible. This is the sort of shit we waste our lives thinking about.

The ground fog tends to get more intense by the second until it seems that the whole world is just what's in your headlights' reach. High beams don't work in fog, they only make things worse. You can go ahead and try them but you'll see what happens, all they do is light up the fog so that it seems even denser. That's kind of a minor paradox, that sometimes you can see farther with low beams than high. All right—and there's the construction and all the flapping TYVEK wrap on houses that if you really do it you'll never see anyone live in. Although it won't hurt, it really will be instant, I can tell you that much. The fields' insects are almost deafening. If the corn's high like this and you watch as the sun sets, you can practically watch them rise up out of the fields like some great figure's shadow rising. Mostly mosquitoes. I don't know what all they are. It's a whole insect universe in there that none of us will ever see or know anything about. You'll notice that Benadryl doesn't help all that much once you're under way. The whole idea was probably ill-conceived.

All right, now we're coming to what I promised and led you through the whole dull synopsis of what led up to this in hopes of. Meaning what it's like to die, what happens. Right? This is what everyone wants to know. And you do, trust me. Whether you decide to go through with it or not, whether I somehow talk you out of it the way you think I'm going to try to do or not. It's not what anyone thinks, for one thing. The truth is you already know what it's like. You already know the difference between the size and speed of everything that flashes through you and the tiny inadequate bit of it all you can ever let anyone know. As though inside you is this enormous room full of what seems like everything in the whole universe at one time or another and yet the only parts that get out have to somehow squeeze out through one of those tiny keyholes you see under the knob in older doors. As if we are all trying to see each other through these tiny keyholes.

But it does have a knob, the door can open. But not in the way you think. But what if you could? Think for a second: What if all the infinitely dense and shifting worlds of stuff inside you every moment of your life turned out now to be somehow fully open and expressible afterward, after what you think of as *you* has died, because what if afterward now each moment itself is an infinite sea or span or passage of time in which to express it or convey it, and you don't even need any organized English, you can as they say open the door and be in anyone else's room in all your own multiform forms and ideas and faces? Because listen—we don't have much time, here's where Lily Cache slopes slightly down and the banks start getting steep, and you can just make out the outlines of the unlit sign for the farmstand that's never open anymore, the last sign before the bridge—so listen: What exactly do you think you are? The millions and trillions of thoughts, memories, juxtapositions—even crazy ones like this, you're thinking—that flash through your head and disappear? Some sum or remainder of these? Your *history*? Do you know how long it's been since I told you I was a fraud? Do you remember you were looking at the RESPICEM watch hanging from the rearview and seeing the time, 9:17? What are you looking at right now? Coincidence? What if no time has passed at all?* The truth is you've already heard this. That this is what it's like. That it's what makes room for the universes inside you, all the endless

---

*One clue that there's something not quite real about sequential time the way you experience it is the various paradoxes of time supposedly passing and of a so-called present that's always unrolling into the future and creating more and more past behind it. As if the present were this car—nice car by the way—and the past is the road we've just gone over, and the future is the headlit road up ahead we haven't yet gotten to, and time is the car's forward movement, and the precise present is the car's front bumper cutting through the fog of the future, so that it's *now* and then a tiny bit later a whole different *now*, etc. Except if time is really passing, how fast does it go? At what rate does the present change? See? Meaning, if we use time to measure motion or rate—which we do, it's the only way you can—ninety-five miles per

inbent fractals of connection and symphonies of different voices, the infinities you can never show another soul. And you think it makes you a fraud, the tiny fraction anyone else ever sees? Of course you're a fraud, of course what people see is never you. And of course you know this, and of course you try to manage what part they see if you know it's only a part. Who wouldn't? It's called free will, Sherlock. But at the same time it's why it feels so good to break down and cry in front of others, or to laugh, or speak in tongues, or chant in Bengali—it's not English anymore, it's not getting squeezed through any hole.

So cry all you want, I won't tell anybody.

But it wouldn't have made you a fraud to change your mind. It would be sad to do it because you think you somehow have to.

It won't hurt, though. It will be loud, and you'll feel things, but they'll go through you so fast that you won't even realize you're feeling them (which is sort of like the paradox I used to bounce off Gustafson—is it possible to be a fraud if you aren't aware you're a fraud?). And the very brief moment of fire you'll feel will be almost good, like when your hands are cold and there's a fire and you hold your hands out toward it.

The reality is that dying isn't bad, but it takes forever. And that forever is no time at all. I know that sounds like a contradiction, or wordplay. What it really is, it turns out, is a matter of perspective. The big picture, as they say, in which the fact is that this whole seemingly endless back-and-forth between us has come and gone and come again in the same instant that Fern stirs a boiling pot for dinner, and your stepfather packs some pipe tobacco down with his thumb, and Angela Mead uses an ingenious little catalogue tool to roll cat hair off her blouse, and Melissa Betts inhales

---

hour, seventy heartbeats a minute, etc.—how are you supposed to measure the rate at which time moves? One second per second? It makes no sense. You can't even talk about time flowing or moving without hitting up against paradox right away. So think for a second: What if there's really no movement at all? What if this is all unfolding in the one flash you call the present, this first, infinitely tiny split-second of impact when the speeding car's front bumper's just starting to touch the abutment, just before the bumper crumples and displaces the front end and you go violently forward and the steering column comes back at your chest as if shot out of something enormous? Meaning that what if in fact this *now* is infinite and never really passes in the way your mind is supposedly wired to understand *pass*, so that not only your whole life but every single humanly conceivable way to describe and account for that life has time to flash like neon shaped into those connected cursive letters that businesses' signs and windows like so much to use through your mind all at once in the literally immeasurable instant between impact and death, just as you start forward to meet the wheel at a rate no belt ever made could restrain—THE END.

to respond to something she thinks her husband just said, and David Wallace blinks in the midst of idly scanning class photos from his 1980 Aurora West H.S. yearbook and seeing my photo and trying, through the tiny keyhole of himself, to imagine what all must have happened to lead up to my death in the fiery single-car accident he'd read about in 1991, like what sorts of pain or problems might have driven the guy to get in his electric-blue Corvette and try to drive with all that OTC medication in his bloodstream—David Wallace happening to have a huge and totally unorganizable set of thoughts, feelings, memories and impressions of this little photo's guy a year ahead of him in school with the seemingly almost neon aura around him all the time of scholastic and athletic excellence and popularity and success with the ladies, as well as of every last cutting remark or even tiny disgusted gesture or expression on this guy's part whenever David Wallace struck out looking in Legion ball or said something dumb at a party, and of how impressive and authentically at ease in the world the guy always seemed, like an actual living person instead of the dithering, pathetically self-conscious outline or ghost of a person David Wallace knew himself back then to be. Verily a fair-haired, fast-track guy, whom in the very best human tradition David Wallace had back then imagined as happy and unreflective and wholly unhaunted by voices telling him that there was something deeply wrong with him that wasn't wrong with anybody else and that he had to spend all of his time and energy trying to figure out what to do and say in order to impersonate an even marginally normal or acceptable U.S. male, all this stuff clanging around in David Wallace '81's head every second and moving so fast that he never got a chance to catch hold and try to fight or argue against it or even really even feel it except as a knot in his stomach as he stood in his real parents' kitchen ironing his uniform and thinking of all the ways he could screw up and strike out looking or drop balls in right and reveal his true pathetic essence in front of this .418 hitter and his witchily pretty sister and everyone else in the audience in lawn chairs in the grass along the sides of the Legion field (all of whom already probably saw through the sham from the outset anyway, he was pretty sure)—in other words David Wallace trying, if only in the second his lids are down, to somehow reconcile what this luminous guy had seemed like from the outside with whatever on the interior must have driven him to kill himself in such a dramatic and doubtlessly painful way—with David Wallace also fully aware that the cliché that you can't ever know what's going on inside somebody else is hoary and insipid and yet at the same time trying very consciously to prohibit that awareness from mocking the attempt or sending the whole line of thought into the sort of inbent spiral that keeps you from ever getting anywhere (considerable time having passed since 1980, of course, and David Wallace having emerged from years of literally indescribable war against himself with quite a bit more firepower than he'd had at Aurora West), the realer, more enduring and sentimental part of him commanding that other part to be silent, as if looking it coldly in the eye and saying, almost aloud, 'Not another word.'

Contributors' Notes

ANN BEATTIE's most recent books are *Perfect Recall* (stories) and *The Doctor's House*, a novel.

"This story was written in Rome, when I was freezing inside the American Academy. I tried to turn my thoughts to a warmer place, and L.A. came to mind. I hardly know anyone in L.A., but I do have friends who live in the Hollywood Hills, and their astonishing backyard became the backdrop for the story. I had little idea what would happen until the possum stopped playing possum, and then the story began to run away as well. To that point, my characters had been playing possum with me, but Keller's relief was my own: suddenly I saw where the story was headed, though I was unprepared, myself, for the violence that preceded the ending."

KEVIN BROCKMEIER is the author of the story collection *Things That Fall from the Sky* and the children's novel *City of Names*. His stories have appeared in such periodicals and anthologies as *McSweeney's, The Georgia Review, The Chicago Tribune,* and *Prize Stories 2000: The O. Henry Awards.* He lives in Little Rock, Arkansas, where he was raised.

"I can date the conception of 'The Ceiling' with rare precision—to Sunday, January 11, 1998. I was flying home from the wedding of my friends Chris and Jen Bertram when I read the A. S. Byatt story 'Dragon's Breath,' a tale about giant worms who descend upon and ravage a village over a period of weeks and months, excavating and devouring it before they slide into the depths of a lake. When I finished the story, I found myself thinking about the bad things in life and how we often fail to protect ourselves from them, or understand them for what they are, even when we see them coming. Perhaps because I was in an airplane at the time, this notion took on the particular symbolic form it did—that of a ceiling which crushes as it falls. My stories often grow from metaphors such as this.

"The next day was the first of the spring semester. I began teaching four sections of remedial English composition—a slow, crushing experience all its own—but the organizing symbol of the ceiling stayed with me, accruing details and characters and eventually an entire town beneath it. I wrote the story after the semester ended, in May and June of 1998. Jenny Minton and Dave Eggers helped me shape it into its final form.

"The muddled partnership of Justin and Melissa is no reflection, by the way, on the marriage of my friends Chris and Jen, which four years later is still a happy one."

EDWIDGE DANTICAT is the author of *Breath, Eyes, Memory, Krik? Krak!, The Farming of Bones,* and *Behind the Mountains,* a young adult novel, as well as a nonfiction book, *After the Dance: A Walk Through Carnival in Jacmel.* She is also the editor of *The Butterfly's Way: Voices from the Haitian Dyaspora in the United States* and *The Beacon Best of 2000.*

"The idea for 'Seven' came to me while I was writing a nonfiction book about carnival in Haiti. I had always wanted to write a carnival story, something like Marcel Camus's 1959 movie *Black Orpheus,* which takes place during carnival in Rio de Janeiro. However, I soon discovered that my own carnival story was unfolding way after carnival had ended, seven years later, as a matter of fact, between a husband and wife who had met during carnival but had to be separated from one another soon after. I was thrilled that this development gave me a chance to use the mock marriage ceremonies that are a part of carnival parades. Since political commentary is also a strong element of carnival, I decided to include mentions of two police brutality cases that had involved Haitian men in New York, where the couple is eventually reunited. For me, 'Seven' is as much about carnival as it is about silence, the type of silence which follows the clamor of exceptional experiences merging over time into very ordinary ones."

CHITRA BANERJEE DIVAKARUNI is the author of the novels *The Mistress of Spices, Sister of My Heart,* and *The Vine of Desire,* and of the short story collections *The Unknown Errors of Our Lives* and *Arranged Marriage,* which won an American Book Award in 1996. She also has four volumes of poetry, the latest titled *Leaving Yuba City.* Her work has appeared in *The Atlantic Monthly, The New Yorker, Zoetrope: All-Story, Ms., Agni, The Best American Short Stories,* and the Pushcart Prize Anthology, among others. She teaches in the Creative Writing program at the University of Houston and divides her time between Texas and Northern California.

"Some stories come to me in a rush, like a celestial deluge. 'The Lives of Strangers,' alas, was not one of them. I've been worrying this story ever since I went on a pilgrimage in the Himalayas in 1985 and met the woman who would become, in her final fictional incarnation, the Mrs. Das of the story. The rest of the story gave itself to me piece by piece— rather grudgingly, I thought—and refused outright to be autobiographical in any way. The only element in it that I can claim as mine is geographical: the Calcutta of 'Lives' is very much the Calcutta I grew up in—harsh, beautiful in unexpected, heartbreaking ways, and ultimately unfathomable."

ANTHONY DOERR's first collection of stories, *The Shell Collector,* which includes "The Hunter's Wife," was published in January. He has received writing fellowships from the University of Wisconsin and the National Endowment for the Arts. He lives in Boise, Idaho, where he is at work on a novel.

"There must have been a plane crash in the news during the time I wrote 'The Hunter's Wife,' because I remember thinking that writing it was like retrieving the pieces of an airplane from the bottom of the ocean and strewing them over the floor of a warehouse and trying to reassemble them. For several months there were two endings, no middle, no clear shape. To finish it I quarantined myself in a 3' × 5' carrel in the University of Wisconsin Memorial Library. I can still remember the sweet, almost perfect relief I felt when it finally came together.

"I'm grateful to Michael Curtis and his staff at the *Atlantic* for their scrupulous edits, and to Larry Dark for including my story in such wonderful company."

DEBORAH EISENBERG's most recent collection of fiction is *All Around Atlantis*. She lives in New York and teaches part-time at the University of Virginia.

"Like all of my stories, this one took a long time to write. And yet for the life of me, I can't remember how it came to be. I certainly didn't set out to write it, or anything of its sort. I think that while I was working on it, it felt like an obstacle that needed to be located and removed or discharged before I could get on to something I'd really want to be doing, whatever that might be. But that, too, is the rule rather than the exception for me. The only specific thing I can recall is that I once saw a very brief conversation between two people who didn't appear to know one another, a strikingly vigorous man in his late middle age and a pretty young woman. The exchange was very correct, casual, and pleasant, and yet I felt that they had both unexpectedly disclosed to me a massive amount of information that I didn't want! So perhaps I just felt a need to pass it on, and the rest of the story followed."

LOUISE ERDRICH's most recent novel was *The Last Report on Miracles at Little No Horse*. This story is part of a book called *The Master Butchers Singing Club*. She lives in Minnesota with her daughters and operates a small bookstore, Birchbark Books, with lots of help.

"'The Butcher's Wife' has been with me for thirty years. When I was eighteen years old, my grandmother told me that she was not related to me by blood, and had nursed my biological grandmother through her final, harrowing illness. Much later, she married my grandfather and became Mom to my father and his brothers. I am so proud that this story was chosen for inclusion here, and would like to dedicate it to my father, Ralph. I see now that one way he has repaired the devastation of the early loss of his mother was to become an extraordinary father to me, and grandfather to my children. Also, he passed on to me several crucial eccentricities of mind without which I would never have become a writer."

RICHARD FORD was born in Jackson, Mississippi, in 1944, and raised there and in Little Rock. He has written five novels and three collections of stories. Among these are *The Sportswriter, Independence Day, Rock Springs, Wildlife,* and most recently, in 2002, *A Multitude of Sins,* from which the story "Charity" is taken.

"I don't remember much about how 'Charity' came to be written. More than likely because I live some in Maine, I just felt a pull to set a story there—something about the lingo and the landscape invited language from me. Plus, stories about removals—characters going or wanting to go someplace new in an effort to improve life—always seem dramatic and to inspire invention as a form of inquiry. Generally, though, I don't enjoy excavating a story's origins. Not only do I almost always remember things wrong (that is, I go on making the story up), but also, breaking stories back down to their component parts and impulses too often makes writing seem mechanistic, when in fact it's not. It's much more adventitious and defiant of tiresome critical archaeology, the point of which is usually not very noble anyway. It's nice to leave the mystery somewhat intact."

DAVID GATES is the author of the novels *Jernigan* and *Preston Falls,* and of the short story collection *The Wonders of the Invisible World.* He writes about books and music for *Newsweek,* and teaches in the MFA Writing Program at the New School for Social Research.

"'George Lassos Moon' began as an image: one of those small metal pitchers they put syrup in at pancake restaurants. The pitcher led to a stoned-out young man playing with it, and to an older woman trying to be patient with him, and to a voice telling about it in some kind of cubist diction, which I overdid in the story's first version. That must have been in 1997 or '98; I went back to the piece and rewrote it early in 2001. Good cop Walter Kirn bought it for *GQ,* then bad cop Michael Hainey asked me if I could cut 3,000 words out of my original ten. He suggested that a good place to start would be the ending—in which you actually found out what happened—and he was right. (Thanks, Michael.) They were both too polite to say I could also lose some slack writing, but I could and did. Just in case anybody's curious, the story of how Carl got arrested is an LSD yarn from back in the day; it probably really happened to somebody. The *Millionaire* question is real for sure. I gave Carl my real laptop, DVDs, antidepressants, and Eddie Bauer coat to help him get started, but after that he was pretty much on his own."

A.M. HOMES's new collection of stories, *Things You Should Know,* will be published this fall. She is the author of the novels *Music for Torching, The*

End of Alice, In a Country of Mothers, Jack, and the short story collection *The Safety of Objects.*

"'Do Not Disturb'—the title comes from the disc you hang outside your hotel door, the flip side is, of course, Make Up Room, which I found quite ironic. It represents one of what I'm calling the California Stories, inspired by time I've recently spent in California. There's a companion piece also in the new book—'Please Remain Calm'—which was a notice I saw in a California elevator, pertaining to what to do in an earthquake. I guess the contrast here is the difference between natural phenomena and unnatural, the stressors that can fracture a marriage."

DAVID LEAVITT is the author of several novels and story collections, most recently *The Marble Quilt,* in which "Speonk" is included. *Florence, A Delicate Case* was published in June 2002 as part of Bloomsbury's series The Writer and the City. He teaches at the University of Florida.

"'Speonk' began in the late eighties, when I was living in East Hampton, New York. One afternoon on a beach, I met an actor rather like Jonathan. For several years he had played a villain on a soap opera, but then he had gotten frustrated with playing a villain, and quit. After his last day on the set, heading out to East Hampton to visit friends, he had gotten on the wrong train and ended up in Speonk, where a truck driver had offered him a lift, recognized him, and insisted on bringing him home to show his (the truck driver's) wife. I found the anecdote intriguing, and wrote down a draft of what would later become the first third of the story. But then I couldn't seem to go anywhere else with Jonathan—I couldn't find a middle or an end to follow my beginning—and so I put the draft away in a box. Where I forgot it.

"Many years and several houses later, while housecleaning, I happened upon the fragment, already titled 'Speonk.' As I read it over, I found myself doubting the original actor's veracity in a way that I had not when I was younger. Suddenly his story seemed full of holes. Had he made it up? And if so, why?

"It was then that I saw where I had to go: away from Jonathan, and into the skepticism that his story provokes in the people to whom he tells it. More than a decade in a box—and then I finished 'Speonk' in three days."

ANDREA LEE was born in Philadelphia and attended the Baldwin School and Harvard University. Her fiction and nonfiction writing have appeared in *The New Yorker* and *The New York Times.* Her books include *Russian Journal,* the novel *Sarah Phillips,* and the story collection *Interesting Women.* Lee lives with her husband and two children in Turin, Italy.

"'Anthropology' came into being as an act of penance for something about which I have always had an uneasy conscience: a *New Yorker* article I wrote years ago about some of my relatives down in Hertford County, North Carolina. The piece, entitled 'Quilts,' didn't actually hurt any feelings, but it had in its general viewpoint a kind of dashing carelessness—I wrote it in my early twenties—and an eagerness to relegate real people to picturesque types, that nowadays makes me cringe. The only person to raise an eyebrow at the time was a perceptive cousin of mine in New York, but he never took me to task as the cousin does in the story—in fact, we've never really discussed it. So the dialogue is between me and me: a fleshing out of one of those fantasies of expiation we all have. In homage to 'Quilts,' I could have called it 'Guilt.' And I must admit, entirely selfishly, that I did feel better after writing it."

DON LEE is the author of the story collection *Yellow* (W. W. Norton), which received the 2002 Sue Kaufman Prize for First Fiction from the American Academy of Arts and Letters. He lives in Cambridge, Massachusetts, and is the editor of the literary journal *Ploughshares* at Emerson College.

"This story is a retort to a poem entitled 'The Possible Husband' by my friend Erin Belieu. She called me when it was published in a magazine and said that she had dedicated it to me, and I was very flattered, until I actually read the poem. I decided I should answer her in kind. I based the big-wave break on a legendary spot called Maverick's in Half Moon Bay, California. I've tried surfing only three times, so I had to rely heavily on research, and found a wealth of great surf literature out there by the likes of Daniel Duane, William Finnegan, and Jon Krakauer. A series of stirring articles about Maverick's that arose after the death of Hawaiian surfer Mark Foo was particularly relevant."

MARK RAY LEWIS: "I was raised in St. Louis and Hannibal, Missouri. I received fellowship support from Stanford University 1998–2002, named in honor of Wallace Stegner and Richard Scowcroft. My wife and I moved to her hometown of Boston last year. I am currently employed by the Design and Construction division of Boston Parks.

"I ruminated on Oral's story for about a year before I wrote it down. At

418 / *Contributors' Notes*

the time I was living alone in a shack under six rather large redwood trees that I referred to as The Grandpas. 'Scordatura' is a word for using a non-standard (alternate, open, or slack key) tuning on a stringed instrument. Hawaiians call it 'ki ho 'alu.' I went with the Italian.

"Many thanks to Tobias Wolff."

ALICE MUNRO lives in Clinton, Ontario, and in Comox, British Columbia. She is the author of several books of short stories, the most recent one being *Hateship, Friendship, Courtship, Loveship, Marriage.*

"'Family Furnishings' is one of those mixtures of personal material and invention that are often, and not accurately, described as 'autobiographical' fiction. As a matter of fact, it's very much like the story that the girl in the story both blames and justifies herself for writing."

JONATHAN NOLAN: "Fitting that I can't remember where it came to me. But on the off chance that it was on the foam mattress on top of Malcolm and Penny Webster's deep freeze, I'd like to thank them for the cows and their copy of *Moby-Dick.* If it was in that hostel in Nelson, I'd like to thank them for bunking me with a lunatic divorcée and for the little pictures of ships bolted to the wall. Then again, it might have been on the floor of my folks' living room—if so, I'd like to thank them for that one sleepless night, feeding and clothing me, putting me through college, etc.

"Thanks, of course, to Lisa Hintelmann for reading it, to David Granger for sleeping on it, and to Adrienne Miller for her expert guidance and gentle touch the first time through. Thanks also to O'Loughlin, Sprague, Arney, Berger, and Glavin, whose voices ring in my ear even as I write this.

"Thanks, Chris, for mounting such an impressive publicity campaign on the story's behalf. Most of all, however, I'd like to thank Emma for turning my tall talk into a career.

"So it's adieu, Earl, or Leonard, Lenny, whatever your name was. I'm comforted by the thought that despite the length of our acquaintance, you won't miss me at all."

BILL ROORBACH, a 2002 NEA Fellow, is the author of five books, including the Flannery O'Connor Award–winning collection of stories, *Big Bend.* Other books are: *The Smallest Color,* a novel; *Into Woods,* essays; *Summers with Juliet,* a memoir; *Writing Life Stories,* instruction. All are in print, with a sixth book, *Temple Stream,* forthcoming from The Dial Press. Bill lives in western Maine with his wife and daughter.

"Juliet and I have been to Big Bend country twice for extended spring vacations. It's a vast desert place with mountains in the middle. In March the temperatures would be in the sixties up high, and over a hundred down at the Rio Grande. There was just something sexy and giant about the place and I wanted to set a story there. I also wanted to try an older person as a protagonist—my previous stories had been about guys my own age or younger. I put the two ideas together and started writing one day in Maine. For a story you need a place and a character, for sure, but then you need something to happen. Martha is what happened in this case. I made her my age and let her take her rings off. She and Dennis did the rest. Someone asked if I wanted to keep going, make this one into a novel. And I do wonder sometimes about what happened next. But I don't want to write the novel because I think Dennis would have to die in it. With just the story he gets to stay alive and have his happy ending."

HEIDI JON SCHMIDT is the author of two story collections, *Darling?* (which includes the story "Blood Poison") and *The Rose Thieves,* and has a novel, *The Bride of Catastrophe,* forthcoming in 2003. She lives with her husband and daughter in Provincetown, Massachusetts.

"'Blood Poison' is a departure for me—a tragic farce instead of a comic one. It was rejected at least fifteen times, and I'm so grateful to *Epoch* for publishing it, and to the O. Henry Awards for choosing it. I started with some bizarre moments I knew and tried to string them together to encompass a whole father-daughter relationship. When I saw I was writing about incest, I knew I wanted it to be completely unsensational—about desperation, not sex. I'm always interested in that borderland between ordinary life and madness, and I was thinking particularly about how hard children work to fill the needs of their parents, often at great cost to themselves, and how this character might exact her double-edged revenge."

DAVID FOSTER WALLACE's most recent book of stories is *Brief Interviews with Hideous Men.* He's supposed to start teaching in the English Department at Pomona College in fall 2002.

"Is it Didion who has that thing about writers always selling somebody out? Or was it Pauline Kael? I always have trouble keeping these two straight, which is strange, since they're about as dissimilar as you can get."

MARY YUKARI WATERS is half Japanese and half Irish. Her stories have appeared in various magazines, and have been anthologized in *The Pushcart Book of Short Stories* as well as this year's *Best American Short Stories*. She is a 2002 recipient of a grant from the National Endowment for the Arts. In the spring of 2003, Scribner will publish her first story collection, *Tales of Stone Faces*.

"'Egg-Face' was an idea born more out of nosiness than anything else. I had originally hoped to discover, in the course of writing this story, what makes a character like this 'tick.' I failed in that respect, but luckily the story found its own direction and was able to take me to another place altogether."

Jurors

DAVE EGGERS is the editor of *McSweeney's,* a quarterly, and has written two books, *A Heartbreaking Work of Staggering Genius* and a novel that at press time was untitled.

JOYCE CAROL OATES is the author, most recently, of the novel *I'll Take You There* (Ecco Press). She is the Roger S. Berlind Professor of Humanities at Princeton University.

COLSON WHITEHEAD's first novel, *The Intuitionist,* won the QPB New Voices Award and was an Ernest Hemingway/PEN Finalist. His second, *John Henry Days,* won the Young Lions Fiction Award and was a finalist for the National Book Critics Circle Award and the *Los Angeles Times* Book Prize. He is also the recipient of a Whiting Writers Award. His journalism has appeared in *Salon, The New York Times, Newsday,* and *The Village Voice,* where he was a television columnist.

Short-Listed Stories

ABBOTT, LEE K., "One of *Star Wars*, One of *Doom*," *The Georgia Review,* Vol. LV, No. 3

A middle-aged high school history teacher and the woman he's having an affair with, who teaches math, are caught in the crossfire when two teenage boys start shooting up the school library.

BIGUENET, JOHN, "I Am Not a Jew," *Book,* March/April 2001

An American who speaks very little German wanders off from the hotel he and his wife are staying in while visiting Germany. He gets lost and ends up in a Jewish cemetery. There he is confronted by a group of skinheads defacing graves and, to save his skin, insists that he is not a Jew.

CHABON, MICHAEL, "The God of Dark Laughter," *The New Yorker,* April 9, 2001

Two boys playing in the woods find the body of a murdered and disfigured clown. The district attorney investigating discovers the existence of two competing cults originating in Armenia, one that worshiped an ancient God of dark laughter, named Yê-Hi, the other that worshiped a God, named Ai, of Unbearable and Ubiquitous sorrow. These competing cults seem to be at the heart of the mystery. (Written by Chabon's alter ego, August Van Zorn).

COOKE, CAROLYN, "The Sugar Tit," *Agni,* No. 53

A forty-year-old woman, home schooled by her pedantic father when she was a child, marries a man who fails at a succession of half-baked businesses and carries on an affair with one of her friends. The couple's financial woes force them to sell off her antiques one by one. And after her husband dies, the woman is forced to approach her father to write a check for her for a sum owed her husband's onetime lover.

DAVIES, PETER HO, "What You Know," *Harper's Magazine,* January 2001

A writer-in-the-schools faces sudden interest in one of his fifteen-year-old students after the boy goes on a shooting spree that begins at home and ends at school, where he kills two classmates before taking his own life. The teacher cooks up a scheme to write a fake story, supposedly written by the student, and sell it for $10,000 and, as research, goes to a gun range to see what it's like to shoot.

DAVIS, LYDIA, "Oral History with Hiccups," *McSweeney's,* No. 6

A woman's account of her plans to adopt the grown daughters of her dead sister and move them into her house with her husband and young son is punctuated by hiccups, expressed as spaces periodically inserted into the middle of words. Like th   is.

DOERR, ANTHONY, "The Caretaker," *The Paris Review,* No. 159

When civil war overtakes Liberia, a thirty-five-year-old man who has always lived with his mother becomes a refugee in the United States. He takes a job as the caretaker of an estate. Once winter comes, he lives there alone and begins to seriously neglect his duties. The owners return, furious with him, and send the man on his way. But he hangs around, living in the woods and establishing a friendship with the deaf daughter of his former bosses.

ERDRICH, LOUISE, "The Shawl," *The New Yorker,* March 5, 2001

In a story told by Native American tribe members, a woman took her daughter and the baby she conceived with another man, leaving her husband and older son behind. The son pursued the wagon and found a bloodied shawl, evidence that his mother had thrown his sister to the wolves. Years later a man tells this story to his son, who one day, tired of the drunken beatings inflicted on him and his siblings, stands up to his father.

EVENSON, BRIAN, "White Square," *Post Road,* **No. 3**

A man suspected of killing his ex-wife and her new husband is interrogated by the police but either refuses to cooperate or is incapable of doing so. He allows the interrogator to represent the victims as a gray square and a black square but will not allow himself to be represented. The inspector is under pressure from his superiors to make progress, but is frustrated in his attempts to do so.

EVERETT, PERCIVAL, "Afraid of the Dark," *TriQuarterly,* **No. 109**

Two horse wranglers go to pick up a horse and the brother of the woman who's sending them. Both turn out to be more ornery than they expected.

FEITELL, MERRILL, "Our Little Lone Star," *Glimmer Train Stories,* **Issue 40**

A sixty-two-year-old woman sets out to drive a car from her home in New Jersey to her daughter, who is attending college in Arizona. She gets caught in a storm outside of Houston and pulls off into a McDonald's. While she is talking to a man she meets there, the woman sees the storm blow over a sign that falls on her car and breaks the windshield. She ends up accompanying the stranger on a short trip while waiting for the car to be repaired.

FRANK, JOAN, "The Guardian," *Faultline,* **Vol. 10**

Two boys are asked by their widower father to help him choose between two women that he is considering marrying. One of the choices is the devoted secretary who has helped take care of the boys since their mother's death. The older brother votes for her, but the younger brother votes for the other woman and the father concurs with him. When their father and his new wife have their own baby, the boys are sent off to separate boarding schools. Later, after his father dies, the older boy, now grown, learns that his father and the secretary, whom he loved like a mother, had been lovers all along.

GAITSKILL, MARY, "Therapy," *Tin House,* Vol. II, No. 3 (Issue 7)

A woman shopping for a birthday present for her mother reflects on the anger she feels toward her former therapist as she searches for the perfect gift.

GODWIN, GAIL, "Largesse," *TriQuarterly,* Nos. 110 & 111

A fifteen-year-old girl, who lives with her mother and grandmother, is invited for Christmas to the Texas ranch of a rich aunt. On the drive to the airport, the girl finds out that she and her mother could have moved in with the aunt when she was little and had an easier, more luxurious life. Once at the ranch, she explores this possibility.

HAMPL, PATRICIA, "The Summer House," *TriQuarterly,* No. 109

A divorced couple reconciles and rents a cabin for the summer in northern Minnesota. They spend their days reading, taking walks, and cooking elaborate dinners. But the wife keeps a secret from the husband— she had been to this cabin before, when she was young, with a boyfriend and his family.

HOOD, ANN, "The Rightness of Things," *Five Points,* Vol. 5, No. 2

A divorced woman who is friends with a woman who has a daughter the same age and with the same name as her daughter, meets a man at the friend's house. They have an affair that leads not to a romance but to a job offer. But there are other consequences to their liaison that come between her friendship with the other woman, who looks like her but is really her opposite in many ways.

HUFF, STEVEN, "Blissful," *The Hudson Review,* Vol. LIV, No. 1

A Seneca Indian returns home to live on the reservation after getting out of jail and claims to be a faith healer, which he half believes is true. The man moves back in with his mother, earns money cleaning motel rooms, and pursues the last woman he slept with before going to jail, even though she is seeing someone else.

JOHNSTON, BRET ANTHONY, "Outside the Toy Store," *Faultline,* Vol. 10

A man runs into a woman he knew years ago, when his daughter was sick and dying. She is married now, with young twins. Their conversation is congenial at first, but eventually his bitterness comes out.

KOHLER, SHEILA, "Death in Rome," *The Antioch Review,* Vol. 59, No. 1

An American writer travels to Rome to spend time with a dying friend, her onetime au pair. The friend, who is Italian, never married, and the woman feels sorry for her because she still lived with her mother until recently and never had much of a life. But she learns something that surprises her and causes her to reconsider her view of her ailing friend.

LAHIRI, JHUMPA, "Nobody's Business," *The New Yorker,*
March 12, 2001

A graduate student falls in love with one of his housemates, a thirty-year-old Bengali woman who has a tempestuous relationship with her Egyptian boyfriend. When a stranger calls and claims to be a lover of the woman's boyfriend, the student must decide whether or not to tell his housemate the truth.

LEAVITT, DAVID, "Crossing St. Gotthard," *The Paris Review,* No. 157

A young man accompanies his aunt and two cousins on a trip through Europe toward the end of the nineteenth century, serving as a tutor to the two boys. He is a classicist of some attainment, but his knowledge is wasted on his cousins. He feels himself deeply attracted to one of them, who is quite handsome but boorish. The family is trying to overcome the loss of the father and a brother. They ride a train crossing the Alps into Italy via the world's longest tunnel, engulfed in darkness, soot pouring in.

LEWIS, TRUDY, "A Diller, a Daughter," *The Atlantic Monthly,*
January 2001

After receiving a wedding invitation from her estranged daughter, a woman puts together an album of notes from her daughter recounting their troubled relationship over the years and hinting at the causes of their problems.

LONGSTREET, K.A., "*Fleurette Bleu,*" *The Georgia Review,*
Vol. LV, No. 1

An affluent Swiss man starts an affair with the housemaid, an awkward country girl, meeting her every Thursday afternoon in a hotel room. He ponders his motives and other issues troubling him in weekly sessions with a psychoanalyst.

MARCHE, STEPHEN, "Garrison Creek," *The Malahat Review*, No. 133

A historian encounters an old ex-priest sitting on the porch of a house and sketching. The man tells him that there is a river, Garrison Creek, buried under the street. The ex-priest had ministered to troops during the war and tells the historian about his experiences. Later, a church burns down and the ex-priest exhorts the historian to look beneath the church's remains, to see Garrison Creek revealed. But the historian cannot see nor hear the hidden river.

MARTIN, VALERIE, "His Blue Period," *Conjunctions*, No. 36

A man remembers his younger days when he lived in a loft in the same building as a soon-to-be-famous painter and his girlfriend, whom the man was in love with. The painter is cruel to the girlfriend and the man has opportunities to save her that he fails to act upon. Later, he encounters the famous painter and gains a different perspective on the past.

McCORKLE, JILL, "Billy Goats," *Bomb*, Fall 2001

A group of children, "too old for kick the can and too young to make out," prowl their neighborhood in a pack, encountering local eccentrics and local legends.

McNALLY, T.M., "Bastogne," *DoubleTake*, No. 25

A man temporarily living in Stuttgart, where his wife is working as a scientist, takes his family on a trip to Bastogne, in Belgium, where the Battle of the Bulge was fought and where his father endured great hardships and lost a leg to frostbite. The man is sick, but his wife doesn't know this yet. He explores the town, recalling his father's stories about the horrors of war.

McNEAL, TOM, "Watermelon Days," *Zoetrope: All-Story*, Vol. 5, No. 4

In 1926, a young woman leaves Philadelphia to make a new life in Yankton, South Dakota. She meets a reporter at the radio station where she works and ends up marrying him. They have a baby, who is her father's delight but tortures the young woman with her constant crying. When her daughter is four, she takes her to the watermelon festival in town and abandons her there while she flirts with a young tramp passing through town.

MORROW, BRADFORD, "Amazing Grace," *Conjunctions,* No. 37

A man who has become a successful inspirational speaker after losing his eyesight regains his vision and discovers that his wife and a friend have been cheating on him and using the money he's earned to live an opulent life. Without letting on that he can see, the man learns that his house and his children are far different than he envisioned them and he engineers his revenge.

ORRINGER, JULIE, "Pilgrims," *Ploughshares,* Vol. 27, No. 1

A girl whose mother is being treated for cancer accompanies her family to the house of "people who eat seaweed and brown rice every day of their lives" for Thanksgiving dinner. There she and her younger brother fall in with a group of wild children playing in an enormous tree house. After a vegetarian meal, the adults meditate together. The children are left to clean up and a terrible accident ensues.

POIRIER, MARK JUDE, "Worms," *The Southern Review,* Vol. 37, No. 1

A young woman working as a reporter in rural Texas falls in love with and marries a man who farms worms. He is the survivor of a childhood tragedy and another tragedy strikes the couple, sending them on their separate ways.

RABOTEAU, EMILY, "The Man with the One-Strong Guitar," *Transition,* Issue 87

Various visitors to a seedy section of New Orleans encounter the title character, and the story behind his circumstances is revealed.

RADER, MARK, "The Round," *Glimmer Train Stories,* Issue 39

A violinist dies during the course of a performance. His soul floats above his body and he watches as various members of the audience react to his death.

ROSSMANN, DAVID S., "Fragments of a First Date," *Colorado Review,* Vol. XXVIII, No. 1

The lines of dialogue between a couple on a first date are presented under various categories (e.g., A Fairly Complete Inventory of Questions), rather than in their natural order and context.

RUSHIN, PAT, "Vow," *American Literary Review,* **Vol. XII, No. 1**

A man decides to stop speaking. After a while, his family and employer ask him to seek counseling. He types up a one-paragraph explanation of his speechlessness, which he says is because he has nothing further to say. Try as they might, no one is able to get him to speak a single syllable. Over time everyone becomes accustomed to his silence. Eventually he dies, but not before uttering one last word.

RUSSELL, MICHAEL, "Simple Machines," *New England Review,* **Vol. 22, No. 3**

A man is called to visit his mother after the death of his eccentric father, an engineer and inventor. His crazy brother, once a successful engineer, lives at the house with their mother and roams the grounds. In the barn is a large project his father was working on up until the end.

RUSSO, RICHARD, "Monhegan Light," *Esquire,* **August 2001**

A man receives a crate from his sister-in-law. Inside it is a nude painting of his wife, who'd died a few years before of cancer. He travels to Monhegan, Maine, and looks up the painter, who had had an affair with his wife and painted her over many years.

SCHWARTZ, LYNN SHARON, "The Stone Master," *TriQuarterly,* **No. 109**

A businessman recounts the story of his trip to a town called M_____. He arrives late and is taken in by a man who tells him a strange story about the town's tradition.

SHARMA, AKHIL, "Surrounded by Sleep," *The New Yorker,* **December 10, 2001**

The older brother of a ten-year-old boy goes into a coma after hitting his head on the bottom of a swimming pool. The boy talks to God about what is going on in his life and tries to get God to reverse what has happened, but to no avail.

SHEPARD, JIM, "Glut Your Soul on My Accursed Ugliness," *DoubleTake,* **No. 25**

A boy in the seventh grade, obsessed with Lon Chaney in *The Phantom of the Opera*, starts signing his papers "The Fist," rather than his name. He does this because he feels ugly and inadequate and he is given detention by his teacher after repeatedly refusing to stop. The boy's parents are on the verge of a divorce over an affair his father is having with a veterinarian.

SHERMAN, RACHEL, "Homestay," *Post Road*, No. 2

Short, titled vignettes tell the story of a Danish au pair brought to a Long Island house as strange to her as she is to the family she works for.

SWENSON, LAURA, "Crazy," *The Kenyon Review*, Vol. XXIII, No. 1

A daughter recounts the particulars of her mother's eccentric but appealing brand of craziness and the effect such behavior can have on children.

TALLENT, ELIZABETH, "Mystery Caller," *The Threepenny Review*, No. 87

The way a male colleague puts his coffee cup down directly on the counter instead of on the saucer reminds a woman of her first husband. She has looked up his phone number and has been calling him periodically for some time, though she never says a word and he never hazards a guess as to who is calling, but instead just lays the receiver down and allows the caller to listen to the sounds of his life.

TESTER, WILLIAM, "The Living and the Dead," *American Literary Review*, Vol. XII, No. 1

A college dropout who has spent two years bumming around Europe calls a stranger in Rome, desperate to find a place to sleep. The stranger turns out to be a handsome young man who takes him in and the two of them become lovers. They go to the coast, where the Italian man's family has a house, and swim into a grotto the emperor Tiberius had once used as an amphitheater. There, they have a fight that brings the relationship to a close.

TILGHMAN, CHRISTOPHER, "Us in February," *Meridian*, Issue 8

A middle-aged man, married with children, imagines an old friend in much the same situation. They had both been in love with the same woman when they were in college, which had ended their friendship. Each had successive relationships with the woman, with his ex-friend winning her in the end—or so he believes.

TUCK, LILY, "Next of Kin," *Epoch,* Vol. 50, No. 3

As a couple is walking out of the church after their wedding, an old man driving past has a stroke, loses control of his car, and crashes into the steps of the church, narrowly avoiding the wedding party. The driver dies and the couple goes on to their reception. Later, during the honeymoon, the bride finds that she can't stop thinking about the man and speculating about his life.

UNGER, DOUGLAS, "Leslie and Sam," *Southwest Review,* Vol. 86, Nos. 2 & 3

A young woman working in a university medical lab gets to know a rhesus monkey named Sam, who has endured numerous experiments and been taught language skills. When she receives the order to euthanize Sam, she reconsiders her job, her relationship with a hotshot medical student, and her future.

WALLACE, DAVID FOSTER, "Another Pioneer," *Colorado Review,* Vol. XXVIII, No. 1

The mythical story of a gifted child born to a primitive tribe is told as it was overheard aboard an airplane.

WHITTY, JULIA, "Jimmy Underwater," *Zoetrope: All-Story,* Vol. 5, No. 3

A scientist studying the chemical defenses of invertebrates in the cold waters of the Antarctic once fell through the ice on a lake as a child and had a near-death experience. His partner on the study is a childhood friend who was there the day he nearly drowned and froze to death.

ZAFRIS, NANCY, "Digging the Hole," *New England Review,* Vol. 22, No. 3

An old woman who worked as an escort for children being committed to a lepers' hospital in Louisiana returns each year to visit a spirited young woman she delivered to the hospital and to whom she feels a strange connection.

2002 Magazine Award:
The New Yorker

The New Yorker has won the O. Henry Award for magazines four times in the six years this honor has been given. It's not surprising that *The New Yorker* would do so well: It pays top dollar for stories and it offers fiction writers the highest profile of any magazine that publishes fiction. As a result, it gets the first crack at the work of many top authors, in addition to scores of other writers who aspire to have their work appear in its pages. But give the magazine credit. Under Editor-in-Chief David Remnick and Fiction Editor Bill Buford, *The New Yorker* has made the most of its opportunities and done a splendid job of pushing the envelope and changing the nature of what a *New Yorker* story is. Rather than simply settle for publishing the work of big-name writers, the editors have made a conscientious effort to seek out fresh work by unknowns. As it did in 2000, the magazine in 2001 devoted a special fiction issue to what it calls debut writers and continued to publish stories by lesser-known writers throughout the year. *The New Yorker* has also shown a willingness to rediscover established writers like Ann Beattie and Arthur Miller. And every so often, we still get a story by Alice Munro or William Trevor. The magazine today offers a more diverse mix of writers from different ages and backgrounds than it ever has before. All the while, the editors have maintained very high standards for the stories published.

This quality is exemplified by the fiction from *The New Yorker* selected for *Prize Stories 2002: The O. Henry Awards:* "That Last Odd Day in L.A." by Ann Beattie, "Seven" by Edwidge Danticat, the Third Prize–winning "The Butcher's Wife" by Louise Erdrich, and "Family Furnishings" by Alice Munro. On the strength of this work, the four stories short-listed for this year's volume, and quite a few additional stories that merited serious consideration for O. Henry Awards, *The New Yorker* was the clear-cut choice for the 2002 magazine award. Other strong contenders included *The Atlantic Monthly* and *McSweeney's*, both with two O. Henry Award–winning stories. Congratulations are due to the editors of these magazines, as well as to those of *Agni, Bamboo Ridge, Conjunctions, DoubleTake, Epoch, Esquire, GQ, Ontario Review, The Oxford American, The Threepenny Review, Tin House*, and *Zoetrope: All-Story*, each of which originally published one story selected for this volume.

The four 2002 O. Henry Award winners bring *The New Yorker's* cumulative tally to 171 stories in the eighty-two volumes of the series, an accomplishment that is particularly impressive considering the fact that *Prize Stories: The O. Henry Awards* was started sixteen years before the first issue of *The New Yorker* hit the newsstands. Congratulations to David Remnick, Bill Buford, and literary editors Roger Angell, Cressida Leyshon, Meghan O'Rourke, Alice Quinn, and Deborah Treisman, as well as to other staff members involved in selecting, editing, and publishing the fiction that appears in *The New Yorker*.

Magazines Consulted

Entries entirely in boldface and with their titles in all-capital letters indicate publications with prizewinning stories. Asterisks following titles denote magazines with short-listed stories. Some magazines have different business and editorial addresses. In such cases, the editorial address is provided here. All information is up-to-date as of the time *Prize Stories 2002: The O. Henry Awards* went to press.

<u>Note to writers who use these listings as a resource for submitting their fiction to magazines:</u> The fact that a publication is included in this section does not imply an endorsement of that magazine by the O. Henry Awards. It simply means that issues were received and the fiction published was read and considered for inclusion in this volume. Writers submitting fiction to a particular magazine are strongly advised to first examine a sample issue.

Aethlon: The Journal of Sports Literature
P.O. Box 70270
East Tennessee State University
Johnson City, TN 37614
Don Johnson, Editor
Biannual.

African American Review
Shannon Hall
St. Louis University
220 North Grand
St. Louis, MO 63103-2007
Joe Weixlmann, Editor
aar.slu.edu/
Quarterly with a focus on African American literature and culture.

AGNI*
236 Bay Street Road
Boston University Writing
Program
Boston, MA 02215
Askold Melnyczuk, Editor
webdelsol.com/AGNI
Biannual.

Alaska Quarterly Review
University of Alaska Anchorage
3211 Providence Drive
Anchorage, AK 99508
Ronald Spatz, Editor
www.uaa.alaska.edu/aqr

Algonquin Roundtable Review
Room B336
Algonquin College
1385 Woodroffe Avenue
Nepean, Ontario
Canada K2G 1V8
Dan Doyle, Editor
roundtable_review@algonquincol-
lege.com
www.algonquincollege.com/round-
table_review
Biannual.

Alligator Juniper
Prescott College
301 Grove Avenue
Prescott, AZ 86301
aj@prescott.edu
Annual.

Amelia
329 "E" Street
Bakersfield, CA 93304
Frederick A. Raborg Jr., Editor
amelia@lightspeed.net
Quarterly.

American Letters and Commentary
850 Park Avenue
Suite 5B
New York, NY 10021
Anna Rabinowitz, Editor
www.amletters.org
Annual.

American Literary Review*
University of North Texas
P.O. Box 311307
Denton, TX 76203-1307
Barbara Rodman, Acting Editor
americanliteraryreview@yahoo.com
www.engl.unt.edu/alr
Biannual.

Another Chicago Magazine
3709 N. Kenmore
Chicago, IL 60613
Barry Silesky, Editor & Publisher
editors@anotherchicagomag.com
anotherchicagomag.com
Biannual.

Antietam Review
41 S. Potomac Street
Hagerstown, MD 21740
Susanne Kass, Executive Editor
www.wcarts@intrepid.net

The Antigonish Review
P.O. Box 5000
St. Francis Xavier University
Antigonish, Nova Scotia
Canada B2G 2W5
B. Allen Quigley, Editor
TAR@stfx.ca
antigonishreview.com
Quarterly.

The Antioch Review*
P.O. Box 148
Yellow Springs, OH 45387
Robert S. Fogarty, Editor
www.antioch.edu/review/
home.html
Quarterly.

Appalachian Heritage
Berea College
Berea, KY 40404
James Gage, Editor
www.berea.edu/ApCenter/
AppHeritage.html
*Quarterly magazine of Southern
Appalachian Life and Culture.*

Arkansas Review
Dept. of English & Philosophy
Box 1890
Arkansas State University
State University, AR 72467
William M. Clements, General
Editor
delta@astate.edu
www.clt.astate.edu/arkreview
*"A Journal of Delta Studies."
Triannual. Formerly* Kansas
Quarterly.

Ascent
English Dept.
Concordia College
901 8th Street S.
Moorhead, MN 56562
W. Scott Olsen, Editor
ascent@cord.edu
www.cord.edu/dept/english/ascent
Triannual.

Atlanta Review
P.O. Box 8248
Atlanta, GA 31106

Daniel Veach, Editor & Publisher
www.atlantareview.com
Biannual.

THE ATLANTIC MONTHLY*
77 N. Washington Street
Boston, MA 02114
C. Michael Curtis, Senior Editor
www.theatlantic.com
*2000 O. Henry Award winner for
magazines. The Atlantic
Unbound site features stories
from the magazine plus Web-only
content, including interviews
with authors, fiction not published in the print version, a
reader forum, and more.*

The Baffler
P.O. Box 378293
Chicago, IL 60637
Thomas Frank, Editor-in-Chief
www.thebaffler.org

The Baltimore Review
P.O. Box 410
Riderwood, MD 21139
Barbara Westwood Diehl, Editor
www.baltimorewriters.org
*Biannual featuring the work of
writers "from the Baltimore area
and beyond."*

BAMBOO RIDGE
P.O. Box 61781
Honolulu, HI 96839-1781
Eric Chock and Darrell H.Y.
Lum, Editors
brinfo@bambooridge.com
www.bambooridge.com
*Biannual journal of Hawai'i lit-
erature and arts.*

Bellingham Review
MS-9053
Western Washington University
Bellingham, WA 98225
Brenda Miller, Editor-in-Chief
www.wwu.edu/~bhreview
Biannual.

Bellowing Ark
P.O. Box 55564
Shoreline, WA 98155
Robert R. Ward, Editor
Six times a year. Newspaper format.

Beloit Fiction Journal
P.O. Box 11
Beloit College
700 College Street
Beloit, WI 53511
Rotating editorship
www.beloit.edu/~libhome/Archives
/BO/Pub/Fict.html
Biannual.

Black Warrior Review
University of Alabama
P.O. Box 862936
Tuscaloosa, AL 35486-0027
Rotating editorship
webdelsol.com/bwr
Biannual.

Blood and Aphorisms
P.O. Box 702, Station P
Toronto, Ontario
M5S 2Y4 Canada
Sam Hiyate, Publisher
Quarterly.

Blue Mesa Review
English Dept.
The University of New Mexico
Albuquerque, NM 87131

Julie Shigekuni, Editor
Bluemesa@unm.edu
www.unm.edu/~bluemesa
Annual.

Bomb*
594 Broadway, 9th floor
New York, NY 10012
Betsy Sussler, Editor-in-Chief
bomb@echonyc.com
www.bombsite.com/firstproof.html
Quarterly magazine profiling artists,
writers, actors, directors, musicians,
with a downtown New York City
slant. Fiction appears in First Proof,
a literary supplement.

Book*
252 W. 37 Street, 5th floor
New York, NY 10018
Jerome V. Kramer, Editor
www.bookmagazine.com
Published six times a year.

Border Crossings
500-70 Arthur Street
Winnipeg, Manitoba
R3B 1G7 Canada
Meeka Walsh, Editor
bordercr@escape.ca
www.bordercrossingsmag.com
Quarterly magazine of the arts with
occasional fiction.

The Boston Book Review
30 Brattle Street, 4th floor
Cambridge, MA 02138
Theoharis Constantine Theoharis,
Editor
BBR-Info@BostonBookReview.com
www.bookwire.com/bookwire/bbr/
bbr-home.html

A book review that also publishes fiction, poetry, and essays. Published ten times a year—monthly with double issues in January and July.

Boston Review

E53-407, MIT
Cambridge, MA 02139
Joshua Cohen, Editor-in-Chief
bostonreview@mit.edu
bostonreview.mit.edu
"A political and literary forum."
Published six times a year.

Boulevard

PMB 325
6614 Clayton Road
Richmond Heights, MO 63117
Richard Burgin, Editor
www.boulevardmagazine.com
Triannual. Sponsors a short fiction contest for emerging writers.

The Briar Cliff Review

3303 Rebecca Street
P.O. Box 2100
Sioux City, IA 51104-2100
Tricia Currans-Sheehen, Editor
Annual.

Button

P.O. Box 26
Luneburg, MA 01462
Sally Cragin, Editor/Publisher
"New England's tiniest magazine of poetry, fiction, and gracious living."
Biannual.

C-Ville

222 South Street
Charlottesville, VA 22902
Hawes C. Spencer, Editor
www.c-ville.com
Weekly newspaper with annual fiction contest.

Callaloo

English Dept.
Texas A&M University
4227 TAMU
College Station, TX 77843-4227
Charles Henry Rowell, Editor
www.press.jhu.edu/press/journals/
cal/cal.html
A quarterly journal of African American and African Arts & Letters.

Calyx

P.O. Box B
Corvalis, OR 97339-0539
Editorial collective
calyx@proaxis.com
www.proaxis.com/~calyx
Triannual journal of art and literature by women.

Canadian Fiction

P.O. Box 1061
Kingston, Ontario
K7L 4Y5 Canada
Geoff Hancock and Rob Payne, Editors
Biannual anthology of contemporary Canadian fiction, often with a theme.

The Carolina Quarterly

Greenlaw Hall CB#3520
University of North Carolina
Chapel Hill, NC 27599-3520
Rotating editorship
cquarter@unc.edu
www.unc.edu/depts/cqonline/
Triannual.

Carve Magazine

P.O. Box 72231
Davis, CA 95617
Melvin Sterne, Senior Editor and Publisher

editor@carvezine.com
www.carvezine.com
Bimonthly Web 'zine with annual print edition, The Best of Carve Magazine.

Center

English Dept.
University of Missouri-Columbia
107 Tate Hall
Columbia, MO 65211
Stephanie Powell Watts, Bob Watts, Editors
web.missouri.edu/~cwp
Biannual.

The Chariton Review

Truman State University
Kirksville, MO 63501
Jim Barnes, Editor
Biannual.

Chattahoochee Review

2101 Womack Road
Dunwoody, Georgia 30338-4497
Lawrence Hetrick, Editor
www.chattahoochee-review.org
Quarterly.

Chelsea

P.O. Box 773
Cooper Station
New York, NY 10276-0773
Richard Foerster, Editor
Biannual.

Chicago Reader

11 East Illinois Street
Chicago, IL 60611
Alison True, Editor
www.chicagoreader.com
Weekly newspaper with occasional special fiction issues.

Chicago Review

5801 South Kenwood Avenue
Chicago, IL 60637-1794
Rotating editorship
humanities.uchicago.edu/review
Quarterly.

Cimarron Review

205 Morrill Hall
Oklahoma State University
Stillwater, OK 74078-0135
E. P. Walkiewicz, Editor
cimarronreview.okstate.edu
Quarterly.

City Primeval

P.O. Box 30064
Seattle, WA 98103
David Ross, Editor
Quarterly featuring "Narratives of Urban Reality."

Clackamas Literary Review

Clackamas Community College
19600 South Molalla Avenue
Oregon City, OR 97045
Kate Gray, Tim Schell, Brad Stiles, Editors
www.clackamas.cc.or.us/clr
Biannual.

Colorado Review*

Colorado State University
Dept. of English
Fort Collins, CO 80523
David Milofsky, Editor
creview@colostate.edu
www.coloradoreview.com
Biannual.

Columbia: A Journal of Literature and Art

415 Dodge Hall
Columbia University
New York, NY 10027-6902

Rotating editorship
arts-litjournal@columbia.edu
Biannual.

Comfusion
304 S. Third Street
San Jose, CA 95127
Jaime Wright, Editor-in-Chief
Wright@comfusionreview.com
www.comfusionreview.com

Commentary
165 East 56th Street
New York, NY 10022
Neal Kozodoy, Editor
editoral@commentarymagazine.com
www.commentarymagazine.com
*Monthly, politically conservative
Jewish magazine.*

Concho River Review
P.O. Box 1894
Angelo State University
San Angelo, TX 76909
James A. Moore, General Editor
www.angelo.edu/dept/CRR/
index.htm
Biannual.

Confrontation
English Dept.
C.W. Post Campus of Long Island
University
Brookville, NY 11548-1300
Martin Tucker, Editor-in-Chief

CONJUNCTIONS*
21 East 10th Street
New York, NY 10003
Bradford Morrow, Editor
www.conjunctions.com
Biannual.

Cottonwood
Box J, 400 Kansas Union
University of Kansas
Lawrence, KS 66045
Tom Lorenz, Editor
cottonwd@falcon.cc.ukans.edu
falcon.cc.ukans.edu/~cottonwd/
index.html
Biannual.

Crab Creek Review
P.O. Box 840
Vachon Island, WA 98070
Linda Clifton, Founding Editor &
Publisher
www.crabcreekreview.org
Biannual.

Crab Orchard Review
Southern Illinois University at
Carbondale
Carbondale, IL 62901-4503
Carol Alessio, Prose Editor
www.siu.edu/~crborchd
Biannual.

Crazyhorse
English Dept.
University of Arkansas at Little
Rock
Little Rock, AR 72204
Ralph Burns and Lisa Lewis,
Editors
www.ualr.edu/~english/chorse.htm
Biannual.

The Cream City Review
University of Wisconsin-
Milwaukee
P.O. Box 413
Milwaukee, WI 53201
Rotating editorship
Biannual.

The Crescent Review
P.O. Box 15069
Chevy Chase, MD 20825-5069
J. Timothy Holland, Editor
www.crescentreview.org
Triannual.

CutBank
English Dept.
University of Montana
Missoula, MT 59812
Rotating editorship
cutbank@selway.umt.edu
www.umt.edu/cutbank
Biannual.

Daedalus
Norton's Woods
136 Irving Street
Cambridge, MA 02138
James Miller, Editor
daedalus@amacad.org
Quarterly journal of the American Academy of Arts & Sciences. Now publishing fiction.

Denver Quarterly
University of Denver
Denver, CO 80208
Bin Ramke, Editor
www.du.edu/
englishDQuarterly.htm

DOUBLETAKE*
55 Davis Square
Somerville, MA 02144
Robert Coles, Editor
www.doubletakemagazine.org
Beautifully produced quarterly devoted to photography and literature.

EPOCH*
251 Goldwin Smith Hall
Cornell University
Ithaca, NY 14853-3201
Michael Koch, Editor
www.arts.cornell.edu/english/
epoch.html
Triannual. 1997 O. Henry Award winner for best magazine.

ESQUIRE*
250 West 55th Street
New York, NY 10019
Adrienne Miller, Literary Editor
www.esquiremag.com
Monthly magazine for men.

Event
Douglas College
P.O. Box 2503
New Westminster, British Columbia
V3L 5B2, Canada
Cathy Stonehouse, Editor
event.douglas.bc.ca
Triannual.

Faultline*
English & Comparative Literature Dept.
University of California, Irvine
Irvine, CA 92697-2650
Rotating editorship
faultline@uci.edu
www.humanities.uci.edu/faultline
Annual.

Fence
14 Fifth Avenue, 1A
New York, NY 10011
Rebecca Wolff, Editor
rwolff@angel.net
www.fencemag.com
Biannual.

Fiction

English Dept.
The City College of New York
New York, NY 10031
Mark Jay Mirsky, Editor
www.ccny.cuny.edu/fiction/fiction.htm
All-fiction format.

The Fiddlehead

University of New Brunswick
P.O. Box 4400
Fredericton, New Brunswick
Canada E3B 5A3
Ross Leckie, Editor
Fid@nbnet.nb.ca
www.lib.unb.ca/Texts./Fiddlehead
Quarterly.

First Intensity

P.O. Box 665
Lawrence, KS 66044
Lee Chapman, Editor
leechapman@aol.com
Biannual. "A Magazine of New Writing."

580 Split

Mills College
P.O. Box 9982
Oakland, CA 94613
Rotating editorship
five80split@yahoo.com
www.mills.edu/580split
Annual. Recently established.

Five Points*

English Dept.
Georgia State University
University Plaza
Athens, GA 30303-3083
David Bottoms, Editor
www.ebdelsol.com/Five_Points
Triannual.

The Florida Review

English Dept.
University of Central Florida
Orlando, FL 32816
Russell Kesler, Editor
pegasus.cc.ucf.edu/~english/floridareview/home.htm
Biannual.

Folio

Literature Dept., Gray Hall
American University
Washington, DC 20016
Eve Rosenbaum, Managing Editor
folio_editors@yahoo.com
Biannual.

42nd Parallel

623 North 51 Street
Omaha, NE 68132
Dan McCarthy, Editor
Editors@42ndParallel.com

Fourteen Hills

The Creative Writing Dept.
San Francisco State University
1600 Holloway Avenue
San Francisco, CA 94132-1722
Rotating editorship
hills@sfsu.edu
userwww.sfsu.edu/~hills
Biannual.

Front Range Review

English Department
Front Range Community
College—Larimer Campus
Ft. Collins, CO 80527
Editorial board
Annual.

Fugue

Brink Hall 200
University of Idaho

Moscow, ID 83844-1102
www.uidaho.edu/LS/Eng/Fugue
Rotating editorship
Biannual.

Gargoyle
P.O. Box 6216
Arlington, VA 22206-0216
Richard Peabody, Lucinda
Ebersole, Editors
gargoyle@atticusbooks.com
www.atticusbooks.com/gargoyle/
gargoyle.html
Published irregularly.

Geist
1014 Homer Street #103
Vancouver, British Columbia
V6B 2W9 Canada
Stephen Osborne, Publisher
geist@geist.com
www.geist.com
*"The Canadian Magazine of Ideas
and Culture." Quarterly.*

The Georgia Review*
The University of Georgia
Athens, GA 30602-9009
T. R. Hummer, Editor
www.uga.ed/garev
Quarterly.

Gertrude
P.O. Box 270814
Fort Collins, CO 80527-0814
Eric Delahoy, Editor
www.gertrudejournal.com
*Biannual. Showcases work by "gay,
lesbian, bisexual, transgender, and
straight supportive persons."*

The Gettysburg Review
Gettysburg College
Gettysburg, PA 17325

Peter Stitt, Editor
www.gettysburg.edu/academics/
gettysburg_review
Quarterly.

Glimmer Train Stories*
710 SW Madison Street
Suite 504
Portland, OR 97205-2900
Linda B. Swanson-Davies, Susan
Burmeister-Brown, Editors
www.glimmertrain.com
Quarterly. Fiction and interviews.

Global City Review
105 West 13th Street
Suite 4C
New York, NY 10011
Linsey Abrams, Founding Editor
*Nifty, pocket-size format. Biannual,
theme issues.*

GQ
350 Madison Avenue
New York, NY 10017
Walter Kirn, Literary Editor
www.gq.com
Monthly men's magazine.

Grain
P.O. Box 1154
Regina, Saskatchewan
Canada S4P 3B4
J. Jill Robinson, Editor
Quarterly.

Grand Street
214 Sullivan Street
Suite 6C
New York, NY 10012
Jean Stein, Editor
info@grandstreet.com
www.grandstreet.com
Quarterly artsy arts magazine.

The Green Hills Literary Lantern
P.O. Box 375
Trenton, MO 64683
Jack Smith, Ken Reger, Senior
Editors
www.ncmc.cc.mo.us
Biannual.

Green Mountains Review
Box A 58
Johnson State College
Johnson, VT 05656
Neil Shepard, General Editor
Biannual.

The Greensboro Review
English Dept., 134 McIver
Building
University of North Carolina at
Greensboro
P.O. Box 26170
Greensboro, NC 27402-6170
Jim Clark, Editor
www.uncg.edu/eng/mfa
Biannual.

Gulf Stream
English Dept.
FIU Biscayne Bay Campus
3000 NE 151 Street
North Miami, FL 33181-3000
Lynn Barrett, Editor
Biannual.

Hampton Shorts
P.O. Box 1229
Water Mill, NY 11976
Barbara Stone, Editor-in-Chief
hamptonshorts@hamptons.com
*"Fiction plus from the Hamptons &
The East End."*

Hanging Loose
231 Wyckoff Street
Brooklyn, NY 11217
Robert Hershon, Dick Lourie,
Mark Prawlak, and Ron Schreiber,
Editors
print225@aol.com
www.hangingloosepress.com
Triannual.

Happy
240 East 35th Street
Suite 11A
New York, NY 10116
Bayard, Editor
Two words: Offbeat quarterly.

Harper's Magazine*
666 Broadway
New York, NY 10012
Lewis Lapham, Editor
www.harpers.org
Monthly.

Harpur Palate
English Dept.
Binghamton University
P.O. Box 6000
Binghamton, NY 13902-6000
Rotating editorship
harpurpalate.binghamton.edu
Biannual. Est. 2001.

**Harrington Gay Men's Fiction
Quarterly**
Thomas Nelson Community
College
99 Thomas Nelson Drive
Hampton, VA 23666
Thomas L. Long, Editor-in-Chief

Hawai'i Pacific Review
Hawai'i Pacific University
1060 Bishop Street

Honolulu, HI 96813
Catherine Sustana, Fiction Editor
hpreview@hpu.edu
Annual.

Hayden's Ferry Review
Box 871502
Arizona State University
Tempe, AZ 85287-1502
Rotating editorship
HFR@asu.edu
www.haydensferryreview.org
Biannual.

Hemispheres
1301 Carolina Street
Greensboro, NC 27401
Selby Bateman, Senior Editor
www.hemispheresmagazine.com
*The inflight magazine of United
Airlines. Monthly. Earn miles while
reading.*

High Plains Literary Review
180 Adams Street
Suite 250
Denver, CO 80206
Robert O. Greer Jr., Editor-in-
Chief
Triannual.

The Hudson Review*
684 Park Avenue
New York, NY 10021
Paula Deitz, Editor
www.hudsonreview.com
Quarterly.

Hurricane Alice
English Dept.
Rhode Island College
Providence, RI 02908
Maureen T. Reddy, Executive
Editor

mreddy@grog.ric.edu
Feminist quarterly.

Hybolics
P.O. Box 3016
'Aiea, HI 96701
Lee Tonouchi, Co-Editor
hybolilcs@lava.net
*Emphasis on Hawaiian writing,
some in local forms of pidgin English.*

The Idaho Review
Boise State University
English Dept.
1910 University Drive
Boise, ID 83725
Mitch Wieland, Editor-in-Chief
english.boisestate.edu/idahoreview/
Annual, innaugurated in 1998.

Image
3307 Third Avenue West
Seattle, WA 98119
Gregory Wolfe, Publisher & Editor
image@imagejournal.org
www.imagejournal.org
*"A Journal of the Arts and Religion."
Quarterly.*

Indiana Review
Ballantine Hall 465
1020 E. Kirkwood Ave.
Bloomington, IN 47405-7103
Rotating editors
inreview@indiana.edu
www.indiana.edu/~inreview/
ir.html
Biannual.

Inkwell
Manhattanville College
Purchase, NY 10577
Rotating editorship
Biannual.

Interim
English Dept.
University of Nevada
Las Vegas, NV 89154
James Hazen, Editor
Biannual.

The Iowa Review
308 English/Philosophy Building
University of Iowa
Iowa City, IA 52242-1492
David Hamilton, Editor
www.uiowa.edu/~iareview
Triannual. Web site features additional fiction and hypertext work.

Italian Americana
University of Rhode Island
Feinstein College of Continuing
Education
80 Washington Street
Providence, RI 02903-1803
Carol Bonomo Albright, Editor
Biannual. A cultural and historical review with a focus on Italian Americans.

Jane
7 West 34th Street
New York, NY 10001
Jane Pratt, Editor-in-Chief
www.janemag.com
Sassy women's magazine. Published six times a year. Annual fiction contest.

The Journal
The Ohio State University
English Dept.
164 West 17th Avenue
Columbus, OH 43210
Kathy Fagan, Michelle Herman,
Editors
thejournal05@postbox.acs.ohio-state.edu
www.cohums.ohio-state.edu/english/journals/the_journal/
Biannual.

Kalliope
Florida Community College at
Jacksonville
3939 Roosevelt Boulevard
Jacksonville, FL 32205
Mary Sue Koeppel, Editor
www.fccj.org/kalliope/kalliope.htm
Triannual journal of women's literature and art.

Karamu
English Dept.
Eastern Illinois University
Charleston, IL 61920
Rotating editorship
Annual.

The Kenyon Review*
Kenyon College
Gambier, OH 43022
David H. Lynn, Editor
kenyonreview@kenyon.edu
www.kenyonreview.com
Triannual.

Kiosk
State University of New York at
Buffalo
English Dept.
306 Clemens Hall
Buffalo, NY 14260
Rotating editorship
eng-kiosk@acsu.buffalo.edu
wings.buffalo.edu/kiosk
Annual.

Krater: College Workshop Quarterly
P.O. Box 1371
Lincoln Park, MI 48146
Leonard D. Fritz, Managing Editor
Quarterly. Features work by writers currently enrolled in college writing workshops.

The L.A. Weekly
6715 Sunset Boulevard
Los Angeles, CA 90028
Sue Horton, Editor
www.laweekly.com
Publishes annual summer fiction issue as part of its Weekly Literary Supplement.

The Laurel Review
Dept. of English
Northwest Missouri State University
Maryville, MO 64468
William Trowbridge, David Slater, Beth Richards, Editors
Biannual.

Literal Latté
61 East 8th Street
Suite 240
New York, NY 10003
Jenine Gordon Bockman, Publisher & Editor
Litlatte@aol.com
www.literal-latte.com
Bimonthly.

The Literary Review
Farleigh Dickinson University
285 Madison Avenue
Madison, NJ 07940
Walter Cummins, Editor-in-Chief
tlr@fdu.edu
www.theliteraryreview.org

Quarterly. An international journal of contemporary writing.

Literary Imagination
Dept. of Classics
221 Park Hall
University of Georgia
Athens, GA 30602
Sarah Spence, Editor
litmag@arches.uga.edu
Triannual review of the Association of Literary Scholars and Critics. Publishes one story per issue.

The Long Story
18 Eaton Street
Lawrence, MA 01843
R. P. Burnham, Editor
TLS@aol.com
Annual.

Louisiana Literature
SLU-10792
Southeastern Louisiana University
Hammond, LA 70402
Jack B. Bedell, Editor
Biannual.

Lynx Eye
ScribbleFest Literary Group
P.O. Box 6609
Los Osos, CA 93412-6609
Pam McCully and Kathryn Morrison, Editors
Quarterly.

The Madison Review
University of Wisconsin
English Dept., Helen C. White Hall
600 North Park Street
Madison, WI 53706
Rotating editorship
Biannual.

The Malahat Review*
University of Victoria
P.O. Box 1700
Victoria, British Columbia
V8W 2Y2 Canada
Marlene Cookshaw, Editor
malahat@uvic.ca
web.uvic.ca/malahat
Quarterly.

Manoa
English Dept.
University of Hawai'i
Honolulu, HI 96822
Frank Stewart, Editor
www.hawaii.edu/mjournal
*Biannual. Beautifully produced
"Pacific Journal of International
Writing" with a special focus each
issue.*

The Massachusetts Review
South College
University of Massachusetts
P.O. Box 37140
Amherst, MA 01003-7140
Mary Heath, Paul Jenkins, David
Lenson, Editors
www.massreview.org
Quarterly.

McSWEENEY'S*
429 7th Avenue
Brooklyn, NY 11215
Dave Eggers, Editor
www.mcsweeneys.net
***Quarterly. Original content also
posted on Web site.***

Meridian*
University of Virginia
P.O. Box 400145
Charlottesville, VA 22904-4145
Rotating editorship

meridian@viriginia.edu
www.engl.virginia.edu/meridian
Biannual, student run.

Michigan Quarterly Review
The University of Michigan
3032 Rackham Building
915 E. Washington Street
Ann Arbor, MI 48109-1070
Laurence Goldstein, Editor
www.umich.edu/~mqr
*Often publishes issues with a theme
or focus.*

Mid-American Review
English Dept.
Bowling Green State University
Bowling Green, OH 43403
Michael Czyzniesjewski, Chief &
Fiction Editor
www.bgsu.edu/midamericanreview
Biannual.

Midstream
633 Third Avenue, 21st floor
New York, NY 10017-6706
Leo Haber, Editor
www.midstream.org
*Published nine times a year. Focus on
Jewish issues and Zionist concerns.*

The Minnesota Review
English Dept.
University of Missouri-Columbia
107 Tate Hall
Columbia, MO 65211
Jeffrey Williams, Editor
Non-Minnesota-based biannual.

The Minus Times
P.O. Box 737
Grand Central Station
New York, NY 10163
Hunter Kennedy, Editor

www.minustimes.com
Published irregularly.

Mississippi Review

Center for Writers
University of Southern Mississippi
Box 5144
Hattiesburg, MS 39406-5144
Frederick Barthelme, Editor
rief@netdoor.com
www.mississippireview.com
Biannual. Web innovator.

The Missouri Review

1507 Hillcrest Hall
University of Missouri
Columbia, MO 65211
Speer Morgan, Editor
www.missourireview.org
Triannual.

Moment

470 41st Street N.W.
Washington, DC 20016
Hershel Shanks, Editor
editor@momentmag.com
www.momentmag.com
Monthly magazine of Jewish culture, politics, and religion. Holds annual short story contest.

Nassau Review

English Dept.
Nassau Community College
One Education Drive
Garden City, NY 11530-6793
Paul A. Doyle, Editor
Annual.

Natural Bridge

English Dept.
University of Missouri-St. Louis
8001 Natural Bridge Road

St. Louis, MO 63121
David Carkeet, Editor
natural@jinx.umsl.edu
www.umsl.edu/~natural
Biannual.

The Nebraska Review

Writer's Workshop
Fine Arts Building 212
University of Nebraska at Omaha
Omaha, NE 68182-0324
James Reed, Fiction and Managing Editor
www.unomaha.edu/~fineart/
wworkshop/nebraska_review.htm
Biannual.

Nerve

520 Broadway, 6th floor
New York, NY 10012
Susan Dominus, Editor-in-Chief
info@nerve.com
www.nerve.com/nerveprint
Print spin-off of the Web site, which features additional fiction. Published six times a year. Features literate erotica.

New Delta Review

English Dept.
Louisiana State University
Baton Rouge, LA 70803-5001
Rotating editorship
english.lsu.edu/journals/ndr
Biannual.

New England Review*

Middlebury College
Middlebury, VT 05753
Stephen Donadio, Editor
NEReview@middlebury.edu
www.middlebury.edu/~nereview
Quarterly.

New Letters
University of Missouri-Kansas City
5100 Rockhill Road
Kansas City, MO 64110
James McKinley, Editor-in-Chief
newsletters@umkc.edu
iml.umkc.edu/newsletters/contents.htm
Quarterly.

New Millennium Writings
P.O. Box 2463
Knoxville, TN 37901
Don Williams, Editor
nmw@mach2.com
www.mach2.com/books/williams/index.html
Biannual.

The New Renaissance
26 Heath Road
Arlington, MA 02474-3645
Louise T. Reynolds, Editor-in-Chief
wmichaud@gwi.net

New Orleans Review
P.O. Box 195
Loyola University
New Orleans, LA 70118
Christopher Chambers, Editor
noreview@beta.loyno.edu
www.loyno.edu/~noreview
Quarterly.

New York Stories
La Guardia Community College/CUNY
31-10 Thomson Ave.
Long Island City, NY 11101
Daniel Caplice Lynch, Editor-in-Chief
Triannual.

THE NEW YORKER*
4 Times Square
New York, NY 10036
Bill Buford, Fiction Editor
www.newyorker.com
2002 O. Henry Award winner for magazines. Esteemed weekly with fiction double issues in June and December. Also won the O. Henry Award for magazines in 1998, 1999, and 2001.

Night Rally
P.O. Box 1707
Philadelphia, PA 19105
Amber Dorko Stopper, Editor-in-Chief
NightRallyMag@aol.com
www.nightrally.org
Triquarterly established in 2000. Web site has a feature that allows writers to report on how their submissions were handled by various magazines.

Nimrod
The University of Tulsa
600 South College
Tulsa, OK 74104-3189
Francine Ringold, Editor-in-Chief
www.utulsa.edu/NIMROD
Biannual.

96 Inc.
P.O. Box 15559
Boston, MA 02215
Julie Anderson, Vera Gold, Nancy Mehegan, Editors
Annual. Sometimes features the work of teenagers produced in workshops sponsored by the magazine.

Noon

1369 Madison Avenue
PMB 298
New York, NY 10128
Diane Williams, Editor
noonannual@yahoo.com
Annual.

The North American Review

University of Northern Iowa
1222 West 27th Street
Cedar Falls, IA 50614-0156
Vince Gotera, Editor
nar@uni.edu
www.webdelsol.com/
NorthAmReview/NAR
Five issues a year. Founded in 1815.

North Carolina Literary Review

English Dept.
East Carolina University
Greenville, NC 27858-4353
Margaret D. Bauer, Editor
BauerM@mail.ecu.edu
www.ecu.edu/nclr
Annual.

North Dakota Quarterly

The University of North Dakota
Grand Forks, ND 58202-7209
Robert W. Lewis, Editor
ndq@sage.und.nodak.edu

Northwest Review

369 PLC
University of Oregon
Eugene, OR 97403
John Witte, Editor
Triannual.

Notre Dame Review

Creative Writing Program
English Dept.

University of Notre Dame
Notre Dame, IN 46556
John Matthias, William O'Rourke,
Editors
www.nd.edu/~ndr/review.htm
*Biannual. Web site offers additional
content.*

Now & Then

Center for Appalachian Studies and
Services
Box 70556
East Tennessee State University
Johnson City, TN 37614-0556
Jane H. Woodside, Editor
cass@etsu.edu
cass.etsu.edu/n&t
*"The Appalachian Magazine."
Triquarterly.*

Oasis

P.O. Box 626
Largo, FL 34649-0626
Neal Storrs, Editor
oasislit@aol.com
Quirky quarterly.

Obsidian III

North Carolina State University
English Dept., Box 8105
Raleigh, NC 27695
Afaa M. Weaver, Editor
obsidian@social.chass.ncsu.edu
"Literature in the African Diaspora."

The Ohio Review

344 Scott Quad
Ohio University
Athens, OH 45701-2979
Wayne Dodd, Editor
www.ohio.edu/TheOhioReview
*Biannual. Ceased publication in
2001 after 30 years.*

One Story
P.O. Box 1326
New York, NY 10156
Hannah Tinti, Editor
www.one-story.com
One story per issue, 18 issues per year.
First published in 2002.

ONTARIO REVIEW
9 Honey Brook Drive
Princeton, NJ 08540
Raymond J. Smith, Editor
www.ontarioreviewpress.com
Biannual.

Open City
225 Lafayette Street
Suite 1114
New York, NY 10012
Thomas Beller, Daniel Pinchbeck,
Editors
editors@opencity.org
www.opencity.org
Annual.

Other Voices
English Dept. (MC 162)
University of Illinois at Chicago
601 South Morgan Street
Chicago, IL 60607-7120
Lois Hauselman, Executive Editor
Biannual with all-fiction format.

THE OXFORD AMERICAN
P.O. Box 1156
Oxford, MS 38655
Marc Smirnoff, Editor
oxam@watervalley.net
www.oxfordamericanmag.com
John Grisham–backed magazine
with Southern focus. Bimonthly.

Oxford Magazine
English Dept.
356 Bachelor Hall
Miami University
Oxford, OH 45056
Rotating editorship
Oxmag@geocities.com

Oyster Boy Review
P.O. Box 77842
San Francisco, CA 94107-0842
Damon Sauve, Publisher
staff@oysterboyreview
www.oysterboyreview.com
Quarterly.

The Paris Review*
541 East 72nd Street
New York, NY 10021
George Plimpton, Editor
www.parisreview.com
Quarterly.

Parting Gifts
3413 Wilshire Drive
Greensboro, NC 27408
Robert Bixby, Editor
rbixby@aol.com
users.aol.com/marchst/msp.html

Partisan Review
236 Bay State Road
Boston, MA 02215
William Phillips, Editor-in-Chief
partisan@bu.edu
www.partisanreview.org
Quarterly.

Paterson Literary Review
Passaic County Community
College
One College Boulevard
Paterson, NJ 07505-1179

Mary Mazzioti Gillan, Editor
Annual.

Phantasmagoria
English Dept.
Century Community and
Technical College
White Bear Lake, MN 55110
Abigail Allen, Editor
Biannual.

Phoebe
George Mason University
4400 University Drive
Fairfax, VA 22030-4444
Rotating editorship
phoebe@gmu.edu
www.gmu.edu/pubs/phoebe
Biannual, student edited.

Pindeldyboz
22-53 36th Street
Astoria, NY 11103
Jeff Boison, Editor-in-Chief
Print@pindeldyboz.com
www.pindeldyboz.com
Debut print issue, summer 2001.
Published irregularly.

Pinyon
Languages, Literature and
Communications
Mesa State College
1100 North Avenue
Grand Junction, CO 81502
Randy Phillis, Editor
Annual.

Playboy
Playboy Building
919 North Michigan Avenue
Chicago, IL 60611
editor@playboy.com

www.playboy.com
Fiction slipped in among "pictorials"
and pics of Hef.

Pleides
English & Philosophy Depts.
Central Missouri State University
Warrensburg, MO 64093
R. M. Kinder, Kevin Prufer, Editors
rmkinder@sprintmail.com
www.cmsu.edu/englphil/
pleiades.html
Biannual.

Ploughshares*
100 Beacon Street
Boston, MA 02116
Don Lee, Editor
pshares@emerson.edu
www.pshares.org
Triannual. Writers serve as guest edi-
tors for each issue.

Post Road*
c/o About Face
853 Broadway
Suite 1516, Box 210
New York, NY 10003
Sean Burke, Publisher
www.aboutface.org
Biannual. Est. 2000.

Potomac Review
Montgomery College
Paul Peck Humanities Institute
51 Mannakee Street
Rockville, MD 20850
Eli Flam, Editor & Publisher
www.meral.com/potomac
Biannual.

Pottersfield Portfolio
P.O. Box 40, Station A
Sydney, Nova Scotia
B1P 6G9 Canada
Douglas Arthur Brown, Managing
Editor
www.pportfolio.com
Triannual.

Prairie Fire
423-100 Arthur Street
Winnipeg, Manitoba
R3B 1H3 Canada
Andris Taskins, Editor
prfire@escape.ca
www.prairiefire.mb.ca
Quarterly.

Prairie Schooner
201 Andrews Hall
University of Nebraska
Lincoln, NE 68588-0334
Hilda Raz, Editor-in-Chief
www.unl.edu/schooner/
psmain.htm
Quarterly.

Prism International
Creative Writing Program
University of British Columbia
V6T 1Z1 Canada
Rotating editorship
prism@interchange.ubc.ca
prism.arts.ubc.ca
Quarterly.

Provincetown Arts
650 Commercial Street
Provincetown, MA 02657
Christopher Busa, Editor
cbusa@mediaone.net
Annual Cape Cod arts magazine.

Puerto del Sol
P.O. Box 30001
New Mexico State University
Las Cruces, NM 88003-8001
Kevin McIlvoy, Editor-in-Chief
Biannual.

Quarry Magazine
P.O. Box 74
Kingston, Ontario
K7L 4V6 Canada
Andrew Griffin, Editor-in-Chief
quarrymagazine@hotmail.com
Quarterly.

Quarterly West
317 Olpin Union Hall
University of Utah
Salt Lake City, UT 84112
Margot Schilpp, Editor
Webdelsol.com/Quarterly_West
*Biannual. Also publishes short shorts
and novellas.*

Rain Crow
P.O. Box 11013
Chicago, IL 60611-0013
Michael S. Manley, Editor
rcp@rain-crow.com
rain-crow.com
First issue published in 2000.

Raritan
Rutgers University
31 Mine Street
New Brunswick, NJ 08903
Richard Poirier, Editor-in-Chief
*Quarterly. Edited by former
O. Henry Awards Series Editor
Poirier (1961–66). Only publishes
fiction occasionally.*

Rattapallax
523 La Guardia Place
Suite 353
New York, NY 10012
Martin Mitchell, Editor-in-Chief
rattapallax@hotmail.com
www.rattapallax.com
Biannual. Issues include poetry readings on CD.

The Reading Room
P.O. Box 2144
Lenox Hill Station
New York, NY 10021
Barbara Probst Solomon, Editor-in-Chief
readingroom@prodigy.net
www.greatmarshpress.com
Biannual.

Red Rock Review
English Dept., J2A
Community College Southern
Nevada
3200 East Cheyenne Avenue
North Las Vegas, NV 89030
Richard Logsdon, Editor-in-Chief
Biannual.

Republic of Letters, (News from the)
120 Cushing Avenue
Boston, MA 02125-2033
Keith Botsford, Editor
rangoni@bu.edu
www.bu.edu/trl
Appears irregularly. Publishes some fiction.

River City
English Dept.
The University of Memphis
Memphis, TN 38152-6176

Rotating editorship
rivercity@memphis.edu
www.people.memphis.edu/
~rivercity
Biannual. Formerly known as Memphis State Review. Themed issues.

River Oak Review
P.O. Box 3127
Oak Park, IL 60303
Marylee MacDonald, Publisher &
Editor
www.riveroakarts.org
Biannual.

River Styx
634 North Grand Boulevard, 12th
floor
St. Louis, MO 63103-1002
Richard Newman, Editor
www.riverstyx.org
Triannual.

Rosebud
P.O. Box 459
Cambridge, WI 53523
Roderick Clark, Publisher &
Magazine Editor
www.rsbd.net
Quarterly.

St. Anthony Messenger
1615 Republic Street
Cincinnati, OH 45210-1298
Jack Wintz, O.F.M., Editor
StAnthony@AmericanCatholic.org
www.americancatholic.org
Monthly magazine published by Franciscan friars with about one story per issue.

Salamander
48 Ackers Avenue
Brookline, MA 02445-4160
Jennifer Barber, Editor
Biannual.

Salmagundi
Skidmore College
Saratoga Springs, NY 12866
Robert Boyers, Editor-in-Chief
pboyers@skidmore.edu
Quarterly.

Salt Hill
Syracuse University
English Dept.
Syracuse, NY 13244
Rotating editorship
salthill@cas.syr.edu
students.syr.edu/salthill
Biannual.

Santa Monica Review
Santa Monica College
1900 Pico Boulevard
Santa Monica, CA 90405
Rotating editorship
Biannual.

The Seattle Review
Padelford Hall
P.O. Box 354330
University of Washington
Seattle, WA 98195
Colleen J. McElroy, Editor
Biannual.

Seven Days
P.O. Box 1164
255 S. Champlain Street
Burlington, VT 05042-1164
Pamela Polston, Paula Routly, Co-
editors

sevenday@together.net
www.sevendaysvt.com
*Free weekly newspaper in the
Burlington, VT, area. Occasional fiction.*

The Sewanee Review
University of the South
735 University Avenue
Sewanee, TN 37383-1000
George Core, Editor
www.sewanee.edu/sreview/home.
html
Quarterly.

Shenandoah
Troubador Theater, 2nd floor
Washington and Lee University
Lexington, VA 24450-030
R. T. Smith, Editor
shenandoah.wlu.edu
Quarterly.

Snake Nation Review
110 #2 West Force Street
Valdosta, GA 31601
Robert George, Editor
Triannual.

Songs of Innocence
P.O. Box 719
Radio City Station
New York, NY 10101-0719
Michael Pendragon, Editor &
Publisher
mmpendragon@aol.com
*Celebrates "the nobler, more spiritual
aspects of Man, the World, and their
Creator."*

Sonora Review
English Dept.
University of Arizona

Tucson, AZ 85721
Rotating editorship
sonora@u.arizona.edu
www.coh.arizona.edu/sonora
Biannual.

South Dakota Review
P.O. Box 111
University Exchange
Vermillion, SD 57069
Brian Bedard, Editor
sdreview@usd.edu
Quarterly.

The Southeast Review
English Dept.
The Florida State University
Tallahassee, FL 32306
Rotating editorship
sundog@english.fsu.edu
english.fsu.edu/sundog
Biannual. Formerly Sundog.

Southern Exposure
P.O. Box 531
Durham, NC 27702
Chris Kromm, Editor
info@southernexposure.org
www.southernexposure.org
A quarterly journal of Southern politics and culture that publishes some fiction.

Southern Humanities Review
9088 Haley Center
Auburn University
Auburn, AL 36849
Dan R. Latimer, Viriginia M. Kouidis, Editors
www.auburn.edu/english/shr/home.htm
Quarterly.

The Southern Review*
43 Allen Hall
Louisiana State University
Baton Rouge, LA 70803-5005
James Olney, Dave Smith, Editors
unix1.sncc.lsu.edu/guests/wwwtsr
Quarterly.

Southwest Review*
Southern Methodist University
307 Fondren Library West
Dallas, TX 75275
Willard Spiegelman, Editor-in-Chief
www.southwestreview.org
Quarterly.

Spinning Jenny
P.O. Box 1373
New York, NY 10276
C. E. Harrison, Editor
spinningjenny@blackdresspress.com
www.blakdresspress.com

StoryQuarterly
431 Sheridan Rd.
Kenilworth, IL 60043
M. M. M. Hayes, Editor
storyquarterly@hotmail.com
Despite its name, an annual.

The Sun
107 North Roberson Street
Chapel Hill, NC 27516
Sy Safransky, Editor
www.thesunmagazine.org
Spirited monthly.

Sycamore Review
English Dept.
1356 Heavilon Hall
Purdue University

West Lafayette, IN 47907
Rotating editors
sycamore@expert.cc.purdue.edu
www.sla.purdue.edu/academic/
engl/sycamore/
Biannual.

Talking River Review
Division of Literature and
Languages
Lewis-Clark State College
500 8th Avenue
Lewiston, ID 83501
Student-run biannual.

Tameme
199 First Street
Los Altos, CA 94022
C. M. Mayo, Editor
editor@tameme.org
www.tameme.org
*Annual. "New writing from North
America." Publishes bilingual fiction
in English and Spanish, the original
language and in translation.*

Tampa Review
University of Tampa
401 West Kennedy Boulevard
Tampa, FL 33606-1490
Richard Mathews, Editor
tampareview.ut.edu
Biannual with hardcover format.

The Texas Review
English Dept.
Sam Houston State University
Huntsville, TX 77341
Paul Ruffin, Editor
Biannual.

Third Coast
English Dept.
Western Michigan University

Kalamazoo, MI 49008-5092
Rotating editorship
www.wmich.edu/thirdcoast
Biannual.

THE THREEPENNY REVIEW*
P.O. Box 9131
Berkeley, CA 94709
Wendy Lesser, Editor
wlesser@threepennyreview.com
www.threepennyreview.com
Quarterly.

Tikkun
60 West 87th Street
New York, NY 10024
Thane Rosenbaum, Literary Editor
magazine@tikkun.org
www.tikkun.org
*"A Bimonthly Jewish Critique of
Politics, Culture & Society."*

Timber Creek Review
3283 UNCG Station
Greensboro, NC 27413
John M. Freiermuth, Editor
*Published quarterly or "whenever
there is enough material to fill a few
pages."*

TIN HOUSE*
P.O. Box 10500
Portland, OR 97296-0500
**Rob Spillman and Elissa
Schappell, Editors**
www.tinhouse.com
Quarterly.

Transition*
69 Dunster Street
Cambridge, MA 02138
Kwame Anthony Appiah, Henry
Louis Gates Jr., Editors
www.transitionmagazine.com

Quarterly. An international review with one or two stories per issue. Founded forty years ago in Uganda. Now published in the U.S.

TriQuarterly*
Northwestern University
2020 Ridge Avenue
Evanston, IL 60208
Susan Firestone Hahn, Editor
Triannual.

The Urbanite
P.O. Box 4737
Davenport, IA 52808
Mark McLaughlin, Editor
"Surreal & Lively & Bizarre."
Published irregularly.

Virginia Adversaria
P.O. Box 2349
Poquoson, VA 23662
Bill Glose, Editor
Empirepub@hotmail.com
www.freshlit.com
Quarterly.

The Virginia Quarterly Review
One West Range
P.O. Box 400223
Charlottesville, VA 22903-4223
Staige D. Blackford, Editor
vqreview@virginia.edu
www.virginia.edu/vqr

War, Literature & the Arts
English and Fine Arts Dept.
United States Air Force Academy
Colorado Springs, CO 80840-6242
Donald Anderson, Editor
donald.anderson@usafa.af.mil
www.usafa.af.mil/dfeng/wla
Semiannual. At ease.

Wascana Review
English Dept.
University of Regina
Regina, Saskatchewan
S4S 0A2 Canada
Kathleen Wall, Editor
Biannual.

Washington Review
P.O. Box 50132
Washington, D.C. 20091-0132
Clarissa K. Wittenberg, Editor
Quarterly D.C.-area bimonthly journal of arts and literature.

Washington Square
Creative Writing Program
New York University
19 University Place, 2nd floor
New York, NY 10003-4556
www.nyu.edu/gsas/program/cwp/wsr.htm
Annual with rotating editorship.

Weber Studies
Weber State University
1214 University Circle
Ogden, UT 84408-1214
Brad L. Roghaar, Editor
weberstudies@weber.edu
weberstudies.weber.edu
Triquarterly. "Voices and viewpoints of the contemporary West."

Wellspring
4080 83rd Avenue North
Suite A
Brooklyn Park, MN 55443
Meg Miller, Editor/Publisher

West Branch
Bucknell Hall
Bucknell University
Lewisburg, PA 17837

Paula Closson Buck, Editor
westbranch@bucknell.edu
Biannual.

Western Humanities Review
University of Utah
English Dept.
255 South Central Campus Drive
Room 3500
Salt Lake City, UT 84112-0494
Barry Weller, Editor
Biannual.

Whetstone
Barrington Area Arts Council
P.O. Box 1266
Barrington, IL 60011-1266
Sandra Berris, Marsha Portnoy,
Jean Tolle, Editors
Annual.

Willow Springs
705 West First Avenue, MS-1
Eastern Washington University
Spokane, WA 99201-3909
Christopher Howell, Editor
Biannual.

Wind
P.O. Box 24548
Lexington, KY 40524
Chris Green, Editor
Triannual.

Windsor Review
English Dept.
University of Windsor
Windsor, Ontario
N9B 3P4 Canada
Katherine Quinsey, General Editor
uwrevu@uwindsor.ca
Biannual.

Witness
Oakland Community College
Orchard Ridge Campus
27055 Orchard Lake Road
Farmington Hills, MI 48334
Peter Stine, Editor
www.occ.cc.mi.us/witness
Biannual.

The Worcester Review
6 Chatham Street
Worcester, MA 01609
Rodger Martin, Managing Editor
www.geocities.com/Paris/
LeftBank/6433
Annual.

Wordplay
P.O. Box 2248
South Portland, ME 04116-2248
Helen Peppe, Editor-in-Chief
Quarterly.

Words of Wisdom
8969 UNCG Station
Greensboro, NC 27413
Mikhammad bin Muhandis Abdel-
Ishara, Editor
*Published quarterly or "whenever
there is enough material to fill a few
pages."*

**Xconnect: Writers of the
Information Age**
P.O. Box 2317
Philadelphia, PA 19103
D. Edward Deifer, Editor-in-Chief
xconnect@ccat.sas.upenn.edu
ccat.sas.upenn.edu/xconnect
*Pronounced "Cross connect." Annual
print version of triannual Web 'zine.*

The Yale Review
Yale University
P.O. Box 208243
New Haven, CT 06250-8243
J. D. McClatchy, Editor
Quarterly.

ZOETROPE: ALL-STORY*
The Sentinel Building
916 Kearny Street
San Francisco, CA 94133
Tamara Straus, Editor-in-Chief
www.zoetrope-stories.com
Quarterly. Published by movie
director Francis Ford Coppola.
Note new address and editor.

Zyzzyva
41 Sutter Street
Suite 1400
San Francisco, CA 94104-4903
Howard Junker, Editor
editor@zyzzyva.org
www.zyzzyva.org
Triannual. West Coast writers and
artists.

O. Henry Award Winners
1997–2002

Lee K. Abbott
"The Talk Talked Between Worms," *The Georgia Review,* Vol. L, No. 2
THIRD PRIZE
1997

Peter Baida
"A Nurse's Story," *The Gettysburg Review,* Vol. 11, No. 3
FIRST PRIZE
1999

Russell Banks
"Plains of Abraham," *Esquire,* July 1999
2000

Keith Banner
"The Smallest People Alive," *The Kenyon Review,* Vol. XXI, No. 1
2000

Andrea Barrett
"Theories of Rain," *The Southern Review,* Vol. 35, No. 3
2000

"Servants of the Map," *Salmagundi,* Nos. 124-125
2001

John Barth
"On with the Story," *TriQuarterly,* No. 95
1997

Rick Bass
"The Myths of Bears," *The Southern Review,* Vol. 33, No. 1
1998

Ann Beattie
"That Last Odd Day in L.A.," *The New Yorker,* April 16, 2001
2002

Pinckney Benedict
"Miracle Boy," *Esquire,* December 1998
1999

"Zog 19: A Scientific Romance," *Zoetrope: All-Story,* Vol. 4, No. 1
2001

Jeannette Bertles
"Whileaway," *The Gettysburg Review,* Vol. 12, No. 1
2000

John Biguenet
"Rose," *Esquire,* January 1999
2000

T. Coraghessan Boyle
"The Underground Gardens," *The New Yorker,* May 25, 1998
1999

"The Love of My Life," *The New Yorker,* March 6, 2000
2001

Arthur Bradford
"Catface," *Epoch,* Vol. 45, No. 3
1997

Kevin Brockmeier
"These Hands," *The Georgia Review,* Vol. LIII, No. 3
2000

"The Ceiling," *McSweeney's,* No. 7
FIRST PRIZE
2002

Judy Budnitz
"Flush," *McSweeney's,* No. 3
2000

Michael Byers
"The Beautiful Days," *Ploughshares,* Vol. 25, Nos. 2 & 3
2000

Ron Carlson
"At the Jim Bridger," *Esquire,* May 2000
2001

Raymond Carver
"Kindling," *Esquire,* July 1999
2000

Michael Chabon
"Son of the Wolfman," *Harper's Magazine,* December 1998
1999

Dan Chaon
"Big Me," *The Gettysburg Review,* Vol. 13, No. 2
SECOND PRIZE
2001

Carolyn Cooke
"The Twa Corbies," *The Gettysburg Review,* Vol. 9, No. 2
1997

"Eating Dirt," *New England Review,* Vol. 18, No. 2
1998

Michael Cunningham
"Mister Brother," *DoubleTake,* No. 14
1999

Edwidge Danticat
"Seven," *The New Yorker,* October 1, 2001
2002

Alice Elliott Dark
"Watch the Animals," *Harper's Magazine,* September 1999
2000

Kiana Davenport
"The Lipstick Tree," *Story,* Summer 1996
1997

"Fork Used in Eating Reverend Baker," *Story,* Spring 1998
1999

"Bones of the Inner Ear," *Story,* Autumn 1999
2000

Peter Ho Davies
"Relief," *The Paris Review,* No. 141
1998

Chitra Banerjee Divakaruni
"The Lives of Strangers," *Agni,* No. 53
2002

Anthony Doerr
"The Hunter's Wife," *The Atlantic Monthly,* May 2001
2002

Andre Dubus
"Dancing After Hours," *Epoch,* Vol. 45, No. 1
1997

Deborah Eisenberg
"Mermaids," *The Yale Review,* Vol. 84, No. 3
1997

"Like It or Not," *The Threepenny Review,* No. 85, Spring 2001
2002

Nathan Englander
"The Gilgul of Park Avenue," *The Atlantic Monthly,* March 1999
2000

Louise Erdrich
"Satan: Hijacker of a Planet," *The Atlantic Monthly,* August 1997
1998

"Revival Road," *The New Yorker,* April 17, 2000
2001

"The Butcher's Wife," *The New Yorker,* October 15, 2001
THIRD PRIZE
2002

Brian Evenson
"Two Brothers," *Dominion Review,* Vol. XV
1998

Charlotte Forbes
"Sign," *New Orleans Review,* Vol. 24, No. 1
1999

Richard Ford
"Charity," *Tin House,* Vol. II, No. 3 (Iss. 7)
2002

Mary Gaitskill
"Comfort," *Fourteen Hills,* Vol. 2, No. 1
1997

David Gates
"George Lassos Moon," *GQ,* December 2001
2002

Tim Gautreaux
"Easy Pickings," *GQ,* August 1999
2000

William Gay
"The Paperhanger," *Harper's Magazine,* February 2000
2001

Thomas Glave
"The Final Inning," *The Kenyon Review,* Vol. XVIII, No. 3
1997

Mary Gordon
"City Life," *Ploughshares,* Vol. 22, No. 1
FIRST PRIZE
1997

"The Deacon," *The Atlantic Monthly,* May 1999
THIRD PRIZE
2000

Elizabeth Graver
"The Mourning Door," *Ploughshares,* Vol. 26, Nos. 2 & 3
2001

Allan Gurganus
"He's at the Office," *The New Yorker,* February 15, 1999
2000

Karen Heuler
"Me and My Enemy," *The Virginia Quarterly Review,* Vol. 73, No. 4
1998

Cary Holladay
"Merry-Go-Sorry," *Alaska Quarterly Review,* Vol. 16, Nos. 3 & 4
SECOND PRIZE
1999

A.M. Homes
"Do Not Disturb," *McSweeney's,* No. 7
2002

Pam Houston
"Cataract," *CutBank,* No. 50
1999

Thom Jones
"Tarantula," *Zoetrope: All-Story,* Vol. 1, No. 1
1998

Murad Kalam
"Bow Down," *Harper's Magazine,* October 2000
2001

Matthew Klam
"The Royal Palms," *The New Yorker,* December 4, 1995
1997

Jhumpa Lahiri
"Interpreter of Maladies," *Agni,* No. 47
1999

David Leavitt
"Speonk," *DoubleTake,* No. 24
2002

Andrea Lee
"Anthropology," *The Oxford American,* March/April 2001
2002

Don Lee
"The Possible Husband," *Bamboo Ridge,* No. 79
2002

Fred G. Leebron
"That Winter," *TriQuarterly,* Nos. 107/8
2001

J. Robert Lennon
"The Fool's Proxy," *Harper's Magazine,* October 1999
2000

Mark Ray Lewis
"Scordatura," *Ontario Review,* No. 54
SECOND PRIZE
2002

Beth Lordan
"The Man with the Lapdog," *The Atlantic Monthly,* February 1999
SECOND PRIZE
2000

D. R. MacDonald
"Ashes," *Epoch,* Vol. 46, No. 2
1998

Ian MacMillan
"The Red House," *The Gettysburg Review,* Vol. 9, No. 2
1997

Reginald McKnight
"Boot," *Story,* Spring 1997
1998

Suketu Mehta
"Gare du Nord," *Harper's Magazine,* August 1997
1998

Steven Millhauser
"The Knife Thrower," *Harper's Magazine,* March 1997
SECOND PRIZE
1998

Rick Moody
"Demonology," *Conjunctions,* No. 26
1997

Lorrie Moore
"People Like That Are the Only People Here," *The New Yorker,* January 27,
1997
FIRST PRIZE
1998

Robert Morgan
"The Balm of Gilead Tree," *Epoch,* Vol. 44, No. 2
1997

Alice Munro
"The Love of a Good Woman," *The New Yorker,* December 23, 1996
1997

"The Children Stay," *The New Yorker,* December 22 & 29, 1997
THIRD PRIZE
1998

"Save the Reaper," *The New Yorker,* June 22 & 29, 1998
THIRD PRIZE
1999

"Floating Bridge," *The New Yorker,* July 31, 2000
THIRD PRIZE
SPECIAL AWARD FOR CONTINUING ACHIEVEMENT
2001

"Family Furnishings," *The New Yorker,* July 23, 2001
2002

Antonya Nelson
"Female Trouble," *Epoch,* Vol. 49, No. 1
2001

Jonathan Nolan
"Memento Mori," *Esquire,* March 2001
2002

Josip Novakovich
"Crimson," *Manoa,* Vol. 9, No. 2
1998

Joyce Carol Oates
"The Girl with the Blackened Eye," *Witness,* Vol. XIV, No. 2
2001

Dale Peck
"Bliss," *Zoetrope: All-Story,* Vol. 4, No. 2
2001

Chaim Potok
"Moon," *Image,* No. 19
1999

Melissa Pritchard
"Salve Regina," *The Gettysburg Review,* Vol. 12, No. 2
2000

Annie Proulx
"Brokeback Mountain," *The New Yorker,* October 13, 1997
1998

"The Mud Below," *The New Yorker,* June 22 & 29, 1998
1999

Gerald Reilly
"Nixon under the Bodhi Tree," *The Gettysburg Review,* Vol. 11, No. 3
1999

Bill Roorbach
"Big Bend," *The Atlantic Monthly,* March 2001
2002

Patricia Elam Ruff
"The Taxi Ride," *Epoch,* Vol. 45, No. 1
1997

George Saunders
"The Falls," *The New Yorker,* January 22, 1996
SECOND PRIZE
1997

"Winky," *The New Yorker,* July 28, 1997
1998

"Sea Oak," *The New Yorker,* December 28, 1998 & January 4, 1999
1999

"Pastoralia," *The New Yorker,* April 3, 2000
2001

Susan Fromberg Schaeffer
"The Old Farmhouse and the Dog-Wife," *Prairie Schooner,* Vol. 70, No. 4
1997

David Schickler
"The Smoker," *The New Yorker,* June 19 & 26, 2000
2001

Robert Schirmer
"Burning," *Fiction,* Vol. 15, No. 1
1999

Heidi Jon Schmidt
"Blood Poison," *Epoch,* Vol. 50, No. 3
2002

Christine Schutt
"His Chorus," *Alaska Quarterly Review*, Vol. 14, Nos. 1 & 2
1997

Sheila M. Schwartz
"Afterbirth," *Ploughshares*, Vol. 24, Nos. 2 & 3
1999

Akhil Sharma
"Cosmopolitan," *The Atlantic Monthly*, January 1997
1998

Carol Shields
"Mirrors," *Prairie Fire*, Vol. 16, No. 4 / *Story*, Summer 1996
1997

Mary Swan
"The Deep," *The Malahat Review*, No. 131
FIRST PRIZE
2001

Maxine Swann
"Flower Children," *Ploughshares*, Vol. 23, Nos. 2 & 3
1998

Kate Walbert
"The Gardens of Kyoto," *DoubleTake*, No. 15
2000

David Foster Wallace
"The Depressed Person," *Harper's Magazine*, January 1998
1999

"Good Old Neon," *Conjunctions*, No. 37
2002

Mary Yukari Waters
"Egg-Face," *Zoetrope: All-Story*, Vol. 5, No. 4
2002

Peter Weltner
"Movietone: Detour," *Fourteen Hills*, Vol. 3, No. 2
1998

W. D. Wetherell
"Watching Girls Play," *The Georgia Review,* Vol. LII, No. 2
1999

Julia Whitty
"A Tortoise for the Queen of Tonga," *Harper's Magazine,* June 1998
1999

John Edgar Wideman
"Weight," *Callaloo,* Vol. 22, No. 3
FIRST PRIZE
2000

Don Zancanella
"The Chimpanzees of Wyoming Territory," *Alaska Quarterly Review,* Vol. 15,
Nos. 3 & 4
1998

Permissions Acknowledgments

"Memento Mori" by Jonathan Nolan first appeared in *Esquire*. Copyright © 2001 by Jonathan Nolan. Reprinted by permission of the author.

"Seven" by Edwidge Danticat first appeared in *The New Yorker*. Copyright © 2001 by Edwidge Danticat. Reprinted by permission of the author.

"The Hunter's Wife" first appeared in *The Atlantic Monthly*. Reprinted with the permission of Scribner, a division of Simon & Schuster, Inc. From *The Shell Collector* by Anthony Doerr. Copyright © 2002 by Anthony Doerr.

"Egg-Face" by Mary Yukari Waters first appeared in *Zoetrope: All-Story*. Copyright © 2001 by Mary Yukari Waters. Reprinted by permission of the author.

"The Possible Husband" first appeared in *Bamboo Ridge*. From *Yellow* by Don Lee. Copyright © 2001 by Don Lee. Used by permission of W. W. Norton & Company, Inc.

"Big Bend" first appeared in *The Atlantic Monthly*. From *Big Bend* by Bill Roorbach. Copyright © 2001 by Bill Roorbach. Reprinted by permission of the University of Georgia Press.

"Charity" first appeared in *Tin House*. From *A Multitude of Sins* by Richard Ford, copyright © 2002 by Richard Ford. Used by permission of Alfred A. Knopf, a division of Random House, Inc.

"Like It or Not" by Deborah Eisenberg first appeared in *The Threepenny Review*. Copyright © 2001 by Deborah Eisenberg. Reprinted by permission of the author.

"The Lives of Strangers" first appeared in *Agni*. From *The Unknown Errors of Our Lives*. Copyright © 2001 by Chitra Banerjee Divakaruni. Used by permission of Doubleday, a division of Random House, Inc.

"That Last Odd Day in L.A." by Ann Beattie first appeared in *The New Yorker*. Copyright © 2001 by Ann Beattie. Reprinted by permission of the author.

"George Lassos Moon" by David Gates first appeared in *GQ*. Copyright © 2001 by David Gates. Reprinted by permission of the author.

"Blood Poison" first appeared in *Epoch*. From *Darling?* by Heidi Jon Schmidt. Copyright © 2001 by Heidi Jon Schmidt. Reprinted by permission of St. Martin's Press, LLC.